FEAR NOT

Sandi,

FEAR NOT

April J Spring

APRIL JOY SPRING

To order additional copies of this book, contact:
Xlibris
1-888-795-4274
www.Xlibris.com
Orders@Xlibris.com
785256

Fear not for I have redeemed you; do not be afraid for I am with you.
Isaiah 43:1

Special thanks to my husband, family and dear sisters in Christ
who read, edited, and encouraged me to keep on writing.

Fear not for I have redeemed you; do not be afraid for I am with you.
Isaiah 43:1

Special thanks to my husband, family and dear sisters in Christ
who read, edited, and encouraged me to keep on writing.

CHAPTER 1

Monday, September 3, 2001

Christina stood transfixed before the full-length mirror in her bedroom. She was anxious—no, more like terrified—about the interview scheduled three hours from now. Getting the job would be exciting and scary at the same time. *I'm not qualified to supervise a cardiac care unit.* She reached up to smooth her hair—which was pretty much a hopeless gesture. *I'll deal with that mess later.* After removing her robe and throwing it on the bed, she paced around the room in her silk pajamas as thoughts and questions raged.

Why am I even being considered for this position, and why did I agree to the interview? My résumé clearly stated I'd only worked part-time in a cardiologist office. Sure, I'd kept the job for five years and learned a great deal, but supervising was never on the agenda. They must be desperate. That's it! They'll realize I'm unqualified and send me on my way. She slipped off her pj's, donned her robe once again, and headed for the bathroom. *Maybe a hot shower will clear my head.* Instead, questions continued to pelt her mind as though they were flowing in the water from the showerhead.

Why am I doing this?

Am I ready to take on a full-time job? After all, I've only been back in Alva for a few weeks. Didn't I want to take some time to get my life in order?

Should I just ease back into the workforce instead of jumping in?

What if this job is an opportunity from God?

She was heading into uncharted waters and wasn't sure if she would sink or swim—and all because Cindy had brought the application forms over a week earlier, which she had filled out and reluctantly returned to her.

Cindy had heard about the job opening on the cardiac floor at the hospital, and being such a dear friend, immediately thought of Christina. She had been so sure that this was a great opportunity … so insistent. *Okay, Cindy, let's see what'll happen. If I sink, you'd better be there with a lifeboat!*

After drying off and returning to her room, Christina grabbed her new pale yellow dress off its hanger and pulled it over her head as she headed back to the mirror.

She glanced at the clock. Seven o'clock. Two hours to go.

"I can do this," she whispered to her reflection. *Then why do I feel like an adolescent schoolgirl dressing for a first date?*

She fumbled with the white, flower-shaped buttons on the dress as she murmured, "I can do all things through Christ who gives me strength." *And man do I need strength and wisdom today,* she thought as she turned sideways, pulling her shoulders back and sucking in her tummy.

"Not bad for a woman who'll be forty on her next birthday," she mumbled to her reflection.

Brushing a strand of curly auburn hair from over her left eye, she sighed as she turned from side to side. The pale yellow made her look washed out and tired. In fact, the best part about the dress had been its price: 75 percent off—only costing her five dollars at the checkout. *How could I pass up such a good deal?* The buttons. She touched one of the flower-shaped buttons marching up the front of the dress. That's why she'd bought it. She shook her head, glancing across the room at the shelf that held Grandma Nichols's button jars, as well as ones she added over the years. Taken in by buttons—again.

Pulling the dress off and tossing it on the bed, Christina pulled out a cream-colored linen pantsuit and then rummaged through her dresser drawers to find her navy camisole.

Finally dressed, she stared at the professional-looking woman in the mirror. "That's more like it. Add a necklace, some earrings, and those cute navy sandals, and you're good to go."

Finally … she could smile. At least she *looked* like a supervisor. That was a start.

⌒

The two men in the van across the street from Christina's house were instantly awake when they heard her voice. Each one grabbed a set of headphones and placed them over his ears. They listened intently, fiddling with volume knobs until they were both satisfied. Ed cocked his head and looked over at Tom.

"Can you hear what she's saying?"

"Something about buttons?" Tom adjusted his bulk in the van seat.

Ed chuckled. "Yeah, that's what I thought I heard." He yawned and stretched.

"You know," he said, smiling, "they've really improved these new bugs. When I first started in the business these things had to be in the same room within a few feet of the person talking or you couldn't hear a thing. Now, you put one in the hall and you can hear what's going on behind closed doors." He paused, nodding his head. "That's pretty cool."

Tom chuckled. "Yep, welcome to the twenty-first century." When a few minutes of silence had passed, Tom asked, "Hey, did I tell you that Eleanor's folks live around here?"

"Yep. You mentioned that yesterday. So where exactly do they live?"

"They have some property about five miles from town."

"You wanna drop by and see them when we finish here?"

"Nah. I don't think they'd be happy to see me."

"Hmm."

"I think it's best to leave things as they are. I don't want to kick a hornets' nest by showing up unannounced."

"Well, you could give them a call."

"Yeah, and say what? 'Hey, I'm in the neighborhood and thought I'd drop by?'"

"Well, yeah."

Tom chuckled and shook his head. "You've never had to deal with irate in-laws, Ed, so you just don't get it. It's not as easy as it seems. There's a lot of turbulent water under this bridge, and I don't want to jump in at this point. Maybe once Eleanor and I resolve some of our issues, I can deal with her parents."

"Okay. I was just thinkin', maybe you could be the one to make the first jump and start getting this thing resolved between all of you—for Tommy's sake, if nothing else."

Tom nodded. "Yeah, well, maybe someday I will, but not yet."

Ed nodded and dropped the subject.

They continued listening as Christina, completely unaware of their presence, finished dressing.

CHAPTER 2

The sunlight filtered through the gauzy curtains that gently wafted in the warm morning breeze, replacing the cool night air in the bedroom. Christina looked at the air conditioner and thought about turning it on but decided to wait until she was ready to leave the room.

She walked over to the open window, lifted the shade, pulled back the curtain, and looked outside.

The sky still had a hint of the early morning peachy glow, even though the sun had been up at least an hour. She loved the fresh, clean smell of a new day and took in a deep breath, savoring the taste and feel of it. She looked around the front yard, across the street, and up and down the sidewalk, not sure what she was looking for but feeling she needed to look all the same. All she saw were a few cars and vans parked along the sides of the street and in driveways. There was an early morning jogger with his golden retriever and a few neighbors out watering their lawns. When she saw no boogeymen hiding in the hedges or behind the trees, she felt foolish for even thinking there might be. *Boogeymen? Where had that thought come from?* She raised the other three shades to let the morning light into the room.

Sighing, she surveyed the familiar surroundings. *My room,* she thought. It had been her childhood bedroom and still had the pale pink flowered wallpaper that she had so carefully chosen when she and her mom had redone it her freshman year of high school, some twenty years earlier. She looked around the once cherished sanctuary. The wallpaper had become faded, torn, and stained in various places; the bare wooden floor, though discolored from years of use, still held an imprint of the rectangular rug that had kept her feet warm in the winter; the shelf over her bed that once held her cherished toys and knickknacks from her childhood now held her collection of button jars. She breathed in and smelled a faint odor of mothballs left over from years of sprinkling them in the attic to deter rodents and the unmistakable old house mustiness left over from years of rodent occupation.

When her father had died three years earlier and she was left with the decision to sell or rent the house, she hadn't been ready to let it go and ended up renting it to a nice young woman with two small children. As fate would have it—or was it God?—she was thankful to have a house to come home to. *Be it ever so humble, there's no place like home,* she mused.

"What you see is what you get," she mumbled as she looked around and sighed.

Closing the curtains and walking over to the mirror again, she was unimpressed with what she saw staring back. She brought her fingers up to her eyes and tried to smooth away the small crow's feet at the corners.

Standing within inches of the mirror she looked closely at her face. It was oval shaped, small boned, and delicate, with a smattering of freckles across the bridge of her nose, full lips, and straight white teeth—thanks to two years in braces and cases of whitening gel. Her blue eyes were big and round—doe eyes, someone had once called them—with long, blondish lashes. Once accentuated with liner and mascara, they were her most appealing asset.

Leaning over and tousling her hair, she attempted to run her fingers through the thick, intertwining curls. She stood, shaking her head, watching as the ringlets bounced and landed in their favorite spots. It seemed no matter how hard she tried to change their destination, they ended up where they started.

As she aged, she appreciated her wash-and-wear kind of hair—no wasted time with blow driers and curling irons.

She glanced at the clock by her bed. Seven thirty.

She had been awake since five after tossing and turning most of the night, fearing she wouldn't hear her alarm and would oversleep. Rubbing her eyes, she thought, *I'm surprised I'm not the least bit sleepy.*

Having already had one cup of coffee soon after crawling out of bed, she was starting to crave another. She yawned and stretched. *Okay, maybe I'm a little sleepy.*

She heard voices and kitchen noises: cupboard doors banging, microwave beeping, refrigerator door being slammed. Her children were up and readying themselves for the day's activities.

She finished with her hair and makeup, closed the window, pulled down the shades, and turned the air conditioner on to the lowest setting. She looked around the room and shook her head. *What a mess.* Boxes were stacked around the walls, books were piled in the corners, and clothes were heaped on the bed. It felt like a reflection of her life: messy and chaotic.

Eventually she would change the wallpaper, repaint, and organize her mess, but for the time being, she derived comfort and a sense of continuity and peace even among the chaos—things she desperately needed after the events of the past two years.

As she turned to leave, she felt a tingly sensation on the back of her neck, as if someone was watching her. She quickly looked around, expecting to see—*what?* She chided herself for having such an overactive imagination. Blaming it on the cool breeze from air conditioner, she looked around one last time and left the room. Entering the kitchen and heading straight for the coffeemaker, she glanced at her three children.

Brad, her lanky, redheaded, freckle-faced sixteen-year-old was busily gathering his schoolbooks and stuffing them in his backpack. He turned around and greeted her.

"Hi, Mom! You look nice." He gave her a quick peck on the cheek. As he opened the back door, he said, "Good luck at the interview, Mom. I'll keep my fingers crossed for you!"

She glanced at the clock and hurried over to the back door.

"Brad! Why are you leaving so early and in such a hurry?"

He stopped and said a little too tersely, "Remember, I told you I was gonna walk Melinda to school today, and she lives two blocks over."

"Oh, yeah. Sorry."

Adjusting his backpack, he shook his head and said, "That's okay. I know you have a lot on your mind." He winked and smiled and then turned to leave.

Christina smiled. *That wink. Just like his dad's.*

She glanced out the kitchen window as he stopped to tie his shoelace and readjust his backpack. Sensing he was being watched, he turned his head toward the window and waved. He then sprinted down the driveway and south on the sidewalk toward Melinda's house.

Melinda? Hmm, she thought, *must be a new girlfriend. Last week it was Sarah who had the honor of being walked to school.* She turned to ask Stacey about Melinda when her twelve-year-old daughter suddenly blurted out, "I have a new friend named Linda. She invited me over after school. Can I go?"

Christina hesitated a moment as she readjusted her mind and mouth from the question she wanted to ask to the answer she needed to give her daughter.

"Well, honey, I'd like to meet her first. Does she live far from here?" She poured herself another cup of coffee, added cream and sugar, and put a slice of bread in the toaster.

"No, she lives over on Birch Street, close to the high school. She's really nice, and I know you'd like her." She paused long enough to take a sip of orange juice and then said, "Her mom's a nurse too." Christina raised her eyebrows and turned to face her daughter as she leaned against the counter waiting for the toast to pop up. Stacey drank the remainder of her orange juice and stuffed the last bite of peanut butter toast in her mouth.

"Does her mom work at the hospital?" Christina asked as she sipped the creamy sweet brew from her favorite "My mom's the greatest" mug Brad had given her for Mother's Day when he was twelve.

Stacey nodded as she swallowed the piece of toast and glanced over at her little brother Nicky, who was engrossed in a comic book.

"Do you know what area Linda's mom works in?"

"Nope, but I can ask her today."

"What's her mom's name? Maybe I can look her up when I finish with my interview." She retrieved the toasted bread and slathered it with butter and strawberry jam from Hansen's farm outside of town. Her mouth watered as she put the plastic lid back on the butter container and screwed the lid back on the jam. She could hardly wait to eat the delicious treat.

Stacey shrugged. "Linda's last name is Lewis, so I'm guessing that's her mom's name, too. I'll find out her first name if you want me to."

"Tell you what," said Christina as she walked over and put her hand on Stacey's shoulder, "I'll pick you and Nicky up from school, and maybe Linda can come with us to Dairy Queen. It's gonna be another scorcher today, and I've been craving a root beer float."

Stacey smiled and nodded. "Mmm. Sounds good." Gathering her breakfast dishes, which included a knife with peanut butter still clinging to the sides, she headed for the sink. Before putting the knife in, she held it down for an anxiously awaiting doggy tongue to prewash.

Christina sat at the table and smiled as she watched Stacey interact with Benji, who was completely absorbed in licking every molecule of peanut butter from the knife.

Stacey had her daddy's coloring: dark blonde hair and big blue eyes with long lashes and skin that tanned to a golden brown. She was maturing into quite a beautiful young woman. Stacey had an open, genuine smile that showed tiny dimples in the corners of her mouth.

Soon the boys would start showing interest in her beautiful daughter, if they weren't already. The mother part of her dreaded that time, because she knew once Stacey crossed the line from being a child to being a young woman with raging hormones, their relationship would also take a turn.

Christina wondered what her daughter knew about boys. Having two brothers gave Stacey a little advantage of understanding the male psyche, but even that couldn't prepare her for the emotional and physical turmoil of raging hormones. *I need to talk to her before long and give her an idea of what to expect.*

She knew David would have been a proud and protective father. Shaking her head and looking down at her coffee cup, she willed herself to regain control of her emotions as she felt a lump well up in her throat and tears sting her eyes.

"That's it, Benji. No more peanut butter," Stacey said as she placed the knife on the stack of dishes in the sink. Looking at her mom, she shrugged and said, "I'll ask Linda if she can come with us." Gathering her books together, she added, "We might have to stop by her house or call and ask her mom, though."

"That's fine," Christina said as she cleared her throat and wiped her eyes. Stuffing the last book in her backpack, Stacey made a face and said, "I heard from some of the kids at school that her mom is sorta weird."

"Oh? What do you mean by weird?"

Stacey grabbed her backpack, slung it up onto her shoulders, and headed for the door. "I don't know for sure. Some of the kids said she's into tarot cards and palm reading. I asked Linda about it once, and she just shrugged and said, 'Yeah, my mom's weird,' and before we could talk any more, the bell rang." Stacey shrugged. "I never thought about it after that."

Christina nodded. "Hmm."

Stacey tapped her brother on the head.

"Hey, Nicky, you need to finish your breakfast. We gotta go!" She leaned over and gave her mom a kiss on the cheek. Christina grabbed her, pulled her close, and returned the kiss.

"I love you, baby girl," she whispered in her ear.

Stacey pulled away.

"You can't keep calling me 'baby girl.' I'm growing up!"

"You will always be my baby girl, and I can call you that until I'm ninety-nine!" Christina replied with a grin.

"Okay, Mom, you win," she conceded with a smirk before adding, "but when you turn one hundred, the name-calling stops."

Christina chuckled and then nodded and held up her hand. "I promise."

Stacey leaned over and gave her another quick hug.

"Love you, Mom, and good luck on your job interview!" Turning to her brother, she said, "Come on, Nicky, if you wanna walk with me!" He ignored her and continued reading his comic book. She shrugged, rolled her eyes, and turned toward the back door.

"Nicky, I'm leaving!" she shouted once more as she walked out the door.

Christina looked over at her ten-year-old Nicholas, who had his nose buried in a comic book. Since he discovered comic books, it seemed that he preferred to live in the fantasy world of Comic Book Heroes, and that troubled her. She understood his need to escape from this world of pain and sadness and didn't discourage his escapism, except when necessary—like now. She walked over, stood behind him, and planted a kiss on the top of his head. Leaning over, she whispered in his ear, "Earth calling Nicholas Sanders. Time to get moving!"

"I know," he mumbled petulantly. Closing his comic book and stuffing it in his backpack, he stood.

Turning and looking up at his mom, he asked, "Can Danny come over after school?"

He had inherited his olive complexion and hazel eyes from her mother and curly dark auburn hair from her. The dimple in his chin and the shape of his nose were the only things that he had inherited from his daddy. Christina smiled and nodded. She knew Nicky and Danny were as close as conjoined twins, and even if she had said no, Danny would still find a reason to end up at their house.

CHAPTER 3

Nicky had met Danny a few days after they had moved into her parents' house. Christina had wearied of his whining of boredom and loneliness and suggested he take Benji for a walk to the corner—maybe, she said, he would see someone he could talk to. Sure enough, as he passed the big white house five doors down, he met Danny.

"Hey, what kind of dog is that?"

Nicky stopped and turned toward the unfamiliar voice.

Danny was sitting on his front porch steps eating a red Popsicle but stood when Nicky stopped.

Danny had bright, orange-red hair that stood out like dandelion fluff, ears that were large for his head and stuck out like stop signs, a nose covered with freckles, and two front teeth so large his lips couldn't connect. He looked like a character from a Norman Rockwell painting.

Patting Benji's head, Nicky answered, "He's a beagle."

Approaching Benji, dropping his Popsicle stick, and wiping his sticky hands on his shorts, Danny said, "Ain't never seen a beagle before." Cautiously reaching out his hand he added, "I like dogs, but can't have one 'cause my mama is allergic. My grandpa has three big dogs, but they live outside. Does your dog live outside?"

"No, he's pretty spoiled. He lives in the house most of the time."

"Does he bite?" He asked warily as Benji sniffed and began licking the sweet, sticky hand.

"Nope. Not people anyways—only fleas. He might lick someone to death, though," he added with a grin.

Laughing, Danny said, "That's funny!" He squatted in front of Benji, held the dog's head in his hands, and looked him in the eyes.

Benji looked back, wagged his tail, and suddenly jumped up, knocking Danny on his butt. Then the dog was all over him, licking his face, neck, and ears as Danny squealed with delight and tried in vain to protect his exposed skin. Nicky, at first surprised and concerned, pulled on the leash, yelling at Benji to stop and trying to get the dog under control, to no avail. When he realized Benji meant no harm and was just excited, he loosened his grip and started laughing. After a few seconds of chaos, Danny stood, wiping his doggy-spit-covered face, neck, and ears on his T-shirt.

"Yuck! That dog's got a lotta spit!"

Nicky continued to chuckle. "I should have warned you to *not* look him in the eyes. Dogs don't usually like that." He patted Benji on the head. "I think he liked the taste of your Popsicle."

Benji wagged his tail as he looked from one boy to the next, panting from the heat and exertion.

"What's your name?" the little redhead asked as he continued to wipe himself off. "My name's Danny."

"I'm Nicky."

"Nicky? Is Nicky short for somethin'? I don't know any Nickys."

"Nicholas."

"Nicholas?" Danny raised his eyebrows and scrunched his nose. "Like Saint Nicholas?"

Nicky rolled his eyes and shook his head, explaining, "My mom's last name before she married my dad was Nichols. They made my name out of that."

"Oh. That's kinda weird," said Danny as he scrunched up his face and shook his head. "I'm named after my grandpa. His name is Daniel James Snyder," he announced proudly.

"That's cool." Nicky shrugged and then added quickly, "Hey, we all gotta have a name, and I guess mine's not so bad. I could've been named …" He paused, thinking. "Napoleon … and people would call me … Nappy."

"Nappy! That's funny!" Danny said as he started giggling, which started Nicky giggling and Benji barking.

"How about Poley?" Danny asked with a snort.

"Or Leony!" Nicky chuckled as he sat on the ground and was greeted with a wet tongue on his face.

"Leony!" echoed Danny, laughing so hard he had to sit.

Both boys ended up rolling on the grass with Benji running between them, barking and licking exposed body parts as they continued making up names.

Nicky returned home about an hour later, so happy and excited that he'd found a new friend. After that encounter, the two boys were pretty much inseparable.

Walking Nicky to the door, Christina said, "I'll call his mom today and see if he can go to Dairy Queen with us."

"Thanks, Mom! Love you!" he said as he hugged her.

She returned the hug and kissed the top of his head, which was to the bottom of her chin. *Wow! When did that happen?* Ruffling his thick, curly hair, she nudged him out the front door so he could more easily catch up with Stacey.

With a slam of the front screen door, she watched as he ran to catch up with his sister, who had stopped to wait for him.

It was difficult to comprehend that the school year had started a couple of weeks ago. Preparing for their new schools had been quite an adjustment for all of them. Brad was in his second year of high school, Stacey was in her first year of middle school, and Nicky was in his last year of elementary school. *Where has the time gone?*

Christina walked over to where her reading glasses, Bible, and devotional book lay on the coffee table in the family room. Desiring to have a few moments of quiet time with God, she picked them up and opened the booklet to September 3. "Is It Spiritual Warfare?" was at the top of the page.

Coincidence? she wondered as she remembered Stacey's comment about tarot cards and palm reading. After reading the short commentary and noting the Scripture reference, she lifted the Bible, allowing a piece of paper to flutter to the floor. Bending down to retrieve it and catching her glasses as they fell from her face, she felt an odd sensation, similar to the one she had experienced in her room. She looked around and glanced out the window to see if anyone was there. All she saw was the pecan tree in the backyard, waving its branches as if to say hello. She shook her head and sighed.

Slipping on her reading glasses again, she read the faded typewritten words: "So do not fear, for I am with you." She turned the paper over and over in her hand. Where had it come from? She didn't remember typing it or putting it in her Bible, but she must have. Right? Benji, sensing his mistress's distress, came over and stood next to her chair. She unconsciously rubbed his ears as she considered the strange feelings she had experienced in her bedroom and in the family room.

Could there be something spiritual going on? Was this a message from God? Could David have somehow crossed the supernatural plane that divided heaven and earth and left her this note of encouragement? Or warning? She frowned, sighed, and put the paper back in her Bible. More than likely, she had typed it, put it in her Bible, and forgotten about it, and the force of gravity pulled it free. Yeah, that made the most sense. But why now?

Noticing the time, she put the books back on the coffee table and stood. She would have to do her Bible study later. It seemed that was the story of her life lately. Anything spiritual was shoved off into a corner, while the rest of her life dictated her actions and kept her focused on other seemingly important events. Benji followed her to the kitchen, and Chloe mewed and wove in and out between her feet, almost tripping her mistress.

"Geez, Chloe!" she said as she pushed the cat out of the way with her foot. She glanced at the clock. Eight thirty. *Okay, I'm doing fine. I have half an hour to get there.*

Christina checked the pets' food and water bowls and gave each a quick pat before grabbing her keys and heading out to the van.

Once inside, she automatically switched on the air conditioner. Even though it was early, the Texas heat had already permeated the inside of the van. She looked at the thermometer on her mirror: eighty-three degrees.

She thought about Michigan and remembered that this time last year, they were wearing sweaters and sweatshirts. She turned the air vent toward her face and enjoyed the blast of cool air. After applying a fresh coat of lipstick, she backed her vehicle out of the driveway.

CHAPTER 4

David

David smiled as he watched Christina retrieve the paper and read it. He hadn't *put* it in her Bible, but he knew it had been kept safely tucked between the pages for several years until the moment it fell to the floor. He thought it was interesting that she hadn't noticed it before now.

He remembered where it had come from, even though she didn't. They had been attending a Bible study about fear, and each participant had been given a piece of paper with parts of Scripture references on them. The students were to line themselves up so the words fit together to form the correct Bible verse. When the activity was complete, she had put the paper in her Bible. He continued to watch her a few more minutes before Jarrod tapped him on the shoulder and told him it was time to leave. In the blink of an eye, he was back in heaven. As he and his new angelic friend walked through the heavenly city, they discussed his particular eternal assignment. David had been given the gift of encouragement on Earth, so he would be traveling between the two realms, encouraging those in need.

Since his arrival in heaven, he had not only visited his family and whispered words of encouragement to them as they slept but had also spoken to a missionary in Brazil who was feeling discouraged. *To think I get to do this for eternity ... sweet!*

CHAPTER 5

When Christina's van was out of sight, Ed and Tom exited their own van and walked up the driveway to the west door of Christina's house. If any neighbors happened to look out their windows, all they would see were two men in gray uniforms with large lettering on their backs stating they were from Mort's Electrical Service. Fortunately for them, the door they planned to enter was hidden from the next-door neighbor by a tall hedge.

Using the key that Tom had copied a week earlier from the extra key ring by the side door, the men cautiously entered the house, making sure no one was home—even though they had watched everyone leave. One could never be too cautious in their line of work.

Benji barked once, for he remembered these men—especially the one who had patted him, scratched behind his ears, and given him doggy biscuits. He followed Ed, anxiously awaiting another biscuit.

Ed loved animals—dogs in particular—and they sensed that, making them trust him and his gentle touch, kind spirit, and, of course, treats. He had a reputation for being the agency's "animal whisperer."

When he knew there were animals involved in an assignment, he always carried treats in his pocket. Some were plain dog or cat biscuits, but others contained tranquilizers in case the animals were ornery. So far, he had never had to resort to the tranquilized ones. He walked upstairs, followed closely by his new friend.

When they had come the previous week to install the bugs, Ed had stayed downstairs talking with Christina's friend Cindy, who was under the impression that they were there to check the house's wiring because of an electrical surge caused by a lightning strike at the power plant south of town. When she inquired when this had occurred, Ed had told her the week before, during a thunderstorm that had passed through the area.

"It stormed last week?"

"It was a brief one that passed on through to Waco late last Sunday night."

She scrunched up her nose and bit her lip as she tried to remember the event. "Oh, yes, I remember! I had to get up and close the window."

Thoughts of Cindy made him smile. She was nice to look at, and he liked her bubbly personality. *I should give her a call soon. If she knew what I really do for a living, however, she'd drop me like a hot potato. Maybe I shouldn't bother, but dang it, she's so hot!*

As he and Benji stood outside Christina's room, he looked down the hall at the closed doors to the children's rooms. Curiosity drew him to see what was behind those doors.

Brad's room had posters of cars and motorcycles and comic books hanging on the walls. He had a nice stereo system and a stack of CDs, which, to Ed's amazement, had several Christian artists, along with classical and oldies. He didn't see any hard rock or heavy metal ones. *Hmm. Pretty impressive.* He raised the corner of the mattress, looking for any magazines or pictures of scantily clad women, remembering his own teenage struggle with that particular addiction. He was surprised and somewhat pleased when he didn't find any.

Entering Nicky's room across the hall, he was met with posters of Scooby-Doo and his friends and the Teenage Mutant Ninja Turtles. There were a couple of stuffed animals on the bed and a PlayStation on a shelf near the floor. Ed walked over and picked up a picture frame containing a photo of a man and little boy. *This must be your dad.* Setting the frame down, he noticed a drawing pad and picked it up. Flipping through the pages, he stopped when he came to a crude drawing of a gargoyle-like creature. *You're either playing some wicked video games, watching some frightening movies, or fighting some pretty scary demons.* He replaced the book and turned to go. He waited for Benji to finish sniffing around the room and then closed the door and headed down the hall to Stacey's room, Benji close on his heels.

He was a bit surprised to find the door open several inches. All the other bedroom doors had been closed. He cautiously pushed it all the way open and jumped when he heard a cat hiss and growl. Entering the room and hoping to make friends with the ball of fur, he reached his hand out and said, "Okay, kitty. No need to get all hissy." After batting at his hand, the calico jumped off the bed and ran under it.

Ed looked down at Benji, who was wagging his tail and looking up expectantly at him. Shrugging, he said, "Guess she doesn't want to be friends."

Looking around the room with its pinks, purples, and posters of teenage actors and singers, he smiled as he remembered his sister's rooms when they were around Stacey's age. "Do all girls go through this stage?" he asked Benji, who had his head under the bed, and his tail sticking out and wagging. Mumbling, he walked over to peruse her bookshelf. "I bet when she reaches puberty, this color scheme will go. If she's anything like my sisters, they kinda went through a dark stage—I guess now it's called goth." Benji looked up at him with his head cocked, wagged his tail once, and barked.

"Shh, Benji," Ed said, reaching down to pat him on the head and hand him a treat. He read the names of a few unfamiliar authors: Frank Peretti, C. S. Lewis, Tolkien. He picked out one of the Frank Peretti books and read the cover page. *Hmm. Pretty interesting stuff about spiritual warfare. I'm gonna have to get this one.* He made a mental note of the title and author. Continuing to peruse the shelf, he saw several books from the Babysitters Club series, remembering that his nieces enjoyed those. *She seems to be well-rounded in the literary department.* Not finding anything else of interest, he closed the door, and he and Benji crossed the hall to Christina's room. Remembering the cat, he stepped back over and reopened the door a bit.

Upon entering Christina's room, the first thing he noticed was the chaos.

"Whoa!" Benji ran in and jumped on the bed as Ed entered and stood with his hands on his hips, surveying the somewhat organized mess. Boxes were lined against the walls, spilling contents onto the floor, which was crowded with books and papers. Her bed was made but had a pile of clothes on it. Benji was walking in circles and pawing at the pile, intending to settle in. Even though he doubted Christina would notice the disturbance, he didn't want to take a chance and shooed the dog off.

Even though the air conditioner was giving off a low hum, he turned it off in case he needed to hear Tom or any other disturbance. *God forbid Christina comes home!*

Squatting down, he pulled out the drawer on the nightstand next to her bed, which contained a few pens, a small flashlight, nail files, clippers, and a journal. He pulled out the journal, sat on the floor, and began to read. The first page was dated July 7, 2001. He smiled as he read the account of the Sanders' arrival in Alva. He flipped through the rest of the journal and stopped to read excerpts here and there. Nothing noteworthy jumped off the pages at him.

Little did Christina know that the agency had a file for each one of the members of the Sanders family, and he had read each one thoroughly. One didn't like surprises in his line of work. After an hour or so, Tom called up to him from the bottom of the stairs.

"Hey, Ed?"

Standing and sticking his head out the door, he answered, "Yeah?"

"How ya doin'?"

"Okay. I found a journal I'm reading through. Nothing of great interest, though."

"Okay. I'm still looking through the CDs. Had to take a break and stretch my legs. I'll get back to them now. Hey, how long you want to stay?"

Ed looked at his watch. "How about another couple of hours? If we don't find anything in that time, we'll either give up or come back another day."

"Yeah. All right, then. I'll see you in a couple of hours.

When the two hours had passed and Ed had found nothing of significance, he stood, stretched, and, making sure everything was back in its proper place (as if that were really possible), headed for the door.

He exited the room and almost closed the door when he remembered Benji and the air conditioner. *That would be a tough one to cover up. I'm sure Christina would totally freak out wondering how Benji ended up in her room and no running air conditioner.* He smiled as he pictured her checking Benji's paws to see if he had grown opposable thumbs.

"Hey, come on, Benji." Benji looked at him but didn't budge.

"Come on boy." Benji wagged his tail but refused to move.

"All right." Ed reached into his pocket and pulled out another dog biscuit. "Ya want a cookie?" he asked enthusiastically. Benji ran to him in a split second, sitting and offering a paw. Ed picked him up, carried him downstairs, and gave him the treat in the kitchen.

When Christina backed out of the driveway and passed by the van with "Mort's Electrical" painted in large letters on the side, she waved at the two men inside. Cindy had informed her of their visit the week before, and she wondered why they were still in the neighborhood. *There must have been a lot more electrical damage than I thought.* She continued her drive toward town, glancing in the rearview mirror in time to catch a glimpse of them exiting the van and walking toward her back door. *Sorry, guys, no one's home.*

CHAPTER 6

When the Sanders family had first moved to Texas from Michigan, Christina would take the kids on adventures, as she liked to call them, around her little hometown of Alva. She would point out places of interest and then attempt to educate her children on the history of the town, often going off on a rabbit trail to share with them a few of her childhood memories. The kids were tolerant and even managed to appear interested when they weren't staring out the window as she rambled on.

She smiled as she remembered one of those *special* days right before school started. They had argued whether to go to the train station museum or the cotton mill. Christina finally flipped a coin, and the train station museum won the toss.

When they walked in, they were greeted by walls covered with pictures of trains and stations located in Texas, dating from the 1800s to a recent picture of the Amtrak station in Dallas. There were shelves and bookcases filled with books and brochures and glass cases that housed model trains from the tiniest matchbox size to ones big as a man's arm.

The grandest feature, however, was the model train set in the middle of the room, which was at least twelve feet square and six feet high. Two trains that could be activated with the push of a button occupied the two levels of train tracks. One's imagination could certainly be piqued while watching the trains pass by the countryside, complete with cows and horses, up and around hills and through tunnels and back through the town, where the townspeople occupied cars, shops, and sidewalks. Whoever had constructed the gigantic display had given a great deal of thought to detail. Everything was to scale, from the size and shape of the trees to the little puppies and kittens in the pet shop window.

Walking out the door, Nicky asked, "Mom, can we come back sometime? I really like this place."

She nodded. "Okay. We'll come back sometime."

He was so thrilled that he could hardly focus on anything else the rest of the day. He talked pretty much nonstop about the trains until Stacey, her fingers in her ears, shouted, "Nicky, stop talking about the trains! You're driving me crazy!" Nicky looked at his sister and at then Brad and his mom, who both nodded their heads. He sighed and mumbled something like "Just sayin' it's really cool." He remained quiet and sulky until after lunch, when Stacey apologized. Her apology came with a stipulation, however.

"When we get home, you can go tell Danny all about the train station. Just don't talk about it anymore around me. Please!"

He nodded and grinned. "Okay. I'll just talk to Danny about it from now on."

As they ate their lunch and discussed their day's adventure, the kids decided that *maybe* Alva wasn't such a bad place to live after all—which was a good thing, since Christina couldn't think of any place she'd rather be at that particular time in her life.

CHAPTER 7

Alva was an old town that had buildings still standing from the horse-and-buggy days. Former hotels, banks, and saloons converted into antique malls and small, eclectic boutiques surrounded the courthouse square. Driving past the many empty store fronts, Christina sighed as she remembered the thriving downtown of her childhood—before the outlet mall and Wal-Mart on the east side of town had moved in and taken most of the downtown business. *Ah, progress.* She passed by Mary's Clothes Garden, the little boutique where Cindy was employed, and noticed the owner flipping over the closed sign to the open side. Her dashboard clock read eight thirty-five. *A little early for them to open, especially since there are no cars or folks to be seen in the downtown area. Maybe they're getting ready for their fall cleanout sale. I'll have to drop in soon and see what treasures I can find.*

Stopping at the intersection, she noticed the magnificent courthouse looming before her. The white sandstone block walls shone like alabaster, and the windows reflected the early morning sun like diamonds. It was like a bulwark: strong, stable, and comforting. It had been built in 1805 and had withstood numerous storms, tornadoes, and lightning strikes and a devastating fire that left it gutted and blackened five years earlier. It had taken the renovators approximately two years to restore it to its original condition, which was an amazing feat considering the amount of damage that had occurred.

Driving through the small, picturesque town brought on a wave of pleasant memories with her childhood friends.

The Fab Four, as she, Cindy, Lisa, and Donna had called themselves, had ridden their bikes all over town until they were old enough to drive cars. Their favorite route took them out to the hospital and over the bridge, where they would stop and wave at people as they drove under. They especially loved signaling to the truckers to honk and would rejoice when they did.

After their little adventures, they would end up at one of their houses and rehash their day as they sat and enjoyed Dr Peppers and Fritos corn chips. *Those were the days! Oh, to be carefree, young, innocent, and naïve once again!*

She thought about how the world and Alva had changed in the past twenty years and realized she would never allow her daughter or sons to ride their bikes as she had once done. One had to just watch the news to know that evil and danger lurked everywhere! She wondered if her fear would stifle her children's sense of adventure.

Probably, somewhat, she concluded. *How could they have an adventurous exploration if they were never allowed to do that very thing?*

She drove past by Lisa's parents' house and thought, *One of these days, I'll have to drop by for a visit.*

She had been so busy unpacking and settling in that she had found little time to reconnect with her childhood friends and their families. Lisa and Donna had kept in touch over the years via e-mail and Christmas letters, but they had grown apart over the years from the distance and busyness of life. Maybe now that she was back home, they could reunite the Fab Four and rekindle the friendships they had all once shared.

As she turned on Parker Street, named after Dr. Matthew Parker, she saw the hospital. She never ceased to be amazed at the monumental size of it.

When she was in Alva three years ago for her dad's funeral, construction had begun on the new addition, but she'd had no idea how large it would be. It went from a plain one-story building in the shape of a square with a beautiful garden in the center to a three-story brick and window tower. *I wonder if it still has the garden.* She had spent many quiet, reflective times there and was looking forward to seeing it again.

She had been a freshman in high school the first time she had entered the garden. She and four other girls who were members of a volunteer group called the Candy Stripers (so named because of the red and white striped uniform they wore) and their director were so mesmerized when they walked through the automatic door from the cafeteria that there was an audible gasp of reverential awe as they turned in circles and looked up and around at the vastness and beauty of the jungle-like atmosphere. She was impressed with the large glass dome that covered the area, keeping it pleasantly warm and humid. As they continued their walk down a pebbled path, they passed a large fountain in the middle. The fountain had three tiers with water trickling down, making a soothing, rhythmical, dripping sound. She noticed the many coins lying on the bottom of each tier and whispered to one of the other girls, "I wonder what they do with all that money."

The director, overhearing the question, explained that the money went to a place called Samaritan House, which helped needy people.

Christina thought that was an admirable thing to do with the money and would occasionally deposit her own pocket change. As they continued their walk around the fountain to the entrance on the opposite side, she noticed the variety of plants. There were several types of cacti, flowering bushes, vines, and beautiful, sweet-smelling flowers. Tucked in four corners of the botanical paradise were seating areas complete with tables and chairs. She vowed from that day on that every lunch hour or coffee break would be spent in that peaceful kingdom.

Geez, I hope they didn't get rid of the garden when they redid this place, she thought as she drove into the parking lot.

Looking up, she could see the reflection of the town and the courthouse in the tall dark windows.

CHAPTER 8

As Christina was driving to the hospital, Mrs. Emma Ferguson, the nursing supervisor, was busy clearing her desk of the clutter that had accumulated the previous week.

She was looking forward to interviewing Christina Sanders. Reading the résumé and realizing the applicant was not qualified for the job, she had set the paper aside in her desk drawer. It wasn't until later in the day when Emma started to file the application that she noticed the maiden name of Nichols. *Christina Nichols Sanders.* That name rang a bell. *Christina Nichols.* The name kept playing in her brain like a scratched record until it finally dawned on her to whom it belonged. She didn't remember very many of the girls that had worked as aides over the years, but this one stood out in her mind.

Christy Nichols, as she preferred to be called about twenty years ago, had been a quick learner and a willing worker and seemed to enjoy pleasing the staff as well as the patients. She had a sweet, sensitive spirit and smiled and laughed easily, making the time working with her a pleasure. Emma had enjoyed watching her mature as she continued to work part-time through her high school years. When she announced to the nursing staff that she would be attending the local college to major in nursing, everyone was pleased. She had all the qualities of a great nurse.

Emma looked at the résumé again and sighed. This applicant didn't have the qualifications to be a head nurse in the cardiac department of the hospital. *Why am I even considering her, and how can I justify any decision to hire her?* According to the résumé, Christina had never worked in a hospital setting, and even though she *had* worked in a cardiologist office for several years—which gave her some knowledge and insight into the cardiac world—that was totally different from a hospital environment. Working in a hospital would be stressful with the long hours, emergency situations, and difficult doctors, nurses, and patients. She wondered how well Christy could cope with the day-to-day stress.

She looked at the other two résumés on her desk: Janet Washburn and Irene Taylor. They were much more qualified than Christy, but she didn't like Janet, and Irene just had another baby and stated that she only wanted to work every other weekend.

Janet had worked part-time for several years as a fill-in nurse in all the areas of the hospital and knew her way around better than anyone. She had proved herself quite capable of handling any situation time and again. Rubbing her forehead, she thought, *So why am I reluctant to just put her in this job?* She couldn't put her finger on exactly what made her dislike Janet, but there was just something not right about the woman. *Something mental or spiritual?* It wasn't as if she had ever been mean or rude to a patient, but she was very opinionated and sometimes short-tempered with the nursing staff and doctors. But there was definitely something wrong with her on a deeper level. Just thinking about her made Emma's skin crawl. She rubbed her arms as she felt goose bumps pop up.

She took a deep breath and blew it out her mouth. Someone needed to fill this spot. *Okay, maybe I should rethink my decision about interviewing Christy for this particular job. Maybe I can find her another job elsewhere in the hospital. But really,* she thought, *there aren't any other jobs available for a registered nurse right now, and the position needs to be filled immediately.* Something inside her head and heart kept telling her to give Christy a chance.

Maybe Janet and Christy could both work part-time? But Janet had stated that she didn't want to work part-time. She needed the extra hours and income to support her and her daughter and was the first to get her résumé in. She was the logical choice.

I have to figure out what to do. I can't justify having two RNs on the cardiac floor at one time—at least not on a permanent basis, she thought as she chewed on her bottom lip. The cardiac unit had six beds, and one RN per shift was plenty. Maybe the gals wouldn't mind working part-time for a while or going to another unit, like maternity, where there were at least twenty-plus patients at all times.

The question still remained: could Christy even do the job? Emma felt in her heart that if she was the same person now that she had been as a teen, she could take on any challenge presented to her. She looked at her watch. Eight fifty. *Christy should be arriving soon.*

She removed her glasses and rubbed her eyes. Her heart and mind were in such conflict. "God, please help me make the right decision," she whispered as she stood and stretched, feeling a throbbing sensation in her temples. She consciously relaxed her mind and body by slowly breathing in and out. The throbbing ceased. She sat back down, opened a medical magazine, and started reading an article about stem cell research and its impact on cardiac patients.

CHAPTER 9

Christina checked her makeup one last time before exiting the van. Walking toward the hospital, humidity in the air and heat bouncing off the pavement, made her break out in a sweat. *Great, there goes my makeup, and my hair probably makes me look like I've got poodle genes!*

She looked up, shading her eyes with her hand as she heard two crows cawing at each other as they flew over her head and disappeared from view. She glanced in the reflective glass and thought, *Yep, my nickname should be Fifi.* She tried to get her ringlets under control by running her fingers through them, but ended up with tangled fingers and ripped-out hair. *Ow! A lot of good that did!*

The thermometer-clock beside the entrance read eighty-five degrees, and it was nine o'clock. *Guess they put it there so people can see the temperature and time when they die of a heat stroke,* she mused as she wiped sweat from her forehead.

The cool air felt refreshing as she walked through the automatic doors of the lobby. Approaching the front desk, she was aware of the many watchful eyes and remembered that in a small town, everything was everybody's business and gossip spread like a wildfire.

"Excuse me," she said to the young woman sitting at the reception desk who looked to be in her early twenties with short spiked blond hair and an eyebrow ring. "Could you direct me to Mrs. Ferguson's office?"

The young woman, whose name tag read Sherry, pointed a long, bright-red, well-manicured fingernail toward the hallway.

"You'll see her office around the corner on the right side," she said with a smile that would make any dentist proud.

"Thank you," replied Christina.

Walking down the hall toward the door labeled Mrs. Emma Ferguson: Nursing Supervisor, she started to relax. The hallway looked familiar even though it had been renovated. She passed the area where nursing station one had been located before the renovation. It now had a gourmet coffee bar with various flavors available and an assortment of juices and cookies as well. There were several people standing around drinking and chatting. She shook her head and smiled. *Wow, even small-town hospitals have coffee bars! Alva is definitely moving up to big-city standards.*

She located Mrs. Ferguson's door and knocked lightly.

"Come in," she heard a female voice answer.

Slowly opening the door and peeking in, she called, "Hello, Mrs. Ferguson?"

"Yes," answered the woman behind the desk as she closed the magazine she had been reading and stood.

"You must be Christina. Come in, dear."

When Christina walked through the door, she saw a short, stout woman who looked to be in her early sixties standing behind a large, mahogany-colored desk. She wore thick glasses and had short gray curly hair, and when she smiled, her cheeks disappeared into dimples and her eyes sparkled.

Put her in a red dress with a white cap on her head, and she could be a dead ringer for Santa's wife, Christina thought as she took the plump little hand that reached out for hers.

She knew instinctively she was going to like this woman, who, oddly enough, looked familiar. Her mind zipped through memory files but couldn't pull up a reference to when or where she had seen her. *Maybe on a Christmas card next to Santa?* She shook her head and stifled a giggle.

"Please sit down. May I get you a cup of coffee or some tea?"

"No thank you," replied Christina as she sat in the chair in front of the large desk.

Nodding, Emma said, "Well, I think I would like a cup of coffee," and disappeared through a doorway in the back of the room.

Christina looked around the small room. There were boxes on the floor with books and papers in them, reminding her once again of the chaos in her bedroom. The mahogany shelves surrounding the room from floor to ceiling were full of books, knickknacks, and framed pictures of children at various developmental stages. *Her grandchildren,* Christina surmised. She did a double take when her eyes passed over a familiar face. *That looks like Steven Dawson.* Her heart did a little flutter. *Why is his picture up there with the other ones?* she wondered.

When Cindy had informed her that Steven was the main cardiac physician at the hospital, she knew she would be seeing quite a bit of him if she was hired—and yes, that pleased and terrified her at the same time.

She had had a crush on Steven all through high school, and even though they never dated or spent any meaningful time together, she had always felt weak-kneed and light-headed when he was around. She was surprised that after all these years her mind and body would react similarly when she thought of or even saw pictures of him. *I wonder what I'll do when I actually see him. I just hope I don't pass out or something. Oh geez, I hope I don't see him today,* she thought as she felt a blush make its way up her neck to her face.

She took in a breath, let it out, and rubbed her now sweaty palms on a tissue she had retrieved from her purse. To get her mind off Steven, she walked over to get a better look at the hanging frames by the door, which held various documents, not really focusing on any of them.

After a few moments, much to Christina's relief, Mrs. Ferguson returned with a cup of coffee, set it on her desk, and took her seat. She adjusted her glasses and picked up the résumé and began to quietly peruse it. She was really revisiting the arguments in her mind about why she shouldn't hire this woman. Christina returned to her chair.

After a few minutes of awkward silence, Christina said, "Excuse me."

"Yes?"

"I was wondering if we've ever met. You look so familiar."

Emma Ferguson smiled and removed her reading glasses.

"I was wondering if you would remember me." She leaned back in her chair. "I knew you when you were a nurse's aide about twenty years ago." Christina raised her eyebrows, thinking, *Twenty years ago?*

"You started working on my unit the summer after your freshman year of high school." She paused, waiting for some sort of recognition. When none was forthcoming, she continued.

"I was the head nurse on station two, when the hospital was a lot smaller. Now it's called unit two, and it's upstairs." Christina nodded, remembering that place and time in her life.

Emma leaned forward in her chair, resting her elbows on the desktop, and put her fingers together, forming a triangle, reminding Christina of the little poem "Here's the church; here's the steeple; open the door, and here are the people."

"I knew you as Christy Nichols." She paused then asked, "I take it you've outgrown the name Christy? You prefer to be called Christina?" Christina smiled and nodded and then squinted her eyes, trying to remember. She remembered working at station two, but still could not place this woman before her.

Emma continued, "My name was Emma Bennett then. My first husband died ten years ago, and I remarried. I've also put on a little weight, and my hair is a lot grayer!" She smiled and a chuckled as she patted her tummy and then put her hand up to her hair.

Christina nodded and smiled as recognition and memories flooded in.

"Of course, now I remember. You used to call me your little pup, because I followed you everywhere. You were my favorite nurse!" She exclaimed. "How could I have forgotten? I'm so sorry."

"That's okay. I didn't expect you to remember me. That was a long time ago and we've both changed—a little," she said, chuckling. Christina smiled and nodded in agreement.

"You taught me so much about nursing." She reached across and took the woman's hand. "It seems those other nurses didn't want to take the time to teach me anything. They just wanted me to run errands for them or clean up some disgusting mess."

Emma leaned back in her chair, shaking her head as she remembered those frustrating moments.

"Yes, I remember. I tried to tell them to be a little more patient with you new girls and explain things more thoroughly, but they didn't want to bother."

"Well, I really appreciated your concern for me." Christina paused and then added, smiling broadly, "You were one of the reasons I decided to be a nurse. I wanted to be just like you."

"Oh, that is so sweet. I've never had anyone tell me that!"

They spent several more minutes reminiscing before addressing the reason they were there. Christina nervously massaged her hands in her lap as she spoke.

"I know I don't have much experience in cardiac care, and I haven't worked in a hospital since my college days, but I really do want this job, and I promise you that I'll do my very best, and I'll study and observe and work as hard as I can to prove that I can do it." She knew she was rambling but couldn't seem to stop her nervous banter.

"Yes, Christina." Emma chuckled. "I have no doubt of your abilities. After all, you were my prize student!" she added with a grin.

"I'd like to hire you because I like you, but I'll admit that I do have some concerns. Working in a hospital *is* very different from working in a doctor's office—long hours, much more stress and drama, not only with the patients, but also with the nursing staff and the doctors."

Christina nodded. These were a few of her concerns as well.

"I was wondering if you'd be okay with working part-time? At least for a while. I have another gal that I would like to fit into the schedule because she's been here longer and has more hospital experience."

Christina nodded, thinking, *Good, I didn't want full-time right now, anyway.*

"Would you be willing to work weekends? Say rotating shifts?"

"Rotating shifts?"

"Some weekends you'd work the seven-to-three shift, and other weekends, you'd work the three-to-eleven. You and another gal would rotate your shifts. I'm trying to get three of you gals into the system."

"Three of us?"

"When I put the word out about this job opening, I only had one lady in mind for the position, but then I received two more resumes, and I'd like to help all three of you. The weekend position just came up, as one of my part-timers had to cut back even more on her hours.

"Hmm," Christina replied pensively. "I'm not sure I want to tie up all my weekends. I have three kids I need to spend time with. They just lost their dad a couple of years ago, and we just moved here three months ago. I feel I need to hang out with them as much as possible for a while longer."

Emma nodded. She knew of Christina's situation from the gossip floating around town but hadn't even taken that into consideration when trying to work out a schedule.

"I was hoping I could work the seven-to-three shift during the week while the kids are in school. Then I could be there for their weekend activities." She sighed.

"Well," said Emma as she rubbed her eyes and reconsidered her options, "let me talk to the other gals and see if I can get you in part-time during the week. I can probably shift their schedules around as well—at least I hope so, 'cause I'd really like to give you an opportunity to work here. I think it'd be a great experience for you."

Christiana smiled and nodded. "I'd like that. But if you can't fit me in, that'll be okay too. To be quite honest, I just put my application in on sort of a whim."

Emma gave her a "What do you mean?" look and said, "Hmm."

Christina smiled and shook her head and explained how her friend Cindy had sort of pushed her into applying. Emma smiled and nodded in acknowledgment.

"I see. So I need to know if you really *want* to work here—or are you just reacting to a dare?"

"Oh, I didn't mean to give the impression that I *wasn't* serious about this. I am. I would *love* to work here. I'm just saying that if it doesn't work out for me to get hired, I'd be okay with that. I'll just resubmit at a later date if it doesn't work out now."

"Okay. I just wanted to be sure. I need to hire people who are dedicated and dependable."

It was Christina's turn to nod her head in agreement. "If I'm hired, I'll be as dependable as I possibly can be."

"Good. That's all I ask of any of my nurses."

Gathering the papers on her desk, she asked, "Can you be here next Monday morning at seven thirty? I'll introduce you to Dr. Dawson, and we'll both go on rounds with him. Then I'll take you on a tour of the hospital."

"Dr. Dawson?" she asked as her heart did a flip.

"Yes, he's the attending cardiac physician in this hospital." She paused and spoke conspiratorially, "Well, he and Dr. Meils, who is still pretty wet behind the ears."

Christina smiled. She had no idea who Dr. Meils was but imagined him to be pretty young and inexperienced if this woman thought he was still "wet behind the ears."

"They'll want to meet you, I'm sure."

Christina smiled nervously, "Well, I'll be looking forward to meeting them as well." *Should I tell her I already know Steven?* She decided not to. *For all I know, Steven won't even remember me, and if he does, he may not want her to hire me.* Her heart gave another flutter. *Oh God, what am I getting into?* She took a breath and released it to calm her nerves, and then said, "I'll be here at seven thirty on Monday." Standing, she asked, "Do you want me to meet you here in your office or in the cardiac unit?"

"You can meet me here. Then we'll go upstairs."

"I have some blue scrubs that I wore for my last job. Is it okay if I wear them?"

"Scrubs will be fine. Seems hospitals have gotten pretty lax and casual about what the nurses wear. As long as it's clean and decent." She smiled and added, "You'll notice that some of the older nurses still cling to tradition and wear their whites, but I personally like all the lovely colors and patterns of the scrubs that the younger gals wear. I find the scrubs to be quite comfortable myself."

Christina smiled and nodded. "Thank you." She reached across the desk to shake Mrs. Ferguson's hand.

"Christina?"

"Yes?"

"I'll call you this afternoon about the schedule."

Christina nodded. "Thank you. I'll look forward to hearing from you. I take it you have my cell number."

Emma looked at the résumé. "Is it 810-555-1912?"

"Yes, Ma'am. That's it."

They stood, shook hands, and walked toward the door.

"I'll see you Monday, then," Emma said as she stood in the doorway and watched Christina walk down the hallway. She headed for her desk, mumbling, "Okay, now I've got to get on the phone and do some fancy finagling to get everyone on the schedule. I sure hope I can pull this off."

CHAPTER 10

As Christina walked down the hall to the exit, she could feel Mrs. Ferguson's eyes on her back. Entering the restroom at the end of the hall, she closed the door and leaned against it. *I can't believe that Mrs. Ferguson hired me, especially considering my lack of experience!* She dialed Cindy's number and told her the good news. Cindy squealed with delight.

"I knew you'd get it!"

Christina couldn't help but pick up on her friend's excitement as she explained. "Well, I think it'll only be part-time, and I may have to work some weekends, but yeah, I got it—unless of course, Mrs. Ferguson changes her mind."

"Hmm. Somehow I doubt that. So did you see him?"

"Him who?" she asked, even though she knew whom Cindy meant.

"You know. Steven?"

Christina felt her face blush. "No. But I'm supposed to meet him Monday and go on rounds with him."

"Meet him? You didn't tell Mrs. ... what's her name?"

"Ferguson."

"Oh, yeah. You didn't tell her you already knew him?"

"Well, no. I'm not sure what this means, but she had pictures of him on her bookshelf. Why would she have pictures of him at all?"

"Maybe they're related?"

"Oh, geez, I hope not! How awkward would that be?" Then she had a memory flash of telling the lady years ago of her crush on Steven. "Oh my gosh!"

"What?"

"If they *are* related, I'll be so embarrassed." She told Cindy about the incident years ago and her friend's reply was so ... Cindy.

"Well, maybe that's a good thing."

"And how could that possibly be a good thing?"

"Well ... if she likes you, she'll put in a good word for you with Steven."

Christina shook her head and smiled. Leave it to Cindy to find a silver lining in any seemingly dire situation.

"Besides," she continued, "think how cool it will be to see Steven after all these years. You've both changed a lot, and maybe now he'll appreciate the woman you've become and realize what a fool he was not to have recognized how awesome you were back in high school."

Christina wasn't sure what to say to that, so she just sighed.

"Well, we were both young and immature then, and even after all these years, the thought of him makes my heart flutter. I'm not sure I'd *want* to have any kind of relationship with him. As I've told you before, I truly loved my husband, and I can't even imagine anyone else in my life at this time."

The line was silent for a moment before Cindy spoke again.

"I understand, but I was just thinkin' …" She let her voice trail off. After all, what else could be said at that time?

Recovering her previous excitement, she said, "So anyway, how awesome that you got hired! Do you think the kids will be excited?"

Christina had recovered as well. How could she be angry with Cindy, who was just being, well, Cindy? She was an idealist who believed in life, love and happiness forever and ever amen, no matter what was thrown in the way.

"I do believe the kids will be happy for me. I'm so nervous about this whole thing, however. It's just happening faster than I expected. I figured she'd look at the résumé, see I wasn't qualified, and that'd be that. But she surprised me. "

"How so?"

"She remembered me from way back when I was in high school and worked as an aide. Guess I made an impression then, and she wants to give me a chance now."

"That is *so* cool."

Christina heard voices in the background.

Cindy whispered, "Hey, I'll call you after work. Gotta go."

"Okay. Talk to you later." Putting her phone back in her purse, she turned in a circle and giggled. She felt like running up and down the hallway shouting, "I got the job!"

Pulling herself together, she glanced at her watch: eleven o'clock. *Wow!* Those two hours had passed by quickly.

She felt her stomach growl. *I'd better get a bite to eat, since I only had coffee and toast for breakfast.* She headed in the direction of the cafeteria but was surprised when she came upon a gift shop. *What the heck?* she thought as she turned in circles. *Where's the cafeteria?*

She walked to the counter and spoke to an elderly woman in a light blue lab coat with the words "hospital volunteer" stitched in red above the left pocket.

"Excuse me."

"Yes?" answered the woman, the word sounding more like "yay-us."

She never gave the Texas accent a second thought until she moved to Michigan and was immersed in theirs for sixteen years. Returning to her native land, she thought the drawl was charming. She couldn't help but smile as she asked, "Could you please tell me where the dining room is?"

Smiling pleasantly as she pointed toward the elevators, the volunteer said, "It's up on the second floor. You get off the elevator and go to the right. You'll see it." Christina thanked her and turned to go. As she reached the door, she turned back and asked the little gray-haired volunteer, "How's the food?"

"Why, Honey, it's the best in town. I'd say it's as good as Zimmerman's Steak House, and everyone in Texas knows how good Zimmerman's Steak House is." She smiled, winked, and nodded at Christina as if she knew exactly what she meant—which she did.

"Okay, then," she mumbled to herself. "Guess I'll just have to go and check it out."

Zimmerman's Steak House had been one of her dad's favorite places to eat, and she, her husband, and their kids could count on eating there at least once during their visits with her parents. The food was excellent, and the portions were large enough to have leftovers the next day.

She boarded the elevator and was impressed with the interior. She ran her fingers along the smooth wood, which looked like oak paneling. *Pretty fancy for a small-town hospital elevator,* she thought as she looked up at the mirrored ceiling and smiled at her reflection. Walking down the hall toward the dining room, she had a feeling of peace descend upon her like a warm shawl. *This is where I belong.*

Entering the cafeteria, she was pleasantly surprised, as the decor mimicked a fine family restaurant. There was a bubbling fountain in the center of the room and various plants hanging and grouped in pots around the periphery. The north wall consisted of large tinted windows and a door wall that led to an outside terrace. The south wall was also made of glass, and as she approached, she realized it looked down on the enclosed flower garden. She smiled as she looked down and saw the familiar three-tiered fountain. *It's still here,* she thought in amazement. The garden looked very similar to what she remembered, except the roof was higher and there were taller trees in among the smaller shrubs. *I definitely need to go check that out,* she thought as she turned around and scanned the room. The white plastic wicker table-and-chair sets reminded her of the set she had left with her friend Linda in Michigan. *I wish I could have brought that with us.* She sighed as she recalled a few other furniture items that weren't able to fit in the moving van. *Oh well, it's just stuff. I can always go buy whatever else we want or need.*

The whole décor screamed "English garden," which seemed a little out of place in this cowboy-infested room with its boots, cowboy hats, and large belt buckles that usually bore some kind of Texas emblem. She couldn't help but grin as she looked around the room and spotted every kind of western garb on every kind of person. When she realized that a few of the doctors wore boots under their scrubs, which looked pretty weird, she crinkled her nose and shook her head. *Nope, I'm not in Yankee land anymore. Welcome to the Wild West! Yeehaw!*

She stood in the buffet line and felt her stomach growl and mouth water as she perused the banquet that was displayed before her.

After selecting her lunch, she took her tray and sat at a table overlooking the enclosed garden, remembering a time many years ago when she shared her table with a young man in this same hospital, two floors down.

CHAPTER 11

Because Dr. Parker had known she wanted to pursue a nursing career, he had hired her on for the summer after graduation as an aide in the surgical department. She had been helping in surgery all morning and was looking forward to a nice, peaceful lunch. Munching on her corn chips and having just opened the paperback she wanted to finish reading before returning to the surgical suite, she was startled when a young man asked if he could share her table. She looked around the crowded room and, seeing there were no other places available, begrudgingly agreed. He set his tray on the table, forcing hers over, pulled the chair out, and sat. She sighed, clearly annoyed, and tried to ignore him by returning her attention to her book. She watched him in her peripheral vision as he prepared his food and drink for consumption. She was both surprised and pleased when she saw him bow his head and pray. He was reverent and unpretentious and, to the casual observer, appeared to be looking at something on his tray. She didn't know very many people besides her pastor and her parents who prayed in public. *Impressive!* Holding her book at nose level, she furtively watched him devour his hamburger like it was his first meal after a week of starvation. They were both awkwardly silent until he finished, wiped his mouth with his napkin, and spoke.

"I see your name tag says 'Christina.' My name's David. David Sanders."

She looked up, slightly annoyed. *Can't he see I'm not interested in a conversation?* She sighed and laid her book down. Her mama hadn't raised her to be rude.

"Hi David, David Sanders," she said with a smirk. "I'm glad you can read. By the way, is David your first and middle names, or were you being redundant?"

"Uh, redundant, I guess," he said with a confused look. "My middle name is Bradley."

She chuckled. "Ah. David Bradley Sanders?"

He nodded sheepishly.

She studied his face. It wasn't drop-dead handsome, but it wasn't hound-dog ugly, either. His eyes had a mischievous twinkle in them and crinkled at the corners when he smiled. His smile was open and friendly, and his teeth were straight and white—a good quality when working with the public. He had a dimple in his chin and a clean-shaven face. He was dressed in a blue oxford shirt and khaki pants, which fit nicely on his well-proportioned, not-too-tall frame. All in all, he was nicely packaged—which was a good thing, because it made his persistence less annoying.

He nodded and smiled. "And your name is Christina …?"

"Nichols."

"Christina Nichols. Nice. Do you have a middle name too? I mean, you know mine, so I thought I'd ask about yours."

She shook her head and rolled her eyes. "It's Dawn."

"Christina Dawn Nichols. That's nice too. I like how it flows."

She gave him a "You're weird" look but said, "If you'll excuse me, I need to finish eating and get back to work."

He glanced at her empty plate and then up to her.

Giving him a look, she said, "I have a cookie," and pulled one out of her sandwich bag.

He smiled and nodded. "Okay. Just one more question."

She rolled her eyes and thought, *Really? Are you going for the most annoying award or something?*

"Where do you work?"

She held up her hands, and, with a look that suggested he was dumb as a fence post, said, "Here."

He chuckled. "Well, I gathered that. I just wanted to know what area you work in."

Christina wasn't sure she wanted to go any further with this getting-to-know-you conversation, so she answered, "If I tell you, will you let me finish eating?"

"Uh, sure."

"I work in the surgical unit. I'm a surgical tech."

"What exactly is a surgical tech?"

Rolling her eyes in frustration, she answered, "I make sure all the supplies are where they should be and get the instruments ready for surgery, and I clean up the mess afterward."

"Sounds interesting. Want to know what I do?"

"Not really."

He ignored her surliness. "I install and repair computers. I also teach hospital personnel how to use them."

She nodded, feigning interest. "Wow. Sounds fun. Not."

He chuckled again, thinking, *Geez, she's cute, but what a peevish attitude.* In spite of her protestations, he continued asking questions, coaxing answers out of her, getting her to relax enough to carry on a decent conversation. By the time she was ready to leave, they had agreed to meet again the next day for lunch, which ended up being less tense.

Christina remembered their conversation clearly. They had spent the whole lunch hour talking, starting with trivial things like the weather and which football team was the best and then progressing to more personal things. She learned that he worked for a computer firm in Michigan and was in Alva to install computers in their hospital and instruct the staff how to use them to their full capacity. He would be there at least another month or two and then probably be sent to "God only knows."

"The company sends me on many out-of-state jobs because I'm single," he stated between forkfuls of food. "I'd love to settle down, 'cause after a while, all this traveling and staying in hotels gets very tiring. Besides, I have enough shampoos, soaps, and lotions to open up my own spa."

She giggled, appreciating his sense of humor.

He sighed. "I haven't met the right girl to settle down with, as of yet." He lowered his head and smiled shyly.

Christina remembered thinking, *Well, maybe I'm the one you're looking for.*

When the computer installation job in Alva was completed, he had asked his boss if there were any other hospital computers in the area he could upgrade. Fortunately for him, the Dallas–Fort Worth area had several, so he was able to stay within driving distance of Alva and would meet Christina for either lunch or dinner. After a couple of months of this informal dating, when it seemed the friendship was turning into something more, she took him home to meet her parents.

The first meal they shared had been a little awkward but pleasant.

"I bet you don't get very many home-cooked meals when you're travelling," Mrs. Nichols had said as she passed him the mashed potatoes.

"No, Ma'am," he replied. "I sure appreciate your cooking and making me feel so welcomed."

Her mom had smiled and winked at her. She glanced at her dad, who just smirked and mumbled something under his breath that sounded a lot like *brownnoser*. David had a monumental task before him to win her dad over, since up to that point, no man had ever been suitable for his daughter. Even though he was a Yankee, he had made a favorable impression on both her parents, and her mother had insisted he come to dinner every time he was in town.

After sharing many meals and conversations with Christina and her parents, David had come to love and respect them. Knowing he would be completing his assignment in Dallas and would be heading back to Michigan for an extended amount of time, he had asked Mr. Nichols for permission to marry his daughter—to which he replied, "It's about time you asked."

Christina, completely unaware of that conversation, was surprised when after dinner he knelt down, brought out a ring from his pocket, and proposed. She had been speechless for a few seconds as the reality of what was occurring sunk in. She then threw herself into his arms, knocking him on his butt, and, amongst laughter and applause from her parents, had accepted.

Her parents and friends had been more than helpful in getting everything ready for a Christmas wedding at the First Baptist Church in Alva, which turned out to be simply elegant, in spite of the lousy weather. An ice storm decided to blow in just as the ceremony began and, by the time it was over, had deposited a quarter inch of frozen water on everything.

The reception had been held in the fellowship center, and after the traditional ceremonies of cake cutting and garter tossing, they left to spend their honeymoon weekend in a nice hotel in downtown Dallas. Needless to say, there wasn't any running to the car and being pelted with rice. It was more like tiptoeing through the tulips, each step carefully calculated to prevent any injured body parts, which would have really stunk. She smiled at the sweet memories.

She and David had had a wonderful life together, and she wondered how she would be able to go on without him. The words to one of her favorite songs played in her mind. *How can I live without you? How can I breathe without you? How can I ever survive? Oh, how can I live?*

Christina was brought back to the present by a loud crashing sound, followed by the mournful wail of a child. A little girl had knocked her tray off the table, and several people were helping the mother clean up the mess. Christina looked at her own cold and congealed plate of food. *Ugh!* Checking her watch, she realized her daydream had lasted for twenty minutes. She wiped tears from her eyes and took a deep breath and blew it out slowly. Then, leaving the tray on the table, she left the hospital.

Meanwhile, unbeknownst to Christina, gossip was spreading like wildfire in the CCU.

Betty, a gray-haired LPN, approached the counter and asked, "Did you hear the latest? A lady named Christina Sanders is gonna be the new head nurse right here in the Cardiac Care Unit." All eyes turned toward her.

"From what I understand," she continued, "Christina grew up here in Alva and used to work in surgery with Dr. Parker. Do any of y'all know her?" There were negative responses all around.

Sandy, one of the younger aides, asked, "How do you know all this?"

"Well, I heard it from my good friend Emma Ferguson, who interviewed and hired her right there on the spot."

"When did this happen?"

"A little while ago," answered Betty a little smugly. "I went down to Emma's office to ask about the schedule for next week, and she said she'd have it as soon as she worked the new gal in.

"I wonder what she's like. I hope she's nice," interjected Sally, one of aides who had been filing her nails when the gossip started.

Leaning on the counter and whispering conspiratorially, Betty asked, "You know who's gonna be mad as a hatter, though?" She looked around at the shaking heads. "Janet Washburn."

There was an audible *aah* as they all looked around and nodded knowingly.

"I remember how badly she wanted that full-time position," said Sally as she made a face. "Man, I wouldn't want to be in that new lady's shoes. Janet's got an awful temper, you know."

Betty looked up and grimaced. "Uh-oh, look who's coming."

"Looks like she already knows," Sally said as she put her file into her uniform pocket and stood. "I'm outta here."

In her haste to depart with Sally, Betty knocked over a stack of file folders, which fell to the counter, knocking over a half-full coffee cup, which not only spilled its contents on the desktop, but also bounced off the padded seat cushion of the desk chair and landed on the recently waxed floors. Sally, trying to catch the cup, ended up slipping on the shiny floor and landed on her knees, hitting her head on the desktop. Fortunately for her, it was a light tap, and she started giggling. Sandy rushed over with paper towels, and the three of them cleaned up the mess a minute before Janet arrived.

"Whew, that was close!" Betty whispered between giggles as she and the other two ladies made a quick getaway down the hall to check on the patients.

From the look on Janet's face and the way she carried herself, it was evident that she had already heard the news and was not the least bit pleased. The other staff members speculated that she had heard it either directly from Mrs. Ferguson or through the hospital grapevine. Like an uncontained river, news traveled quickly in a hospital of that size. No matter—the cat was out of the bag, and there would likely be some sort of consequence

Janet plopped in the desk chair, which squeaked in protest, and felt a warm, damp sensation on her behind. She stood and looked at the wet spot on her derrière and seethed with anger. She looked around the area and, finding it vacated, growled, "Great! Just what I need to make my day even better!" After placing tissues on the chair to soak up the remaining liquid, she headed to the nurses' lounge to change into a dry pair of scrub pants.

Pulling out a dry chair and sitting at the counter, she thought, *I have a right to be good and angry!* To give the appearance of being productive while her inner self raged, she grabbed a chart off the counter and opened it. *I put in my application long before Christina Sanders, and Mrs. Ferguson knew I wanted to have that full-time position! I read that woman's résumé, and it's evident she doesn't have any hospital experience. The old witch hinted that if I didn't want to share my schedule with Christina, I could always work in the labor and delivery unit. Yuck! I hate labor and delivery! Listening to those women moan and groan and scream—I'd go crazy. Besides, I'm the most qualified for this job. How dare she give* my *job to someone else? I've practically worked my butt off for her—all those late hours, double shifts, and stacks of paperwork! It's not fair!* Like an angry child after a tantrum, she sat, crossing her arms, and scowling, daring anyone to say anything to her.

She heard the dinging of a call button, interrupting her mental rage-fest, and looked up to see Sally approaching.

"Sally, Mrs. Abernathy needs something."

Sally stopped midstride, happy to have somewhere else to go besides the nurses' station. She could tell by Janet's scowl, red face, and surliness that it would be in her best interest to avoid being in the same vicinity—the woman had that pre-erupting-volcano look about her.

CHAPTER 12

As Christina drove toward her home, she let the tears flow. *I wonder when I'll be able to think of David and not shed any tears.* Not wanting to return home yet, she decided to drive to the cemetery and spend a few quiet moments talking to her dead parents. On her way there, she passed her house and noticed the Mort's Electrical Service van still parked in front and briefly wondered why it was still there. *Shouldn't they be done by now?* She decided to have to talk with a couple of her neighbors and find out what's going on. As far as she knew, she didn't have any electrical problems. *Since I'm right by the house, I wonder if I should stop and let Benji out.* She looked at the dashboard clock. Twelve forty-five. *If I do stop, I won't have time to go to the cemetery—and I need that time with my folks.* She shook her head and continued driving. *Benji will be fine for another hour or so. After my cemetery visit, I'll stop by the house, let him out, and then take him with me to get the kids. He'll love getting the special doggy ice-cream cone from Dairy Queen.*

⁓

Her van and a red pickup truck were the only two vehicles in the vast cemetery. A couple of men were shoveling dirt onto what looked like a newly dug grave. She parked in front of her parents' gravesite and sat for a few minutes looking around at the incalculable number of tombstones and markers. Thousands of folks had lived and died, and all that remained was a marker reminding those who followed that this too would be their fate. She shuddered to think that someday she would be a faint memory in her children's and grandchildren's minds. Her own children barely remembered her mom and dad, even though she tried to keep their memory alive with stories and pictures. *One's life truly is a wisp of smoke—here today, gone tomorrow. How utterly depressing,* she thought as she sighed and exited the van.

Looking over at the men who had finished their task and were loading what looked like a dead bush onto the bed of the truck, she thought, *I'm glad they were filling in a hole instead of digging one, and I'm glad they're loading a dead tree instead of a dead body.* For some reason, she felt a little relieved. *One less death. Well, unless you count the bush.*

Sitting on the hard ground, she busied herself with pulling out any dead or dying plants around the tombstone while having a conversation, all one-sided, with her folks. After a few minutes, she was sweating profusely and needed a drink. Unwilling to leave the area, she sat in the van and enjoyed the cooling effect of the air on her skin as the sweat evaporated. Sipping from her water bottle, she briefly thought about her parents' funerals—both simple, yet well attended.

The Nichols family had lived in the Alva area for generations, and both her folks had grown up within the city limits, resulting in an overflowing attendance of friends and relatives at both funerals.

She looked at the tombstones marking her parents' graves, reminding herself again how short our lives are on this Earthly plane. Her mom had been sixty-five years old when she died from a tenacious form of colon cancer. Her dad had been sixty-eight when he had passed on three years later from what the coroner called natural causes—but Christina knew it was from a broken heart.

Sitting in the cool van, she laid her head back, closed her eyes, and let her memory take a trip back in time.

When her mom had called to inform Christina of her impending surgery for a bowel obstruction, Christina and the children had flown down to be with her during the recuperation time. It had been a shock to all involved when the surgeon informed them he had removed a cancerous section of her bowel, her reproductive organs, and one kidney. Her mom had been left with a hole in her abdomen that allowed her bowel to empty into a bag—known as a colostomy.

As Christina helplessly watched her mom go from a vibrant, full-bodied woman to a shriveled, weak bag of bones in a three-month period, she felt physically and emotionally drained. She had begged her mom to fight the cancer with chemotherapy or radiation, but the strong-willed woman would have none of it. She wanted to let nature take its course, knowing that any intervention would just delay the inevitable and would undoubtedly make her feel worse. The cancer had been aggressive and unrelenting. Toward the end of her battle, she allowed Christina to give her the pain medication and humbly accepted the embarrassing but necessary care that came with having a colostomy.

If it hadn't been for her childhood friend Cindy and a few other former high school friends who stepped in and took the kids to different activities during those long, draining days, she wasn't sure if she or they would have come through it all with their sanity intact.

When her mom passed peacefully in her sleep one Sunday morning, three months after her initial surgery, Christina was sad but also relieved to have an end to her mom's suffering.

David had taken a two-week vacation and had driven to Texas to be with his family during that difficult time. He had been such a tower of strength, stepping in and helping with funeral arrangements, organizing and explaining the paperwork to her dad, and keeping everyone occupied while she went through her mom's belongings and packed up or donated them.

The first couple of years after his wife's death, her dad had kept busy gardening, cleaning, and doing odd jobs for a few of the widowed ladies in his neighborhood, convincing everyone that he was coping well. Their visits to Texas, his visits to Michigan, and the many phone conversations in between led Christina to believe that he had adjusted well to his loss.

Christina had suggested on several occasions that he come back and live with them in Michigan, but he adamantly refused.

"How can I leave this home that your mom and I shared for so many years?" She understood and quit asking.

On the eve of her mom and dad's fiftieth wedding anniversary, he went to bed with his wife's picture clutched in his hands and didn't wake up. Delores, the home-care helper, found him the next morning and, after calling the police, called Christina with the news. Although deeply saddened, she wasn't completely surprised.

She and David had made as many arrangements via phone as they could before travelling once again to Alva to lay her daddy to rest next to her mama.

There were times, especially around holidays and birthdays, she missed her parents so much her heart ached. She had finally adjusted to their deaths and was putting it in its proper perspective when David died. Too much death in such a short time made her heart feel as if it would never mend—because the scars kept getting ripped open.

CHAPTER 13

She opened her eyes a moment and looked at her watch, took a sip of water, and allowed her mind to replay the memory of David's accident, death, and funeral.

Since his death in that dreadful car accident, the emotional side of Christina's life had been like a roller-coaster ride. Some days, she coasted along, doing her daily routines without any emotional upheavals—and then *wham,* the least little comment or memory would start the tears flowing, making it difficult, if not impossible, to function.

It had been a beautiful sunny March morning—a welcomed reprieve from the previous week's dreary, rainy, cold weather, which was typical for Michigan. When David's alarm buzzed, she rolled over and pulled the covers over her head. She didn't usually get up with David in the morning, preferring to stretch out on his side of the bed and doze until her alarm went off an hour later. She and David had an unspoken understanding that started when they brought Brad home from the hospital: she got up with the babies during the night, and he wouldn't bug her about getting up with him in the morning. She had planned to change that little habit once the kids got out of diapers, but old habits are difficult to break—especially when there isn't a real incentive.

That particular morning, however, she felt a nervous kind of energy, and her mind refused to drop back off to sleep. As David showered, she crawled out of bed, dressed, and ran downstairs to prepare him a surprise breakfast. Pouring the coffee and buttering the toast, she looked out the kitchen window and noticed hints of spring. Daffodils and crocuses were poking green heads up through the dark earth, and a flock of birds feasting at the feeder included a couple of robins, which weren't there last week. She loved witnessing the earth wake up from its long winter nap as the ground and sky seemed to come alive with critters jumping, crawling, fluttering, or buzzing to the plants poking up through the soil and bursting forth in colorful buds, flowers, or leaves. *What a glorious time to be alive!*

David had been rendered speechless when he entered the kitchen and saw a lovely breakfast set before him.

"Miracles really do happen!" he commented, pulling a chair up to the table. As they enjoyed their early morning time together, discussing work, kids, and finances, their conversation turned to plans for their garden.

"I would love a large assortment of vegetables this year," she had said as she sipped her coffee.

"What did you have in mind?"

You know, the usual stuff: carrots, green beans, squash, tomatoes, lettuce, radishes ..."

"Whoa! I only have a half acre set aside for a garden. Are we planning to feed a third world country or something?"

She shook her head. "I don't mean plant a field of each item. I just meant a few of each."

He reached over and patted her hand. Smiling, he said, "I know. I was just messin' with you. We can definitely do a little of each."

"Okay, as long as it isn't as big as last year! Geez, that was almost too much to handle."

Shaking his head, remembering all the work and time they had invested to cultivate it and then process the bounty, he added, "I know. We still have enough canned and frozen veggies to feed the state of Texas."

She rolled her eyes and thought, *Not Texas, but definitely Rhode Island.*

When they finished eating, David stood, saluted, and stated that he had to "march forth" to work. At first she didn't get the joke, and gave him a confused look.

He repeated, "March forth," nodding his head toward the calendar. She then realized that he was referring to the date, March 4. She thought that was pretty silly and giggled and shook her head.

Smiling, she said, "David, you're as nutty as peanut butter."

"Yeah, I know. Good thing you love peanut butter," he said over his shoulder as he headed upstairs to brush his teeth and shave.

As he completed his morning tasks, she put the dishes in the sink. She had just wiped the table off when he came back to the kitchen to pray with her before leaving for the day. Prayer was the strong glue that held their marriage together, and on the rare occasions they weren't able to have that special time, her day seemed to be more frazzled.

As they stood by the front door, preparing for his departure, David took her in his arms and held her close for a few moments, both of them enjoying the warmth, smell, and feel of each other. He whispered that he loved her, kissed her softly on the lips, and walked out to his car. She stood in the doorway watching as he opened the door and climbed in. Before turning the key, he waved one last time, winked, and smiled. She felt a wave of love wash over her and wished they had time for another kiss.

"Thank you, God," she whispered. "He's such a wonderful man." Waving and smiling, she watched as he backed out of the driveway and disappeared around the corner.

Heading upstairs, Christina passed by the kids' bedrooms and peeked in—each one was sleeping peacefully. She decided to wake them after she showered and dressed.

Once they were up, dressed, and fed, she drove them the three miles to the elementary and middle schools, which were conveniently located next to each other.

Walking back into the kitchen after dropping the kids off, humming a tune she had heard on the radio, and planning out her day, she jumped when she felt the buzzing in her pocket and heard the musical ring tone of her phone.

Digging it out, she answered cheerily, "Hello?"

"Mrs. Sanders?"

"Yes." Thinking it was a telemarketer, she rolled her eyes in annoyance.

"Mrs. Sanders, this is Susan Edwards from Saint John's Hospital. Is David Sanders your husband's name?"

"Yes," she answered, leaning against the counter and gripping the phone tighter, her pulse making a sudden jump and her knees weakening.

"David Bradley Sanders?"

"Yes, what's this about?"

"Mrs. Sanders, your husband has been in an accident. You need to come to the hospital."

"What?" she exclaimed. "What kind of accident? Is he all right? How bad is he hurt?" Her pulse was galloping like a runaway horse. Sitting in a nearby chair, she asked, "Which hospital did you say?"

"I can tell you this," the nurse answered calmly. "He was involved in a multivehicle collision around Eight Mile Road, and even though his injuries are extensive, he's stable right now, and I promise we'll answer any other questions when you arrive. You should get here as soon as possible, however. He's in the emergency ward in Saint John's Hospital on Seven Mile and Moross. Are you familiar with that area?"

"Uh, yeah. I've been there a couple of times."

"Okay. We'll be waiting for you ... and Mrs. Sanders?"

"Yes?"

"Please drive carefully, and be assured you husband is in good hands."

"Okay, I'll be right there." Her hands were shaking so badly that when she tried to put the phone back in her pocket, it slipped from her hand, landing with a loud crack on the tile floor. Picking it up quickly, inspecting it for any damage, and finding none, she slipped it into her jean pocket, thanking God that it wasn't broken. She couldn't imagine being phoneless at this crucial time. A feeling of fear enveloped her, and her knees buckled. She began to fervently pray: "Dear God, please let him be all right! Let me get me there quickly and safely."

Grabbing her purse and jumping in her little Tracker, she maneuvered in and out of traffic, zipping through the yellow lights, only slowing at stop signs—making the normally forty-five minute ride in thirty.

She pulled her car into a parking spot close to the door, jumped out, ran through the entrance to the nearest counter, and breathlessly inquired of her husband's whereabouts. She was immediately escorted into his room and inhaled sharply when she saw wires and tubes running in and out of every orifice and limb. He looked like some kind of freak show marionette.

"Oh, David," she whispered. "What happened to you?"

She sat by his bed and took his hand. He moaned and turned his bandaged head toward her.

His eyes fluttered open, and he whispered, "Hi. You're here."

She kissed his forehead. "Hey, baby, what happened?"

He whispered weakly, "Had an encounter with a semi. It won." Closing his eyes again, she felt his body relax and his breathing deepen as he drifted off to sleep. A few minutes later, his body jerked, and he opened his eyes, looked to the foot of the bed, and whispered what sounded like, "Not yet."

"I'm here, honey." She kissed the back of his hand lightly and felt tears trickle down her cheeks and over her lips, tasting the saltiness as they dropped onto David's hand.

He smiled and then spoke so softly she had to put her ear next to his mouth.

"Christina, I love you, and I will through eternity. Tell the kids I love them, and please remain strong in your faith."

"David, you can tell them yourself when you see them," she said through her tears, but he had already drifted back to sleep.

A doctor came into the room to check David's vital signs and adjust the medication in his IV.

"Mrs. Sanders, I'm Dr. Rosenbaum, the ER resident."

She took his extended hand, which was thick but surprisingly soft and gentle, and weakly shook it, asking him to please explain what had happened and how badly David was injured. He took her by the arm, guiding her into the hall.

Dr. Rosenbaum was a short, stout man with thinning gray hair. He wore a pair of thick-lensed glasses, which reminded her of David's safety glasses he wore to keep sawdust out of his eyes. Seeing her eyes fill with tears and the worry etched on her face, he sighed as he felt compassion fill his heart. Speaking softly, he told the story.

"According to an eyewitness, David had stopped at the intersection at Eight Mile and Gratiot and started to turn south, when a semi, which had lost power to its brakes and couldn't stop, hit the driver's side of his car."

He looked down the hallway, nodded at a nurse who was pointing to her watch, and then returned his gaze to Christina. She was holding one hand over her heart as if to protect it from a sharp dagger, and the other was over her mouth as if to keep a scream from escaping.

He continued, "There were other cars involved, as the drivers, trying to avoid the accident, slammed on their brakes, causing a chain reaction. A few of the other drivers were injured, but David was the one that took the full impact." He paused and sighed. "His injuries were very extensive, and it didn't help that it took them nearly an hour before they could cut him out of the tangled mess and get him here."

Tears trickled down her face as she listened and pictured the accident in her mind.

He finished by saying, "These first twenty-four hours will be the toughest. If he makes it through, he'll have a fighting chance."

Christina nodded, wiped the tears from her eyes and face, thanked him, and returned to David's room.

Dr. Rosenbaum watched her go in and then turned and walked back down the hall toward the nurses' station. He sighed, knowing it would take a miracle for David to pull through, having been nearly pulverized. In his twenty-five years as an ER resident, he had witnessed plenty of miracles, proving to him there had to be a higher power at work. "I sure hope this higher power smiles down on you, David," he whispered as he continued down the hallway.

Christina sat by David's bed, vaguely aware of the heart monitor's beeping, and watched the IV drip, drip, drip its life-sustaining fluid into David's arm. Imagining how the accident occurred, playing the tape over and over in her mind, she was vaguely aware of a nurse coming in to change the catheter and IV bags.

When her mind returned to the present, she realized a few phone calls needed to be made. Standing and stretching, she looked down at David's battered and broken body. His relaxed face and body looked peaceful as he slept, oblivious to the pain and his surroundings—making her thankful for strong sedatives.

As an RN, she knew the road to recovery would be a long, painful, and difficult one. Placing her hand over his heart, she said a prayer, and then, leaning over the railing, she kissed him on his right cheek—the only part of his face not swathed in bandages.

Whispering, she said, "I'll be back in a few minutes. I love you."

Knowing she couldn't use her cell phone in the hospital, she looked for the nearest exit sign, which was down the hall and around the corner. She stepped outside. The first called was to the church to put David's name on the prayer chain and ask for the pastor to come by. Then she called her friend Linda and asked her to get the kids from school. Feeling emotionally and physically drained, she decided to get a cup of coffee and a snack before heading back to David's room. As she turned the corner near his room, she heard "Code Blue in ER 101!"

It took her a second to realize that was David's room number. She dropped her coffee in a garbage container, ran the rest of the way to his room, and was quickly blocked and pushed aside as nurses and doctors ran in with a crash cart. She stood in the doorway and watched in misery as they busily worked on her husband's limp body.

"Please God, please God, please God, don't let him die!" she repeated over and over like a mantra. Time seemed to have slowed down and everyone seemed to move in slow motion as she watched and listened, hearing bits and pieces of the doctor's orders.

"Two hundred amps. Clear!" She jumped as she watched David's body jump.

"Three hundred amps. Clear!" Again, David's body jerked. She didn't realize how hard she was biting her knuckle until she tasted blood. Glancing over at the heart monitor, she was encouraged as the wavy lines were replaced with normal cardiac patterns.

Dr. Rosenbaum put on a sterile gown and gloves as he entered the room and asked, "Vitals?"

The nurse standing next to the bed holding David's wrist and looking at the monitor said, "His pulse is 150 and weak, and his blood pressure is eighty over thirty. His oxygen level is at 85 percent."

Dr. Rosenbaum lifted David's eyelids and shone a light into them, checking for a reaction, and then donned his stethoscope and listened to his heart and lungs.

"I want blood gases and a complete blood workup. Is he bleeding anywhere?" The nurses rolled David up on his side to check for any blood underneath. There was none.

He leaned over and spoke into David's ear. "Come on, David! Don't you give up now!" Seeing no reaction from his patient, he shook his head and said, "He must be bleeding internally. Bring me a syringe. I want to check his abdominal cavity for blood."

A nurse handed him a large syringe with a long needle. The doctor pierced David's abdomen and withdrew a syringe full of bright-red blood.

"Dang it!" he murmured. "Hang another unit of packed cells and call the OR. We need to open him up stat!" One nurse took the syringe from him as another was on the phone to the operating room. Dr. Rosenbaum and the emergency team stood in silence as they watched the monitor, waiting for word from the OR and staff. An eternity seemed to pass, but in reality it was only a few seconds. The occasional blips of heart rhythms were replaced by a wavy line, which quickly became flat, setting off the insistent whine of the alarm until someone reached over and turned it off.

Dr. Rosenbaum started shouting orders again, and once more, everyone went into action to save the dying man before them.

It was then that he looked up and saw Christina standing in the doorway. He asked the nearest nurse to take Christina out into the hall.

"Honey, I know you want to be close, but it'll be best if you just stay out here until we get him stabilized."

"Okay," mumbled Christina. "Let me know when they take him up to surgery?"

"Sure, Honey. I'll keep you posted."

"Thanks."

From that point on, Christina blocked out the commotion around her and concentrated on praying, vaguely aware of Pastor Jim's presence. After a few moments, he gently took her arm and guided her to a chair in the waiting room. They sat quietly, each in their own thoughts and silent prayers to an omnipotent God who would either choose to spare David's life or take it. With her head bowed, she felt an odd tingling sensation flow through her and knew that David had passed on. She looked up and over to Pastor Jim, and with an anguished look on her face, she whispered, "Oh, no, David's gone." He stood and walked over to her chair and knelt, asking, "What makes you think that?"

"I just had the oddest feeling, like something … passed through me."

Tears streamed down her face as she recounted the morning her mother died.

"I had been sleeping, and I felt something warm on my cheek. I thought at first it was my dad trying to wake me up, but when I opened my eyes, the room was empty, and I felt all warm and tingly. It was like she came into my bedroom and kissed me good-bye. When I went downstairs to check on my mom, she was gone. I felt that same sensation a few minutes ago." She looked around the room as if expecting to see David's ghost.

He cocked his head and gave her a look that said he didn't fully comprehend. Needing to check on David's status, she stood and turned just as Dr. Rosenbaum came in to tell them that David had indeed passed on.

"I'm so sorry, Mrs. Sanders. We did everything we possibly could. The injuries were just too extensive."

She gave Pastor Jim a look that said, "See? I told you he was gone." He nodded like he understood, which of course he didn't. He had heard and read of such things but had never personally experienced such an event. *Can the dead reach out and touch us?*

Expecting Christina to break down and cry or get hysterical, both men were surprised when she did neither. She calmly asked if she could see David. Dr. Rosenbaum motioned for an RN to come and take Christina into the room. Closing the door quietly, she gave the grieving woman privacy with her husband.

Christina went to the bedside and took David's hand, which was surprisingly warm. *I figured it'd be cold by now,* she thought as she surveyed the still body of her beloved. Except for the bandages, casts, IV lines, and complete stillness, he looked as if he were merely sleeping and would wake and give her one of his million-dollar smiles. It was difficult to comprehend that the person before her was the same one who had hugged, kissed, and winked at her just a few hours ago.

She felt a sob work its way up from her chest and let the tears flow as she crawled on the bed beside him and laid her head on his chest. She traced his lips with her finger. She would never see that beautiful smile again or feel his gentle kiss. She touched his closed eyes gently. She would never gaze into those amazingly blue eyes and see that special wink meant only for her. She would never feel his soft, gentle caress or hear his funny jokes. She would never hear his reassuring breaths in the night or feel his heart beating under her fingertips.

She wept tears of deepest sorrow as the reality of her loss sunk in, the bed shaking with her sobs. She felt as if something in her had shattered and realized she would never be the same—as if a piece of her soul had died with David.

Sometime later, the RN came in and whispered that she needed to take care of the body and clean the room. Christina nodded, gave David one more kiss, and whispered, "I'll see you again someday, my love."

CHAPTER 14

The day she said her final good-bye to her soul mate, the sky had been amazingly blue and absent of clouds, and the air was comfortably cool—a perfect day for a funeral.

David had always expressed his desire to be buried on such a day and often said, "A funeral is sad enough without rain or cold weather adding more gloom to it." She was thankful that God had honored his desire.

The church had been full and overflowing into the foyer, with people of every age and race, many whom she had never seen or met before.

"At least seven hundred people," someone had said.

There were so many flowers. The sweet smell wafted out of the building like an invisible aromatic fog. She hadn't realized how many lives David had touched until she looked around the crowded church.

Nicky and Stacey sat on her right side with Brad on her left. Holding hands, they listened intently as the pastor conducted the service, telling of David's faithfulness and love for his family and God's creation. He finished the elegy by quoting David's favorite verses from Proverbs: "Trust in the Lord with all your heart and lean not on your own understanding. In all your ways acknowledge Him and He will make your paths straight."

Many people went to the podium and gave sweet and thought provoking testimonies of how David had impacted their lives, but when David's older brother, Robert, told of some of their childhood shenanigans, the audience couldn't help but laugh.

David had wanted his funeral to be not a sad occasion, but one full of hope and celebration, and she was thankful his brother had honored that wish with his wonderful sense of humor and story-telling ability.

When the praise and worship team sang "Finally Home," there wasn't a dry eye in the building. When they came to the chorus and sang, "But just think of stepping on shore and finding it heaven! Of touching a hand and finding it God's! Of breathing new air, and finding it celestial! Of waking up in glory, and finding it home!" People stood and started clapping and cheering. Even though she was sobbing, she couldn't help but smile and picture David waving at her from that distant shore.

The pastor closed the service by saying, "Even though we have lost a beloved brother on this earthly plane, if you know Jesus as your Savior, you will see David again in heaven."

Wiping her eyes and looking up toward the casket, she was shocked to see David smiling and waving at her. She blinked, thinking she was imagining things, but when she glanced at her children and saw the grins on their faces, she realized they could see him as well. She smiled and lifted her hand to wave, but in a blink, he was gone.

Whispering, she said, "He's okay, and we're gonna be okay."

At the gravesite, her knees felt weak and her whole body trembled as she watched the casket being lowered into the ground. The pastor concluded the internment ceremony by saying, "David Bradley Sanders will be gone forever from this world, but not from the minds and hearts of those who loved him."

After the funeral, family and friends met back at the house for food and comforting fellowship. The children tried to be sociable, but after eating, they excused themselves and escaped to their own rooms to silently grieve.

CHAPTER 15

David

When David regained consciousness in the ambulance after the near-death encounter with a semi, he saw what appeared to be an angel standing at his feet and assumed it was there to take him to heaven. He was sure he wouldn't make it to the hospital or see Christina and his children again. When he woke in the hospital and saw her standing by his bed, he was surprised and pleased. Looking past her toward the foot of the bed, he could see the angel that had appeared to him in the ambulance. It was a beautiful transparent creature that seemed to glow from within its human male form. David watched in wonder as the medical staff, completely unaware of his presence, passed right through him. The angel smiled and spoke to him telepathically, never moving his lips.

"Hello, David, my name is Jarrod. I am your assigned companion." He assured David that he would be seeing Jesus soon and that everything would be all right here on earth. David felt a warm peace enfold him and was vaguely aware of the pain, monitors, and tubes running from his body. His spirit was willing to go with his assigned companion, but looking over at Christina, his earthly flesh felt sad and heavy. He didn't want to leave *her*. Tears trickled down his face. Christina looked so worried.

Seeing the tears, she grabbed a few tissues and wiped them away. Leaning down and kissing his face, she asked if he hurt or needed any medication.

He whispered, "No, I'm just glad to see you."

She took his hand and held it gently at her heart. After telling her he loved her and the kids, he closed his eyes and drifted off to sleep but woke when Christina left the room.

Jarrod watched her depart, and then turned to David and said, "It's time." David rose from the bed and joined his companion, causing the alarms to sound. The human and the angelic being watched as the medical staff tried to revive the limp body. As he took one last look at his earthly vessel, he was surprised that he had no desire to return to it. He and Jarrod walked out to the waiting room, where Christina and Pastor Jim waited. David gave his wife a kiss on the cheek, and then the two spiritual beings left the hospital.

Asking if he could see his kids one last time, he was pleased when and the angel took him to his home in what seemed like a split second.

David saw several of his friends gathered in the kitchen and dining room and floated through them to where his children sat in the den on a sofa, pretending to watch a program on the television. He kissed each one on the cheek, and smiled as each one reacted differently. Brad absently rubbed the area thinking a fly had landed on it. Stacey waved her hand in front of her face, batting at an unknown annoyance. Nicky looked right at David and whispered, "Dad?" David jumped back. Realizing no one was there, and thinking it was his imagination, Nicky sadly turned his attention back to the television.

"It's all right," assured the angel, placing his hand on David's shoulder. "Children are usually more sensitive to the spiritual realm. It's not unusual for them to engage in conversations with us. Seems the older they get, the less they can see or hear us."

"Did he really see me?" David asked as he watched his children.

Observing the Sanders children, Jarrod answered, "No. He just sensed your presence."

"Will they be all right?" As soon as the question left his mouth, his spiritual eyes were opened, and he saw three celestial beings, one standing behind each child. They looked at David and smiled. He nodded a greeting and smiled back.

"Come, David. We must go now. There is a great party awaiting your arrival, and we don't want to keep our host waiting."

In an instant, David was traveling through a dark tunnel toward a brilliant light. *So this is the dark tunnel and bright light people have talked about over the ages. Cool.*

CHAPTER 16

David had been allowed to attend his own funeral, which had pleased and surprised him.

"Humans can attend *any* funeral, even their own, if they so desire."

They stood by the casket, invisible to the family and friends who paid their last respects. David hadn't realized he knew so many people.

Jarrod explained that all through our lives, God brings people in and out—kind of like weaving a basket. "You may see them just every once in a while, but there is a connection that will last forever. You have touched many lives, David. Many of these folks wouldn't be here if you hadn't intervened."

Confused, David asked, "Who? Why?"

"You see that man over there? Mr. Hanson?" Jarrod pointed to a middle-aged man who was blowing his nose into a handkerchief.

David nodded.

"Remember about five years ago, his company laid him off, and his wife was planning to leave him and take their two kids if he didn't find a job right away?"

David nodded again.

"He was making plans to kill himself."

David gave him a shocked look.

"I was the one that whispered his name in your ear, and you felt inclined to call him. After talking and praying with him, you went and talked to your boss, who hired him the next week." David smiled and nodded.

Jarrod continued, "He is making more money now than he did before, and he and his wife have reconciled and will be celebrating the birth of their first grandchild in a few months."

David remembered the time and incident but hadn't thought it was that important.

"There are many more stories like that one, David, but I'm not going to tell you now. Someday soon, it will all be crystal clear to you."

David was touched by his wife and his children's sorrow as he watched them cry.

"I wish I could touch them. Or at least tell them I'm okay."

Jarrod bowed his head and then raised his hand and pointed at Christina and the children.

"David, wave at then. They can see you."

David waved and smiled at his wife and children, wondering if it was truly possible to cross the supernatural boundary. Even though the revelation lasted a few seconds, David was thankful that the boundary was indeed crossable. He could see that Christina and the kids had been comforted by his appearance.

"Will I be able to see them again?"

Jarrod smiled. "Yes. I'm sure there will be many more occasions for you to visit them."

"Will they be able to see me?"

"Only if the Father allows it. All things are possible through Him."

CHAPTER 17

Christina looked at her watch. Three o'clock. The trip down memory lane had taken longer than she expected. It was time to get the kids from school and take them to Dairy Queen as she had promised. She dug her cell phone out of her purse and dialed Denise, Danny's mom.

As she pulled the van in front of the elementary school, Danny and Nicky came running up.

"Can he come?" Nicky asked as he opened the van door.

"Yep. Hop in."

"Are we gonna go pick up Stacey and Brad?"

Pulling into traffic, she said, "We'll pick up Stacey and then swing by the high school and see if Brad wants to go with us."

A car horn blared.

"Sorry!" She mouthed as the driver passed by.

Pulling the van in front of the middle school building, she saw a large group of kids milling about, but she didn't see Stacey.

"Hey, guys, do you see Stacey?"

"Isn't that her over by the steps?" Danny asked, pointing to a group of girls.

"Yep, I think so," she said as she drove the van slowly to the west side of the building.

"Who's that dark-haired girl with her?" Nicky asked, pointing to the girl walking next to Stacey.

Christina smiled and answered, "That must be her new friend Linda."

"She's pretty," Nicky said matter-of-factly.

She glanced in the rear view mirror and saw the two boys giggling and poking each other in the ribs. As Stacey and the dark-haired girl approached the van, Christina lowered the window.

Pointing to her friend, Stacey said, "Hi, Mom. This is Linda."

Linda was a beautiful child with long, straight, thick black hair that glistened in the sunshine and cascaded over her thin shoulders and down her back. She had a delicate, heart-shaped face with a cute little button nose right in the center, and her brown eyes were so dark, the pupils could barely be distinguished. They were framed by long, black eyelashes that would make any female jealous, and her full lips—they were perfect as well. Yep, she was definitely a beauty.

"Hi, Linda. Did you get to ask your mom if you can come with us?"

Shrugging, she said, "My mom said I can't today. Maybe some other day, though. Thanks for asking me."

Christina smiled and nodded. "Okay. Can I at least drive you home?"

"No, that's okay. I only live a block over."

Stacey gave her a quick hug and said good-bye as she entered the van.

Pulling out in traffic once more, Christina said, "I guess we'll go by and ask Brad if he would like to come with us." Glancing over at Stacey, she said, "I like your friend. She seems like a very sweet girl."

Stacey smiled. "Yeah, she's really nice. She gets teased about being so shy, though." She paused and made a face. "Some of the girls can be so mean."

"Oh, I'm sorry to hear that."

Christina understood how cruel kids could be, and how words could hurt. She endured a great deal of teasing in middle school because of her freckles.

Reaching over and patting Stacey on the leg, she said, "I'm glad you've chosen to be her friend." She pulled into the high school parking lot. Noticing the many groups of students, she added, "Now, let's see if we can find Brad."

Looking out the window, Stacey said, "I just saw him a few minutes ago with Melinda. I called out to him, and he just waved and kept walking." She added with a smirk, "I don't think he would be interested in going with us."

"Ooh, Brad's got a girlfriend!" Danny said in a singsong voice, joined by Nicky.

In her firmer mama voice, Christina said, "All right, you two, enough!"

With a smile and a wink, she looked at Stacey, who shook her head and rolled her eyes.

Sure enough, Brad declined the invitation to Dairy Queen, stating he was planning to walk Melinda home and would see them all later.

Before walking away, he called out, "Hey, Mom, could you bring me a chocolate shake?"

Smiling and nodding, she answered, "Sure, anything else?"

"Nope. Thanks, Mom."

She watched as he walked over to Melinda, took her books, and turned to wave at them. That was her cue to leave.

That evening as they were preparing dinner, Christina told her children about the job acceptance. They all cheered and did high fives. Brad asked about her schedule.

"Well, I thought I'd know by now, but I guess I'll find out for sure on Monday when I go in for orientation."

Setting the napkins and cups on the table, Nicky asked, "Orientation? What's that?"

"Mrs. Ferguson, the lady who interviewed me, will take me on a tour of the hospital and to the cardiac unit, where I'll meet the staff that I'll be working with. She'll also explain the hospital rules and make sure I understand everything my job will require."

"Oh, okay," he said as he nodded his head in understanding.

"I hope I can work the seven-to-three shift, but it all depends on another nurse and what she plans to do. I'm low man on the totem pole, so I'll get whatever is left over. I may have to work some weekends too." Sighing, she added, "So … it may be a little crazy around here until I get used to working again."

They all seemed satisfied with that bit of information. After the dinner dishes were done and everyone went to finish homework or watch TV, Christina made a call to her friend Cindy.

CHAPTER 18

Brad

As Brad sat on his bed trying to focus on his English assignment, he thought about the past two years, where they had been, and where they were now. It had been quite an emotional roller-coaster ride for them all, especially his mom. She had been through so much, and yet here she was, happy and going back to work. *I'm not sure how I feel about that. I'm not sure she'll be strong enough physically and emotionally to handle the stress of work and home. I'll have to keep an eye on her. I definitely don't want her to go back into that deep, dark depression she fell into after Dad died.*

He remembered being so scared, thinking he was going to lose her too, and was thankful his aunt Linda came to the rescue and brought his mom back from the brink of death.

Aunt Linda. She wasn't really his aunt, in the genetic sense, but she was the closest thing to one that he'd had since he had been old enough to talk. She and his mom had been like sisters, sharing in all the ups and downs of raising kids and living life. Of all the people he missed in Michigan, she and her family were at the top of the list.

He could hardly believe it had been two years since his dad's death. Sometimes he felt like he was living someone else's life, and at times he wished that were true: His dad would still be alive, and they would all still be in Michigan. Not that he hated living in Texas—he just preferred the familiarity of Michigan and all the good memories and friends he had left there.

Thinking about the homecoming game coming up in October, he wished his dad could be there to watch him play. His dad had played football and soccer in high school and had been an avid fan of both sports. The trophies his dad had won were now shelved alongside his own trophies he had earned over the years.

Brad felt an ache in his heart and tears sting his eyes. Sometimes he just wanted to pitch a full-blown hissy fit and rant and rave against the unfairness of it all, but he knew it would do no good. His dad would still be gone, and he would still be in Texas, and life would *still* go on for the Sanders family. Being the oldest male in the family, he felt a strong need to protect them and secretly vowed to do whatever it took to do just that.

He took a deep breath, and letting it out slowly, wiping his eyes, and straightening his shoulders, he refocused on the book in front of him.

CHAPTER 19

Saturday morning, Christina received a call from Mrs. Ferguson informing her that she had talked to the other two nurses. One of them, Janet Washburn, would be helping her learn the procedures and routines of the new job.

"Christina, will you be able to work all five days next week to familiarize yourself with everything? Because after that you'll be on your own."

"Yes, barring any unforeseen complications, I can be there every day. Will it be from seven to three?"

"Yes. The first half hour this week, you'll be meeting with Dr. Dawson and me to go over patients' histories and charts. The next week, however, you'll meet with the nurses that first half hour to go over the previous night's notes."

"Oh, okay."

"And Christina, would you be okay with working on Mondays, Wednesdays, and Fridays? You can have the weekends off, except in the case of an emergency when you might have to fill in."

Christina agreed with the terms and, after disconnecting, thought once again, *What am I getting myself into?*

She shared the information with the kids, who were more excited than she would have imagined.

After breakfast, they all piled into the van and went to the outlet mall to look for another set or two of scrubs and supportive tennis shoes that she knew she'd need.

The kids, who were allowed to bring a friend along, were excited about checking out the stores. Nicky brought Danny, Brad brought his friend Eric, and because Linda wasn't able to come, Stacey invited another girlfriend named Carmen. Knowing they would keep an eye on each other, Christina wasn't as nervous about leaving them on their own as she went in and out of the different stores trying on uniforms and shoes.

The area along the highway was quite different from when she had lived there as a child, and sometimes she had to remind herself where she was. Never in a million years would she have pictured an outlet mall in Alva—Dallas, Ft. Worth, Waco, for sure, but not Alva. There were over eighty-five stores and a dozen or more eating establishments within the two-mile radius—which just boggled her mind.

Because of its proximity to the junction of I-35 East, which came from Dallas, and I-35 West, which came from Fort Worth, Alva was the chosen site for the mall. It was also a convenient stopping place for fuel, food, and facilities before heading down to Waco, Austin, San Antonio, and other towns along the I-35 corridor.

She and the kids had spent several hours browsing through the many clothing and shoe stores. At the end of the day, each member of the Sanders family had something new to add to their wardrobe.

Christina found scrubs and shoes in a place called Uniforms R Us, a small store tucked in between Metal Works and Leather Goods. She had chosen pastel blue and aqua-green tunics and matching pants with extra large pockets in the front for her notebook and pen, which would undoubtedly be her constant companions in the training days to come. The shoes, more expensive than she had hoped, were white with extra arch support, which gave the impression of walking on air.

During lunch at one of the diners, Christina listened and asked questions to better acquaint herself with her children's friends.

By doing so, she learned that Carmen was from a family of six. She had two older sisters and a younger brother in third grade. Her dad, George, was a mechanic at the local Chevrolet dealership, and her mom, Ruby, stayed home and wrote articles for the local newspaper.

"What's your sister planning to major in at A&M?" Christina asked after taking a sip from her Dr Pepper.

"Well, besides being a stripper to earn her tuition, she wants to be a vet 'cause she loves animals."

The shocked look on Christina's face was priceless. *A stripper?* Carmen and the other kids burst out laughing.

"Let me explain. When my parents called to ask how her classes were going that first semester, she told them that she decided to take classes on how to become a professional stripper and was working at the local strip club to earn a little extra cash. My sisters and brother and I laughed so hard as we watched our parents' reaction. We knew she was joking, but she was so convincing that they almost had a coronary and threatened to come and get her and make her switch to the local college. She let them believe this little lie for a few hours before calling them back and telling them the truth. They almost didn't believe her. All us kids had to swear that she was kidding."

Still laughing, Stacey said, "Oh my gosh! That's hilarious!"

Christina giggled and looked at each of her children as she pointed a finger and said, "Don't you even think about pulling something like that on me. I probably *would* have a coronary!"

They responded by smiling and shaking their heads and saying, "Never."

Once the giggling stopped, Christina asked, "How about your other sister, Maria? What does she want to do when she graduates?"

"I don't know," she answered as she scrunched up her face. "She says she just wants to get married and have babies."

"I see," answered Christina, nodding. "Well, that can be an honorable profession. There aren't many women wanting to do that anymore."

"Yeah. That's what my mom says. She also tells Maria that she has to go to college at least two years to get some kind of degree, 'cause she might have to support herself someday."

Christina sighed and nodded. "Yeah, that's good advice. I don't think *any* kind of education is ever wasted." Carmen nodded and took a sip of her soda.

"How about you, Carmen? What do you want to be when you grow up?"

"I'd like to do something in the medical field—maybe a nurse or doctor or something. I'm not sure yet."

Christina nodded. "Well, I'm partial to the nursing field, and I know there's a need for good nurses."

Carmen nodded and munched on a fry.

Christina directed her attention to Eric.

"So Eric, what do you want to do with your life when you graduate?"

He cleared his throat before answering. "I'd like to go into sports medicine. I plan to go to Texas A&M too."

Danny interjected, "I want to be a fireman when I grow up!"

"Me too—or maybe a policeman," added Nicky.

Smiling, Christina said, "That's great! Those are two honorable professions."

Popping another fry in her mouth, Carmen asked, "Brad and Stacey, what do you want to do when you grow up?"

Brad answered first, "I plan to get into some kind of computer engineering field—maybe work for the government or some company like my dad did." Carmen nodded, took a bite of her sandwich, and then looked at Stacey.

"I want to get into fashion design or acting so I can make lots of money and help the poor people."

Christina smiled and nodded. Even though she'd heard some of those desires before, she wanted to continue encouraging them.

"Wow, sounds like you all have some pretty big goals. Good for you! Just remember when you're fussing about taking tests and homework, it's all for a good cause."

Nicky and Danny made faces. Danny stated emphatically, "I hate homework and tests!"

Reaching over and tousling Danny's hair, Eric said, "Unfortunately, that's part of life—and the foundation for a good education and a good job in the future," *Wise words from one so young,* thought Christina. While discussing the children's futures, someone else was mulling over plans for Christina's future.

As they gathered the refuse, the kids joined forces and begged her to take them to a movie.

"So no more shopping?"

In unison, they answered, "No way!"

Being the good and somewhat gullible mom, she took them to see an action-packed thriller featuring an actor who was famous for doing all his own stunts. In a day of stunt doubles and computer graphics, this man was unique in his seeming ability to defy gravity and fly through the air unassisted like a bird. She had marveled at his daring and reckless abandon and wished she could tap into those resources.

CHAPTER 20

Even though her days and evenings had been full of activities, Christina's spirit felt restless and empty. There was a void in her heart, as if the universe had opened up and swallowed a part of her. Something was missing, but she couldn't identify it. It wasn't just the empty spot in her heart that David had occupied; there was a longing for something more.

When Stacey asked about going to church the next morning, Christina, lost in her own thoughts, was caught off guard by her daughter's question.

"What? What did you say?"

"Church. Are we going tomorrow? We haven't gone since we've been here, and I was wondering if maybe we could go. Carmen and her family go to the First Baptist Church, and she asked me to come tomorrow. Isn't that the church you used to go to?"

"That's it!" Christina exclaimed. "That's what's missing!" She hit her hand on the steering wheel.

Looking totally perplexed, Stacey asked, "What are you talking about, Mom?"

"Well, I've had this kind of empty feeling inside, like something wasn't quite right, but I couldn't put my finger on it." She slapped her palm on her forehead.

Turning the van into the driveway and pulling into the garage, she said, "I can't believe it's taken this long for me to figure it out."

Frowning, Stacey reached over and patted her mom on the arm.

"It's okay, Mom. You've been busy unpacking." She looked back at her brothers as if to say, "Help me out here, guys." She wasn't totally sure what her mom was talking about or why she was acting so weird.

Brad reached up from his seat directly behind his mom and patted her on the shoulder, not understanding her sudden outburst any more than Stacey.

Sitting behind the steering wheel, Christina continued to mull over the idea of attending her childhood church. It wasn't as if she hadn't *thought* about going to church since moving in a couple months ago. When Saturday would roll around, she *thought* about getting up for Sunday services but just couldn't get motivated. There were boxes to unpack and things to sort through. *Lame excuses.* Chewing on her bottom lip, she mulled over the real reason she didn't want to attend *that* church.

Turning off the ignition, she turned in her seat to face the kids.

"I guess I miss our church up north. I enjoyed the praise and worship and the pastor and all our friends. They were like family." Shrugging, she continued, "I don't think I'd feel that here, but then again, I haven't been to *that* church since my mom and dad passed on. For all I know, it could be different. Anything is possible."

The kids nodded in agreement.

"I do kinda miss going to Sunday school," stated Nicky as he undid his seat belt. "My teacher, Mr. Rogers, always made it fun at our old church. I wonder if the teacher here will be as fun as Mr. Rogers."

Brad added, "I wonder if they have a big youth group." Looking at his sister, he asked, "Remember how huge the one was at our other church?"

Stacey nodded, "Yeah, about a hundred kids! I wonder how many of the kids from school go here."

Christina interjected, "Well, I'd think quite a few. Alva isn't that big. You said your friend Carmen and her family attend the First Baptist Church?"

Stacey nodded.

"And what about Linda?"

"She says they go to church in some barn out in the country."

Removing the keys from the ignition and unfastening her seat belt, Christina said, "Well, we won't know if we'll like it if we don't get involved."

Nicky was already out the door.

She looked at Brad and Stacey, who were exiting the van, and said, "Hey, let's plan to get up and go tomorrow. We can check it all out then. Okay?"

They looked at her and smiled.

"Sure, Mom." Stacey answered.

Brad nodded in agreement, and then they both raced to the back door, joining their brother, who was struggling to keep their very excited beagle from knocking down his young master.

She remained in her seat for a few more minutes, thinking. *Well, if we don't like it, we can always go somewhere else. There are a lot of different churches to choose from. We don't have to go back to the First Baptist Church. Just because I grew up there doesn't automatically make it mandatory that I return. Does it?* She felt a twinge of guilt.

Mom and Dad will probably turn in their graves if I don't go back to their church, she thought as she gathered her things and joined her kids.

As Christina fell exhausted into bed that night, she thanked God for such a great day and quickly drifted into a deep sleep.

I'm running. From what? Don't know. Something big and black. Dog? No, it has wings. Monster! Run! Hide! Quick, over the fence. Into the building. Hide in the cabinet. Heart racing. Can hear it approaching. Hear it breathing. Smells foul. Quiet! No sound. Is it gone? No. Can still feel its presence. It's waiting. "God help me!" I scream over and over.

Waking, she throws her covers off and sits up. Sweat trickles down over her closed eyes. She reaches up with a shaky hand to wipe it off. Putting a hand over her heart, she feels it pounding and realizes her gown is drenched.

"Am I awake or still asleep?" she asked. Taking deep breaths and calming herself, she woke up fully. "Whew!" She blew out air and then reached over to turn on the bedside light. "Ow! Too bright!" She turned it off, and her eyes adjusted to the dim glow of the night-light. *Geez, I gotta pee!* Her hands were trembling, and her legs felt weak. She steadied herself, took care of business, and then crawled back into bed. It took a long time to fall back to sleep. No more monsters. Or so she thought.

CHAPTER 21

David, Jarrod, and *her* guardian angel, Michael, stood by Christina's bed and watched as she wrestled with the demon in her dream. As soon as she called out to God, Michael grabbed it by the neck and threw it back to hell—thus ending the nightmare.

David looked at Jarrod and asked, "Why are Christina and the kids having to wrestle with demons in their dreams?"

"Sometimes the Enemy of man finds it more effective to attack believers when they are most vulnerable."

"Why did Michael wait so long to get rid of it?"

Jarrod shrugged. "We are not allowed to interfere in a person's life until they call on our Father or Jesus, who then gives us permission to act."

"Hmm," replied David as he shook his head. "I sure have a lot to learn about this spiritual realm."

Jarrod nodded. "You do indeed, my friend." He touched David's shoulder, and they were instantly transported back to heaven.

CHAPTER 22

Dr. Steven Dawson sat across the desk from Emma Ferguson on Saturday morning before heading upstairs to check on his patients. They were drinking coffee as they caught up on hospital and family business.

Steven was Emma's only nephew, and even though they worked side by side and disagreed frequently, they had a deep love and respect for each other.

Draining the last drop of cold coffee from her cup, she asked, "Steven, do you know a Christina Sanders?"

He frowned and shook his head. "No, should I?"

"How about Christy Nichols? Does that ring a bell?" She knew it should because of their history together.

He thought for a moment and then smiled. "Oh yeah, I went to high school with a girl named Christy Nichols. She was a year younger than me." He paused and then grinned and said, "She had a *major* crush on me."

Emma rolled her eyes and smiled. "Yeah, I remember."

Her children had kept her apprised of all the drama that occurred at school, *especially* any dealing with their cousin. Steven's sister and Emma's daughter were best friends, and goodness, those girls could talk. Emma learned more than she ever needed to know about those kids in high school.

He leaned back in his chair and thought for a moment before saying, "Didn't she marry some guy from Minnesota or Wisconsin or someplace up north? Why are you asking?"

"She lived in Michigan, but she moved back here in July. I've just hired her as a part-time nurse on the Cardiac Care Unit for the morning shift."

He raised his eyebrows. "Really? I didn't know she was back in town. Why didn't you tell me before now?"

"I didn't mention it before now because I didn't make the connection between Christina Sanders and Christy Nichols until right before I interviewed her."

He nodded and said, "Hmm. Why did she move back *here?*"

"Her husband died in a car accident a couple of years ago, and since her parents' house never sold, she decided to move back home."

"Oh, I didn't know that," he said, placing his coffee cup on her desk. Sitting back in his chair, he asked, "Didn't she have a couple of kids? I remember one summer a few years ago, she brought her little guy into the emergency room with a gash on his forehead—seems he had a run-in with the coffee table."

Emma smiled and nodded.

Looking at the paper before her, she answered, "Yes, she has three. According to her résumé they are ten, twelve, and sixteen."

"Wow, that old, huh?" He sighed as he processed the idea that over twenty years had passed since he had attended high school, and most of his former classmates were married and had children—a few had grandchildren.

Maybe if I'd worked harder at my first marriage, or maybe if I'd tried harder at maintaining my previous relationships, I'd have a family too. Maybe there's still hope—I'm only forty. His thoughts trailed off, ending with the conclusion *Maybe I'm just not good marriage material.*

Bringing his mind back to the present, he said, "Bummer. Poor kids." He retrieved his cup, took another sip of coffee, and then added, "Poor Christy. Must be tough trying to raise three kids without a husband."

Emma nodded in agreement.

He shook his head and frowned, trying to imagine working and raising three children alone, and realized he didn't have a clue as to how women and some men managed it. The whole concept of marriage and children was as foreign to him as the concept of understanding the female population.

"Yep," she replied, quietly remembering her sadness at losing her own husband.

He said thoughtfully, "I'm surprised she would move back after being gone for so long. It's not as if she has family to come home to. Why would anyone *want* to move back to Alva? There's certainly not a lot to offer around here."

Emma gave him a look that questioned his sanity. "*You* moved back here."

He sighed and nodded. "Yeah, well, I have family here."

She smiled and nodded then reached across the desk and patted his hand. "And quite a wonderful one if I do say so!"

Steven's sensitive spirit and generous heart were two qualities that Emma admired in her nephew. He loved and cared for his parents, who were in their mid-seventies, and in his spare time, volunteered his services at various events around Alva. She knew he would do his best to help Christina feel at home and do well in her job. *Why wouldn't he? And if he doesn't, I'll tell his mama, and she'll kick his butt!*

She looked at her nephew and noticed the graying hair at his temples. *When did that happen?* Life was passing too quickly. Steven had just turned forty, and if he wasn't careful, he would end up a lonely old man. She didn't want that kind of life for him. *He's a great man who deserves a great wife and great kids. Right, God?*

They were sitting in silence for a moment when he said thoughtfully, "Christy was a nice girl. Not my type, though."

Smirking, Emma said, "So I've heard."

Steven raised his eyebrows. "And what exactly have you heard?"

Smiling and waving her hand as if shooing a fly, she said, "It's not important."

"Yeah, well, anyways," he said, slightly flustered. "I haven't seen or heard about her since the emergency room visit."

"She starts on Monday. Do you want to meet her and help her out?" She asked as she stood and stretched.

He looked startled. "Meet her? Help her? What? Me? How?"

"Hold on, Steven. No need to get all worked up!" she said with a grin as she put a hand up. "I just thought maybe you two could get reacquainted and you could at least help her get to know your routine. She hasn't worked in a hospital setting, so I'm sure she'll be very nervous." Pausing, she looked at him and pointed a finger. "And I don't want you being all macho and scaring her." He looked surprised and mouthed, "What?"

"You know how you can get sometimes."

"What does that mean? How I get sometimes?" he asked, a little miffed.

She raised her eyebrows and gave him a look.

He sighed and sat back smiling and nodded.

"Touché. All right, I promise not to bite her head off the first day or so."

"I'm sure she'll be relieved," Emma said sarcastically, rolling her eyes and shaking her head as she carried the coffee mugs to the sink. She looked over at her nephew as she rinsed the cups. He had leaned forward in his chair and was reading Christina's résumé.

Steven was a little over six feet tall, with thick, light brown hair intermingled with gray, giving him a distinguished, professional look. He had clear, sky blue eyes that could freeze someone with an icy glare or melt one's heart with warm compassion. With the professionally whitened teeth, dimples, well-proportioned muscular body, and charming personality, she understood why the ladies, even those close to her age, would practically swoon when he walked by. Steven, however, seemed oblivious to his impact on the opposite sex, focusing his energies on being the best cardiologist in Alva.

"Do you think she's qualified to work in the cardiac unit?" he asked, closing the folder with the résumé.

Emma sat in her chair before answering, "Well, not really, but my gut feeling is that she'll do just fine."

"Your gut feeling?"

Hesitating, knowing her explanation wouldn't make much sense, she said, "Well, yeah. I guess one could call it intuition. You see, she worked at my station as an aide for three years when she was in high school and, during that time, proved herself to be not only dedicated, but also willing to learn." Sensing he was about to protest, she put her hand up and continued, "I know that was a long time ago and it's not much to go on and it doesn't make sense now, but I honestly think she's the right one for the job."

He gave her a confused look.

"That was twenty years ago!" he exclaimed. "You said she's never worked on a cardiac care unit before?"

She shook her head, saying, "But she *did* work for a cardiologist for five years. That's something."

"I don't get your reasoning here," he said as he shook his head and ran his fingers through his hair. He had worked with inept nurses before and dreaded the idea of doing so again, even if it was Christina.

She shrugged, not knowing how to explain her gut feeling any better.   .

"How can you possibly know that she'll do a good job? People's lives will be in the balance, Aunt Emma! She *has* to be able to think and act quickly." He sighed heavily.

"Look, I know you're concerned. I am too. I don't *know* how she'll do under stress, but I'm telling you, I just have this feeling she's the one I should hire."

He mumbled, "I know, your *gut* feeling."

"I'll have a couple of the other nurses working alongside her for a while until she feels comfortable going alone." She paused and sighed before continuing. "Steven, she's an intelligent, compassionate woman who needs a chance to prove herself—not only to us, but to herself as well."

He sighed again and shook his head. "Well, I hope you're right about this."

They sat in silence a few minutes, and then he asked, "What about Janet Washburn or Irene Taylor? Didn't they apply for the job? I know they're both qualified."

You would have to bring them up! Sighing and nodding, she started to speak when he interrupted.

"I've worked with Janet for the past several years. She seems to be the best candidate as far as I'm concerned. Why are you passing her up?"

She leaned forward and said, "May I be honest with you?"

"Of course."

"Well, I just don't like Janet Washburn. There's something creepy about her." *It feels good to finally tell someone what I really think.*

He raised his eyebrows in surprise.

"Creepy? Like what?"

"I can't put my finger on it." Leaning back in her chair, she continued, "Maybe her attitude—the way she relates to the patients and other staff. She always seems angry about something." Putting her hands up as if in surrender, she said, "She just doesn't have the compassion and gentleness in her spirit that I sense in Christina."

"Well, that's interesting." He leaned back in his chair, made a triangle with his fingertips, and placed them under his chin.

"I've never had any problems with Janet. She's always done what I've asked, and although she isn't what I would call a gentle person, she is thorough." He furrowed his brow, thinking. "Hmm. What about Irene?"

"Well, I think she's all right and probably would be a good candidate, but she has two small children and just had another baby—I don't believe she'd be as reliable.

Besides, she said she'd be happy just working weekends and as a sub." She folded her hands on her desk and shrugged, not knowing what else could be said.

He leaned forward, placing his hands on her desk. "Well, I guess you'd know best in this matter. Seems like you've thought it through, and I don't think I'll be changing your mind." He stood and walked toward the door and then turned to face her.

"I need someone on the cardiac floor who can keep up with me, follow orders, and care for the patients as if they were their own family members."

"I don't think you'll be disappointed, Steven."

"I hope you're right, Aunt Emma." He walked out the door.

CHAPTER 23

Dr. Dawson walked down the hallway, mulling over the conversation with his aunt. Her decision to hire Christina, who obviously wasn't qualified, had been quite a shock. Through the years, his aunt had proven to be wise in her character assessments and hiring decisions, so what about Christina made her wisdom take a step back?

He let his mind wander back to his high school days as he boarded the elevator.

Christina had been in his band class, and he would occasionally pass her in the school hallway—other than those times, he rarely interacted with her. He knew she was nice and cute but hadn't felt inclined to spend any significant time with her. She just wasn't the type of girl he wanted to hang out with or date—she wasn't a cheerleader or in the popular crowd.

He shook his head and frowned as he exited the elevator and headed for the cardiac unit. He hated to admit that *maybe* at times he could be a bit rude—or, okay, a jerk.

He had never taken the time to get to know her during those three years they had attended school together, and he now regretted it. *Things might have turned out differently if I had just taken the time. Maybe I would have fallen in love with her instead of Tammy. Hmm, actually, falling in love with anyone besides Tammy would have been a good thing.* He shook his head, dislodging those thoughts. He didn't want his mind to go there. *I wonder how many other opportunities have passed by because I didn't take the time to investigate further. Well, I can't live my life worrying about what-ifs. Only God knows for sure what would have happened.* He sighed.

CHAPTER 24

"Dr. Dawson, line fifty-two. Dr. Dawson, line fifty-two." The announcement brought him out of his thoughts. He walked to the nurses' station and picked up the phone, punching the numbers five and two.

"Hello? Dr. Dawson speaking." There was a slight pause as he listened.

"Yes, Dr. Spears, I remember him. What are you calling about?"

The conversation lasted several minutes while Janet Washburn watched and listened. She wanted to speak to him about the nursing position, but as he replaced the receiver, he turned and headed for the elevator, ignoring her completely.

Grumbling, she said, "Dang it! Every time I *need* to talk to him, he's either coming or going somewhere!"

Filing her nails, Sally Jean said, "Well, he's an awfully busy doctor."

Janet gave her an irritated look, replying sarcastically, "Thank you, Miss I-can-state-the-obvious!"

Sally rolled her eyes and continued filing. "I'm just sayin' …"

Janet raised her hand before Sally could say anything further.

Sally Jean, in her early twenties and recently hired as an aide, annoyed Janet with her effervescent and chatty personality.

Ding! Ding! rang one of the bells at the nurses' station. Janet glanced at the switchboard, which had the room numbers lined up in neat little rows like tiny mobile homes in a trailer park. Number 102 was lit.

"Sally Jean, Mrs. Edwards in 102 needs assistance. Please go."

Making a face and returning the nail file to her pocket, she answered, "All right. I swear, she is the crankiest old woman I've ever been around! I tried telling her a few jokes, and she didn't even crack a smile."

Probably because she's deaf as a june bug, thought Janet as she rolled her eyes. "Did you check to see if her hearing aid is in and turned on? Sometimes she takes it out or turns it off."

Giggling, Sally Jean said, "I didn't think of that!"

Janet shook her head, rolled her eyes, and thought, *Of course not. All those blond jokes could be about you.* Janet looked at her watch. Two thirty. After another half hour she would be finished with her shift and could go home. She looked forward to changing into her comfy sweats and spending quality time with her daughter, Leelee.

The name on her daughter's birth certificate was Linda Lenore Lewis, but when Linda was a baby, Janet gave her the nickname Leelee and very rarely addressed her by her given name. As Janet thought of her daughter, her heart gave a light flutter.

Leelee was a beautiful, intelligent, sensitive, raven-haired twelve-year-old. Desiring to educate her daughter about the cruelty of others and how to protect her heart, body, and mind from those who may try to abuse them, she at times came across as harsh and strict. She hoped she had at least another year or two before Leelee would rebel and start pushing against the carefully erected boundaries and begin questioning her authority.

Janet sighed. She hated having to work so many hours, but the bills had to be paid. Time was slipping by like sand through her fingers.

CHAPTER 25

"Janet?" Sally Jean called as she approached the nurses' station.

"Janet?" she called a little louder when there was no response the first time.

"Oh, what?" Janet answered, shaking her head and focusing her attention on Sally Jean.

"Did you want me to empty Mr. Garland's urine bag before I leave?"

Janet gave her a look that said, "Are you stupid or what?"

She sighed and rolled her eyes, and, speaking as if to a child, said, "Of course. Didn't they tell you in the training class that the bags are always measured and emptied and the IV's are checked, and everything is written down on the clipboard at the foot of the bed at the end of a shift?"

Giggling, she answered, "Oh, yeah. I guess I forgot."

Janet shook her head. "How long have you been working here, Sally Jean?"

"A couple of weeks."

"Oh, seems longer," Janet mumbled under her breath.

"What? Did you say something to me?"

"No. Just go do those measurements and write them down so we can go home."

Janet sat at the desk and chewed on her thumbnail. *What am I gonna do? I can't just let Christina waltz in and take over—not after everything I've done and worked for.* She was deep in thought when Sally Jean returned and reported that her duties were completed.

"I'm gonna clock out now, unless you have something else for me to do."

Janet mumbled an "Okay" but was vaguely aware of her leaving. An idea began forming in her mind, and she smiled as it started taking shape. She had a few days to work on her plan before Christina walked onto the floor.

CHAPTER 26

Sunday morning arrived with a loud clash of thunder, waking Christina from a deep sleep. Thinking it was a noise from her dream, she rolled over and started to doze, only to be shaken awake by another loud, cymbal-like sound. She bolted out of bed and ran to close the windows in the bedrooms just before a hard rain blew in and pelted against them. She had forgotten how intense a Texas thunderstorm could be. As the lightning blazed across the sky and thunder shook and rattled the old house, Benji came running into her room to hide under her bed, followed closely by Chloe, who jumped on the bed and burrowed under the covers. She was amazed the kids had slept through that initial thunder crash and her subsequent window closings. As she sat on the bed listening to the wind, thunder, and rain hitting the windows, she heard Nicky call out for her. She glanced at the clock: five thirty.

She went to Nicky's room and told him he could join her in her room. Grabbing his pillow and stuffed puppy, he followed. Just as they were settling in, she heard a knock on her bedroom door.

"Mom? Can we come in?" Brad and Stacey asked in unison over a clap of thunder.

"Sure, come on in."

Good thing I've got a king-size bed, she thought, watching her kids settle under the covers. Turning on the room fan to drown out the storm's noise, she too was able to settle and drift off to sleep. Benji came out from under the bed and nestled amongst the four pairs of feet, shivering and whimpering quietly as he sensed more than just a thunderstorm brewing.

When the alarm went off at seven o'clock, Christina fought with her body, which wanted to stay in bed, and her mind, which wanted to stay awake. Fortunately, her mind won. She sat up, rubbed the sleep from her eyes, stretched, and went to the bathroom. When she returned to wake the kids, Stacey was sitting up, rubbing her eyes, and yawning.

"Mom? Are we still going to church today?"

"That's the plan," said Christina, covering a yawn and fighting the urge to crawl back in bed. Stacey nodded and said, "Good."

"If we're gonna go, young lady, you'd better get up and get movin'," she said patting her daughter's cheek. Walking to her closet and grabbing her thick cotton robe, she added, "I'll go make breakfast while you take a shower. How do pancakes sound?"

She looked at her sleeping boys. Brad was on his back with his arms and legs akimbo. Nicky was curled on his side, holding his stuffed dog under his chin. Her first thought was *That is so cute*; her second one was *I can't remember the last time I washed that nasty little thing.*

He had slept with that raggedy little bundle of fur since his daddy gave it to him five years ago, and she wondered if he would ever outgrow the habit. Crawling over her brothers and out of bed, Stacey whispered, "Awesome! We haven't had those in a long time!"

On her way to the bathroom, she called out, "Do we have any more shampoo?"

"It's in the cabinet on the second shelf," whispered Christina as she closed the door to the bedroom, not wanting to wake the boys. "Stacey," she called before heading down the stairs, "when you're finished, please wake your brothers."

"Okay, Mom."

As Christina prepared breakfast, she looked out her kitchen window. There were several small branches lying in the driveway, and rain was dripping from the leaves. The birds were singing loudly, and she could hear a couple of squirrels chattering about something.

The neighbor's gray cat was barely visible in the bushes by the garage, but she could see his tail swishing and twitching like a cobra dancing in front of a charmer. If the squirrels had known he had no intention of chasing them, they wouldn't have wasted their time and energy. The cat, however, did seem to derive pleasure at getting them all fussed up.

She smiled as she remembered Inky, one of their cats in Michigan. Early one morning, she was awakened by the sound of blue jays making such a racket that she thought the cats were having some of their flock for breakfast. She went to see what all the commotion was about, and there was Inky, curled up in the bird feeder sound asleep. He was oblivious to the scolding he was being given by the surprised and indignant birds. She quickly ran in to get her camera and immortalized that Kodak moment, which she framed and hung in the hallway with all the other family pictures, including snapshots of all the pets they ever had.

Animals were always an interesting creation to watch. *Better than TV most of the time,* she thought as a smile played across her lips.

If she hadn't experienced the intensity of the early morning storm, she would have wondered if it had all been a dream. Everything seemed normal. Little did she know that her whole concept of normal at that moment was about to take a huge nosedive.

Once the kids were showered and dressed, they came down to the breakfast nook and feasted on pancakes and sausages. Christina enjoyed the chatter as they gave their accounts of the storm and how it had affected their sleep.

The kids were anxious about attending the church and Sunday school classes.

Not knowing who would be there or what to expect, Christina had to admit that she too felt a little fearful and nervous.

As the family rode the short distance to church, they were amazed at the amount of damage the storm had inflicted on the properties up and down the street.

Having once witnessed the aftermath of a tornado and the devastation it had left behind, she wondered if one had passed over during the early morning storm. Neighbors were out picking up limbs and other debris that had been dumped in their yards and waved as the Sanders family van drove by, its occupants gawking at the mess.

Pulling into a parking spot in front of the large, red-bricked church, Christina experienced wave after wave of memories.

Walking up the brick sidewalk and stopping at the steps in front of the large white columns, she thought of David and their wedding day.

It had been a cold December day, and the church had been packed with family and friends. The ceremony went smoothly, and before she knew it, was kissing her Mom and Dad good-bye and heading out the door and down the steps to jump in her new husband's classic black GTO. She sighed. *Who would have imagined I'd be back here under these circumstances?*

Noticing his mom had stopped at the steps, Brad turned and saw her standing with her eyes closed. "Mom? Are you okay?" Brad asked as he touched her arm, bringing her back to the present.

"Oh, yeah, I'm fine. Just having a nice memory."

He smiled and nodded—she did that a lot lately.

As she walked in the door, another memory resurfaced. She could picture herself as a child, running through the hallway and being reprimanded by her mother. She closed her eyes for a second time and took in a deep breath, releasing it slowly. Oh, how she missed her mom and dad, and the carefree innocence of childhood. How she wished she could turn back the hands of time for just a little while and recapture some of those precious moments.

Looking down the long corridor, wondering where the classrooms were, they were approached by a little old lady who looked a lot like the wicked witch from a fairy tale. She held out her hand, which looked like it should have held a poison apple. Christina was pleased that it didn't.

"Christy? Christy Nichols? Is that you, dear?" asked a voice that sounded like it had been scoured by sandpaper.

When Christina answered in the affirmative, a shriveled little hand took hers, and the face leaned forward and kissed her on the cheek, catching Christina off guard. It had been a long time since she had been kissed on the cheek—especially by a strange little troll-like lady.

Trying not to sound flustered, she said, "Oh, hi."

Patting the hand she still held and trying desperately to remember the name of the woman in front of her, Christina just smiled her best smile.

Looking at each one of Christina's children, the gravelly voice asked, "Are these your children?" Her bright, clear blue eyes squinted behind thick lenses. Christina smiled and nodded.

"My goodness, they've grown so much! I haven't seen you or your children since your daddy's funeral five years ago!" She reached over and patted Nicky on the head. He squirmed and shifted from foot to foot.

"I heard you had moved back to Alva, but I wasn't sure if I should believe it since I haven't seen you here at church."

Christina felt a twinge of guilt. As she began to reply, she felt a bony arm encircle her own, guiding her down the corridor. The children followed silently behind.

"You know Christy, your mama and daddy were very dear friends of ours, and we sure missed them when they passed away. Did you know Burt went to be with the Lord last year?" She stopped and looked up at Christina, eyes looking huge and owl-like behind the lenses.

Now I remember, thought Christina with relief. *Ellie and Burt Sterling. Mom and Dad's domino-playing friends.*

"No, I'm sorry to hear that."

Patting Christina's arm, she said, "Oh, that's okay. He was dying of lung cancer and was just so tired of the pain." Christina felt Ellie's hand tighten on her arm as she continued. "He would say every night, 'Ellie, please pray that God will take me home tonight.' Well, after six months of suffering, his prayer was finally answered." With a smile and faraway look in her eyes, she said, "He just went to sleep and never woke up. I sure miss him, but I know I'll be joining him soon." She sighed, refocusing her attention on Christina.

"By the way, dear, what brought you back here to Alva?"

Ellie listened intently as Christina shared about David's death and a condensed version of the past few months. When she had finished speaking, Ellie took her hand in hers and said, "You poor little thing. I had no idea. I just sort of lost contact with everyone and everything since Burt's illness and death." Patting Christina's hand, she said, "If I can help in *any* way, please let me know."

"Well," answered Christina sheepishly, "you can help right now by telling us which classes we should be attending." Ellie chuckled and proceeded to point everyone in the direction of his or her Sunday school class. Christina reached down and hugged Ellie and told her she would keep in touch.

Walking to her class, she thought about Ellie and Burt Sterling. Her mom had once commented that when she and her dad had first started attending the church soon after their marriage, Ellie and Burt had taken them under their wing—becoming spiritual parents, so to speak. Over the years, her parents had attended Sunday school classes and Bible studies led by the older couple. Although Christina knew the Sterlings, she never had serious dealings with them. They were just another couple who came over to play dominoes with her folks.

Ellie has to be in her nineties, thought Christina, doing the math in her head.

Wow! That little lady is old enough to be my grandma, she thought as she found her classroom. *My how the time flew.*

She sat in the back of the classroom and looked around, hoping to see someone as obviously unattached as she was. *Surely there's another single lady in this room.*

All she saw were couples in their mid to late forties and fifties. She felt like an orange in a basket of apples. Sighing, she tried to focus on the lesson being taught, but her heart felt heavy and lonely. Before the class dismissed, while the teacher was praying, she quietly slipped out and headed for the bathroom. Not realizing how difficult it would be to reinstate herself into the Christian community as a single person, she had been emotionally unprepared.

Where do I fit in? She felt so disconnected and alone. Tears started forming, and she felt a sob trying to work its way out when the bathroom door opened and a teenage girl came in. Wiping her eyes quickly and avoiding eye contact with the teen, she rummaged in her purse for lipstick. Applying a fresh coat, she forced herself to smile before leaving the room.

CHAPTER 27

Her children met her at the back entrance of the sanctuary after the dismissal of their classes. Brother Ken Jones—church leaders in Alva were addressed as *brother* or *sister* instead of *Mr.* or *Mrs.*—greeted them at the door, wearing his usual attire: a black suit, white shirt, and bright blue tie. Christina wondered if it was the same outfit he had worn through the years. Surely not. He probably had a whole rack of black suits and bright blue ties in his closet. Her thoughts trailed off as a look of surprise and recognition registered on his face when he handed her a bulletin. Taking her hand in his, he commented on how lovely she looked and how glad he was to see her and her family. He looked ancient. She remembered him as a large man with a big, toothy grin and hands that seemed to be the size of shovels. The man before her was stooped over and barely taller than she, and his hands were shriveled and crippled with arthritis. He wore thick glasses, and his head had little wisps of gray hair. She felt sad as she realized he probably wouldn't be around much longer—like Ellie.

She wished certain people didn't have to get old and die, because they added so much life, love, and beauty to the earth, and their passing would leave a void that could never be properly filled.

As Christina surveyed the sanctuary, it seemed as if nothing had changed in the past twenty years. The walls were still a creamy white, the carpet and pew cushions were a muted red, the six candelabras were still a shiny brass with about thirty light-bulbs illuminated in each, and the large, tall windows still had the painted white shutters that kept the hot Texas sun out.

She had always loved the simple but elegant look of the sanctuary and was glad there had been no major renovations over the years. Sometimes consistency *was* a good thing, especially to someone who'd had her share of changes.

Looking around the large room that could easily seat five hundred folks but contained half that many, she saw several familiar faces. The Swanson family, sitting in the same row they had sat in twenty years earlier, looked pretty much the same; a few more wrinkles and gray hairs and a couple additional members were the only obvious changes.

Mr. and Mrs. Miller, who had to be in their mid-eighties, were present with their handicapped daughter Melissa. Melissa had been diagnosed with multiple sclerosis when she was twenty-five, and after twenty years of battling the disease, looked as if she was in her last stages of combat. She looked thin, pale, fragile, and tired. Melissa, feeling she was being observed, raised her head shakily and focused on Christina. She smiled lopsidedly, and then her head dropped back down, making her look as if she were in a perpetual prayerful posture. Christina had smiled back and made a tiny waving motion with her fingers. *I can't believe Melissa is still here! I figured she would have passed on years ago. I'll have to talk with the Millers after the service,* she thought as she continued to scan the room.

Even though there was a smattering of older familiar faces, she was happy to see many young couples and small children present. As she turned her attention to the bulletin, she saw an announcement for the teens to meet in the basement after the service. She touched Brad's arm and showed him the announcement. He nodded and smiled, taking the bulletin and showing it to Stacey, who whispered, "Can we go?"

Christina smiled and nodded.

The service wasn't as lively as she was accustomed to, but the pastor gave a wonderful message entitled "Why Does It Have to Hurt So Much?" It was about Paul's life and the pain and suffering he endured to be God's servant. She glanced over at her kids: Brad seemed to be listening and taking notes, Stacey was doodling in her notebook, and Nicky was drawing cars and army scenes on the back of a letter written by one of the missionary families the church sponsored.

By the end of the message, Christina was in tears—not so much because she was sad, but because she finally realized that God knew *exactly* what she was going through and had a purpose for it. During the final song, Christina prayed and promised God she would strive to be a better-committed servant. She asked for protection, wisdom, and peace in her family's lives. Little did she realize how difficult it was going to be to keep that commitment.

When the service ended, Christina and Nicky walked around the sanctuary. She reacquainted herself with the townsfolk as the two older kids met a group of their friends and headed for the basement. The Millers, who were pleased to see her, insisted she tell them about the events that led her back to Alva. As she recounted her story, several other people joined the circle. *To save time, I should just stand up at the pulpit and share my story with everyone,* she thought as she repeated parts of her story to the newcomers.

Within a week or so, she knew that *everyone* in town would know the story of the Sanders family. Gossipy news travelled fast in a town that small. Once everyone in the immediate area heard the story about her family, the conversation changed to the topic of the early morning storm.

Mrs. Miller asked, "Did y'all get any damage from that storm this morning?"

Christina shook her head. "No, but it sure sounded scary."

"I heard on the news this morning before church that there was a tornado spotted."

Several of the folks standing in the circle gasped.

A lady Christina didn't recognize asked, "A tornado? Are you sure?"

"Where was it? Did it touch down anywhere?" Christina asked.

"Well, from what I heard, it went over the east side of town, and there was some damage over on Maple Street."

"I heard the sirens and had everyone go to the basement," said a young mother with a baby on her hip.

Christina said, "I didn't hear any sirens."

Patting Christina's arm, Mrs. Miller said, "Well, honey, if you had your windows closed or the air conditioner on, you may not have heard them."

Or if you're a deep sleeper, Christina thought.

"As far as I know, no one was hurt, but a couple of roofs were blown off. The rest of the town was untouched," Mr. Miller added as he put his arm around his wife's shoulders.

Wow! I can't believe I slept through all that! Christina thought as she listened to their comments. *We should take a walk down the street after church and see if the neighbors need help cleaning up the debris.*

Stacey and Brad met her in the sanctuary, and after saying good-byes to everyone, the family headed to the van. She heard a crow's caw and looked up to see one on top of the church steeple. *Seems like everywhere I go, there's a crow. Weird. I don't remember there being so many crows up in Michigan,* she thought as she crawled into the driver's side of the van and started the engine.

Stacey and Brad told of their meeting in the basement, and Christina asked if the bowling lanes were still there.

"When I was a teen, our youth group painted the basement in wild colors and reopened the three-lane bowling lanes that had sat dormant for several years."

"Yep, the lanes are still there, and the walls are still pretty colorful, *and* there's a big screen TV—and I'm talking several-feet-wide big. There's several video games, a snack bar, Ping-Pong tables …" He paused to take a breath.

At this point, Stacey, evidently excited and impressed as well, added, "And a stage with a keyboard and drum set!"

"I think it's gonna be a lot like our youth group up in Michigan! I can hardly wait to come Thursday night!"

Christiana smiled and asked, "What time Thursday?"

Stacey looked at Brad who answered, "Seven."

"Good." She glanced over at Nicky, who was looking out the window.

"Hey, Nicky, you want to go to the Wednesday night program?" She asked as she touched his leg.

He shook his head and made a face. "I don't think so. I didn't see anyone I knew from school at church." He continued looking out the window.

Christina raised her eyebrows in surprise. "You mean you were the only one from your grade in the Sunday school class?'

"No. There were other kids there my age. I just didn't know them," he answered quietly.

"Well, I'm sure you'll get to know them all eventually. Why don't you go

Wednesday night and check it out? You could even ask Danny to come along." She paused, waiting for a response. Getting none, she continued, "Maybe you'll like it. If not, I won't make you go again."

When the words left her mouth she felt a little twinge of guilt, wondering if she should even give him a choice. Because of his somewhat shy and cautious temperament, he had difficulty making friends, and her mother's heart was concerned he would feel awkward or miserable.

He would be in the youth group with Stacey the next year, anyway, and she knew he would enjoy that much better. He could afford to take a year off if he needed to.

He shrugged and said, "Okay."

CHAPTER 28

After church, they shared a basket of steak fingers, Texas toast, and gravy—her favorite comfort food—at a place named Jack's Chicken Shack.

Christina asked if they had heard anything about the storm that morning and was met with negative responses.

"Why?" Stacey asked as she dipped her French fry into the gravy.

Christina shared with them the information she'd received concerning a tornado.

"No wonder there was so much stuff on the lawns and street this morning," Brad said as he chewed on a piece of toast.

Dipping a steak finger in the gravy, Nicky said, "I'm just glad it didn't get our house."

"Yeah," agreed Stacey. "All that thunder and lightning was scary enough."

"Mom, have you ever seen a tornado?" Nicky asked as he chewed the morsel of meat and gravy.

She told them of the time she and her mom were driving home from Fort Worth when they saw a tornado in the distance. The kids sat wide-eyed as they tried to imagine what it was like.

"It was scary," she said as she gathered the garbage on the table.

"I think it would be cool to see one," said Nicky.

"Hey, remember that movie about those storm chasers?" Stacey asked, wiping the remaining crumbs into a pile. Christina nodded.

"Yeah, that was a cool movie," added Brad

Giggling, Nicky said, "I liked the part in that movie that had the cows floating through the air. Did you ever see cows fly, Mom?" he asked.

She chuckled and said, "No, can't say that I've seen a flying cow. I have seen a horse fly, however." At first they looked puzzled, then Nicky broke out in laughter. "I get it!" he exclaimed. "I've seen a house fly, but I've never seen an elephant fly!" He added remembering a line from one of the Disney movies.

Brad and Stacey shook their heads and rolled their eyes at their mom. She grinned back at them.

"Hey, guys, when we get home, how about we change clothes and walk down the street and see if we can help the neighbors clean up their yards?"

"That'd be cool," said Stacey.

"Yeah. That'd be fun," added Nicky enthusiastically.

As he scooted out of the booth and stood by the table, Brad said, "Yeah, okay. I've got some homework to do, so I don't want to be gone very long. I also told Melinda I'd help her with her math homework this evening."

Christina nodded. "Okay." She looked at her watch. "By the time we get home and change, it'll be two o'clock. Why don't we work till around five? Would that give you enough time, Brad?"

He nodded. The other two kids gave her nods as well.

"I just remembered that I need to read a chapter in my world history book," stated Stacey as she slapped her forehead.

"You'll have plenty of time to do that as well." Christina looked at Nicky and asked, "Do you have any homework?" He shook his head and answered, "Nope."

"Well, we best get going if we're gonna do everything." They deposited their litter in the trash bin and headed for the door. The lady in the booth across from them lowered her head and avoided eye contact as they walked by. Christina had noticed her earlier watching them as they ate and chatted. She recognized her as one of the employees at the hospital but couldn't remember what department. She had planned to say hi, but when the lady deliberately avoided eye contact, she decided not to. *Obviously, she doesn't want to chat,* thought Christina as they walked out the door. During the ride home, Nicky asked, "Mom, who was that lady that kept staring at us?"

"Which lady?"

"The really big one in the booth next to us. Every time I'd look over, she'd be looking at us. Do you know her?"

"Oh, that lady. Well, I recognize her from the hospital, but I don't *know* her. I think she works in the housekeeping department." *Poor thing. She's so overweight, she must be miserable in this heat.*

"She sorta creeped me out," he said, crinkling his nose.

"She was probably trying to remember where she had seen us before."

Nicky nodded. "Yeah, maybe."

The mysterious lady was forgotten as they arrived home, ran in to change clothes, and headed out to help their neighbors.

Later that day, after helping clean up branches and roof debris, Brad and Stacey went to their rooms to do homework, and Nicky went to his room to play a video game.

Christina called her friend Linda and enjoyed a wonderful time of friendly chitchat. She then called Cindy, Lisa, and Donna and made plans for a luncheon get-together the following Saturday. As she was settling down to read a suspense novel, the phone rang. David's Mom, bless her heart, called at least once a week to chat with her and the kids. Once they caught up on the week's activities, they talked of plans for Thanksgiving, which was still several weeks away.

As Christina reflected on the day, a smile played across her face. All in all, the day had turned out to be quite a blessing. They had met several of their neighbors, and the decision to attend church felt like the beginning of a great new phase in their lives.

"Oh, shoot!" she exclaimed as a thought occurred to her. "I forgot to ask the neighbors about the electricians." She made a mental note to ask someone the next day.

As Christina was talking on the phone, unbeknownst to her, the woman from the restaurant was writing down her observations for the day: Sanders family went to church, had lunch at Jack's Chicken Shack, went home, helped neighbors clean yards. *A perfect little family,* she thought.

"Well, they don't seem like bad people," she mumbled as she closed the journal. The man on the phone had told her to follow them, record their activities, and report to him. She'd been doing this for a week now, and to be honest, the Sanders family led a pretty dull life. She found her cell phone and made the call.

CHAPTER 29

Monday

Christina woke at 5:00 a.m., unable to sleep any longer. A sense of impending doom surrounded her spirit like an invisible fog. Climbing out of bed and heading to the bathroom, she showered and dressed in her new uniform, and still the feeling persisted. There was a nervous energy that made her hands shake and her body feel like a thousand bees were coursing through her veins.

"Must be first day's work jitters," she mumbled to herself as she massaged lotion into her trembling hands. Deciding to do her hair and makeup later, she went downstairs and started the coffeemaker. Walking into the family room, she found her Bible and reading glasses next to her new recliner, which she sat in. The small piece of paper that had fallen out the previous week was still in there, tucked tightly in the forty-third book of Isaiah. She decided to read the page—again.

"Fear not, for I have redeemed you; I have summoned you by name; you are mine." As she read this, her pulse quickened. She continued to read. "When you pass through the waters, I will be with you; and when you pass through the rivers, they will not sweep over you. When you walk through the fire, you will not be burned; the flames will not set you ablaze. For I am the Lord, your God, the Holy One of Israel, your Savior." She stopped and reread the verses and then scanned down to verse five. "Do not be afraid, for I am with you." She almost dropped the Bible as she felt goose bumps start from the top of her head and travel to her toes. It seemed like God was speaking directly to her.

She closed her eyes and prayed. "Okay, Lord, I'm not sure what all this means, but I'm gonna trust you to take care of us. The verse says I shouldn't be afraid of anything, and yet I struggle with fear of the unknown."

She continued to pray for her family and David's, friends in Michigan and Texas, and her children and their friends, until she heard Brad's alarm go off, surprised that it had been an hour. As she said her amen, she felt peace enfold her like a blanket. Yawning, she thought, *I would love to cuddle up on the sofa and go back to sleep for a couple of hours.* She shook her head and forced herself up and into the kitchen, where she prepared another cup of coffee and set out cereal and bowls for the kids.

As she ascended the stairs, she heard activity from the bedrooms and couldn't help but smile. Another day awaited the Sanders family, and she wondered what interesting treasures it would hold. Returning to her room, she applied her makeup, attempted to brush her hair, and took one last look at her reflection. She went to each child's room, giving hugs, kisses, and a brief prayer with each, and then, with a nervous excitement, she headed out the door to begin a new and challenging job, trusting that Brad would make sure everyone left the house on time.

CHAPTER 30

Nicky

Nicky headed for the bathroom soon after his mom left his room. Being the youngest, he was always the last to use the facilities. He took a quick shower and, after drying off, looked at himself in the mirror. He was thin enough to count his ribs. He tried to make the muscles pop up on his arms as he flexed them but to no avail. Pushing his hair out of his eyes and leaning into the mirror to get a better look at his face, he inspected his teeth and touched the dimple in his chin—the one characteristic of his dad that had been passed on. He didn't like the smattering of freckles across his nose, even though his mom said they'd go away as he matured. Noticing the dark areas under his eyes, he tried rubbing them away, but the grayish color returned as soon as he stopped. *It looks like someone socked me in the eyes!* Grabbing his T-shirt and putting it on, he thought, *I just want to go back to bed and sleep without any monsters chasing me. I'm so tired.* He sighed, knowing there was no way his mom would let him stay home, especially if he wasn't running a fever or throwing up. He finished dressing and headed downstairs. Stacey had poured a bowl of cereal for him, which he made a face at and declined—food wasn't very appealing lately either. She scolded him for wasting food and not eating.

Setting the bowl on the floor for Benji to eat, she said, "You're gonna get awfully hungry in a couple of hours."

Nicky shrugged. "I'll be okay."

"Do you have any money so you can buy a snack?"

"Yeah, I have a couple of quarters." He jingled the change in his pocket.

She reached into her backpack, pulled out her change purse, and handed him four more quarters. "Here," she said as she handed him the change and returned her purse to the backpack.

He took the money and put it in his pocket, knowing he probably wouldn't use it. "Thanks."

"Come on, guys, it's time to go," Brad said as he threw on his varsity jacket.

Stacey looked at her little brother and frowned. *Something's going on in that brain of his, and I'm not sure what it is. He's been acting kinda weird the past few days.* She wondered if anyone else had noticed the dark circles under his eyes or his lack of an appetite. She'd have to mention it to her mom tonight. She put her arm around Nicky and gave him a quick hug.

"You're a neat kid, little bro."

He gave her a crooked smile and rolled his eyes.

CHAPTER 31

Christina arrived at the hospital by six thirty, anxious to be on time. She sat in the parking lot and listened to the radio until six forty-five, and then, with sweaty palms, she left her sanctuary and headed to Mrs. Ferguson's office, where she and Dr. Dawson were having a cup of coffee.

Her heart almost leaped out of her chest as he smiled and reached out his hand to take hers. Feeling weak in the knees, she willed herself to remain standing and her hand to stop shaking as she reached out and took his—which was warm and soft.

Smiling, he said, "Good morning, Christina. How are you today?"

She thought, *Well, now that I'm standing in front of you, I'm scared spitless, not to mention sweaty-palmed and weak-kneed, and my heart is about to burst out of my chest.* But what she said was "A little nervous, but fine. And you?"

He nodded and smiled. "I'm doing well today. It's nice to have you on board." He pointed to a chair in front of his desk, and she sat.

"Why don't we have a cup of coffee, and I'll go over today's schedule?"

She agreed, even though she'd already had two cups and wasn't sure another would settle into her nervous stomach. He brought a cup to her along with a tray containing creamer and sugar packets, which she graciously accepted.

As Steven explained the schedule of the day, she lost track of his words and just watched his facial expressions. His clear blue eyes and radiant smile were mesmerizing, and she remembered why she had been attracted to him through high school. He was so cute then, but now that he had matured, he was quite handsome. *Not quite drop-dead gorgeous, but pretty close.*

She was quickly brought back to the moment, when he asked if she had any questions. *How could I, since I haven't heard anything you've said?* She shook her head, feeling her face flush, and said, "Uh, not right now. I'll probably have some later, though."

Smiling and nodding, he said, "Okay then."

Standing and donning his white lab coat and stethoscope, he walked to the door.

"Ladies," he said as he held it open for them.

Mrs. Ferguson entwined her arm with Christina's, and the three of them headed up to the third-floor Cardiac Care Unit.

Mrs. Ferguson introduced her to the CCU staff, and they all seemed happy to have her there—except one named Janet. Once she had been introduced, she avoided any further contact. When Christina would glance in Janet's direction, she would be met with a scowl.

I wonder what that's all about.

As they walked around the CCU, he introduced his five patients and, after a quick exam of each, gave a brief medical history.

Boarding the elevator, he said, "We'll go over each chart in detail after lunch. Have you had a chance to tour the hospital?"

"I've only seen the cafeteria. I just haven't had a chance to do a thorough investigation. I figured once I start working, I can tour it in small increments."

He glanced at his watch.

"We have a couple of hours before lunch. You wanna see it now?"

"Yeah, that'd be great. Are you sure you have time?"

"Yep. I cleared my schedule for the day 'cause I wasn't sure how much time I'd be spending with you."

She gave him a surprised look. "Well, thanks. I appreciate that."

The next couple of hours passed quickly as they walked the halls of each floor and met the staff in each area. The last places they visited before lunch were the labs and laundry facility located in the basement. She was amazed at the complexity of both areas.

Leaving the lab, he asked, "So what do you think?"

"I'm almost speechless. I didn't realize this hospital had such a large lab facility. When I worked here years ago, it was just a small room next to the surgical ward."

Steven smiled. "Well, when the board decided to remodel and expand, the lab was one of the first areas to be considered. The other doctors and I joined together and made a list of what we wanted, informing them that our lab was inefficient and that it was expensive to be sending our lab work out to Dallas all the time. Sometimes we needed immediate results and couldn't get them or wouldn't hear back for a day or more. I can't tell you how frustrating that was. Since we would be taking in more patients, it seemed logical to have our own updated facility."

Christina nodded in agreement. "That laundry facility is huge too. How many more beds were added with the addition?"

"About three hundred."

"Wow. No wonder there's so much laundry. I didn't realize there were that many additions."

"Yeah. This place has filled up quickly, and even as big as it is, we still have to send folks to Dallas, Fort Worth, or Waco because of bed shortages."

"Hmm. Well, I'm impressed."

Steven smiled and nodded, glancing at his watch again.

"You ready for lunch?"

She nodded and rubbed her stomach.

They boarded the elevator once again and headed for the second floor.

While dining, they reminisced about their high school days. He brought her up to date on a few mutual acquaintances and his own life.

"I'm currently dating a lady from Waco named Anika Marouf. She's a psychology teacher at Baylor University and is doing research on the influence and power of prayer in the healing process."

Christina gave him a surprised look and felt her face flush. *Cindy failed to mention that he was dating someone.* She ate her salad as he continued speaking, hoping he hadn't noticed her surprise and—what? Disappointment?

"We don't see each other very often because of conflicting schedules and distance, but I'm definitely attracted to her. She's on a business trip to New York and will be back on Friday morning." He took a sip of tea before continuing. "I'm planning to pick her up at the Dallas–Fort Worth Airport and bring her back to Alva to stay with a girlfriend, and then I'll take her home on Sunday." Taking a bite of his sandwich, he asked, "Would you like to meet her?"

Christina was shocked when she felt a twinge of jealously grip her gut.

"Uh, sure I'd love to meet her."

"Good. I'll see if I can arrange it. If not this weekend, then I'm sure there will be other opportunities." Christina smiled and nodded.

After lunch, they returned to Steven's office and perused the patients' charts, discussing each one at length. He left for a cup of coffee as she continued to study one of them. Standing in the doorway of the little break room, he watched her for a few seconds.

She hasn't changed much over the years, except that she has matured into an attractive woman. He watched as she pushed a strand of curly auburn hair from her eyes. *I like her hair. Why wasn't I attracted to her back in high school? Oh yeah, I wasn't thinking with the right brain during that time in my life. She was such a quiet, sweet, and good girl, and honestly, not sexually attractive at all—definitely not my type at that time. But now, I'm a different person with a different perspective on life. She, however, still has that same sweet spirit, calmness, and level-headedness that I remember from high school. She radiates a confidence that I didn't notice back then.* He felt something stir deep within his spirit. *Whoa!* he told his inner being. *I can't be attracted to her, 'cause I already have a girlfriend. Remember?*

Christina looked up to see him staring at her. Blushing, she smiled and said, "What?"

"Do you want any coffee?" he asked quickly to cover the awkwardness of the moment.

"Sure, but I take a ton of cream and sugar."

He nodded, remembering the morning's meeting and how she had totally defiled her coffee. He brought a tray loaded with packets. She smiled and nodded as he set it on the desk in front of her.

"Thanks, I think this might be enough."

"Well, I wasn't sure how much a ton was, so …" His voice trailed off. "Sorry, guess I went a little overboard."

She waved her hand. "It's fine. You may be surprised at how much of this I *will* use. I think I like the *idea* of coffee—not the coffee itself."

He watched in amazement as she poured about six packets of sugar and creamer into her cup. "I like the aroma and warmth—and a sweet, creamy hint of coffee flavor," she said, stirring the light brown brew.

He smiled and shook his head. He was a one-packet-of-sugar black coffee drinker and couldn't understand why anyone would pollute such a perfect beverage.

They sipped coffee and discussed the rest of the week's schedule, finishing up at around three.

Once she was gone, he walked around the room, feeling a profound loneliness that he hadn't felt for quite some time. *What is going on?* he wondered. *Surely I'm not developing feelings for this woman.* As he drove home that evening, he couldn't help but drive by Christina's house, feeling like an adolescent schoolboy trying to get a glimpse of his secret crush. Pulling into his own driveway, he thought, *Get ahold of yourself, Steven!* Later that evening, he called Anika, and thoughts of Christina were dispelled for the night.

CHAPTER 32

Christina arrived home about fifteen minutes before her children walked in the back door. She had had time to feed the animals and check the mail. In the bundle were flyers announcing several sales and a couple of letters from friends in Michigan. The one that caught her eye though was an envelope addressed to Mr. David Sanders.

That's strange, she thought. *Who would write to him now, two years after his death?* The return address said Washington, DC.

Just as she started to open it, she heard her children in the driveway and decided to check it out later. She perused the rest of the mail and then set it all aside as her children entered the back door. She greeted each one with a hug and kiss and asked about their day. As she poured milk and sat out cookies, Stacey excitedly told her about the Christmas play tryouts.

"I think I have a good chance at getting the lead part. A girl named Angie tried out too, but I think I did a better job."

Sitting at the table and munching on a cookie, Christina asked, "When will you know if you got the part or not?"

"We should know by Friday. I hope we know tomorrow. I really want the part, and I don't *want* to wait that long," Stacey said between bites of cookie and sips of milk.

Christina asked what the play was about, and as Stacey described it, Nicky quietly slipped away and went to his room. Christina was vaguely aware of his disappearance.

Brad announced, "I made an eighty-five on my history test."

Christina reached over and patted him on the arm. "Good for you, Brad. History was never one of my strong subjects."

"Now I have to study for an algebra test on Wednesday," he said, popping the last bite of cookie in his mouth.

"Now that I think about it, algebra wasn't one of my strong subjects either," Christina said thoughtfully.

Stacey stopped midbite and asked, "So Mom, what *were* your strong subjects?"

Christina thought for a moment before answering. "Hmm. I guess English, science, and band. Anything to do with remembering dates and numbers—well ..." She let her words trail off.

Stacey said, "I'm not fond of math and history either, but I *do* like my drama class!"

Christina inquired about Brad's grade status so far and was reassured that he was doing well. As the two older Sanders children munched and talked, Christina thought about the letter. It was like an itchy mosquito bite, demanding attention.

"Mom?" she heard her daughter say.

"Yes, Stacey?"

"I've noticed that Nicky is acting kinda weird lately."

"What?"

Wiping her mouth on a napkin, she restated, "Nicky. He's not acting like himself lately."

Brad nodded and said, "Yeah, he seems kinda depressed or sick or something."

Christina looked around. "Where is he?"

Nodding her head toward the stairs, Stacey said, "He left a few minutes ago. Probably went to his room. He's been spending a *lot* of time in his room the last few days."

Christina thought about that. She had been so busy getting ready for her new job that she hadn't paid close attention to Nicky.

"Brad, has he said anything to you?"

"Well, I know he's been complaining of being tired lately. I noticed this morning that he had dark circles under his eyes. I asked him if he was okay, and he just said he was tired."

"He seemed fine over the weekend. He enjoyed the shopping trip and seemed to enjoy church yesterday and was okay when we were helping the neighbors."

"Yeah," said Stacey, "but remember when we came home yesterday after cleaning up? He went right up to his room and napped the afternoon away."

"Well, we all took naps," Christina countered.

"Yeah, but he took a *three*-hour nap, Mom." Stacey raised her eyebrows as if challenging her mother. "That's *not* normal for Nicky."

Christina slowly nodded and sighed.

Looking across the table, she said, "Thanks, guys, for bringing this to my attention."

Standing, Brad said, "Mom, I need to get upstairs and start studying. If you need help with dinner, let me know."

"Thanks, Brad. Stacey, could you grab the laundry baskets and take them up?"

"Sure, Mom."

CHAPTER 33

Christina stood outside Nicky's door and said a silent prayer before knocking. Getting no response, she quietly opened it and whispered, "Nicky?" It was eerily quiet and dark with the shades drawn. She saw a lump on the bed and, realizing it was her son curled up in a little ball sleeping (or pretending to do so), put her hand on his forehead. It was warm and damp. She listened to his deep sleep-induced breaths. Sighing, she bent over to kiss him on the cheek, noticing the stuffed puppy tucked under his chin. She walked over to his desk and, seeing his drawing pad, opened it. Thumbing through the pages, she smiled as she saw cars, trucks, boats, and army soldiers, but she stopped abruptly when a demonic-looking face seemed to jump off the page at her. She carried the book to the hallway where the light was brighter and was shocked at the terrifying picture that had been crudely drawn with dark pencil lines. Red eyes and sharp teeth defined the creature's face, and curved claws on the ends of long bony fingers looked as if they were reaching out to grab someone. She wondered if this creature was haunting Nicky's dreams. *Maybe that's why he's so tired. I'd be tired too if I had to fight something like this at night.* Looking closer, she saw the words "Daddy, help me" written over and over amongst the dark lines. She felt a pang in her heart as tears flooded her eyes. *What should I do now? Should I get him into counseling?* She replaced the drawing tablet on the desk, kissed her son on the forehead, and prayed a hedge of protection around him before then heading downstairs to prepare dinner. She needed to talk to someone about this and decided to call her in-laws after they had eaten.

While Christina was preparing dinner for her family, Lula sat on her couch drinking Dr Pepper while anxiously awaiting a call from her boss. She hadn't heard from him in a couple of days and wanted to report her observations. She had almost had a heart attack when she saw Christina and Dr. Dawson walk into the laundry room at the hospital. That was the *last* place she'd expected to see Christina.

Thank God I saw them before they saw me! Christina would have surely recognized me from the restaurant yesterday. I've gotta be super careful. If she finds out who I am, I could lose my job at the hospital! If all goes according to plan, I'll be sittin' pretty soon and won't have to worry about a stupid hospital job. As she sat thinking about the last couple of days, the phone rang. It was the boss.

CHAPTER 34

Sitting around the dining room table, Christina watched as Nicky pushed his food around his plate and made feeble attempts at eating. Even though he had slept a couple of hours, he still had an exhausted look about him.

"Nicky, are you feeling all right?" she asked, concern etched on her face.

"My tummy hurts" was his reply.

As thoughts of bullying and possible abuse ran through her mind, she asked, "Nicky, is everything all right at school?"

He quietly nodded without looking up as a tear made its way down his cheek. Stacey and Brad stopped eating and looked from their brother to their mother, with "See what we mean?" looks on their faces. She nodded. Knowing he wouldn't open up yet, she changed the subject and started asking Stacey about her friends and Brad about his job at Safeway.

"You haven't mentioned Carmen in a while. Everything okay between you two?"

"Oh, yeah. We just don't see much of each other in school. I'll see her at church on Sunday for sure."

They continued chatting as Nicky sat with his head resting on his hand, stirring his food around his plate. Every now and then, she noticed him slip a piece of food down to Benji's eagerly awaiting mouth.

After dinner, as her kids loaded the dishwasher, she went to the den and sat in her recliner for a few minutes of quiet reflection and prayer for wisdom. She noticed there wasn't the usual sibling banter going on and knew that Nicky's dark mood was the reason.

Once the dishes were loaded and she heard Nicky walk upstairs, she followed. He was sitting on his bed looking at the picture of his dad and him taken two summers ago. When his mom walked in, he slipped it under his pillow. She sat at the foot of the bed and sighed. Not knowing what to say or do, he remained quiet with his knees up and his arms wrapped around them.

After a few quiet moments, Christina asked him what was going on and why he wasn't eating. A minute or two of silence passed before Nicky finally opened up. It was as if an emotional dam had ruptured and words poured out of his mouth as he shared his fears and concerns with her. He told her of the recurring nightmares and his fear of going to sleep and how he missed his dad and longed for those special times they had together, knowing they would never come again.

He reached down to where his backpack lay beside the bed and dug out a paper and handed it to her. Tears continued to stream down his face as he said, "I'm so stupid." She unfolded the math paper and saw a bright red F on the top. "I'm trying so hard, and I just don't get it! I'm such a retard!"

After showing her the math paper, he crawled to the corner of the bed next to the wall, wrapped his arms around his knees, rocked his body, and bowed his head as he talked. "I just want you and Dad to be proud of me, like Brad and Stacey. I'll never be as smart or athletic or outgoing as them."

Christina sighed and said, "First of all, you're *not* stupid or a retard. Sometimes it just takes longer to catch on to some of these math concepts. If you're concerned that I or even your dad would be disappointed in you, then you need to throw those thoughts out the window! There is *nothing* you could do that would diminish our love or pride in you. As far as Brad and Stacey go, they have their own fears and shortcomings as well. In fact, the whole human race is defective in one way or another." He looked up at her and frowned, not sure he totally believed what she was saying.

"There will *always* be someone better, smarter, prettier or handsomer, more talented, more athletic, or more outgoing—you get the idea?" He nodded.

"The thing is, we just need to focus on what we're good at and excel in that area. Everything else will eventually fall into place." He wiped his nose on his sleeve and had stopped crying and seemed to be listening. She felt tears well in her eyes as she continued. "God made us all so differently so we could work together and accomplish his goals for the human race."

"What goal?" he asked, scooting closer.

"First of all, God wants us to love and worship him. Then we are to help our fellow man. If we all thought the same or had the same talents, it would be pretty boring around here."

"Or crazy. Can you imagine a whole world filled with Dannys?"

She smiled. "Well, it would be fun, but nothing would get accomplished."

"Exactly!" he said, grinning. "I like Danny as a friend, but sometimes I wish he would be a little more serious."

Sensing that she had said enough, she opened her arms, and he dove into them. He was too big to sit in her lap, but he snuggled in close and with her arm wrapped around his shoulder, they sat for a few quiet moments.

"I hope you don't mind, but I was looking through your drawing pad and noticed a pretty scary picture. Want to tell me about it?"

Nicky looked down at his hands, chewing his bottom lip. "Well, no one was supposed to see that picture, but I guess it's okay if you did." He looked up, worry etching his face. "Sometimes when I fall asleep and dream, that monster chases me. I call out for Daddy, but I can't find him. I usually wake up then. I'm too scared to go back to sleep sometimes."

"Hmm," she said in response. "How long has this been going on?"

He shrugged. "I dunno, maybe about a week."

She pulled him into a hug and kissed the top of his head. "I'm sorry you're having such scary dreams. Maybe we can pray together before you go to sleep?"

Shrugging, he said, "I guess it couldn't hurt."

She lifted the covers for him to crawl under and tucked them around his body, wondering if he would sleep after having such a late nap. She kissed him on the forehead and said a short prayer of protection.

Maybe this talk will set him back on the right track. Not knowing what else to do she said, "Maybe your math teacher can help tutor you or have another student help you with the math concepts."

He shrugged and said, "Yeah, maybe."

Standing and heading for the door, she turned and said, "Nicky, if the teacher can't or won't help you, Brad, Stacey, or I will help."

He smiled a crooked little smile and said, "Thanks, Mom. I love you."

"Love you too, babe." She blew him a kiss and closed the door.

About an hour later, he wandered downstairs, poured himself a bowl of cheerios, and came into the den where she was reading a book, Brad was working on the computer, and Stacey was busily cutting and pasting pictures on a poster board for a science project having to do with agriculture across the United States.

He shrugged as he looked at his mom. "I couldn't sleep."

She smiled and nodded.

Looking at Stacey's project, he asked, "Can I help you cut and paste?"

She looked warily at him. "Okay, as long as you don't spill any cereal on my poster."

He set the bowl on a nearby table and, sitting cross-legged next to her, picked up a pair of scissors.

"What do you want me to cut out?" he asked as he looked around at the piles of magazines and papers.

As Stacey explained what she needed, Christina went back to reading her book, feeling hopeful that Nicky would be all right.

That evening, right before sending the kids up to bed, Christina called David's parents and brought them up to date on the events in their lives.

"Oh my goodness," said Ruth, David's mom. "I had been planning to call you in a few minutes."

"Wow! Guess great minds *do* think alike! So what are you and Dad up to?"

Ruth told her of their large garden and its bountiful supply and how she was canning and freezing and sharing with her friends and neighbors.

"Christina, I wish I could send you some of this stuff! It's times like this that I really miss you and the children."

Christina nodded in agreement. She too missed the sweet corn, fresh red tomatoes, green beans, and especially the zucchini and yellow squash. The markets around Alva had their share of fresh produce, but it wasn't the same. The sweet corn wasn't as sweet, and the other vegetables just didn't look, smell, or taste as wonderful as Ruth and Dan's. *Maybe I'm just prejudiced.*

Christina knew how much time, energy, and love went into the production of such a grand garden, as she and David had tried several times on a much smaller scale. As Ruth described the garden, Christina pictured the white picket fence surrounding it, the archway covered with morning glories, and the neat rows of marigolds and veggies. She could feel her mouth watering as Ruth told of all the tomatoes she was making into salsa and sauce. She promised to save a few jars for Christina and the kids and to bring them when they came for Thanksgiving.

"Mom, I was thinking that maybe we could come visit y'all for Thanksgiving. We're all getting pretty homesick to see you and Dad and Robert and Joyce and their families, not to mention our friends up there."

Ruth exclaimed, "Oh, honey, that would be wonderful! I know everyone would love to see you too."

Christina continued her thoughts. "I get a week vacation from work, and the kids have a week off, so I think we could swing it. Now that Brad can drive, we can take turns, so it won't take as long and be so tiring."

Ruth was smiling as she said, "Dad will be thrilled when I tell him."

She called the kids in and handed the phone to Stacey, listening as she told of her recent activities.

"And Grandma, you and Grandpa need to come see me in the Christmas play at church. I got the part of Mary! I've also tried out for the play at school. I'll know in a couple of days if I get the part or not. No, it won't be too much to be in both plays. Okay, I love you too. Here's Brad."

"Hey, Grandma and Grandpa, thanks again for the two plane tickets for my birthday. I still don't know when I'll be able to get away or who'll come with me. It'll probably be next summer." He paused. "Yeah, her name's Melinda. She's really cute and sweet. You can meet her when you come down in December." He paused again, and Christina left the room to see if Nicky wanted to speak to his grandparents. He jumped up from the floor where he had been pasting a picture of a cow onto Stacey's poster board and went in just in time to hear Brad say his good-byes. He handed his little brother the phone.

"Hi, Grandma!" he said, trying to catch his breath. "Benji says hi too. I like school all right. I have a best friend named Danny and we do lots of things together." He paused. "We Rollerblade and play in his tree house. I hope to get a bike for Christmas, 'cause I've sorta outgrown the one I have." He paused. "I'm almost to Mom's chin now, and I grew a whole shoe size and two sizes in my pants! I now wear a size twelve." He talked a few more minutes, said his good-byes, and handed the phone back to Christina. She couldn't help but smile as she took the phone.

Ruth asked, "Wasn't today your first day at the hospital?"

Christina related how nervous she had been and how it had all felt like a dream.

"Well, Dan and I will be looking forward to seeing you at Thanksgiving, and we'll make plans to come down over Christmas. We wouldn't want to miss Stacey's plays. It sounds like you all are adjusting well."

"Yes, it's been a *long* year, but we're finally seeing the light at the end of the tunnel." *A very long and dark tunnel.*

"Well honey, we love you and will talk to you again next week."

"Mom, before you hang up, I do have something I need to talk to you about." She told them about Nicky and his moodiness. Ruth listened quietly and then let out a sigh.

"I think you're doing the right thing. Seems David would get in his moods as well, and they would pass after a few days. We just talked and prayed together and tried to find solutions to his problems, just like you're doing."

"I sure hope this phase passes soon. If not, I'll get him into counseling."

"That sounds like a good idea. We'll keep him in our prayers in the meantime." There were a few seconds of silence as each woman processed the information.

"Christina, if you need anything, and I mean *anything*, please don't hesitate to call us. We love you all *so* much."

"Love you too." They said their good-byes.

CHAPTER 35

Once the kids were in bed, Christina called Cindy and told her about her first day of work and asked about the electricians.

"I know you were here the day they first showed up—a couple of Saturdays ago when we went to Dallas. You said you came to check on Benji and they approached you? You were going to tell me more, but we got interrupted and never finished. I forgot about it until I saw *that* van again today. I figured they'd be done and gone by now."

"They're still there?"

"Yeah. Kinda weird, huh? I meant to ask the neighbors yesterday but forgot."

Cindy replied, "Hmm. That *is* kinda weird, especially since there doesn't seem to be any electrical problems anywhere else." After a brief pause, she continued. "They seemed legit. I still have the business card in my purse. Do you want me to get it?"

"Not now. Maybe I'll look at it tomorrow. What did they do and how long did they stay?"

"Two of them looked around the house, supposedly checking the wiring, while I talked to the other guy. Ed. Did I tell you he is drop-dead gorgeous?"

Christina chuckled. "Only a million times. You two went for coffee a after that, didn't you?"

Cindy sighed. "Yeah. He is so hot."

"Okay. I get that. He didn't seem the least bit suspicious? What about the other two guys?"

"Like I said, they all seemed legit. They were very polite, and the time I was with Ed, he seemed the perfect gentleman. He did ask a few questions about you and the kids, which I thought was a bit odd at first, but he said he just wanted to know about my friends."

"Hmm."

"What? You think something shady is going on? Like maybe they're *not* who they say they are? Like they're *really* jewel thieves or something like that and are checking out the neighborhood so they can come back and rob everyone?"

Christina chuckled. "Well, now that you mention it, maybe so. I was actually thinking along that line. I was thinkin' maybe they were thieves of some sort, but then I don't think they would stay in the area for so long if they were just checking out possible targets."

Cindy sighed. "Yeah, you're right. And besides, Ed just seems so darn nice. I can't picture him stealing from anyone."

"Okay. Tell you what. I'll ask Danny's mom if she's seen or heard anything about an electrical problem in the neighborhood. In the meantime, you should be cautious with this Ed guy. Remember, looks can be deceiving."

"Yes, ma'am. Did I mention that he is hot?"

Christina giggled. "Good night, Cindy. Oh, wait. I forgot to tell you that Steven has a girlfriend."

"Get out! Seriously? Well, I'll be danged. I didn't know that."

"I figured you would have given me a heads-up if you had known."

"Well, yeah. Sorry, honey. Guess you two just aren't meant to be together."

"Yeah, that's what I'm thinking. Good night."

That night she dreamed that Godzilla was in the water and heading for one of the ports in Michigan. She was standing on the boardwalk and could see him coming and was screaming for David, because she had lost sight of him. People were running and screaming as huge waves headed for shore. She woke as a large wave nearly engulfed her.

"Lord," she whispered as she turned over and tucked the covers under her chin, "please protect us." As she was drifting off to sleep once again, she remembered the envelope sitting on her dresser. "Oh, dang it! I'll just have to wait till the morning."

CHAPTER 36

While Christina had been working, Ed and Tom made another attempt to find the missing documents. They knew she would be gone all day, so they were very thorough. Ed picked up where he left off in Christina's bedroom, being careful to replace papers, knickknacks, and clothes where they had been. Tom was busy with the computer. After a couple of hours, Benji started barking and ran to the side door. Ed and Tom went into high-alert status, thinking someone may be coming in. When he heard the mailbox cover click into place and saw the mail carrier walk away, Tom breathed a sigh of relief. "Hey, Ed. It was just the mailman."

"Whew! I was afraid we were gonna have a confrontation."

"Yeah, me too! I had my stun gun out and everything! I'm gonna check through the mail and see what interesting things there may be."

"Let me know if there's anything important—like a special sale at Wal-Mart," he mumbled as he returned to Christina's room.

Tom was surprised when he saw a brown five-by-seven envelope with David Sanders' name on it and a return address from Washington, DC.

"Well, I'll be danged! Hey, Ed, she got something in the mail from Washington, DC. Wanna come down and take a look with me?"

"Sure. I'll be right there."

Looking the envelope over, Ed said, "Well, we'll just have to open it up and check it out." He pulled out his pocketknife and carefully peeled the flap back.

As Ed extracted the paper, Tom said, "I'll be surprised if this is what we're looking for."

They both laughed as Ed showed him a picture of George and Laura Bush in a dance pose, both smiling at the camera. At the bottom of the picture it read, "To Mr. David Sanders: Thank you for your support. Together we can build a single nation of justice and opportunity. Warmest regards, George Bush."

Ed replaced the picture and resealed the envelope and then returned it to the mailbox with the other items.

Glancing over at the computer screen, Ed asked, "How are things going?"

"They have a lot more files and programs than I anticipated." Pointing to the box on the desk, he said, "There's a shoebox *full* of CDs I need to look through. It would really help to *know* what to look for. I just hope I know it when I see it."

"Yeah, me too. I'd like to wrap this thing up today and get out of here. The more often we're here, the more likely someone will see us." He turned and headed back upstairs.

After about an hour, when Ed was thinking of taking a break and getting some ice water, he heard a whoop from the den.

"Hey, Ed!" called Tom. "I think I found it!"

Ed closed the lid to the box he was sorting through and headed downstairs.

Walking in the room, he asked, "What did you find?"

"I found this CD labeled 'David.' Let me show you what's on it." He scrolled down the page. "At first, I thought it was just some of his work-related stuff, but look here." Ed looked over Tom's shoulder at the computer screen.

"Most of the following information doesn't make any sense, and I'm pretty sure it really is work related, but I did notice the name Ackbar Al-Zahid. Now, why that name would be on this disc is indeed a mystery."

"Huh. That is strange. That name sounds familiar."

"Well, it should. He's been on the top ten list of terrorists to watch for."

Ed nodded. "That explains that, but why would David have his name on any of his stuff?"

"Good question. I'm gonna just confiscate this CD. Do you think they'd miss it?"

"I bet they don't even know it's here. I have a feeling Christina doesn't use the computer much, and the kids would probably think it was their dad's work stuff and wouldn't be interested."

Removing the disc, Tom said, "I wonder *why* David made this CD. Surely, he would know his family wouldn't know what it was or what it meant."

"But if it's *so* important, why keep it hidden in a CD? I know he was working for the government tracking down terrorist cells, but why would he have kept *any* information? He would have been taking quite a risk if anyone in the agency knew he had this—whatever *this* is. Obviously, it was meant for someone else, besides the ATO, FBI, or CIA.

Ed answered thoughtfully, "Maybe it was meant for us."

"Hmm, well, that's a possibility, I guess. But why, and why not before now?" Tom turned off the computer and began putting the CDs and other papers back in their proper places.

Ed left the room, leaving Tom with questions and no answers running through his head. "I'll go up and make sure everything's in order. Then we can get out of here and head back to Dallas."

David checked on each of his children and watched as they slept.

"They are so precious to me," he said to Jarrod.

"Yes, I know."

"I've noticed a lot of activity in the spiritual realm. Anything going on that I should be aware of?"

"Nothing you have deal with. Michael and Gabriel are gathering the troops to do some kind of battle, and I've heard a few of the guardians say that Father has asked them to prepare some extra rooms. Whenever there is a battle on Earth, the guardians have to build more rooms to welcome the newcomers."

"How many rooms are we talking about?"

"Not sure. I heard as many as five thousand."

"Wow! Will my family be safe?" he asked as he transported to Christina's bedside.

"As far as I know." He looked at David. "If they were to be called home, do you think they're ready?"

David nodded. "Yes. I believe they are."

"Good."

Christina moaned and called out David's name. He reached out and touched her head, and she immediately calmed and went back into a deep sleep.

CHAPTER 37

On Tuesday, Christina almost cried when the alarm rang. She smacked the snooze button with her hand. Not wanting to get out of bed, she pulled the covers over her head and tried to think of excuses for not getting up. None came to mind. The alarm rang a second time. *Okay.* She sighed and forced her weary body out of bed and into the shower.

Leaning her head against the wall and letting the hot water cascade down her neck and back, she wondered if the recurring nightmares about fires, floods, falling buildings, and monsters chasing her were some kind of omen. Her head continued to throb even after a hot shower with the bar of soap that promised to refresh, revitalize, and wake her up. She took a couple of pain relievers and headed downstairs for a steaming cup of coffee.

Glancing out the window on her way to the refrigerator, she noticed the clear blue sky. *It looks like another beautiful day. I wonder what the temperature is.* She checked the thermometer by the back door. Seventy-eight degrees. *Nice!*

Once her head cleared and she wasn't so bleary-eyed, she thought about the day's schedule. She was looking forward to seeing Steven again. It had been a pleasant experience working with him and reminiscing at lunch. Hopefully the day would go as well as the previous one.

Once the kids were up and ready for school, she headed out the door, arriving at Steven's office in time to share a cup of coffee with him and Mrs. Ferguson.

Christina was informed that a new patient was admitted the previous night. He was diagnosed with a blockage in his carotid artery, and Dr. Dawson had done an emergency angioplasty. Mrs. Ferguson opened the chart and read the ER and surgical reports, the blood test results, his latest vital signs, and the plan for his care over the next several days.

Closing the chart, she said, "So ... seems like he's stable for now."

Steven nodded. "We'll continue monitoring his intake, output, and vitals as usual—and of course the incision site."

Christina looked at Steven and asked, "Any other patients I need to know about?"

"I think I'll be dismissing Catherine Watson today. Her vitals are good, and her blood work came back within the normal parameters. There are no signs of infection around the pacemaker incision."

Christina remembered Catherine, a fifty-year-old mother of four teenage boys who worked part-time as a piano instructor. She had come into the outpatient surgical ward three days ago to have a new pacemaker installed. She complained of feeling feverish and nauseated and was soon diagnosed with a systemic infection, originating where her previous pacemaker was located. Once the infection was under control with IV antibiotics, the new pacemaker was installed. She had been kept overnight as a precaution.

Glancing at the clock on the wall, Christina set her mug on the desk, stood, stretched, and stated that she needed to get upstairs and do her briefing for the next shift. She took the charts from Emma, said her good-byes, and left. Steven smiled and said he would see her in a few minutes.

Gathering up the coffee mugs and walking to the sink, Emma asked, "Steven, what do you think about Christina?"

"You mean as a nurse or as a person?"

"Both."

"Well, she seems to be doing all right as a nurse—but then she's only been here one day. And I like her as a person."

She nodded and smiled.

"Why do you ask?" he asked warily, remembering times when his aunt had tried to set him up with women.

She shrugged and said casually, "Oh, just wondering."

He frowned at her. "Don't you even think about playing matchmaker, Aunt Emma."

"Whatever would make you think I would do such a thing?"

He rolled his eyes and sighed. "Besides, I already have a girlfriend, remember?"

"Of course you do, dear." She turned her back to him, hiding a smile.

He shook his head and scowled. He loved his aunt dearly, but sometimes she just had a sneaky way about interfering in his life.

CHAPTER 38

When Christina and Steven entered Mr. Davis's room an hour later, time seemed to stand still. They watched his TV in stunned silence as a plane flew into the Twin Towers of the World Trade Center, followed closely by a second. Christina felt her knees buckle as she watched the subsequent collapse of the two buildings in horror. She sat in the nearest chair, unable to speak, hot tears stinging her eyes before cascading down her cheeks. She looked at Dr. Dawson, who had gone pale and was leaning against the doorjamb. As they were trying to grasp the magnitude of the devastation, news reports came in that the Pentagon had been attacked as well.

Mr. Davis's heart monitor alarm went off with a loud, ear-piercing ringing, and it took a couple of seconds for Christina and Dr. Dawson to react. The pulse indicator had jumped from a steady one hundred beats a minute to an erratic 150 beats. Dr. Dawson ordered a sedative, which he administered through the IV line. Once their patient was visibly calm, they went to check on the other five patients on the unit. Fortunately, there were only two others who had watched the news and were upset enough to need sedation.

Once the patients were settled, and before leaving the floor to offer his services elsewhere, Dr. Dawson called the staff together for a meeting.

"I need everyone to be ready for *any* emergency. Once the news gets around about the towers, I have a feeling there'll be a lot of stress-related heart problems. You witnessed how these patients reacted, and that's in a controlled environment. Just imagine how folks with preexisting heart problems may react. Anyway, we just need to be ready."

Each staff member nodded in agreement.

Boarding the elevator, he was surprised to hear a code red was announced over the public address system—which meant that all medical personnel were on high alert and couldn't leave the building until it had been lifted with the announcement of a code green. Christina and the other nurses and aides just looked at each other and shook their heads. Not knowing how long they would be required to stay, each one started making phone calls—some to set up child care, others to let family members know the situation.

Christina, feeling anxious and wanting to speak to her children but not wanting to disrupt their class time, called each of the schools, only to be answered by busy signals.

The week before school started, she had given each of her children an emergency cell phone that would only dial her number or 911. She was relieved when she felt the first buzzing in her pocket and saw that the call was from Stacey.

"Mom?"

"Hey, baby. You all right?"

"I'm okay. They're sending everyone home. Can you come get me?"

"I can't 'cause I have to stay at the hospital, but I'm gonna call Cindy and see if she can come. If not, I'm sure Brad will check in and he'll come get you." She felt her phone buzz again. "Gotta go, babe. Brad's calling."

She disconnected Stacey and answered Brad.

"Mom?"

"Hey, Brad. I just spoke to Stacey. She's pretty upset. I told her you'd come get her. I can't leave the hospital anytime soon. In fact, I'm not sure when we'll be able to leave. We're on high alert right now."

"Okay. What about Nicky?"

"I'm gonna call Cindy to see if she can pick y'all up, then swing by and get Nicky. If she can't, then could you and Stacey get him?"

"Sure, Mom. I just can't believe this is happening! Kinda makes me scared. You don't think these terrorists will attack anywhere else, do you?"

"I don't know. If they're crazy enough to pull this off, they may do something more, or worse."

"Geez, Mom. I don't know *what* could be worse! Please come home as soon as you can."

"I will, honey. I don't want to be away from y'all either, and if I could, I'd leave right now."

"I know. You'll let me know if Mrs. Murray will be getting us?"

"Yep. I'll probably have her call your cell phone so you can pick a place to meet. If you can get away, why don't you walk down and sit with Stacey until you hear from me or Cindy?"

"Mom?"

"Yeah?"

"Love you."

"Love you too, babe."

When Christina disconnected, she had to take a few deep breaths to regain control of her emotions. The mother hen in her wanted to gather her chicks and hide them under her protective wings. Instead, she called Cindy.

"I just heard about what happened from one of the customers. Oh my God, Christina! Who would do such a horrible thing?"

"I don't know, but I do know I want my kids to be safe, and I can't be there right now. Can you please get them and bring them here, or have them come to your work or take them home and be with them till I can get home?"

"Oh my God! I need to get Samara! She's probably scared too!"

Christina heard a noise in the background.

"Okay. I just asked Mary if I could go, and she said she would close the store for the afternoon. She doubts anyone will be in the mood to shop after all this. You want me to call Brad and have him get all the kids together?"

"Yeah. I told him to expect a call from you. He's walking down to the middle school to sit with Stacey. He could probably get Samara too. You'll have to go by and get Nicky. I'll call the school and let them know you'll be picking him up. I gotta go. I'll call you later."

"Don't worry Christina. I'll take care of everything."

"Thanks."

Christina and her staff breathed a sigh of relief when a code green was announced at three o'clock. When one of the afternoon nurses and two of the aides called in sick, she and two of the aides reluctantly volunteered to stay until the night shift came in. *Can't leave the patients to fend for themselves.*

She called home to check in on everybody. Cindy assured her that everyone was fine, but her children were anxious to speak with her.

"Here's Nicky."

"Hey, Mom. When are you comin' home?"

Christina explained the work situation.

"That's not fair! We need you here!"

"I know, and I'd love to be there, but these people need me more. I promise I'll be home as soon as I can."

Nicky sighed. "Okay. Here's Stacey."

"So you won't be home for a while?"

"No. I have to stay awhile longer. Maybe y'all can come here? Let me say hi to Brad. Then I want to talk to Cindy again."

"Okay, Mom. Love you."

"You too."

"Hey, Mom. I only heard a little of the conversation, but I gather you're not gonna be home for a while?"

"Right. A couple of aides and nurses called in sick, so I volunteered to stay and help, otherwise they'd be shorthanded."

"Hmm. Seems kinda weird for them to call in sick. I bet they just wanted to stay home with their families."

"That may be true, but it doesn't really matter *why* they didn't come in. These patients still need to be cared for."

"I know. It just stinks that you can't be here with us."

"Yep. But life isn't always fair."

"Yeah."

"Hey, thanks for being so helpful today. I appreciate you caring for your sister and brother."

Brad let out a sigh. "Yeah. You wanna talk to Mrs. Murray now?"

"Yep. Thanks."

Christina and Cindy made plans to bring the Sanders kids to the hospital to see their mom. Christina met them in the cafeteria, and they shared a McDonald's dinner.

"How late do you have to work, Mrs. Sanders?" Samara asked as she dipped a French fry in ketchup and popped it in her mouth.

"At least until eleven, when the next shift is supposed to start. After going over all the nursing notes and checking the medications and all, I should be out of here by eleven thirty."

Cindy said, "Why don't Samara and I stay the night? That way, if you do have to work later, someone will be there for the kids. Is that okay with you, Christina?"

"Oh yes, absolutely! I like that idea. How about y'all?"

Stacey, Nicky, and Brad all nodded in agreement, and Samara shrugged.

"Okay. It's settled. Brad, would you please get the bedding in the upstairs linen closet for Cindy and Samara when y'all get home?"

"Sure."

Good-byes were said, and Christina breathed a sigh of relief. She didn't have to worry about her kids and could totally focus on her job. She passed by the emergency room and saw that each chair held a body, either in distress or for support. She overheard two nurses discussing the number of folks being brought in for anxiety attacks and heart and breathing problems.

I'd better get back up to the floor. I won't be surprised if some of these folks end up there. As she rode the elevator to the third floor a thought came to her.

I wonder if all my nightmares of fires, floods, earthquakes, and monsters were God's way of warning me of this horrible event. Well, maybe the nightmares will stop—unless there's more to come. Oh Lordy, I hope not!

Christina, thinking about the possible implications of her dreams, walked into the medication room to prepare the evening meds and was surprised to see Dr. Dawson standing at the sink. She gasped and put her hand to her chest. "Geez, you scared me!"

Getting no response, concern overwhelmed her. Forgetting protocol, she reached out and put her hand on his trembling back.

"Steven? Are you all right?" He was holding his face in his hands and taking deep breaths in an effort to regain control of his emotions.

"I can't reach Anika! She won't answer her cell phone, and the phones aren't working at the hotel she was staying in." He paused to catch his breath and looked at her with panic in his eyes. "It was only a couple of blocks from the World Trade Center."

With more confidence than she felt, she said, "Oh, Steven, I'm sure she's fine. She'll call you as soon as she can. Can I get you anything? A drink of water? A sedative?"

"No." He smiled and shook his head. "I'll be fine. I just need to get myself together before I go back out there. I'm so tired, and after all the events of today and not being able to reach her—well, it just hit me hard, and I sorta lost it."

"I can understand, but hopefully everything will be fine." She patted his arm. "I'm gonna check on Mr. Davis. Then I'll come back to get the meds ready to pass out. You stay as long as you need to." She left him standing in front of the sink, splashing cold water on his face.

"Thanks, Christina," he called out, but the door had already shut.

CHAPTER 39

Christina was so exhausted when she returned home around midnight that she stripped out of her scrubs and fell into bed, not even bothering with makeup removal or teeth brushing. The next morning she awoke at eight and jumped out of bed, thinking she had overslept. Stumbling to the bathroom, she remembered it was her day off.

"Thank you, God!" she muttered as she splashed cold water on her face.

She didn't hear the kids but did hear the television. *That's weird. Why is the TV on?* She ran downstairs to see if perhaps the kids had left it on and was shocked to see Cindy, Samara, Brad, and Stacey sitting on the couch watching the news on the television. They still had their pj's on.

"Good morning. What's goin' on?"

"School's been cancelled," announced Brad as she entered the family room.

Samara added, "Every station is showing news about the Twin Towers and the Pentagon."

The death tolls were being discussed, and video clips were being shown from every angle. There was also footage of another plane crash in Pennsylvania and speculation as to its cause. She stood in stunned silence as the reality of it all came crashing down on her. There were *thousands* killed and missing.

She thought about Anika and wondered if she was among the dead. She said a quick prayer on her behalf and for the victims and their families. Tears streamed down her cheeks, and Cindy handed her a tissue from the box in her lap. Christina could see that she had been crying as well. After wiping her eyes and blowing her nose, she sat in between Brad and Stacey and drew them close to her, kissing each one on the cheek. They returned the hugs and snuggled close.

"We missed you, Mom. Are you all right?" Brad asked, looking at his tired and rumpled mother.

She nodded wearily. Cindy stood and asked if she would like some coffee and toast.

"Thanks, Cindy, I'd like that."

"Where's Nicky?" she asked no one in particular.

"He's still asleep," answered Stacey. "He stayed up till eleven because he was afraid to *go* to sleep, and kept asking for you. Brad put a sleeping bag on the floor next to his bed and told Nicky it would be like camping out. He went right to sleep after that."

"That's great, Brad. Thanks," she said, pulling him into a hug.

Nicky was up by the time they were ready to eat breakfast. Sitting in a circle and holding hands, they prayed for the families of the victims and for the leaders of the country and their families, all needing comfort, protection, and wisdom during this critical time.

Cindy and Christina cleaned up the breakfast dishes while the kids went their separate ways to clean up and dress for the day. Then everyone returned to the den and watched as the president addressed the nation.

Around 10:00 a.m., Christina called the CCU to see if she was needed. She was informed that everything had settled and all the nurses and aides were present, and although her concern was appreciated, they'd see her on her next scheduled day. She was relieved, as she felt the need to stay home and recuperate from the previous day and night's drama.

CHAPTER 40

Tom and Ed sat in their boss's office on Tuesday morning discussing plans to return to Alva when it seemed all hell broke loose. People were running and yelling, and phones and alarms were ringing.

"What the heck?" Tom said as he jumped up and went to the office door.

Their boss, Henry Steil, walked in, threw a folder on his desk, and then turned to address the two agents.

"Gentlemen, we have a huge problem." He walked over and turned on the TV. No words were needed as they all three watched the Twin Towers collapse.

"Oh … my … God!" Tom said as he sat in the nearest chair.

Ed looked in shocked horror at his boss. "Is this for real?"

Henry nodded and sat in the chair behind his desk as Ed paced around the room, wanting to ask a thousand questions but unable to get his mouth to work.

Tom finally said, "How could this happen?"

Henry let out a long sigh. "I wish I knew."

"What are we gonna do?"

"We've put every government building on high alert, grounded all planes, and put the president, vice president, and their families in undisclosed protection. The air force has planes in the air, and all the other armed forces are on standby."

Tom's thoughts went immediately to his son and ex-wife, and he shot up a prayer on their behalf, vowing to call them as soon as possible.

Ed stood by the door chewing on his thumbnail as Henry talked. Thoughts of his mom and sisters flooded his mind, and he had to push them back. The rational part of him knew they were safe, but his emotional side wanted to run and gather them together and hide in a cave somewhere till there was no more danger.

There was a knock on the door. Henry motioned for the young man to enter. "Sir, there will be an emergency meeting for all the personnel down in the auditorium in thirty minutes."

Henry nodded and looked at his watch. "Thanks, Kyle. We'll be down soon."

Ed shook his head and ran his fingers through his hair. "Never in a million years would I have thought this could happen. Not in America! Not on *our* soil! I'm so angry I want to punch someone!"

Henry held his hand up. "I know exactly what you mean. I'm still in shock, and

I don't know whether to feel angry or afraid. I'd like to go kick some butt too, but I'm not even sure whose to kick."

"I just want to see my kid and hold him," mumbled Tom. There was silence in the room as all three men thought of their loved ones.

Holding the door open, Ed said, "All right, guys, guess we'd better head on downstairs."

CHAPTER 41

The rest of the week had been a physically and emotionally challenging time for Christina and her family. Even though people were encouraged to get back to their normal routines, it was as if their feet had been kicked out from under them, and they were having difficulty getting up. Christina used her two days off to contact family and friends via Internet or phone, feeling the need to connect and be reassured that everyone was fine and easing her troubled mind.

School had resumed on Thursday, much to her kids' dismay, as they all wanted to stay home, where they felt most secure. According to the news media, the nation was still on high alert, and many government buildings, schools, malls, arenas, and airports remained closed, stranding travelers around the world.

Normal TV programming was put on hold as each station continually carried pictures, videos, and testimonies of folks who had either survived the catastrophes or were missing loved ones. The radio DJs seemed to play more patriotic songs and did interviews with government officials and local residents who had been affected by the Twin Towers tragedy or the airplane crashes.

Trust and security had been replaced by fear in the hearts and minds of the American people, and life would never be the same. Once it had been revealed that Middle Eastern Islamic terrorists were responsible, it seemed all Middle Easterners were scrutinized more closely. Christina thought of the Islamic family in Alva who owned the convenient store and gas station and wondered how they were being treated. The few times she interacted with them, they seemed courteous and kind, and she never heard anything negative concerning them. She hoped they wouldn't be treated disrespectfully.

She also thought of the few doctors and nurses in the hospital who looked Middle Eastern with their dark skin, eyes, and hair, and wondered if they too were Islamic and if their loyalty to America would be questioned.

Geez, she thought, *here I am sorta profiling. I never even thought about people's nationality or wondered about loyalty until now.* She was reminded of how the Japanese were treated during World War II and asked God to please not let that happen again. *I'll be so thankful when all this turmoil passes and we can get back to a normal life.*

CHAPTER 42

When Christina arrived at Steven's office Friday morning, she was met by Mrs. Ferguson.

"I think you need to go on up and handle things on your own today. The nurses from the night shift will fill you in on what needs to be done, and there'll be another RN and a couple of aides on the floor with you."

Panic and worry were etched Christina's face, and her hands began to shake. Mrs. Ferguson shook her head and smiled. "You'll do fine, dear. There are only three patients on the floor, and if you need anything, I'll just be a phone call away."

Inside, Christina felt like a wiggly bowl of Jell-O, but she managed to say, "Oh, good," while her mind was reeling. *I'm not ready to be on my own, but what choice do I have? What could possibly go wrong?*

During the elevator ride to the third floor, she did a few deep breathing exercises to calm her nerves and shot a prayer up to heaven, asking for help to not screw anything up—or, worse yet, kill anyone!

Exiting the elevator and heading for the nurses' station, she was surprised to see Janet Washburn sitting at the desk. She had heard several negative comments about the woman's disposition and felt her trepidation go up a notch at the thought of working with her. She took in a deep breath and released it before speaking.

"Hey, Janet, are you working on this floor today?"

Looking up and giving Christina a look that said, "Well, duh," she said, "Yeah. Mrs. Ferguson didn't tell you?"

"She said there'd be another nurse, she just didn't say who it would be. I'm glad you're here." *I would have preferred anyone but you.* "I'm not sure I'm ready to run everything on my own, being this is my second week and all."

Janet nodded. "Well, Mrs. Ferguson figured you might need a little help and asked me to come in. I'm only supposed to step in if you need advice or something. She wants you to do everything as if I wasn't here." *Let's see how incompetent you really are,* she thought as she gave Christina a tight smile.

Christina nodded and sighed. "Well, okay. Nothing like jumping into the deep end to learn how to swim," she said as she leaned on the counter to steady herself. Janet stood looking at her expectantly. "We need to have a short staff meeting in five minutes in the conference room. Could you please tell the other gals?"

Janet nodded and looked around, and, seeing no one in the vicinity, said, "I'll go get them."

Christina gathered the charts and headed for the meeting room.

Once everyone had arrived, she asked if there were any new patients admitted during the night and what the status was. Satisfied she was caught up on the news from the previous shift and had an idea of the agenda for *her* shift, she dismissed the staff and busily prepared the medications to be distributed in the next couple of hours.

After checking on his patients, Dr. Dawson left the hospital for the weekend, or so Christina thought. He informed her that his associate, Dr. Timothy Meils, would be on call if an emergency arose and should be coming onto the floor soon to go over the charts with her.

Christina felt a strange emptiness as she waved good-bye and watched Steven board the elevator. She wouldn't see him again until Monday morning. She hoped their friendship would continue to evolve, even if Steven was romantically involved with Anika. She felt that little twinge of jealousy again as she thought of them together. *Stop it!* she told herself. *He wasn't interested in you years ago, and he isn't interested in you now.* She sighed. *I know,* she replied to her inner self. *Just be happy. You're friends. If you weren't, your job would be a lot more difficult.*

Dr. Timothy Meils, known as Dr. Tim to his patients, was fresh out of medical school and looked all of sixteen. He had blond hair that was closely cropped, blue eyes, and rosy red cheeks with deep dimples. His nose was well proportioned for his thin face—not too big, and not too small—and he had a pleasant smile that accentuated his dimples. He wasn't quite six feet tall and had delicate features. His hands were slender and his fingers were long, like one would expect on a piano player, and though he wasn't beefy, he was muscular—wiry and lean, like he rode a bicycle everywhere.

Approaching the counter, he called, "Excuse me."

Christina looked up from the chart she was writing in. "Yes?"

"Are you Christina Sanders?"

She nodded.

"Dr. Dawson said I needed to speak with you about his patients."

"Oh, yes, you must be Dr. Meils." He nodded and smiled. "Let me get those charts for you, and we can go into the conference room and discuss them." Christina gathered the charts and called Janet over.

Janet *wanted* to dislike Christina and tried to find fault with her but had difficulty mustering any ill feelings toward the woman. She wondered how she could discredit this interloper and not get caught. Then she had an idea.

"I need to go over these charts with Dr. Meils. Can you please keep tabs on the unit until I get back?"

"Okay."

"Thanks so much. This shouldn't take long."

"Take as long as you need," she said sweetly.

Once Christina was out of sight, Janet picked up the chart Christina had left. She looked around and, seeing no one in the vicinity, took her ink eraser and went to work on the papers in front of her. She was just finishing her handiwork when Christina returned to the desk to retrieve the forgotten chart.

Smiling and handing the chart over, she said, "I was just going to bring this in to you." Janet was counting on the changes to go unnoticed. As the day progressed, it became evident that they were.

As far as Christina was concerned, the day went well and was at times even a little boring. The three patients survived, and the staff was helpful. The two aides and the LPN took the time to explain procedures, show where items were kept, and bring her snacks and drinks—except Janet, who seemed to deliberately avoid being in her presence. Ending her shift and turning everything over to the afternoon staff, she thought, *I think I'm gonna like it here.*

Walking toward the elevator, her thoughts were interrupted as Janet called out, "Hey, Christina, Dr. Dawson wants to speak to you."

She gave a surprised look, thinking he should be gone, and headed back to the nurses' station, taking the phone from Janet.

"Hello?"

"Christina, can you come by my office before you leave?"

"Uh, sure. I'll be there in a few minutes."

"Great! I'll see you then."

Replacing the receiver, she shook her head in disbelief. *I thought he'd be gone by now. Why on earth would he want to see me?*

She had no idea that Steven had heard from Anika. He had been withdrawn and uncommunicative, secluding himself in his office most of the time, worrying and fretting and calling everyone he knew who might know how to reach her.

Tapping lightly on the partially opened door, she called, "Steven, you wanted to see me?"

He walked over and pulled her into the room, closing the door behind them.

"Yes! I heard from Anika!" he said cheerily. "The reason I hadn't heard from her sooner was that she's been in the hospital." Christina watched as he paced around the room.

She was feeling a little … what? *Awkward? Jealous? Certainly not jealous. And yet—no, I won't even consider that emotion. Not now.* She refocused on what he was saying.

"She said she was hit on the head by a falling brick or chunk of concrete as she was running away from the area. She and her friend were about a block away from the building when they heard the plane and then the impact. She said at first they just stood there in shock, but when things started falling from the sky, they turned to run and had gotten a few yards when she felt the impact and went down. She says after that, she doesn't remember anything. Her friend was able to pull her into an alcove of a building, thus protecting them from falling debris and possible death. It was utter chaos for several hours as falling objects, thick smoke, and the noise of people screaming and sirens blaring kept rescue workers from finding them.

Christina gasped. "Are they both all right now?"

"Yeah, thank God. Anika had to get ten stitches and had a concussion, but she'll be fine. Her friend ended up getting a few stitches on a deep gash in her knee where she must have knelt on a piece of glass or sharp rock when she bent down to check on Anika. She told Anika that she didn't even know she had the cut and was surprised when they told her she needed stitches. Anyway, Anika plans to head for home tomorrow as planned," he said cheerily.

"Oh my gosh, Steven! I can't even imagine how horrible it would be to be in the middle of all that! It looked terrible on TV, and I'm sure that doesn't even do the whole thing justice—the dust, the smoke, the smells, the noise. That certainly doesn't translate through the lenses of any camera." She took a breath. "Whew! I'm so glad she's okay. I understand how worried you were for her. I'd feel the same way if I had a friend who I knew was possibly in the middle of all that horror."

"Yeah, I didn't realize how much I cared about her until I thought I had lost her."

Christina smiled and felt a twinge of sadness in her heart. She knew that feeling so well and could certainly empathize with him.

"How is she getting back? I know there are no planes flying now."

"She and another gal from Dallas that she met in the hospital are renting a car and will be driving back to Dallas. I'll meet her there and drive her back here, where she'll spend the night with another girlfriend. If all goes well, I'll have her back in Waco Sunday afternoon.

She smiled and nodded. "Good." Feeling a little awkward and not knowing what else to say, she said, "I need to head on home."

"Oh, yeah. Sorry. I just needed to tell you about Anika." She nodded again and then said, "Yeah, thanks for telling me. I'll be seeing you." On her way out to the parking lot, she thought about Steven and Anika. *Am I really jealous of this lady I've never met? And if so, why? I have no claim on Steven. I don't want to waste my time with thoughts of Steven. He is obviously not interested in me in any romantic way—just like in high school. And really, why did I even think he would be?* She sighed and exited the building.

CHAPTER 43

Ed and Tom looked at their superior, stupefied.

"You know, guys, since Tuesday's events, it's been decided to stop the investigation into the Sanders situation. There are bigger fish to fry than that. Besides, the last CD you gave us proved to be quite valuable."

Ed started to protest, but Henry put his hand up.

"I know it seems y'all have been on a wild-goose chase with this whole thing, but as I said before, I'm not the only one who makes these decisions."

"Okay, so I guess we'll go back one more time to get the bugs?"

Henry nodded. "Yep. This assignment has been terminated as of today."

Placing his hands on his desk, he stood. He was a large man, thanks to too many hamburgers, French fries, and hours sitting behind a desk. He looked older than his fifty years with bags as big as suitcases under his eyes, thinning gray hair, baggy jowls, and a double chin. When he stood, the effort made him short of breath, making Ed wonder when he would keel over with a heart attack. The guy was a walking time bomb.

Ed asked, "Can we at least take the direct approach this time?"

"What do you mean?" Henry asked, sorting through papers on his desk.

"I'd like to walk up to the door and introduce ourselves to Mrs. Sanders, tell her why we're there, and ask permission to retrieve the bugs. She seems like a reasonable lady." He looked at Tom, who was nodding in agreement.

Henry sat back down with a grunt, steepled his fingers, and considered the scenario.

"Okay. Because of the 9/11 thing and our time schedule and ongoing terrorist threats, go ahead and try it. I want this thing to be resolved ASAP." He sat back down causing his chair to creak and groan as if in agony.

"You don't think she'll freak out at the thought of y'all being in her home in the first place?"

Tom considered this and said, "You know, he's right, Ed. Maybe we should just do as we have been. Sneak in under her radar." Ed thought a moment and then nodded in agreement. "All right. I just have this nagging feeling that we're gonna get caught."

"Guess that's always a possibility, but you gotta get those bugs out," said Henry, shaking his head.

Tom and Ed sighed and nodded, resigned to one last trip to Alva.

Standing and stretching, Ed asked, "When do you want us to go?"

"Well, today is Wednesday. Why not drive down to Alva on Friday?" their boss answered as he adjusted his walrus-sized body in his chair, not bothering to stand this time. Both agents nodded.

"Good." He held out his meaty hand. Tom and Ed took turns shaking it.

Ed had conflicting feelings about returning to Alva. He was hoping to see Cindy again. He missed her exuberant personality and yeah, her good looks. His heart was heading dangerously close to the love territory, and that scared him. If they did continue to see each other, he would have to be honest about who he was and what he did for a living. She would probably hate him for lying to her. *To pursue or not to pursue? I can't worry about that now. I have a job to do. I'll just have to wait and see what paths will open up to me.*

As the two men boarded the elevator, Tom asked, "So you ready to head back down to that little town of Alva?"

Ed grunted and nodded. "Yeah, sure." He sounded about as enthusiastic as if he was going to get a tooth extracted.

"You gonna try to hook up with that woman again? What was her name? Candy? Sandy?"

"It's Cindy. And yes, I would like to see her again."

"So what happened between you two?" Tom asked as they exited the elevator and entered the lobby of the large FBI/CIA/ATO Headquarters in Dallas. Ed was silent as they walked through the lobby and out to the parking lot where they had left their van.

Once inside the van, he answered. "We've just had coffee. Nothing serious."

Tom raised his eyebrows. "Really? Could have sworn there was more to it. You actually seemed happy for a while."

Ed looked at him and frowned. "Look, I've told you before, I can't get serious with anyone when I have to lie to them about who I am and what I do. That's no way to build a relationship."

Tom held his hands up in surrender. "Okay. I just thought you and she hit it off. I mean, you look *good* together." He started the engine and backed out of the parking space.

Ed sighed. "Maybe if I see her again, I'll just be up-front and honest. If she's okay with that, then maybe we can pursue a relationship."

Tom nodded. "That's a lot of maybes." He looked over and grinned as he pulled into the early morning Dallas traffic. "You really like this gal, don't you?"

Ed nodded and turned his head to look out the window. He thought, *Yep, I think I'm fallin' for this gal, and that scares the bejeebies out of me!*

As Tom pulled the van up to his apartment complex, Ed asked, "Hey, why don't we head down to Alva Friday afternoon? I've got a couple of loose ends I need to take care of."

"Sure. All right. I wouldn't mind a little free time myself. Maybe Eleanor will let me take Tommy for the day." He smiled as he thought of his six-year-old son. "I haven't seen him since last Sunday. "

"How's Tommy doing?" Ed asked, delaying his exit from the van as he sensed his friend wanted to talk.

"He's growing like a weed. Say, did I show you his latest picture?"

"No. I haven't seen one in a while."

Tom reached for his wallet and pulled out a small photo of a grinning, redheaded little boy missing a front tooth. Ed smiled as he looked at the picture. "He sure is a good-looking little guy." Grinning, he added, "Must take after his mom."

Tom reached over and hit him on the shoulder.

"I'll have you know, he's the spittin' image of me when I was that age."

Ed looked at him, shocked. "Oh, come on. You were *never* that cute."

"So you say. Just ask my mama." Both men laughed. Ed knew Tom's mom and knew she would think her baby boy was the most handsome man on the planet.

Ed handed the photo back to Tom and asked, "So how are things working out between you and Eleanor?"

Tom shrugged. "I guess as well as can be expected. At least she doesn't hate my guts like Irene does."

His first wife, Irene, had been difficult, if not impossible, to please. She would *always* find something to complain about. They had only been married six months when he came home and found her having an affair with her therapist, who she insisted was the *only* man that truly loved and understood her. *Yeah, right,* thought Tom as he remembered Irene saying that about the lawn maintenance man, the man at the car wash, and the young man at the checkout counter at Safeway.

He moved out after that encounter, hoping she would come to her senses. When he realized she wouldn't—or couldn't—he filed for divorce. He lost track of her once she married a used car salesman from El Paso.

Eleanor, on the other hand, was a great lady. He felt a deep sadness when he thought about how their divorce came about. They had been so much in love and had a wonderful marriage and were thrilled when Tommy was born. A couple of years after his birth, however, Eleanor had a miscarriage in her fifth month, which left her emotionally scarred.

She and Tom had been driving home from a New Year's Eve party, and even though he had been drinking, he insisted he was sober enough to drive. The alcohol had significantly affected his reaction time, so by the time he saw the red light and stopped the car, they were in the middle of an intersection that another car was zipping through. He could still hear his wife screaming, the tires screeching, and then the loud crash. Everything else was blurry. There were flashing lights, shouts, blood, glass, and sirens.

When he regained consciousness in the hospital the next morning, he asked about his wife. It was then that he learned she had lost their baby girl. He wept bitterly and swore he would never take another drink. She said she could never forgive him, and that was the beginning of the end of their marriage, ending in divorce the next year. Feeling guilty, he let her have everything she asked for, even their son. She was generous in giving him partial custody, agreeing that he could see his son anytime as long as he called in advance and plans hadn't already been made. She had never been vengeful or spiteful but was always kind and respectful of him, and he wished with all his heart that she would forgive him and they could get back together again—if nothing else, for the sake of their son whom they both loved. He knew the separation was difficult for him. She still had an air of sadness about her, and that pained his heart.

He took the little picture of his son, kissed it, and returned it to his wallet. Ed reached over and patted his friend on the shoulder. He knew Tom still carried a truck full of emotions when it came to Eleanor and Tommy. Tom sniffed, wiped his eyes and nose, and said a little too heartily, "Well, you go and have a good night now. I'll see you again Friday around noon."

"Yeah. I'll see you then."

As Ed watched the van drive away, he let out a sigh. He and Tom had been working together for several years and had become tight as friends and partners. Both men knowing they would lay their life on the line for each other. Tom had been there for Ed when his wife, Celina, had died, and for that, he was eternally grateful. He still held out hope for Tom and Eleanor.

A few months after the divorce, he was able to talk to Eleanor, and she had informed him that she didn't hate Tom. In fact, she still loved him and always would—she just couldn't bring herself to forgive him for the accident. Until she could get past that, she couldn't be with him, because he was a constant reminder of her loss.

As he thought of the two people who meant so much to him, he lifted his face toward heaven and said, "God, I know I don't talk to you often, but if you could please, help Eleanor heal and forgive Tom, and help Tom be the man that you want him to be. God, they're so miserable without each other. And God, I don't know what to do about Cindy. I think I'm falling in love with her. Please give me wisdom. Thank you. Amen." Ed entered his apartment and called his mom.

CHAPTER 44

During the drive home from the hospital, Christina recapped the uneventful day in her mind. The three patients were stable, and she was sure they would all make it through the weekend without any complications. She had thoroughly gone over the charts with Dr. Meils and the next shift of nurses, and everything seemed to be in order.

She then let her mind drift to Janet. She wasn't sure what to think about her. Even though she wasn't friendly and one didn't get a warm and fuzzy feeling being around her, she was efficient and thorough when doing her job.

Janet gave off an air of confidence and control, which some may have considered arrogant and pushy. Having felt intimidated after meeting and working with her the first couple of days, Christina could understand why the other staff members deliberately avoided Janet. Because she had taken the job Janet wanted, Christina was concerned there would be resentment, but so far, everything seemed to be going smoothly. *Well, hopefully it will continue that way. I don't think it would be wise to get on the negative side of that woman.*

Little did she know, beneath Janet's efficient exterior lived a bitter, angry, envious, and revengeful woman.

CHAPTER 45

Tom arrived at Ed's apartment at two thirty Friday afternoon. After throwing a duffel bag into the back area of the van, Ed climbed in.

"Say, buddy, how was your day off?" Ed asked as he adjusted his seat belt. "Did you get to go to the zoo with Tommy?"

Tom chuckled. "Yeah, and you know what?" He looked over at Ed grinning.

Ed shook his head and raised his eyebrows.

"Eleanor went with us."

"No kiddin'? So tell me what happened." He reached over and patted his grinning buddy on the shoulder.

Ed loved to hear Tom's New York accent, which became more pronounced when he was excited about something—making it easy to judge his moods. He listened, smiling as Tom rambled on about his day with his son and his ex-wife. Ed was so glad Eleanor was giving Tom a chance. That was the first time they'd spent any significant time together since the divorce three years earlier. *Maybe God did hear me after all.*

"And you know what she did when I dropped them off at the house?" he asked excitedly. Ed put up his hands and shrugged. He didn't have to say anything, because Tom was on a roll. He knew he wouldn't be able to get a word in even if he tried.

"She asked me to come in! Can you believe it?"

"Did you?" Ed asked, noticing the sudden change in Tom's mood.

"No. I *wanted* to," he said emphatically, "but I was afraid I'd do or say something stupid and spoil the whole day, so I said, 'Not this time.'"

"What did she say?"

"She smiled, nodded, and said okay."

"Hmm."

"Yeah. I can't believe I walked away. But you know what? It felt good. I really think I did the right thing." He looked over and Ed and smiled.

After several minutes and miles had passed, Ed asked, "So when will you see them again?"

"I'm not sure. My schedule's pretty full until the end of the month. I plan to see them over Thanksgiving for sure. So enough about me—what did you do?"

Ed sighed and adjusted himself in his seat. "I went to see my mom and two of my sisters."

"Yeah? How's your mom doin'?"

"She's doin' great. She's gonna turn sixty next month." He shook his head. "Hard to believe my little mama is getting old. Of course, she doesn't act old." Chuckling, he said, "I bet she could still take me down!"

Tom laughed too. He knew Ed's mama and agreed that she was one feisty senior citizen.

"So which sisters did you see?" Tom asked after taking a drink from his thermos of coffee.

"Nadine and Stephie. Nicole couldn't make it. She was teaching."

"Say, how old are those girls? I haven't seen them in a while."

"Nicole is the oldest. Hmm ... " He paused, thinking. "She's thirty-five, Nadine is thirty, and Stephie is the baby. She's twenty-five."

"So how many nieces and nephews do you have now?"

Ed had to stop and think once again. He didn't see his sisters or their families often and tended to lose track of the names and numbers of their offspring.

He closed his eyes and mentally pictured each one and named them.

"Let's see. Last time I counted there were six. Nicole has two, Nadine has three, and Stephie has one and is pregnant, so that will make seven."

"Wow. Must be lots of fun at Christmas with all those kids around."

Ed blew out some air. "Yeah, a real madhouse, let me tell you."

Both men grew silent, thinking about their lives and their families. Before entering Alva, they stopped for lunch at a Dairy Queen in Waxahachie.

Back on the road again, Tom asked, "What kind of name is Waxahachie? Is it some kind of Indian name or what? And what could it possibly mean?"

"I think it's an Indian name. A lot of places around the state are either Indian or Mexican names." He paused, rolling the word around in his mind. "It is a weird name, though, isn't it? Wax-a-hachie, and I don't have a clue as to its meaning. Almost sounds like 'wax a hatchet.' Maybe there was an axe or hatchet involved somewhere."

Tom nodded and grinned. "Maybe. I kind of doubt it, though."

"Yeah? Well, we can always check the Internet."

Tom nodded again, and he considered doing just that when he returned home. He found, to his surprise, that he really *did* want to know so he could share that information with his son.

They pulled into Alva around three thirty and decided to go check out a few stores in the outlet mall. After a couple hours of walking around, they ended up in a toy store and purchased a few items for Tommy and Ed's nieces and nephews. They had dinner at Pizza Hut and then decided to go check on Christina and her family.

Knowing the Sanders family would all be heading out to the football game in an hour or so, the men would have adequate time to remove the bugs.

CHAPTER 46

Monday had started a little off-key when the first thing Christina did as she crawled out of bed was step in cat puke. It seemed Chloe had decided to deposit a hairball and her last meal right beside the bed. After grabbing a few tissues and trying not to gag, Christina cleaned it up, plunked it in the toilet, and flushed. She was surprised when it didn't go down but continued to swirl in the bowl. She ran downstairs to retrieve the plunger from the downstairs bathroom and twisted her ankle on the last step. Fearing the toilet would overflow, she gritted her teeth against the pain and continued on her mission. Once the toilet was unclogged, she sat on the floor and massaged her tender right ankle.

After standing and tentatively putting weight on her foot and finding it strong, she took a deep breath, let it out, and continued her morning routine. The rest of the morning went well—except for the milk carton that fell out of the fridge and spilled half its contents onto the floor, the light bulb that went out as Stacey was taking a shower, and the garbage bag that ruptured and spilled its contents onto the driveway as Brad was taking it out to the garage. Amazingly, everyone left the house on time without any other physical damage to body or belongings.

On her way to work, she thought about the weekend's events. Friday night, they had attended Brad's football game, and even though Alva lost by several points, it had been fun hanging out with her friends.

She chatted with a few of her old high school buddies and caught up on events that had occurred in their lives since graduation, along with gossip about other classmates. Some of the stories she heard made her shake her head. *People can do some of the stupidest things,* she thought.

On Saturday they went to the zoo in Waco along with Lisa and her children. Lisa had been one of the Fab Four during High School, and over the years, she and Christina had grown apart. The ride there had been filled with laughter and chatter as the kids played various games and she and Lisa caught up on the past several years.

Lisa informed her that they were in the process of adopting a couple of kids from Guatemala.

"Oh my gosh! So when did this all come about?" Christina asked.

"We applied last year, and we went to the orphanage and talked with the officials and met the kids—a boy who's four and his sister who's six. Oh my goodness, Christina, they are the cutest kids!"

"When will they be here, and how are your kids dealing with this?'

"We should be able to get them in the next six months, and the kids are so excited. Sarah is already buying little accessories—hair clips, jewelry and even some clothes."

"That's awesome. She always was the mothering type. I remember you telling me about her dressing the cats and bunnies in baby clothes and carrying them around."

Lisa giggled. "Yeah, the animals didn't appreciate it much, though. I was a little concerned that she might be jealous. She just turned fourteen, and being the oldest and only girl, she's been the princess all her life, but she's okay with it. She even offered to share her room, but I think we'll let her keep hers and put Elliana in the boy's old room."

"Elliana? That's a pretty name. Oh my goodness! I just realized you'll have six kids. Wow! How are you gonna fit two more kids in your house?"

Lisa nodded. "I know! Well, we remodeled the attic and added a dormer, so we'll make that into room for the boys. It'll accommodate four boys quite nicely. The twins are already setting toys aside for their new brother, Rico."

"How old are the boys now?"

"Jessie just turned eleven, and the twins are eight."

"Where have the years gone? Seems like yesterday they were all toddlers!"

Lisa glanced in the rearview mirror before saying quietly, "I know! It really hit me when I had to start buying bras and female products for Sarah, and then Jessie's voice started cracking!" She giggled. "The first time it happened, it caught us both by surprise, and he put his hand over his mouth and turned beet red. Then we both started laughing."

Christina smiled. "Yeah, I remember when Brad's voice changed. It was pretty funny at times too. He'd be talking normally, then *bam*, it would squeak or change octaves. He would get quite embarrassed."

They both sat in silence a few minutes, and then Christina said almost in a whisper, "Stacey hasn't crossed that bridge yet, but I think it'll be soon. Her moods have been crazily unpredictable, and I had to get her a bra last week."

"Let me warn you that when it happens, she'll change. Toys will be exchanged for boys."

"Yeah. I know. I kinda dread it." A few miles passed before she said, "I think it's awesome that y'all are adopting. How come I haven't heard about this till now? I don't remember anything about this in your Christmas letter."

"Well, we weren't sure if everything would fall into place and didn't want to be telling everyone and then have to retract everything."

Christina nodded. "Okay. I can see that."

Lisa smiled and nodded. "I'm so excited. It's so difficult to not buy every cute outfit or toy I see. We've still gotta keep an eye on our budget. I know that all our bills will increase significantly. Tom's business is doing well right now, and I've been considering a part-time job somewhere, so we should be fine."

"Do the other gals know?"

"Donna does, but I haven't talked to Cindy in a while, so I don't think she does. She and I don't travel in the same circles, and besides, she was always more your friend than mine."

Christina nodded. "Yeah, but I'm sure she'd want to know too."

"Oh, yeah, I plan to tell her next time I see or talk to her."

"Is it okay if I tell her?"

"Yeah. You'll probably talk to her before I do. So how are things going with you now that you've moved back?"

Christina brought her up to date on her life since moving back home.

As Lisa's van pulled into the parking lot, they spotted Donna and her three boys standing in front of the large gate that marked the entrance of the zoo.

After quick hellos and hugs all around, Donna asked about Cindy, and Christina explained that she and Samara had gone to Dallas to care for Cindy's mother, who had come down with a stomach virus. Otherwise they would have been there as well.

It had been a beautiful, clear, warm September day. The zoo was spread over a couple thousand acres, and after hours of walking and a couple of train rides, they had enjoyed *most* of it. The highlight of the trip had been the polar bear exhibit, complete with ice and snow. Lisa's children were awestruck by the antics of the bears as they watched them through a Plexiglas tunnel. Donna's boys had been to the zoo before, and even though they enjoyed the bears, they weren't nearly as excited as the Davis children. Christina's kids couldn't help but compare the Waco zoo's polar bear exhibit with the Detroit exhibit—both were quite impressive.

The three moms had packed picnic lunches, and the whole gang enjoyed them under a large pecan tree in front of the monkey exhibit. It was a pleasure to see how well the kids interacted and seemed to enjoy each other's company even though there were age differences. Christina had enjoyed reacquainting herself with Lisa and Donna. They had e-mailed and sent Christmas cards through the years to keep in touch, but there were so many subjects that weren't discussed through letters—like some of the stories she'd heard at the football game. When the kids finished eating and had left the moms to clean up, Christina casually said, "Did you know that Bo Jessup and Janie Smith were caught in a compromising position in the back of Bo's truck by Janie's teenage son?"

Lisa giggled. "Really? When did that happen? And who told you?"

"Kristy Wilms—used to be Smith—told me the other night at the football game. She said it happened last year, and Janie's son is still not talking to her."

"Well, who would have thought!" Donna commented as she gathered her children's trash.

"I know it's not nice to gossip, but I just had to get that out of my head. Been thinkin' about it since last night. I feel so bad for all of them—Bo's wife, Janie's husband and kid." The other two gals nodded.

Donna said, "So, I'm curious. Where were they caught?"

"Out by the water tower. You know, one of the famous make-out places in Alva?"

Lisa giggled and nodded. "Oh yeah, besides behind the grandstands at the football field?" Donna and Christina gave her a shocked look.

"Oh come on! Don't tell me you never went there?"

Christina shook her head and said innocently, "I have no idea what you're talking about."

"Me neither," Donna added. "I was a good girl and never went parkin' with a boy."

Lisa looked at her friends, who burst out laughing.

"Actually," said Christina, "I liked the spot behind the baseball dugout at the park."

"Oh yeah, I forgot about that place!" Donna added with a giggle.

Lisa shook her head. "You two."

They all embraced and did high fives.

"The Fab Four!" they said in unison.

Christina said, "It is so nice being together again—except for Cindy. I'll bring her up to date on everything when I see her again."

Christina asked if they remembered Brother Stan Hart, one of the youth ministers they had during high school. They did.

"Wasn't he the one who did those musicals during the summer?" Lisa asked.

Donna nodded. "Yep. The girls were all crazy about him."

"Yeah, 'cause he was the whole package," Christina said with a smile.

"Oh yeah. I remember. He had dark hair, brown eyes, a hot body, and a killer smile. What wasn't to like?" Lisa said, taking a sip of lemonade before continuing. "I remember begging my mom to let me be in the musicals and then begging her to let me attend your church. She was okay with the musical part, but a 'good Catholic girl' didn't just switch churches."

Christina looked at her with raised eyebrows. "Didn't you drop out of the Catholic Church when you married Tom?"

"Yeah. My mom was angry with me for so many years and brought the subject up at every family get together. She'd say things like 'Can you believe my Lisa has turned her back on the church?' Then she'd make the sign of the cross. As if the Catholic Church were the only *true* religion! She thought we were involved in some kind of cult when we started attending a nondenominational church."

"Has she stopped bugging you?"

"Yeah, she finally gave up and realized that after twenty years, she wasn't gonna change my mind. In fact, she's even attended our church on a few occasions."

Christina and Donna gave her surprised looks. "Really?" Christina asked as she looked around for her children. All the children were playing catch with a Frisbee in a green grassy area close by.

Nodding her head and grinning, Lisa said, "Really, and I even think she liked it, but she'd never admit that. Once a Catholic, always a Catholic, as far as she's concerned."

"Hey, getting back to Brother Hart—isn't it funny that the pastors down here are all called brothers? We just call them pastors up in Michigan. Anyway, didn't he marry one of the gals from the youth group?"

"Yeah," said Donna. "I think she was a senior, and her name was, uhm ..."

"Wasn't it Brenda Watson?" Lisa offered.

Surprise etching her face, Donna said, "Yeah, that's it. How did you ever remember that?"

"She and my brother were both seniors, and he had a major crush on her. That's the only reason I'd know at all. After all, we were just lowly sophomores and didn't travel in those upperclassmen circles."

Christina chuckled and nodded.

"Hey, do y'all remember that one night during a performance, the tape broke right in the middle of one kid's solo?" Lisa asked as she took a sip of water.

"Oh yeah! That was awful," stated Donna. "I felt so sorry for that kid. He almost panicked, but I think he handled it pretty well."

Christina nodded in agreement. "I remember his ears turning a beet red."

Laughing, Lisa added, "Yeah, but not as red as Brother Hart's."

"Nope. That look of panic on his face was priceless, though, as he hurried to the sound room to see what had happened." She paused, remembering the incident. "I remember a few minutes of total silence, and then everyone onstage and in the audience started whispering," said Donna as she nibbled on a cookie.

Christina added, "Yeah, it was a good thing Brother Hart had a backup tape. Too bad we didn't have CDs back then. That would have been a lot easier."

"Isn't it amazing how far technology has come in twenty years?" Donna asked. They all nodded in agreement and continued reminiscing as they began packing up the remaining lunch items.

Christina smiled and nodded. After loading the wagon with the picnic items, the three moms walked over and joined their children, who were gleefully watching the antics of the monkeys in the exhibit.

When it was time for good-byes, the group had difficulty saying them. They were the last remaining people in the parking lot, and when the lights came on, they finally entered their vans and drove off. The drive home was much quieter as the children dozed off. Brad and Sarah were the only ones awake the entire trip home, and Christina could hear them whispering and stifling giggles. She and Lisa enjoyed the quiet and would occasionally make a comment about the day's events, both expressing their desire to do this again someday soon.

CHAPTER 47

Christina walked across the parking lot, looking up at the clear azure sky. Stopping and turning her face toward the early morning sun, she closed her eyes and took in a lungful of the fresh, clean air that had a tinge of autumn coolness in it, reminding her of Michigan and all she'd left there. She could feel sadness so large and dark trying to enfold her in its deadly embrace and may have let it, had it not been for the car horn that startled her back to the present. She shook her head to rid her mind of the fog that was penetrating its borders.

Smiling, she waved at the driver, wondering if he thought she was crazy. As the car passed by, the driver, who looked to be in his seventies or eighties, waved and smiled. Gnarled, thin hands gripped the steering wheel as his body leaned into it, his eyes barely peeping over the dashboard.

How in the world can he see out of those thick glasses propped on his nose? When their eyes met and he smiled, she felt as if he knew *exactly* what she was doing, as though he had done the same thing on many occasions. She imagined him saying, "Don't you worry, darlin'. There's nothin' wrong with standin' out in a parkin' lot, lookin' toward heaven. Do it all the time. Nope, nothin' at all wrong with that."

It had certainly been a weird morning, and she wondered if it would get weirder. She hoped not. She let out a sigh and headed into the building, saying good-bye to the beautiful day.

Listening to the nurses' report from the previous shift, she found her thoughts drifting to Steven. He was usually the first one in the conference room, and he hadn't arrived yet. She wondered how his weekend with Anika had been.

The head nurse from the previous night finished her report, and everyone gathered their information sheets and headed out of the room, some for the nurses' station, others for the nurses' lounge. Christina sat in the quiet room for a couple of minutes and said a prayer for Steven.

Dr. Dawson finally made an appearance about an hour later, looking and acting as if his thoughts were elsewhere. He wasn't his usual good-old-boy self and seemed annoyed that he had to be there at all.

He listened halfheartedly as Christina related the previous nights' information about his patients. His eyes had a faraway look in them and a sadness that touched her soul. He kept rubbing them and would blink quickly as if trying to rid them of the images that were being played behind the lids. It didn't take a genius to deduce that his weekend had not gone as well as he had hoped.

The curious side of her wanted to pry and ask blatantly what had happened, but the cautious side of her said it wasn't the right time—*He'll talk to me when it is.* She hated having to be patient and wait for things to happen. It made her all nervous and fidgety inside and out. She would find herself biting her nails or twisting her hair around her fingers—which she was doing now. Even worse, her stomach and bowels would react noisily, causing embarrassment, making her more nervous, and intensifying her reactions. She had to consciously stop the cycle before it got completely out of control. *That's all I need—for Steven to hear my gurgling gut. Then again, maybe it would lighten the mood.* She mentally slapped herself and got her thoughts and nervous tics under control before Steven was even aware of her discomfort. Of course, with the mood he was in, she doubted he would notice anything, except maybe an earthquake.

Nope, patience is not one of my stronger virtues. I wonder if God enjoys giving me little tests to try and strengthen it. She was relieved when he left the unit to return to his office. She didn't like all that negative energy she was feeling when he was near, and neither did her body, she realized as she felt a gurgling building up in her gut.

After work, she walked by Steven's office to see if he was in. He was sitting in his chair with his back to the door, looking out the window. She stood outside the door, wondering if she should enter or not, and decided to let him be.

She said a quick prayer for him and headed home, where she was greeted by Benji, who was so excited that he piddled on the floor at her feet. Realizing what he had done, he immediately went into his don't-beat-me posture with his ears down and his tail between his legs. She chuckled. He looked so pitiful. She took his face in her hands and asked, "Benji, have I ever beaten you?" He avoided eye contact. "You silly dog." She picked up his trembling body and took him outside. Once he had completed his elimination job, he came bounding up to her, all misconduct forgotten, ready to play. She chuckled as she scratched behind his ears. He ran in circles, barking as she tossed his favorite tennis ball across the yard. *Oh, to have such a short memory and a fun-loving spirit,* she thought as she tossed the ball a few more times. He had happily retrieved the ball, bringing it back to her and dropping it at her feet until it was just too soggy and slimy for her to pick up. He actually looked disappointed as she urged him to come in the house, minus the tennis ball. He stood stubbornly in the doorway, looking at her, then at the tennis ball, and then back to her, as if to say, "I'm not coming in without my ball." She couldn't help but chuckle.

She knew what would bring a smile to his face and make him forget about the ball. Returning with one of his favorite peanut-butter-flavored doggy biscuits, the tennis ball was dropped and quickly forgotten.

Chloe, not wanting to be neglected, wove her body around and through Christina's legs, nearly tripping her on the way to the kitchen. Christina reached down and picked up and snuggled the purring cat, assuring her that she too was loved.

Chuckling, she remembered a joke she had received through her e-mail a few days earlier that had made her laugh out loud.

It read: "A dog looks at its master and thinks, 'He gives me food, water, love—he must be God.' A cat looks at its master and thinks, 'He gives me food, water, love—I must be God.'" She smiled and thought, *It's funny how cats and dogs are so different from each other. Kind of like the human race—each one having their own unique look, temperament, thinking pattern, life choices. It boggles the mind to think that no two creatures, animal or human, on God's planet are exactly the same.*

As she was placing Chloe's bowl of water on the floor, her phone rang. She answered to hear Cindy's excited voice on the other end.

"Hey, girlfriend, whatcha doin'?"

"Hey yourself. I just walked in the door and was takin' care of the animals. How was your weekend with your mom? Is she over her flu?"

"Yeah, she's doin' fine. We got in late last night, and Samara got up this morning complaining of a stomachache. She wasn't running a fever and had no other symptoms, so, bad mother that I am, I made her go to school. I guess she's okay 'cause she didn't call for me to come get her. Hopefully, that nasty bug'll just pass us by. So how was your weekend with the girls?"

Christina told of the trip to the zoo and her conversations with Donna and Lisa. "Did you know that Lisa's family is adopting two little kids from Guatemala?"

"Oh my gosh! That's awesome! When will that happen?"

Christina filled her in on the details and then said, "We sure missed you and Samara. Lisa said she thought she saw you talking to some big, good-looking guy outside your store last week. I pretended ignorance 'cause I thought you'd like to tell that story yourself."

"Aww, thanks Christina. You have such good control of your tongue. If it had been me, I would have blurted everything I knew, and then some."

Christina chuckled. "Believe me, it wasn't easy keeping what little I knew to myself."

As they continued to chat, Christina's phone buzzed, indicating a new call was coming in. Not recognizing the number, she decided she'd better answer it.

"I'm sorry, Cindy. We'll have to talk later. I have a call coming in I need to answer. I'll talk to you later."

Cindy said good-bye, and Christina switched the phone to the next call.

"Hello?"

"Christina?"

Putting the cat on the floor, she answered, "Yes."

"Christina, this is Mary Kelly, the head nurse for the afternoon shift on the Cardiac Care Unit."

"Oh, yes, Mary. What can I do for you?" she asked as she leaned against the counter.

"Well, I'm not sure, exactly. There's been a problem with one of the patient's medication orders. Seems that Mr. Wilson's drug order never made it down to the pharmacy on Friday. He's been without his Atenelol all weekend. I just now caught the oversight and called Dr. Dawson."

Christina's heart started galloping and felt as if were trying to escape the confines of her rib cage. *Why hadn't the oversight been caught that morning when she passed out the medications? How could she or Steven have missed its absence?*

Atenelol was a beta-blocker prescribed for Mr. Wilson after his heart attack to decrease his blood pressure and regulate his heart rhythm by relaxing the blood vessels in and around the heart. Dr. Dawson prescribed it for all his post-heart-attack patients, because it was the drug of choice to increase survivability after such a traumatic event.

"Are you sure?" She knew the question was rhetorical. Why else would she be calling if she wasn't sure? "'Cause I remember him writing the order and putting it in the chart. I sent it to the pharmacy as soon as we finished rounds." She paused, remembering the events clearly.

"Well, it isn't in the chart, and I called the pharmacy, and they never received an order."

"I don't understand what happened." Christina started twisting a ringlet of hair around her trembling fingers. "Is Mr. Wilson all right?" She asked anxiously.

"Mr. Wilson is doing amazingly well, even without the medication. His blood pressure was slightly elevated over the weekend and yesterday, but all in all, he doesn't seem any worse off, but Dr. Dawson would like to speak with you. Do you think you could come back to the hospital around five and meet Dr. Dawson in his office?"

"Oh, um, sure," she said nervously as she looked at the clock on the counter. It read four thirty, and she knew the kids would be home any minute. "Are you sure I need to come *back* to the hospital? Couldn't I just talk to him on the phone?"

"He said he wanted to speak to you in person. Sorry."

"Tell him I'll be there."

"All right, I'll let him know. Thank you." The line went dead, but it was a few seconds before Christina was able to lay the phone down. What on earth was going on?

She thought about Friday and all the orders she had copied and filed and pharmacy slips she had sent and was absolutely, positively sure she had written Mr. Wilson's down in the chart and had sent an order to the pharmacy. *So, that being the case, what happened to it?*

Nicky and Stacey walked in the back door at four thirty-five, calling for her. Brad had walked to the Safeway store right from school for his shift, and she would have to remember to pick him up at eight. She went to greet her children and was shocked to see blood on Nicky's T-shirt.

"Nicky, what happened?" she asked as she knelt in front of him.

"I had a nosebleed today," he said, smiling. "It's no big deal."

"Looks like a big deal," she said, alarmed by the stains on his shirt. "When did it happen?"

"Right before school let out. I was putting my backpack on when Randy Jenkins bumped into me with his. It hit me right in the nose."

"Ow!" she said. "Must have hurt."

"Yeah, a little, but I didn't cry!" he said proudly. Christina smiled and nodded approvingly. "Even when it started gushing blood." He giggled. "You should have seen Randy's face, though. I thought he was gonna pass out or puke or somethin'. His face turned so white!"

"What did you do?" she asked, picturing him standing in front of his locker while people stood around watching blood drip from his nose and pool at his feet.

"Well, I dropped my books and bag and ran to the bathroom and got lots of toilet paper and stuffed it in my nose. Mr. Hill, the gym teacher, came in and told me to pinch the place on my nose between my eyes and hold it tight for at least five minutes and put my head back like this." He demonstrated what he had done. "Anyways, it quit bleeding, and when I walked outside, Stacey was waiting for me." He looked at his sister and smiled. "She nearly freaked until I told her what had happened." Christina looked at her daughter and raised her eyebrows.

"Yeah, it kind of freaked me out when I saw the blood. I was ready to clobber whoever had caused it." She smiled and patted Nicky on the head.

Christina smiled and drew him into a hug. "I'm glad you're okay. Now why don't you give me that shirt, and I'll put it in the washer?" He took it off, handed it to his mom, and then ran up the stairs with Benji following close behind.

Heading for the laundry room, she asked, "So, Stacey, how was your day?" She feared what she might hear.

"My day was great! How about yours?" she asked, looking in the fridge and pulling out a Dr Pepper.

"You don't *even* want to know," Christina said as she walked behind her daughter and wrapped her arms around her shoulders and kissed the top of her head. "I need to go back to the hospital for a meeting in a few minutes. Could you fix a salad and sandwiches for you and Nicky?"

"Sure. Why do you have to go back?"

"Oh, there's been some misunderstanding that I need to help sort out."

Stacey shrugged. "Oh, okay."

As Christina drove to the hospital, her palms began to sweat, and her heart fluttered in her chest, like a bird desperately trying to escape a net. *Why am I so nervous? I did my part. The orders must have been misplaced. That is the only logical explanation. Surely Steven will understand. Or will he? Considering the mood he was in this morning, he might just decide I'm more trouble than I'm worth and just fire me. God, I hope not! Could he? Would Mrs. Ferguson have a say in it? Maybe she thinks I'm inept too and wants to get rid of me!* She took a deep breath and let it out slowly.

Okay. No matter what happens, I will not let it break me. I'll be mature and handle this maturely—whatever that means.

She hated confrontations, but more than that, she hated disappointing people. She hoped with all her heart that Steven wouldn't think any less of her as a nurse or a friend.

When she reached Dr. Dawson's office door, she stood for a minute, taking a few deep breaths and trying to calm her anxious heart.

Lord, she prayed, *please help clear this up. I don't know what's going on, but I need your help in this matter.* She took in a deep breath, let it out slowly, straightened her shoulders, and lightly knocked on the door. At least her hands had stopped shaking, but her pulse was about fifty beats above normal.

"Come in," she heard a familiar voice say.

Opening the door, she saw Dr. Dawson at his desk, perusing a pile of paperwork. He looked up and smiled when she entered. *A smile's a good thing, right?* Sitting in a chair across from him was Mrs. Ferguson, who also smiled at her. *Two smiles. Good?* She thought as she closed the door.

"Christina, thanks for coming back in. I hope this isn't too much of an inconvenience," said Dr. Dawson. Christina shook her head. "Good, come on in and have a seat." He motioned a come forward movement with his hands. She and Mrs. Ferguson exchanged greetings as Christina sat down in the empty chair next to her.

Dr. Dawson leaned forward with his elbows on the desk and looked at her for a moment before he spoke. *What do I see in his eyes? Compassion? Pity? Anger? No, not anger. Disappointment?*

Clearing his throat, he began. "Christina, how do you like working here?"

Why is he asking me that? Is he planning to fire me? Her pulse quickened and her palms dampened as she answered, "I like working here. It's been a bit of a challenge getting back into the swing of things, but all in all, it's been fine."

He nodded. She sat up straighter in her chair and held her hands together to keep them from shaking and looked him in the eyes—such intense blue eyes. She looked down at her hands.

"I bet it's difficult working and taking care of three kids."

She frowned and looked into those eyes again. *What is he getting at? Does he think I can't handle both jobs?* She felt herself becoming defensive.

"It's not so bad. The kids are old enough to take care of themselves, at least most of the time, and they help around the house. I'm only working three or four days a week, and on those days, I spend a few minutes with them in the morning, and I get home a few minutes before they do in the afternoon, so I really don't miss much time with them."

He nodded and smiled. "Do you like the gals you work with up in CCU?"

She nodded. "I haven't had any problems with *any* of the nurses or aides." Shrugging, she added, "Everyone seems to get along all right."

"But do you like them? Do they like you?"

She was beginning to feel flustered and answered a little too harshly, "I guess I like them. I don't know any of them very well to form an opinion one way or the other—and I don't know if they like me or not."

She started nervously twisting the ring on her finger where her wedding band used to be. Dr. Dawson sat back in his chair and looked thoughtfully at her. She cocked her head and frowned.

"Why are you asking me these questions, Steven?"

He smiled. He liked that she used his given name.

"Well, I'm genuinely concerned about you. I just want to know if you're happy here. I've found that if people like where they are working, they perform their jobs better."

She frowned again, not sure where all this was leading. It had to be about the missing medication. Did he think she screwed up because she wasn't happy with her job? Well, she didn't screw up, and she was happy with her job status, thank you very much. Why doesn't he just get to the point and stop beating around the bush?

"I was wondering if you could explain what happened with the medication order for Mr. Wilson."

Bingo! she thought.

He cleared his throat and pushed an open folder across the desk toward her. She took it and looked at the page. There was a written account for Friday, but her entry about the medication was strangely absent. She shook her head and sighed, not fully comprehending the whole thing. She looked over it once again, hoping she had overlooked something—but no, nothing had changed.

She took a cleansing breath before commenting and looked at Steven.

"Like I told Mary Kelly, I distinctly remember you writing the order on the pharmacy slip, putting it in the chart, and then, when I returned to the station, I wrote your order in the chart and sent the slip to the pharmacy. Now, what became of it after that?" She put her palms up. "I have no clue."

"I see," he said as he made a steeple with his fingers and swiveled in his chair to face the window behind him. The two ladies exchanged glances, and Mrs. Ferguson reached over and patted Christina's hand. Christina gave her a halfhearted smile and looked at the back of Steven's chair. *What is he thinking? Does he think I'm incompetent? Is he planning to fire me and is trying to figure out how to say it?*

He was silent for a moment and then turned around and unexpectedly said, "Well, it's a good thing Mr. Wilson is doing so well. The atenolol was prescribed more as a precautionary measure. As you know, it's what I prescribe to *all* my post myocardial infarction patients. Fortunately, he was on other medications that basically did the same job as the atenolol, so he wasn't in any real danger of another attack. Now, if it had been one of the other medications or, God forbid, *all* of the medication orders that went missing, then I would have been a lot more concerned." He paused a moment before continuing. "As it is, it sounds like a case of misplaced paperwork." He put his palms down on the desk and stood.

Christina looked up at him, wondering if that was it. She came all the way to the hospital fretting and sweating bullets, and all he had to say was "Looks like misplaced paperwork"?

"What?" she asked, perplexed, her confusion turning to anger. "So that's it?"

"Yep. I guess that's it. Hopefully it won't happen again." He smiled and nodded at Mrs. Ferguson. She smiled, nodded, and stood.

"Guess I'll be getting on home now," said the older nurse as she patted Christina on the shoulder, winked at Steven, and walked toward the door.

Christina missed the wink. She remained seated, kneading her damp palms, not believing this was the end of the meeting. Something just didn't seem right.

"Steven, is it all right if I stay a few more minutes? I'd like to talk to you." *You can't just brush me off without a good explanation, mister,* she thought as she watched Mrs. Ferguson leave the room.

He smiled. He had hoped she would stay. He needed to talk to her.

"Sure." He waved as his aunt exited the office and then sat behind the desk again.

"Steven, or Dr. Dawson?"

"Steven is fine."

"You seem to be taking this situation, um"—she paused a second and waved her hands—"lightly." She cocked her head, looking into those captivating eyes. Swallowing hard, she continued, "I thought surely you'd be more upset."

"I don't see any reason to make this a big deal," he said as he looked straight into her eyes and smiled. Her heart skipped a beat. "There's been misplaced orders and paperwork over the years, and fortunately the items are found or realized before any patient is put in danger." He gave a crooked smile. "I haven't lost a patient yet because of misplaced paperwork. I have a great staff of nurses who keep close tabs on me and my patients to avoid any, um, tragedies."

Then why did you call me here if it's not big deal? She wanted to scream but instead said, "Maybe not, but this isn't the first time something like this has happened since I've been here, and I'm concerned that you may think I'm inept at my job." She leaned forward. "Remember last week, Anita Simpson's blood work came up missing after I had put it in the chart? I even had witnesses who saw me put it in there."

"Yeah, but if I remember right, one of the nurses found it on the floor under the desk."

"True, but—"

"So Christina, do you think there's a conspiracy going on?" he said in a mocking tone as he put his fingers up, indicating quotes. "Ooh, let's see if we can get that new girl fired by messing with the charts."

She looked at him and frowned, feeling defensive and angry. *How dare he mock me!*

"I don't think that's funny, and I don't appreciate you belittling my concern," she said coolly and calmly. She put her hands on the desk, leaning forward. Confrontational.

"And what *if* someone is messing with the charts? Patients could be at risk, not to mention that *my* reputation is on the line." She glared at him for a moment before leaning back in her chair, crossing her arms across her chest, staring at him—waiting for a response.

He stared back for a moment and then leaned back in his own chair and raised his eyebrows, thinking, *This gal has some spunk. I never would have thought she could be so bold. I like that.* He held his hands up as if to surrender.

"I apologize." He leaned forward, meeting her gaze, and softened his facial expression and his voice.

"You're right. *If*—and that's a big *if*—someone is messing with the charts, then we should see a pattern. Why don't we keep this under wraps and see if any more papers go missing? If someone is doing this, then I doubt they'll stop, especially if they think they're getting away with it."

She sighed and uncrossed her arms, lacing her fingers together in her lap.

"All right. But I have to say, this makes me more than a little nervous. I don't want to come off looking incompetent."

He shook his head and smiled. "You are anything but incompetent. All I hear from Mrs. Ferguson and the rest of the staff is how wonderful you are and what a great job you're doing."

She raised her eyebrows in surprise. "Really?"

Leaning forward and nodding, he said in almost a whisper, "I think a lot of folks are surprised that a Yankee could do such a good job."

She smiled, rolling her eyes and shaking her head. "Well, remember, I was a southern gal before I was a Yankee. Those southern roots gotta count for somethin'."

He chuckled and nodded his head. "Yeah, they should count for somethin'."

After a few seconds she looked up and asked him how things were between him and Anika.

Leaning back in his chair and looking up at the ceiling, he said, "It's over between us."

She couldn't cover her shock and blurted out, "What? What do you mean it's over? What happened?" She caught herself. "Oh, I didn't mean to be nosy." *Yes, I did.* "If you don't want to talk about it, that's okay." *Please tell me everything!*

He looked at her and sighed.

"When I went to meet her in Dallas, she seemed happy to see me and we had a wonderful time together. We went to dinner, and we laughed and talked. Then I drove her to her friend's house here in Alva, and I went home. The next day on the drive back to Waco, she was very quiet, and when I asked what was wrong, she said she had some important decisions to make and needed to think things through. I dropped her off at her apartment and came on back to Alva. She called me late Sunday night and said she had made her decision." He paused and shook his head.

"I had no idea what she was talking about, so I asked what it was. I was so shocked when she said she was going to move to New York and help a friend of hers run a counseling center for the 9/11 victims." He paused and gave Christina a perplexed look.

"I asked if we could still see each other, and she said she didn't think it would be a good idea. She has a lot to do before she leaves and doesn't want our relationship to go any further than friendship." He sighed. "So there you have it, in a nutshell." He rubbed his face with his hands.

"I'm so sorry, Steven," she said, leaning forward and placing a hand on his arm. Inside, her heart was doing flippity-flops. *Why? Not totally sure, but I have a suspicion that it has to do with that unresolved high school crush thing.*

"I suspected something was wrong between you two because of your behavior today, but I didn't want to pry."

"I know I was kind of a jerk today. I was just having trouble wrapping my mind around it all." He rubbed his eyes with the heels of his hands and then laid them back on the desktop. "It's just that I thought *maybe* she was going to be the right one, and her announcement just threw me for a loop." Their eyes met. Hers was showing sympathy, his despair. "It hurts to be rejected, you know?"

She nodded. "Yeah, I know." Remembering how she felt so long ago when he had rejected her, she wanted to say: "What goes around comes around, buddy." Instead, she reached across the desk and put her hand on top of his.

When her skin touched his, she felt that electric current again, flowing through her hand, up her arm, around her heart, and down to her toes. She removed her hand from his and returned it to her lap.

"So, hey, let me tell you about my morning." She told him about her crazy day, which brought smiles and laughter to both of them, breaking the tension. They discussed how weird the last week had been and what lay ahead. He had a couple of angioplasties and bypasses scheduled, and she had the usual load of paperwork and motherly duties.

Looking at her watch, she said, "Um, I need to go pick up my son from Safeway." She stood and gathered her jacket and purse. Actually, she had another hour, but she felt their time together had come to an end.

"Oh, okay," he said, nodding. "Thanks again for coming. I'll see you tomorrow," he said as he stood and walked her to the door.

"Oh, I won't be in tomorrow. My new schedule started today, and I'll be working Mondays, Wednesdays, and Fridays with an occasional Saturday thrown in."

"Oh, okay. Then I guess I'll see you Wednesday."

When she left, he leaned on the doorjamb and watched as she turned the corner. *Was it my imagination, or did I feel some sort of connection when her hand touched mine?* He pondered this as he stepped back into his office. *Get a grip, man!* He looked at his watch. Seven o'clock. Desiring to stop by the gym before going home, he grabbed his duffel bag and looked around the office once more. The paperwork on the desk could wait. He turned out the light and closed and locked the door, mentally saying good-bye to the hospital until the next morning.

CHAPTER 48

During the drive to Safeway, Christina thought about the conversation she and Steven had shared. Had he called her to his office as an excuse to tell her of his breakup with Anika? He certainly didn't seem concerned with the paperwork issue, at least not as concerned as she was. She felt a smile run across her lips as she thought of their few moments alone together. *Did he feel the electric current too? I doubt it.*

She walked into Safeway and spotted Brad at one of the checkout lanes, bagging groceries for a young mother whose toddler kept trying to climb out of the shopping cart seat in spite of the restraining belt around his waist. She smiled and waved as she grabbed a shopping cart.

Might as well pick up a few things while I'm here, she thought as she headed down an aisle, trying to remember what they needed—a difficult task, as her mind kept returning to thoughts of Steven. By the time she had finished wandering aimlessly up and down the aisles, picking up items here and there, and placing them in her cart, Brad was waiting at the checkout lane, ready to bag her groceries and head home.

During the short drive, she asked, "So, Brad, how do you like working at Safeway?"

"Well, I've only worked a couple of days so far, but I like it okay."

"Is your boss nice?"

Brad nodded and said, "Yeah, he's okay too."

"I noticed a couple other young people working there. Do you know any of them from school?"

"Not really. Frank, the other bagger, graduated last year, and Sandy, the cash register gal, is a senior this year. I've seen her at school, but we don't travel in the same circles."

"Oh. Do you think you'll be able to handle work and school okay?"

"Mom, I'm only working twelve hours a week. Surely I can handle that."

She looked at him and smiled. "Well, you say that now, but you may be singing a different tune when finals come around."

He shook his head. "I'll be okay."

She nodded and said, "Okay." *I sure hope so, son.*

Once home and everyone was settled into their nightly routine, Christina called Cindy.

"Okay. Tell me what's going on with you and that Ed guy," she said as soon as Cindy answered her phone.

Giggling, Cindy said, "No 'Hello, how are you?'? Just 'Tell me about this Ed guy'?"

"Okay. Hello. How are you? Now talk."

"Well, last week he was coming out of the coffeehouse as I was going in. We recognized each other and started talking. We ended up going back in together and having another cup of coffee."

"Really? Is that *all* that happened?"

"Christina! What are you implying? Never mind. And yes, that is *all* that happened. He did ask for my phone number and asked if he could call me and maybe get together again."

"Well, that's interesting. I know you thought he was hot the first time you met him. What do you think now that you've gotten to know him a little better?"

"Well, he's definitely still hot—and I mean drop-dead-gorgeous, ice-melting, built-like-a-tank, and smooth-as-honey-from-a-honeycomb hot."

"Whew! Okay. Sounds a bit risky to me, knowing your history with men and all."

"Christina! Really. You can sure put ice water on things. I didn't say I was gonna have sex with him or anything, but dang, if I were able to choose—I'd definitely choose him!"

"Okay, Cindy, calm down. We'd better end this conversation, or we're both gonna need cold showers. I'm glad you were able to reconnect, but please take it slow. I worry about you. Sometimes you can let your heart and body rule over your mind and common sense."

"Yes, Mother. I hear you loud and clear."

"Cindy, I don't mean to offend. I just love you so much and don't want to see you hurt again."

Cindy sighed. "I know. I love you too, but please keep your fingers crossed or say a prayer or whatever you can do to help this work out between Ed and me."

"Okay, honey, I'll say a prayer for you. Talk to you tomorrow. Sleep well." Christina disconnected and laid the phone on the end table by her chair.

Cindy, Cindy, please be wise, she thought as she headed up the stairs to prepare for bed.

CHAPTER 49

Because of the small incidents at work, Christina worried more, slept less and found herself becoming increasingly irritable at home, many times snapping at the kids for offenses that would normally just frustrate her.

She yelled at Stacey for forgetting to hang her scrubs when she unloaded the dryer; Christina had to redry them or wear them wrinkled.

Brad forgot to put the garbage cans out for the trash men one morning, and Christina dragged them out and proceeded to spill the contents of one by the curb, revealing to the world what the Sanders family had consumed, bought, or used the past week. Brad had to endure his mother's wrath and ranting and ended up late for school as he obediently cleaned up the mess.

A few days later, when Nicky had neglected the litter box, Chloe, in protest, decided to do her business on the floor in front of the dryer—right where Christina set the laundry basket. Fortunately, she had realized her mistake when she smelled the distinct odor as she lifted the basket to carry it upstairs. When Nicky returned from school, he had to not only deal with an irate mother, but also wash the laundry basket and clean out the litter box.

Maybe someday I can laugh about these incidents, she thought. But because of her fragile emotional, physical, and mental state, she ended up lashing out at those closest to her.

The kids, not used to their mom being cranky, picked up her negative attitude and started nitpicking at one another, causing temper flare-ups and much arguing. After a week or so of this irritating behavior, Christina had had it. *Enough already!* She called a family meeting after dinner and, after some finger pointing, accusations, and angry outbursts, was able to discuss her own issues and ask for some kind of resolution. She apologized for her negative behavior and told them she needed help because she was so drained emotionally, physically, and even mentally.

"I have to get used to working again and running a household." She paused and sighed as she looked at each child. "I know I've been a bit witchy lately, and I apologize, but geez, kids, I really need your help to keep everything operating smoothly around here. I know y'all think I'm like a supermom"—which elicited grins from each of them—"and I thought I was too, but lately, I realize that I'm not." Looking down at her hands, she added, "Much to my surprise." The kids smiled and shook their heads.

Brad spoke first. "These past few months have been really hard on all of us, but you're right, Mom, we do need to work together to make life easier. I don't like all this … negativity. I can't focus on my schoolwork if I'm mad at Stacey or Nicky or even you, Mom." Stacey and Nicky nodded their heads in agreement.

"Yeah, I feel like my stomach and gut are all tied up in a knot, and sometimes I don't even want to come home 'cause I'm afraid someone's gonna yell at me about something I did or didn't do," added Nicky.

"Yeah, me too," said Stacey as she made a face.

Christina reached out and took each child's hand.

"Okay. Thanks for being so open and honest. I promise to work on my attitude, if y'all will promise to work on yours." They nodded in agreement. Handing them pencils and a piece of poster board, she said, "Good, then why don't y'all work together and make a job chart so you won't forget what needs to be done? Oh, don't forget to put me on it as well. Just 'cause I'm your mom, that doesn't mean I won't forget my duties every now and then. I'm gonna go get a glass of iced tea. Anyone want anything while I'm up?"

Stacey and Nicky asked for a Dr Pepper, and Brad asked for apple juice. She smiled and stood, feeling a wave of dizziness pass through her. She sat back down until the spots before her eyes and the feeling that the room was spinning passed.

Brad, noticing her behavior, asked, "Mom, are you okay?"

She blew out a lungful of air. "Yeah, I think so. I guess I stood up too quickly." She shook her head, clearing out any remaining dizziness, and stood slowly, leaning on the table for support. Everything was fine.

"Yep. I'm good."

Brad watched as she walked out of the room. Stacey gave him a "What's wrong?" look, and he just shook his head and returned his attention to the chart they were making. When Christina returned a few minutes later with the drinks, Stacey, with her brothers' help, had drawn up a work chart.

Christina knew Brad was maintaining a 4.0 grade point average by studying several hours each evening and, not wanting to put any added burden on him, asked if he could, besides doing his own laundry, help with the dinner dishes in the evenings he wasn't working at the local Safeway store. He agreed and volunteered to keep up with the yard work on the weekends as well.

Stacey, wanting to prove herself to be responsible as well, agreed to do her own laundry and help with the vacuuming and dusting on Saturday mornings.

"Oh, Mom, I forgot to tell you that I'll be babysitting Danny and Annabelle every other Saturday night so their parents can go on a date."

Christina raised her eyebrows in surprise. "When did this come about?"

"Mrs. Snyder called this afternoon and asked about my availability. She said she'd pay me seven dollars an hour!"

"Wow. That's generous. I know Danny's ten. How old is Annabelle?

"She's five."

Christina nodded her approval. "What do you plan to do with all that money you'll be making?"

"Well, I'd like to keep a few dollars for spending, but I want to save the rest so I'll have money to spend for Christmas."

Christina couldn't help but smile as she said, "That sounds like a great plan. If you want, we can go to the bank and set up a savings account for you. I'm pretty sure they have a special one for kids—at least the bank up in Michigan did."

Stacey thought for a moment and then said, "Yeah, I guess that would be better than me putting it in the piggy bank Grandma gave me. I won't be tempted to get into it if it's in a real bank."

"When will you start babysitting?"

"Next Saturday. Mrs. Snyder said they want to go to dinner and a movie, so it'll be about four or five hours."

"Well, good for you," said Christina with a smile, feeling quite proud of her daughter.

Looking over at her youngest son's troubled face, Christina asked, "So Nicky, what do you want to do to help around here?"

"Well, I was thinkin' that maybe I can take care of the animals."

Brad interjected. "Hey, you already do that. You gotta come up with something else, little brother."

Nicky frowned at Brad. "I haven't finished."

Brad held up his hands. "Sorry."

Christina shook her head. "Go ahead and finish, honey."

Nicky sighed. "I know I can't do a lot, but I can make sure the animals have food and water *before* I leave for school *and* when I get home *and* clean out the cat box at least every other day instead of just on Saturdays *and* I can keep all the waste baskets emptied." Nicky nodded and sat back. When Christina was sure he was finished, she nodded and said, "Well, okay. That sounds good."

She looked at the list of jobs next to each child's name and was pleased and thankful for their willingness to help, but she wondered if it would be enough. It was more difficult being a single working mom than she could have imagined. When she had worked before, David had been around to take over some of the household responsibilities and decisions, lessening her stress. Now, she was on her own. She silently apologized to all single, working mothers she had ever had a negative thought about. She wasn't sure she could maintain the three-or-four-day job status and was starting to rethink her decision.

I wonder if I could cut back on my hours. Maybe I should only work a couple of days a week, or maybe every other weekend. She sighed. She didn't want to give up yet. *Maybe I should make an appointment for a physical,* she thought wearily. It had been at least five years since her last one. *Maybe I'm starting menopause. Oh yeah, just what I need—hot flashes, mood swings, irregular periods. That'll certainly make life easier—not!*

The woman listened halfheartedly, making appropriate remarks as the man on the other end of the phone ranted and raved about the 9/11 event. He had called in the middle of her favorite game show, and try as she might, she couldn't follow his thoughts. He wasn't making any sense, but she knew better than to hang up—he may get angry and not call her back or follow through on his promise to give her money. She had done everything he'd asked so far: watch the Sanders family, keep tabs on their activities, and report back to him. What he did with the information was no concern of hers. He ended his monologue by saying, "Remember, I want Christina gone by Christmas."

She agreed but didn't have a clue how she was going to successfully pull that off.

CHAPTER 50

October

As summer progressed into fall and the air had a crisper feel to it in the mornings and evenings, the Sanders family continued to adjust to their new life. The first Saturday in October, Christina and Stacey searched the boxes in the basement and came up with the fall decorations. Christina had a grand collection of pumpkins, which were put on the porches, up the stairs, and in every nook and cranny. She also had colorful leaf garlands, scarecrows, apples, and other miscellaneous fall decorations.

Standing with her hands on her hips, Stacey surveyed the front two rooms and said, "Mom, you and Aunt Linda are the only two moms I know who go all out decorating for the seasons."

"Yeah?" Christina asked. "I can hardly wait to decorate this place for Christmas." Looking around at their handiwork and smiling, she imagined how pretty it would look with Christmas garlands and lights in place of the fall items.

"Oh, *please* hire someone to help you!" Turning in circles and waving her arms, she said, "I'll be too exhausted from putting this stuff away!"

"So … does that mean you're volunteering to help put this stuff away when the time comes?" Christina asked playfully.

"Ugh. No!" Stacey replied as she rolled her eyes, and dramatically wiped her brow. "I need a Dr Pepper. You want one?"

"No thanks, but I would like an iced tea," Christina said as she watched her daughter head for the kitchen. "Stacey?"

Stacey stopped in the doorway and looked at her mom. "Yeah?"

"Thanks."

She shook her head and smiled. "Yeah, no problem."

Christina sat on the couch, sipping her iced tea, and thought of her dear friend Linda.

She and Linda and their husbands had spent many wonderful hours together before David had died—the two men sharing computer interests while the women talked of household duties, kids, and medical topics.

As the years passed, Linda gave birth to two children: Haley and Joshua, who were now eighteen and fourteen. Christina had her three children, and Linda, being an RN on the obstetrics floor, had been there to assist with each birth. The kids referred to Linda and Mike as aunt and uncle, and her kids did the same to her and David. They were family. Linda was, in every sense, the sister that Christina never had.

Linda had also been there to listen and council her through the emotional struggles with her parents' deaths and especially when David had died. Christina briefly thought of that time and said a quiet thank-you to Linda for helping her and her family get through those terribly difficult days.

The second week following David's death, Christina fell into a cavernous well of depression. The mere thought of getting up and dressing was exhausting. She had done well those first few days while people were there to help, but once everyone left and the kids went back to school and she was alone in the big empty house, her mind and body had a meltdown. The first day the children left for school, she went back to bed and was there when they returned home in the afternoon. She forced herself to get up and fix them dinner and pretended that she was well. When the dinner things were put away, she found herself ascending the stairs and crawling back in her comfy bed, where David's smells still lingered.

This became a pattern, and it finally got to the point where she didn't even bother getting up in the morning or evening and would only venture to the bathroom to do her toileting. Food and liquid had lost all its appeal, and the weight started sloughing off like dead skin. At first the kids were tolerant, but when they saw their mom wasting away before their eyes, they became alarmed, and Brad called his aunt Linda.

"Aunt Linda?" he had sobbed into the phone.

"What is it, honey?" she asked with concern.

"My mom won't get out of bed," he said between sniffles and sobs.

"What do you mean?"

"She just sleeps all the time and lays in bed and cries and won't eat or drink and she's lost a lot of weight, and she won't fix us food or go get us any and the cabinets and fridge are getting empty, and I have to get Stacey, Nicky, and myself ready for school and out to the bus on time." He paused and caught his breath, and she could hear him blow his nose.

"I don't know what to do," he said, sniffling.

"Brad, how long has this been going on?"

"About two weeks. At first, we just figured it was sorta normal, 'cause she was missing Daddy so much, but now …" He paused, gaining control of his shaky voice. "We need help, Aunt Linda." He let out a sigh, and there was silence for a minute as she thought about what to say and do.

"Oh, honey, I'll be over in a few minutes."

"Thanks, Aunt Linda. We're so worried about her."

As an idea popped into her head, she said, "Tell you what. I'll stop by Burger Palace and get you guys some hamburgers. How does that sound?"

"That'd be great." He thanked her again and replaced the receiver.

Linda sat for a few minutes and thought about Christina. She had been so busy with work and her own family's needs that she had neglected her friend. She had called a couple of times, and Christina had sounded fine over the phone, but she should have listened better and made time to go visit. Then she would have picked up on the signs of depression and … and … and … *I need to stop beating myself up and go take action. I can't undo the past, but I can surely change the future.*

When Linda arrived at the Sanders house, Nicky met her at the door.

"Hey, Aunt Linda."

She pulled him into a hug. "Hey yourself." Setting the bags of food on the counter, she asked, "Are you hungry?"

"Yeah, I'm starved," he said enthusiastically, reaching for the kid's meal bag.

"Hey Brad and Stacey," she called, "dinner has arrived."

They came in from the den. Stacey ran into her arms, and Linda pulled her close and hugged her.

"Why don't you guys eat in the family room while I go check on your mom?"

They agreed, gathering their bags of food and drinks and heading that way while she turned and headed up the stairs.

Arriving at Christina's door, she tapped lightly. Hearing no response, she opened it slowly and poked her head into the darkened room. The odor hit her first, causing her nose to crinkle—a mixed smell of unwashed head and body. *She must not have bathed in a while* was her thought as she flipped on the overhead light and approached the bed.

"Christina?" she whispered, tapping lightly on the lump of covers.

"Hmm?" came the muffled reply.

"Christina, it's Linda. I need to talk to you. Can you get up please?"

The lump moved. "Can't we talk another time? I'm so tired." Moaning, she pulled the covers tightly over her head, turning away from the voice and curling into a ball.

Linda sighed and with a determined gesture grabbed the covers and pulled them off her friend.

"What are you doing?" Christina responded angrily as she reached for the covers and pulled them back around her.

It was then that Linda saw the reason for Brad's concern. Christina had indeed lost weight, making her look like a stick-figure character.

The dark circles under her eyes, matted oily hair, and rank breath and body odor were definite clues of depression. Linda knew if she didn't intervene quickly, Christina would just curl up and die. She had seen several women over the years suffering from postpartum depression—getting close to the point of no return before their families intervened. For a few of them, it was a touch-and-go situation as medical staff and families struggled to bring them back from the brink of death. She hoped she would be able to help Christina without having to call in outside help.

"Christina, you need to go take a shower. You stink," she said matter-of-factly.

"Linda, leave me alone! I just need to sleep. I'm *so* tired," she mumbled as she pulled the covers back over her head and buried herself in them.

"Sorry babe. Can't do that." She reached once again for the covers and struggled with a weakened Christina before finally winning the tug-of-war. She threw the covers on the floor and with a quick movement grabbed for the sheets. Another tug-of-war ensued, and she won again. By then Christina was livid.

"How dare you come in here and do this!" she hissed.

Linda frowned sympathetically and said, "I know you're angry with me now, but you've got to get yourself under control." She sighed once again and said calmly, "If you don't get out of bed, take a shower, eat, and drink something, I'll have to call an ambulance." Christina gave her an "I can't believe you said that" look. "I'll do it, Christina. I don't want to, but I will. Your well-being is more important than what you think of me."

Christina breathed hard, frowning as tears streamed down her face. She sat in the middle of the bed with her feet curled under her, balled her fists, and crossed her arms over her chest. She looked like a small child throwing a temper tantrum. Linda shook her head, speaking softly as she sat on the side of the bed.

"Christina. Honey." She reached for her hand, but Christina scooted further away.

Linda nodded slightly and started again. "Christina, when was the last time you ate?"

Christina shrugged but continued to glare at Linda.

"When was the last time you showered?" Again she shrugged.

"Tell you what. You go take a shower, and I'll go make you some dinner."

Christina shook her head and said emphatically, "I don't *want* to take a shower, and I don't *want* to eat!"

Linda suppressed a smile as she was reminded of a time when her daughter had said the same thing when they were fighting about the evening meal ritual. She had wanted to watch cartoons instead of sitting at the table to eat. It had been an ugly battle, but Mom had won. Of course, her daughter had been around four at the time. Linda stood.

"Okay. Guess we'll have to do this the hard way." She reached out for Christina, who tried batting her hands away and scooted to the far corner of the bed.

"Christina! Stop behaving like a bratty child!" she said sternly, reaching for her again and grabbing an arm.

"Ow!" Christina cried out, wrenching her arm free and rubbing the area that had been grabbed. "Leave me alone, Linda!"

"I will *not* leave you alone! You need to go take a shower and eat something."

She lowered her voice, afraid the children would hear and come running upstairs in defense of their mother. "Do you want to end up in the hospital? Or, worse yet, do you want to die? Is that what you want?" Christina continued to glare, tears streaming down her face as Linda stood looking down at her with her arms across her chest, trying desperately to remain calm. She took a breath and let it out slowly, silently asking for God's help. She wanted to reach out and slap some sense into her friend but opted to stand with her hands tucked firmly and safely in her armpits. Tears filled her eyes, blurring her vision, and she batted her lashes to clear them. She didn't trust herself to release her hands just yet to wipe them away.

In a very controlled voice, she said, "As your friend, I can't just let you waste away. I love you too much." She then felt tears stream down her own face and watched as Christina buried her face in her hands and sobbed. She continued more softly, relaxing her body and grabbing a tissue from the box by the bed, wiping the tears from her face.

"Think about your children, Christina!" she said pleadingly as she reached out to touch Christina's arm. "They're scared. They've lost one parent and are afraid of losing another. Don't do that to them."

Christina shied away from her friend's touch, but something inside her broke as she thought about her children. *My poor children.* Part of her did want to die. The thoughts *Maybe they would be better off without me* and *A lot of good I'm doing them anyway* flitted across her mind. Part of her was shocked that she could even think such things. Before David's death, she had always been a positive, life-loving person. *Before David's death. Before a part of me died. Before …*

Being a nurse, she knew the signs of clinical depression and knew that was what she had, but a part of her wasn't willing to let it go. There was a part of her that was—and she hated to admit it—happy being miserable. She was so lonely and miserable without David and didn't want to face life without him, but the thought of her children being taken away and raised by someone else made her realize how selfish she was being. Linda was right. It would be devastating for them if they lost her too—especially because of her own choice. It was one thing to lose a parent because of an accident, but to lose one because they chose death over them—well, that could cause irreparable damage to the spirit. She wiped a hand across her face, smearing tears and snot. Linda reached over and grabbed a few tissues from the nightstand and handed them to Christina, who took them, blew her nose, and wiped her eyes and hands. She let out a big sigh.

"All right," she said angrily. "You win. I'll go take a shower, but I don't want anything to eat."

Linda nodded and said a silent thank-you to God.

As Christina showered, Linda finished stripping the bed, put new linens on, grabbed up the smelly pile, and took them to the laundry room. She checked on the kids, who were watching a game show called *Street Smarts*. She quickly opened a can of tomato soup and made a grilled cheese sandwich. When she could no longer hear the shower, she threw the bedding into the washing machine. When she heard

Christina slam her bedroom door, she put the food on a tray, said a quick prayer for strength, and headed up the stairs. She didn't bother knocking. She opened the door and wasn't surprised to see Christina wrapped in her robe, curled up on top of the bed with a towel wrapped around her wet head, facing away from the door.

"I brought you a little bite to eat," she said as she set the tray on the nightstand.

Christina turned over, tears streaming down her face.

"You washed the bedding, didn't you?" she asked between sobs.

Linda looked at her, perplexed. "Well, yes. It was very smelly."

"I didn't want you to wash the pillowcases. They still had David's smell on them."

Linda sighed and looked at her friend sympathetically.

"I'm so sorry, honey," she said, taking her friend's hand, "but everything smelled so dirty. I had to wash it all."

Christina continued to cry quietly. Linda handed her more tissues and sat with her, feeling her own tears cascade down her cheeks. She was at a loss for words. After a few minutes she said, "Christina, you have to eat. Even if it's just a couple of bites." She picked up the soup bowl and handed it to her. "Please," she pleaded.

Christina blew her nose again, wiped her swollen eyes, shuddered, and finally ceased her crying. She looked at Linda and sighed.

"All right. I'll eat a couple of bites." She took the bowl and spoon and tested the soup's temperature before cautiously putting it in her mouth. Before she realized it, she had eaten the remainder of the soup.

Lifting the plate from the nightstand and handing it to Christina, Linda said, "Here, try a couple of bites of the sandwich too." She watched as her friend ate the few bites she promised. When Christina finished, Linda patted her on the hand and said, "Okay, you can rest now, but I'll be back in a few hours to check on you again." She leaned over and kissed her forehead. Christina grabbed Linda's hand.

Yawning, she said, "Thanks for the food." Removing the towel from her head, she turned over and buried herself in the covers. Linda gathered the food items and headed downstairs. That had been the turning point.

It had been a difficult recovery for Christina as she dealt with her loss, but Linda was there for her and the children on a daily basis, either physically or by phone, until Christina was able to fully function.

Linda insisted that Christina and the children go for counseling and even took them when Christina would try to back out with flimsy excuses. After about six months of therapy, she woke one morning and didn't feel the heavy burden of grief she had been carrying around like a huge bag of garbage. It was as if someone had come and just picked it up and tossed it away. She was sure she knew who that someone was.

It had been an extremely difficult time for all of them as they worked through their grief, anger, and frustrations, it was but well worth the pain and time it had taken.

As Christina thought about her dear friend and all the drama she had put her through, she wondered if she would have done the same thing—if she would have endured the verbal and emotional abuse. There were a few times on the way to or from the counseling sessions when Christina would feel such anger and frustration, she would verbally lash out at her friend—and then, feeling such remorse for having done so, would cry for hours. Linda just took it in stride, realizing it was part of the healing process.

Christina hoped that if she was ever put to the test she too would pass. She would call Linda that evening and express her appreciation once more and catch up on the events of the past couple of weeks.

She stood, looked around the room, and started cleaning up the mess that she and Stacey had made.

CHAPTER 51

A few mornings later, Christina sat in her overstuffed easy chair, sipping a warm cappuccino and watching the birds and squirrels at the feeder, and reflected on the past few months. She wrote in her journal.

"The kids all seem to like their schools and most of their teachers and are passing with As and Bs.

"Nicky is learning how to play the trumpet, and even though my ears feel like they're going to bleed because of the strained or missed notes, he is making progress. He's doing better in his math class, especially after we talked to the teacher and explained that he may need a little extra help every now and then.

"Stacey joined the drama team in middle school and earned the title of 'Drama Queen' by her classmates and teacher. She has the lead parts in the upcoming Christmas plays at school and church. I hope she can handle learning all the lines for both plays. She's pretty energetic and more organized than I was at that age, so she'll probably be fine.

"Brad is playing quarterback for the Eagles football team and is thoroughly enjoying it. We're still not sure what happened out on the field last Friday night but are calling it a miracle. How one minute he appeared to have sprained his fingers and the next minute they were healed is still a mystery. Whatever happened, it sure has increased his faith.

"He seems to be handling work and school and extra activities well— even the girls who come and go in his life. He has taken on the role of oldest male in the family very seriously and helps me keep everything running smoothly. I just hope and pray that I keep everything in balance and don't become too dependent on him. I have to remind myself that he's only sixteen.

"I'm still worried about the situation at work. I just don't understand why things keep getting misplaced. I'm still feeling quite tired and am going to make an appointment for a physical. I need to ask Steven whom I should choose for my primary care doctor.

"Steven and I are getting along very well. Cindy keeps hoping we'll end up together. I don't know. I have mixed feelings about all of this. I like Steven, but I can't help but feel weird when I think of us together in the future. I still love David, and he will always be in my heart. I'm not sure I'll have room for anyone else, especially in an intimate way. I'm leaving this all up to God. He'll have to change my heart and mind before I could ever think of any kind of commitment.

"Cindy has a new man in her life. I haven't met him yet, but she seems quite taken by him. I do hope she's careful. She's had her heart broken too many times."

CHAPTER 52

The previous Friday night, she had been ready to run on the field when Brad didn't get up after being tackled. He lay in the middle of the playing field on his side, writhing in agony. She ran down to the sidelines as the coach and first aid team went to assess his injuries. She hadn't realized she was holding her breath until she saw him walk to the sidelines holding his right hand, which was wrapped in gauze. She let out a cry of joy that he was able to walk off the field.

The previous week, a young man from the opposite team had been carried off the field on a stretcher and loaded into an ambulance. The spectators were informed at the end of the game that he had a broken ankle and a mild concussion.

When Brad walked off the field, the crowd stood cheering and clapping with relief. Their star player was all right—nothing more serious than two sprained middle fingers on his right hand.

He *was* a lucky guy, for if it had been more serious, the mother lion in her would have come out and would have pulled her cub out of the line of danger. *Of course, Brad wouldn't have forgiven me for a very long time if I had.* The team had become very important to him, and he wouldn't want anyone to do anything that would jeopardize that relationship—not even his mom. The rest of the game had continued without him as he sat on the sidelines watching, feeling frustrated, as his teammates did their best but lost the game anyway.

When Christina met him at the gate, expecting him to be in pain and misery, she was surprised to find him in neither state. He was actually grinning and waving his right hand around, minus the bandage. Either he hadn't really sprained his fingers or a miracle had taken place. His fingers that had been injured seemed to have healed themselves—or were supernaturally healed.

As she sat in the chair remembering the event, she still had a difficult time wrapping her mind around it. God did work in strange ways; that was a fact. But why then and why that way? Perhaps she would never know the answers, but wasn't that what faith was all about? Trusting God when things just didn't make sense?

CHAPTER 53

Brad lay in bed that same morning, thinking about the weird incident on the football field the previous week. He had thought about it often since then but couldn't logically explain any of it. He remembered leaving the field after he injured his hand, seeing his mom cheering and waving, and hearing the crowd clap and yell, and then sitting on the bench on the sidelines, trying to make sense of what had just transpired. He was hardly aware of the rest of the game and the fact that the opposing team had scored the winning touchdown, so focused was he on trying to figure out what had happened to him on the field.

As he was running toward the opposing team, in his peripheral vision he saw a bright light, but when he turned his head toward it, all he saw was another teammate running beside him. When he looked forward again, the young man that was about to plow into him had a strange darkness encircling him, like a shroud. *Was I hallucinating?* Just as the shrouded guy was about to tackle him, the bright guy reached over and pushed Brad out of the way. Both guys tumbled and fought, but Brad lost his balance and landed on his fingers, spraining them. When the medics came to the field, he looked around for the two strange team members among the guys surrounding him but didn't see them anywhere—but he could have sworn he saw his dad standing on the sidelines by his mom. *Did I imagine it all? Was I having an awake dream, or am I just losing my mind? Who can I talk to about this? Mom would understand, but would anyone else?*

By the end of the game, Brad's fingers had been completely restored. His coach had a difficult time believing it and kept asking Brad to show him his fully functional appendages. He even called the medic over to confirm that the healing had taken place.

When Brad met his mom after the game, she was speechless when he showed her his unbandaged hand. All she could say was "Wow!" Later, when he told her about the strange encounter on the field, they decided that he had been on the receiving end of a miracle. *But why?* he wondered as his alarm clock sounded. He reached over to hit the snooze button, stretching and wiggling his strong, healthy fingers.

By the time school had started the following Monday, the story of the Friday night football game miracle had made its rounds through the town. When he walked on the school campus, fellow team members, cheerleaders, and a plethora of students surrounded him, wanting to see and touch his healed fingers. Although he enjoyed the extra attention, it was a little unnerving as well.

He had always considered himself to be a strong Christian but hardly ever talked about his faith, God, or the possibility of miracles. He hadn't given the spiritual world much consideration until the Friday night incident. It wasn't that he *didn't* believe in angels and demons or heaven and hell; he just didn't think about it often. He hadn't had a need or desire to think about or to try to understand it—until now. He decided do some research to better understand the spiritual world and how it interacted with the earthly one.

That evening and the ones following, he searched the Internet for stories about miracles, angels, demons, and unexplained phenomena. He also searched his Bible and found a verse that seemed to jump off the page at him. He was looking through the book of Ephesians and came across the verse in book six verse twelve: "For our struggle is not against flesh and blood, but against the rulers, against the authorities, against the powers of this dark world and against the spiritual forces of evil in the heavenly realms." That verse started him searching his Bible for other related verses. He remembered memorizing Romans 8:38 in Sunday school when he was twelve: "For I am convinced that neither death nor life, neither angels nor demons, neither the present nor the future, nor any powers, neither height nor depth, nor anything else in all creation, will be able to separate us from the love of God that is in Christ Jesus our Lord." He kept searching and was amazed at the number of Scriptures in the Bible that referred to angels and demons.

He shared his findings with his mom, who encouraged him to discuss them further with the senior pastor or the youth minister. He had an appointment with the youth minister on Wednesday afternoon after school and hoped he would be able to shed more light on the subject. His alarm rang again, and he forced himself to crawl out of bed.

Stepping out of the shower, Brad realized too late that there were no clean towels for him to use. He went to the bathroom door, peeked out, and seeing no one leaned over the upstairs rail and called to his mom.

"Mom, could you bring me a towel, please?"

Christina jumped when she heard Brad's voice, realizing she had dozed off. She called up for him to repeat his request, then headed to the laundry room, grabbed the basket of fresh towels and clothes, and headed upstairs, her mind continuing to wander. She had the day off and started mentally listing all the things she wanted to get done.

She heard a squeal and then Brad's voice.

"Geez, Stacey, you're supposed to knock before just barging into the bathroom!"

"I didn't just barge in! The door was partly open! How was I to know you'd be naked?"

Christina ran up the last few steps and handed a clean towel into Brad through the partially open door.

Grabbing the towel, he said, "Thanks, Mom. This smells good."

"Sorry, Brad," Stacey said as she went back to her room.

Brad came out of the bathroom with the towel wrapped around his waist, looking sheepishly at his mom and shaking his head. She bit her bottom lip, stifling a smile and a giggle. It was hard to believe that a few years ago, the kids had all showered together and thought nothing of it. Now, however—well, it was a good thing that maturity and modesty stepped in when it did.

As she folded the laundry and put it away, she thought about the previous night's discussion with Brad and smiled.

"Mom?" he called as he hung his jacket on the coat rack.

"Yes, Brad." She had gone into the kitchen to throw a bag of garbage from the van into the waste can and peeked in the family room to see Stacey and Nicky engrossed a movie.

Leaning against the door frame in the kitchen and munching on a carrot, Brad asked, "How do you know when you're in love?"

Why are you asking?" she asked as she leaned against the kitchen counter.

"I just wondered. A lot of kids at school say they're in love." He crossed his arms over his chest. "My friend Paul says he loves Jenny." He walked over, picked an apple off the counter, and took a bite out of it. "How can he know for sure if it's love?"

Putting her arm around his waist and turning him, she said, "Let's go sit in the front room."

They sat on the couch. She pulled her feet under her and laid an afghan over her lap on one end, and he draped himself like a blanket on the other end, one long arm over the back of the couch and the other holding the apple, his legs spread out in front. *He has to be close to six feet,* she thought as she looked at his lean body.

"Okay." She sighed and rubbed her forehead. "How do you know when you're in love?"

He nodded. She took a deep breath, released it and asked, "Well, what do *you* think?"

"I don't know. I haven't really thought about it," he answered as he leaned forward, put the apple core on the coffee table, and rubbed his palms on his pants legs.

"Well, you must have been thinking about it a bit to have asked me the question."

"Okay, you're right." He smiled sheepishly, rubbing his hands together.

"There's this girl I really like. She's cute, funny, and *so* sweet. When I see her, my heart flutters, I get weak in the knees, and I can feel my ears getting red. I get really clumsy and can't even talk." He paused, looking perplexed. "Is that what love feels like?"

She looked into those intense blue eyes as her thoughts rambled: him as an infant, his first steps, his first days of kindergarten and middle school—and now high school and girls! *Geez oh Pete! Where did those years go?*

She had about a thousand other thoughts zip through her head in the few seconds before she was able to respond to his question.

"Wow. Those are some pretty intense feelings. Have you ever felt that way before?"

"No."

She thought about the few girls he had walked to school and wondered if his heart had been stirred by any of them.

"Have you sat down and talked to her?" she asked, hoping he would tell her the name of the mystery girl.

Blushing, he said sheepishly, "Well, no, not really. I mean, we say hi and stuff, but nothing serious."

Well, it isn't any of the girls he walks to school. Who could it be?

"I'm too nervous. What if I say something stupid? I'm afraid she'll think I'm a dork or something." He looked worried.

She nodded, remembering when she had felt the same way about Steven Dawson.

"Well, Brad, I may be wrong, but I think you're feeling infatuation, which is different than the feeling of love. Granted, they're similar, and sometimes it's hard to tell the difference, but usually time takes care of that."

"Okay, I don't mean to sound dumb, but what is infatuation?"

"Infatuation, my dear son, is a feeling of intense like."

"What? Intense like?" he asked, confused.

She sighed. "Okay, let me see if I can explain this." She thought for a moment. "Say there are qualities of a person that you really admire—like her funny personality or cute looks, the way she walks or talks." He nodded. She continued, "The difference between infatuation and true love is that true love goes beyond looks and personality and other outward appearances."

He looked confused again. "You see *past* all that outer stuff and really see her spirit—her true self," she said. "All the good and bad stuff."

"Like?"

"You're not gonna make this easy for me, are you?"

He grinned and shook his head.

She sighed. "Okay. Let me see how else I can explain this. Let's say at school she seems aloof and maybe even snobby, but at home she writes poetry, composes music, helps with her siblings, and maybe even volunteers for her church's activities. On the outside she seems one way, but when you get to know her, there's a whole 'nother side you were unaware of and quite honestly like. There's a commitment you feel. Like you would do anything and everything to please and protect that person. When you get to know the person on a deeper level and still like everything about them, then infatuation can progress to love."

"Oh, so if I start talking to her and she responds, and we get to know each other and start liking each other, that can lead to love?"

"Well, yes, that is possible." She paused. "But you have to understand that it may be more complicated than that."

He looked down, chewing on his thumbnail, trying to wrap his mind around the whole concept.

She added, "And please don't get having sex and being in love confused. They don't always go hand in hand." She noticed his cheeks and ears blush. He nodded slightly.

"Brad, you're still young, and I don't think at this point in your life you need to be worrying about whether you are in love with someone or not. Why not just enjoy being *everyone's* friend? Just have fun and enjoy your teenage years." She leaned over and cupped his chin in her hand and looked him in the eyes.

"Believe me, you'll have plenty of time after graduation and college to find a wonderful life partner."

They sat in silence together on the couch for a few minutes, each wondering if there was more that needed to be said. *Should I tell him about how his dad and I met and fell in love? No, I'll wait for him to ask. This is all about him right now.*

Brad sighed and stood. "Yeah, you're right." He put his hands in his pockets and shrugged. "It's just that so many kids are feeling pressure to *have* a boyfriend or girlfriend. I just don't want to feel—different. I mean, Melinda and I are friends, but not boyfriend and girlfriend, although most people think we should be." He paused and looked at her, bewildered. "You know what I mean?"

She looked at his tall, lanky form and tried to imagine him as a grown man. *When did he turn from a little boy to a young man?*

"I know." She nodded and sighed. She reached out, and he took her hand.

"It's hard to stand alone. Just trust God to bring the right girl into your life at the right time."

He looked at her with raised eyebrows.

"Yeah—right. Thanks, Mom." He leaned over and kissed her on the cheek before walking from the room.

"Hey, Brad!" she called as he turned the corner. He poked his head around the doorframe.

"Yeah?"

"Are you gonna tell me who this girl is?" He smiled and shook his head and then left her sight. *You stinker!* She smiled, remembering her first big crush and how she wouldn't have told her folks for a million dollars. She'd find out sooner or later. She heard him walk up the stairs and close the door to his room. Then she heard the stereo. Stacey and Nicky came in to kiss her good night before they too headed up to bed.

She sat on the couch for a few more minutes rehashing the conversation, hoping she had said the right thing. She missed David. He needed to be here to talk to his son about these manly things! She felt an anger rising from deep within her. Was she mad at David? *Yes. He shouldn't have died and left me alone.* She balled her fists and hit the cushion next to her. *Why? Why? Why?* She knew there would be no answer.

She wiped her eyes, stood, turned the light off, and headed up to bed.

David shook his head and looked at Jarrod. "I wish I could reassure her that she's doing a great job. She said everything I would have."

Jarrod nodded.

"Will she get past the anger?"

"Of course she will. It takes humans varying amounts of time to process all their feelings. I've found that those with a strong faith and good family ties do much better. They don't grieve or stay angry as long as those without that support system.

"Sometimes Father lets the saints talk to their loved ones through dreams. Let me ask Him if you can speak to Christina as she sleeps."

David smiled and nodded. "That'd be great."

As Christina crawled in bed and was pulling the covers up, her cell phone rang. She looked at her watch. Ten o'clock. *Who would be calling me this late?* She grabbed the phone, praying it wasn't a relative or friend in need, and looked at the display face. Not recognizing the number, she answered tentatively, "Hello?"

No answer.

"Hello?"

Click. The line went dead.

"Well, that's weird. Must've been a wrong number." After looking at the number one more time and realizing it was a local area code, she thought, *I guess I could call it back, but honestly I'm too tired to care.* Instead, she laid it on her nightstand next to the bed, turned off the light, and pulled up the covers.

Janet put the phone down quietly and smiled. Christina wouldn't recognize her number, so she doubted she would call her back, and if she did, Janet would recognize her number and be able to pretend to be someone else. She smiled sardonically. She had called just to unnerve Christina. Give her something else to worry about.

That night, Christina had had a very strange dream.

"Christina! Christina! Wake up!"

"Hmm?" she asked sleepily.

"Christina." The voice spoke firmly.

"David?" She asked sleepily.

"Yes, it's me. I need to tell you something."

She sat up in bed, rubbing her eyes with balled fists like a child. She automatically glanced at the clock. One eleven.

"What are you doing here? You're not supposed to be here." She looked around the room. It was bathed in a white light. David seemed to shine and reflect the light as well. She rubbed her eyes again. "David, what's going on?" she asked as she came fully awake, sitting up and pulling the sheet around her neck.

"Christina, don't be afraid. I need to tell you something important." He stood beside the bed and put his hand on her face. She felt a tingling sensation—warm and full of love.

She reached up and put her hand over his and leaned into it.

She felt warm tears stream down her face.

"I've missed you so much," she said between sobs. "Why did you leave me?"

"Oh, Christina, my love, I know this has been very difficult for you." He stroked her hair, and she felt him kiss the top of her head. She closed her eyes and basked in the warmth of his love. It was similar to the feeling of being snuggled in a warm downy blanket in her mother's lap, but oh so much more intense. She wanted to stay there forever.

"You're doing a great job with the kids. I'm so proud of you. I need to remind you to stay strong and keep your faith."

She felt him pull away and opened her eyes to see the light fading.

"David! Don't leave me!" she wailed.

"Christina, I'll always be near you. Remember to keep your faith and trust God. Do not fear anything. Everything will work out. I promise. I love you, and tell the kids I love them too!"

Sobbing and calling out to him, she watched as the room became dark again, except for the blinking numbers on her clock, which still read one eleven. How could that be? Had time stood still? Her heart felt as if it would rupture with grief. She lay down and curled into herself, shivering and weeping. Her angel put his hand on her head, and she fell into a deep, peaceful sleep.

The next morning she awoke refreshed, knowing she should remember the dream she had, but for the life of her, she couldn't. She lay in bed trying to remember what it was. *Something about David.* It was like a fog dissipating into the atmosphere of her conscious world. *I can remember him telling me something, but for the life of me, I can't remember. God, if you're trying to tell me something, you'll have to help me remember.* After a few minutes of trying, she gave up and crawled out of bed.

CHAPTER 54

David

David was truly enjoying his new heavenly body. He could come and go wherever he wanted with just a thought, and he loved being in the presence of angels.

When he had arrived in heaven, he was met by a multitude of heavenly beings, as well as his grandparents and other friends and relatives who had passed on before him. The intense love he felt emanating from them was nothing compared to what he felt when Jesus pulled him into a hug. It had been more wonderful than he could have ever imagined in his earthly body and mind. His spirit soared with ecstasy as he hugged his Redeemer and felt the love and warmth that radiated from the Son of God. As he held on to Jesus, in his mind he had asked when he would see the Father and was assured that soon he would see Him, but it wasn't the right time yet.

In his new body every sense had been intensified—every emotion was stronger. The only emotions that seemed to be absent were grief, worry, and anger, which became evident when he thought of his family. All those earthly cares were gone, and he felt an indescribable peace when he thought of Christina and his kids.

He was surprised to learn that he didn't have to eat or drink to survive; his heavenly body could either be solid or spirit, depending on where he was or what he was doing; he could only visit earth and his family with God's permission; and in heaven there was no such thing as time. The only way the saints were aware of time passing on the earthly plane was when they went to the viewing room and looked down on the events taking place. In that special place, they could pray for their loved ones, asking God to send someone to intervene on their behalf. Sometimes God would let the believers and their guardian angels go for a visit to warn or encourage their loved ones, like David had done in Christina's dream. Neither saint nor angel was allowed to interfere with the free will of the individual.

David was aware that there was a battle going on for his family, but he wasn't sure to what extent. He was able to witness the demon trying to hurt Brad during the football game and was thankful when Brad's guardian angel stepped in and protected as well as healed his son. He had asked Jarrod if he knew the outcome of the situation with his family, but he said that only God knew such things.

Janet had been observing Christina's work habits during the past month. The patients loved her, and the staff seemed to respect her. *Why does she have to be so stinkin' perfect?* Janet hated Christina and everything about her: size-eight body, naturally curly auburn hair, size-six shoes, and everything in between, including her sickeningly sweet personality.

Why with all the kids in the middle school did my daughter have to befriend Stacey?

When Leelee came home from school and told her about her new friend Stacey, Janet almost blew a gasket. She wanted to scream and shout, rant and rave, and forbid her daughter from any association with Stacey Sanders, but instead, sat in shocked silence as her daughter talked on and on about her wonderful new friend. Inside her mind, however, she was thinking up ways she could disengage her daughter from this friendship. *Why her? Why now?*

Janet had *no* idea that this battle in her mind was not only mental and emotional, but extended into the spiritual realm as well. Hers and Christina's lives, as well as their children's, were hanging in the balance between good and evil.

CHAPTER 55

In addition to being homesick for Michigan friends and missing David, Christina was having trouble at work. The past few days' events were enough to make her question her sanity. A few orders had been lost or misplaced and had caused her concern, but the one that troubled her most was pertaining to Mr. Johnson. Dr. Dawson had told her during rounds to give him nitroglycerine tablets orally if he started having chest pains. She remembered vividly writing it down on his medication sheet, but when she went back later to check if his prescription had come up from the pharmacy, there was nothing documented. She asked the other nurses about it, but no one seemed to know anything. She had to call Dr. Dawson to get a new order written. Even though he said he didn't mind and told her to never hesitate to call him if she had any other problems, the tone of his voice said he was a bit miffed.

She had been working with him for six weeks and still felt like an adolescent schoolgirl when he was around—all nervous and sweaty. She tried to appear calm and in control but would occasionally belie her confidence by dropping pens or papers. He intimidated her whether he meant to or not—her problem, not his. He was just being himself, oblivious to the turmoil he was causing in her mind and body.

Lula was stuffing another load of sheets in the washer when her cell phone buzzed in her pocket.

Pulling it out and recognizing the number, she looked around the laundry room to make sure no one was listening and then answered it.

"Hello?"

"Have you been administering the drug as you were instructed?"

"Yeah, but I don't think it's working. She's not acting any different."

"It takes a little time to build up in the system. You should be seeing some results in the next few days."

"So, what should I be looking for?"

"Don't worry. You'll know. The less I tell you, the less you'll be held accountable if you ever get questioned."

"Um … so can I call you when something happens?"

"No! Don't even think about it. I'll be getting rid of this phone anyway after we talk. I'll know when something happens, so you don't need to worry."

"Um, okay." She stood a few seconds listening to dead air and then put the phone back in her pocket.

I sure hope I don't get in trouble, she thought as she started the washing machine.

CHAPTER 56

The weekend for homecoming was coming more quickly than Christina had anticipated. She had been so focused on work and home activities that when Cindy called to ask about her plans for the big twenty-year reunion the next weekend, she was surprised that it had slipped her mind.

"Christina, we talked about this a couple of weeks ago. Remember?"

"I'm sorry, Cindy. I've just been so busy and I'm so tired lately that I've hardly had time to think about anything." She paused, catching her breath and retrieving a pen and paper. "Okay, tell me the schedule again."

As Cindy went over the list of activities planned for the next weekend, including a pregame dinner on Friday night, after-game dance and gathering at a local night club, and a baseball game at the park on Saturday, Christina could feel herself getting weary.

"Samara is so looking forward to going to the park. She seems to think there will be some hot boys there." Giggling, she said, "Remember when we used to get excited about boys?"

"What do you mean 'used to'?" Christina asked with a chuckle.

"Christina!"

"Okay, not boys now, but I can appreciate a good-looking man just about any time." She caught herself smiling as Steven's face popped into her mind.

"Maybe there'll be some single guys there we can flirt with," said Cindy, a hint of mischief in her voice.

"Speaking of guys, how are things going with you and Ed? You haven't mentioned him lately."

"I haven't seen or talked to him in a while. He's always so busy going back and forth to Dallas or Waco or wherever he's called. I just don't understand why he has to travel so much. I'm trying to convince him to come to the homecoming activities with me, but I don't know. He's pretty noncommittal."

"Hmm. I'd like to meet him someday, if at all possible. If he's as hot as you say he is, I'd like to enjoy the scenery too!"

"Christina! You never cease to shock me!"

"And you, me."

"So what's going on with you and Steven?"

Christina sighed. "Yeah, well. I'm not sure *what's* going on in that department."

"You want to talk about it?"

"No. It'll all work out eventually. Maybe we're just not meant to be together." She sighed again. Perking up, she asked, "So what do you have planned for us?"

"What do *you* want to do?" All businesslike, she asked, "Do you want to go to all the activities, or just some of them?" She paused, waiting for an answer, and then quickly added, "Donna said they'd be going to the game but wouldn't be able to go to the activities on Saturday. Lisa said her family will go to the game and the park on Saturday."

"Well," replied Christina, "I think I'd like to go to the dinner, but if no one else wants to go, then we could just go to the game. I don't really want to go to the after-game activities. It'll probably run late, and I'm just not into that whole drinking and dancing stuff." She paused and then said quietly, "Guess I've turned into quite a fuddy-duddy as I've gotten older."

"Hmm." Cindy nodded in agreement, which thankfully Christina couldn't see. Her dear friend had *never* been the party girl type, unlike herself, who wouldn't miss one. She hoped her disappointment didn't come through when she said, "Well, that's okay. I'd like to go to the after-game activities, and I was wondering if Samara could spend the night at your house."

"Of course she can!"

Samara had a natural gift for the piano and would sit for hours practicing and composing. When Christina had the rare opportunity to listen to her play, her spirit would be transported to another time and place.

She would catch herself feeling envious of this child who could take anything, in any genre requested or set before her, and make it sound as if she had been practicing for hours. Her hands would seemingly float across the keys, and the music emanating from the instrument would be both melodious and almost magical.

I hope I can convince Samara to play so I can justify having the piano for something other than a knickknack shelf and dust collector.

CHAPTER 57

The week of homecoming was very stressful. Between work duties, home obligations, and feeling so rundown and exhausted, Christina couldn't work up enough energy to get excited about the upcoming event. The thought of attending *all* the activities that were planned made her want to take a nap.

The kids, on the other hand, could hardly wait till Friday night's game. From the moment they arrived home Monday afternoon till they left the following day and on all the days after, that was pretty much all they talked about.

Brad had been at football practice every afternoon for the past couple of weeks, gearing up for the big event. The Eagles were to play against their rival team, the Burleson Broncos. Alva had played against Burleson at every homecoming for the past thirty or so years and had only lost a couple of games during that time.

Christina remembered how excited she and her girlfriends would be during the week of homecoming. The four girls would meet at her house, make banners for the pep rallies, and talk about boys and the sock hop that was planned the Saturday night after the big game, which they would usually attend together. *Such fond memories.* Remembering stirred a desire within her to attend and recapture those feelings, but her exhaustion was overwhelming, and she wondered how she would make it through *any* of the events planned for the weekend.

She had started noticing dark circles under her eyes about a week earlier, and even though she applied moisturizer and makeup, they remained, looking as if she had been in a boxing match—and lost. She also noticed several bruised areas on her hips and thighs and upper arms. *I don't remember bumping into anything that may have caused them, but I must have. Bruising just didn't spontaneously occur. Did it?*

According to the Internet, it did under special conditions: blood diseases, cancer, and certain medications. She didn't fit any of those criteria, so she deduced it must have been caused by clumsiness.

She caught herself nodding off a few times during the day on Monday while writing in the chart, and that anytime she stood abruptly, spots would dance across her eyes and a wave of queasy dizziness simultaneously would engulf her, forcing her to sit and close her eyes until it passed.

She had started her period that morning, and it had been heavier than usual, making her wonder if she could be anemic—she had many of the symptoms. If so, that would explain the dizziness and tiredness. As she drove home that afternoon, all she could think about was her nice, cozy bed.

Once home, she cared for the animals, wrote the kids a note telling them she was upstairs taking a nap, and headed up to her bed. She removed her shoes and, being too tired to remove her uniform, crawled under her soft downy blanket and laid her head on her soft pillow. *If my period is this heavy next month, I will definitely have everything checked out,* she thought as she closed her eyes and succumbed to the warm darkness.

She awoke an hour later with her underclothes and uniform completely soaked with blood. *What the heck!* She thought as she stripped off her soiled clothing and bed sheets. *Okay, this is not normal, at least for me,* she thought as she went to the bathroom to take a warm shower. Standing under the warm stream, she watched in amazement as blood trickled down her leg and into the drain. She felt weak, shaky, sweaty, and nauseous all at the same time. Turning off the shower, she sat on the tub floor until the symptoms passed.

"Mom? Are you okay?" Stacey called from the other side of the bathroom door.

"I will be in a few minutes. I'm gonna need to go back to bed for a while. Could you and Brad fix something to eat?"

"Sure, Mom. Are you sure you're okay?"

"Yes, honey. I'm fine." *No, I'm not. This is scary. I've never bled this much before. If this continues, I'm gonna have to go to the ER. God, I don't want to do that!*

After drying off and cleaning up, she threw an old blanket on the bed, thanking God her mattress was waterproof, and lay down. She didn't wake until her alarm went off the next morning. The bleeding had relented somewhat, and she was just passing large clots. Fortunately for her, she didn't have to go in to work and was able to lie around and doze off and on all day. She did manage to wash the bedding and her clothes and put a casserole together for the kids' dinner, but other than that, it was a pretty unproductive day. Cindy called that evening.

"Hey, Christina, you doin' all right? Samara heard from Brad that you weren't feeling well."

"I'm okay, I think. I'm having a *very* heavy period, and it's kicking my butt. All I've done today besides a load of laundry is doze off and on."

"Is it getting better? Do you need to go to the ER?"

"It seems to be slowing down somewhat, but I'm so weak and shaky. Say, what's the name of your ob-gyn?"

"It's Dr. Kim. She's awesome. I think you'd really like her. She's gentle, kind, and a good listener. I'll get her number for you. You need to see her ASAP 'cause somethin' ain't right."

Christina sighed. "Yep. I need to see someone about this. I don't think I can survive another month of this."

The friends chatted a few more minutes, ending with Cindy giving Christina Dr. Kim's phone number.

CHAPTER 58

The decision to have a thorough physical was made for Christina, when on Wednesday morning she passed out in front of Dr. Dawson and the whole nursing staff as she stood to go on rounds with him. Everyone in the small meeting room gasped as she hit the table with her chin, landing with a crash as her arm hit the metal folding chair and her head hit the tiled floor. Blood immediately flowed from her chin, soaking her top and dripping on the floor, and a bruise where her head had made contact with the unrelenting floor started to swell before anyone moved. The nurses were in shock at seeing her fall, and it took a few seconds for the incident to register in their minds. Dr. Dawson was the first to move and immediately started shouting orders. The nurses and aids went into action, moving the chair and table out of the way and retrieving the necessary equipment to soak up the blood and apply pressure to the bleeding wound.

"Christina?" Dr. Dawson said as he lifted her eyelids and checked her pulse, which was weak and rapid. One of the nurses from the night shift checked her blood pressure. "Ninety over fifty," she said with alarm as she removed the cuff from Christina's arm, which was starting to bruise where it had been. Dr. Dawson frowned as he watched the bruise grow larger. *What the heck?* he thought as a wave of panic passed through him.

"Get a gurney!" He ordered.

Janet stood in the corner, watching the whole incident with a detached curiosity.

"Hmm, wonder what's wrong with her?" she whispered to the nurse standing next to her. The nurse shrugged and shook her head before leaving the room to get the gurney.

Janet decided she had better pitch in and look busy. *Wouldn't want anyone wondering why I'm not being helpful.* Trying not to smile as a thought passed through her head, she grabbed a handful of paper towels.

Maybe this will put Christina out of commission for a while. Maybe she'll decide not to come back to work, and I'll get my well-deserved job back.

As she was lifted onto the stretcher, a trickle of blood flowed from under Christina's uniform, which caused Steven's heart to take another leap.

"Let's get her down to the emergency room!" he shouted as he grabbed the gurney and headed for the elevator. Mary Kelly, the nurse who had taken Christina's blood pressure, followed alongside the gurney.

Symptoms and diagnoses ran through his mind as he and Mary raced down the hall, pushing and pulling the gurney into the elevator. Even though it was only three floors down and around a corner, the trip to the emergency room seemed to take a lot longer than it should have. Under normal circumstances, it would only seem like a blink of time, but in this crisis, time seemed to slow profoundly. Steven found himself hitting the number one button several times as if that would make the elevator go faster.

Mary gave him a look that said, "You know, hitting the button won't get us there any sooner."

He sighed and shook his head and then focused on Christina. He took her hand, which was limp and cold, and felt for a pulse—still rapid and weak. He tucked it under the sheet. Mary reported her blood pressure reading.

"Ninety over fifty. Her pulse is 130. Hasn't changed much." Hanging the stethoscope around her neck, she removed the blood pressure cuff. He nodded slightly. *Still too low,* he thought as possible causes raced through his baffled mind.

He looked at the nurse sharing the elevator. Her name tag read Mary Kelly. His mind wandered for a second. *I knew a couple of Kelly kids in high school. I wonder if she was one of them or is related. She looks around the right age and has a vaguely familiar face.* He was about to ask if they had been in high school together when the elevator door opened. Thoughts of Mary vanished like fog on a sunny morning. His focus returned to Christina.

Christina was vaguely aware of someone calling her name. She tried opening her eyes but couldn't find the strength to do so. She just wanted to sleep. She smiled as the blackness enveloped her once again.

Steven was worried. *What on earth is wrong with her?* He had noticed that she looked more tired than usual on Monday but had attributed that to the new job adjustment. He knew being a single mom and working part-time could put extra stress on an individual but usually not to the point of collapse. *And the bleeding. What was that about?*

When they entered the emergency room, he was almost reluctant to turn her over to the attending physician—even though they were friends and he trusted him as a doctor. He wanted to take care of her himself. He wasn't exactly sure why. He felt a need to watch over and protect her. From what, he wasn't sure of either. He paced outside her room until the attending physician came out to speak with him.

"Steven," he called as he walked toward the nervously pacing man.

"What's wrong with her, Jim?"

Steven stood with his arms folded across his chest, listening intently as Dr. Jim Harrison explained the preliminary findings on Christina.

"Well, I'm not exactly sure. I ordered a complete blood panel, and it hasn't come back yet. She has all the classic signs of anemia: the low blood pressure, increased pulse rate, pale pallor, dark circles under her eyes. She's menstruating and there seems to be quite a heavy flow, which may be a contributing factor, but …" He paused as he wrote something down. "I'm calling in Dr. Kim for a consultation." Steven nodded. He knew and respected Dr. Kim. She was the best ob-gyn on staff.

"But what?" Steven asked as worry etched his face.

Dr. Harrison continued, "I've stitched up her chin, which continues to bleed, and I had to lance the hematoma on her forehead because it wouldn't stop bleeding and was becoming quite large. It too continues to seep around the stitches. We've put pressure bandages on the wounds, but …" He looked at Steven and frowned. "I'm very concerned about the lack of clotting and amount of blood loss for such small injuries. She's got a large bruise on her arm where you said she hit a chair as she fell?" Steven nodded.

"She has several more on her body, probably sustained in the fall as well." He paused, shaking his head. "Do you know if she has a bleeding disorder or is on any medication that might thin her blood?"

Steven shook his head. "She hasn't said anything to me about that." He paused, his mind running through all their previous conversations. He sighed and shook his head. *Why would she tell me? Health issues were never brought up in our conversations.*

"I don't know, Jim. I'm not her primary care doctor."

"Well, do you know who is?"

"Sorry, I don't. We've never discussed anything along those lines. Isn't it on her application or health file?"

"I'll have to look. I want to check out her list of medications and any other health issues as well. In the meantime, I've ordered blood and platelets to help with clotting."

"Are you planning on admitting her?" Steven asked as he looked toward the gurney that held Christina.

"Yes, of course. I want to know why she keeps losing blood and keeps fading in and out of consciousness. She may have a concussion. I've ordered a CT scan to rule that out."

He closed the chart, patted Steven on the shoulder, and started to walk away.

"Steven, I'll let you know as soon as I know anything." Pausing, he turned back. "Oh, yes, is there anyone we should call?"

"Well, her kids, I guess," he said, rubbing his hand over his eyes and sighing, "but I'm not sure who to call to get in touch with them." He shook his head. "I'll check with Mrs. Ferguson. She'll know." He shook hands with his friend and, turning to walk away, said, "Let me know as soon as you know anything, Jim."

Dr. Harrison, who had his back to him, nodded and waved. He wondered if anything was going on between Steven and Christina. *Why else would Steven be so concerned?* He smiled. It would be nice to see his friend find a good woman and settle down. He had heard only good things about Christina. *Well, I'd better get to the bottom of her problem, if there is any hope for the two of them.* He continued his walk to the lab. The sooner he had her blood results, the sooner he could know how to proceed.

Steven had known Jim Harrison for several years and respected and admired his ability to respond quickly and efficiently in emergency situations. Jim had a private family practice but rotated with three other doctors on a monthly basis in the emergency room. Steven was glad he had been there. The other doctors were equally qualified, but Steven didn't know them as well and knew they wouldn't have kept him in the loop concerning Christina.

Dr. Dawson checked on the unconscious woman once more before returning to the third floor to resume his rounds. He stood at the foot of the bed and watched as she slept peacefully. The heart monitor beeped a steady 120 beats a minute, and her breathing was regular. She looked so small and pale under the white sheets. The fluorescent lights caused her bruises to look vividly dark and frightful. He felt a painful twinge in his heart. He took a breath and let it out, gaining control over his emotions, which seemed to indicate that he was starting to have strong feelings for this woman. *Is that why I've been avoiding her lately? I'm afraid of my feelings? Afraid she wouldn't feel the same? Afraid of rejection?* He unconsciously nodded. Yep, that was it.

He was falling for Christina and was afraid she wouldn't feel the same, especially after the way he had treated her in high school. He walked over to the side of the bed and took her delicate and cold hand in his. He leaned over and whispered in her ear, "Hang in there, Christina. We'll find out what's wrong. You'll be better in no time." He placed his hand on her forehead, which felt clammy and cold. He glanced up at the IVs to make sure they were working properly and then turned to go, unaware that his actions had been observed by one of the workers in the area.

Janet had been waiting for his return to the third floor and had to keep fighting the smug smile that wanted to make its way to her lips. She inquired of Christina's condition and was annoyed when he seemed to be so anxious about her. They walked around the unit checking on his six patients, but he was quieter and more tense than usual. A couple of his patients commented that he looked tired and asked if he was feeling all right. He smiled, patted their hands, and said he was just fine, but Janet knew better. She knew he was worried sick about Christina. The frightful thought came to her: What if Christina wasn't going to recover? What if she died? Her pulse quickened, and she had to take a few deep breaths to calm herself. He turned to face her as he opened a chart and started writing in it.

"You all right, Janet?"

"I'm worried sick about Christina. Do you think she'll be all right? Do you know what caused her to black out?"

He stopped writing in the chart before him and looked at her. She seemed genuinely concerned, which surprised him if the rumors floating around the hospital were true.

"I think she'll be all right. She's pretty bruised. Dr. Harrison just needs to discover why her blood isn't clotting normally. Then that can be dealt with." He sighed and gave a wistful smile. "Hopefully, she'll be back to work by Monday."

Janet sighed and nodded as well.

"Yeah. I hope so. She'll be missed. She's a good nurse."

Steven cocked his head and looked at Janet, surprised to hear that comment come from her mouth. The scuttlebutt around the hospital indicated there was some hostility on Janet's part concerning Christina's position. Their eyes met for just a second, and then Janet looked away and started stacking charts.

Steven pretended to write, but his thoughts wandered elsewhere. He thought about the few dates he had been on with Janet two years ago. He liked her. Besides being beautiful, she had a great sense of humor once one could get past the tough, all-business exterior she donned when she was working. He knew she didn't make friends easily because of her chosen persona, and he felt a little sorry for her. She had such a rough life growing up and didn't readily trust people, especially men. She rarely let her guard down to let people know the real Janet who cried at sappy movies and loved her daughter to the moon and back. He hadn't seen that tender side in a very long time, making him wonder if he ever would again. He also wondered what had happened to make her so unhappy.

He felt that Janet had wanted their relationship to develop into something more, and maybe it would have if Anika hadn't come into his life and turned his heart upside down—and now this thing with Christina and his budding feelings for her. Try as he might, he just didn't have romantic feelings for Janet. He was pretty sure his name would be on her untrustworthy list.

Only time could heal broken hearts and dreams. He watched her as she stacked charts and organized papers and wiped down counters, impressed by her professionalism, and again wondered why she had been passed over for the full-time position on the cardiac floor. He knew she would have done an excellent job. She would have made sure that everything and everyone would have been in the proper place, unlike poor Christina, who seemed to keep losing things.

Oh, well, I have to trust my aunt in this matter. What had she said? Oh yeah, she just didn't like Janet—something about her that gave her the willies. He smiled. His aunt had a sixth sense about people and was usually right in her assessment of them. For the life of him, he couldn't understand how she did it. He was a clueless male when it came to the intuitive side of the human nature. He just accepted people the way they presented themselves, oblivious to any underlying negative karma or deceit on their part.

Janet gathered the charts and returned them to their appropriate slots. Dr. Dawson finished writing, handed her the last chart, thanked her for going on rounds with him, and then turned his back and walked away.

Janet watched Steven walk toward the elevators. She liked how he swaggered a little when he walked, like a cowboy coming in from a long day on the range. She liked everything about him: his looks, his personality, and the fact that he was a doctor. *Why can't he feel the same about me?*

They had gone on a few dates and had enjoyed each other's company. He had even kissed her on their last date. If Anika hadn't shown up, she felt pretty sure their relationship could have gone on to higher levels—maybe even marriage. *And now Christina.* She could tell he had feelings for her. *What am I going to do about her?*

She had to stifle a smile as she thought about the morning's events. *Who would have thought that such a minute amount of heparin could cause such a great amount of bleeding and so quickly?* She had timed it perfectly. She knew Christina had started her period, because several days earlier she had asked if Janet knew where the women's products were kept in case she needed them while at work. She was sure the amount she had snuck into her coffee the past few mornings wasn't enough to be fatal, but it would be enough to put Christina out of circulation for a while—maybe enough time for her to work a little magic on Dr. Dawson. *I just don't understand how a couple of drops—okay, maybe twenty give or take a few—over the past week could work so quickly and cause so much bleeding.* Maybe Christina has an underlying blood disorder. *I'm gonna have to do some research on the subject, for surely the five drops in this morning's coffee couldn't have caused such a spontaneous reaction. Could it?*

CHAPTER 59

Dr. Jim Harrison read Christina's lab results. Her pregnancy test was negative, so he knew she wasn't having a miscarriage—one less thing to worry about. As he perused the other numbers, he stopped at the ones that had been highlighted. Her clotting time was way off. The APTT, or activated partial thromboplastin time, which evaluated all the clotting factors in the blood by measuring the time required to form a fibrin clot, indicated that her blood finally formed a clot after five minutes. It should have formed within a minute. *That's not good.* Several reasons zipped through his head: acute leukemia, hepatic disease, presence of heparin, and a blood disorder. He then looked at her hemoglobin level. It should read between twelve and sixteen, but hers read six. Her hematocrit level was down as well. *What the heck is going on?* He continued scanning the paper. Her Prothrombin time was up, and her red blood cell count was down, which he expected, considering the amount of blood she lost and was still losing. He would order more blood work every hour to keep tabs on these levels.

No wonder she took a nosedive, he thought as he called the lab and ordered a unit of packed red blood cells and platelets before she went for her CT scan. He didn't think she had a concussion, but because of the head-to-floor impact and the amount of bleeding, he wanted to be absolutely sure. He asked the lab tech on the other end of the line if any of the other results had come through yet. She assured him someone would bring them as soon as they were finished. It would be interesting to see what the drug and toxicology screen showed. He left his office and headed to the emergency room, where Christina was still being held until her CT scan was done and she was taken upstairs to an awaiting room.

"Dr. Harrison?" a female voice called from the end of the hallway.

Dr. Harrison turned around to see a young lady in a lab coat heading in his direction. He stopped and waited for her to catch up. She was probably in her twenties, with brown hair pulled back in a ponytail, fair skin, and big blue eyes. Her name tag read Megan Wright, not beautiful, but cute in a tomboyish kind of way.

"Yes?" he replied once she was in speaking distance.

"Here are the results of the other lab tests you asked for. I think you'll be interested in the numbers on page two."

"Thank you," he said as he took the papers from her. She turned and walked back toward the lab. He wondered if his twenty-two-year-old son knew her. *Maybe I could arrange a meeting. It's about time that boy got a girlfriend.* He shook his head and looked at the paper in his hand. He flipped the top page over and was indeed surprised at what he saw. He decided he had better do a little research into Christina's medical history.

Christina awoke in the X-ray department as they were moving her from the gurney to the X-ray table. She tried to sit up but was quickly advised to lie back down.

"What happened? Why am I here?" she managed to ask.

"You had a little accident, and we need to do a CT scan of your head. You need to lie still now." The young man placed a neck wedge under her neck, tucked the sheet around her body, put a strap across her abdomen, and asked her to lie still. As she lay there with her eyes wide-open, trying to remember what accident he was talking about, he noticed her furrowed brow. He patted her hand reassuringly.

"We'll talk about this later. Okay? Right now you need to relax."

Christina managed a weak smile and a slight nod. She closed her eyes and before she knew it was being lifted back onto the gurney.

While she was being scanned, a room was being prepared for her on the second floor. After the attendants rolled her into the room and helped her into bed, Cindy walked in the door.

"Girl, what happened to you?" she asked as she rushed over to the bed and gave Christina a hug.

"I'm not sure, but I think I passed out. I haven't been able to get a straight answer from anybody." She yawned and rubbed her eyes, wincing when she ran her hand across her bandaged forehead.

"What are you doing here?"

"I got a call from Mrs. Ferguson." She laid her purse in the nearest chair and sat on the bed next to Christina. "She said you had an accident and I was the first name on the list of people to call." She took Christina's hand in hers. It was cold. "So, here I am," she said with a sigh.

"What time is it?" Christina asked as she shakily tried to sit up. Feeling a wave of dizziness and nausea envelop her, she lay back down.

"It's one o'clock," Cindy said as she looked at her watch. "Can I get you anything?"

Looking at the IV in her arm, realizing she had a catheter, and reaching up to feel the padded gauze on her head and chin and the bandage on her arm, Christina sighed and said, "I guess they're gonna keep me overnight, so I'll need my toiletries and a gown." She frowned. "I really hate these hospital gowns."

"Yeah, I can imagine," said Cindy, smiling. "They are a little breezy and ugly. Maybe we could come up with a better design and definitely better colors," she said, shaking her head and making a disgusted face.

"I feel like I've been hit by a truck," Christina said as she closed her eyes to stop the room from spinning. "I wonder what happened." She opened her eyes and looked at Cindy, hoping for a clue. Getting none, she closed her eyes again.

Cindy shrugged, giving her friend a sympathetic smile. "No offense, honey, but you *look* like you've been hit by a truck."

Christina winced. "That bad, huh?"

Cindy nodded. "So what happened?" she asked. She shook her head. "I mean, just tell me what you remember."

Christina recounted her morning.

"I didn't feel very well this morning when I got up. Remember our conversation last night?"

Cindy nodded. "I'm surprised you came in at all! I would have stayed home in bed."

"Well, I thought I could make it through the day, but obviously not. I only had a cup of coffee because I was feeling a little nauseous." She paused for a moment, trying to remember anything else that might be important, but nothing else came to mind.

"The last thing I remember was standing up to leave. That must have been when I blacked out—probably from the loss of blood and low blood sugar."

Cindy nodded in agreement, not knowing what else to do.

"Looks like you hit your chin on the way down and bounced your head on the floor." She made a face. "You're gonna be *so* sore tomorrow. It's a good thing you can get some drugs, 'cause honey, you're gonna need 'em." Cindy instinctively started rubbing Christina's cold hand between her two hands.

"Man, I'm already hurting. I dread tomorrow." Christina looked around for the nurse's call button and, finding it pinned to the top of her bed sheet, pressed it. A nurse came into the room soon after.

"May I help you, Mrs. Sanders?" she asked politely as she came over to the bed and checked the IV and the insertion site and then glanced down at the catheter bag—things Christina normally did for other patients.

"My head really hurts. Could I have something for the pain?"

"Let me check and I'll be right back." Smiling sympathetically, her eyes scanned the room and her patient once more before leaving the room.

Cindy leaned over and gave her friend a kiss on the cheek. "Guess I better get going."

Christina grabbed her hand.

"Cindy, could you please be there when the kids get home, and would you mind staying the night? I know they'll be so worried—especially Nicky. He's still reeling from his dad's death and may freak out when he hears that I'm in the hospital."

"Oh, honey, don't you worry about a thing. I'll bring them by around suppertime if you want."

Glancing at her watch, she continued, "I have to get back to the store. Mary gave me a longer lunch break so I could check on you, but I need to get back ASAP. We just got another big shipment of fall dresses, purses, and shoes that need to be unpacked, priced, and displayed."

Christina smiled and nodded, knowing Cindy loved it when new items arrived. She was able to pick and choose a few items for herself and Samara before anyone else—one of the many perks the employees enjoyed.

"Well, have fun, and if you find anything that I might like, please set it aside as well," Christina said as she gritted her teeth against the pains that were coursing through her body.

"I'm gonna go and let you rest. I'll be back later." Cindy leaned over and hugged Christina one more time. The skin on her cheek felt so cold and clammy, and she looked as white as the sheet she was lying on—except for the large purple bruises on her face and arms.

She was worried sick about her dear friend, who was normally healthy and perky, and was determined to talk to the doctor in charge. She wanted to know the details and diagnosis of this bizarre incident that had put her friend in that hospital bed. After tucking a blanket around Christina and giving her hand one more squeeze, she turned to leave.

Christina smiled and dreamily. "Thanks," she said as she closed her eyes.

Cindy closed the door quietly and headed for the nurses' station. Leaning on the counter, she cleared her throat. When one of the nurses approached, she spoke.

"Excuse me, but I was wondering if you could tell me the name of the doctor taking care of Christina Sanders?"

The RN, whose name tag read Marie Davis, smiled and said pleasantly, "Dr. Harrison is currently in charge of Christina's care. Are you a relative?"

"No, but we're practically sisters. Well, I'm her best friend. We've been friends since elementary school." Marie raised her eyebrows and gave her a look that said, "And your point would be?"

Realizing that their history together didn't matter, Cindy shook her head and put up her hand. "Sorry. I'd like to speak with him, if I could?"

Marie smiled. "Well, he should be up here in a few minutes to check on her. If you'd like to wait in the waiting room, I'll let you know when he arrives." Pulling a pen and small notebook from her pocket, she asked, "What's your name?"

Cindy looked at her watch before answering, "It's Cindy Murray, but dang it, I don't have time right now. Maybe I can see him later or tomorrow?"

"He'll be in the hospital till around five, and he'll be in tomorrow morning around seven. Maybe you can catch him at one of those times, or you could probably call his office and make an appointment."

Chewing on her bottom lip, Cindy considered her options and realized there was no way she could get back to the hospital by five. Sighing, she said, "Okay. I'll try to catch him tomorrow."

Marie nodded and patted Cindy's arm. "Your friend will be fine. I promise we'll take good care of her."

Cindy gave her a crooked smile. "Yeah, I know. Thanks."

Marie watched Cindy walk toward the elevator and then picked up Christina's chart and looked over the latest lab results. Shaking her head, she thought, *I've never seen anything like this before.*

While preparing to leave the CCU, Janet went into the nurses' break room to rinse and replace her mug and saw Christina's mug still sitting on the counter by the sink. Her pulse quickened and her hands shook as she realized that mug, which contained convicting evidence which could put her in jail, had been sitting there all day. With a shaking hand, she reached over to retrieve it and noticed it was still full of coffee—and heparin. *What the heck?* Then it dawned on her: Christina never drank the heparin-laced coffee. As she poured the offending liquid down the drain and thoroughly washed and rinsed the cup, her mind revisited the morning's events, remembering that Christina had been in a hurry and had—*what?* She forced herself to relax. Taking in a few cleansing breaths and closing her eyes, she emptied her mind to retrieve the memory.

Christina had walked in a few minutes late, complaining of tiredness and oversleeping, headed to the nurses' lounge, and donned her lab coat. Then Janet handed her the cup of coffee as she entered the staff meeting room.

She had taken a sip and set it down on the table next to her charts and never picked it up again. So she hadn't drunk the laced coffee this morning. She stood at the sink, rubbing her face with her shaking hands as thoughts zipped through her mind. *What happens next? Should I continue my quest, or would this be the last straw? I guess I'll just have to pretend that I'm as surprised and distraught as the other staff members.*

"Janet? Are you all right? You look pale as a ghost." Sally Jean said as she walked over to the sink to wash her hands.

Janet moved over and said, "I was just thinking about Christina and all that happened this morning."

"Oh, wasn't that just awful? That poor lady. I sure hope she's gonna be all right. I sure do like her."

Janet nodded. "Yeah."

Putting a hand on Janet's arm, she asked, "Are you sure you're okay?"

Janet nodded. "I'll be all right."

"Well, okay. I gotta go. Are you gonna take Christina's place on Friday, since I doubt she'll be up to comin' back to work?"

"Probably. I'll have to check with Mrs. Ferguson."

"I'll see you tomorrow or Friday?"

"Yeah, I'll be in tomorrow. I'm working a couple of extra days this week, covering Jenny Jones's spot till she comes back from vacation, and now I guess I'll be covering Christina's spot as well."

"Oh, well, that explains why you were here today. I was wonderin'." She grabbed her purse from under the sink and said, "Guess it's a good thing you are. Otherwise we wouldn't have a nurse in charge."

Janet nodded. *Yes, indeed. Who would be the nurse in charge?* "I'm sure Mrs. Ferguson would have called someone else in," she said as she dried the cups and hung them on the hooks.

The girl giggled and, tightening her ponytail, said, "Oh yeah, I guess she would have."

Janet watched Sally Jean walk down the hall with her ponytail swishing from side to side and thought, *Bless your heart, you are about as dumb as a stump.*

She took a deep breath and sighed. *I've either been dealt a lucky hand, or someone or something is looking out for me.* She gathered her belongings and headed home.

CHAPTER 60

Dr. Harrison checked the computer file on Christina Sanders and couldn't come up with a logical explanation why she would have a blood thinner in her body. She didn't have any heart disease or any clotting disorders.

So, how did the heparin get into her system? Did she take it accidentally, or was it given to her by some other means? It wasn't a large amount, but it was enough to wreak havoc with her clotting ability during her menstruation. Was that a coincidence? *Get a grip, Jim!* he told himself. *You've been reading too many detective novels. Surely there is a logical explanation for all of this.*

Should I have a chat with Steven and see what he thinks? Not being sure what Steven and Christina's relationship was at this point, he wasn't convinced it would be wise to bring him in on the decision making. Steven certainly seemed concerned, but was that as a friend, or did it go beyond that? He'd have to investigate further before sharing too much with his colleague. After all, Christina was his patient, not Steven's.

I need to call Dr. Kim and see what she thinks about a possible surgical intervention if the bleeding isn't under control by midnight. Hopefully, once the heparin is out of her system and the transfusions and blood clotting drugs start working, her body will start repairing itself, and normal clotting will take effect again. What a strange case this is turning out to be, he thought as he picked up the phone to call Dr. Kim.

~~~

Christina was reaching for the call button again when Marie Davis walked in. Christina tried to sit up. "Would you like me to raise the head of the bed?" Marie asked as she reached for the control apparatus.

"Yes, thank you." Shakily shifting her body as the head of the bed began to elevate, she asked, "Could you answer a few questions for me before you give me the medication?"

Marie reached over and plumped the pillows behind Christina's head. "Sure. What do you want to know?"

"First off, what happened to me?"

The nurse leaned over and spoke conspiratorially, "I wouldn't normally tell a patient everything I'm gonna tell you, but since you work here, I figured it wouldn't matter. I know if it was me in that bed, I'd want to know."

Christina smiled and nodded. "Thank you."

"So, according to your chart, you passed out and hit your chin on the table, your arm on a chair, and your head on the floor. You were rushed to the emergency room, where it was discovered that you were not only bleeding from your chin and head, but elsewhere as well. Your hemoglobin count was very low. Dr. Harrison ordered a unit of blood, a CT scan of your head, and a GYN consultation. You were then sent up here." She smiled and took a breath. "That's it in a nutshell."

"Wow," Christina said. "No wonder I feel like I've been beat up." Yawning, she asked, "So, Dr. Harrison is taking care of me?"

Marie nodded.

"Will he be in soon?" she asked as she gently rubbed the bruise on her upper arm, which was beginning to itch.

"He's supposed to come up as soon as he gets the rest of your lab work."

"Maybe I should wait on the pain med. I need to talk to him."

"If you'd like, I could just give you some Tylenol instead of the Demerol. At least it would take the edge off. Or if you can wait a little longer …"

She waited as Christina weighed her options.

"I think I'll wait a little longer. If he doesn't come in the next hour, then I'll go ahead and take the pain medication and hope I can be coherent when he *does* come in."

"All right, honey. Is there anything else I can do for you? Do you need any water, or …"

Before she finished her sentence, Christina asked, "Why do I have a catheter? And when can I get it out? I hate these things!" She squirmed and moved the tube so it wasn't pulling on her delicate tissues.

"I think they put the catheter in because you were unconscious and incontinent in the emergency room, *and* because you were bleeding so heavily they wanted to monitor all your intake and output." She paused and made a sympathetic face. "At least that's what I think. Guess you'll have to ask Dr. Harrison when it can come out."

Christina sighed. "Okay. I just hope I don't get a bladder infection from this thing."

"I've heard cranberry juice is good for preventing bladder infections. You want me to order it with your dinner tray?"

Christina nodded. She wasn't fond of cranberry juice, but if it helped her avoid a bladder infection—*Bring it on.*

Marie left the room, and Christina closed her eyes, trying to focus on other things besides the catheter—which was causing a burning sensation—and the dull throbbing of her chin, head, and arm. The only thing that came to mind was the little song she sang as a child: "Jesus Loves Me." She smiled as she hummed the tune, drifting in and out of consciousness.

Marie came in and administered the Demerol. *Has it already been an hour?* she wondered as her eyelids became heavy.

She was in the middle of an interesting dream when she was awakened by a patting sensation on her arm, followed by an unfamiliar male voice.

Struggling to open her eyes, she looked into the face of who, she assumed, was Dr. Harrison.

"Hello, Christina." He took her hand, which was surprisingly cold. *I won't be able to take an oxygen reading with them this cold,* he thought, before saying, "I'm Dr. Harrison. Seems you've had a pretty rough morning."

She nodded and found it difficult to focus. He pulled a chair beside the bed but, instead of sitting, put the chart on it and took her wrist and checked her pulse. Fast and steady at 120. He then took her blood pressure—eighty-six over sixty. Still low, but better than it had been. He checked her eyes and the elasticity of her skin. She wasn't dehydrated, thanks to the IV. He asked her to squeeze his fingers and was amazed at her weakness. He lifted her arm and asked her to hold it up as long as she could. That lasted all of about five seconds before it dropped back to the bed.

"I'm sorry," she mumbled. "Guess I'm pretty wimpy today." Her mouth felt like she had a huge ball of cotton stuck in it. "Excuse me, Dr. Harrison, could you get me a sip of water? I can barely talk."

He smiled and handed her a cup of water with a straw in it. She drank greedily.

Looking into his intense hazel eyes, she said, "You'd think I wouldn't be so dry and thirsty with this IV, but I am."

He took the cup and replaced it on her bedside table before sitting in the chair next to the bed. "It's probably the Demerol. One of the side effects is dryness of the mouth."

She nodded. "Oh yeah."

"Your condition baffles me, and I need to ask you a few questions determine why you passed out and why your blood isn't clotting properly." He leaned back in the chair and crossed his legs.

He had a page of questions about her and her family's medical history, her diet, medications, supplements, daily activities, and sleeping habits. As he documented her responses, she took those opportunities to look him over.

He looked to be in his late fifties, with a receding hairline and bald area on the back of his head. He had gray hair at his temples, in his mustache, and in his goatee. He wore glasses that kept slipping to the end of his nose when he looked down to write and that he kept pushing back up with his right index finger. He was about six feet tall, with a few extra pounds around the middle. "Love handles" her mom had called them when her dad started putting on extra weight. He didn't strike her as the type of man who did much physical activity, except maybe hit and chase a golf ball around.

He wore a silver wedding band on his left hand and what looked like a college ring on his right ring finger. She could see the collar of a white polo shirt under his lab coat, black slacks, and black socks and loafers.

Once finished with the questions, she asked if she could ask him a one of her own.

He smiled and said, "Of course."

With a pleading look on her face, she asked, "When can I get this catheter out?"

He smiled and spoke as he wrote on the chart. "Now that you're conscious and strong enough to go to the bathroom, I can order its removal."

Grasping his hand, she said, "Thank you. So what did the rest of my tests show, and why are you referring me to an ob-gyn?"

"Well, the good news is that you don't have a concussion, and you're not pregnant."

She gave him a confused look.

"I had a pregnancy test run to make sure you weren't having a miscarriage. I couldn't very well ask you."

She smiled. "Guess not. 'Cause I would have told you that would have been impossible. I haven't been with a man since my husband died two years ago."

He smiled and nodded. "The only abnormal results were the blood clotting times and hemoglobin."

Wincing in pain she said, "Hmm." Adjusting her body in the bed, she added, "And you don't have an explanation for that?"

"No, not yet. To answer your question about Dr. Kim, she is the ob-gyn on staff here. She's an excellent physician, and I'm sure you'll be pleased with her. From what I hear from my patients, she's very gentle and has a comforting presence."

She nodded.

"The two things that concern me the most," he continued, "are the amount of blood loss and the amount of time it takes for your blood to clot. It's as if you've been taking a blood thinner." He paused slightly before asking, "Have you?"

He felt justified in asking, because in his profession, he had witnessed people taking things to either get medical attention or commit suicide.

"No, I've listed everything that I take. Is there anything else that could have caused this? A hormone flux of some kind? I may be starting menopause."

"I've never heard of anything like this happening because of hormones. I'll run a complete hormone level test, just to get some baseline numbers. In fact, there are several other blood tests I'd like to run as well." He closed the chart and stuck the pen in his pocket. "I sure hope we can get to the bottom of this." Standing, he patted her hand and said, "Wouldn't want it happening again."

"Right!"

He headed for the door and then turned. "Dr. Kim will be in to check you soon, and we'll see if you need another unit of blood. I also want to check your clotting time again. It looks like you've passed the crisis point, but we need to be cautious until we figure out this mystery."

She nodded, gave a weak smile, and yawned. Her eyes felt heavy. She found the control button and lowered the head of the bed. Within minutes, she was asleep.

Christina was awakened by a woman's voice and a gentle nudge on her shoulder. "Christina?"

"Yes," she answered, which actually sounded more like "yeth." Her mouth felt dry and cottony again, and her tongue stuck to the roof of it. She slowly opened her eyes and focused on a pretty Asian woman.

"Hello, Christina, I'm Dr. Kim. I need to do a pelvic examination to see how things are going. I'll have someone come get you and take you to an examination room. Okay?"

"Okay" was all Christina could get out before Dr. Kim exited.

An orderly came in with a wheel chair within minutes of Dr. Kim's departure.

"Mrs. Sanders?" he asked as he looked at the chart. He was a young African American man, heavy-set and probably in his mid-twenties, and spoke with a slow drawl. "Melvin Jones" was on his name tag.

"Yes," she answered nervously, dreading the next procedure.

"I need to take you down the hall to an examination room. Do you have a robe?"

"No, but I could put another gown over this one, and that should be adequate." Hospital gowns, being so generic with the one-size-fits-all tailoring, left arm holes big enough for an elephant's leg and the bottom area wide open, and even though she was used to seeing other people's bottoms, she wasn't ready for the world to see hers.

"I'll go get you another gown," he said, turning to leave.

Pointing to a chair in the corner, she said, "Excuse me, sir, but there's one on the chair over there."

"All right." He walked over, retrieved the gown, and handed it to Christina. "Do you need help?"

She shook her head.

Nodding, he turned his back while she did her best to slip it on. With the IV, she couldn't get her right arm through the sleeve, and her left arm was swollen and painful to move. She was sweating by the time she slipped the gown over her shoulders. *Oh well, this will have to do,* she thought.

He helped her to a sitting position, which started a chain reaction—dark spots floating across her vision, stomach lurching, and head hurting, all within nanoseconds of each other. She realized she was going to be sick and said so. Looking worried, he insisted she lie back down until the episode passed.

"I'll be right back."

She closed her eyes, focusing on her breathing and willing her body to calm down so she wouldn't vomit. She felt her gown grow damp with perspiration and shivered as cool air passed over her. Needing the blanket at the foot of the bed, but fearing the nausea, she sat up slowly and took a couple of deep breaths. She was then able to reach for the blanket without vomiting and wrapped herself in its soft embrace. She turned on her side and, breathing in and out slowly, wondered if she would ever feel normal again.

The male aide, followed by a nurse whom Christina hadn't met yet, came in and asked if she would like an anti--nausea drug. Christina wanted to refuse but, knowing she wouldn't make it through the next exam without it, reluctantly agreed.

The nurse left and returned with a syringe of Compazine. Within a few minutes, Christina was transferred to the exam room without fear of losing her stomach contents on herself or others.

Dr. Kim was indeed gentle and efficient. She removed the catheter, much to Christina's relief, and within the hour, the examination was done and she was back in her room.

"I never thought I'd be happy to crawl into a hospital bed," she said as she maneuvered herself into a comfortable position and Melvin pulled her covers up and tucked her in.

Smiling, he said, "I hear that a lot."

As soon as he closed the door, she closed her eyes and gave in to the warm blanket of sleep that enfolded her.

CHAPTER 61

Cindy went straight home from work and made phone calls to Lisa, Donna, and Christina's in-laws. She then texted Samara to walk over to the Sanders house after school instead of going home, adding, "I'll explain when you get here." Once the calls were made, she headed over to Christina's house. Arriving and letting herself in, she was greeted by a nervously barking Benji. Realizing it was Cindy, he began licking her hand and wagging his tail.

She giggled, returning his affection by rubbing behind his ears.

"You are such a good boy—a lousy watchdog, but such an adorable boy."

If dogs could smile, he was giving her a toothy grin as his whole body wagged with excitement. He followed her into the kitchen, watching as she checked his and Chloe's food and water bowls. She opened the refrigerator door, perusing its contents, deciding what could be thrown together for an after school snack. She chose sliced apples and peanut butter.

She walked through the house feeling uneasy. Goose flesh popped up on her arms and a prickly sensation made its way down her spine—as if she was not alone and intruding.

Okay. This is weird, she thought as she looked at Benji, who didn't seem the least bit concerned. She shrugged.

"All right, Cindy, get ahold of your imagination," she mumbled while glancing at her watch.

"So what do we do now for the next hour, Benji?" He cocked his head and wagged his tail. He didn't have an answer.

Deciding she had too much nervous energy to read the books she had brought, she glanced around the room, hoping to find something else of interest. Seeing books, papers, and clothes scattered here and there, she grabbed an empty laundry basket by the stairs and began filling it with the errant items.

She found the vacuum and took care of the downstairs rooms and then lugged it upstairs and did the kid's rooms and the hallway. She walked into Christina's room and stopped. Looking around at the piles of papers, books, boxes, and clothes, not knowing if they were being packed or unpacked, she decided there wasn't enough floor space to bother vacuuming.

"Whew. What a mess!" she mumbled and almost turned around and walked back downstairs, overwhelmed by the immensity of the chaos. Instead, she took a deep breath and blew it out slowly.

Looking at Benji, who looked as perplexed as she felt, she said, "Oh, what the heck," and started stacking the books and papers nearest the bed.

She changed the bed linens and put the soiled clothes and linens in the laundry basket, which she took down after she vacuumed the small area around the bed. As she began loading the laundry into the machine, the Sanders kids and Samara walked in the back door.

"Hey, guys!" she called from the basement.

"Mrs. Murray?" Brad called out, surprise filling his voice.

"Yeah, I'll be right up."

Brad, Stacey, and Samara looked at each other and shrugged. Nicky ran to the bathroom followed closely by Benji.

Cindy came up the stairs carrying a full laundry basket. Samara hurried over and took it from her mom and gave her a quick hug and kiss on the cheek.

"Mrs. Murray, what are you doing here?" Stacey asked, pouring herself a glass of cold water. Samara took the basket and sat it at the bottom of the staircase before returning to the kitchen.

"Where's Nicky?" Cindy asked, avoiding the question.

"He's in the bathroom. What's going on?" Brad asked with an edge of wariness to his voice. "Is mom all right?"

Nicky walked into the kitchen, wiping his wet hands on his pants. *Why use towels when you've got pants?* "Where's mom?" he inquired, walking over to stand by Brad, who put a protective arm around his shoulders.

"I don't know how to tell you this except to just tell it." She took a deep breath and blurted out, "Your mom's in the hospital."

All three Sanders kids gasped, and Stacey choked on her water. Once it was determined that she'd be okay, they each asked simultaneously, "Why? Is she hurt? Is she all right? What happened?"

Cindy put her hand up to silence them. "Okay! Okay! Shhh, and I'll tell you!

"She had a little accident at the hospital." She made quick eye contact with each child. "She passed out and hit her head, but she's okay. They just want to keep her there overnight to make sure she doesn't have a concussion."

Clenching his fists and fighting back emotions, Nicky said, "I wanna see my mom."

Stacey walked over and stood by her brothers and, looking at Cindy, said, "It'll be all right. We'll go see mom in a minute. Right?"

Cindy nodded.

Brad gave Cindy a skeptical look, sensing there was more to the story than she was sharing, and asked when they could leave.

"Let me call your mom and see if she's ready to see y'all."

When they arrived at the hospital, Cindy and the kids immediately boarded the elevator, and Nicky punched the button for the second floor. When the elevator doors opened, he made a beeline for his mom's room, not waiting on the rest of the group. He was so excited to see that she was alive and smiling that he ran and threw himself into her outstretched arms. *Sometimes he acted like a six-year-old,* Christina thought. She grabbed his face in her hands and kissed his forehead and cheeks.

"Hey big guy, how are you?"

Wiping his eyes, he pulled away and said, "I'm okay now, but what happened to you?" He looked around at the IV, the bruise on her arm, and the bandages on her chin and head. He was so cute with his furrowed brow and frown, she almost laughed.

Brad and Stacey came over to the bed and gently hugged their mom. Christina scooted over so Stacey and Nicky could sit beside her, while Brad stood by her head, his hand lightly touching her hair.

Samara and Cindy whispered a greeting and did a finger wave when they entered but stood by the door while the Sanders children greeted their mom.

"Mom, please tell us what happened," implored Stacey.

Christina gave them a condensed version.

"I just passed out after sitting for a while. On the way down, I hit my chin, head, and arm. Probably just low blood sugar because I didn't eat any breakfast." She smiled and tried to make light of the event. She glanced over at Cindy, making eye contact and telepathically saying, "Don't say anything." Cindy nodded slightly and smiled. She knew exactly what Christina meant.

Christina then changed the subject and started inquiring about the kid's activities at school. Brad saw the eye contact his mom made with Cindy and knew instinctively that something more was going on than they were willing to admit. He would have to question Mrs. Murray when the other kids went to bed, if he wanted the truth—which he did.

They all shared dinner together, even though Christina's consisted of a cup of chicken broth, Jell-O, and apple juice. She was surprised she didn't get liver or beets to build up her blood—or maybe even spinach. *Wasn't that what Popeye ate to give him strength?* Even though it was difficult, she tried to be thankful for the meager amount of liquid food, thinking she could have had *nothing* to eat, allowing the IVs do the nourishing.

During the oppressively silent drive home from the hospital, Cindy cheerily asked, "So are y'all looking forward to the homecoming weekend?"

All three Sanders children and Samara answered affirmatively.

"Do you think Mom will be out of the hospital by then?" Nicky asked.

"Oh, you bet! Your mom is tough, and I know she wouldn't want to miss the homecoming game."

She glanced back and winked at Brad. He smiled and nodded.

"Yeah, Nicky, Mom won't miss my first homecoming game." He put his hand up for Nicky to give him a high five. He did.

"Hey, Nicky, why don't you and Stacey help me make a poster for the pep rally?" Samara asked from the passenger side of the van.

"Could we?" Stacey asked, looking over at her little brother who was nodding eagerly.

"Sure. Mom, can we stop by our house so I can run in and get the poster and markers?"

"Of course, honey, we needed to stop any way to get our pj's and clothes and stuff for tomorrow."

Samara gave her a puzzled look.

"We're staying at the Sanders house tonight."

"Oh, yeah. Sorry, I forgot." She paused a minute before asking, "Can we bring Sasha? She'll get really lonely if we're not there." She gave her mother a pleading look.

"Oh." Cindy sighed. "I guess so."

Stacey said with a chuckle, "I'd better put Chloe in my room and shut the door. Those dogs will terrorize her."

CHAPTER 62

The head nurse for the evening shift came in to check Christina's IV, change the bandages, and give her Demerol to ease her discomfort so she could sleep. A few minutes later, an aide came in to help Christina prepare for bed. Feeling light-headed and weak, Christina was grateful for her presence as she helped her to the toilet and stood by as she brushed her teeth. When she crawled back into bed, the aide, Angela, fluffed her pillow, added an extra blanket, and lowered the head of the bed. Just as she was exiting the room and Christina was beginning to relax and float off to dreamland, the door opened.

Poking his head in, Dr. Dawson said, "Hi, Christina. Is it okay if I come in for a few minutes?"

Surprised and pleased, she said, "Sure."

Turning over, she reached for the button to raise the head of the bed once more. Being very self-conscious of her appearance, her hand automatically went up to her hair as she tried to fluff it up a bit. Knowing she looked like death warmed over didn't help her in the self-confidence department.

Oh well, there's nothing I can do about my looks now, she thought as she watched him cross the room.

He pulled a chair to the side of her bed, sat down, and then asked how she was and quizzed her about her day's activities, smiling as she recounted her embarrassment with the hospital gown.

"Dr. Kim checked me out and says everything looks normal. I won't have to have a D & C or hysterectomy, thank God." She shrugged, adding, "I really like her." Suddenly feeling chilled, she reached for the blanket folded at the foot of the bed. Steven, seeing what she wanted, quickly retrieved it.

"I hear good things about her," he replied, tucking the blanket around her body and under her chin.

Wincing as she turned on her side to face him, she said, "Tell me about your day."

Smiling, he answered, "Well, after our little excitement this morning ..." He paused and looked at her. "You know, you scared the crap out of me!"

"Sorry."

He broke eye contact for a second and looked down, absently turning the class ring around and around on his finger.

"What I meant to say was that you really scared *all* of us."

She smiled and said, "Well, I thought y'all needed a little excitement. It's been too dull around here lately."

He smiled and nodded. "Well, it certainly was exciting." He put his hand over his heart. "But please don't do it again. You almost gave me a heart attack when I saw you hit the table and then the floor." He looked down again and said quietly, "It happened so fast I didn't have time to react, or I would have caught you." She smiled at his verbal chivalry. He looked into her eyes.

"It's been a long time since I've seen someone bleed so much and so quickly from such a small gash."

Wanting to break the emotional tension she felt building, she rubbed her chin and said playfully, "Hey, it wasn't so small. It took *ten* stitches!"

"Okay. Maybe not so small," he conceded, shaking his head and smiling. "Anyway, Dr. Harrison and I are concerned about the amount of blood you've lost today. I'm sure he's talked to you about the test results?"

She nodded. "He said it looks like I had some blood thinner in my system, but I don't know how it could have gotten there. I don't take any blood thinners."

"Yeah, that's what he told me. Do you think we should do some investigating? Maybe get the police involved?"

"Wait. What? Why are you discussing my health issues with him? You're not my primary doctor. And police? Really?" she asked incredulously. "What on earth for? I'm sure this was just a fluke. Maybe my body chemistry is just going whacky. I'm probably starting menopause." She paused as she fluffed her pillow. He put his hand up to speak, but she kept talking. "You know how weird the body can get when a woman is going through menopause?"

Steven waited a second to be sure she had finished before speaking.

"First off, Dr. Harrison and I are friends, and you and I are friends, and it just seemed natural to discuss *your* health issues as two professionals. I wasn't trying to pry; I was just concerned. Secondly, you're kinda young to be going through menopause. Besides, I have *never* heard of this kind of thing happening to *any* woman during menopause. And thirdly, this is such a bizarre situation that maybe we should think of the possibility of an outside source being responsible. "

"Are you sure?"

"About …?"

"About the menopause thing?"

"Christina, you're only thirty-nine, and Dr. Harrison said your hormone levels are perfectly normal for a woman your age. There are *no* signs of menopause." He sighed. "This is not a normal situation by any means." They both were silent for a few seconds.

Finally, she asked, "If it's not hormones and it's not because of any medicine I'm taking, then that leaves the questions of what, who, and why? Who would want to hurt me like this and why? And what did they use, and how long was it used? Was this a one-time dose, or has it been going on for a while? So many questions, so few answers!"

Steven shook his head. "I can't even imagine anyone wanting to hurt you, but if there is someone out there who caused this, we'll find out, and justice will be served."

She smiled slightly. "You sound like a lawyer." Mocking him, she repeated, "Justice will be served."

He smiled and nodded and then sighed.

Christina looked into his tired eyes. She hoped he wasn't on call and could go home and get a good night's rest. She shook her head.

"So Steven, enough about me. Tell me about your day."

He took her hand and looked into her eyes. Her heart did a flip-flop as she felt a tingle of electricity flow through her body and felt her face flush. *Geez, I hope these lights are dim enough that he can't see me blush! What is he thinking? He's been holding my hand for a long time!*

After a few seconds, which seemed like minutes, she retrieved her hand and tucked it under the covers. He sat back in the chair and began to tell her of his day.

"Mr. Walters took a nosedive, and we almost lost him. It took us twenty minutes to stabilize him."

"Is he all right now?"

Steven nodded slightly.

She remembered Mr. Walters, eighty-five and thin. The right side of his face was droopy and weak because of a stroke a couple years ago, making it difficult to understand what he was saying. He was always apologizing for having to wipe the drool that kept sneaking out the right corner of his mouth. Dr. Dawson had recently done an angioplasty on him, and in spite of his age and handicap, he was recovering nicely and hoping to go home next week. She was sorry to hear that he had had a setback. Christina shook her head and said quietly, "He is such a nice, gentle man; I know his wife and daughter will be saddened to see him lose ground in his recovery. Hopefully he'll pull through with a minimal amount of damage."

"I wish his family would put a DNR on his chart. I don't think he could go through that again." Looking down at his hands, he added, "I know *I* don't want to go through that again." He continued quietly. "We did CPR on him for fifteen minutes. He has bruises on his chest and the couple of cracked ribs that cause pain when he breathes."

Christina reached out and patted Steven's hand.

"Maybe I can talk to his family when I get back. It's difficult for a family to sign the do-not-resuscitate paper. It finalizes their hopelessness, and they know there's no turning back." Remembering how her dad and she had cried when they signed her mother's paper, she felt a wave of sadness wash over her and had to take a cleansing breath.

Dr. Dawson brought her up to date on the remaining three patients on the cardiac floor, and she struggled to keep her eyes open. When the nurse came in to check on Christina's IV and offer her a sleeping pill, she was almost relieved and had to stifle a yawn. Steven stood, noticing how pale, helpless, and vulnerable she looked, and felt a light flutter in his chest.

Taking her hand and patting it, he said, "Well, I gotta go and let you rest. Sleep well, and I'll see you tomorrow morning before rounds."

When he took her hand and looked into her eyes before leaving, she felt as if her heart would beat out of her chest. She thought maybe he was planning to lean over and kiss her, and she held her breath in anticipation, hoping he couldn't hear or see her beating heart under her thin gown. With a shaking hand, she reached up and tucked a strand of hair behind her ear and wished he would just leave and quit looking at her. But then again, she didn't *want* him to leave. Smiling, she squeezed his hand and thanked him for coming. He didn't kiss her, but she could tell by the way he hesitated that he wanted to.

It took a few minutes for her heart to return to normal. She smiled as she remembered their few minutes together. *Why am I so attracted to him? Does he feel the same attraction? Doubtful.* That was her last conscious thought as she drifted off to sleep.

Steven left Christina's room and headed straight for the nurses' station and asked for her chart. He paused a moment before opening it. He didn't have any legal right to look at it, but as a coworker and friend, he felt he had an ethical right to. *Oh well, what is she gonna do if she finds out I've been reading her chart? Sue me? Right.* He couldn't help but smile as he opened the chart. Once he looked over the list of medications, nurse's notes, and the lab results, he replaced the chart and headed for Dr. Harrison's office, hoping his friend would still be in.

Jim Harrison was putting papers in his briefcase when Steven knocked on his door.

"Hey, Steven, come on in. You're just the guy I wanted to talk to. I tried calling earlier, but your line was busy."

Not bothering with pleasantries, Steven crossed the room and asked, "You got a few minutes?"

"Yeah, okay. I was just clearing off my desk before heading home." Dr. Harrison put the briefcase on the floor and sat in his chair and then pointed to the chair opposite the desk. Steven sat.

"So, let me guess. You're here about Christina?"

Steven nodded. "I'd like to discuss her case with you."

"Now Steven, you know I can't tell you everything. In fact, I shouldn't be discussing this with you at all—doctor-patient confidentiality and all."

"Really, Jim? You know I can get the information without you telling me. All I have to do is *look* at her chart, which I just did. It would just save me more time if you could give me your honest opinions about her case." He raised his eyebrows and looked seriously at his friend and colleague.

Jim sighed and smiled. "All right. You already looked at her chart?" He shook his head. "You, my friend, are treading on some thin ice legally, not to mention ethically. Did she give you permission?"

Steven shook his head.

"You know she could go after us both if she wanted to?"

"I know, Jim. It's okay. I'll deal with her. Right now we need to work together and solve this mystery."

Jim sighed. "Okay. Here." He retrieved his copy of Christina's chart from the desk drawer and opened it to the lab section. Handing it to Steven, he pointed to the highlighted numbers.

"Whew!" Steven said as he looked at the numbers. "What do you think this means?"

"Well, it could only mean one thing. She ended up with blood thinners in her body somehow, either accidentally or on purpose." He sat back and steepled his fingers. "I hate to even consider an attempted murder theory, but I'm not sure how else this could have happened."

Steven sighed and furrowed his brows as he continued to read the information before him. "I hate to think someone deliberately gave her heparin, but I guess it's a possibility." He then shared with his friend about the misplaced papers, orders, and medications that had been directly connected with Christina.

"If someone is out to discredit her—or, God forbid, kill her—then we *do* have a serious problem on our hands."

Dr. Harrison nodded.

After closing the file and placing it on the desk, Steven sat back in his chair and sighed. "What do you think we should do about this?"

"What *we* should do about this? I don't think *we* should do anything. I'll continue monitoring Christina's health, and if you really think there's a conspiracy, maybe *you*"—he pointed to Steven—"should keep close tabs on her and see if there's any sort of pattern. If there is, *you* might want to consult the sheriff."

"You're right. You shouldn't get involved." He paused, thinking through the situation. "Are you going to be her primary care doctor now?"

"Well, she hasn't exactly asked, but I guess I am by default, unless she says otherwise."

"I'd like you to be. That way if anything out of the ordinary happens again, we'll both be attuned to it." Steven stood. "I'll encourage her to choose you as her doctor." He reached out to shake his friend's hand.

"Thanks, Steven. I'd like that. She's a great gal, and I hope and pray nothing else out of the ordinary happens to her."

CHAPTER 63

Lula gathered the laundry from the cart and quietly loaded the washer, listening as two coworkers discussed Christina's case.

"I heard she drank some poison and had a bad reaction," said one lady, who was of Mexican descent.

"Well, I heard she tried to commit suicide and took some rat poison, which made her blood not clot. That's why she almost bled to death," commented an African American woman. "I had to go clean up the room and pick up the laundry. There was so much blood everywhere! Oh my goodness! I don't know how she survived so much blood loss!"

The Mexican lady said, "I know! I saw all the sheets and towels you brought down. I thought maybe someone had been in a bad car accident."

"Do you know what room she's in? I'd like to go take a look at her. I hear she's as pale as a ghost!"

"She's in room 212. I saw her, and she *is* pale, but what looks really bad are all those bruises! She looks like she's been in a train wreck!"

Making a sign of the cross, the Mexican lady said, "I heard about those! Man oh man! I'm glad it's her and not me."

Lula couldn't help but smile and shake her head. Things were going as planned. She hadn't heard from her boss about the situation yet, but she was sure he'd call her soon. He'd want some kind of progress report.

The two coworkers finished loading their machines and walked out of hearing distance.

That's okay. I heard enough, she thought as she unloaded sheets from the dryer.

⁓

Watching Christina sleep, David asked Jarrod, "Why did this have to happen?"

Shaking his head, Jarrod answered, "I don't know, my friend. Sometimes one thing has to happen so that something else can happen."

"Hmm. Well, how can I keep her safe if things like this happen before I'm even aware of it?"

Jarrod shook his head and put a hand on David's shoulder. "It's not your job to keep her safe."

David nodded. "Yeah. I know. I guess it takes a while for this human side of my mind to give in totally to the mind of God."

"A lot of saints struggle with that. Some take longer than others to totally let go. See, God even lets you humans have free will here."

"Has anyone ever rejected God while here in heaven?"

Jarrod smiled and shook his head. "No. People are given a choice while down on earth to accept or reject God. Once that decision is made, their eternity is sealed. As I said, because of free will, God lets the person decide when they want to totally let go of earthly thoughts."

"Hmm. And I thought when we died, we would just automatically forget or reject our human thoughts."

"Well, some folks do, but as I said, some folks take longer."

"Okay. Guess it's gonna take me a while to get used to this heavenly stuff."

Jarrod smiled and nodded.

CHAPTER 64

The next couple of days were pretty uneventful for Christina. By Friday, her blood count had returned to normal, her appetite was back, and her head ceased throbbing. Dr. Harrison dismissed her from the hospital that morning, with strict orders to take it easy.

"You know I'm planning on going to the homecoming game, right? It's Brad's first homecoming game, and I'm determined to be there, even if I have to ride in a wheelchair!

He smiled and nodded when he realized he wasn't about to talk her out of it. He wrote a prescription for pain meds and antibiotics, emphasizing once again the need for her to rest.

"You aren't out of the woods yet, young lady. I don't want you back in my ER because of a nosebleed or any other kind of bleed. Understand?"

Saluting him, she said, "Yes, sir!"

Handing her the prescription, he said, "So your son is playing in the game tonight?"

She nodded.

"Well, I was planning on going. Maybe I'll see you there?"

She smiled. "I hope so."

Cindy came to pick her up that morning and was very solicitous—to the point of annoyance.

"Cindy! Sit down," Christina had finally said when her friend continued to flit about nervously in the hospital room, waiting for Dr. Harrison to sign the dismissal paper.

"I can't help it, Christina. I just don't know if you're *ready* to go home yet. And here you're talkin' about going to the football game! Are you sure you're up to it? I mean, I won't be upset with you if you don't go."

"I'm fine. My blood levels are all back to normal, and my head doesn't hurt. I'm fine. Really," she said, trying to sound convincing as she rubbed her sore arm. "Dr. Harrison said I can go to the game as long as I take it easy." Smiling, she added, "In fact, he said he'd probably be there too, so I really have to behave! Besides, wild horses couldn't keep me from the game, 'cause I need to see Brad play." Cindy shook her head and sighed.

Christina paused, thinking about how much strength she would have. "I doubt if I'll make it to the Saturday park thing, though. I'll have to wait and see how I feel then."

"Oh, honey! Don't you even *think* about goin' to the park on Saturday! You just need to stay home and rest and get stronger."

Cindy reminded Christina of her mother and how she had fussed and fretted over her after she ended up having a C-section with Nicky.

"Cindy! Please don't worry so. I'm a big girl. I'll be careful and only do what I feel comfortable doing. Now go and see if those papers have been signed."

The trip home had been more exhausting than Christina could have imagined. Walking up the stairs to her bedroom just about did her in. She undressed and climbed into bed, thinking she would just take a little snooze. Two hours later, she awoke to a full bladder and a quiet, empty house.

Chloe had been sleeping on Christina's hip, and when she turned onto her back, the cat protested loudly and jumped off the bed. Benji had been sleeping at the foot of the bed and, when he realized his mistress was awake, walked up and gave her a kiss on her cheek.

"Benji, yuck, you have a nasty case of doggy breath!" She grabbed his head and rubbed behind his ears and then told him to get down. She sat up and put her feet on the floor, getting her bearings and letting the little wave of dizziness pass before standing up.

"Cindy?" she called downstairs. Silence. *She must have gone home. Good, I'll have a few minutes of peace and quiet before the kids come home.* She smiled and headed for the bathroom with Benji close behind.

As she sat on the toilet and looked over at the tub, she imagined what a nice hot soak would feel like. She reached over, turned on the water, added some bath salts, stripped out of her sweatpants and shirt and ever so slowly and carefully climbed in.

"Ah, just what the doctor ordered," she said as she sighed contentedly and closed her eyes. The hot water felt so good on her tired, achy body. After a few minutes, she held up her left arm and looked at the bruise. Because of the blood thinner, when her arm hit the table, the tissues began to immediately swell with blood, and her arm almost doubled its size. The bruise had been an ugly purple color, extending from her wrist to under her arm pit, and even though it was dissipating nicely, turning a light greenish-yellow, it was still very tender and swollen at the point of impact between her wrist and elbow. She figured that after a couple of weeks it would be back to normal.

Her mind started going over the events of the past few weeks, and she started seeing a pattern that disturbed her. *Am I really being paranoid and everything is just a case of bad luck, or is someone out to destroy me? Maybe there's a logical explanation for everything, but for the life of me, I can't figure it out.*

Steven was concerned when he heard that Christina had been dismissed. Because of a pacemaker replacement he had to perform that morning, he was unable to see her before she left, and he was determined to call her in the afternoon once everything had been completed.

He went into his office and dialed her number. It rang five times before her voice mail kicked in. An automated voice said, "You've reached the voice mailbox of Christina Sanders. Please leave a message."

He said, "Christina, this is Steven. Just calling to see how you're doing. Sorry I missed you this morning. I had surgery. Please call me." He disconnected and sat thinking about her, wondering why no one answered the phone. *Isn't Cindy there with her? Should I go check on her? I wonder if she's all right. Maybe she's passed out somewhere.* Then his imagination went crazy, and he pictured her at the bottom of the stairs, helpless and bleeding. He stood and was grabbing his keys when the phone rang.

Grabbing it out of his pants pocket, he answered, "Hello?"

"Steven?"

"Yes. Christina?"

"Yep, it's me."

"Thank God you're all right," he said a little more enthusiastically than he meant.

"Why wouldn't I be?" she asked.

"Well, when no one answered your phone …" He paused, reining in his emotions. "Anyway, I was just concerned."

"Oh, that's sweet, but really, I'm all right. I was soaking in a nice hot tub when the phone rang."

"Oh, sorry if I disturbed you."

"No, you didn't. It was time to get out. I was starting to prune up."

"I figured Cindy would be there."

"Me too, but I just found a note on my mirror that says she had to get Samara from school and she'd be back to pick me up for the game."

"Hmm." There was an awkward silence as each tried to think of something engaging to say.

"So Steven, are you going to the homecoming game tonight?"

"I hadn't really thought about it. I'm assuming you'll be there?"

"Well, yeah. This is Brad's first homecoming game, and I wouldn't miss it for the world! Do you remember how exciting homecoming was when we were in high school? All the marching band practices and pep rallies?"

He chuckled. "How could I forget that? I remember getting so mad at that one kid who seemed to forever get his right and left turns confused."

"Oh yeah, didn't Mr. Johnson paint a big *R* and *L* on each hand?"

"Oh, I forgot about that! Yes, he did. And I think that kid never forgot again!"

"Do you remember his name?"

"Not right off the top of my head. I'd have to look in the annual. Didn't his family move the next year or so?"

"I think so. I wonder what profession he chose."

"Probably a band director!"

She chuckled. "Wouldn't that be ironic?"

There was a pause in the conversation before Steven asked, "Are you sure you're up to the game?"

"I think so. If I feel sick or faint, I can always come back home. Cindy will be there, and I *know* the kids will keep a close watch on me. Dr. Harrison said he'd be there as well. So with all that attention, I doubt if I'll have any worries."

Before he realized what was coming out of his mouth, he asked, "Would you like to go with me?"

"What?" she asked, not sure she had heard correctly.

"I was wondering if you'd like to go to the homecoming game with me," he said, a little hesitancy in his voice.

Christina realized this was what she had waited for all through her teen years, often fantasizing of going to the homecoming game and dance with Steven, and never experiencing it. Now it was a possibility, and—*How awkward was that?* Once her shock subsided, she was able to say, "Oh, Steven. Thank you for the offer, but I've already made plans with the kids and Cindy." She quickly added, "If you'd like, you could meet us there and sit with us."

"Oh, well, if you've already made plans, then I don't want to intrude." He had felt an ache and loneliness in his heart since his breakup with Anika and wanted to make a connection with someone. *No, not just someone—Christina.*

Sensing the special moment had passed, Christina made an effort to regain it by saying, "We could meet at the gate around seven. I'd love for you to meet my kids." There was silence for a few seconds as he thought of his options: stay home and be lonely and miserable, or go to the homecoming game and enjoy Christina's company. The answer was obvious.

"Well, if you're sure I won't be intruding."

She smiled. She had never heard him sound so nervous and vulnerable.

"No, Steven, you won't be intruding. So I'll see you at seven?"

"Okay. I'll be there." He disconnected and felt his pulse quicken. He had three hours before he was to meet Christina and her children, which left him feeling as nervous and awkward as a teenage boy going on his first date. He made a couple of phone calls and cleared his desk before heading out the door.

Christina put her phone down and couldn't believe what had just transpired. *Steven Dawson actually asked me out!* She didn't want to read too much into the invitation, however, so she told herself he was just concerned about her health and wanted to keep an eye on her. *Yeah, that's it.* Her heart, though, was having an argument with her mind and was trying to convince her that he *really* was interested after all these years. She pushed those thoughts aside when she heard her children enter the house.

CHAPTER 65

The homecoming game was fun and exhausting for Christina. Steven had joined them, as well as Cindy, Samara, Lisa and her kids, and Donna and her family—Brad's own cheering section on the fifty-yard line.

As the announcer said, "Number thirty-six, Brad Sanders, scores a touchdown for the Alva Eagles," the crowd went wild with clapping, yelling, and foot stomping. The announcer then added, "Brad is new to Alva this year and has proved to be a great asset to the Eagles football team."

Christina noticed Steven's glances off and on during the game and tried to ignore them, but every now and then their eyes met and she would have to hold on to Cindy's arm for fear of becoming too weak-kneed to stand.

By the end of the game, she admitted to feeling quite tired and weak and was more than willing to have him put his arm around her shoulders and walk with her to the sidelines to meet with Brad.

"Hey, Brad, congratulations on winning the game! I'm so proud of you!" He smiled sheepishly as he walked into his mother's awaiting arms.

"Thanks, Mom. I can't believe we won!"

As they stood by the sidelines, his coach came up and patted him on the shoulder. "Locker room in five, Brad."

"Sure, Coach. Be right there."

"Hey, Brad, before you go, I want you to meet Dr. Dawson. Remember I told you he was the cardiologist at the hospital?"

Brad extended his hand, and he and Dr. Dawson shook hands.

"Nice to meet you, sir."

Steven nodded. "Yeah, me too."

"Mom, a group of us are going to the dance afterward. What time should I be home?"

"I'd like you home by midnight. Y'all have a busy day planned for tomorrow as well, and you'll need to rest up."

He leaned over and gave her a peck on the cheek. "Thanks, Mom. See you later!" He turned and ran to catch up with his teammates, who hoisted him up on their shoulders. Christina grinned as only a proud mama could.

She and Steven walked to the van, where they were met by Cindy, Samara, Stacey, and Nicky, who were excitedly talking about the game and the Eagles' victory. Once everyone was seated and buckled, Steven reached in the window and patted her on the arm, saying, "Thanks for letting me sit with y'all." He looked in the backseat and told the kids he enjoyed meeting them, and they said the same back to him.

As they exited the parking lot, Christina looked in the side mirror and watched as Steven turned and walked to his car.

She glanced at Cindy, who was grinning like the Cheshire Cat.

"What?"

Cindy continued to smile and shake her head, saying in a singsong voice, "You like him, and he likes you."

"Cindy—really?"

"I'm just sayin ..."

Christina was sound asleep by the time they pulled in the driveway twenty minutes later. Cindy hated waking her, but there was no other way to get her inside. With Cindy and Stacey's help, Christina crawled up the stairs, changed into her pj's, and climbed into bed. She smiled as Cindy reached down to hug her and kiss her on the cheek. "See, I *knew* you and Steven would hit it off." She pulled the covers up to Christina's chin. "I saw how he was lookin' at you durin' the game."

Christina shook her head. "Oh, Cindy, I'm sure he's just concerned about my health." She yawned and closed her eyes.

"Yeah, right. That explains the whole arm-around-the-shoulder thing," Cindy mumbled as she turned off the light and closed the door.

Once Cindy was convinced her friend would be okay, she left Samara in charge of the two kids and headed to the country club for the after-game reunion dance. She was hoping Steven would be there so she could talk to him about Christina. He wasn't. Attending without her girlfriends or a date, she felt profoundly lonely, even with a room full of people. She thought about Ed and wondered where he was and what he was doing, wishing he were there with her.

Deciding not to torture herself any longer than necessary, she was back at Christina's by midnight, just in time to let Brad in and hear about his own after-game dance. He, at least, had attended with a date and had enjoyed his time there.

Once the kids were all settled into bed, she pulled out the hide-a-bed in the den and fell into a fitful sleep.

CHAPTER 66

Saturday morning had a crisp bite to it and started out cloudy and threatening rain, but by noon the sky had cleared and the temperature had reached seventy degrees.

"Hey, Mom, are you ready yet?" Leelee called as she grabbed her sweater off the hook by the door.

"Be there in a minute!" Janet stood in front of the bathroom mirror trying desperately to rein in her emotions. She breathed slowly in and out and clenched and unclenched her fists. If she hadn't promised her daughter they'd go to the park, she would have gladly stayed home. She didn't feel like being sociable, because she was still reeling from last night's events.

I can't believe Steven actually sat with Christina and her family! I asked him on Monday if he wanted to attend the football game with Leelee and me, and he said he doubted he'd even go.

I guess he's a liar too. Why can't people just be up-front and honest? If he didn't want to go with me, then he should have said, "Janet, I don't want to go with you," but no, he gave me some lame excuse, and fool that I am, believed him! Maybe I shouldn't just get rid of Christina—maybe I should get rid of him too. Having them both out of the picture would certainly make my life easier.

"Mom!"

"I'm coming!" Janet ran her fingers through her hair, checked her makeup, and dabbed a little perfume behind her ears.

"You look nice, Mom. Is that a new sweater?"

"Thanks, Leelee, and yes, it is a new sweater. Do you like the maroon color? I figured it'd be an appropriate color for today."

Leelee nodded. "I love it! Can I borrow it sometime? Better yet, can you get me one like it? It'd look great on team spirit day."

Janet smiled. "I'll see if I can find another one. If not, you can have this one."

"Thanks, Mom. We'd better hurry or we'll be late for the pie-eating contest. It starts at ten."

Janet looked at the clock on her phone. They had ten minutes.

The house was so quiet once Cindy left with the kids for the planned activities and afternoon picnic at the park, Christina didn't even crawl out of bed until noon.

She enjoyed a leisurely brunch of yogurt and fruit, a hot shower, and a few minutes reading in her suspense novel before dressing and then called Danny's mom and asked if she would be willing to drive her to the park.

"Why, of course, Christina. Nicky told us what happened to you. I'm glad you're home." After a few more minutes of chitchat, Christina disconnected and then gathered her sweater, purse, icepacks, pills, and a pillow to sit on as she waited for Denise to arrive.

The ride to the park was short, but Christina took the opportunity to inquire about Denise's family and learned that five-year-old Annabell could tie her shoes, Danny had lost another tooth, and her husband had had to go to Houston on a business trip. Her mom and dad, whom they lived with, were doing well and were planning a fortieth anniversary trip to Hawaii.

"Oh, that's so nice. David and I had talked about doing an Hawaii trip for our twenty-fifth anniversary but didn't make it that far."

Denise reached over and gently patted her on the leg. "Well, sometimes life just doesn't seem fair."

Looking out the window, Christina mumbled, "Don't I know it."

Denise let Christina out by the bleachers and declined the gas money that was offered.

"Honey, don't you even think about paying me. You're not only my neighbor, you're my friend, and I wouldn't think of taking your money."

Christina smiled sheepishly and said, "Aw, thanks."

"Are you gonna need a ride home?"

"No, but thanks for asking. Cindy will bring us back to the house."

She joined her family around four o'clock to watch a baseball game that Brad, Samara, and Cindy were participating in. Because they were too young to play, Stacey and Nicky opted to stay in the stands with their mom. They stood and cheered when Cindy hit the ball and ran to first base, but when Samara hit the ball out of the park, allowing all the filled bases a safe slide into home, the crowd went wild. Christina was so caught up in the excitement of the moment that she wasn't even aware when Steven came and stood by Nicky. When she glanced over and saw him, her heart did a triple beat. She was shocked, amazed, and thrilled all at the same time.

"Hey! What a nice surprise!" she said in greeting.

He smiled. "Hey yourself! You doin' all right?" Nicky voluntarily moved directly behind his mom so Steven could stand next to her.

Smiling and looking up, she said, "I'm doing great!" She felt her heart do another triple beat. *Ouch! If I keep having this reaction every time I see him, I'm gonna end up with a coronary!*

He was wearing a maroon sweatshirt with an eagle in the middle surrounded by the words "Alva Eagles," jeans, and tennis shoes. He also wore a maroon baseball hat that had the Texas A&M emblem on the front.

"So are you here to check up on me?" she asked, smiling as she took a sip of water from her Evian bottle.

"Well, of course. What kind of doctor would I be if I didn't keep close tabs on my, um …" He paused, trying to come up with something clever. "What do I call you? Patient? Friend? Nurse? Former band member?"

She giggled. "Friend will suffice." She playfully hit him on the arm. "Thanks, Doc." She then turned her attention back to the game. Nicky and Stacey looked at each other and rolled their eyes. *Grown-ups are so weird.*

When Janet saw Steven exit his car and head for the ball diamond, she left her place in the stands and started walking toward him. She had every intention of diverting his attention from Christina by convincing him to sit with her, but he hadn't even looked in her direction. Like an eagle spotting its prey, once Steven saw Christina, his eyes were for her only, and he closed the distance in a matter of seconds—faster than Janet could reach him.

She was livid as she watched their playful exchange. She turned and walked back to where her daughter was patiently waiting. Taking her daughter's hand, she led her to the opposite side of the playing field so she could keep an eye on the cozy little couple.

"Come on, Leelee, let's sit on *this* side of the ball field."

"But Mama, I see Stacey over there. Can I go sit with her?"

Janet sighed. "When the teams change positions, then you can go sit with Stacey."

Leelee, being a compliant child, nodded and said, "Okay."

Janet watched in amazement and disappointment as Christina interacted with Steven and the people around her. She was laughing and joking and seemed to be enjoying herself in spite of her appearance and handicap. Janet would have never gone out in public if she looked as hideous as Christina—puffy purple eyes, bandaged chin, and arm in a sling. She chuckled as a thought passed through her head: *Put a bolt in her neck and she could be Frankenstein's monster's twin sister.*

"Mom, Stacey is motioning for me to come join her. Can I?"

"It's 'may I join her,' not 'can I.'"

"Sorry. May I go join her?"

"All right, it looks like the teams are getting ready to switch. Be back here as soon as the game is over."

"Okay, Mama."

Janet watched as Leelee, flapping her arms and waving, ran over to Stacey, reminding her of a little caged bird being set free. She wondered how much longer it would be before Linda's true identity would be revealed. Janet was prepared to keep up the ruse indefinitely, hoping her daughter would do the same. When Christina put the two names together and came up with the truth, well ... Janet would cross that bridge when she got there.

When Linda arrived, Stacey asked permission to go to the concession stand for drinks. Christina agreed and ordered bottled water, and Steven asked for a Coke as he handed a ten-dollar bill to Nicky.

Reaching for her purse, Christina said, "Hey, you don't have to pay for that."

"I know, but I want to. It's no big deal, and besides, I'm the doctor, and I get paid the big bucks. Surely I can afford a couple of drinks."

She smiled and shook her head. "All right, big spender. I'll concede this time, but next time, it's my treat."

He bit his bottom lip to keep from smiling and then saluted her.

"Yes, ma'am."

Christina watched as the kids took off running toward the concession stand and disappeared into the crowd. She then turned her attention back to Steven.

"So, did you go to the dance after the football game?" Looking across the field and spotting Brad, she waved.

"Nope. Remember, the class reunion dance was for your class, not mine."

"Oh yeah. Sorry." Smiling smugly, she said, "I forgot you're a year older than me."

"Yeah, thanks for the reminder."

Christina stood and stretched, wincing at the pain in her arm.

"You okay?"

"Oh, yeah. I just forget sometimes that this arm is still so sore."

She saw Cindy wave and waved back. The teams were changing places. Cindy and Samara were on opposite sides in the outfield. Brad was stationed at first base, pounding his fist in his glove to soften it in preparation for any wayward balls. As the game began again and the spectators took their seats, Christina reached for her sweater, wincing once again at the effort. Steven assisted as she gently and slowly put her left arm in the sleeve.

"Thanks. You know, I'm glad it's my left arm and not my right. Sure would cramp my style and make me even more dependent on others." She let out a sigh. "It's frustrating enough as it is."

Steven thought about the time he had broken his right arm when he was twelve and how physically and emotionally challenging that time of mending had been. He hated relying on others to do things for him.

If Christina's arm had broken during the fall, he knew in his gut she wouldn't be at the ballpark—or anywhere, for that matter. With her blood's clotting inability, she would have probably bled out before any kind of treatment could be implemented.

"What? You mean you don't like being waited on hand and foot?"

She looked at him, shaking her head, and said emphatically, "No, I don't. Even though I was my parents' one and only daughter, I don't have a princess complex."

He laughed. "Good. I was married to a princess once. Not a pleasant experience."

"Yeah, I think being a princess is highly overrated. A queen however, I could get used to that!" He smiled and shook his head. She looked around the concession stand for her own little princess. Seeing the kids heading back with drinks and popcorn in their hands, she breathed a sigh of relief. If they had been gone any longer, she would have sent Steven to check on their whereabouts.

Stacey handed Steven his Coke, and Nicky gave his mom her water and a bag of popcorn. As they sat eating, drinking, and watching the game, Christina let her mind wander through her memories.

She remembered Steven's first wife, Tammy. During high school, she had been a cheerleader and ran with the popular kids—not the nerdy little band squad. She was the epitome of a healthy all-American girl with her long blonde hair, tanned skin, and big blue eyes. She reminded Christina of a Barbie doll—big chest and all.

Tammy had been very materialistic and proud of it, flaunting her newest clothes and jewelry to anyone who'd look or listen. Christina hadn't liked her—not because of her looks or possessions, but because she was often cruel in her words and actions toward people whom she deemed poor, ugly, or ignorant. Christina surmised that she and her friends must have fit into one of those categories, because Tammy and her friends never acknowledged their existence, unless by accident.

A few years later, when Cindy sent her the newspaper with pictures and an account of Steven's wedding, she was very surprised and disappointed to read that he had married the girl.

During one of their phone conversations, Cindy had informed Christina that the couple had divorced and Tammy had married a rich oilman and lived out near Lubbock on his large ranch.

Christina remembered thinking, *Good riddance. Hopefully she's happy now that she can have everything she wants.* Cindy also informed Christina that Steven had taken the divorce pretty hard and had gone through a depression for a while.

She glanced at Steven who was intently watching the game, and thought, *Well, for a guy with a heart that's been broken at least twice--by Tammy and Anika, he seems to be doing okay.*

Stacey asked if she and Linda could go hang out with a couple of friends from school. Christina agreed, warning her to stay in the immediate area.

"Hey, Nicky, you wanna come along?" Linda asked as Stacey grabbed her hand to lead her away.

"Nah, I'll just stay with Mom. I wanna see who wins the game."

The girls waved as they headed to a group of kids by the concession stand.

"You sure you don't wanna go?" Christina asked, watching Stacey leave the area.

He nodded. He was content to stay close to his mom and keep an eye on her new friend. He wasn't sure what he thought about this Dr. Dawson guy. Not wanting anyone taking his dad's place but wanting his mom to be happy, he felt conflicted. Dr. Dawson *seemed* like a nice enough guy, and he *seemed* to genuinely care about his mom, and she *seemed* to like him. *Hmm, maybe I ought to give him a chance.* Then, like a typical ten-year-old, dismissed the idea and refocused on the game, which ended about an hour later with a tied score. Members of both teams shook hands, high-fived, and patted each other on the back. Christina looked around for Stacey and Linda and, not seeing them immediately, asked Nicky to go look for his sister.

"Nicky, if you don't see her by the concession stand or swings, just come on back."

"Okay, Mom."

While waiting for the kids to return, she and Steven stood talking to other classmates and their families, explaining over and over why she looked like she had been in a train wreck. She figured that by the end of the day, everyone in Alva would know why she looked like an anatomy lab reject. Nicky returned about five minutes later without Stacey.

"I can't find her or Linda anywhere. I even asked some of those other kids she was hanging out with, and they don't know where Stacey is."

Christina was concerned but not alarmed, as she knew twelve-year-old kids tended to forget time and place when they were with friends.

As the park became less congested with people and vehicles, she began to look around nervously for signs of the missing girls. When Brad and Samara approached, she asked them to walk around the park and look for the girls. They took off toward the play area, calling Stacey's name.

She sat on the bleachers, fidgeting nervously while Nicky and Steven went to the opposite side of the park, searching and calling as well.

Cindy and Lisa joined her and tried to keep her calm as they discussed the homecoming game and the day's activities.

Wincing as she looked into Christina's battered face, Lisa asked, "How are you holding up?"

"I'm exhausted. I wish those girls would get back so we can go home. I need to lie down."

Cindy patted her hand and said, "They'll be here soon, I'm sure. I don't think Stacey would go very far." After a few more minutes of idle chatter, she saw Brad, Samara, Linda, and Stacey walking toward her from the creek area. Christina excused herself from the group and hurried toward the children. She dismissed the other three kids and focused her anger on her daughter.

"Where have you been, young lady?" she demanded, trying to control the urge to shake her.

Shrugging, Stacey said, "Linda and I went down by the creek. Her mom said it was all right."

"Didn't I tell you to stay in the immediate area?"

"Yeah, but it was boring. We just wanted to go to the creek and look for turtles."

"Why didn't you come ask or tell me where you were going?" she asked a little more calmly.

"I don't know. I guess since her mom said it was all right, I figured you'd think it was all right too." She sighed and looked down. "I'm sorry."

Christina let out a big sigh and pulled her into a hug.

"Am I in trouble?"

"No, not this time. But if it ever happens again"—she looked her daughter in the eyes—"you can bet you'll be in big trouble." Stacey nodded.

Christina asked, "Why do you think I'm so upset and angry with you?"

In a singsong voice and with plenty of eye rolling, she answered, "You're upset because there are bad people out there who get some kind of sick pleasure in kidnapping and hurting children. That's a parent's worst nightmare."

Stacey had heard those words at least a hundred times during her lifetime. Christina put her arm around her daughter's shoulder and kissed her on the forehead.

"That's right, babe. You need to remember that, in case you're ever tempted to go with someone you don't know very well."

Stacey nodded.

"Come on, kiddo. Let's go home." Stacey leaned into her mom and put her arm around her waist. "I love you, Mom. I'm sorry I worried you."

Christina smiled and squeezed her, feeling tears stinging her eyes.

"Yeah, I know."

Janet sat in the car with Linda and watched as Christina and her family stood talking to Dr. Dawson and a group of their friends. She felt a twinge of jealousy. She didn't have any friends to speak of. She knew people from work and church, but she never socialized with anyone. She had trust issues. She had been hurt and betrayed so many times in her life that she never felt comfortable with another human being—except her daughter. For her, the relationship she had with Linda was enough for now. She poured her heart and soul into her child. Her welfare was the main reason she wanted to find a good man to love them both and to provide stability and financial help. That was why she wanted Dr. Steven Dawson—he was the perfect man as far as she was concerned. She just needed to get Christina out of the picture.

As Janet drove out of the parking lot toward home, Linda asked, "Mom, why don't you ever go talk to Mrs. Sanders? She's such a nice lady."

The question took Janet by surprise. "What?"

"Mrs. Sanders. Why aren't y'all friends like Stacey and me?"

"Uh, well, why are you asking?"

Linda scrunched her eyebrows and said, "Well, you just seem kinda lonely. I never see you with any friends, and it just makes me sad that you don't have a best friend like I do."

Janet shook her head and glanced at her daughter.

"Oh, honey, I'm doing all right. I have friends at work, and that's enough for now." She patted her on the leg. "Besides, I have you."

"Oh, Mom, I'm just a kid. You need a grown-up girlfriend or boyfriend." She smiled and bit her bottom lip and arched her eyebrows.

Janet sighed. "You, little missy, don't need to worry about my social life. You have plenty to worry about in that noggin of yours." Linda rolled her eyes. "So, what do you want to do tomorrow? I have the day off and I thought we could go do something fun."

Twirling her hair and chewing on her bottom lip, Linda said, "Hmm. Let me think about it, and I'll let you know."

Janet nodded, thinking, *I wonder how much longer I can divert her attention away from mine and Christina's relationship.*

CHAPTER 67

Christina felt strong enough and asked if she could return to work the following Friday, nine days after the strange bleeding incident at work. The bruised area on her left arm was turning interesting shades of yellows, greens, and blues, and she could extend and rotate it with very little discomfort.

Dr. Harrison had removed the stitches from her chin and forehead on the previous Wednesday and said that if her blood levels were normal and she felt up to it, she could resume all her normal activities the next week.

"Does that mean I can go back to work?"

"Only if you feel up to it, and only if you promise not to lift more than five pounds—at least until we're absolutely sure your blood work is stabilized."

Putting her fingers up like a Girl Scout, she reluctantly agreed.

"Okay. I do solemnly swear to abide by your rules."

He smiled and patted her on the shoulder.

"Good, 'cause I have spies everywhere, and I'll know if you've disobeyed."

"Oh? And what will you do if I do?"

He grinned and stood to go. "For me to know and you to find out—if you dare." Winking, he said, "I'll see you in a week."

She nodded.

Lula felt the phone buzzing in her pocket and pulled it out. The number was unlisted. *Must be the boss man,* she thought as she pushed the answer button.

"Hello?" she said sheepishly, afraid—of what? That he would reach through the phone and throttle her? She almost giggled at the thought as a cartoon image flew through her mind.

"Ms. Halsey?"

"Yes."

"I understand that you did your best to get rid of Christina, and obviously it didn't work, so I have another assignment for you."

Lula listened intently, smiling and nodding and answering, "Yes, sir," and "No, sir," when appropriate. She had to always remember her manners when speaking to the boss man. Her mama didn't raise a fool. She remembered her words well: "You always pay extra special attention to the way you act and speak when dealing with a person who is smarter and richer than yourself."

"So Ms. Halsey, do you understand everything I asked you to do?"

"Uh, yes, sir."

"Good. The items you will need will be in on your porch steps this evening."

"You know where I live?" she asked, biting her thumbnail.

"Of course I do. I know everything about you."

Lula inhaled sharply and looked around, wondering if she were being spied upon this very minute.

"Not to worry, Ms. Halsey. You do as I've instructed, and you will get your money and can leave this little dumpy town."

Lula nodded and, realizing he couldn't see her, said, "Yes, sir. I'll do my best."

CHAPTER 68

While recuperating at home, Christina caught up on her e-mails, letters, and cards. Looking through boxes of photo discs, she downloaded and printed several pictures of David and the kids and put them in her scrapbook albums. Sitting on the floor in her bedroom, she sorted through the boxes that had been sitting around the perimeter since they moved in—three months ago.

Every now and again, she would bump her arm or stand too quickly and feel the painful repercussions of those actions, which would start her thinking and worrying all over again.

God, I hope this is all over. I hope whatever or whoever did this won't do anything else. I hope and pray this was a one-time deal.

During that week of recuperation, her friends had been quite solicitous of her and the kids, bringing meals and running errands for them, even though she could have done most of those things herself.

She was proud of the way the kids had pitched in to help with the laundry and the other chores she usually did, and although it had been a nice vacation—except for the soreness—by the end of that week she was getting antsy and anxious to return to work.

Steven called on Thursday evening to check on her progress, and she told him all she had accomplished.

"That's great. Weren't you complaining a few weeks ago about not having time to do those things?"

"Yeah."

"Well, maybe this is God's way of slowing you down and allowing you to get those things done."

"I don't think God works like that, but it's a nice thought. I guess good can come out of evil."

"Hmm. Okay. Anyways, you wanna go out for lunch on Saturday? We could even catch a movie if you're feeling up to it."

"Wow. Uh, maybe. I'm still looking pretty freakish. I'm not sure I'm ready to go out in public, and besides, if I do go out, I want to go to the hospital."

"Hospital?"

"I just wanna go see how things are and check on the patients and talk to the nurses. I love my kids and friends, but I'm kinda missing my work buddies."

"You're not planning to work, are you?"

"Probably not. I think I'll just drop in. Dr. Harrison said I could drive now and resume my normal activities, so I'd like to do something normal."

"Hmm. Well, if the doctor said it was okay, how can I argue with that?"

"Exactly."

"Okay. If we can't go out, can I at least come by to see you? I've kinda missed your beautiful Frankensteinish face."

"What? Now that's not very nice."

He chuckled. "I know. I was teasing, of course. You have a beautiful face under all those bruises and scabs."

"Really? If you're gonna be mean, I'm gonna hang up."

"Not until you tell me if I can come by."

She sighed. "I'll see you tomorrow at the hospital, and if you have an attitude change and say only *nice* things to me, we'll see about going out."

He chuckled. "Good night, Christina."

"Night David—oops, I mean Steven." *Thank God he hung up before hearing that slipup. David must be thinking about me. Oh, wait, can people in heaven think about us here on earth?*

"Yes, Christina, we can," answered David as he kissed her good night.

Friday morning during breakfast, Christina informed the kids of her plans to drop by the CCU for a visit, assuring them she felt strong enough and showing them how well she could move her arm.

Stacey said, "But Mom, your face is still all bruised. Are you sure you won't scare the patients?"

Christina replied, "My dear, that is why makeup was invented. You'll be surprised how well I can cover up these bruises."

Stacey rolled her eyes and made a face like she didn't really believe her mother could pull it off.

"I don't know, Mom. It would take a can of spackle to cover up those bruises."

Christina gave a shocked look and gently punched her daughter on the arm. She made a pouty face and said, "Between Dr. Dawson's and your negative comments about my appearance, my self-esteem has just bottomed out!"

Getting up from her chair and hugging her mom she said, "Oh, mom, I was just teasing."

"Gotcha! I wasn't upset. Actually, you have a valid point. I do look kinda Frankensteinish, as Dr. Dawson said."

Stacey gasped and said, "He said that? That you were Frankensteinish?" When Christina nodded, Stacey burst out laughing hysterically, joined quickly by her two brothers.

"Hey, I'm right here! Not nice to laugh at your mom!" Then she joined in the giggle fest.

Once everyone settled, she explained that she wasn't going to work, only observe and catch up on the latest hospital news.

Finishing her coffee, she said, "Well, I gotta go get ready, and y'all need to get a move on." She gave each child a kiss and a hug.

When Christina walked into the staff room and took a seat, silence filled the room—everyone was shocked but happy to see her as they smiled and did finger waves.

Janet paused in her presentation and said, "Welcome back, Christina. I didn't realize you'd be here today."

Christina smiled and nodded and glanced around the table.

"Just pretend I'm not here, 'cause I'm just here to hang out. I was getting bored at home and missing y'all."

Dr. Dawson was sitting across the table, and her heart did a triple beat when she saw him. He smiled and nodded a greeting. After a moment of awkward silence, everyone refocused on Janet, and she continued the presentation.

Once completed, everyone gathered around Christina and welcomed her back and expressed their concern for her—even Janet, not wanting to give the impression that there was a problem between her and Christina.

Christina expressed her appreciation to Janet, who smiled and said that although she wasn't used to working full-time, it had been a nice change.

Dr. Dawson stood in the doorway and watched. When everyone had dissipated, he walked over to Christina and asked if she felt strong enough to be there. She turned to face him and replied a little too tersely, "If I didn't think I could handle being here, I wouldn't be here."

Steven looked shocked for a second and then smiled. Putting his hands up in surrender, he said, "Yes, ma'am, I think you'll be just fine."

She rolled her eyes and said, "Sorry, I just want things to go back to normal."

Raising his eyebrows and clearing his throat, he replied, "Normal, huh?"

She made a face and shook her head.

"I know. I may be rushing things a bit."

Shaking his head and smiling, he said, "You think?"

Checking his watch, he asked, "Do you want to go on rounds with Janet and me?"

She nodded, looking around for Janet, who was gathering the charts. Walking over, she asked if she could help by carrying a couple of them. Janet smiled and handed her the two largest ones. Christina frowned and thought, *The two biggest ones? Really? Is this a test or something because you don't think I'm strong enough and are trying to make a point? Well, I'll show you.* She hated to admit that the two large charts did hurt her arm, and she had to shift them from one spot to another, but she was determined not to let Janet see her sweat.

After all five patients had been checked and orders given, Dr. Dawson excused himself, saying he had some business in Waco to take care of. Christina walked with him to the elevator, and before leaving, he took her hand in his and gave it a squeeze.

As they waited for the door to open, she asked, "I don't mean to be nosy, but what business do you have in Waco?"

"Yes, you are being nosy. It's personal."

He didn't want to tell her that he was helping Anika pack up the last of her belongings for her move to New York and that he would be saying good-bye, possibly for forever. He was concerned that his emotions would get the better of him and didn't want to take the chance of losing control, so it was best to say nothing.

She grimaced. "Sorry. Will you be home tomorrow? You had mentioned lunch and a movie?" The door opened and he put his hand out to keep it there.

"If all goes well, I'll be home this evening. Can I call you then and we can make plans?"

She smiled and nodded. "Okay. Have a safe trip."

Nodding and smiling as well, he boarded the elevator.

"Talk to you later," he said, waving as the elevator door closed.

She smiled and did a finger wave. Feeling a chill on the back of her neck as if someone touched her lightly with cold fingers, Christina turned.

"Oh, Janet, you scared me. I didn't know you were there."

"Obviously," she said through clenched teeth as she gave her a glare that could freeze hell before turning to head back down the hall.

If looks could kill, I would definitely be dead meat, thought Christina as she watched Janet walk away, wondering *why* she had reacted so strongly. Not having a clue and giving her the benefit of the doubt, she thought, *Maybe she's just having a bad day.*

Seething with anger and jealousy, Janet walked away from Christina and Dr. Dawson, mentally chiding herself for allowing her emotions to get the best of her. If looks could kill, and sometimes she wished they could, Christina would have been dead in a heartbeat, allowing her to carry out her plans to win Dr. Dawson's affection without any distractions.

As Janet contemplated what had transpired, she began planning her next course of action. *What will it take to get rid of the pesky interloper once and for all?*

A smile crept across her lips as an idea took root. *I know what I need to do,* she thought as she squared her shoulders and headed back to the nurses' station, determined to finish her shift in peace even if Christina's presence was like a splinter under her skin—annoying and painful

Hannah Isbell, one of the aides, was busy writing in the charts when Christina approached the desk. Not looking up, she asked, "Are you and Dr. Dawson dating?"

"Excuse me?" Christina stammered, leaning against the counter for support.

Hannah chuckled.

"Forgive me. I've never been known to be subtle. I just couldn't help but notice somethin' goin' on between you two."

Hannah was in her early sixties, stout with short salt-and-pepper hair, a round face, eyes that twinkled, and an infectious smile and laugh.

Christina had worked with her a couple other times when she had filled in for absent aides, and had enjoyed her sense of humor and positive outlook on *everything*—never having a negative thing to say about anyone or anything.

Remembering their first conversation, when Hannah had introduced herself, Christina smiled.

"I live with my husband of forty years, have four grown children, all married and living all around Texas, ten beautiful grandchildren, two golden retrievers named Molly and Marvin, and a dozen or so cats. We live out on old Brandon Road on five acres with several pecan trees. So if you ever want any pecans, come on out and get 'em."

She thought at the time, *Anyone who had been married that long, loved dogs, cats and kids, and was willing to share their pecans couldn't be bad.*

Feeling her face and neck flush, she stammered, "Well, we used to know each other in high school, and we're just kinda reconnecting. We're not dating … yet." She gave a crooked smile. Hannah nodded knowingly.

Returning her attention to the paperwork but continuing to smile, she said, "I see."

Christina appreciated Hannah's open, honest, and sometimes bold way of cutting through any erected barriers to get to the root of a problem and felt any information given would be respected, but she wasn't ready to spill her guts yet.

Not wanting to get into a discussion about her feelings for Steven, she cleared her throat and said, "Um, do you mind if I take the charts you've finished and read them in the nurse's lounge?"

"Not at all. By the way, did anyone figure out what caused your bleeding?"

Christina sighed and set the charts on the counter. Shaking her head, she said, "Somehow I ended up with heparin or rat poison or something like that in my body, which destroyed my clotting factors. The rest is, well, history."

Hannah nodded. "That's weird. I had heard something to that effect, but I just wanted to make sure it was the truth and not gossip. You know how rumors can spread around here."

Christina smiled and nodded. *Yes indeed.* "I'm pretty sure my situation has become the topic of many conversations since this kind of event rarely happens."

Shaking her head, Hannah answered, "Rarely? More like never!"

Christina shrugged, shook her head, and held up her hands. "Right now, it's still a mystery. Obviously someone put it in my food or drink, but who and why? Well, we just don't know."

Hannah sighed. "I can't imagine someone deliberately hurting another person in such a strange manner."

"I know. It just doesn't make any sense."

"Well, if I hear anything at all about this, I'll be sure to let you know."

"Thank you, Hannah. I'd appreciate that. It's nice to know someone is looking out for me." She turned and headed for the nurses' lounge to read the charts.

Hannah watched Christina walk toward the lounge and thought, *I hope she and Dr. Dawson do connect. They make a cute couple. She's so sweet and he's just … wonderful. Whoever did that to that poor girl needs to get caught and punished.*

Christina busied herself with reading the rest of the charts and bringing herself up to date on the patients, their procedures, and their medications.

Janet and three aides busied themselves caring for the five patients, passing out medications and documenting their activities.

When Christina returned the charts to their appropriate slots after scanning through them, she saw Janet leaning on the counter and asked if she was all right.

She answered, "I'm having my monthlies, and not feeling quite up to par." *A good lie*, she thought as Christina nodded knowingly. *Really, you're presence is making me sick.* She wanted to yell but instead took a cleansing breath to calm her emotions.

The rest of the day was uneventful. At one time or another, almost everyone had asked if she was okay and if there was anything they could get or do for her. They were aggravatingly solicitous as they kept reminding her to sit down and take it easy. Beginning to resent their concern, she was glad when their shift ended and the reports had been given to the afternoon staff. Gathering her belongings, she headed for the elevator. As the door began to close, she spotted Janet heading her way, put her hand in the doorway, and called out, "Janet, you want to ride down with me?"

She could have sworn the woman scowled before answering.

"Sure, thanks."

Once the door closed, she asked, "Janet, did I do something to tick you off?"

Janet inhaled and tensed. "Why do you ask?"

"Well, maybe because you're scowling at me and you've been snippy with me all day. You said you were having your monthlies, but I think there's something more going on."

Janet sighed, looking away, not ready for a confrontation, but Christina continued, "I've thought about it all day, but nothing comes to mind as to *why* you'd be angry with me."

Janet turned and looked at her for a moment, wanting desperately to unleash the venom that was in her heart and mind. Instead, she smiled and said, "Christina, I'm not angry with you. I told you I'm having my period, and sometimes I get cranky." She shrugged. "Sorry if I gave you the impression that I was mad at you."

The bell rang, indicating that the elevator had arrived at the first level. Janet left quickly, almost running for the exit. Christina stood for a moment before leaving the elevator. *Something isn't right with that woman. There is more to this than she's letting on.* Sighing, she thought, *Well, I can only do so much.*

Exiting the building and entering her toasty van, she headed for home, stopping at the Qwik Mart for bread and milk.

CHAPTER 69

After arriving home that Friday afternoon and caring for the animals, Christina, realizing she only had a half hour before the kids came home, wanted nothing more than to sit in her easy chair and read another chapter of her suspense novel. She poured a glass of iced tea, grabbed her book, and settled into her nice cozy chair, trying to stay focused on the words in front of her but finding her mind wandering to thoughts of David and Steven, comparing the two men—who, in reality, were nothing alike. *Why then was I so attracted to both of them?* Coming up empty, she took a sip of her tea and refocused on the novel. She was halfway through the chapter when she heard voices yelling for her.

She was up from her easy chair heading to the back door to open it as Stacey ran into her arms.

Crying and holding her abdomen, she said, "Mommy, my tummy hurts!" Christina knew something was definitely wrong, because Stacey hadn't called her "Mommy" for a couple of years.

Nicky followed close behind, dropping the two backpacks on the floor, and breathlessly said, "She threw up twice on the way home." He made a face. "It was gross!"

Christina's mother and nurse alarms went off simultaneously. Feeling her daughter's forehead, which was hot and clammy to the touch, she said, "Why didn't you call me? I would have come got you."

Between gasps of pain, Stacey answered, "I thought it would pass."

Leading her daughter into the family room and sitting her on the couch, she asked, "Honey, when did you start feeling sick?"

Putting a pillow under her child's sweating head, she went into the bathroom for a cool, wet washcloth.

"It came on really quick, right before the last bell rang. I thought it was because I ate a hotdog for lunch and it didn't agree with me." She paused as she accepted the cloth that Christina handed to her. Wiping her forehead and then placing the cloth under her chin, she said, "Ooh, I think I'm gonna be sick again!" She jumped up and, with one hand over her mouth and the other clutching her stomach, ran to the bathroom as Nicky stood in the doorway helplessly watching his sister sit on the floor in front of the toilet, retching. As far as he could tell, there was nothing left in her stomach, and her dry heaves shook her whole sweat-drenched body.

Christina kept wiping her daughter's forehead with a cool cloth and pulled her hair back from her face.

Doubling over and crossing her arms across her abdomen, she cried, "Oh, Mommy, my stomach hurts so bad!"

Nicky ran upstairs, followed closely by Benji, returning a few minutes later with Stacey's pillow and blanket from her bed.

Stacey smiled weakly and said, "Thanks," as she was guided back to the couch.

Christina had Stacey lie stretched out on the couch as she pressed her abdomen and asked, "Honey, does it hurt when I press here?" Stacey inhaled and grimaced. "Yes." Panting, she pulled her knees up and turned on her side, crying softly. Benji sat on the floor next to the couch whimpering, not sure what he could or should do. Stacey pulled a shaky hand out from under the blanket and patted him.

"It's okay, buddy." He looked at Nicky and then back to Stacey and lay with his head on his paws.

Christina found the thermometer, and put it to her temple. After a few seconds, it read 103. Stacey started shaking and, her teeth chattering, said, "Mom, I'm freezing! How can I be freezing if my temperature is so high?"

"That's just the body reaction to the fever. Don't worry. You just snuggle under that blanket, and I'll be right back."

Concern etching his face, Nicky asked, "Mom? You want me to get another blanket for her?"

"Yes, honey. Thanks."

Nicky had never seen his sister this sick, and it scared him. As he ran up the stairs to retrieve another blanket, a sudden vision of his sister lying in a coffin flitted through his mind. He tripped on the last step and stifled a sob. "God," he whispered, "don't let Stacey die. Please." He felt a hot tear run down his face, and he quickly wiped it away. Grabbing a blanket out of the hallway closet, he ran back down the stairs, shook it out, and gently tucked it around her shivering body.

"Thanks," whispered Stacey through chattering teeth.

Not knowing what else to do, he then sat on the floor beside her and held her very hot hand. Chloe curled up on Stacey's feet, and Benji lay by Nicky with his head on his lap. Nicky unconsciously rubbed the whimpering dog's head.

Christina called Cindy.

"Hey, Cindy. I have a very sick girl on my hands, and I need to take her to the hospital. I was wondering if you and Samara could come stay with Nicky while I drive her there."

"Oh my gosh! What's wrong with her?"

"Well, it could be the flu, but quite honestly I think it's appendicitis. She has all the classic symptoms."

"I'll grab Samara, and we'll be right over."

"Thanks."

She then called Brad, who was at the pregame practice.

"Hey, Mom, what's up?" he asked, sounding winded.

"Brad, I need to take Stacey to the ER. I think she may have appendicitis."

He was silent for a moment and then with concern in his voice asked, "Do you need me to come home?"

"No, that's okay. Cindy and Samara are coming over to watch Nicky. You just go ahead and finish your practice and game. I'll call you when I know anything."

"Okay, Mom. Tell Stacey I'll be praying for her. And Mom?"

"Yes?"

"Um, tell her I love her too."

"Okay, honey, I will. I love you, and I'll call you later."

"Love you too, Mom."

When Brad replaced the receiver, he went immediately to his coach, explained the situation, and asked if he could leave after the warm-up practice.

"Tell you what, Brad, let's finish up here, and I'll drive you home. The game doesn't start for another hour or so."

"Coach, could you just drive me back to the school? I left my bike there, and I can just ride it home."

"Are you sure? 'Cause it's no problem to just drive you the extra couple of blocks home. I'd offer to take your bike too, but I brought the two-seater convertible." Brad nodded, thinking, *Some day, I want a convertible like the coach has.*

"Nah, I need to have my bike for tomorrow anyway."

His coach dropped him off, saying, "Good luck—don't worry about the game," as he drove off. Brad unlocked the chain, dropped it in his backpack, and jumped on his bike, peddling the few blocks home as fast as his legs would allow.

This would be a good time to have a motorcycle, he thought.

When Cindy and Samara arrived, Christina bundled Stacey in the blankets, and she and Cindy helped her walk out to the van. She walked slowly, doubled over and stopping every few feet to brace against the pain that was coursing through her abdomen, reminding Christina of her own reactions to labor pains so many years ago.

Cindy insisted on driving them to the hospital, and Samara volunteered to stay with Nicky, who was angry and disappointed at not being able to accompany them. As Cindy backed out of the driveway, Nicky waved miserably.

Putting her arm around his shoulders, Samara said, "Come on, Nicky, we'll go see what's on TV, or if you want, we can play a game." He sighed and, taking one last forlorn look at the retreating vehicle, followed Samara into the den.

Christina and Stacey sat in the back seat as Cindy drove like a race car driver to the hospital, making the five-minute ride in three.

Christina was both surprised at and pleased with the efficiency of the ER staff. Stacey was whisked into an examination room and within the hour diagnosed with appendicitis. Christina had to keep wiping her eyes in order to sign the surgical release forms.

From the time Stacey arrived home to the time she was in the recovery room, four hours passed. Brad had just arrived at home and was sitting with Samara and Nicky when Cindy returned.

"How is Stacey?" he asked as soon as she walked in the back door.

She held up her hand. "She's fine, Brad. She did have her appendix out. She's in the recovery room right now."

Giving her his best pleading look, he asked, "Can I borrow your car? I just need to see my mom and Stacey—to make sure they're okay."

She cocked her head and gave him a quizzical look. *Didn't I just say she's okay?* she thought. "I probably shouldn't since you just recently got your license, but okay. *No* speeding, and *please* watch out for the other guy! Your mom's probably gonna kill me!"

"It'll be okay, Mrs. Murray. I'll explain it all to her."

She reluctantly handed him the keys to her cute little red Chevy Camaro convertible and watched as he backed out of the driveway and disappeared down the street.

Nicky and Samara stood next to her and watched.

"He'll take care of your car, Mom."

"I know. That's not the only thing I'm worried about."

Samara nodded, and they both looked at Nicky, who was staring out the front door, seemingly lost in his own world of worry.

CHAPTER 70

Brad carefully parked Cindy's car and then ran the short distance to the hospital entrance. Approaching the desk, he asked one of the clerks, "Is there a Stacey Sanders here?"

As she was looking on the computer screen, his mom approached.

"Brad, what are you doing here? And *how* did you get here?" she asked, looking around the room for Cindy or someone else who could have brought him.

"Mrs. Murray let me borrow her car."

Christina looked surprised and nodded. "Well, that was nice of her," she said, remembering Cindy's protectiveness of her red Camaro and Brad's brand-new license.

"Is she all right?" he asked his weary mother as he pulled her into his arms. She nodded. When he saw how tired she looked he asked, "Are you all right?" She nodded again.

"What about your game?"

"The coach said not to worry. My spot would be covered by Micky Simms."

Christina nodded. She knew that Micky, having scored a few touchdowns in the past couple of games, was a good choice to take Brad's place for the quarterback position.

Worry etched on his face, Steven Dawson walked into the emergency room, looking for Christina. Approaching her, he said, "Christina, what's this I hear about Stacey? Is she all right?"

Christina felt tears well in her eyes again and motioned for him to go into the hall with her.

"Mom, I'm gonna get a Coke, and I'll be in the waiting room if you need me."

She nodded.

In the hall, not knowing exactly what to do, Steven put his arm around Christina's shoulder and pulled her into an embrace.

At first she was surprised and almost pulled away, but then relaxing a bit, allowed herself to be comforted. After a few seconds, she regained her composure and did pull away. He handed her a handkerchief from his pocket. *How is it that men always seem to have clean hankies? Do they carry spares for damsels in distress? And it is clean and pressed! Did men never use the handkerchiefs themselves and if not, why have them?* These thoughts raced through mind as she took it and wiped her eyes, taking half her makeup with it. *Dang it, now I need to go check my makeup!* she thought as she started to hand the soiled cloth back to its rightful owner.

He held up his hand. "No, you might need that again."

Again? Does he know something I don't? Okay, I'm being totally paranoid.

She took a breath and let it out. "I thought you were in Waco."

He nodded. "Well, I was, but the business I had to take care of took less time than I had anticipated. I came back here because I forgot a magazine I left in my office. In fact, I had just walked in the door when I overheard one of the nurses say that Stacey had been admitted. I came right over." He paused, catching his breath. "So what happened?"

Christina ran her fingers through her hair before responding.

"Stacey came home from school throwing up and running a 103 fever and complaining of a stomachache. At first I thought it might be a flu bug, but when the pain became more intense, I suspected appendicitis." She blew her nose into the once pristine hankie.

"I thought I should bring her in just to be on the safe side." She wiped away the moisture beginning to pool in her eyes. *Why am I so dang emotional? Kids have their appendixes out every day, and none that I know of ever died. Died? Why am I thinking like that?* She took a breath to steady her nerves. Steven stood across from her, empathy etched in his face. He wanted so badly to make everything all right again. That was what he did. He fixed things. But now, he was helpless. He couldn't fix this. He felt a strange ache in his heart as he watched Christina's attempt to regain control over her emotions.

Christina released a sigh.

"She did indeed have appendicitis and is now in surgery." She sniffed and wiped her nose, leaning against the wall. "I'm sorry. I'm blubbering like a baby."

"It's okay. You've had a rough couple of weeks—now this." He took her hand and held it in both of his, close to his heart—which she thought was kinda weird. *Should I pull my hand away? This is not how I expected him to act. Why is he acting this way? Probably a rebound effect. This is just weird. Nice, but weird.*

"I'm sure Stacy will be fine, though. Who was the surgeon?"

"I think it was Dr. Carmichael. Isn't he the pediatric surgeon?"

"Oh, yes, Aaron. He's a great doctor," he said, nodding, still holding her hand. "Has he come in to talk to you yet?"

"No, not yet," she answered as she gently disengaged her hand from his.

"He sent one of his assistants out to inform me that Stacey was headed up to the operating room. She said he'd be out later, that he had another emergency to attend to when he finished with Stacey."

Looking around the crowded emergency room, he said, "Yeah, for some reason, it seems to be a busy night here. I'm surprised you got in so quickly."

"Well, I think it helped that Stacey was screaming and throwing up. That got their attention."

"Yeah, I hate emergency rooms and all the drama involved. That's one reason I didn't want to be an ER doctor." He shook his head. "I prefer a little calmer atmosphere, where I'm in control."

She smiled and nodded. She felt the same way most of the time, except now, where she had absolutely no control of anything.

A nurse in surgical garb walked in the waiting room and called out, "Mrs. Sanders?"

"Yes," Christina replied as the nurse approached.

"Your daughter is Stacey?" she asked, looking at the chart in her hand.

"Yes."

"We've moved her to the recovery room. If you'd like, you may go see her for a few minutes. She's still pretty groggy."

"Oh, yes! Just let me tell my son. Then I'll be right with you." Turning, she asked, "Oh, can he come in as well?"

The nurse looked over to the teen talking on his phone.

"Well, why don't you go in alone? He can see her once she's in a room."

Christina nodded. Steven said, "Let me know if you need anything." He reached over, squeezed her hand, and turned to leave.

Christina hurried over to Brad, telling him of the situation. She followed the nurse to her daughter's bedside and was taken aback by how fragile the child looked in the hospital bed with the IVs and heart monitor hooked up. She sat by the bed and took the small, cool hand in hers and rubbed it, saying a silent prayer.

The recovery room nurse came in, checked Stacey's IV and vitals, and then tried to rouse the sleeping child. Stacey groaned and started to cry when the nurse put a cold cloth on her face and told her to wake up.

"Mom? Mommy?" she cried as she opened her eyes and looked around the room.

Christina took her hand again. The nurse left the room.

"I'm right here, honey."

"What happened?" she asked groggily.

"You had to have your appendix out."

"Am I gonna be all right?" she asked as she yawned and rubbed her eyes.

"You're going to be just fine. They'll be moving you up to the children's ward."

"Do I have to stay here?" she whined.

"Yes, honey, just for the night, I think."

"Will you stay with me?"

"Yep, I'll be right by your bed."

"Hmm," she mumbled as she dropped off to sleep.

Steven came by again before leaving for the night. "How's our girl doing?" he asked as he came over to the bed and looked at the sleeping child.

Our girl?

"She's doing as well as can be expected," she said, sighing and rubbing her eyes.

He nodded. "I'm not sure what I'll do about work tomorrow," she said worriedly. Then she perked up. "Oh wait, tomorrow's Saturday. Whew! I don't have to work."

He smiled and nodded. "Good for you. You might want to give Mrs. Ferguson a call about Monday, though. I doubt Stacey will be ready for you to leave her alone."

"Oh, right. Thanks. I'll call her first thing tomorrow."

He turned to leave. "Well, guess I'd better head on home. Do you need anything?"

She shook her head. "Thanks for stopping by."

Remembering that Brad was still in the waiting area, she went to inform him that his sister was recovering nicely and would probably be going upstairs.

"Can I peek in?"

Nodding, Christina said, "Sure. She's still asleep and won't realize you're here, though."

"That's okay. I just want to see her."

He walked over to the bed and took his sister's hand. "Hey sis, just want you to know you have a lot of folks rooting for you. You get better soon, okay?" She was unresponsive, but he was thankful he had a chance to see her anyway. Walking with his mom to the exit, he said, "Well, I guess I'll go on home to relieve Samara and Cindy. I need to get some homework done and hopefully be in bed before midnight."

She smiled and hugged him. *What a great young man he was turning into.*

"Hey Brad?" she called as he turned to go.

"Yeah?"

"Could you ask Cindy to bring my toothbrush and pillow and Stacey's stuffed bear?"

"Sure. You need anything else?"

"I don't think so. I'm sure if I need anything, the hospital will give it to me."

"Okay. See you tomorrow."

"Thanks, son." Brad smiled and waved as he exited the building.

"Mrs. Sanders, we're going to move Stacey to her room now," a nurse said as she unlocked the wheels and started moving the bed. "I'm taking her up to the new pediatric ward on the second floor."

"Good. I toured the ward a couple of weeks ago. It's really nice," Christina said, gathering Stacey's belongings.

"Yeah, it's about time this hospital had a children's ward. It was difficult having the kids and adult patients on the same floor."

Holding the elevator door open, Christina said, "I'm sorry, I didn't get your name."

"I'm Becky. Becky Cyrus. No relation to Billy Ray, unfortunately," she said with a smile. Christina nodded.

"Here we are. Second floor. Let me give the chart to the nurse in charge, and we'll get Stacey set up in a room."

By the time Stacey was settled in, it was well past ten o'clock. Christina called Cindy's cell phone, which went to voice mail. She left a message, hoping Cindy would get it before making the trip up to the hospital.

"Cindy, it's too late for you to come up tonight. I'll make do with what I have. The nurses are very helpful and have set up a cot with pillows and gave me a toiletries bag with everything I need."

As soon as she hung up her cell phone rang. It was Cindy.

"Hey, Christina, it's a good thing you called me, 'cause I was just heading out the door. I wasn't sure how I'd get this stuff to you, but I figured I could bribe someone to take it up there. How's Stacey doing?" she asked. Christina brought her up to date on her daughter's condition. Cindy said she and Samara would spend the night at the house with Brad and Nicky.

"Not that Brad wants us to. He assures us he's old enough to be home with Nicky. But I figured if Nicky wakes up scared or something, it'd be good if an adult was there."

Christina smiled and nodded. "Thanks, Cindy. I appreciate your concern." After talking a few more minutes, they hung up and readied themselves for bed.

CHAPTER 71

They parked the now plain tan van—no more Mort's Electrical decal on the side panel—next to the curb a couple of houses down from the Sanders'. They were setting up their monitoring equipment one last time when they saw Brad coming toward them on his bike—like a bat out of hell.

"What the …?" whispered Ed as he nudged Tom, and they both watched in surprise as he turned into the driveway and rode out of sight, presumably putting his bike in the garage. Ed gasped as he recognized the red Camaro in the driveway.

"What?" Tom asked.

"It's her."

"Who?"

"Her. Cindy. She drives a red Camaro."

"Wonder what she's doin' here."

He looked at his watch. Six thirty. The sun was just starting to drop out of sight, casting long shadows on the ground from the houses and surrounding trees. It would be dark in another hour or so, and the football game should begin around that same time. *Why was Brad home?* According to their surveillance and monitoring, this was the last game of the season, and Brad would be participating. He was usually at the pregame practice at this time. Something out of the ordinary was definitely going on. They sat in silence, watching the well-lit house, seeing shadows passing by the windows. Ed and Tom both looked at the monitors at the same time.

"Quick, turn them on," Tom said as he placed the earphones on his head.

Ed reached over and grabbed his own earphones with one hand, and as he placed them on his ears, he used the other hand to turn on the receivers for the bugs. All they heard was static and muffled voices. Tom frantically turned the knobs, but to no avail.

A few minutes later, Brad ran out, jumped into Cindy's car, backed it out of the driveway, and drove past them, headed for—they weren't sure, because they couldn't understand what was being said.

Turning the knobs, Tom asked, "You think we should follow him? See where he's goin'?"

Ed thought for a moment. He didn't *want* to leave the house with Cindy in it, but what good would it do to just sit and watch the house? Apparently, the bugs were malfunctioning. He couldn't just go up to the door and say, "Hi, I was just in the neighborhood and thought I'd drop by and check on y'all."

Yeah, that would go over like a lead balloon. After the initial shock of seeing him, she'd probably slap him—hard—for not calling her. And yeah, he'd deserve it, but then he'd have to explain everything, and it just wasn't the right time. *When will it be the right time?* he wondered. *After all this stuff is over? Maybe? No, definitely. If I want to continue this relationship, I have to be up-front and honest with her.* He sighed. *Man, I dread that time.*

To Tom he said, "Sure. Wouldn't hurt to see where the kid's headed, especially since he's drivin' *her* car—with a new license—and seems to be in such a hurry."

They started the van and followed Brad and were surprised when he pulled into the hospital parking lot. Tom pulled in and parked a few cars down from the Camaro and watched as Brad quickly exited the car and ran to the entrance.

Turning the engine off, Tom said, "Wonder who he's gonna see."

"Yeah. Me too."

"Do you want to go in and check things out, or should I?" Tom asked.

"I think it'd be best if you did. I don't want to be seen around here yet. Someone might recognize me as the guy who was with Cindy. I tried to be discreet, but you never know. Seems in these small towns, everybody knows everybody else's business."

"Yeah. Okay. I'll be back in a minute."

Ed watched from the dark interior of the van as Tom sauntered up to the entrance of Alva Community Hospital. Once he had entered and was out of sight, Ed reclined his seat and closed his eyes. Thoughts ran through his mind like a current of electricity. One thought would lead to another and then another. It was difficult to stay focused, and pretty soon he drifted off to sleep. He was jolted awake when he heard Tom beating on his window.

"Hey, Sleeping Beauty, let me in."

"Oh, yeah, sorry," Ed said as he shook the cobwebs from his brain and unlocked the door.

"So who was young Bradley visiting?" Ed asked as he rubbed his eyes.

"Well, seems baby sister had to have her appendix out."

Ed sat up. "Really?" Straightening his van seat and buckling his seat belt, he asked, "Is she all right?"

"I guess so. I only heard bits and pieces of the conversation between the mom and the kid."

"Well, that might put a damper on our plans for this weekend," Ed said wearily. "How are we gonna get into the house if everyone is there?"

"Yeah, right." Tom ran his hand over his face. "Well, I'm all for goin' back home and comin' back next week. What do you say?"

"Sounds good to me. Fire up the engine, captain."

Tom gave Ed a look that said, "What?"

Ed laughed.

"Captain?" Tom shook his head. "Where do you come up with that stuff?"

"Don't you ever watch *Star Trek*?"

"Oh, yeah. *Star Trek*." He said and grunted.

As they drove back to Dallas, Ed asked, "Say, Tom, do you ever think about God?"

Taken aback by the question, Tom said, "What?"

"Do you ever think about God?"

"What kind of question is that?"

"A simple one, really. I sometimes think about God and wonder what he's like. Don't you ever wonder?"

"What's goin' on here? Why are you getting all philosophical?"

Ed chuckled. "I'm not getting philosophical." He grinned. "I'm not even sure what that means."

It was Tom's turn to chuckle. "Me neither. I think it has to do something with religious thinking. I just heard it on one of those religious shows once. Nice big word, though, isn't it? Phil-o-soph-i-cal," he said, pronouncing each syllable. Ed smiled and shook his head.

"Anyway, back to my question. Do you ever think about God?"

"Well, yeah. I guess everybody does at one time or another. Why are you asking? You sick or something?" Furrowing his brow, he looked at his friend.

"No." Ed sighed and looked out the window. "I just wonder how someone or something could create such a vast universe and all the creatures that live on this planet, including us humans." He looked over at Tom, who was intently staring at the road.

"I went to church as a kid and learned about God and Jesus and the Holy Spirit, and at one time I knelt at the altar and promised I would serve him." He sighed heavily. "I've wandered so far from that promise, and I'm not sure if I know how to get back there. I don't know *if* God would even accept me back." He sighed. "I've done some pretty awful things these past few years." He thought about the men he had tortured and killed and the women he had used and lied to. He was quiet for a moment and then added, "If I was God, I don't think I'd accept me back."

"Whew," said Tom as he blew air through his lips. "Okay. First of all, I'm not all that great myself, but from what I understand about God, he's pretty forgiving. Do you remember that story in the Bible about King David and how he sinned by getting some other guy's wife pregnant and then having that guy killed in battle to cover up his sin?"

"Yeah, vaguely," answered Ed, frowning.

"Well anyway, David cried out to God for forgiveness, and God forgave him."

"Wait a minute. Didn't God kill the kid that he and that woman had? That doesn't sound very forgiving to me."

"Okay, the kid died. Sin always has some kind of consequence. But the *main* thing is God forgave him. There are other stories too about how people did bad things and asked for forgiveness and God forgave and even blessed them. Like Abraham."

Ed sighed again. "Yeah, that was then. What about nowadays?"

"Look, I don't claim to be a Bible scholar, and it's been a long time since I've even opened one, but when Eleanor and I were married, we attended church regularly." He paused, putting his thoughts together. "I seem to remember a Sunday school class we attended that taught about salvation—what it is and how to get it."

Ed looked at him, motioning with his hand for him to continue.

"Anyway, if I remember right, there's a verse in the Bible that says something like, 'God loved the world so much that he gave his son Jesus to die on the cross in our place, and anyone who believes in Jesus won't die but will have eternal life."

Ed perked up. "Hey, I remember that verse." He cleared his throat and then proceeded to recite John 3:16. "For God so loved the world, that he gave his only begotten Son, that whosoever believeth in him should not perish, but have everlasting life."

"Yeah, that's it. I knew I didn't quote it right, but I had the main idea."

"Yeah, you did. Man, I'm surprised I remembered that verse. It's been at least twenty or more years since I've even said it." He looked over at Tom and smiled. "I had to recite it so I could get a sticker on a chart and win a prize. I think it was a Snickers bar."

Tom smiled and nodded. "Yeah, I remember having to memorize Scripture as a kid. Funny how those memories come up when you least expect them."

Ed nodded in agreement.

"Back to your question. Will God forgive you? Yes, I believe he will. The thing is, you have to *ask* him and then *believe* he will." Tom slowed the van, put his blinker on, and exited the freeway.

"Where are you going?" Ed asked, looking out the window.

"Man, I gotta go. And I need another cup of coffee. My thermos is empty."

Chuckling, Ed said, "Oh, okay. I was afraid you were gonna take me to a church or something."

"That's not a bad idea. I'm sure we could find a good little southern gospel church around here."

"That's okay. We'll save that for another time."

The two men did their business, bought a few snacks for the remainder of the trip, and rode the last half hour or so in silence, each thinking about what the other one said.

CHAPTER 72

As Christina tossed and turned and pounded and wadded the pillow, trying to get comfortable in her small cot next to Stacey's bed, she thought about their trip to Texas—the events that led up to it and the day they arrived.

They had arrived at her childhood home on July 7, the hottest day of the year, reaching 110 degrees in the sun. As Christina stepped out of the air-conditioned van into the Texas heat that day, she felt as if her breath had been being sucked out with a giant vacuum.

"Mom, I'm boiling!" fussed Stacey as she exited the van carrying a mewling, squirming Chloe, who wanted nothing more than to use her litter box, eat her cat chow, and stretch out completely. She had had enough of traveling in a cramped cat carrier for almost three days. Stacey stood under a nearby tree holding the cat and looked at the house. Her mind had two predominant thoughts: *It's too hot here. I want to go back to Michigan!*

"It's too hot!" Nicky whined as he grabbed the leash that held Benji, their two-year-old beagle.

"So, is this as hot as it gets?" Brad asked as he walked around the van and stood by his mother. Christina gave him a look.

He held up his hands. "I'm just sayin …"

"All right!" Christina responded, exasperated by the whining and complaining. "I *know* it's really hot right now, but we need to get inside and turn on the air conditioners. We can unpack the van once it cools down out here."

"Yeah, like maybe in December," she heard Brad mumble under his breath as he reached into the van to retrieve his backpack. She stifled a smile.

Benji pulled on his leash, dragging Nicky with him.

"Hey, wait a minute, Benji. We can't go into the neighbor's yard!"

The dog stopped, turned around, and looked at Nicky as if to say, "Why not?"

"Come on, boy. We need to get inside, or my brain's gonna fry!" Nicky gently pulled on the leash as the dog sniffed the nearby trees and bushes, familiarizing himself with his new surroundings, and reluctantly acquiesced after quickly watering the brittle grass. Panting, his tongue hanging out and dripping drool, he followed his young master up the steps to the front door.

Before walking up the sidewalk to unlock the door, Christina stood by the van and looked at the old two-story Tudor-style house. She felt a wave of nostalgia wash over her that made her feel dizzy, as though she was looking over a railing of a tall building.

Closing her eyes for a moment, she regained her equilibrium and instantly relived a precious memory. In her mind's eye, she saw Brad and Stacey as small children riding down the sidewalk on new tricycles that Nana and Papa had bought them for Christmas. Her mom and dad were standing on the porch laughing and waving as the two little pedalers raced toward their videotaping dad. She opened her eyes and sighed. She saw a shadow go across the yard and heard a cacophony of noise overhead. Shielding her eyes from the bright sunlight, she looked up to see several crows circling above. *That's interesting,* she thought. *What was it that grandma said about crows? A crow on your roof meant trouble was coming, a crow in your house meant death was coming, and if a crow walked on a grave, someone in that family would die soon.* Of course, they were old wives' tales, and she didn't hold any value to them. Nevertheless, she felt uneasiness in her spirit as she headed up the sidewalk to the porch where her three sweltering children stood. She looked up once again to see that the noisy birds had continued their journey and sighed in relief. *Thank God none landed on the house.*

"Come on, Mom, we're dyin' here!" Nicky whined.

As she approached the house, digging in her purse for the key, she heard the low whine of an air conditioner and looked over to see the one in the front window was running. *Thank God!*

She turned the key in the lock and pushed open the large, heavy wooden door. They were met with a blast of cool air.

"Hey, Mom, who turned on the air conditioner?" Nicky asked as he entered the large living room.

"Hmm, my friend Cindy must have," she answered, wiping sweat from her brow with the hem of her T-shirt. She was so thankful that she had thought to call the gas, water, and electric companies to turn everything on before they had left Michigan; otherwise it would have been a very hot, stuffy, and miserable weekend. She was also glad that she had sent a key to Cindy so she could let the movers in, turn at least one of the air conditioners on, and make sure everything was in working order.

She looked at her watch. Two o'clock. She had talked to Cindy that morning when they had left the motel in Texarkana and informed her they would be arriving sometime in the next four to five hours. She must have come right over and turned on the air conditioner for them. *What a great friend,* she thought.

Cindy had informed her two days earlier that the moving van with their many possessions had arrived, and she had told the men where they were to be distributed.

Walking into the big house, they were met with stacks of boxes and furniture. Christina dreaded going upstairs for fear it was just as crowded as the downstairs rooms.

"Oh man, we're never gonna get this all sorted," commented Stacey as she let out a lungful of air and looked around the living room. Chloe jumped from her arms and ran through the maze, disappearing into an adjoining room. Nicky unhooked Benji's leash, and the happy dog ran after Chloe, stopping every now and then to sniff boxes along the way.

"Mom? Is this *all* our stuff?" Nicky asked, dumbfounded, as he too surveyed the large, crowded room.

"Whoa!" was all Brad could say as he walked to the middle of the room where the paths met to form a T and looked around. Furniture and boxes were piled in every nook and cranny and along walls, with just enough space for a person to walk between them and travel from room to room.

When Christina took a deep breath, she realized that even though the air was cool, it had that stale, old-house smell. She was sure the walls were full of mice and their droppings, and the attic probably had bats and guano. *Yuck!* Making a face, she thought, *No telling how many bug carcasses we'll find in and around the windows or in the corners.* She knew that Texas had a much larger and more diverse bug population than Michigan, and she would have to get used to the ever-present arachnids and creepy-crawly things once again.

"Well," she said to no one in particular as she nodded and exhaled. She wiped the fine sheen of sweat from her forehead with the bottom of her T-shirt again.

"In answer to your questions—yes, Nicky, this is all our stuff." Turning to Stacey, she said, "Yes, we will get this all unpacked. It'll take some time, but we can do it." She said this with more confidence than she felt. She looked at Brad, smiled, and shrugged. He nodded, knowing exactly what she meant. This would be a monumental task.

She looked at their flushed, sweaty faces and shook her head, thinking, *My poor little Yankee kids—they're gonna have a hard time adjusting to this heat.*

"Let's not stand around complaining!" she said, feeling sweat trickle down her sides from her armpits. Now she wished she had asked Cindy to turn on *all* the air conditioners. Being so used to the mild Michigan summers, she had forgotten how hot Texas would be in July. She had reasoned that one air conditioner would be sufficient in making the house cool enough. *Foolish,* she chided herself.

"Brad, please go into the family room and turn on that air conditioner. Stacey, run upstairs and turn those on as well. Nicky, find bowls and give the animals water and food, and find a litter box for Chloe."

The kids busied themselves with the tasks at hand while she maneuvered around the boxes and found the air conditioner, checking to see if it was set to the coldest and highest fan settings. It was. She looked around and sighed. It would be a monumental task indeed to get everything unpacked and organized. She remembered how tiring and time-consuming it had been to sort through and pack everything for the move to Texas. Even though they had had a huge garage sale and disposed of or donated many items, she was still amazed at the amount of things that ended up in the moving van and were now here in these front rooms.

"Hey Mom? Which room is mine?" Brad asked as he walked in, followed by Benji, who quickly turned and chased Chloe into the kitchen. Nicky, not really caring about the room situation, followed the pets.

Stacey came bounding down the stairs.

"I want the room in the front," she stated emphatically.

"Hey, that's not fair, that's the biggest room!" Brad responded, glaring at his sister, who made a face at him.

Wanting to diffuse an impending argument, Christina held her hands up and said, "You know what? We can discuss this later. Why don't we just unload a few more things from the van and then go get a bite to eat? I'm starving, and a restaurant will be a lot more comfortable than this place!" She looked at her two children, who were glaring at each other. "Maybe by the time we get back it'll be cooler and we can unload the rest of our stuff and decide on rooms."

"Hey Mom, there's food in the fridge and ice in the freezer!" Nicky shouted from the kitchen.

That Cindy. What a friend, she thought as she headed into the kitchen to get a cold glass of water, followed by Brad and Stacey, who kept making faces and poking each other in the arm. She found a note attached to the fridge with a Texas-shaped magnet painted with bluebonnets, the Texas state flower.

Knew you wouldn't have time to do much shopping, so I hope this helps get you through the first couple of days! Call me as soon as you get in!

Love you! Cindy

Cindy had been Christina's friend since their first day of kindergarten, and as the years passed, their friendship had blossomed and grown like a strong oak with deep roots that had withstood the storms and trials that life had thrown at it; time and distance proved to be no match for their sisterly bond.

Mom and kids, each holding a tall glass of ice water, stood in the kitchen and discussed what to do for dinner. Even though Cindy had left sandwich meat and salad fixings, the Sanders family agreed that they wanted a hot meal in a nice sit-down restaurant. They were tired of fast food and sandwiches, which had sustained them on the long trip down.

Christina rummaged through her purse, found her cell phone, and gave Cindy a call, asking her to meet them for dinner at the Golden Corral Restaurant out by I-35. What a fun time it had been to reconnect.

Christina's last thought before finally drifting off to sleep was *I wonder what we'd be doing now if we hadn't moved here.*

Lula had heard the gossip and had a difficult time believing her luck. The boss had said she needed to do something with the children, and she had thought long and hard and was about to put her ideas into action when lo and behold, the little girl ends up in the hospital. Now she just needed to think about the other two kids and plan something for them. Christina was going to get tired of all the stress eventually, and then maybe she'd give up and move back to Michigan. That's what the boss man wanted—just to be rid of her.

Lula didn't usually work the late shift, but the supervisor called and said one of the girls had called in sick and asked if she would be willing to work. *Of course I'll work!* Time-and-a-half-pay was a much-needed blessing—she had bills to pay. Maybe the gods were smiling down on her, 'cause here she was, in the hospital at the same time the Sanders were. Curiosity was encouraging her to take a peek at the little girl.

She liked kids and was having quite a struggle in her mind as to how she was going to scare Christina without harming the children. The oldest boy would be the most challenging. As she was emptying trash bins and straightening up the emergency waiting room, she had caught a glimpse of him talking on his cell phone. He was tall and lanky, and she easily outweighed him by about 150 pounds—but he was all muscle, which might present a problem.

She stopped at the utility room, emptied her garbage containers, and reloaded her maintenance cart before heading up to the second floor.

CHAPTER 73

D r. Aaron Carmichael tapped lightly on the door and came into the room on Saturday morning, waking Christina.

"Mrs. Sanders?"

"Yes?" she answered groggily as she rubbed her sleep-filled eyes. She was shocked at what she saw standing before her. Dr. Carmichael was the most handsome man she had seen in a *long* time. He was tall, muscular, and tan with dark hair and eyebrows and big brown eyes with lashes to die for. *Middle Eastern descent?* she wondered. He wore wire-rimmed glasses and sported a goatee. She caught herself staring and had to shake her head to bring her focus back on what he was saying.

With a Middle Eastern accent, he said, "You're daughter is doing remarkably well."

Stacey awoke and rubbed her eyes. She clutched the stuffed bear that Steven had given her the Christmas before he died.

Christina wondered how it had gotten there and learned later from Cindy that Brad had insisted that she take it to his sister that night. He had said emphatically, "She needs her bear, Mrs. Murray. If she wakes without it, she'll freak out. If you don't want to take it, I'll do it." She had relented and left him with Samara and Nicky while she drove to the hospital and gave the bear to an aide, insisting she take it to Stacey's room. Sometime after Christina had drifted off to sleep, the bear was delivered as promised.

"Good morning, young lady. I need to listen to your lungs and heart." Stacey frowned, nodded, and put the bear on the pillow beside her head.

He paused as he set the chart on the foot of the bed and put his stethoscope on Stacey's chest.

"Sounds good. I need to check your bandage. May I?" She nodded again. He pulled the sheet down and checked her bandage, probing gently around the incision area. Stacey winced but didn't cry out. Smiling, he asked, "How are you feeling Stacey?"

"Pretty good, considering I just had my appendix out last night."

"Well, would you like to go home this afternoon? That is, if you don't start running a fever or start spurting blood." He grinned and gave her a wink.

Giving him her most pitiful look, she said, "Yes, please."

He raised his eyebrows and smiled.

"Good, then I'll sign the papers." He patted her on the leg and looked at Christina, who was running her fingers through her hair, trying not to look like she just woke up. *Goodness he's gorgeous! He looks like he could be a model for GQ.* He took her breath away. *Why haven't I noticed him before? The hospital isn't that big.* She caught herself looking at his left ring finger. It was surprisingly naked.

"Say, aren't you the nurse who passed out a couple of weeks ago and ended up in the ER?"

"Yeah, that would be me," she said as all hopes of trying to impress him deflated like a balloon.

"Are you doing all right now?"

She wasn't sure if he was asking out of concern or just kindness. It didn't matter—she liked his voice.

Nodding and clearing her throat, she answered, "I'm fine, thanks. She asked, "So my daughter can go home today?" She wondered if her eye makeup was smudged and if she looked as bad as she imagined. *Where was a mirror when you needed it?*

"Yes, barring any complications," he said as he finished writing in the chart. He patted Stacey's leg and then looked at Christina and couldn't help but smile. When he first walked in, he hadn't paid much attention to her, as he was focused on his patient, but now, he really *saw* her. He liked what he saw. His first thought was *Wow, she's cute—smudged makeup, crumpled clothes, and all.*

"Well, thank you, Dr. Carmichael," she said as she reached out to shake his hand.

His hand, encircling hers, was warm, soft, and gentle. They stood for a few seconds, neither one wanting to break eye contact. She felt her heart flutter. *Wait a minute,* she thought. *What about Steven?* She broke eye contact first and removed her hand from his.

He cleared his throat before saying, "Stacey may leave anytime after one." He stopped in the doorway and turned around. "Oh yes, call my office and set up an appointment for next week. I need to make sure she's healing well." He smiled and waved at Stacey, who was grinning and waving back at him. When he was gone, Stacey said, "Wow, he's hot!" Christina looked at her daughter with a shocked expression.

"What? Just because I'm a kid doesn't mean I can't appreciate good looks."

Christina smiled and nodded. "You're absolutely right. He is hot." Stacey giggled.

Whew! I need to find out more about him, Christina thought as she poured glasses of water for Stacey and herself.

Saturday morning, after Stacey had a breakfast of juice and Jell-O and kept it down, Christina left her to go home, take a shower, and change clothes, promising a quick return. Stacey was content to watch TV and doze off and on until the nurse came in and informed her that she would have to walk up and down the hall twice before she could be dismissed. No amount of whining or protesting deterred the nurse from her duty. She *did* agree, however, to give Stacey two pain relievers and came back within the hour to help her up. Surprised that it hadn't hurt as much as she had anticipated, she did the laps around the hallway and was pleased when the nurse stated she was ready to pack up and head home.

Christina arrived as the lunch trays were being distributed. Stacey had the option of eating what was on the tray, which looked like some kind of broth and more Jell-O and juice, or waiting until she was home, where she could have real food, like mac and cheese. She opted for the later.

During the drive home, Stacey asked, "Mom, why is all this stuff happening to us?"

"What stuff, honey?"

"You know. Brad's hand, your accident, my appendix. That stuff."

"Well, I'm not sure I have an answer to that, babe. Sometimes stuff just happens." She looked over at her daughter, who was chewing on her bottom lip, brows furrowed, seriously considering this.

"Why do you ask?" she asked as she turned the van onto Elm Street.

"Well, I just don't understand why all this is happening. Seems since we've moved here weird things have been going on." She looked over at her mom with concern on her face. "I just hope nothing bad happens to Nicky. He's the only one left who hasn't been hurt."

Christina's heart jumped, and she gripped the steering wheel. She'd thought about that and prayed for Nicky's protection, but when her daughter expressed concern as well, the possibility frightened her.

"Well, we'll just have to pray for his protection."

"Yeah." Not looking or sounding convinced, Stacey turned her head toward the widow, concern still etching her face.

Stacey recovered from the surgery quickly and wanted to return to school on Monday, but her mom insisted she stay home the rest of the week to completely mend.

"Honey, it's only been three days. What if someone accidentally bumps into you or you trip and fall, or, or …"

In a voice that sounded a bit whiney but resigned to her sentence, she said, "Okay, Mom. I'll stay home a while longer, but the whole week? I need to at least go to some of the play practices."

All Christina could say was "We'll see how the week goes. I'll go by the school and pick up your assignments in a little while. That should keep you busy."

"Could you maybe pick up some DVDs too? There's nothing but soap operas on during the day, and they're *so* boring!"

Christina smiled. "Okay, I'll swing by Blockbuster and pick up a couple. Anything in particular?"

"Anything with animals in it."

"Okay. I'll see what I can find."

Christina returned an hour later with a bag full of books and papers and two DVDs about a dog named Beethoven. Stacey was happy about the movie choices, but not so much about the homework assignments.

CHAPTER 74

Christina reluctantly left Stacey on Wednesday to work a few hours until a replacement nurse could arrive. Leaving her with a list of emergency numbers and promising to call every hour or two to check in, she gave her a kiss on her forehead and a hug. Closing the door, she waited until she heard the click of the lock before heading to her van.

When she walked onto the floor, she was informed that Mr. Walters, the eighty-five-year-old cardiac/stroke patient had died a few minutes before her arrival. She immediately went to his room and was met by his grieving widow and daughter. Embracing each of them, she told them how sad she was to have lost such a wonderful man. "Is there anything I can do to help?" They thanked her and reassured her that all the details had been taken care of, as they had both prepared emotionally and financially for the inevitability of his passing.

Christina left them to do the morning report with the nursing staff and go on rounds with Dr. Dawson, who looked visibly shaken by the loss of his patient. There were five patients on the ward, so rounds took about an hour, and when they finished, Steven asked Christina to join him for a cup of coffee in the nurses' lounge. As they sat across from each other at the long table, he pulled out a chart.

"Christina," he began, "I'm very concerned about Elizabeth Hadley."

Elizabeth was a fifty-one-year-old lady who had come into the ER the previous night complaining of chest pains and shortness of breath. The ER staff had done preliminary tests and found she had had a mild heart attack—if one could call any heart attack mild.

"Her blood pressure was up, and her breathing seemed more labored this morning. I'm going to start her on some new medication. I'd like you to keep close tabs on her." She nodded. "Check her vitals every hour for the next twenty-four hours, and if there are *any* changes, let me know as soon as possible." She nodded again. "I'm scheduling her for a cardiac catheterization tomorrow morning. I suspect she's got a few clogged arteries, given her symptoms and her size."

Elizabeth weighed close to three hundred pounds, Christina guessed. He glanced through the other charts in front of him. "I think everyone else is pretty stable. I'm dismissing Mr. Palmer." She raised her eyebrows and wondered why he hadn't mentioned it to his patient when he saw him earlier. He read her thoughts, adding,

"I didn't tell him earlier because I wanted to check the latest lab results. They came back within the normal range."

"Oh, good," she said as she nodded again. "Anything else?"

"I think that's it. If anything changes, I'll let you know."

Smiling, she said, "And I'll let you know if there are any changes at this end."

"By the way, how's Stacey doing?"

"She's recovering nicely." She smiled and added, "Going crazy from boredom and wants to go back to school." She looked at her watch. "I need to call and check in on her."

She pulled out her cell phone and made the call. Steven watched her facial expressions and heard the motherly concern in her voice.

He could feel his emotions and mind sliding toward that abyss called love, and he was feeling helpless to stop them. He had no idea that Christina felt the same way. Christina was quite relieved when the substitute nurse, Gina, came in at noon and she could leave to be with her daughter.

"I'm so sorry I couldn't be here sooner, but I had to take my mother to the dentist. We made that appointment a few months ago, and I just couldn't bring myself to cancel it."

Christina smiled and nodded. "That's fine. I'm just glad you could come in now. I want to get back home to my daughter. She just had her appendix out last week, and even though she insists she's fine, I don't want to be gone for very long."

Concern etched Gina's face. "How old is your daughter?"

"She's almost thirteen and quite independent."

Gina looked relieved and said, "Oh, okay. We'll go over these charts, and then you can scoot on home."

While on the elevator, she called Stacey and asked if she wanted anything.

"I'd really like a Dr Pepper and some Fritos if it won't be too much trouble."

"I'll stop at the Qwik Mart and be right home."

CHAPTER 75

On Friday of that week, Christina took Stacey for her post-op checkup with Dr. Carmichael, who seemed pleased to see them both

I at least look better than at our first meeting, she thought.

After doing a thorough examination of Stacey, he stated that she was recovering well and could return to school and most of her activities the following Monday.

"No running, jumping, or lifting heavy objects, though," he had said as he palpated the incision site.

Stacey smiled and nodded in agreement. "I promise I'll be careful."

"Do you have any plans for Halloween?" he asked as he stepped away from the examination table and picked up Stacey's chart.

Stacey smiled and answered, "Yeah, we're gonna have a harvest party at our church."

"A harvest party? What's that?" he asked, looking over at Christina.

She was about to answer when Stacey jumped in with the explanation.

Pulling her shirt down and pants up and with excitement filling her voice and face, she said, "Instead of going trick-or-treating, we'll have a big party for the kids in the basement of the church. We're gonna have pony rides, face painting, which I'll be doing, games, and lots of food."

Dr. Carmichael raised his eyebrows and smiled. "Sounds like fun. Are the ponies going to be in the basement too?"

Stacey giggled. "No, they'll be outside on the lawn along with a couple other games."

He nodded. "I was wondering how they would get the ponies down the steps. Can anyone come, or do you have to be a member of your church?"

"Oh, anyone can come," Stacey answered. "Do you have kids?"

"I have a little five-year-old girl."

"Oh, she'd love it!" She looked at her mom. "Wouldn't she, Mom?"

Christina nodded and smiled. "Yeah, I think she would."

"What time will all this be taking place?"

Stacey looked at her mom and frowned, not sure of the starting time.

Christina looked in her purse and pulled out a flyer.

"Here, Dr. Carmichael. This has all the information on it." She handed the bright yellow flyer to him. He glanced at it, folded it, and put it in his pocket.

"Thanks. I'll see if Sammie would like to go. It sounds like fun."

Christina and Stacey smiled and nodded. As father and daughter walked away, Christina said, "Well, we hope we see you and Sammie at the party."

During the drive home, mom and daughter talked about the harvest party to be held the next Monday night and went over the list of items they needed to purchase. They made plans to go shopping the next morning and would start decorating the church basement that afternoon. Christina had a list of volunteers who would help set up the booths and decorate on Saturday evening and finish the rest of the preparations on Sunday afternoon, giving them time to make any last-minute purchases or adjustments.

CHAPTER 76

Halloween day arrived with a blustery cold front, causing some of the straw and decorations to blow into the neighboring lots.

Fortunately, by the time the party started, the wind had calmed, and the temperatures had risen to a comfortable fifty degrees.

When Christina had mentioned the Halloween activities in passing one Sunday morning back in August, she had no idea that some of the ladies would take those ideas, add a few of their own, and turn the church parking lot and basement into what looked like an old-fashioned barn—complete with ponies to ride and animals to pet.

Stacey volunteered to do face painting, adorning cheeks and sometimes hands with pumpkins, cats, bats, and balloons. Brad helped organize the bowling teams, making sure there were equal numbers on each team, showing the participants how to keep score, and handing out prizes to the winning groups. Nicky ran the ring-toss game, which involved getting plastic bracelets over the tops of pop bottles. He had a grand time showing people how easy it was to accomplish.

As Christina helped in the snack bar area, she would occasionally look around the room, catching glimpsing of her children and being filled with joy as she saw the looks of pleasure on their faces. There were over one hundred children and parents in attendance, giving the basement a carnival-like atmosphere with its various game booths, bright colors, music, and ceaseless movement. The teens of the church ran most of the booths, which included fishing for treasures in a kid-sized pool, bobbing for apples, searching for pennies in a pile of hay, and various relay races. What Christina didn't realize was that she and her children were being observed as a cat watches its prey before pouncing.

As people left, there were a plethora of positive comments, most of which mentioning doing it again the next year. The teens and adults who had volunteered to run the booths and games stayed to clean up, informing Christina they had a great time and wished they had thought of something like this before.

As Christina was wiping the counter, putting the excess food in containers, and ridding the area of garbage, Dr. Carmichael and his little girl walked up. Christina looked up, pushing a strand of hair from her eye, surprise showing on her face.

Wiping her hands on her jeans, she said, "Oh, hi!"

"Mrs. Sanders, I just wanted you to know that Sammie and I *really* enjoyed this evening." The little girl smiled broadly and nodded her head.

"So this is Sammie?" she asked, smiling back at the little girl, who had her daddy's skin and hair coloring and pale green eyes that she surmised must have come from her mother.

"Yes," Dr. Carmichael answered as he smiled adoringly at his daughter.

"Forgive me, but I didn't even know you were here. There were so many people I didn't even see y'all arrive."

"Oh, we came a little later than we had planned. I had an emergency at the hospital I had to take care of. I'm just glad we made it at all." He looked around the room, amazement etched on his face. "Did you do all this?"

"Oh my goodness no! I just gave some ideas that I brought from Michigan. We used to do this at our church every Halloween."

He nodded. "Well, I think this is gonna be a big hit. Wouldn't be surprised it if ends up in the papers."

Christina smiled and nodded. "I would like to see it grow into a yearly event. It's a great way to reach out to the community."

They were interrupted by a small voice. "Daddy, I'm tired. Can you hold me?"

Aaron reached down, picked up his daughter, and kissed her on the cheek as she wrapped her arms around his neck and laid her head on his shoulder. Christiana's heart swelled, and she felt tears sting her eyes. It was such a tender moment—this big, gorgeous man being so tender with his daughter.

"Well, I'd better go and put this sleepy little princess to bed."

Christina smiled and nodded. "I'm glad you had a good time. It was nice meeting you, Sammie."

Sammie smiled and gave a little princess wave. Christina watched as they walked down the hall, thinking, *I really like Steven, but I wouldn't mind getting to know Dr. Carmichael a little better.* She shook the thought out of her head and finished cleaning the counter. She didn't see the older man leave with Dr. Carmichael.

Christina, her children, and the youth pastor were the last ones to leave the building, making sure everything was picked up, swept up, put away, and turned off.

Christina and her kids were looking forward to the next year and excitedly discussed ideas for improvement during the drive home. All in all, it had been a wonderful night—until they arrived home.

As Christina drove the van into the driveway, the headlights illuminated a box on the front porch. Anxious to see what it was, Nicky jumped out of the van and ran to the front, followed closely by Stacey and Brad. Christina was gathering paraphernalia from the back seat when she heard Stacey scream. Dropping her things, she ran to the front of the house, where Stacey was shaking and being held by Brad. Nicky was squatting next to the box and poking its contents with a stick. Christina looked at

Brad, who nodded toward the box. She inhaled sharply when she saw what was inside: a dead rat covered in blood.

"Mom, it's not real!" exclaimed Nicky as he picked the rubbery rat up by the tail and showed it to her. In the dim porch light it had looked *very* real, especially with the fake red blood dribbled on it. Stacey pulled away from Brad and moved closer to Nicky. She started to giggle.

"It looked so real! It scared the crap out of me." Realizing what she had said, she added, "Sorry, Mom," and then reached out to touch the creature with her finger. Christina sighed and nodded—she certainly couldn't punish her child for expressing the same sentiment she felt.

Brad shook his head in amazement and asked no one in particular, "Why would anyone leave that on our porch?"

Christina picked up the box and looked inside, noticing a note with her name on it. Thinking this was a joke, she opened the paper. It read in bold, childlike letters:

Christina: This could have been real; this could have been one of your pets or one of your kids. Go back to Michigan. You are not welcome here!

Christina gasped as she read it once again. She then folded it and put it in her jeans pocket.

Her brow furrowed, Stacey asked, "What does it say, Mom?"

Not wanting to alarm her children, she said with a nervous giggle, "Oh, it just says 'Trick or treat'! Probably some silly kids put it there."

Brad, sensing his mother's evasiveness, gave her a questioning look. She frowned and shook her head and mouthed the word *later*. He nodded.

"Okay, you guys, it's late, and I'm bushed. Let's go to bed."

She was met by protests.

Putting the rat in the box, Nicky whined, "Aw, do we have to?" He held the box close to his chest. "Can I have the rat, Mom?"

"Absolutely not!" she said firmly. "It's going straight into the garbage."

"I think it's cool," he said quietly.

Patting him on the shoulder and holding her hand out for the box, she said, "Sorry buddy, but it's just too ugly and scary for me to have in the house. I'll have nightmares if I know it's nearby."

Nicky sighed and handed the box to his mom.

Once Stacey and Nicky were settled in bed, Brad approached his mother, who was pacing back and forth in the family room.

"Okay, you want to show me the note?"

She sighed and dug the note out of her jeans pocket and handed it to him. He read it. Chewing his bottom lip and frowning he asked, "Who do you think sent this?"

"How should *I* know?" She shrugged and then plopped down in her recliner. He sat opposite her on the couch.

Reading the note again before handing it to her, he asked, "What should we do about this?"

"I think I'll show it to Steven. Maybe he can help me decide if it's something I should take seriously."

"Why *wouldn't* you take it seriously? It was only a couple of weeks ago that you had that blood thinner found in your body, and nobody seems to know how it got there. I'd say someone is out to get you, Mom."

She rubbed her eyes and considered the possibility.

"Well, we can't do anything about it tonight. Let's go to bed and worry about it tomorrow." They knew, however, that they'd worry about it all night.

As she was crawling into bed, the phone rang.

"Hello?" she answered, wondering who would be calling at ten o'clock.

"Christy?"

"Yes." *It has to be Lisa. She's the only one who still calls me Christy.*

"Hey, this is Lisa. I hope I'm not calling too late."

"Oh, hey, girlfriend. I was just crawling into bed, but that's okay. We can still talk. What's up?"

"You know those two girls we talked about from high school, Bonnie and Janet?"

"Yeah?" Sitting up in bed, she asked, "Did you find something out about them?"

"Well, I talked to Dana, and she said that Bonnie works as a legal secretary at a law firm in Dallas. No one seems to know what happened to Janet. After high school, she just sorta disappeared. Maybe she changed her name?"

"Hmm. Good to hear Bonnie is doing well. Hopefully Janet is living a good life somewhere."

"Yeah. Look where we've ended up." She paused for a beat and then asked, "So what's been happening in your life since we talked last?"

Christina realized they hadn't talked in a couple of weeks, so she told her of Stacey's appendectomy and the incident with the rat.

"Oh my gosh, Christy! I'm so sorry all that's happened to you. Is there anything I can do for you?"

"Well, you can pray for our protection. Seems a lot of weird things have been happening lately. Makes me feel a bit paranoid."

"Yeah, I can see why. I'll certainly be praying for you and the kids."

"So how are things in your family?"

"Can't complain. Sarah was on the honor roll, and the twins, well, they're typical eight-year-olds—full of spit and vinegar!"

"How's Tom's job as a small claims lawyer going?"

"He's working hard as usual. He's got a new hobby, though."

"What is it this time?" She smiled, remembering that Tom always had a new hobby.

"He's taken up wood carving."

"What is he carving?"

"He's working on a life-sized duck right now. It looks pretty good."

"What's he gonna do with the duck once it's finished?"

"He says he wants to use it as a lure out in the back tank. I think it's taking longer than he anticipated, so this may be the only one he does."

"Does he still play golf and racquetball?"

Lisa laughed. "Yeah, but not as often as he did. He's got a couple of new clients, so his free time is limited."

Christina yawned. "How's the adoption process going?"

"Slow, but steady. The agency should be contacting us pretty soon about our passports and the shots and legal documents we'll need."

Lisa yawned as well, saying, "I know it's late, so I'll let you go. I just had to let you know about the girls. Maybe we can get together soon."

"I hope so. I miss seeing you and the kids. "

"Yeah, me too. Hey, I haven't talked to Cindy in a while. How's she doin'? She have any new men in her life?"

Christina smiled and said, "What can I say? She's Cindy. Seems she always has a new man in her life." She chuckled. "Actually, there is a new guy, but she doesn't see him often. She says he's just busy all the time. Other than that, she's doing great."

Lisa chuckled. "Cindy was always sort of a wild card. I like being around her, though. You just never know what's gonna come out of her mouth."

"Yeah, that's the truth," Christina said with a smile and a nod.

"Well, I gotta go, babe. I'll talk to you soon. Let me know if you find out who put the rat on your porch." She added with a giggle, "Maybe Tom could sue them."

"Yeah, wouldn't that be something? Winning a lawsuit over a rubber rat!" She couldn't help but chuckle as well. "Well, thanks for calling and telling me about Bonnie and Janet."

They disconnected, and Christina lay in bed a few minutes, thinking about the two girls and wondering what had happened to Janet. Before dropping off to sleep, she prayed a hedge of protection around herself and her family.

CHAPTER 77

The next morning, when Christina's alarm went off, she heard Stacey calling for her. Jumping out of bed, she immediately went to her daughter's room.

Approaching the bed, she asked, "Hey, babe. Why are you awake so early?"

Stacey was on her side facing the door with her knees drawn up.

"Mom, it hurts when I pee. And I feel like I'm gonna puke."

Christina sat next to her on the bed and put a hand on Stacy's forehead. She felt a little warm.

"When did all this start?"

"I got up to go pee about an hour ago, and it hurt. I didn't want to wake you 'cause I thought it would be okay, but when I went again a few minutes ago, it hurt worse."

Christina nodded. "Sounds like you have a bladder infection. I need you to urinate in a cup, though, so I can check to see if there's any blood or floaters in it. I also want to take your temp."

Stacey made a face. "Pee in a cup? Blood? Floaters?"

Her mom nodded. "I know it's not pleasant, but I need to see if there are signs of an infection. If so, I need to call Dr. Carmichael about dropping the sample off or making an appointment for you."

Stacey moaned.

"In the meantime, you need to drink a lot of water today to flush out your kidneys and bladder."

"But then I'll have to pee more, and it'll hurt," Stacey whined.

Christina smiled sympathetically. "It might at first, but it'll feel better later." She patted her daughter's leg. "How about I give you a pain reliever and go fix you a cup of cocoa? I know you don't like to drink anything cold on an empty stomach."

Her daughter yawned. "Can I just have the Motrin? I'd like to go back to sleep now."

Christina considered the request and then said, "You can go back to sleep *after* you have a few sips of cocoa. You need to get some liquids in you."

Stacey sighed. "Okay. But I might be asleep when you come back up."

Christina smiled and patted her leg.

"That's okay. I'll just have to wake you up."

Stacey moaned again. "Man, I was just starting to feel good again."

"I'll go get a cup, and you get up and go in the bathroom and try to pee in it."

"All right," she said, making a face and crawling out of bed to head to the bathroom.

Christina put the thermometer on Stacey's temple, which read a slightly elevated temperature. Stacey gave her a urine sample, which did indeed have floaters in it, drank her cocoa, and had fallen back to sleep—the Motrin having eased her discomfort—by the time Christina went downstairs to make her phone call to Dr. Carmichael. He said she could just drop the urine sample off at the lab, with the understanding that if there was an infection, he would have to see Stacey. Christina was okay with that, as she wanted to stop by the hospital anyway to talk to Steven about the previous night's events. Christina arrived at the hospital and took the urine sample straight to the lab.

"Can you check this out and get the results to Dr. Carmichael?" she asked as she handed the plastic container to the lab technician, whose name tag read Kellie.

"Sure. Could you please fill out some paperwork first?" Kellie asked, handing Christina a clipboard and a pen. Christina filled in the appropriate answers, handed the clipboard and pen back to Kellie, and thanked her. She looked at her watch. *Steven should be finished with his patients by now,* she thought as she headed for his office.

She knocked on his door and was pleased when she heard his voice.

"Come in." He looked up from the paperwork in front of him and was surprised to see Christina. "Hey, I thought you had the day off."

"I do, but I had to stop by the lab. I think Stacey has a bladder infection, and Dr. Carmichael asked me to bring in a urine sample."

"So you decided to come visit me?"

She smiled. "Well, I have something I'd like to discuss with you, if you have a few minutes."

He looked at his watch. "Yeah, my schedule is pretty light today. Mostly I'm just catching up on reading and paperwork." He motioned for her to sit. "So what's on your mind?"

She told him of the previous night's events and showed him the note. He was shocked and worried at the same time.

"What do you think I should do?" she asked chewing on her thumbnail.

"I think you should take this to the police."

"What could they do? Check for fingerprints?"

"Maybe. At least they'd be aware of the threat and if anything else happens, they'd be more apt to do a full investigation."

Feeling the sting of tears in her eyes, she said, "I'm worried that this lunatic might try to hurt my kids."

Steven pondered this and then said, "Probably not. It seems this is more of a threat to you personally."

She looked up at him as a tear trickled down her cheek. "Do you think it's someone here at the hospital?"

Leaning back in his chair and crossing his arms over his chest, he said, "I never thought of that, but I guess it's a possibility."

"I just don't know what to do, Steven. It's been a crazy few months since we moved back here. First, all the missing paperwork, then my accident, then Stacey's appendicitis, and then this threat. Makes me a bit nervous to get out of bed each day wondering what'll happen next."

Steven nodded slightly. "Yeah, it's like you have a dark cloud over you, threatening to rain or hit you with lightning at any given moment."

She couldn't help but smile, because that's exactly how she felt, but she hadn't been able to put her feelings into words.

"I wish I had better answers for you, but I'm just as baffled by all this as you are. I guess I'll just have to say—please be careful, and don't trust anyone."

She smiled slyly. "Not even you?"

He grinned. "Especially not me."

Christina's cell phone vibrated in her pocket. "Excuse me, Steven. I have to get this." He nodded and began stacking papers and magazines in a pile as she talked.

"Hello?"

"Mrs. Sanders?"

"Yes."

This is Dr. Carmichael. I just received Stacey's lab results from the urine sample you brought in this morning. Her urine showed blood and a mild infection. I want to start her on some antibiotics. When did her symptoms start?"

"She said when she got up to urinate around five this morning."

"Is she having any pain?"

"Just some burning and a little cramping. I gave her some over-the-counter pain meds before I left. She went right to sleep, so I guess it worked."

She could sense him smiling. "Well, okay. If her symptoms get worse, you'll have to bring her in. I don't usually give prescriptions to patients without seeing them first, but I'll make an exception in this case."

"Thanks, Dr. Carmichael. I thought the sooner we get the urine checked, the sooner she can start treatment. If you *want* to see her, I can bring her in later."

"No, that's okay. You did the right thing. If she doesn't improve in twenty-four hours, though, I definitely need to see her."

Christina nodded. "Okay. Thank you, I'll come pick up the prescription if you want."

"I'll just call it down to the pharmacy and you can pick it up later."

"Thank you, doctor."

As she started to hang up, he said, "Christina?"

"Yes."

"Could you meet me for lunch in the cafeteria? Say around noon?" She looked at her watch. Ten thirty.

"Is there something else you need to tell me about Stacey?" she asked apprehensively.

"No, I'd just like to talk to you—get to know you better."

"Oh," she answered, surprised. She looked at Steven, who had walked over to his file cabinet and was rummaging around in it. He was probably listening in but was trying not to look or act like it.

"Can we meet tomorrow? I don't want to leave Stacey any longer than necessary."

"Oh, sure. How about lunchtime tomorrow?"

"Um. I guess that would be okay."

"Good, I'll see you then."

She disconnected and furrowed her brow. *So he wants to get to know me better? How about that? Now there's a fine specimen of a man,* she thought as she smiled.

"Everything all right?" Steven asked when she returned the phone to her pocket.

"Well, Stacey definitely has a bladder infection. Dr. Carmichael will start her on antibiotics, and he wants to have lunch with me."

Steven looked surprised. "Lunch? Really? Did he say why?"

"Yep. He said he just wanted to talk and get to know me better."

"Huh."

She shrugged. "I guess I'll have lunch with him tomorrow."

Steven furrowed his brow and nodded.

"Dr. Carmichael seems nice. What do you think of him?" She asked.

"He's a nice guy. His wife was killed a couple of years ago, and he's been a single dad since then. He's great with his patients and their families." *And I don't want you to start dating him,* he thought, but didn't say.

She frowned. "His wife died? What happened?"

"She was in an automobile accident. A drunk driver, I think. Their little girl, Sammie, was only three at the time. It just about devastated Aaron. If it wasn't for his little girl, I don't think he would have recovered so quickly."

"Wow! I had no idea. Good to know, though. Thanks." Looking at her watch, she said, "The prescription should be ready by the time I get down to the pharmacy, and I need to get home. I've already been gone about a half hour. I don't want Stacey to wake up and be alarmed that I'm not there."

Steven nodded. "Okay. Guess I'll talk to you later."

He walked her to the door, and she gave him a finger wave. "Later."

Once she had the prescription, she drove to the Qwik Mart and picked up a bottle cranberry juice and then headed home, unaware that she was being photographed and her actions documented.

Gently waking her sleeping daughter, she told her the results of her urine test.

"Dr. Carmichael says you definitely have a bladder infection, and he gave me a prescription for you to take. So here's the pill and a glass of cranberry juice for you to drink."

"I don't like cranberry juice," she whined, making a face. "It tastes so sour. Why do I have to drink it?"

"Cranberry juice is a great remedy for bladder infections. The acid in it makes your urine unfriendly for bacteria. Besides, this is strawberry and cranberry blended together. I think it tastes yummy."

Stacey took the pill, popped it in her mouth, took the cup of juice, and guzzled it down.

"Hey, you're right. This does taste yummy. Can I have some more?"

Christina smiled and took the empty glass. "Have as much as you like." Kissing her on the forehead, she said, "I'll go get another glass for you."

When she returned, she told Stacey about her phone conversation with Dr. Carmichael.

"So you're gonna have lunch with him tomorrow?" she asked, wiping away the pink mustache from the juice with the back of her hand.

Christina nodded.

Stacey smiled and nodded. "That's cool. He's *so* hot!"

Christina lightly slapped her daughter's leg. "Yes, but we shouldn't go around saying that."

"Why not?"

"It just doesn't sound ... I don't know ... respectful?"

"Okay. So why did he ask you to lunch?"

"He says he just wants to talk to get to know me better."

Stacey smiled and nodded. "Wow, you're becoming quite popular. Now you have *two* doctors wanting to date you."

Christina smiled and shook her head. "Just a nice lunch. That's all."

"Yeah, right."

"I'm gonna do some laundry." Heading downstairs, she asked, "Do you want some lunch?"

She wasn't about to discuss her dating relationships with her twelve-year-old daughter. It was disturbing enough that her daughter was referring to the older man as *hot*.

"I'd like a peanut butter and jelly sandwich and some potato chips and maybe a Dr Pepper."

Christina nodded. "Do you want to come down, or you want me to bring it up?"

"I'll be down in a few minutes," she said as she crawled out of bed and headed to the bathroom.

CHAPTER 78

The next day, Christina kept looking at the clock, anticipating the time when she would be able to meet Aaron for lunch. She found it difficult to focus, as her mind kept playing different scenarios involving the two charming men in her life. *If I had to choose between them, could I? Why am I even thinking along those lines? I don't even know Aaron. Just because he's handsome that doesn't mean he won't be boring—or, worse yet, a jerk. I'm getting way ahead of myself.*

She glanced at her watch. *Time to go.* As she stood in the elevator, she realized her pulse had increased, her palms were sweaty, and her stomach was growling. *Nerves or low blood sugar? Probably a little of both.*

Lunch with Aaron Carmichael was pleasant. He was not only drop-dead handsome, but he was quite charming as well—pulling her chair out for her to sit, paying attention as she spoke, and helping clear the table when they were finished. He was soft-spoken and had an air of reservation about him—like he was afraid to show any strong emotion. He kept asking her questions about herself and her family, and it wasn't until later that she realized she didn't know very much about him except the fact that he was a widower with a five-year-old daughter.

Their time together was cut short when his name was announced over the intercom to report to the pediatric ward, stat. He hurriedly asked if they could have lunch again tomorrow, and she said maybe. Christina called Cindy on the way home.

"Hey, you think you could come over after work?" she asked, pulling in the driveway.

"Yeah. Everything okay?"

"Oh yeah. I just want to talk."

"Is it okay if Samara comes too?"

"Of course!"

When they arrived, Samara headed up to Stacey's room, and the two moms went in the family room. As they sat on the sofa drinking iced tea, Christina told her of the previous night's events and showed her the note.

Cindy gasped. "Who on earth would do such a wicked thing?"

Christina sighed as she took the paper back from Cindy.

"I haven't the foggiest idea. But it kinda scares me."

"Well, yeah. I can see why. I'd be scared too. What are you gonna do?"

"I don't know. Do you think I should just ignore it?" She held the note up. "Steven suggested I get the police involved."

"I think Steven is right. I think you *should* get the police involved and let them know of the other weird things that have been happening." She sat her drink on the coffee table and scooted closer to her friend. Taking Christina's hands in hers and looking into her eyes, she said, "Christy, I'm worried about you. You look tired, and I know you've got to be worried sick about all this and how it will affect your kids. Heck, I'd be going nuts!" Christina nodded.

"Why don't we call Larry at the police department? He's a good friend of mine. He'd be willing to help get to the bottom of this, *and* he would be discreet if we asked him to." Christina was silent for a moment as she considered the suggestion.

She sighed. "All right. I guess it wouldn't hurt to get another professional opinion."

"I'll make the call right now, if that's okay?"

Christina nodded.

Cindy patted her friend's hand and leaned over, grabbing her purse off the floor. After rummaging through it and finding her phone, she began dialing.

Christina pulled her feet up under her bottom and pulled an afghan down around her shoulders. She suddenly felt chilled. She listened as Cindy asked for Larry. Cindy smiled and gave her a thumbs-up sign as she started explaining the situation to the policeman on the other end of the phone line. When she closed the phone with a snap, she smiled and stated that Larry would be over in a few minutes. Christina let out a loud sigh and nodded.

The ball was rolling, and there would be no turning back now. She was scared, but relieved that others were taking this threat seriously and that it wasn't just paranoia on her part.

Watching Cindy return her phone to her purse, she said, "So tell me again who this Larry guy is." Cindy smiled and tilted her head.

"His name is Larry Clifton. He's the police chief of Alva, and he's just a long-time friend."

Christina raised her eyebrows. "Nothing more?"

Cindy retrieved her and Christina's iced tea glasses, smiled playfully, and said, "Nope, that's it." Then she turned and headed toward the kitchen.

When Larry arrived, Christina was upstairs changing into a pair of maroon sweat pants and matching sweatshirt—her favorite lounging outfit. She heard him and Cindy talking downstairs and heard Cindy offer him a glass of iced tea. He had a deep voice with that smooth Texas drawl that she loved to hear coming from a man. Something about the way they said *ma'am* and *darlin'* when talking to a woman made her think of her dad and the warm feeling she would get when he spoke those words to her and her mom.

Larry stood when Christina entered the room and offered his hand in greeting. He was tall and lean, standing at about six and a half feet.

"Howdy, ma'am," he said, taking her hand in his large, scarred, calloused one—unlike the hands of the doctors she knew. He had thinning brown hair that seemed to have a permanent indention of a hat ring that encircled his head above his ears. His face told of hours spent in the Texas sun—leathery brown and etched with deep lines, especially around his clear, Montana-sky-blue eyes that seemed to twinkle when he smiled. Her eyes traveled down to his nose, which, although big, wasn't disproportionately large, and then to his mouth and teeth, which she expected to be tobacco stained but to her surprise were not. *I thought all Texas cowboys chewed, smoked, or dipped tobacco.* She smiled. *Guess not.*

After introductions, they sat, the ladies on the couch and him in the chair across from them. He took out a notebook and pen and leaned toward them as he asked questions. Christina showed him the note. He looked it over and frowned.

"May I keep this, ma'am?"

"Of course."

"Have you had any other threats?"

Christina shook her head. "Not like that."

Cindy blurted out, "Tell him about the hospital stuff."

"Hospital stuff?"

She told him of the misplaced orders, the odd little things that she couldn't explain, and the bleeding incident. He sat up straight and asked why she hadn't notified him sooner.

Nervously massaging her hands, she said, "I didn't think any of that stuff was related, until now. I can sort of see a pattern, and it scares me."

"Well, yes, ma'am, I can see how it would. Seems like the incidents are becoming more personal and dangerous, especially since your life was threatened."

"At first I thought the whole fainting and blood thing was just a fluke—a freak act of hormones or chemicals in my body." She looked over at Cindy, who was nodding and motioning for her to keep going. "But then when the heparin showed up, I knew someone had given it to me somehow." She gave him a bewildered look. "I just can't begin to imagine *who* would want to hurt me. I get along with *everyone* at the hospital, and I haven't encountered any strange people around here—at least that I'm aware of."

He nodded. "Well, ma'am, I would like to do some investigatin' on my own, if you don't mind."

"You do what you have to do." Balling her fists, she said, "When someone starts threatening my family …" She paused, not continuing the sentence. Drawing in a calming breath and releasing it, she said, "Well, anyway, they need to be stopped."

"Yes, ma'am, they do." He stood and held out his hand, which she took again, but this time he covered hers with both of his. Looking up, she smiled shyly.

Patting her hand, he said, "We'll get to the bottom of this. I promise." Cindy watched the interaction and smiled. If anyone could solve a mystery, it was Larry.

She had known him for several years, and they had shared a brief romantic encounter several years ago.

They had met in a bar on the outskirts of Alva. Both were celebrating a recent divorce, and after drinking a little too much, had ended up in a cheap motel room. This meeting, drinking, and sleeping together was fun and exciting for a while, but after several encounters, they both realized there was no depth to the relationship—no *real* chemistry between them. They parted as friends and remained that way through the years. She had even attended his second marriage ceremony. Unfortunately, because of some jealousy issues, she and his second wife didn't get along.

Cindy stood and gave him a hug. Christina smiled. He looked like a giant next to her friend, who seemed to disappear as his big, long arms engulfed her. Christina wondered if something had gone on between them that Cindy had failed to mention. Larry donned his large cowboy hat and headed for the door. *Well, that explains the hat ring,* Christina thought as she smiled and waved when he looked back one last time before entering his car.

Once Larry left, Christina turned to her friend.

"Is there something between you two?"

Cindy laughed. "Uh no. Not now."

Christina looked at her with a quizzical expression.

Cindy pulled her to the couch, and they both sat.

"Okay, I'll tell you the story about Larry and me."

She told Christina of hers and Larry's brief romantic involvement, which didn't surprise Christina at all, knowing Cindy's history with men.

"So we have a special bond, but nothing more will come of it, I'm sure." She smiled. "Besides," she said with a laugh, "as jealous as his wife is, she'd probably hunt me down and shoot me!"

Christina smiled and nodded. "So why haven't I heard of him before now?"

"Well, the whole thing was a bit embarrassing, and I didn't want you to think badly of me. Besides, you were super busy with your own life."

Christina shook her head and sighed. "Cindy, I would *never* think badly of you. You are who you are, and I love you unconditionally. You can tell me anything, and it won't change my love for you. I might not agree with your choices, and I'll tell you so, but I would *never* turn my back on you."

Now it was Cindy's turn to sigh. "I guess I've always known that, but the thing with Larry was a long time ago, and it doesn't matter anymore. So let's just let it go, okay?"

"Sure. Okay, it's gone. By the way, did he go to school with us? 'Cause he looks very familiar."

"No, he graduated from Cleburne."

Shaking her head, she said, "Hmm. I could have sworn I've met him before." Shrugging, she dismissed the idea. Changing the subject, she said, "You'll be interested to know that I had lunch with Stacey's doctor today."

Curiosity piqued, she answered, "Oh, really? So tell me about him."

Christina said, "Well, where should I start? You know that saying 'tall, dark, and handsome'?"

Cindy nodded.

Smiling, she said, "He fits all three categories."

"Ooh, tell me more."

"Remember when Stacey had her surgery?"

"Of course."

"Well, I had never met Dr. Carmichael until the morning after her surgery. Let me tell you, when he came to talk to me, I thought I was gonna swoon."

"Swoon?" Cindy giggled. "I haven't heard that expression in a long time."

"Anyway," she continued, smiling, "he was drop-dead gorgeous."

"So is he married?"

"No. He told me over lunch that his wife died in an automobile accident two years ago."

"Does he have any kids?"

"He's got the cutest little five-year-old girl."

"Oh? So you've met his kid?"

"Yeah, they showed up at the harvest party at church the other night, and he introduced us."

"Interesting." Cindy said nodding. After a brief hesitation, she said, "How sad for her, though—losing her mommy at such a young age."

"I know. But he told me she was adjusting pretty well. His parents live close by, and they keep her when he's at work."

"He sounds dreamy—almost too good to be true."

Christina sighed. "Yeah. I really liked him, but I also like Steven."

"Ooh, torn between two lovers?"

Christina slapped her friend's arm and said, "No! First of all, they aren't my lovers, and second, I'm *not* dating Dr. Carmichael."

"Would you?"

"Would I what?"

"Would you date him if he asked you out?"

Christina made a face and thought about that. "Maybe. I don't know. Depends."

Cindy giggled and shook her head. "Depends on what?"

"Depends if Steven asks me out first and if we click or not."

Cindy nodded her head. "Okay, but I think you should date *both* guys and make an evaluation then."

Christina smiled and nodded. The thought did appeal to her. Maybe she *would* do that.

She slapped her hands on her thighs and stood.

"Hey, why don't we grab the kids and go out tonight? I don't feel much like cooking."

"Sounds good to me. Where do you want to go?"

"I don't know. Let's see where the kids want to eat. Then we'll decide."

"Okay. I need to go home and feed the dog, then meet you back here?

Christina nodded, walked her to the door, and gave her a hug.

"I love you, Cindy. You've been such a great friend. I don't know what I'd do without you."

"Hey, the feelings are mutual," Cindy said as she returned the hug.

"See you later!" she said, waving as she drove away in her little red Camaro.

CHAPTER 79

A week later, on the first Saturday morning in November, which happened to be very cold and rainy, Christina went out to start her van and discovered a flat tire. She clenched her fists, muffled a scream, and stomped her feet. *Why now?* She kicked the tire, which did nothing to it but did hurt her big toe. When she reached down to massage the throbbing appendage, she leaned far enough out of the garage to get drenched with the run-off from the roof. She stood up, shook her head, releasing her drenched ringlets of the icy water, took a deep breath, and blew it out angrily. She said to no one in particular, except maybe the angels who might be standing around, "This isn't funny!" Muttering, she went back into the house to dry off.

Brad was standing at the sink when she came back in. "What's wrong, Mom? Why are you all wet?"

She told him of the little incident with the tire and the rain. As she headed up the stairs to change clothes, she muttered, "I have to call in to work and tell Steven that I'm going to be late. He's going to be irritated, because he's expecting two cardiologists from Dallas in a couple of hours and needs me there to help him get his paperwork organized." Brad couldn't help but smile as he listened to her mumbling as she stomped up the stairs.

The hospital administrators decided to add more cardiac testing equipment and wanted Dr. Dawson to talk with the representatives from Dallas to get a feel for how much it would cost and what would be required to operate and maintain it all.

Christina knew it was a *very* important meeting and started to panic when she realized she might miss it if she couldn't get a ride.

Steven was counting on her. He had asked her a couple weeks before if she would help him the morning of their visit, because he wouldn't have much time before then to prepare. She had promised she would be there bright and early.

Saying a quick prayer, she called Steven, who was concerned but not angry, much to her relief. She then changed out of her wet clothes, called Cindy, explained the situation, and asked for a ride. Cindy said she could drop her off at the hospital on her way to work but wasn't sure she could pick her up. Christina said she'd try to get a ride home from someone, maybe even Steven, but she really needed to get to the hospital ASAP.

Thank you, God! She whispered as she entered Steven's office about an hour before the arrival of the men from Dallas, giving them plenty of time to get the paperwork, which had detailed drawings and questions, organized and ready to present.

After a lengthy question-and-answer time, the visiting cardiologists left with a promise to keep in touch, and Dr. Dawson promised to present the information and money matters to the hospital board within the next week or so. When they left Steven's office, Christina sighed and slumped into the chair across from him.

Smiling, he asked, "How about celebrating our ability to pull this off? I make a pretty good cup of coffee. Want some?"

"I thought you'd never ask!" she said, massaging her temples.

"If I remember right, you like a *lot* of cream and sugar?"

She nodded.

"Would you like me to fix it for you?"

"No, that's okay. I'm pretty finicky." She walked over to the coffee bar and started pouring cream and sugar into the very black liquid.

"My husband always accused me of liking the *idea* of coffee." She poured a little of the coffee out to make more room for the extra cream she needed to add. "David liked his strong and black and wondered why I bothered drinking it when I polluted it so." She smiled at the memory.

Steven took a sip of his coffee and said, "Aah. Good and strong." He watched, slightly amused, as she changed her coffee from dark black to a light creamy color. When finished, they walked back to the seating area next to his desk and sat across from each other.

"I used to drink mine with cream and sugar years ago, but when I was in med school, I learned to drink it black and strong, and I got accustomed to it that way. At times we were required to work twenty-four- to thirty-six-hour shifts, and after about twenty of those hours we lived on adrenaline and caffeine."

"Whew!" responded Christina. "I don't think I would've made it!" *If I don't get at least seven hours of decent sleep, I'm a walking zombie.*

"I've never understood why med students are required to go through such torture. I can't see how it benefits them or the patients." She sipped the sweet brew. "I'm glad we weren't required to do that in nursing school."

"I don't understand it either. Very rarely will I stay up more than eighteen hours, and *only* if I have a very critical patient—but even then I can catnap." There was an awkward silence as they both sipped their coffee.

He leaned forward, their knees almost touching. Her heart gave a flutter, and she felt light-headed as she looked into his clear blue eyes. Noticing that her hands were beginning to shake, she sat her coffee cup on the desk, fearing she might drop it.

"How are you feeling these days?" he asked, looking at her chin.

"Pretty good, actually. I think I've fully recovered from my little accident." She put her hand up to her chin and rubbed it, feeling the bumps from the stitches.

"Good. It's too bad we never figured out where the heparin came from."

"Yeah, the more I think about it, the more nervous I become. What if someone really is out to get me? I often wonder if something like that will happen again." She paused, reclaimed her coffee cup, and took a sip. She looked into her cup and spoke softly.

"I just hope that *if* someone is out to hurt me, they don't decide to attack my family as well." She paused, looking up at Steven with concern etched on her face. "Or instead of."

He nodded and sighed, leaning back in his chair. "Well, I don't know what to think. It's hard to imagine someone trying to hurt you. I mean, who would want to do that?"

"I've racked my brain and can't come up with any possible suspect. Maybe it was a one-time thing just to get my attention or scare me." She paused and smiled sardonically. "It worked."

They both sat silently for a few minutes, sipping the remainder of their coffee. Steven stood, picked up the mugs, and gave her a look that asked, "Do you want more?" She shook her head and watched as he walked to the coffee room. Standing, she stretched and walked over to the wall that held all his certificates of accomplishments.

Pouring himself another cup, he said, "You know, this is nice. We haven't talked for quite some time." He walked in and sat, quietly watching as she read the twenty or so plaques and framed certificates that told of his various accomplishments over the past twenty years.

As she read, she couldn't help but be amazed at the number of nonmedical awards. She turned, smiling, to face him, and pointed at the award that read "Volunteer Fireman of the Year." "What's this about?"

He chuckled, shaking his head. She returned to her seat.

"Ever since I was a kid, I wanted to be a fireman—and a doctor, as well as an actor and a few other strange things." She smiled and nodded knowingly, thinking of her own childish aspirations.

"Well, when I moved back here to open my practice, which started out very small and left a *lot* of time on my hands, I decided to fill those extra hours with something productive. I took some classes on how to be a volunteer fireman, and after working with the guys for a couple of years, they gave me that award."

She nodded as she sat and said, "Hmm, interesting. Did you get to save anyone from a burning building?"

"Yeah, actually, I did. Only once, though."

Leaning toward him, crossing her legs and, resting her left elbow on her knee and her chin on her hand, she said, "Tell me about it." He proceeded to tell her how he and the other firemen were called out to a barn fire. When they arrived, the farmer and his two boys were trying desperately to get the horses out. As the father ran back in for the last horse, a beam fell on his leg, trapping him in the inferno. Steven and his buddy Mack went in and were able to pull the farmer out and rescue the horse before the whole building collapsed.

"It was pretty intense there for a few minutes." Making a face, he added, "I've never been so scared in my entire life. I can look back on that time and honestly say it was an awesome experience. If I had time, I'd go back and do more volunteering." He sighed and shrugged, saying with a crooked smile, "Maybe when I retire."

"I think that's pretty cool." She paused a moment and then added, "My son Nicky would be impressed. He's talked a few times about becoming a fireman. Maybe you should tell him that story."

Steven smiled broadly. "Maybe one of these days I will." Rubbing his chin, he asked, "So he wants to be a fireman?"

Christina nodded.

"Say, do any of your kids want to be doctors?"

She chuckled and shook her head. "Sorry. Stacey wants to be an actress. And believe me, she's halfway there." Leaning back in her seat, she asked, "Did I tell you she was voted Drama Queen by her classmates?"

Steven shook his head and smiled. "No kiddin'?"

"Nope, she can really put on a performance when she has to."

"What about Brad?" Steven asked, sipping his coffee.

"Bradley," she said as she paused to think. "I don't think he knows what he wants to do. He's mentioned going into computer design like his dad, but really, I don't think he's thought very seriously about it lately. Right now, he's busy keeping his GPA up, working part time at Safeway, playing football, and, of course, enjoying the company of girls."

Steven nodded knowingly. He remembered those wonderful, carefree days of being a teen. Of course, at the time they had seemed stressful and tedious. Had it really been twenty years? Because he had what some folks called a photographic memory, learning facts, figures, and other facts in academia had been as easy as drinking water. His counselors during those four years had encouraged him to go into engineering, medicine, or some other scientific field. It wasn't until his second year of college that he decided on a medical major, and during his third year of medical school, the field of cardiology.

After a moment of silence, he said, "I don't have any patients scheduled for this afternoon. Why don't you tell me what's been happening in your life since … say, high school." He leaned back and grinned.

Christina smiled, giving him a quizzical look. "Are you sure you want to hear about *everything* that's happened since high school? That's covering a lot of years, you know!" She chuckled. "It could take hours!"

"Well, okay. Don't tell me everything, just give me a condensed version." He smiled and winked at her. She thought, *Man, he winks like David.*

She blushed. "Okay, here goes …"

Christina recounted the story of how she had met David in that very hospital, their move to Michigan, the children, the deaths of her parents, the various jobs she had, David's death, and her decision to return to Alva.

As she talked, he watched her intently, nodding, responding appropriately with facial expressions and body language. When she would pause, he would ask probing questions to keep her talking, enjoying the sound of her voice.

When she had finished telling her story, she sighed and said, "Okay, it's your turn."

He shook his head and said, "No, not this time. My life certainly hasn't been as exciting as yours. I'll tell you about it another time." He looked at his watch as he stood and stretched. "Gosh, the day is half gone. Do you have any plans for this evening?"

"Well sort of. I was thinking I'd like to go through the remainder of the boxes in my room that contain letters and paperwork that I haven't been able to get to." She shook her head and made a face. "I really dread going through it all. A lot of it is David's work-related stuff and old cards and letters from him." Sighing, she looked down at her hands in her lap. "I think I'm finally ready to start closing the door on that part of my life."

He nodded sympathetically. He knew it was hard to lose a spouse, but a death was much more difficult than a mutually agreed upon divorce.

"It's like this box of papers is the last puzzle piece, and I haven't been able to complete the picture because I can't seem to put that last piece in."

She felt tears sting her eyes and batted her lashes to keep them from completely forming and running down her cheeks.

His heart ached for her. He reached over, took her hand, and patted it.

"It's gotta be so hard for you. David sounds like he was a great guy."

She nodded, not looking at him, but continuing to stare at her hands.

He said gently, "As difficult as it is, it's something that needs to be done."

She nodded again and said quietly, "I know."

"Tell you what," he said, patting her hand. "When you get finished, why don't you give me a call, and we'll go out for dinner or dessert of coffee or something."

She smiled and looked up at him. "That's sweet of you. I'll see how I'm doing, and if it's not too late, I'll give you a call."

He patted her hand again and smiled.

"Alrighty then. The sooner you go and get started on that stuff, the sooner you'll be finished." *And the sooner I'll see you again.* He extended his hand and helped her stand.

"Thanks, Steven." She smiled and turned to go.

"Christina?"

She turned back to face him.

"Uh, be careful."

She cocked her head and smiled. "Okay."

She thanked him again, for being interested and caring and for the cups of coffee.

He replied in a comical way, "Oh, shucks, ma'am, t'weren't nothin'!"

She couldn't help but laugh. Now *that* was the Steven Dawson she knew and loved! *Loved? Careful, girl.*

Halfway down the hall, she stopped. "Dang it, I forgot. I don't have a ride home." She turned around and reentered Steven's office.

"Excuse me, Steven?" she said as she stepped into the room. He was washing the coffee mugs and turned when he heard her voice.

"Yes? Are you all right?" he asked, drying his hands on a towel and approaching her with a concerned look on his face. She thought that was so cute.

Smiling, she said, "Yes. I'm fine. I just remembered that I don't have a ride home, and I don't have my cell phone with me. I must have left it on the bed when I changed clothes. May I borrow your phone to call Cindy to come get me?"

"Nonsense. I'll drive you home."

"No, I don't want to be a bother, really. Cindy said she'd come get me." *Well, what she said was that she probably couldn't come get me, but I don't want Steven to think that I planned for him to take me home.* "I'll just give her a quick call."

"Christina, don't bother her. I'll take you home. It's not like you live a long way from my house." He went back to the sink. She smiled.

"Let me finish here. Then we'll go."

"Can I help you?" she asked, and he handed her a dishtowel.

CHAPTER 80

Stacey spent Saturday morning lounging around in her bedroom reading while Nicky was in his room playing video games. Brad had called a couple of his friends over, and they had changed the tire on the van for his mom. When finished, they all hung out in Brad's room. Stacey could hear them laughing even though the music from his stereo was loud enough to make her bed vibrate. *Mom wouldn't like that if she was home,* she thought as she found her CD player, put in her favorite CD, and put the earphones in to drown out her brother's music. She wondered what teenage boys talked about. *Probably girls.* She shook her head and went back to reading her book.

In reality, Brad and his friends hardly ever mentioned girls. They talked about the latest movies, video games, cars, and motorcycles. Brad's friend James had a cool Honda 150 that he rode around on the back of his property. Brad was just itching to take it for a ride someday. As his friends talked, his mind drifted. *Maybe I should start saving for a street bike instead of a car. It would be cheaper and wouldn't require as much gasoline as a car. I'll have to run that past Mom, though. I'm not sure how she feels about motorcycles since we've never discussed them. It might be a tough sell if she has bad feelings about them. Oh well, nothing ventured, nothing gained.*

Stacey sat on her bed reading and unconsciously petting a purring Chloe on her lap. She was on the last chapter of the first book in the Chronicles of Narnia series, *The Lion, the Witch, and the Wardrobe.* Her dad had read this book to her and her brothers the winter before he died and had explained that even though Aslan was a lion, he was a very good, kind, and wise lion and was not to be feared—unless you were the White Witch or her followers. She had loved hearing about the kids' adventures in Narnia and decided that now that she was older, she would reread the series.

She was determined to finish the chapter before her mom came home but paused in her reading when she thought she heard the house phone ring and turned down her CD player to listen. Not hearing anything further, she shrugged, turned the volume back up, and continued to read. Benji, who was lying quietly at the foot of her bed, suddenly sat up, cocked his head as if listening, and then started to bark. She stopped reading and went to the door. Benji was right behind her and started scratching the door to get out. She opened it, and he ran down the stairs, barking. She stood in her doorway listening. *Maybe Mom's home.* Sighing, she closed the door and returned to her book when she heard Danny's voice.

"Hey, anybody home?" She didn't bother getting up, knowing that Danny would head straight for Nicky's room.

Nicky sat in front of his Nintendo PlayStation, pushing buttons with his thumbs and watching intently as the characters jumped and scurried across the screen, gathering their treasures before the opposing team was able to. So intense was his concentration that he jumped when he heard a knock on his door.

"Yeah?" he said, pausing the game and standing.

"Hey, Nicky, it's me, Danny. Can I come in?"

"Sure!" he said excitedly, rushing to the door and meeting his friend halfway through it. He reached out and hit him on the arm. "What are you doing here?"

"Well, I tried calling, and no one answered the phone, and I remembered you said you'd be home all day, so I thought maybe I should come down and check on y'all."

Nicky nodded. "Oh, sorry about the phone. We can't hear it when we have our doors closed," he said, walking over and closing his again. "Can you stay a while?" Nicky asked, heading for his Nintendo game.

"Yeah. I gotta call my mom, though. Let her know y'all are okay. I can ask her if I can stay a while."

"Okay. I'll come downstairs with you while you call. I need to get a drink anyway."

After a few minutes, they were back upstairs in the enclosed room, battling each other on the game screen.

Christina arrived home and was annoyed when she saw the back door standing wide open. "What the …" Entering and closing the door, she stood in the kitchen a moment and listened. The phone began to ring. She called out, "I'll get it," as if anyone could hear her over the loud music coming from upstairs. She set her purse on the counter and picked up the receiver after the third ring.

"Hello?"

"Christina?" a scratchy female voice inquired.

"Yes?"

"Christina, this is Ellie Sterling from church."

"Oh, yes, Ellie. It's so nice to hear from you. How are you doing?"

"Well, I'm just fine, but I called to ask how you and the children are doing."

"We're doing quite well, Ellie. I'm getting used to working, and the kids are adjusting to their schools." She paused, sensing there was more to this phone call than a simple "How are you?" "Is something wrong?"

"Well, dear, I woke up during the night last night from an awful dream, and I can't even remember what it was, but you and your kids kept coming to my mind. I prayed for you, but I've just been thinking about y'all all day. Thought I should call and make sure everything's all right."

"Hmm, well, we've had a few little things happen that have been stressful, but nothing really drastic. I do appreciate your concern, however, and prayers on our behalf are always welcome."

"All right, dear. If you need anything, please feel free to call me. I have a lot of free time on my hands these days."

"Thank you, Ellie. I'll keep that in mind. Again, thank you for your concern and prayers. I'll see you at church tomorrow?"

"Well, Lord willin' I'll be there. Have a good night, dear."

"You too." She replaced the receiver. *That's interesting. I guess it's good I still have a landline or I would have missed Ellie's call. Maybe I'll keep it for a while longer.*

Benji came in and gave her a doggy kiss on her hand. She reached down and scratched his head. The music from Brad's room made her insides vibrate. She took off her wet coat, hung it on the coat rack, and headed up the stairs, followed closely by Benji.

Coming to Stacey's door first, she knocked quietly, thinking her daughter might be sleeping. She was still recovering from her surgery and tired easily. She was surprised when the door opened and Stacey stood there smiling.

"Hi, Mom."

"Hey girl, how are you?" she asked as she hugged her child, who was nearly as tall as she.

"I'm okay." Lightly patting her incision area, she said, "Still feeling a little sore and tired, though. I thought I'd be back to my old self by now. This is taking a lot longer to heal than I thought it would."

"Well, honey, it usually takes a good three months to recover from surgery."

"Three months!" she said with disgust, walking back in her room and sitting on the edge of her bed. "It's been a month!" Pounding her fists on the bed, she said, "I hate being like this! I can't even do my dance routines for the play yet. The teacher says *maybe* I can start back practicing in another week or so, after she gets a doctor's note saying I can."

Christina sat by her daughter and put an arm around her shoulders, pulling her close and kissing the top of her head. "I know this is hard for you right now, but the time will pass quickly, and before you know it, you'll be back in full swing."

"Mom, the play is only six weeks away. I don't know if I can learn *all* the dance routines by then."

"Oh, baby. You're a quick learner, and I'm sure your friends will help you learn them in plenty of time. I think you worry too much."

Stacey looked at her mom, rolled her eyes, and sighed. "Okay, maybe you're right. It'll all work out. I guess I'm just not as positive about things as you are."

Christina hugged her again and then stood to go. Standing in the doorway, she asked, "Is Nicky in his room?"

"Yep. He and Danny. I think they're playing Nintendo."

"Oh. Okay. I'm gonna say hi to them."

"Do you want me to help you with dinner?" Stacey called out before the door completely closed.

"Maybe later. I want to work in my room for a little while. Thanks." Knocking on Nicky's door, she heard two voices say in unison, followed by a giggle, "Come in!" She opened the door.

"Hey guys, just wanted you to know I'm home." Looking up, they smiled, nodded, and said, "Okay." Then they quickly turned their attention back to the screen.

She closed the door, shaking her head and smiling. *They are so cute.*

She walked across the hall to Brad's door and knocked loudly. All of a sudden it became quiet. Brad opened the door, thinking it was Stacey or Nicky, and said a little too harshly, "Yeah?" He was taken aback when he saw his mom standing there and quickly changed his demeanor. "Oh, hi, Mom."

She gave him a stern mom look. "Your stereo is a bit too loud. Could you turn it down a notch?" She then looked in the room, saw the other two boys, and said hi to them.

"Hi, Mrs. Sanders," they said in unison as they waved.

"Sorry about the noise," said the one named Billy, who sat nearest the door. She smiled and nodded.

Brad made a face and said, "Yeah, sorry about the noise. I'll take care of it."

"Okay," she said and turned to go, hearing the door close quietly behind her. She walked down the hall and opened the door to her room, allowing Benji to enter and jump on the bed. She sat beside him, removed her shoes, and lay back on the soft surface, enjoying the few moments of quiet before getting up to conquer the remaining boxes around the room. Benji lay down beside her, resting his head on her belly.

"Oh, Benji, you're such a sweet boy," she said as she rubbed his soft ears. After relaxing to the point of sleepiness, she jumped up, startling Benji, who let out a *woof.*

"Sorry Benji. It's okay. I just need to get up or I'm gonna fall asleep."

She changed into her sweats, looked around the room, and decided to start unpacking the box nearest her. She was tired of her room looking like a storage unit with boxes and clothes and things piled around the fringes.

The first box contained winter items—hats, mittens, gloves, scarves, and heavy sweaters—which she knew wouldn't be needed in the warmer Texas winters. *I should have sold them in the garage sale or donated them, but chose to hang on to them for what reason?* She wasn't 100 percent sure—maybe nostalgia. Several of the items belonged to David and the kids when they were younger. She shook her head and started sorting through the pile, telling herself to keep one favorite pair of mittens or gloves for each kid and one of David's things. The rest would go to Salvation Army. *There are people who need these items more than we do.*

She continued sorting, catching herself remembering moments when the items had been worn. It was especially difficult to put aside the wool sweaters that she and David had shared. He used to tease her by saying she bought *him* sweaters that *she* could also wear—which was partly true. She always bought sweaters in the colors that would not only complement him but also add a nice touch to her wardrobe as well.

Putting one of the sweaters to her nose and inhaling David's woodsy, musky scent, she just couldn't bring herself to part with it.

Instantly a memory of David and the kids wrestling in the snow the winter before he died flooded her brain. It was the middle of December, and about ten inches of snow had fallen during the night. The whole area was officially snowed in, including the schools, David's office, and the cardiologist Christina worked for. The sky had been a crystal clear azure blue, and the sun glinted off the freshly fallen snow like it was made of diamonds. After eating a late breakfast, they all bundled up in their snow gear and headed out to sled down the hill at the back of their property. The kids had built a snow fort in one of the deep ditches next to the fence line while she and David built a snowman and -woman in the front yard. Later that day, the kids built replicas of themselves next to the snow couple.

It had been a glorious day that would be etched in her memory forever. Feeling the familiar stinging in her eyes, she quickly put the sweater aside. She didn't have time to get lost in any more memories.

After she sorted through a couple more boxes, she heard a knock at her door.

"Come in," she said, wrestling with the lid as she stuffed one more sweater into an overstuffed box.

She heard her door open and turned to see two boys standing in the doorway.

"Mom," Nicky said, "we're hungry." She glanced at the clock by her bed and was shocked that two hours had passed since she entered the bedroom—she had only managed to sort through three boxes. She sighed and comforted herself, thinking, *They were large boxes.*

She reached out with her hands, and Nicky and Danny grabbed them and helped pull her to a standing position. She brushed herself off and looked around the room. *Am I ever going to finish this?* Sighing, she told the boys to go on down to the kitchen—she needed to take care of a couple more items. She heard them run down the stairs, followed by Benji. She folded the treasured sweater, placed it in a large Ziploc bag on her bed, and left the room.

CHAPTER 81

On the way home from dropping Christina off, Steven remembered an important article he had been reading that morning while waiting for Christina. A friend from college had written about a new thermal-imaging scanner designed to detect any amount of plaque buildup in the arteries in and around the heart. He had placed it in his desk drawer when Christina walked in and had forgotten about it until now. He wanted to go home and have a hot shower and relax but knew it would gnaw at him like hunger pangs until he finished reading it.

He drove past his house and circled back to the hospital.

As he sat behind the desk and looked through the drawer for the magazine, he heard a knock at the door. *Who on Earth could that be?*

"Come in."

"Dr. Dawson?"

"Yes," he replied, looking up to see Janet Washburn. Her beauty always captivated him—the raven hair that was graying at the temples, big brown doe eyes, and full lips. His eyes did a quick inventory of her well-proportioned body as well, and he felt a stirring in the pit of his stomach. As attractive as she was, however, she seemed a little worn around the edges. She didn't light up a room when she walked in like Christina did. *Christina? Why am I comparing Janet to her?*

"Janet? What are you doing here? I didn't think you worked on Saturdays."

She smiled as she crossed the room, "I don't usually, but one of the nurses on the cardiac floor went home sick, so I came in to finish her shift."

Steven nodded. "Oh. So what brings you down here?"

"Here is the file you wanted on Mrs. Jacobs." She handed the folder to him and lightly touched his hand as he took it. He felt a tingle of electricity when their skin met. He jerked and looked surprised.

"Oops! Must be a bit of electricity in the air!" she said, smiling demurely and biting her bottom lip as she withdrew her hand.

"Yeah, must be," he said as he rubbed the tingling area. He suddenly felt warm and uncomfortably crowded. Standing, he took a couple of steps toward the door, putting more distance between them.

"Um, thanks, Janet. You didn't need to bring it by today. It could have waited till Monday."

She waved her hand and furrowed her brow as if to say, "It's no bother."

"Do you want me to go over any of the information with you?" she asked in a silky smooth, sultry voice, batting her long lashes and moving closer.

Sidestepping and putting his desk between them, he answered, "Uh, no, that's okay. I'll look them over later." She stood there a minute looking him over. *Gosh, he's so dang handsome! I'd do just about anything to make him fall in love with me.*

She noticed his quick jerky movements as he straightened the papers on his otherwise orderly desk. Stifling a smile, she noted, *I make him nervous. That could be a good thing. It could mean he's interested but doesn't know how to express it.* She felt a slight smile twitch her lips.

Realizing he wasn't going to engage in any further discussion and not knowing what else to do, she sighed and turned to go. Looking back over her shoulder as she reached the door, she said, "Call me anytime if you need anything." She winked, smiled, and glided out the door.

Dr. Dawson let out the air that he was unconsciously holding hostage. *That was weird!* he thought. He sat at his desk, pondering what had just taken place. Had Janet really come on to him, or was it just his imagination? Whatever it was, there was no denying his body had betrayed him by reacting to the visual and sensual stimuli. It was definitely a good thing they weren't working close together for an extended amount of time, especially when she turned on the charm.

He sighed, retrieved his magazine, and headed home. He envisioned taking a hot shower (no, maybe a cold one would be better), drinking a hot cup of coffee, and then curling up in his favorite easy chair to finish the article. He hoped Christina would call when she finished her unpacking so they could spend more time together.

As Janet left Dr. Dawson's office, she paused outside his door and smiled. He had definitely reacted to her presence. She knew she had that effect on men when she wanted to. Of course, the little spell she'd cast the previous night must have helped a bit. She was pleased that her effort to rattle him had been successful. Maybe tonight he would be dreaming of her instead of Christina. *Christina.* She was really getting on her nerves. No matter what she did to make her look incompetent, she always came through the crisis with hardly a nerve frayed. Steven and his aunt kept covering for her, making Janet wonder how long they would continue that. *Well, I'm gonna have to continue my efforts to either get Christina flustered enough to quit or, better yet, make Dr. Dawson angry enough to recommend she be fired.* She smiled, liking the idea of Christina being fired.

On her way out the door, she stopped by the gift shop to purchase a little charm for her daughter. Her thirteenth birthday was coming up in a week, and she wanted to get her something special to mark this momentous occasion. She sighed. *Hard to believe it's been thirteen years since I gave birth to my precious daughter,* she thought as she looked at the charms displayed under the glass countertop. The charm she selected was a sterling silver 13 with a diamond in the center.

On Linda's first birthday, Janet had bought a little heart locket and put her daughter's picture in it. On her second birthday she purchased a number 2 with a teddy bear next to it. Each year thereafter, she purchased another charm. On her tenth birthday, she purchased a bracelet and presented the charms and bracelet to her daughter. Linda was rarely seen without it, pleasing her mother immensely.

When Janet arrived home, she found her girl curled up on the couch, so engrossed in a book that she barely acknowledged her mother's presence. Janet walked over and planted a kiss on her daughter's head. Leelee closed her book and smiled up at her mother.

"Hey, Mom. How was your afternoon?"

Janet plopped down next to the girl and drew her into her arms.

"It was all right. I went to the bank, the post office, and then the hospital." She paused and sighed. "It's better now that I'm home. What did you do this afternoon?"

"Oh, the usual—watched TV, did my laundry, cleaned my room, and just sat down with this new book."

Janet looked at the cover: *This Present Darkness* by Frank Peretti.

Picking it up to read the back cover, she asked, "Where did you get this?"

"Stacey let me borrow it. It's all about angels and demons and how they interact with us humans. It's pretty good so far, but I've only read the first chapter."

Reaching over and taking the book from her mother, she laid it on the couch between them.

Janet wasn't sure what to say or how to react. She didn't believe in angels or demons. She thought the whole idea of unseen beings that did our bidding was a bunch of hogwash created by people who needed a reason to explain things they didn't understand—although there were things that happened from time to time that even she couldn't understand. She believed that there was a great cosmic energy field that was accessible to anyone who understood how to tap into it.

She had believed in God at one time in her life, when she was little, but he hadn't been there for her when she needed him to protect her from her father and others who had taken advantage of her through the years. *Why should I believe in a heavenly Father whom I can't see or hear when I wasn't been able to rely on my earthly one? It's easier to rely on myself and the earthly powers within my grasp.*

"So Leelee, what do you think of demons and angels? Do you think they're real?"

"I don't know." On a sigh, she said, "Never really thought about it before. Stacey and I have been talking a lot about God and stuff lately, though. Makes me kinda wonder about it."

"Stacey Sanders?" Janet asked, even though she knew the answer.

Leelee nodded.

Not wanting to make an issue of it, she sighed and said, "Hmm. Well, we *all* have to make our *own* decisions about God—what he is and if he even exists."

"Mom?"

"Yeah?"

"What do *you* think about angels and demons and God?"

Janet rubbed her face with her hand and sighed.

"Honey, let's talk about it at another time. I just remembered I need to run to the grocery store for a couple of items." Standing, she asked, "You want to come with me?"

Her daughter nodded, stood, and stretched.

"Good, I'll be out in a minute." She headed for the bathroom.

Janet closed the door and leaned against it. "Whew." She blew out the air in her lungs. She had hoped to avoid the whole God thing for a few more years, or, better yet, all together—kinda like how she wanted to avoid the sex talk. Some things just couldn't be avoided.

Her plan had been to introduce Leelee to the art of spell casting on her thirteenth birthday. That was when *she* had first learned to cast spells and use nature and cosmic energy to do *her* bidding. She knew Linda was pretty levelheaded and mature for her years and would be able to understand and not misuse the power she could gain from such knowledge. She smiled as she thought how happy and surprised Linda would be to receive the books she had purchased for her.

CHAPTER 82

As Christina was washing the dinner dishes, the phone rang. Drying her hands on the dishtowel, she answered it.

"Hello."

"Mrs. Sanders?" a male voice heavy with a drawl inquired.

"Yes."

"Mrs. Sanders, this is Larry Clifton, the police chief."

"Oh, yes, Chief Clifton. I remember."

"Mrs. Sanders, I hate to bother you at this time, but I was thinking about you and wondering if anything else unusual has happened this week."

Christina smiled and chuckled slightly. "Well no, except for the flat tire on my van this morning. We've had a pretty good week all in all."

"That's good to hear. I've done some checking around and haven't come up with any suspects in the rat incident, but I have several people keeping their eyes and ears open. *Someone* is bound to slip and admit to the prank, and then the mystery will be solved."

"So you think it was just a prank?" she asked, feeling it was more ominous than that.

"Well, yes, at this time I do. If there haven't been any other threats or mischief, then I think we can assume it's nothing serious."

Christina sighed. "Yeah, you're right. I guess I've gotten a little paranoid, especially with the incidents at the hospital and then the Halloween thing. I'm sure you're right and I'm making too big a deal of all this."

"Well, ma'am, I don't want you to feel that we aren't concerned about you and your family. As I said, we'll keep our eyes and ears open for any leads. You just hang in there and continue doing what you normally do, but please don't hesitate to call me if anything out of the ordinary happens "

"Thank you, Larry—I mean Chief or Mr. Clifton."

"That's okay, ma'am, you can call me Larry. Any friend of Cindy's is a friend of mine."

"Okay, then thank you, Larry. I'll call if anything weird happens."

When she placed the phone back on the counter and thought about the Halloween incident again, she knew beyond a shadow of a doubt that it was an intentional act to scare her—which it did. Now if she could just figure out *who* would do such a thing, she could confront them and find out why.

As she returned to the dirty dishes, the house phone rang.

She called out, "Stacey, can you get that?"

"Sure, Mom … Hello? Oh, yes, just a minute." She handed the phone to Christina, who had to wipe her hands again before taking it. "Some guy," she whispered as her mother took the phone.

"Hello?"

"Christina, it's Steven."

"Oh, hi!" She slapped her forehead with her palm. "I was supposed to call you when I finished in my room. I'm sorry, I completely forgot."

"I was wondering if we could go out for some coffee and dessert."

Christina looked at the clock over the sink. Seven thirty.

"Wow, I didn't realize it was so late."

"That's okay. I figured you were busy and forgot—that's why I called you. So are you free to go for some coffee?"

Smiling, she said, "I'd like that. I could use the break."

"Okay. I'll be over in about fifteen minutes. Do you think the kids want to come along?"

"That's nice of you to ask, but I think they'd rather stay at home. There's a good movie on they want to watch."

"Okay. I'll see you in a few minutes."

Christina told the kids she was going out for coffee with Dr. Dawson and then ran upstairs, changed clothes, checked her makeup, and ran her fingers through her hair, noticing her shaking hands.

She willed herself to slow down and take a few calming breaths. As she was walking down the stairs, she heard the doorbell ring.

"Mom!" called Nicky. "It's Dr. Dawson."

CHAPTER 83

E d and Tom decided to head back to Alva the following week, once they knew the Sanders family would be back to its normal routine. They arrived Saturday night and checked into a room at the Holiday Inn, deciding to have dinner at the Black-Eyed Pea. The waitress had just arrived to take their order when Ed looked across the room and saw Cindy. As he looked in her direction, she looked in his, and their eyes met, causing them both to gasp. Her eyes were as big as saucers, and he was sure his looked like a deer caught in headlights. He nodded at her, and she smiled, blinking a few times as if to clear her vision. He held up a finger to let her know he would be over as soon as he had finished ordering his food.

She was so stunned at seeing him that she just stared, unblinking, until a waitress came to refill her coffee cup. It was only then that she looked down at her cup and felt as if she was going to be sick. Her heart started doing a tap dance against her ribs, and her stomach felt as if it wanted to jump out of her throat. As she picked up her coffee mug, her hand was shaking so badly she had steady the cup with the other one to avoid spilling the contents onto the table.

Once Ed had ordered his medium-well steak, a baked potato, and green beans, he sauntered over to Cindy's table.

"Hey, darlin', fancy meetin' you here."

Cindy looked up at him with a half smile and said, "Yeah, fancy that."

"Do you mind?" he asked as he motioned to the seat opposite her. She shook her head and sighed.

"So what's a fine gal like you doin' in a place like this?"

She rolled her eyes and shook her head. "Really? That's the best line you can come up with?"

He grinned. "Okay. How are you?" he asked as he adjusted his bulk into the booth.

"Fine. And you?" she asked, trying to keep her voice steady.

"I've been busy. That's why I haven't gotten back to you. We've been doing a lot of out-of-town work lately. Long hours."

"Yeah, right," she said as her eyes bore into him.

Gosh, he hated when women did that. It was as if they could look right into his mind and soul and know everything he ever did or planned to do.

"Let me see your hands."

"What?"

"Let me see your hands," she said again.

Ed put his hands on the table, and she took them, turning them over and examining each digit. "Hmm."

"What?" he asked as he withdrew them.

"I was just checking to see if your fingers were broken or injured."

"Why?"

"'Cause if they had been injured or broken, then I would understand why you haven't picked up the phone and dialed my number. But being they are perfectly fine, I guess you haven't called because of some other reason." She looked at him with her eyebrows raised.

Ed felt uncomfortable at her boldness and squirmed in his seat. He looked around the room and then lowered his head and spoke almost in a whisper.

"I'm sorry." He sighed and rubbed his eyes with his hands. *How can I tell her without really telling her?*

Tom watched the interchange between Ed and Cindy and wondered what they were saying. He couldn't hear them but could read their body language, and both seemed to be tense and uncomfortable, which made him a bit uncomfortable. He wasn't sure what would happen next, having witnessed similar situations where the woman would get hysterical or angry and start yelling, screaming, and crying—or, worse yet, throwing things. He sure hoped that wouldn't be the scenario with this situation.

Keeping her voice low and calm, she asked, "Do you really think 'I'm sorry' is good enough?"

He shrugged, sighed, and said, "You're right." To avoid meeting her eyes, he looked at his hands. *I have to tell her something. Anything but the truth. At least not here and now.*

"My workload has been heavy and intense. My boss has been on my back about meeting deadlines." He looked up, only to see her staring at him with her head cocked and eyebrows raised. She wasn't buying any of it.

"Okay. So you say you've been intensely busy. That still doesn't explain *why* you haven't called. Maybe I'm being a dumb blonde about all this, but I thought we had something. I believed you when you said you enjoyed my company and would call me. Not that I sat by the phone waiting." She looked down at her hands and fidgeted with her rings.

Ed sighed heavily, lowering his eyes and feeling bad about disappointing her. *Gosh, I really am a jerk.* He reached across the table and took her small hands in his. She looked up, and when their eyes met, that spark of electricity flowed through them again. She inhaled sharply, her eyes widening. She knew he felt it too as his hands tightened around hers.

"Look, I want to be totally honest with you, but I can't right now. I *do* like you and I *do* enjoy your company, that's no lie, but ..." He paused, trying to think of the right words to say.

"But what?"

"Cindy, when this assignment is over, I promise I'll tell you everything you need to know."

"Look, the *only* thing I need to know is whether you want to continue this relationship. I don't want to wait around wondering if you're gonna call or show up unexpectedly. I don't want to play any games. Been there, done all that, and I'm getting too old to play."

Ed nodded and smiled. "No games. I *do* want to continue seeing you, and I *will* call you more often. It's just—right now I can't commit to anything but this job assignment."

"When will you be finished with this job?" she asked, removing her hands from his and reaching for her coffee.

"Hopefully soon. Tom and I ..." He nodded in the direction of his partner. She glanced that way and nodded. "We have to tie up some loose ends around here. Then we should be done."

She looked at him, wondering for the thousandth time if he was being honest or leading her on like most of the other men in her life had done. As she gazed into his big brown eyes, she felt her heartstrings twang. *If I let myself fall for him and he hurts me, I swear I'll never let another man near my heart,* she thought as she sighed and nodded. He certainly looked genuinely remorseful, and she decided to give him one more chance.

"All right. In the meantime, please keep in touch." She reached over and patted his hand, asking, "Can we see each other again this week?"

He shook his head. "I'm sorry. Like I said, until this job is finished, I can't have any distractions."

She slowly nodded. "Okay. Guess you'd better get back to your table. I see your food has arrived, and mine is getting cold."

He smiled and took her hand and kissed it. She felt weak with desire.

Standing, he said, "I'll call you next week."

She nodded and smiled as she watched him walk away. Her heart raced, and her stomach did flip-flops. She looked at her plate of food and suddenly lost her appetite. As the waitress passed by, she asked for her bill and a box. She couldn't be in the same room as Ed and not be *with* him.

When Ed returned to his table, Tom asked how things went. He gave him a quick synopsis and dove into his food. Tom watched in amazement. Nothing ever seemed to affect Ed's appetite—well, except when Celina died and Ed lost thirty pounds.

Ed's back was toward Cindy's table, and he was unaware of her departure. Tom saw her leave but didn't bother telling Ed. They finished their meal and headed for the Holiday Inn, where they discussed their plans for the week.

Ed sat on the bed and leaned his head against the headboard.

"We'll follow the same plan we did before. When Christina and the kids leave for the day, we'll just go in and get those bugs."

Tom said, "Okay," and headed for the bathroom, where a nice, hot shower was waiting for him. As Ed listened to the water running and Tom singing a very poor rendition of "Summer in the City," he thought about Cindy. He had been shocked to see her, causing his heart to do a back flip. He hoped he had handled the situation properly, not wanting to hurt her—or, worse yet, cause her to distrust or dislike him. He knew if he wanted to continue a relationship with her, he needed to be up-front and honest about who he was and what he did for a living.

He played different scenarios in his mind about how he might approach the subject and how she might react and, not liking any of them, sighed. He needed some supernatural intervention. Listening, he heard the shower stop, knowing he only had a few minutes. He sat up in bed and put his head in his hands.

"God, I know I don't talk to you often enough, but I would *really* appreciate a bit of wisdom and maybe some of your divine intervention in this thing between Cindy and me. I'm just not sure what to do." He heard Tom open the door and quickly said. "Thanks, God. Amen."

"Were you talking to me?" Tom asked, drying his hair with the white fluffy towel.

"Nope." Ed didn't want to discuss his spiritual dealings with Tom. He swung his feet off the bed and stood.

"Could have sworn I heard you say something."

"All right, I was talking to God."

"Really?"

Ed nodded. "Yeah, really."

Tom stared at him a moment, nodded, and said, "That's cool."

Heading to the bathroom door, Ed asked, "Hey, did you leave any hot water for me?"

"I doubt it." Tom chuckled as the bathroom door closed.

Fortunately for Ed, there was plenty of hot water, which he basked in to ease the tension in his neck and back.

CHAPTER 84

As Christina sat in the pew Sunday morning, trying desperately to concentrate on what the pastor was saying, she couldn't help but let her mind wander back to the previous night's events. After Steven's phone call, she had told the kids of her plans to go out for coffee and dessert with him. They were surprised and pleased, and Stacey gave her opinion on what she should wear.

"Mom, those new jeans you bought and that striped turtleneck sweater look really good on you. I think you should wear those."

She did, and Steven noticed and commented on how nice she looked. He took her to a cute little coffee shop in downtown Alva called Rosie's. She had never been there, although she had driven by on several occasions and promised herself that someday she would visit. Who would have thought it would be with Steven?

The coffee shop was located on a side street across from the courthouse and next to the post office. It had been someone's home at one time and had been converted into a cozy place to enjoy not only coffee, but also teas, fruit drinks, and a variety of pastries and desserts. During the lunch hour, it also offered little sandwiches and a choice of homemade soups. There were couches and tables in the front two rooms, and the larger dining room had a fireplace containing a beautiful fire that gave the room a warm glow and feel. There were couches and large, overstuffed chairs in front of the fireplace, which was so inviting, reminding her of how she and David used to curl up on the sofa in front of their own fireplace in Michigan.

Fortunately for her and Steven, the room was empty, and they were able to sit on the couch and enjoy both the fire and each other's company in privacy. As they sipped their coffee and nibbled on spice cookies, Steven finally opened up and told her his life's story since high school, some of which she already knew—going to Texas A&M for his medical degree, marrying Tammy, divorcing Tammy, and, of course, working as a volunteer fireman. What she didn't know was that he and Tammy had had a baby girl who had been born two months premature and died soon after birth. As he told her of his daughter's birth and death, she could see tears brimming his eyes, which he quickly wiped away before they escaped down his face.

"I think that may have been one of the reasons our marriage broke up," he said, rubbing his eyes. "Tammy wasn't the same afterward. She just kind of closed up emotionally to me, and I guess I did the same. I dealt with my grief and rejection by throwing myself into my work." He sighed and took a bite of cookie and a sip of coffee.

"We just kept building walls between us, and pretty soon, we realized neither one of us had the energy or inclination to bring them down." Christina nodded sympathetically. He leaned forward with his arms resting on his legs, holding the coffee mug in his hands.

"What was her name?" she asked after a brief silence.

"Whose name?" he asked, looking at her with a confused expression.

"Your daughter's."

Smiling, he said, "Oh. Abigail."

"Abigail. That's a nice name." After sipping the last drop of coffee from her mug, she set it on the table beside the couch. She reached out to put her hand on Steven's back but withdrew it before making contact.

"She was so tiny and fragile." He set his mug on the coffee table and cupped his hands.

"She fit right in the palm of my hands. I often wonder who she would be and what she would look like," he said wistfully. "She'd be sixteen this year. Old enough to drive." He shook his head. "Hard to imagine."

Christina nodded. "Yeah, I know. Hard to believe Brad is driving now."

"That's right. Your son is sixteen, isn't he?"

"Yep. And believe me, it's scary."

He nodded, remembering his own parents' concern when he started driving alone.

They sat silently for a few moments, both lost in their thoughts about what was and what might have been.

He turned and took Christina's hands in his, looking her in the eyes.

"Christina, I was just thinking about what a jerk I was to you in high school. I want to apologize for that behavior and hopefully prove to you that I've changed."

She smiled and shook her head.

"Steven, you don't have to apologize or prove anything. That was a *long* time ago. We all did and said things that were unkind." She paused and, moving her hands to her lap, said, "I know I could write a book about my indiscretions."

"What? Not you."

"Yes, me." She looked at him, confused. "You don't think I made mistakes?"

"Well …"

"What?"

"It's just …" He sighed. "It's just that you seemed like such a *perfect* little Christian girl. It's hard to imagine you doing or saying *anything* that would hurt anyone."

She shook her head. "Well, I certainly wasn't perfect, and I'm sure I hurt my share of people over the years."

"Name one time," he said, challenging her.

She stopped to think for a moment. "All right. One time one of my friends was being picked on, and instead of stepping in to defend her, I just walked on by, pretending I didn't know what was happening."

He shook his head. "That's it?"

She sighed and looked at him. "Well, I still feel bad about that," she said defensively.

"See, you were almost perfect."

"I was not!" she stated emphatically.

"Okay, then tell me of another incident."

She thought for another moment.

"Okay. There was this one time I reported a girl for shoplifting—sort of." He raised his eyebrows. She waved her hand and continued.

"My girlfriend and I were in Wal-Mart. I was talking to one of my friends and her boyfriend, who worked there as a security guard." She paused a second. "Wait a minute," she said as a thought hit her. "I remember now. Larry Clifton was my friend's boyfriend. I thought I remembered him from somewhere. Gosh, that was over twenty years ago. Hmm. How about that?"

Steven looked at her and asked, "So what happened next?"

"Oh, sorry, I was lost in a memory."

He smiled and nodded, motioning for her to continue.

She did. "I saw some girl either take something out of or put something in her pocket. It looked like a necklace or bracelet. Anyway, as I watched her, our eyes met, and she shook her head and had a pleading look in her eyes, asking me to not say anything. I didn't, but the guy saw me looking at her, and he turned his head in time to see her with the jewelry. Before I knew what was happening, he had rushed over and grabbed her hand. She looked at me, and I'll never forget those eyes. First there was that look of betrayal, and then, as she was being led away, she looked over her shoulder and glared—such intense hatred in those eyes." She shuddered. "I think she thought I told the security guard, but I didn't. I wish I could have told her that." She was quiet for a moment. Steven reached over and took her hand.

"I felt so bad about that. I never knew the girl or what happened to her. I hope she didn't get into too much trouble."

He patted her hand. "I'm sure she's fine and has probably forgotten about the whole incident. If those are the *worst* things you've done, then you're still pretty saintly, as far as I'm concerned."

She made a fist and hit him on the shoulder.

"Ow!" he said rubbing the shoulder with exaggerated care. "Okay, I take it back. You're *not* a saint." He grinned. "And I guess you're *not* perfect." He put his hand over his heart. "Sure messes with my image of you all these years, though."

"What do you mean by that?"

"I guess one reason I didn't ask you out, and I know some other guys felt the same way, was that you always seemed so sweet and innocent and untouchable." He looked at her with a crooked smile.

She shook her head and chuckled. "And here I thought no one asked me out in high school because I was ugly or weird or something."

"Oh no! You were adorable. I just think us guys felt intimidated by you."

She gave him a confused look. "Intimidated?"

"Maybe that's not the right word." He sighed, frustration building in his voice. "Okay. At that age, most of us guys just wanted to … you know."

She shook her head, feigning ignorance, enjoying his discomfort.

"We just wanted to see how far we could go with a girl."

She nodded knowingly, remembering the stories her girlfriends had told her.

"Anyway, there were some girls we just knew wouldn't allow any of that behavior, and you were one of them. So we just figured, why bother?"

She stifled a giggle. "Oh, I see. So let me get this straight. You would have dated me if I had had a reputation for being easy?"

"Uh, well …" He made a face and nodded. "Probably."

She laughed.

"I know! Sounds pretty lame, doesn't it?" he said, scratching his head.

"Yeah, just a bit." They both chuckled.

"I sure hope my son doesn't think of girls that way," she said taking a sip of cool coffee.

"I'm sorry to say this, but he probably does—you know, raging hormones and all."

She nodded. "Guess I'll need to have a talk with him, hmm?"

He nodded and smiled. "Anyway," he said, taking her hands again. "I wanted to let you know that I'm sorry I was a jerk."

She nodded slightly.

"So, maybe we could do this again sometime?" he said, looking at her hopefully.

"You mean share our deepest secrets?"

He laughed. "Not really. I thought maybe we could spend more time together. I really enjoy your company."

"I'd like that too. You're not so bad to be around either."

A blonde girl who looked to be about sixteen cleared her throat and said, "Excuse me, may I take your cups?"

They both looked up and said simultaneously, "Yes."

Christina looked at her watch.

"Good grief. It's ten. I need to get home." They stood, and he helped with her jacket. On the way home, they talked a bit about work and what was on the agenda for the next week. He walked her to her door, took her hand, and kissed it.

"Thanks, Christina. I'll see you bright and early Monday morning." He turned and left as she entered the quiet and dark house, assuming the kids had already gone to bed, or at least to their rooms. She was glad. She would have a few minutes to unwind and rehash the evening and plan the next week's schedule.

"If you would please stand and turn to page 104," she heard a male voice say, interrupting her thoughts. She shook her head and brought her mind back to the present. She looked around and saw people standing and turning their hymnals to the appropriate page. The organ started playing "Just as I Am," and she stood, amazed that she had missed the entire sermon because of her thoughts of Steven. Smiling, she joined in the singing.

CHAPTER 85

Sunday morning, Steven awoke from a dream about teaching his daughter to drive. He thought it interesting that she looked like Christina's daughter. He fixed a cup of coffee, retrieved the paper from the front porch, and sat in his easy chair enjoying both. His mind kept returning to thoughts of Christina, and he finally put the paper down and let his mind wander back to the previous evening. He had truly enjoyed their time together. She had a great sense of humor, and he liked the way her laughter bubbled up and her eyes almost disappeared when she smiled.

He remembered the different subjects they had covered and thought it sweet that she was still concerned about a couple of girls she felt she had wronged. *She didn't even know one of the girls, for goodness' sakes.* His mind started to wander, and he wondered if people held grudges for twenty years—which made him wonder if that girl was still holding a grudge and maybe was involved with Christina's threats. He sat up in his chair. *Could it be possible? How can I find out who that girl was?* He thought of his friend Larry at the police station and reached for the phone.

Christina and the kids drove through Dairy Queen on the way home from church and purchased a few hamburgers, fries, and Dr Peppers. She didn't feel like preparing a meal, and the children all had homework to do before their youth group meeting that night. As they entered the house, her phone started ringing. Christina dug in her purse and answered it on the fourth and final ring before it would go to voice mail.

"Hello?"

With a catch in her voice, Cindy said, "Christina, can I come over and talk to you?"

"Cindy? Are you all right?"

"Not really," she answered between sniffling and blowing her nose.

"Sure, honey, come on over. Or would you rather I come over there?"

"No, I'll come over to your house, if that's okay. Samara wants to ask Brad about some math homework."

"Okay. I'll see you in a few minutes."

When she disconnected, she called for Brad.

"Cindy's coming over in a few minutes and bringing Samara, who needs help with math. I think we're going to need some privacy, so if you could take any phone calls and handle the kids, I'd really appreciate it. I don't want us to be interrupted."

"Sure, Mom," he said, hiding a smile as he took a bite of his hamburger. "Is everything all right?"

She shrugged and handed him her phone. "Probably. We just need to have some girl time." Brad nodded and left the kitchen. Christina hurriedly ate her burger and fries, drank her Dr Pepper, and cleaned up the mess before Cindy arrived.

When Cindy walked in, Christina gave her a hug and took her up to her room while Samara joined the Sanders kids in the family room.

Putting her arm around her shoulders and leading her to the bed, Christina said, "Okay, Cindy, tell me what's wrong."

Cindy buried her face in her hands and cried. "I should have told you a long time ago, but I just wasn't sure if things would work out."

"Told me what?"

Cindy blew her nose and wiped her eyes. Christina hadn't seen her friend this upset in a very long time. Cindy was not a crier—a screamer and a yeller, but not a crier—so this was serious.

"Remember that guy Ed I told you about?"

"The hot one?"

"Yeah, him."

Christina nodded. "Yeah, what about him?"

"Well, I was really falling for this guy, and I thought he was falling for me. Then all of a sudden he quit calling. I hadn't heard from him in a couple of weeks, so I had just about given up on him, then bam! I saw him at the Black-Eyed Pea last night!"

"Did you get to talk to him?" Christina asked, her curiosity growing.

"Yeah, but not for long," she said, nervously twisting the tissues in her hand.

"What did he say? Did he tell you why he hadn't called?"

"He said he's been very busy." She paused and looked at her friend pleadingly. "Come on, Christina, how much time and effort does it take to pick up a phone and call someone?"

"Did he seem happy to see you?"

"I think he was more shocked than happy."

Christina sighed, not knowing what to say. They sat in silence for a few minutes, Christina replacing the worn tissues with fresh ones.

"What's Ed's last name?"

"Flores."

"Flores? That sounds Mexican. Is he Mexican?"

"Maybe. He's got dark features. Does it matter?"

Shaking her head, Christina said, "Not really, just curious."

"Oh gosh, Christina, he's so perfect!"

"Well, from what you've said about him, I can see why he'd be attractive to you. He sounds almost too good to be true."

"I know. Maybe he is. Maybe he really works for the mafia or something."

Christina frowned and made a face. "I doubt that."

Cindy sighed. "Yeah. Probably not." She blew her nose again.

At least she's stopped crying, thought Christina, rubbing her friend's back.

"What do you think I should do?"

Christina's first inclination was to tell her friend to suck it up and get over him, like she had all the other guys in her life, but she knew that would be too harsh. "What do you want to do?"

"Well, I want him to fall in love with me, get married, and live happily ever after."

Christina nodded and smiled. "Not asking for much, huh?"

Cindy shrugged and smiled slightly.

"Hey, if I'm gonna dream, it might as well be big. Isn't that what you always say?"

"Have you fallen in love with him?" Christina asked, knowing the answer. Cindy had never been this upset over a guy before. All the other men who had come and gone had made her sad or angry, but never distraught. She was usually over them the next day. This relationship had to be more serious, which made Christina's heart ache for her friend.

Cindy nodded slightly. "I think so." She looked at her friend. "It sure feels like it. He's all I think about lately—well, besides Samara and work." She waved her hand and made a face. "You know what I mean."

Christina hugged her friend.

"Cindy, you've had more experience in the man department than I have, so I'm not sure I can give you any sound advice."

"But?"

"But I would say, keep your options open. If he calls and wants to work on the relationship, then go for it. If he doesn't"—she paused, carefully choosing her words—"then try to get over him and go on with your life."

Cindy's shoulders drooped, and she sighed.

"I don't want to get over him," she whined. "I'm getting too old to be playing games. I want to settle down. I want to be loved!" she said emphatically. "Do you know how long it's been since I've truly felt loved?"

Christina shook her head slightly.

"It's been way too many years! In fact, I can't remember ever feeling loved, except maybe when I first got married, and that was short-lived. Stan loved himself and other women more than me and Samara."

A tear trickled down her cheek, which she promptly wiped away. She stood and paced around the room.

"I know I've had several relationships in the past few years, but I always knew deep down that nothing would come of them. I was just lonely and wanted some male companionship, if you know what I mean." She looked at Christina, who smiled slightly and nodded.

She knew exactly what Cindy meant, for she had also desired male companionship, missing the intimate times that she and David had had. She understood the depth of Cindy's desire, but she and Cindy didn't have the same ideas about intimacy. Cindy thought of it as more of a recreational activity, and Christina believed it to be a sacred marriage act and wouldn't think of indulging with anyone outside of marriage, no matter how desperate she became.

Christina stood and walked over to her friend and put her arms around her, pulling her into a hug.

"Oh, Cindy. I don't know what to say. Do you mind if we pray about it?"

"That's what I thought you'd say."

Christina made an "Oops, sorry" face.

"I guess I can be pretty predictable."

Cindy returned the hug and then pulled away.

"Hey, that's why you're my best friend. You're like the anchor, and I'm the rocking boat." She wiped her nose and ran her fingers through her hair. "Look at me. I'm a mess!" She walked over to the mirror and, using a tissue, wiped the smudge under her eyes. "You'd think I was some teenage schoolgirl." She paused, giving Christina a bewildered look. "My daughter behaves better than I do! And she's only fourteen!"

"Cindy, don't be so hard on yourself. You're acting like any red-blooded woman who's felt rejected." She walked over to stand behind her friend and embraced her. "You're tough. That's why you're my best friend. I know you're a fighter and a winner. This will all work out. You'll see."

Cindy smiled and nodded, clearing her nasal passages once more. "Yeah."

Christina walked over and sat on the bed, patting a spot next to her. Knowing Cindy felt uncomfortable at the mention of prayer and was avoiding it, she decided she wouldn't pray *with* her at that moment, but *for* her later. Cindy sat next to her fiddling with the tissues in her hand.

Smiling, Christina asked, "Hey, can I tell *you* something that will put a smile on your face?"

Cindy cocked her head and squinted. "Okay."

Christina told her of her coffee date with Steven. When she finished, Cindy squealed.

"See, I knew you two would eventually hook up! So when's the next date?"

Christina shrugged. "Don't know yet." She heard her cell phone ring but ignored it, knowing Brad would take the call.

"Mom!" she heard him call up the stairs.

She opened her door. "Yes?"

"There's some doctor on the phone for you. I thought it might be important."

She gave Cindy a "I don't know who it is" look and told Brad to bring her phone up.

"Hello?"

"Christina?"

"Yes."

"This is Aaron Carmichael."

"Oh, hi, Dr. Carmichael." She smiled and looked at Cindy, who had a perplexed look on her face.

"Christina, please call me Aaron."

"Sorry, Aaron." She could sense him smiling.

"I was wondering if you'd like to go out to dinner with me this Friday night."

She was too shocked to speak and looked at Cindy, who mouthed *What?*

After a few seconds of awkward silence he said, "Christina?"

She gathered her wits, cleared her throat, and responded, "Oh, I'm sorry. You just caught me off guard."

"Oh, I apologize. I haven't had a chance to talk to you since our lunch, so I thought maybe we could get together and talk some more."

"That sounds like a great idea. Can you hang on a minute while I check my calendar? The kids have so many activities lately that I never remember what they're up to unless I check the calendar first." She put her hand over the receiver and pointed to her purse, which had her day planner in it. Cindy handed it to her, and she flipped the pages to Friday. It was clear. She wasn't sure she wanted to go out with Aaron or wait for Steven to call and ask her out. She decided she had better take her own advice and keep her options open, informing him that she had nothing planned.

"Good. Can I pick you up at six? There's a new restaurant in Dallas I'd like to take you to." He paused, and she could hear papers rustling. "Do you like Japanese cuisine?"

"Oh yeah, I love it!"

"Great. Then I'll see you at six on Friday."

"Okay. Six it is. Thanks."

"No, thank you."

"Hey, I'll see you at the hospital this week, right?" she asked before disconnecting.

"Probably, but the pediatric unit is full, and I have several surgeries scheduled, so if I don't see you this week, I'll see you Friday night."

She stood with the phone in her hand, trying to comprehend what had just transpired. *Why on earth am I agreeing to see Aaron Carmichael when my heart is being pulled toward Steven? Oh yeah, options.*

Cindy squealed when Christina told her of her date for Friday.

"I've got to meet him. He sounds so hot!"

Christina rolled her eyes. "Gracious, Cindy, you think just about any male is hot."

Cindy huffed. "I do not! Just the ones who really are," she said, smiling playfully.

Christina shook her head. "You're hopeless."

"Girlfriend, you'd better be careful. You'll end up with a reputation as the town flirt."

"Oh, God forbid!" Christina said with mock horror as she put her hand on her forehead, causing both to giggle.

"So what are you gonna do if Steven calls and asks you out?"

"I'll cross that bridge when I get to it. In the meantime, I'm gonna enjoy the attention I'm getting." Smiling and cocking her head, she said, "Besides, Steven doesn't have any claim on me. Yet." Noticing the time, she said, "Cindy, I need to bake some cookies for the kids to take to their youth meeting tonight. You want to help?"

"Sure. Are we using slice and bake or the kind you pull apart?"

Christina shook her head. "Nope, we're gonna bake them from scratch."

"Scratch?" Cindy asked.

Christina caught the look of disgust on Cindy's face before heading down the stairs, wishing she had a camera.

CHAPTER 86

While Christina was dealing with the Cindy crisis, Steven was busy talking to his friend Larry.

"So Larry, do you remember being there at Wal-Mart and catching that girl shoplifting? Do you think that gal from Christina's past could be involved in her present circumstances?"

"Steven, I appreciate your concern, but it's highly unlikely that someone would keep a grudge for so long over something so trivial, especially if they didn't know each other. And to be quite honest, I don't remember the incident at all. Maybe if I sat and thought about it, but right now, I'm drawing a blank. Maybe Christina just thought I was the guy there—although now that I think about it, I did work for the security team around that time."

"I know it's a long shot, but is there any way you can check the records and find out who the girl was?" Steven asked, sounding hopeful.

"Well, it may take some digging; after all, it's been twenty years. I suppose I could check the files and see what pops up." He stopped for a minute and wrote himself a note. "Everything is on microfilm now, which reminds me, do you think you could narrow down the time? What month and year?

"I'll try," Steven said, rubbing his chin, wondering how he could get the information without alerting Christina of his intentions.

"If I don't have specifics and have to look over a two- or three-year period, it'll take a lot of extra time. Are you willing to pay for that?"

"Of course. Just send me the bill," Steven said smiling. "And Larry?"

"Yeah?"

"Don't let Christina know you're doing this."

"Yeah. Okay. I'll keep it under wraps. After all, it's a *very* big long shot."

"Thanks, buddy. I owe you one."

Chuckling he answered, "Yep, you'll owe me a lot by the time we're finished."

"Yeah, right."

"Talk to you later," the police chief said as he replaced the receiver, thinking, *What have I got myself into now?*

CHAPTER 87

Monday morning, Christina awoke with thoughts of Cindy and her mystery man. While mixing and baking the cookies, Cindy had opened up and revealed more about Ed, which made him seem like the ideal man. He was handsome, had a good job, and came from a close-knit family. *What more could one ask for?*

Slipping on her robe and heading down the stairs for her morning cup of coffee, she thought, *I sure hope and pray things will work out for Cindy and Ed, 'cause darn it, she deserves a wonderful man in her life.* As much as she loved and respected Cindy, she knew she wasn't very wise in the men department. *She has certainly had her share of users and abusers.* She sighed. *Lord, please don't let this one hurt her.*

As the coffee brewed, she let Benji out and took a deep breath of the clean fresh air. Looking up at the clear blue sky and realizing it was going to be another beautiful day, she thought of her friends in Michigan, who were bracing themselves for an early snowfall. She fed Chloe, who was winding herself in and around her legs, let Benji back in, and then took her cup to the family room to sit in her recliner. A few seconds later, Chloe jumped in her lap and began purring and kneading her chest through her fuzzy robe.

"You silly cat," she said, petting the cat from head to tail. Chloe arched her back and continued purring and kneading until she'd had enough, curled into a ball, and went to sleep on Christina's nice, warm, fuzzy lap.

Sipping her coffee, she picked up her devotional book and turned to the appropriate date. It was titled *I've Fallen and I Can't Get Up!* She chuckled as she read an account of the author's experience with falling back into her old, annoying, and sometime sinful behavior and related it to her own struggle with negative attitudes.

She heard Brad's and Stacey's alarms and looked up to the ceiling as she heard footsteps and running water, imagining her children preparing for the day. She smiled contentedly and closed her eyes in prayer.

The sound of her daughter's voice as she ran down the stairs brought Christina out of her reverie.

"Mom?"

"I'm in the den, Stacey."

Rushing in to where her mother sat, she said, "Mom, you wouldn't believe the dream I had right before I woke up!"

Laying her book on the table beside her, she focused on her daughter's smiling face.

"Tell me about it."

"It's kinda weird and may not make as much sense when I tell about it, but it made sense in my dream."

Christina nodded. "Yeah, dreams are like that."

The two boys joined them in the family room and listened intently as Stacey told of her dream.

"I had been chosen by a group of people to go after a couple of lions that had escaped from the zoo. I was kinda scared, but I remember saying to myself, 'When I am afraid, I will trust in God.' Anyways, I had to find these lions, and I had people following me telling me I could do it. Then I found the lions lying up in some bleachers, like at a stadium or auditorium or someplace like that, and the female lion was pregnant, and someone in the crowd said, 'Wow, it looks like she has millions of babies in there.' And I said, 'Well, maybe not millions, but certainly a lot.'"

Nicky said, "That's it?"

"Well, there was a little dog in it, and I remember telling someone to not let it out of the building or the lions might eat it. Then, when I found the lions, the male had blood on his face, and I said, 'I think he ate the puppy.'"

Nicky smiled and said, "Cool." She made a face at her brother.

"So Stacey, what do you think it means?" Brad asked as he walked over to the couch and sat.

"Well, I was hoping y'all could help me with the interpretation. I feel like it means something, but I'm not sure."

Christina pondered it for a moment and then spoke. "I think it means that you have been chosen to do something big, and the lions represent that big, fearful thing you have to conquer."

"Hmm. I guess that's possible."

Brad added, "Yeah, I think it's something that you're afraid of, something you think is really scary, but once you confront it, you'll find that it isn't so bad after all."

"Maybe. Like the Christmas plays I'm gonna be in. Everyone says I'll do well, but I'm kinda scared to get in front of everyone, especially doing the dancing part. I'm so afraid I'll forget something 'cause I haven't practiced as much as the rest of the group."

Christina patted her daughter's leg and said, "Well, whatever it means, I'm sure God is trying to tell you to not be afraid." She paused a moment as a new idea surfaced. "Remember Aslan the Lion from the Narnia series?"

Stacey nodded.

"Everyone was afraid of him until they met him, spent some time with him, and got to know him. Sometimes things seem scary but aren't so much once they are understood." Christina pulled her daughter into a hug.

"Yeah. That all makes sense. Maybe I dreamed of lions 'cause I just finished the book about Narnia and Aslan." She stood and said, "I think this dream will stay with me for a long time. It was so real!"

Standing and stretching, Brad added, "I've had some pretty interesting dreams since we've been here."

"Yeah, I've had some really scary dreams too!" Nicky said as he headed for the kitchen.

"Hmm. Me too." Christina whispered, leaving the recliner and heading to the kitchen with the kids to find something for breakfast.

"Well, maybe God is trying to tell us something—or they're just dreams, our subconscious trying to work out the emotional ups and downs of our conscious mind."

All three kids gave her a "Huh?" kind of look.

She just smiled and shook her head. "Let's get breakfast."

David smiled as he watched the interchange between Christina and the kids. He knew *why* the dream had been sent—Jarrod had told him—and was surprised they all hadn't been sent that dream or a similar one, as they would be facing some major "lions" soon.

CHAPTER 88

Janet woke from a fitful sleep as her alarm buzzed incessantly in her ear, breaking the spell of her dream, in which she was being chased by a huge, black, winged creature and was about to be caught and devoured. *If it had caught me, would I be alive to tell about it, or would I have died in my sleep?*

These kinds of dreams had been invading her sleep on a nightly basis lately—ever since Christina came into her life. *What does that mean? Why am I being pursued by these hideous-looking monsters?*

She lay on her side facing the clock, watching the seconds tick by, thinking about how miserable her life had become since her nemesis's arrival. Granted, it hadn't been any Cinderella story with a handsome prince coming to her rescue and them living happily ever after before that, but at least she wasn't so tired and frustrated all the time. She didn't understand *why* things weren't working out in her favor. She had used all the right tools for spell casting, and yet Steven and Christina weren't responding as expected—like there was an opposite force at work. She wanted to discuss this problem with someone, but didn't trust anyone else—not even the twenty or so people in her circle of believers.

Rolling on her back, putting her hands under her head, and crossing her legs at the ankles, she let her mind wander back to the meeting she and her daughter had attended the previous day. The group, consisting of eight family groups, including herself and Leelee, called themselves the Enlightened Ones.

The meeting was held in an old barn on a hundred-acre parcel of land owned by Mr. and Mrs. Clark, who were also the leaders.

They and their two children and grandchildren were responsible for obtaining information and passing it on to the rest of the members. The group was run like many churches, with singing, collection offering, and teaching. The elder Mr. Clark spoke each week, passing on words of wisdom and information regarding the latest health concern and its remedy, as well as the best ways to manipulate one's own environment and destiny. Mrs. Clark taught the children about using the tools nature had provided, and her son and daughter and their spouses led the singing and discussion groups.

She and Leelee had joined the group about a year earlier after overhearing a couple of ladies at the local bookstore talk about it. Wanting to connect with people who had similar beliefs, she decided to give it a try. In the beginning, as she discovered new ways to tap into the power within, there was a feeling of excitement, but lately, that feeling was lacking. Something was missing, but she didn't have a clue as to what it could be.

She remembered seeing a book on the library shelf about dream interpretation and decided to swing by and pick it up after work. She also decided to invest in a dream catcher after overhearing one of the members tell how she had had nightmares, but once she hung it over her bed, the nightmares stopped.

She sat up and stretched, looking out at the darkness beyond the window across from her bed, and thought, *What have I got to lose? I can't keep functioning on so little sleep.* As she entered the bathroom, she caught a glimpse of her reflection in the mirror above the sink and gasped.

Goodness, girl, you look old today, she thought as she stripped down and entered the shower, letting the hot water cascade down her body, temporarily washing her cares away.

Steven dressed for the day, looking forward to seeing Christina again. He liked her smile, her laugh, and the sparkle in her eyes. Well, gosh, when he thought about it, he just liked her whole being. *Is there anything about her that you don't like?* He asked himself. A resounding *nope* was what he heard in reply. He smiled. *Could I be falling in love with you, Christina Sanders?* The rational side of his brain—or was it his heart?—said *No way!* The irrational, emotional side said, *Oh, yes, you are!* He chuckled as he pictured two little imps sitting on each shoulder whispering these answers in his ears.

Remembering that she and her kids were a package deal, he thought of them and realized they hadn't had an opportunity to spend any quality time together. If he wanted the relationship with their mother to grow, which he did, he needed to make that a priority. He felt his heart flutter as he envisioned Christina, the children, and himself as a family. *Whoa! Don't you go rushing into this!* he reminded himself, bringing his thoughts under control. As he drove to work, he started thinking about activities that the whole gang could do together.

CHAPTER 89

As mom and daughter enjoyed breakfast together, Janet handed Leelee the birthday package, singing "Happy Birthday" as she presented it. Leelee smiled and took the small package, knowing what was inside: another birthday charm. Her mother had given her similar ones on every previous birthday, which made it difficult to act surprised when she opened it.

"Thanks, Mom," she said as she took the silver charm from the jewelry box. Removing her bracelet, she added the new charm and then replaced it on her wrist. She had thirteen charms now, and as she shook the bracelet on her arm, it made a neat jingling noise.

Janet took her daughter's hands in hers.

"Honey, now that you're thirteen and an official teenager, I was wondering if you'd be interested in learning about tarot card reading and casting spells?"

Her daughter's eyes lit up. "Yeah!" she said excitedly.

Janet smiled and nodded. "Well, I have a couple of books that you can read. Then I'll show you more things that *I've* learned along the way." She stood, walked into the living room, and returned with two books, placing them in front of her daughter. Linda happily accepted them and started turning pages as Janet stood behind her, kissing the top of her head. The one about tarot cards had pictures and explained what each one represented and how to interpret them. The other was about casting spells.

"Honey, I've got to finish getting dressed. You have about twenty minutes before you need to leave, so watch your time." Smiling, she leaned down and kissed her on the cheek and turned to walk toward her bedroom.

"Okay. I will." Turning pages, she thought, *I'm gonna show this to Stacey.*

As Linda walked to school, she not only thought about the books her mother had given her, and the interesting information held within, but also about Stacey's possible reaction to them. *Would she be interested in them, or would she find them offensive?* She and Stacey had been talking recently about God, angels, demons and different religions, and Stacey was very opinionated about her beliefs. Linda had just finished reading *This Present Darkness* the previous night and had several questions to ask Stacey. *Do angels and demons truly exist? And if so, are they involved in our lives on a daily basis? Is there really a war between them for man's souls? Was there honestly a man named Jesus who was God's son, and did he really die on the cross? Is heaven a real place? If so, is Jesus the only way there?*

She had never thought about all those things before, and now that her mind had opened up to them, she found it all a bit confusing. She didn't feel comfortable talking to her mother about it, and she wasn't sure why. *Maybe because when the subject of religion is broached, Mom always seems angry and defensive and changes the subject.* She felt she was at a crossroad in her life now that she was thirteen—no longer a little girl, but not an adult either. She sensed this was going to be a very confusing and frustrating time in her life, and she needed to think about her future and what she wanted to do and be.

CHAPTER 90

Filling in once again for a nurse with a sick child, Janet drove the familiar route to the hospital, thinking about her daughter. She was happy that Leelee seemed interested in magic. She had feared that Stacey had turned her against the ancient arts. She thought about the question her daughter had asked: "Do you believe in God and angels and demons?" She didn't think so, but then again, she *did* believe in some sort of power source, and she believed in spiritual guides. *Would they be considered angels or demons?* In her mind's eye, she pictured them being just a form of light with the vague shape of a human—kind of like in the movie *Cocoon*. Those creatures were sweet and gentle and had a human form that glowed with transparent light. Yep, that's how she pictured her guiding spirit. She had never seen it, even though some of the people in her group had claimed to have seen theirs. She certainly didn't think the guiding spirits were evil or demonic. When she called on her spirit, she always felt a soothing presence. How could she feel so good if her spirit was evil? Surely she would be able to tell if it was evil, right? What exactly was evil? Wasn't one man's evil another man's redemption?

Some people considered her form of religion evil, calling it witchcraft. She chuckled. *I'm not a witch, for goodness' sakes, even though I do read the Wiccan manual. I'm not in a coven, and we don't wear long robes or sacrifice animals. We don't call on Satan or any other demonic spirit. Our spiritual guides, which aren't good or evil, are helpful. We do cast spells like those considered witches, but I certainly don't cast spells to hurt people, only to change their minds about something or change the course of events. If people did get hurt, like that one time, then it was their own fault for not heeding the warnings. We just use what the earth provides, and what's wrong with that?*

She thought of Steven Dawson. *My spells aren't meant to hurt him—just make him fall in love with me and not Christina.* She furrowed her brow and chewed on her thumbnail. *I can't understand why my spells aren't working. I've done everything the books say to do, and yet he seems to prefer her. Maybe it'll take more time.* She sighed. *Patience, girl.* Pulling into the parking lot in time to see Christina exit her van, she let out a loud "Ugh!" As she gathered her belongings, she whispered, "Please don't let her see me."

As Christina walked toward the hospital entrance, she heard a crow caw and, turning to see where it was, spotted Janet exiting her car. She stopped and waited for her to catch up. Janet sighed when she saw her waiting. It was inevitable that she saw her nemesis, but she had hoped for a few more minutes of peace and quiet before entering the workplace and having to deal with Christina. As she approached, Christina smiled and waved. Janet returned the wave, clenching her teeth, because the smile just wouldn't come to her face.

"Hey, Janet, filling in for someone again today?" Christina asked as she held the door open, feeling the cool air drift across her face.

Janet nodded and, with great effort, managed a halfhearted smile.

"How are you doing today?

Not really wanting to continue the small talk but not wanting to be rude either, she answered, "I'm fine, and you?"

Christina sniffed and coughed. "I'm fighting some allergies, but otherwise I'm fine."

Janet nodded. "My allergies act up in the spring and fall."

"Mine are usually seasonal too, but we just turned the furnace on this weekend, and since that came on, I've been really stuffy. I guess I should get all those ducts vacuumed out. No telling how long it's been since they've been cleaned." She took a tissue out and blew her nose. "Sorry."

As she and Janet entered the elevator, they heard a male voice call out, "Hold that, please."

Janet reached over and pushed the Door Open button, and a couple of seconds later, a smiling Dr. Carmichael entered. "Good morning, ladies."

"Good morning, Dr. Carmichael," they both responded right before Christina had a sneezing fit.

He looked at her, concern etching his face. "Are you all right?"

"Allergies," she answered, wiping her nose.

"Are you taking anything for them?"

Sniffling and wiping her nose and eyes, she said, "Just some over-the-counter stuff. Doesn't seem to be working very well, though."

"You look pretty miserable. How about if I get you something else a little stronger and bring it up to you?"

"That would be nice, being I have to work all day and would rather be home in bed."

"Are you sure it's allergies and not a cold or flu?"

"Well, I'm not running a fever and the drainage is clear, and this is how I act when the seasons change. So, yeah, I'm pretty sure it's just allergies."

He nodded. "Okay." The elevator door opened on the second floor, and as he exited, he said, "I'll bring that medicine up in a while." She nodded and smiled.

"Thanks."

Janet raised her eyebrows. "Do you and Dr. Carmichael have something going on?"

Christina chuckled. "No. He's Stacey's doctor."

Janet nodded. "Well, he seemed awfully concerned."

Christina shook her head. "He's just a nice guy."

Janet thought, *Hmm, maybe I can help that relationship along.* She smiled and nodded. "He is a nice guy. He's had it tough the last couple of years, though."

"What do you mean?"

"You don't know?"

Christina shook her head. "Know what?"

"His wife died two years ago in a car accident out on I-35."

"Oh, yes, I heard about that."

"Yeah." She paused and then added, "He has a five-year-old daughter, too."

Christina nodded. She knew that too.

"Must be tough being a single dad. He always seems so cheerful though."

"Yeah, well, it's only been in the past couple of months that he seems happier." Janet paused for a moment, looking at Christina. "Maybe he's got a girlfriend."

Christina furrowed her brows. "I don't think so," she replied, thinking about their plans for Friday night.

Janet looked at her. "No? How would you know?"

The elevator door opened, and the ladies exited. Christina shrugged. "I don't."

The morning went well. There were no new admittances and no emergencies. A couple of the patients were discharged, leaving only four on the floor, and they were all stable.

Dr. Meils went on rounds with Christina and Steven. She noticed he was spending more time with Steven the past couple of weeks. When asked about his presence, he answered, "I've decided to do my residency here and moved to Alva two weeks ago. I enjoy working with Dr. Dawson, and we make a pretty good team."

Dr. Dawson smiled and said, "I like having him around. It frees me up a bit. I was getting pretty tired of being the only cardiac physician in Alva."

Christina smiled and nodded. She was glad he had more free time also. Maybe they could spend that extra time together.

True to his word, Dr. Carmichael brought up a prescription to Christina.

Handing her the bottle, he asked, "When did you take the other medicine?"

She looked at her watch. "Let's see. Um, I think around five. I woke up all stuffy."

He looked at his watch. "Well, wait at least another hour or so before taking one of these. If it still doesn't help, maybe you should be checked for a sinus infection."

She smiled warily and sighed. "Thanks. This won't make me sleepy, will it?"

He shook his head. "It's not supposed to, but then everyone reacts differently."

She made a face as she stifled a yawn. "I don't need any encouragement. I already feel like I'm running at half speed."

He smiled and patted her arm. "I know that feeling."

The phone rang, and one of the nurses handed the receiver to him. He listened and said, "Yeah, I'll be right there."

He passed the receiver back to the nurse, shrugged, and said, "Duty calls."

Christina smiled and nodded. He turned to leave and then stopped and turned back. Christina was still watching him.

"Drink plenty of water today. Should help with the stuffiness and make you feel better."

She saluted him and said, "Yes, doctor."

He chuckled and then turned and walked briskly down the hall and around the corner to the elevator. She smiled and took a tissue and blew her nose. She was looking forward to Friday night.

As Christina sat at the nurses' station and read through the charts, she felt as if she were being watched. When she glanced up, she noticed Janet looking back at her from across the counter.

"Do you need something, Janet?"

Shrugging, she said, "No."

"Okay," Christina said, returning her attention to the chart in front of her.

Janet didn't move but continued to stare. Christina closed the chart and looked up once again into Janet's troubled face.

"Obviously something is bothering you. Do you want to talk about it?"

Janet sighed. "I just wonder how you do it."

Christina furrowed her brow. "Do what?"

"How you manage to work, take care of three kids, and still have time for a social life. I can barely make it through a week without collapsing. I mean, Friday comes, and all I can think of doing is curling up on the couch to watch TV."

"I know what you mean. Some nights that's exactly what I do. I'm just thankful the kids are old enough to help around the house, *and* they're pretty independent, so I don't have to do a lot for them."

Janet smiled and nodded, speaking softly as she scribbled on a piece of paper.

"Yeah, well, it's just interesting that after all you've been through, you have enough energy to ..." She paused and looked Christina in the eyes. "Date." There, she said it.

Christina shook her head, not sure she should even validate the statement. After all, it wasn't Janet's business if she dated or not. They weren't friends, so she didn't feel any obligation to explain or justify her behavior. She cocked her head and thought about what to say. *Do I sense a little jealousy? Maybe. I don't know Janet well enough to make any conclusions.*

"I appreciate your concern, Janet, but I'm feeling better now."

Janet nodded and shrugged. Obviously, Christina wasn't going to talk about her social life. *That's okay. I'll find out sooner or later what's really going on.* She put her pen in her pocket, wadded up the piece of paper she had been scribbling on, and stuck it in her pocket with the pen.

"Well, that's good," she said before walking down the hall to the restroom.

Christina tried to refocus on the chart in front of her but kept thinking about Janet, who seemed like such a lost soul. Granted, she was drop-dead gorgeous, but there was something missing. She had a haunted look in her eyes, like she had suffered something horrendous and hadn't fully recovered from it. There were no visible scars, but Christina suspected that there were invisible ones. She vowed to herself and to God that she would make a stronger effort to befriend Janet. In the three months she had been working at the hospital, she had heard nothing positive about the woman. Words like *rude, angry, intimidating, standoffish, stuck-up, selfish,* and *mean* were used when people would speak of her. Even though she had experienced a couple of those attributes from the woman, she still felt that underneath that tough exterior was a hurting, vulnerable woman screaming to be noticed and loved. She said a quick prayer asking God to help her break through that hard shell.

She turned her attention back to the chart in front of her, noticing that the pink lab slip that should have been there from Friday morning was missing. *Not again!* She remembered putting it in the chart after detaching the white portion and sending it down to the lab. *So where is it?* She flipped through the pages and looked around the desktop. Sometimes slips were tacked on the bulletin board, so she turned her chair to look. It wasn't there. *Oh man, not again!* she thought as panic started to grip her heart.

"Sarah?" she called to the LPN sitting at the opposite end of the desk.

"Yeah?"

"Have you seen Mrs. Abernathy's pink lab slip? I put it in the chart on Friday and can't seem to find it."

"No, I haven't seen it. Did you call the lab? Maybe it got sent down with the white one. Sometimes they stick together."

"I distinctly remember putting it in the chart." She shook her head. "I'll call the lab anyways. Thanks." She picked up the receiver and punched in the numbers.

"Lab. Jeanie speaking."

"Hi, Jeanie, this is Christina Sanders from the cardiac floor. I was wondering if you could find Mrs. Lucille Abernathy's blood work slip. I seem to have misplaced the orders."

"Sure. When were they ordered?"

Christina heard papers being shuffled in the background.

"Last Friday."

"I don't see them in front of me, but hang on, I'll be right back." She was put on hold and listened to some piano music as she waited.

Suddenly the music stopped and she heard a click.

"Christina, I've looked around, and I don't see any orders for Mrs. Abernathy. Are you sure they were sent down last Friday?"

"Well, yes. I sent them down myself after Dr. Dawson handed the order to me."

"Sorry. I'll keep looking, and I'll call if I find them."

"Thanks." Christina replaced the receiver. *It's happening again.* She thought maybe the other times were flukes, but not now. Either she truly was losing her mind, or someone was sabotaging her work.

She opened the chart and flipped the pages back to Friday's entry. She noticed a smudge and upon closer examination realized that something had been erased. Her heart skipped a beat as she read the entry. Where it should have read "Dr. Dawson ordered a chemical profile" was replaced by "Dr. Dawson stated patient is doing well." Upon closer examination, she realized that it wasn't even her handwriting—a close imitation, but not hers. *What should I do now?* she thought. She felt sweat trickle down her sides from her armpits. Just then, the phone rang, making her jump.

"CCU. Christina Sanders speaking."

"Hey, Christina, it's Steven." Her heart jumped.

"Have you got the lab results for Mrs. Abernathy? I was looking over her meds and think I'll try her on something else."

Trying to keep the panic she was feeling out of her voice, but failing miserably, she said, "Steven, we need to talk."

"What? Why?" he asked, feeling there was more to her desire to talk than just normal chitchat.

"I just need to talk to you about something important. Can I come down to your office?"

"Sure, come on down. I don't have anything scheduled for the next half hour."

Christina replaced the receiver, picked up the chart, told Sarah she would be right back, and headed for the elevators. She passed Janet on the way. Noticing the chart in Christina's hand, Janet asked if everything was all right. Christina nodded, not wanting to talk to anyone and entered the elevator.

Janet walked up to the counter and asked Sarah what was going on with Christina.

Sarah shrugged and answered, "Don't know. She said she'd be back in a few minutes is all I know."

Janet nodded and asked, "Do you know which chart she took?"

"I think it was Mrs. Abernathy's. She was asking about some lab work that was missing."

Janet felt her heart skip a beat. When Sarah turned her back, she reached in her pocket and pulled out the missing lab slip. She had removed it on Friday with the intention of making Christina look incompetent. She quietly slipped it into another chart.

She would pretend to discover it when Christina came back. She smiled and looked up to see Sally Jean staring at her. *Had she seen anything?*

"Do you need something, Sally Jean?" she asked, trying not to sound nervous.

"I need Mrs. Abernathy's chart. I need to put this intake-output paper in it." She waved the paper for Janet to see.

"Here, let me take that. I'll just stick it up on the bulletin board, and when the chart returns, I'll put it in."

Sally Jean smiled. "Thanks. That would be great."

She handed the paper to Janet, turned, and headed back down the hall, her blonde ponytail bouncing from side to side as she walked. Janet wasn't worried about Sally Jean. Even if she had seen her put the paper in the chart, she wouldn't have given it a second thought.

She checked the four heart monitors above the desk and, noting that they were all producing normal readings, went into the break room for a cup of coffee. As she sipped the dark brew, she heard one of the monitor's alarms sound. She set the coffee cup on the counter and quickly returned to the station to see that one of Mr. Johnson's four leads was flatlining. The other three were producing normal blips, spikes, and waves, even though the rate had increased from his normal eighty-five beats per minute to over one hundred. *One of the leads must have come unattached.* If anything more serious was happening, the other three would be showing signs of distress as well. She walked briskly to his room and found him sitting up in bed, trying to unsuccessfully reattach the missing lead. He was sweating profusely, and his face was flushed.

Entering the room, she said, "Mr. Johnson, let me help you with that." She snapped the lead back on and put her hand on his shoulder, gently pushing him back to a semi reclining position.

"I'm sorry," he said breathlessly. "I had to go to the bathroom and it popped off—like to have scared me to death when the alarm sounded."

Janet patted his arm. "It's okay. Happens all the time." She checked the monitors. His pulse rate was still over one hundred. She took his blood pressure, which was high as well—*probably due to the stress of the situation,* she thought. She handed him a cup of water and some tissues to wipe his face and then asked him to lie back, close his eyes, and concentrate on taking slow breaths.

"Next time you need to go to the bathroom," she said quietly as she took the empty cup, sat it next to the pitcher, pulled the sheet up around his chest, checked his IV, and laid his arms across his ample belly, "please call us. Someone will come help you."

He nodded and smiled with his eyes closed. "I just didn't want to bother anyone," he said quietly. She patted his arm again.

"I know, but right now, you need to let your heart heal, and you don't need any more stress. Besides," she added conspiratorially, "that's why we are paid the big bucks. We do the grunt work, and you just get to lounge around."

He opened his eyes and gave her a big toothy grin, nodding, and said, "Oh, yeah."

She put fresh water in the flower vases and folded the gowns on the chair across the room. By the time she was ready to leave the room, his pulse was back down, and his blood pressure had returned to the normal range. She patted his hand, which felt warm and dry, and left the room. He was drifting off to sleep. On her way back to the desk, she checked in on the other three patients. All was well.

CHAPTER 91

While Janet was dealing with Mr. Johnson, Christina was showing Steven the chart.

"See?" she said as she pointed to the smudge on the paper in front of him.

"That's where something has been erased and this other entry written over it." He scanned down the page and pointed to her signature.

"That's my signature at the end of the page, but Steven, that is not my handwriting there," she said defensively. He squinted as he looked closely at the paper.

"I can see where it's smudged, but are you sure you didn't write that?" He pointed to the words in question. "'Dr. Dawson states that patient is doing well.' I'm not sure what it said before, but this seems pretty accurate."

"I think what it said before was that you ordered a complete blood panel. I remember you ordering it, and I wrote it in the chart. Then I wrote out the order and laid it on the desk to send down to the lab."

Steven nodded, remembering the moment. He had indeed ordered a complete blood panel.

"That's what's missing. It's not documented, and the lab slip is missing," she explained once again.

Steven rubbed his chin and then removed his glasses and rubbed his eyes. Sighing, he said, "Well, Christina, I don't know what to make of this." He sat back in his chair and laid his head back on the cushioned headrest. She stood next to him with her arms folded across her chest.

"Don't you see? Someone is out to discredit me!" She threw her hands up in the air and started pacing around the room. "This same kind of thing happened a few weeks ago, but I didn't have any evidence of foul play. It just looked like I misplaced the orders. Now I can prove that someone else wrote in that chart."

He looked at her bewildered face and felt pity for her.

"I'm not sure how you can prove it. It would take a handwriting analyst to see the difference between your writing and that there," he said, pointing to the writing in question.

"Well, then, let's get one," she said with determination in her voice.

Steven smiled and nodded. "I'll see what I can do."

She smiled and leaned over and hugged him. "Thanks."

"You know what this means, don't you?" he asked as he handed the chart back to her.

She furrowed her brow. "What?"

"If there *is* foul play as you have suggested, it means that someone who has access to the charts and medical information is behind all this."

She sucked in air and put her hand over her mouth.

"Oh my goodness, you're probably right." She sat down in the chair across from him, her mind whirling. Faces of coworkers zipped past her mind's eye. *Who could be so mean-spirited to cause me such turmoil, emotionally and physically? And put the patients' lives in danger?* She didn't have a clue but would certainly start looking at her coworkers with a different perspective.

Steven reached over and took her free hand in his.

"I'm going to call Larry and have him come look at this and get his opinion as to where we go from here. In the meantime, you just go on about your business as if nothing is wrong." He took the paper in question out of the chart and laid it on his desk by his phone.

She nodded. "I just want to get to the bottom of this and be done with it. I want my life to get back to normal." She sighed and gave him a bewildered look. "Is that too much to ask?"

He smiled and shook his head. "No, it isn't. And I think we'll get to the bottom of this and find out why it's happening."

She nodded and sighed. Looking at the clock above Steven's head, she said, "I need to get back to the floor. I've been gone longer than I anticipated." They both stood, and he walked around the desk and drew her into his arms, resting his chin on top of her head. She put her arms around his waist, enjoying the moment. She was intensely aware of his steady heartbeat, his breathing, and his manly, Old Spice smell. She felt her own pulse quicken. *Goodness it feels good to be in his arms.*

Steven felt a warm glow throughout his body and after a few seconds decided that although it felt good to have Christina in his arms, he had better let her go, or he may ruin the moment by doing something stupid like kissing her. He kissed the top of her head instead, and pulled away. The instant she felt him relent, she too released her hold and stepped back, crossing her arms in front of her chest. For an awkward second they looked into each other's eyes, both realizing that their relationship had just taken another step past the boundary of mere friendship.

She reached down and retrieved the chart from his desk, holding it protectively to her chest.

"Thank you, Steven, for helping me with this." He relaxed and leaned back, resting his backside on his desk. Cocking his head and giving her a crooked smile, he said with his best Texas drawl, "Oh, shucks, ma'am, I'm always willin' to help a lady in distress."

She smiled and shook her head. "You're nuts, Steven."

He nodded. "Yep, that's what I hear."

She shook her head again, glancing at the clock. "I've really gotta go."

He walked with her to the door and put his hand on her shoulder. "I'll be up later and let you know what Larry said."

She nodded. "Okay, see you later, then." She headed down the hall toward the elevators.

Steven closed the door to his office and headed for the phone.

CHAPTER 92

Once on the elevator, Christina thought about what had transpired in Steven's office. *Goodness, I feel like a giddy schoolgirl.* She was thankful that he was her ally, and by the way things were progressing, he was becoming more than just a friend. *Am I ready for that? Maybe.*

When Christina arrived at the CCU station, Janet was standing at the counter. "Anything happen while I was gone?"

Janet told her of Mr. Johnson's episode with the monitor.

"Mr. Johnson is a very independent man, and I'm sure it pains him to be waited on," Christina said as she thought of the fifty-eight-year-old ex-linebacker for the Dallas Cowboys, "especially to go to the bathroom." Shaking her head, she added, "Guess we'll have to keep close tabs on him. He's likely to try getting up on his own again."

Janet nodded in agreement and then, looking at the chart in Christina's hand, asked, "Is everything all right?"

"I'm not sure." Christina answered as she looked at Janet and set the chart on the countertop. "Do you remember seeing a lab slip for Mrs. Abernathy from last Friday?"

Janet felt her pulse quicken. "Hmm. I don't think so. Why?"

"Well"—she sighed—"seems I must have misplaced it." She sat at the desk and began perusing the paperwork that had come up from the lab.

Janet walked around and retrieved the intake-output paper for Mrs. Abernathy and put it in her chart. She turned to Christina and said, "Things have a way of turning up around here. Remember that one X-ray we were looking for, and it turned up behind the filing cabinet? How it got there"—she shrugged—"nobody knows."

Christina smiled and nodded. They had looked for the X-ray for two days before discovering it.

"And," continued Janet, "that lab slip a couple of weeks ago turning up in one of the lab tech's pockets." She chuckled. "So I wouldn't worry too much. It'll probably turn up in the craziest place."

Christina nodded. "You're right Janet. In the meantime, though, Dr. Dawson requested more blood work, so if you'll let me know when the results come up, I'd appreciate it."

Janet nodded.

When the other nurses and aides came to the desk, Janet asked each one if they had seen the missing lab slip, but no one had. *Hopefully, one of them will come across it, because it might be a little suspicious if I find the slip,* she thought as she began stacking charts.

As Christina worked through the day, she couldn't help but be suspicious of each person she came in contact with. She watched Sally Jean walk around the hall and listened as she interacted with the patients and other staff. Christina dismissed her as a suspect because of her age and naïveté. She didn't think Sally Jean had a mean bone in her body.

She looked over the counter at Brenda. She was the oldest aide there, and hardly a day went by that she didn't announce to someone that she had "been working at this very hospital since it had first opened over forty years ago." Christina couldn't imagine her doing anything that could get her fired or, worse yet, ruin her reputation.

"Christina?"

Christina's thoughts were abruptly interrupted.

"Yes?" She answered looking up into the worried face of Sarah Stevens, the only LPN that did swing shifts. She worked two day shifts and two night shifts during the week and would occasionally fill in when someone would call in sick. She had short, straight, gray hair, big blue eyes that were magnified behind her thick-lensed glasses, and a beautiful smile with perfect white teeth accentuated by dimples in both rosy cheeks. She had a quiet, compassionate spirit, which endeared her to the patients and staff. Christina was told that she had been married for a couple of years before her husband was killed in Vietnam. She never remarried, and vowed to honor his memory by helping others.

"Could you please look at Mr. Wilson's IV? The area around the needle looks quite red and swollen."

Christina stood and stretched. "I'll get a new needle and line and join you in his room in a second. In the meantime, why don't you go ahead and remove it and put an ice pack on the area?"

Sarah nodded and headed back to Mr. Wilson's room.

Christina entered the supply room and flicked on the light. As she rummaged through the IV supplies, something fell to the floor. Bending down to retrieve the object, she lost her balance, and as she regained it, her foot kicked the object under the shelves. She tried reaching under the metal shelving unit, but it was too close to the floor for her hand or arm to fit under. She put her head on the floor and peered under the shelf. It was dark and full of cobwebs and other creepy things, but she did see that the object in question was a medicine bottle. She sat back on her knees wondered what she could use to retrieve it. Looking around and not seeing anything useful, she stood and picked up the IV supplies and decided she'd have to come back later for the bottle. She left the room and headed for Mr. Wilson's room. When she entered, Sarah and Mr. Wilson were laughing about something. She smiled as she headed for the bed.

"Hey, Mr. Wilson. How are you doing today?" she asked as she set the IV supplies on his bedside tray, lifted the ice pack from his hand, and inspected the swollen puncture site.

"Well, I'm much better now that that thing is out," he said as he pointed to the dangling IV line. "That was hurting like a son of a gun!"

Laying his hand back on the bed and returning the ice pack, she said, "I can see why."

"Do I have to have another one?" he asked as he looked over at the IV needle and tube on the tray.

Christina sighed and made a face.

"Yeah. Sorry." She patted his arm. "I'm sure Dr. Dawson will have it removed as soon as you are well enough. In the meantime, it's giving you medicine and nutrition that will help heal your heart."

He sighed and nodded. "I know. I just hate being so dependent on this stuff. Do you know that I have *never* been in the hospital, until last week when I had my heart attack?"

Christina raised her eyebrows. "Wow! That's pretty amazing." She walked around the bed, bringing the IV equipment with her.

"Yeah." He nodded slowly. "My wife only went to the hospital to have our two boys. She was a strong woman, that Frannie."

"Was?" Christina asked cocking her head as she set the equipment on the bedside stand.

"Yeah. She died a year ago. Went in to wake her up for her morning coffee." He smiled crookedly. "I started taking her a cup of coffee each morning after I retired. I was always up earlier and let her sleep while I had my coffee and read the paper. Then I'd take her in a cup, and we'd sit and talk about what we would do for the day." He sighed. "I sure miss those times. Anyway, when I went in and tried to wake her, she wouldn't wake up. I felt for her pulse, but couldn't find one. She was so cold, and I knew she was dead, but I pulled the covers up on her anyway." He wiped at a tear as it trickled down his cheek. "I called 911, but by the time the paramedics got there she had already been dead for a few hours." Another tear trickled down his cheek, and he quickly wiped it away. Sniffling, he added, "Guess that's the best way to go." He looked up and smiled slightly. "In your sleep."

Christina gave him an understanding nod. "I'm sorry for your loss, Mr. Wilson." She patted his hand and asked, "Do your boys live close by?"

He smiled. "Yep. Down by Hillsboro. Tommy has a farm out on Brandon Road, and Leslie has a farm out on Whitney Highway."

"That's nice that they're close by."

He nodded.

"Do you have grandchildren?" she asked as she palpated a large vein in his arm and wiped the puncture area with an alcohol swab.

"Oh yeah. I have eight."

Christina raised her eyebrows and smiled. "Wow, that's awesome." Sliding the IV needle in the vein, she said, "This might hurt a bit."

He inhaled and winced but sighed and chuckled when she finished.

"Boys and girls?" she asked as she opened the IV line and adjusted the flow.

With a smile on his face, he answered proudly, "Four boys and four girls."

Watching her put tape on and around the needle and tubing, he commented, "The last nurse who did this must have poked me four or five times before it finally went in. I was about ready to do it myself." Nodding his approval, he said, "You did a good job, young lady."

Cleaning up the area around the bed, she smiled and said, "Thanks."

Noticing a picture frame that held a professional photograph of eight smiling children dressed in colorful outfits and ranging from a toothless baby to a teenage boy wearing braces, she asked, "Are these your grandchildren?" He nodded and proudly pointed to each one, telling the child's name and age and which son they belonged to.

Christina smiled and commented on how cute each one was.

Sarah removed the ice pack from Mr. Wilson's other hand and put a dab of antibiotic cream and a Band-Aid on the bruised area. She patted it and tenderly put it under the sheet and straightened the covers. She lowered the head a little, fluffed his pillow, and offered him a drink of water.

"Mr. Wilson, call me if you need anything or if this IV starts hurting," Christina said as she walked toward the door.

He nodded as he sipped his water through a straw being held by Sarah.

Christina left the room and immediately crossed Sarah off her suspect list.

She returned to the nurses' station and recorded the incident with the IV in Mr. Wilson's chart.

When she reached over to pick another chart off the stack, two pieces of paper fluttered to the floor. She reached down to retrieve them and was shocked to see that it was Mrs. Abernathy's blood work order. She looked at the name on the chart: Arlene Davies, Mrs. Abernathy's roommate. She leaned back in her chair and thought. *Was it possible that I put them in her chart by mistake? If so, why would they turn up now? Why didn't someone find them before now? No. I distinctly remember putting the pink slip in the chart and the white one in the basket that goes down to the lab, so how did they get here? Unless someone put them there to make it look like I'm inept. Like I forgot. Like I made a mistake.* She sighed. *Okay. If that's the case, then I had better be more alert and careful with all my paperwork.*

Janet walked up to the desk and smiled slightly when she noticed the lab request. "So you found the lab slip? Where was it?"

"It was in Mrs. Davies's chart."

Janet nodded slightly. "Interesting."

Christina nodded slightly as well. "Yes, interesting."

Janet shrugged. "Well, I told you it'd probably turn up in the strangest place."

Christina nodded again. "Yep, that's what you said." *Could Janet have done this and all the other things? She certainly had opportunity, but what about her motive? Why would she want to hurt or discredit me? Is she still angry about the job situation—after all this time?*

Janet noticed Christina staring at her and raised her eyebrows. "What?" she asked.

Christina shook her head. "Sorry. I was just wondering how those papers could have ended up in Mrs. Davies's chart, that's all."

Janet shrugged. "It's a mystery. That's for sure. Speaking of Mrs. Abernathy, I should probably go check on her." Turning her back and walking away from the station, Christina missed the sardonic smile that crossed Janet's face.

She really is a strange woman, thought Christina as she turned her mind back to the charts in front of her.

CHAPTER 93

Dr. Aaron Carmichael sat at his desk staring at the pile of papers. He knew he should be sorting through them but just couldn't stop thinking about Christina. He knew he was acting irrationally—he hardly knew the woman—but he couldn't help it.

After his wife died, no other woman had attracted his attention as Christina had. Remembering how he had felt the first time he saw her made his breath catch and his heart flutter.

He had done an emergency appendectomy on Stacey the previous night and had walked into the hospital room to check on his patient, waking both mother and daughter. He had been so focused on Stacey that he hadn't paid close attention to Christina until he had finished his examination. Then he looked at her.

She hadn't struck him as drop-dead gorgeous or anything like that, but she was so darn cute, with her big blue eyes and curly auburn hair. Even though her eye makeup was smudged and she looked tired and rumpled and still had fading bruises, there was something about her that attracted him. Here it was, weeks later, and he still couldn't pinpoint what it was that struck a chord in his heart. She was so totally unlike his wife.

Tabitha had been tall, thin, blonde, and drop-dead gorgeous. She had modeled for Elite and Ford and had even been in a couple of commercials for beauty products.

They had met at a charity dinner for a new children's wing in Chicago where her father was the guest speaker and head of the organization that was sponsoring the fundraiser. She had been at the bar ordering a drink when, unbeknownst to her, Aaron approached to order his own drink. Turning around quickly, she bumped into him and spilled her drink on his tuxedo. Embarrassed, she turned to grab a napkin and then slipped and lost her balance. He had reached out and caught her by the hand before she hit the floor. It had been an awkward moment for both, but they ended up laughing about it over another drink. The rest of the evening was spent in private, intimate conversation.

Within a year they were married, and a year after that had a beautiful daughter named Samantha. Their life had been a fairy tale until Tabitha was killed by a drunk driver on her way home from a photo shoot in Fort Worth. He put his head in his hands and let his mind go back to that night.

He had just put three-year-old Sammie to bed and was sitting at the computer reading an article about gallbladder disease in obese children when the phone rang. As he reached for it, he heard Samantha scream. Jumping out of his chair and ignoring the ringing phone, he ran to his daughter's bedroom. She was sitting up in bed screaming for her mother. He ran in and picked her up and tried to soothe the hysterical child. She kept asking, "Where's Mommy?" He tried to tell her that mommy would be home soon. She kept saying, "No, Mommy's here. Where is she?" He didn't understand why she kept insisting she saw her mommy. He carried her around the house, showing her each room and assuring her that her mommy wasn't there, that she was on her way home. She finally calmed down, and he was able to put her back to bed. As he kissed her forehead, which was damp with perspiration, he wondered what had brought on such an episode. When he was sure she was sound asleep, he returned to his study. Hearing a beeping noise, he realized that in his haste, he had knocked the receiver off the cradle. He replaced it and jumped when it rang.

"Hello?"

"Dr. Carmichael?" the male voice asked.

"Yes."

"Dr. Carmichael, this is Sheriff Lane Mason of the Tarrant County Police Department. Is your wife's name Tabitha?"

"Yes," he had said as his heart did a double tap and his hands started to shake.

"Dr. Carmichael, your wife has been in an accident, and we need you to come to the hospital. She'll be taken to the Fort Worth Medical Trauma Center. Do you know where that is?"

Fearing the worst, he answered, "Yes. How badly is she injured?"

The sheriff hesitated for a moment. "Dr. Carmichael, she isn't doing very well. Her injuries are extensive. You need to get here as soon as possible."

"I'm on my way!" he said as he slammed down the phone and rushed into his daughter's room, scooped her up, blanket and all, and headed for the car. He strapped his sleeping child into her car seat and drove like a maniac to the hospital. He hadn't been thinking clearly or he would have called his mother to come over to watch Sammie, but time was ticking away, and he didn't think he could afford any delay. He was amazed that Sammie slept through the whole trip, only waking when they arrived at the hospital.

On the way, he had made a call to his mother and asked her to meet him so she could care for Sammie. She agreed and was waiting for him when he walked in carrying the fussing child. He quickly handed her off to his mother and headed for the emergency department, where Sheriff Mason greeted him. He sensed the news would be tragic when he saw the dismal faces of the policemen, firemen, and medical staff. Choking back a sob, he asked about his wife's whereabouts. A middle-aged nurse came and quietly escorted him into a room. There lay Tabitha on a gurney, covered by a white sheet. She looked so pale and still. He walked over and took her hand. It was cold to the touch, but he put it up to his mouth and kissed it. He felt tears stream down his face as he leaned over and kissed her mouth. It too was cold. There were bruises and gashes on her face where the window glass must have cut her. He lifted the sheet to see what other damage had been done to his beautiful wife and inhaled sharply as he saw her broken and mangled legs and bruised and distended abdomen. Sobs racked his whole being, and he fell to his knees.

CHAPTER 94

Aaron jumped when the phone rang, and, wiping tears from his eyes, he reached for it, clearing his throat as he spoke.

"Hello?"

"Dr. Carmichael?"

"Yes."

"This is Mrs. Stanford from the elementary school."

What now? I don't need another interruption in my day, he thought as he gripped the receiver.

Ever since her mother's death, Samantha had gone through periods of clinginess. She would pretend to be sick or deliberately hurt herself so he would end up staying at home and giving her extra attention—good for her, but not so much for him and his patients. After the fifth time, he decided he couldn't continue playing that game and keep his practice, so he had taken her to a counselor and was informed that she was going through normal grieving adjustments and would eventually stop with the manipulative behavior. The past couple of months *had* been better with less clinginess and whining. *So what now?*

"Yes, Mrs. Stanford. Is Sammie all right?"

"Well, Dr. Carmichael, it looks as if she may be coming down with chicken pox. I noticed a few bumps on her face, and then I looked at her belly and there are a few there as well."

Aaron sighed and rubbed a hand over his face.

She continued. "There have been a few cases this past month, so it wouldn't surprise me if that's what it is." There was a pause as Aaron reviewed his options. "Dr. Carmichael, do you want to come get her, or should I call your mother?"

His parents had moved from Dallas to Alva soon after Tabitha's death, to be closer to Aaron and Sammie. Their presence had been comforting during those turbulent times of adjustment, and he found himself relying on them more often as his patient load and work hours increased.

"No, I'll come get her so I can check her over. Thank you for calling."

"All right. She'll be waiting in the office."

Replacing the receiver and sighing, he shot a prayer up to heaven expressing his gratitude that it wasn't anything more serious—like a biting, kicking, screaming tantrum.

Pressing the buzzer to call in his secretary, he was pleased when she responded promptly. He gathered the file folders, handed them to her, and said, "I need to go get

Sammie from school. Could you please reschedule my patients, or, better yet, see if Dr. Seltzer can take them? I think I only have a couple of consultations this afternoon."

Dr. Daniel Seltzer, a thirty-two-year-old recent graduate of Baylor Medical School, had been hired the previous year to work with Dr. Carmichael. Aaron had been the only pediatric surgeon before that, and even though his workload had been steady, it had increased over the past couple of years when Alva had a population growth due to the new outlet mall. He hadn't minded the long hours in the beginning—the less time he spent at home, the less time he thought about Tabitha—but Sammie needed him, forcing him to put aside his selfish reasoning.

He went before the board of directors and asked for an assistant or another pediatric surgeon to be hired, or he would start sending cases to Dallas or Fort Worth. Not wanting to lose patients or money, the board had started interviewing right away and within a short time had hired Dr. Seltzer.

Aaron liked the young man, who was eager to learn and full of energy, reminding him of himself at that age. He had a positive rapport with the children and their parents as well. Dr. Dan would be qualified handle the two or three consultations scheduled for the afternoon—two tonsillectomies and one ear tube placement. *Nothing serious.* Hopefully, by tomorrow, he would be back to work, and Sammie would be with Grandma, being comforted and spoiled as only a grandma could do.

After scrawling a quick note to Christina and dropping it off at the CCU nurses' station, he headed for his car. He would call Christina that evening when everything had stabilized.

While driving to the school, the plans for Friday night occupied his mind. Having shared his parents' forty-fifth wedding anniversary meal at a restaurant called Two Dragons and being quite impressed with the atmosphere and food, he wanted to share that experience with Christina. Sammie raved for several days afterward about how awesome it was when the chef prepared their meal right in front of them. He knew she would be disappointed and possibly angry when she realized she would not be going with them.

If the rash was indeed chicken pox and it ran its usual course, Sammie would be out of the contagious stage and feeling like her usual frisky self by Friday, and he wouldn't feel guilty about leaving her for the evening. He would call Tabitha's mom, who lived on the outskirts of Dallas, and see if she would be willing to watch her granddaughter for the night. *A night with Nana beats a dinner at the Two Dragons—right?* he thought.

After Tabitha's death, he found he had to make a conscious effort to keep in touch with his in-laws. *Why is it so hard to see them more often? Probably because when I see them, I see Tabitha, and that makes my heart hurt.* His mother-in-law, bless her heart, called him at least once a week to check up on him and Sammie and offer her time for babysitting. This past year, when he had to be in Dallas for a meeting, he would drop Sammie off with a quick hello and good-bye, avoiding any intimate conversation. *One of these days, I've got to get past this,* he thought. Feeling a pang of guilt wash over him, he sighed as he pulled into the parking lot, found a space right in front of the school entrance, and went in to retrieve his child.

CHAPTER 95

Christina rubbed her fingers over her tired eyes. *I need a cup of coffee,* she thought as she looked at her watch. *One thirty—only a couple more hours to go.* She took the allergy medication that Aaron had given her around eleven, and it had helped clear up her stuffiness, but she still felt sluggish.

Lack of a good night's sleep didn't help. *I wish I could just go lie down and take a little nap,* she thought as she covered a yawn with her hand.

Looking around the station and finding it empty of caregivers, she raised her hands over her head and, standing on tippy toes, stretched as far as she could. *I should start seeing a chiropractor again,* she thought as she rotated and stretched her neck hearing and feeling the pop and crack of those bones and joints. She looked at the heart monitors before leaving the station to pour a cup of coffee. All was well.

Seeing there was only a little sludge left in the bottom of the coffee carafe, she rinsed it out and prepared a fresh brew. While waiting, she remembered the medicine bottle that had fallen under the shelving unit in the medication room. She unlocked the door, flipped on the switch and bent down to look under the shelves. The bottle was still there, along with a plethora of cobwebs. Looking around and spotting an IV pole, she retrieved it and pushed it under the shelves, managing to tap the bottle and move it out to the side of the unit. Reaching over for it and wiping off the cobwebs, she was surprised when she read that it had once contained heparin. It was a tiny bottle that when full would have contained about five cc's—but now contained only a drop or two. *Hmm, that's interesting. Wonder how that got there? It shouldn't have been on the shelving unit. It should have been locked in the medicine cabinet, or disposed of in a hazardous waste container.* She turned it around, looking at it from all angles and considering the possibilities of its presence there. *Could it be the same heparin that made me sick?* She shook her head. *Probably not. What are the odds of finding the bottle that contained the very medicine that had almost killed me?* She instantly thought about the possibility of fingerprints, realizing too late that her careless handling of the container probably smudged any evidence. She held the bottle between her finger and thumb anyway, hoping to salvage something significant. Standing, she returned the IV pole, found a tissue, wrapped the small vial in it and slipped it into her pocket. She would show Steven later and ask his opinion. Returning to the lounge area, she waited for the coffee to finish brewing.

As she leaned against the counter waiting for her cup of energy, she watched as

Janet walked to the counter, took a piece of paper out of or from under a chart, slip unidentified paper into her pocket, replace the chart, and walk away.

I wonder what that was all about.

She finished her coffee, rinsed the cup, returned it to the cup rack, and then walked over to the counter and picked up the chart that Janet had opened. Flipping through the pages, it appeared as if nothing was out of place. *What was the mystery paper—a lab slip, prescription order, a new doctor's order? Guess I'll either have to wait and see what it was or just ask Janet straight on.* She replaced the chart in the file cabinet and sighed. Realizing it had been a couple of hours since she checked on the four patients, she slipped on her lab coat, put her stethoscope around her neck, and walked around the unit.

Janet had noticed Dr. Carmichael on the floor earlier and was curious as to the reason for his visit. He seemed to have been in a hurry as he slid a piece of paper under the chart on the counter. When he had left, she went over to the counter and, not seeing anyone, pretended to be reading the chart but had found the paper and stuck it in her pocket. Now, away from prying eyes, she opened the paper and read.

Dear Christina, Sammie has come down with the chicken pox, so I may not be around much the next couple of days, but I will get in touch to discuss our plans for Friday. Till then, Aaron.

Janet couldn't believe it. Not only was Christina fooling around with Dr. Dawson, she was dating Dr. Carmichael as well. *Did this woman have no decency? Common sense? How could she string two men along like that?* Then another thought occurred to her. *If Christina and Dr. Carmichael hooked up, that would leave Steven available. He will feel hurt and rejected, and I can be there to comfort him.* She smiled. *Okay, maybe this could be a good thing—something I want to encourage.*

Folding the note and putting it back in the envelope, she returned it to the counter. Surely Christina couldn't miss it, with her name so boldly written on the envelope. *I'll just casually mention that I saw Dr. Carmichael and that he left a note for her.* She smiled again.

Janet walked into the utility room and picked up a fresh set of bedding for Mr. Simpson, whose IV had come apart, leaking fluid and blood all over his bed as he slept. With his blood thinners, he could have easily bled to death had she not checked on him when she did. Thinking about how things could have turned out differently, she turned to exit the room and bumped into and nearly tripped over a laundry cart.

"Geez oh Pete! Where did that come from?" she asked as she bent to retrieve the sheet that had fallen from her arms.

"Sorry. I didn't know you were in there," said a voice from behind the cart. Janet looked up into the woman's smiling face and noticed how round it and the rest of her was. *Wow! I may never complain about my weight again!*

"Um, okay," Janet said as she retrieved the sheet from the outstretched hand and then hurried down the hall.

Lula entered the laundry room and looked around for the small vial she had left earlier that day after setting it down to pick up a towel that had fallen from the shelf, promptly forgetting about it.

She had been mentally beating herself up all morning because of her carelessness.

How could I be so stupid? If anyone else finds that, I could be in big trouble. Turning in circles, moving contents, and looking frantically on each shelf and not finding the missing vial, she almost cried. She slapped herself on the forehead, and, wiping her eyes, she took a deep breath to calm herself.

"What am I gonna do now? The boss man will be so mad."

Not knowing what else to do, she restocked the shelves with bedding materials and towels and turned to go, nearly bumping into Christina.

Avoiding eye contact and hurrying past, she said, "Excuse me."

Before Christina had time to respond, the woman had grabbed her cart and rushed away down the hall.

Christina shook her head. "Sorry," she called out to a retreating back. *Well, alrighty then. Wonder why she's in such a hurry.*

When Janet walked into Mr. Simpson's room and watched the snoring man, she wished she could end his suffering. *I could just put the pillow over his face. No one would be the wiser. The way my luck has been going lately, something would backfire, and I'd get caught. Then who would take care of Leelee?*

She whispered, "Sorry, Mr. Simpson, guess we'll just have to wait for the death angel to come claim you." As she reached for his pillow, she added, "I hope for your sake it's soon." She watched as he opened and closed his mouth, adding saliva to the parched tongue and cheeks. She sighed and shook her head.

Poor guy. As she went about the task of changing his linens, Christina walked in. Surprised, Janet nearly dropped the bundle of wet sheets.

"Hi, Janet. Need help?"

"Uh, no. I've got it under control."

"What happened?" Christina asked as she surveyed the wet, bloody sheets.

"His IV came loose. Good thing I caught it when I did, or he could have bled out."

Christina nodded, concern showing on her face.

"Do you think he bled enough to warrant a CBC?"

Janet shook her head. "No, it just looks like a lot because of the IV fluid, but really it's nothing to be concerned about. Believe me, I've seen more than this, and it's always been fine."

Christina nodded, not fully convinced. She walked over to Mr. Simpson's bed and took his hand, which felt surprisingly warm. She had expected it to feel cold, like so many other patients on the unit. Feeling his forehead, which also felt warm, she asked, "Have you taken his temperature?"

"I took it about an hour ago. It was 99.6—nothing to be alarmed about."

Putting her stethoscope in her ears, she listened to Mr. Simpson's chest. "Would you please take it again?" His heart rate seemed elevated. Taking the blood pressure cuff from the wall and wrapping it around his arm, she pumped it up. Listening to the steady *thump, thump, thump* of the heart as the air escaped through the valve in the cuff, she was surprised that his blood pressure was high: 150 over 95. She turned to Janet, who was still standing in the doorway.

Returning the cuff to the wall unit and replacing her stethoscope around her neck, she asked, "What was his last blood pressure reading?"

Janet shrugged, "I can't remember exactly. The chart's at the foot of the bed."

Walking over and retrieving it, Christina looked at the numbers and nodded.

"Well, it's been running high all last night and today. I'm gonna call Dr. Dawson and inform him. He might want to increase his medication. In the meantime, go ahead and take his temperature to make sure we're not dealing with an infection as well." She lifted the sleeping man's eyelids and shone a penlight in each, checking for reaction time.

"Good. No stroke," she mumbled as she patted Mr. Simpson's cheek and called his name. He tried desperately to open his eyes, managing only a slit before closing them completely again.

"Has he been this unresponsive all day?" she asked Janet, who was standing at the foot of the bed waiting for further instructions.

"Pretty much. I can't wake him."

"Hmm. He should be more responsive by now. I'll mention that to Dr. Dawson as well."

Janet nodded in agreement.

The two ladies left the room and went their separate ways—Christina to make a call to Dr. Dawson, and Janet to dispose of the soiled linens and get a thermometer.

CHAPTER 96

Dr. Dawson stretched, twisted his back, and rolled his neck, hearing the satisfying crack and pop of bones and joints. He had had a very busy morning monitoring stress tests, performing heart catheterizations, and meeting with patients and families regarding upcoming surgeries and had just finished an angioplasty when his pager went off. He felt the familiar buzzing in his pocket and reached for it, immediately recognizing the number—his office. He removed the gloves, face mask, hair net, and outer sterile gown, throwing them in a receptacle near the door before heading for a nearby phone. His heart jumped when his receptionist stated that Christina wanted him to call her back regarding a patient. He hadn't spoken to her, except about patients, since their coffee date and was beginning to miss her company. Checking his watch and realizing he had an hour or so to kill before his next appointment, he headed up to the cardiac floor to speak to Christina personally.

Reading through Mr. Simpson's chart, she noticed an envelope with her name on it out of the corner of her eye. Curiosity getting the upper hand, she pushed the chart aside and reached for the envelope, surprised and pleased to see the note was from Aaron. Smiling, she tucked the note back in the envelope and quickly put it in her pocket as Steven approached the desk—which didn't go unnoticed. He gave her a curious look.

"Is everything all right?" he asked, noticing the blush travelling from her neck to her face.

"Sure," she answered quickly. "So what brings you up here?"

"You called, wanting to discuss one of the patients?"

"Oh yes." She took a calming breath and reached for Mr. Simpson's chart with shaking hands, willing them and the rest of her body to settle down. *Why am I so flustered? I have nothing to hide from Steven—or do I?*

"Are you sure you're all right?" he asked with growing concern.

"Really, I'm fine. It's just been a long day."

He nodded, not truly convinced that that was the reason behind her nervousness.

"So which patient are you concerned about?"

She told him about Mr. Simpson's high blood pressure, elevated temperature, and unresponsiveness. She followed with the chart as Dr. Dawson made a beeline for his patient's room. After checking him over, Dr. Dawson wrote out a prescription for IV antibiotics, increased his blood pressure medication, and lowered his dosage of Valium.

"If he doesn't improve within, say, a couple of hours after all this is implemented, please give me a call. He may have another blockage somewhere or a more serious infection brewing."

When they exited the room, he pulled her aside.

"Christina, are you sure everything is all right? You seem nervous or anxious about something."

She assured him that everything was fine. *How can I tell him that I'm going on a date with his best friend? He'll probably find out anyway, but I don't want to tell him yet. Why am I feeling guilty? I'm a grown woman and can date anyone I choose, so why the guilt?*

Noticing Janet for the first time since leaving the patient's room, she said, "Oh, hi, Janet. Is everything all right?"

Janet stood for a moment, glaring at the two of them as thoughts raced through her mind. Realizing what she was doing, she shook her head.

"Oh, uh, yeah. I just wanted to let you know that Mrs. Abernathy was asking for you." She looked back and forth between Dr. Dawson and Christina, sighed, and said, "Guess I'll see you at the desk."

Steven watched as she walked away and then turned and smiled at Christina.

"She's an interesting lady," he said.

"Yep, she sure is. Did it look like she was glaring at us?"

"Oh, I don't know if I'd use the word *glare*, but she certainly did look shocked to see us together."

"Maybe I'm getting a little paranoid, but sometimes she gives me the creeps."

Steven chuckled. "Well, I'm sure she's harmless."

She nodded and gave a halfhearted smile.

Looking around and seeing they were the only two people in the hallway, he casually asked, "Are you doing anything Friday night?"

She was caught off guard and stammered, "Oh, um, I already have plans."

Obviously disappointed but undeterred, he said with a sly grin, "Oh, all right. Well, what about Saturday or Sunday?"

She thought for a second before replying, "I don't have any plans yet for Saturday, except to catch up on housework."

"How about we go to a movie?" He smiled and raised his eyebrows and then added, "We could take the kids too if you want."

She smiled and shook her head and then lightly patted him on the arm.

"Tell you what. Let me see what the kids have planned, and I'll see how my week goes and how much housework I can get done. Then I'll give you a definite answer."

He frowned slightly and nodded. Leaning down and kissing the top of her head before she could react, he said, "Alrighty then, guess I'll have to wait for an answer."

He chuckled and turned to go. With his back to her, he waved his hand as he walked to the elevator, leaving her standing there, dumbfounded.

What the heck was that about? Smiling and shaking her head as she watched his retreating back, she thought, *Darn it, why does he have to be so cute? How could any gal in her right mind resist that?* Shrugging and sighing, she headed for Mrs. Abernathy's room. Reaching in her pocket for a pen and feeling the small wrapped bottle, she chided herself. *Oh, shoot! I was going to tell him about the bottle I found. Guess I'll try to catch him before I leave today.*

Janet was livid. She knew she was losing any ground she had established with Steven. *I can't understand why he isn't interested in me. I'm much prettier than Christina, I'm a dedicated worker, and I've always shown him respect. What does Christina have that I don't? Why aren't the spells I cast working?* She left the desk area as soon as Christina approached, fearing that if something were said, she would lose control and tell her what she really thought of her.

CHAPTER 97

During the drive home, Janet replayed the scene between Christina and Steven and felt her anger and resentment build. By the time she entered her house, rational thinking was gone. *Christina has to go once and for all—but how? I will have to take some time to meditate on that.* She went to her room, closed the door, took a couple of books from her shelf, and sat on the bed.

That's where Linda found her when she came home from her piano lesson.

Rapping lightly on the closed door and then poking her head in when she heard a muffled "Yeah?" she asked, "What ya doin', Mom?"

Glancing up from the book she held in her hand, she answered, "Just doing some research." Cocking her head, she asked, "So how was your lesson?"

Linda did a one-shoulder shrug and said, "Okay. I got a new song to work on for the recital in May called 'Für Elise.' It looks pretty hard."

"Well, you have plenty of time to learn it." Glancing at the bedside clock and picking up her pen and notebook, she said, "I need to get back to work here."

Noticing the scattered books on the bed, watching her mom scribble something in a notebook, and realizing her mom wasn't in an attention-giving mood, she asked, "You want some ice tea or something?"

"No. I'm all set. Why don't you go fix yourself something to eat? I need to keep at this for a while longer."

"Okay." Quietly closing the door, she stood thinking a moment before heading to the kitchen. *I wonder what that's all about.* Then, like a typical thirteen-year-old, she shrugged and headed to the kitchen. As she prepared a salad, she did think of her friend Stacey and wondered what she was up to.

As Christina walked into the kitchen, almost tripping over Chloe and Benji, who were competing for her attention, her cell phone rang. She rushed over to the counter and dug into her purse, finding her phone on the fourth ring.

"Hello?" she answered breathlessly.

"Christina?"

"Yes." Recognizing her mother-in-law's voice, she added, "Oh, hi, Mom."

"Are you all right, honey?"

Christina pulled up a stool to sit on. Chuckling, she said, "Oh, I'm fine. I just got home and was running to get to the phone. I almost tripped over Benji and Chloe."

Ruth let out a relieved sigh. "Okay, because you sounded a bit winded."

"So what's up?" Christina asked as she picked up Chloe, scratching her ears and feeling the cat's body relax and vibrate as she began to purr. Benji lay at her feet, thumping his tail on the floor, waiting patiently for his portion of attention.

"Well, are you and the kids all right? I mean *really* all right?"

Christina made a face. She was the second person to ask this in the past twenty-four hours.

"Well, yeah. Why?"

"Oh, I just had an awful dream last night about you and the kids and woke up worried and anxious all day."

"Really? What was the dream about?" she asked, curiosity growing within her. Chloe, deciding that she had had enough attention, jumped from her lap and ran to the kitchen, followed closely by Benji. Christina smiled as she watched them go. Even though they were two completely different species, they seemed to derive pleasure from each other's company.

"I can't remember it exactly, but something about y'all being chased by something dark and scary. I kept calling out for you, but I kept losing sight of you and the kids." She paused and chuckled. "It doesn't sound so bad when I tell it, but I woke in a sweat and just terrified that something bad was going to happen to you all. I just can't help but worry about you, especially after that incident at work."

"Hmm. Well, we're okay so far." *Should I tell her about the threatening note? No. No use making her more anxious.*

"Are you sure you're fully recovered from that accident?"

"Oh, yeah. I'm totally fine now."

"Well, good."

"You know, Mom, you're the second person to call and say they had a bad dream involving us. Kinda makes me wonder if God is trying to tell us something." She reached for a pen and paper and began doodling.

"Really? Who else called?"

Christina told her of the phone call from Ellie. Both women were silent for a few seconds. Finally, her mother-in-law asked quietly, "Christina, do you mind if I pray for you and the kids?"

"Of course not," she said quickly. "I'd really appreciate it. I'm starting to feel a little nervous about all this." She laid the pen down and closed her eyes.

Ruth said a quick prayer, and they said their good-byes. When the call was disconnected, Christina sat for a few minutes reflecting on the past couple of days. All of a sudden the dream she had had about David came to her mind.

He had said, "Christina, stay strong in your faith," making her wonder what that meant. *Why would I need to stay strong in my faith? Was he warning me of impending doom?* Not feeling any lightning bolt of insight from heaven, she let out a sigh and headed for the kitchen to fill the animals' empty bowls. The thought crossed her mind that she should wait for Nicky to come home and do his job, but when she saw Benji lying on the floor with his chin resting on his empty food bowl and Chloe sitting patiently in front of hers, she couldn't help but give in and feed them. In appreciation, Benji thumped his tail and Chloe purred as she filled each bowl. They had trained her well.

As she stood in front of the open fridge door deciding what she could throw together to make a decent meal, the phone rang again. Grabbing a head of lettuce, a tomato, and a bowl and butting the refrigerator door shut, she picked it up on the third ring. She was pleasantly surprised to hear Aaron Carmichael's voice on the other end.

"Hey, Christina. Just wanted to touch base with you about Friday night."

"Okay, but first off, Aaron, how's your little girl?" she asked as she sat at the table, cradling the phone between her shoulder and ear, ripping lettuce into bite-sized pieces. He explained that the child did indeed have chicken pox, but fortunately for her, it was a mild case.

"She should be fine in a couple of days."

Christina related how she had gone through that phase with each of her three children and twice with Stacey.

"Twice? It's unusual for a kid to have chicken pox more than once, especially if the first case was intense."

"I know! Can you imagine Stacey's anger at having to go through it again? She was one very crabby little girl." Chuckling, she added, "I was so glad when she went back to school. I'm not sure either one of us would get through another week without someone getting hurt!"

Clearing his throat, he asked, "Can I pick you up at six o'clock Friday evening?"

"Okay. That'll be fine."

"Also, if you don't mind, I'd like to take Sammie and drop her off at her grandparents' house. Then we can have dinner at the Two Dragons Japanese restaurant in Dallas."

"That sounds great! I'd like to see Sammie again."

When she set the phone on the counter, she felt a pang of guilt in her heart. Here she was, going out with Aaron on Friday night and Steven on Saturday night—both attractive, caring, intelligent, and available. *Steven has a great sense of humor, but does Aaron? He seemed pleasant on the few occasions we've spoken, but can he compete with Steven? Do I want him to compete with Steven?* She would find out on Friday night. She sighed and spoke to Benji, who was looking up and wagging his tail.

"Well, Benji, I sure hope I don't have to choose between the two of them. At this point, I guess I'd still choose Steven, only because I've known him longer." Benji snuffed and shook his head as if to agree. She patted him on the head, and his tongue reached out and found her hand.

"You're a good dog, Benji," she said as she moved the bowl of lettuce and began cutting up vegetables for the rest of the salad.

CHAPTER 98

When Cindy returned home from her nail appointment on Tuesday afternoon, she retrieved the mail from the mailbox, sorted through it, and found an envelope addressed to her in unfamiliar handwriting. Noticing no return address in the upper left corner, she turned it over to see if there was a return address there. There wasn't. She started to rip it open when Samara walked in.

"Hey, Mom," she said dully as she sighed and slowly walked over to her mother and gave her a halfhearted hug.

"Hey yourself," replied Cindy, noticing her daughter's depressed mood. Dreading what she might hear, she tucked the letter in her jeans pocket and asked, "What's wrong, honey?"

Throwing herself onto the sofa, the petulant girl answered, "I had an awful day."

Cindy walked over and sat next to her daughter, pulling her close. "Tell me about it."

Instead of telling her mom about her day, she asked, "Mom, do you think I'm pretty?"

Surprised, Cindy stated emphatically, "Why, of course you are, honey. Why would you ask that?"

Samara sighed and wiped her eye before the tear that was forming made its way down her cheek. "Are you just saying that 'cause you're my mom, or do you honestly think I'm pretty?"

Cindy stood, pulling her daughter up with her. "Well, let me see." Turning her around and pushing her hair from her face, she gave her daughter a once-over body scan with her eyes. Samara was petite and was just starting to blossom into a woman. Her big blue eyes with dark eyebrows and eyelashes and olive complexion were from her father, and her small nose, full lips, and straight teeth were from her mom. She had been blessed with flawless facial skin and, if lucky, wouldn't have to deal with teen acne, like so many other girls her age.

"Well," said Cindy as she stood with her hands on her hips, "other than that big ole wart on the end of your nose, I'd say you're just about perfect."

"Oh, Mom!" said Samara as she put her hand up to her face, crossing her eyes and looking down to the end of her perfect little nose. "Do you really think it's that noticeable?"

Waving her hands in the air, she answered, "Well, duh. I suppose we could go have it removed, but personally I kind of like it, especially with the big black hair growing out of it." She cocked her head and tried not to smile but felt a giggle forming in her belly.

Striking a pose and showing her mother her profile, she said, "It is kind of attractive, isn't it?" Both giggled.

Composing herself, Samara said, "Seriously, Mom. Am I what you'd call pretty?"

Cindy put her arms around her child and hugged her. "Yes, my darlin', you are indeed pretty." Then, trying unsuccessfully to stifle a giggle, she added, "Warts and all."

Samara shook her head and pulled away to look into her mother's eyes. "Then why don't the boys like me?"

Cindy put her at arm's length. *Oh, boy,* she thought. *Not the boy thing.* She had a feeling that was what all this was leading up to but had kinda hoped it wasn't.

She sighed. "Okay, baby, let's sit back down and talk about this."

After a few minutes, it was obvious that Samara was concerned about one boy in particular. It wasn't that *all* the boys didn't like her. In fact, there were a few who were vying for her attention. It was just this one boy, whom she wouldn't reveal, who had her doubting herself. Cindy tried reassuring her that she just needed to give the boy time to get to know her, and if he was smart, he'd befriend her—and then who knew where that would lead?

"Samara, do you and this boy ever talk to each other?"

Samara nodded. "Well, yeah. I mean, we know each other and say hi and stuff, but nothing ever serious." She sighed. "Ooh, I get so frustrated. I want to talk to him, but I get all nervous and then I clam up and can't think of anything to say—or, worse yet, I say something stupid."

Hoping to discover the identity of this mystery boy, Cindy asked, "Is this boy in any of your classes? Does he have a name?"

"No, he's not in any of my classes, 'cause he's a sophomore, and yes, he has a name, but I'm not telling you, so don't try to wheedle it out of me."

Cindy raised her eyebrows. "Wheedle?"

"You know what I mean!" Samara said with her arms folded across her chest.

Cindy nodded and chuckled. "Oh, I see, a mysterious older man." *Way too old!* she thought. *Okay, maybe not too old—he would be maybe a year or two older than Samara. Still. She is only fourteen and won't even be allowed to date till she's sixteen. So yes, he is too old for her daughter.* What she said was "Hmm" as her mind ran through the short list of young men she knew who were sophomores. Brad Sanders popped into her mind. He certainly fit the bill: cute, sophomore, someone Samara knew but was shy around. *I wonder if he's the object of my daughter's affections. I can just about bet that wild horses couldn't drag that out of her, at least not now. She's probably afraid*

I'll say something to Christina, who'll say something to Brad—and what if I did and I was wrong? Guess I'll find out sooner or later.

She smiled. "Well, baby, I'm not sure what to tell you except to just be yourself. Don't compromise your beliefs or values for any guy at any time. If he's the right one, he'll like you just the way you are without trying to change you."

They sat quietly on the couch for a few minutes, Cindy's arm around Samara's shoulders and the girl's head on her mom's shoulder, absorbing what was just said. Then Cindy broke the silence by saying, "Oh yeah, and remember—you can't date till you're sixteen."

Samara rolled her eyes. Standing, she leaned down to give her mom a hug and kiss on the cheek. "Thanks, Mom."

"For what?"

"You know. You're the best mom ever. And maybe someday I'll let you know *who* this mysterious man is."

Cindy nodded. "Well, that's something to look forward to."

Samara shook her head and smiled. "I need to go do some math homework. I'll just make myself a salad and eat in my room if that's okay."

Cindy nodded. "Yeah, that's fine. Don't forget to let Sasha in. She's been in the garage all day."

"Oh yeah. I almost forgot about her!" She headed for the garage, and Cindy could hear Sasha yipping and Samara giggling and could imagine the little dog jumping with glee. When Samara returned with the wiggling bundle of fur, the dog jumped down and made a beeline for Cindy. Before she could fend her off, the excited dog covered her other mistress with doggy kisses.

Trying to catch the wiggling mass of fur, she yelled, "Samara, please get her off me!" Samara was giggling as she reached for Sasha.

"Sorry, Mom. She just can't help herself."

Cindy sighed as she wiped her face with her hands.

"I know. She gets really lonely cooped up all day, but doggone it, I hate when she licks my face!" She stood and walked to the bathroom to wash the spit-covered areas. "You'd think she'd be too old to have so much energy—she's nearly seven." She paused as she dried her face and hands.

"What's that in human years?" she called out to her daughter.

"It would be around forty-nine years," Samara said as she snuggled Sasha, who had calmed considerably. "Wow, that *is* old!" she added, smiling at her mom, who had just recently celebrated her fortieth birthday.

Cindy, realizing the connection, frowned and shook her head.

Walking by and rubbing the dog's ears, she said, "All right, maybe she's not *that* old, yet. I bet she's got a few good years left in her."

Samara headed to the pantry and filled a bowl with dog food. Setting Sasha down in front of the bowl, she smiled as she watched the dog gobble the food as if it were her last meal. Cindy watched for a moment and then said, "I'm gonna sit and read the mail then do some laundry and catch up on my e-mails." Samara looked up and nodded. "Okay."

Cindy returned to the couch and sat down, picking up the stack of envelopes and flyers. As Samara walked by, she said, "Why not make enough salad for the both of us? I just bought some ham and cheese yesterday you could add."

Samara waved her hand and said, "Sure, Mom, in a little while." She entered her room with a now satiated Sasha and closed the door. Soon Cindy heard a female vocalist singing in the background.

She smiled and stretched out on the couch. *Aah, it feels good to get off my feet.*

Setting the mail on the floor, she leaned her head back and closed her eyes for a few seconds. As she felt herself drifting off to sleep, she remembered the envelope in her pocket and was instantly awake. She retrieved the wrinkled envelope, ripped it open, and, with shaking hands, pulled out a folded piece of paper. *Why am I so nervous?* She opened the paper and started reading.

Dear Cindy,

It was so nice seeing you the other night. I understand your frustration and anger with me for not getting in touch with you. I want to continue seeing you, but right now isn't a good time for me to pursue this. The job I'm doing requires my full attention and all my extra time. When I'm finished with it, hopefully we can continue where we left off. Please forgive me for any hurts I may have caused.

Ed

Cindy read the letter a couple more times, hoping to find some kind of hidden messages between the lines—there were none. She returned it to its envelope and then to her pocket. He had pretty much written the same words he had spoken to her in the restaurant, but it still touched her heartstrings to think he would take the time to write and reaffirm his desire to see her again. She sighed. *Dang it! How can I be angry with him when he goes and writes me such a nice note?*

"Dang it! Dang it! Dang it!" she said as she pounded her fist into the couch cushion. Her mind was telling her to forget him. *He's a loser, like all the other guys in your life. He doesn't really care about you. He just wants to use you.* But her heart retaliated and said, *No, he's a great guy who really cares about you and your feelings, or he wouldn't have sent the note.* She chose to believe her heart. She stood, took a deep breath, let it out, and headed for the laundry room, where she was met with piles of dirty clothes. Later on, she would call Christina.

CHAPTER 99

When Ed and Tom were sure that Christina and the kids had vacated the house, they quickly and quietly entered using the same key Ed had used before. Benji, determined to protect his family's home, greeted the men with a cacophony of barks. Ed reached in his pocket, found a dog biscuit, and handed it to the wary dog. Benji sniffed the treat and the hand that held it, recognized both, and gently removed the biscuit. Ed reached out and scratched the dog's ears, causing instant tail wagging. Benji happily retreated to the family room, where he promptly ate the biscuit, and ran back for another one as Ed was heading up the stairs.

"Goodness, Benji, didn't you get enough to eat today?" He handed the pooch another biscuit and told him to leave them alone, as they had work to do. Benji went back to the family room, buried the biscuit behind the cushion on the couch, and then ran back up the stairs to lie on the floor next to Ed.

"I'm gonna hit the head and then start retrieving the bugs."

Ed nodded. "Don't forget to put the toilet seat back down," he called from the top of the stairs.

He heard a muffled "Yep."

Looking up at the light fixture where the bug was hidden, he heard the toilet flush and then the familiar bang of the toilet lid hitting the toilet. He chuckled. *Wonder if he's ever broken a toilet lid.*

Benji wagged his tail, walked in a circle three times, and plopped down. Sighing and laying his chin on his front paws, he watched Ed with big brown eyes.

Smiling, Ed decided right then and there that he needed a dog.

The men worked diligently for the next hour, clearing the house of any bugs.

Tom had just finished screwing the last light bulb in when his heart did a triple beat. Had he heard a car door slam? He listened intently, and there was a noise that sent adrenaline rushing into his system. He heard a door opening. It sounded like the back screen door. He quickly retrieved his tools and quietly moved to a hiding spot behind the door in the bathroom off the family room. He wished he could warn Ed but didn't want to give himself or Ed away if at all possible. He heard the back door open and a female voice call.

"Hey, Benji! Where are you, you useless watchdog?"

Hearing his name, Benji jumped up and barked all the way down the stairs, and Ed quickly and quietly entered the closet in Christina's room. Realizing he had left his tool bag on the bedside nightstand, he debated on whether he should get it or leave it where it was. If this was Christina, she would wonder where it had come from. He heard the female voice talking to Benji and realized it was Cindy. He made his decision to retrieve the bag just as he heard her start up the stairs. *Darn it,* he thought as he grabbed the bag and hid on the opposite side of the bed, away from the door. If he were lucky, she wouldn't come around to that side. He wondered if Tom had heard her and was hiding somewhere. *Of course he is.* Tom had been in this business longer than he and knew how to make himself practically invisible. It was amazing how quickly and quietly that man could move in spite of his size and weight.

He and Tom had been trained to move like cats and become as ghosts, which became an asset in times like this. He steadied his breathing, which slowed his heart. *What was Cindy doing here?* He held his breath as she entered the room.

"Hey, Benji, where's Chloe?" Ed could see her feet from his vantage point and hoped she wouldn't look under the bed for the missing cat. Chloe, who was curled up on Stacey's bed, heard her name and came sauntering in.

"There you are!" Cindy said as she laid something on the bed, bent down, and picked up the purring ball of fur. Ed heard the distinct sound of plastic being crinkled. *What was she doing?* Then she told him—well, not him exactly, but Benji. Women, God bless them, tended to think out loud, which was a benefit for some men who knew how to listen.

"Benji, I'm going to hang these clothes in the closet, and then I'll go down and get you and Chloe a treat." Ed almost sighed. Good thing he had moved out of the closet. He whispered a silent thank-you to God as he heard the rattling of the plastic and the sound of metal coat hangers being pushed aside.

"There," she said. "I'll have to call Christina and tell her I picked up the cleaning. That'll be one less thing she has to worry about."

She picked up Chloe, whom she had deposited on the bed while she hung the clothes.

"Come on, Benji," she said as she walked toward the hallway. Ed peeked under the bed and saw Benji's feet by the door. He silently whispered, *Go on, Benji. Don't let her know I'm here.*

"Come on, Benji, if you want a treat," Cindy said as she started down the stairs. Benji heard the word *treat* and took off after her. Ed let the air slowly out of his lungs.

"Thank you, God," he whispered. When he heard her in the kitchen, rummaging through the cupboards, he left his hiding spot. He stood by the door listening and smiling as he heard her speaking to the animals. He had almost relaxed, thinking the crisis was over, when he heard Benji bark and run toward the family room.

"What is it, Benji? Do you want out?" she asked as she followed the dog into the family room. He heard her opening the door to the backyard and calling for the dog. Benji stood his ground and continued barking in front of the bathroom door. She made a frustrated face and sighed.

"Benji, there's nothing in there." Ed heard her walk over to the door and fling it open. He knew he had to do something. He and Tom couldn't afford discovery. He stealthily went down the carpeted stairs, avoiding the fifth one that creaked. He reached in his jeans pocket and retrieved a small vial and a handkerchief. Quickly unscrewing the top and putting a few drops of the aromatic liquid on the handkerchief, he returned the vial to his pocket. He hoped he wouldn't have to use it. He quietly went through the dining room carefully avoiding squeaky floorboards and furniture. He heard Benji run into the bathroom sniffing and growling. It was then that Ed knew where Tom was hiding. He pushed thoughts of Cindy out of his head and went into CIA mode. Before she had time to open the closet door, he snuck up behind and put the handkerchief over her nose. She tried to scream and clawed at his hand, but he held her firmly, keeping her face away from his. Benji started barking and growling and backing away, as if he didn't know what to do, confused by Ed's behavior. Cindy went limp after a few seconds, and Ed scooped her up in his arms. She felt light as a feather and looked so peaceful and beautiful. He felt tears sting his eyes and quickly blinked them away. Tom exited the closet and let out a big sigh.

"Whew! That was too close," he said as he looked at the sleeping beauty.

"Now what are we gonna do? You know she'll call the police."

Ed sighed and looked around. "Why don't I put her on the couch, and we'll just take our stuff and leave."

Tom shrugged. "I guess that's all we can do."

Ed nodded. "Yeah. The police won't find anything out of the ordinary, anyway. I mean, we both wore gloves and put everything back in its place, so what have we got to worry about?" He gently laid Cindy on the couch and covered her with a blanket. Benji cautiously walked over and sniffed the sleeping lady. Ed reached out and scratched the nervous dog behind the ears.

"It's okay, Benji. She's all right." Benji looked up at Ed and slowly wagged his tail and then jumped on the couch by Cindy's feet.

"Come on, Tom. Let's go before she wakes up. I didn't use very much chloroform. No telling how long she'll be out."

Tom nodded and looked around the room, making sure everything was in order. The two men left the Sanders house as quietly as they had entered it—like ghosts.

In her dream, something heavy was on her chest, and she couldn't breathe. She awoke with a start and sat bolt upright, knocking Chloe to the floor. She rubbed her chest, feeling a warm spot where the cat had lain.

"Oh, it was you Chloe," Cindy said as she rubbed her face with her hands, wondering why she was on Christina's couch. The cat jumped back on the couch and started kneading the blanket on Cindy's feet. Cindy felt a cold sweat break out on her face as a wave of nausea hit her. She ran to the bathroom just in time to empty her stomach contents into the toilet. She sat on the floor trembling and weak as the nausea subsided and her memory returned.

CHAPTER 100

Christina was sitting at the table in the meeting room finishing her charting for the day when Janet summoned her to the phone. Thinking Steven or Aaron might be calling, she was surprised to hear Cindy's hysterical voice on the other end.

"Christina, I'm at your house, and someone was here!" Then, between sobs and blowing of her nose, she told her friend the story of dropping off the cleaning, Benji's barking, and someone drugging her, and her waking on the couch. Christina's heart raced, and her hands shook as she held the receiver.

"Cindy, did you call Larry?"

She heard a hiccup and a sniffle before Cindy answered. "No, not yet. Guess I'm not thinking straight. I automatically called your number first. Guess I should have called 911. That was really stupid of me …" She continued to ramble and Christina said, "Cindy! It's okay. When you hang up, call him, and I'll be home as soon as I can."

"Okay," she heard her friend say in a scared-little-girl voice.

"Are you sure whoever it was is gone?"

"Yes. It's quiet as a tomb here, and Benji doesn't seem to be nervous."

"Do you feel safe enough to stay there, or would you rather go home?"

Cindy sighed and paused for a moment as she considered her options.

"I'll be okay. I'll stay here and wait for Larry and you."

"That's good, honey. I'll be home within the hour." She replaced the receiver and stood thinking for a moment, chewing on her thumbnail. *What should I do next? Should I call Steven or Aaron? Maybe I should just leave and let someone else finish my charting. No. No one else could do that.* She took in a calming breath and slowed her mind. *Okay. First things first.* She looked at her watch. She had about an hour before her shift change. *I could call the head nurse for the next shift, explain that I have a family crisis and have to leave early, and ask her to come in early. Then I could call Steven and possibly Aaron. No, not Aaron—he isn't aware of the events that have transpired over the past month.* She chewed on her thumbnail again.

At least the kids won't be home for a couple of hours. Hopefully, the excitement will be over by then. No use getting them all upset and paranoid. I have enough paranoia for the whole town of Alva right now. As she headed back to the meeting room to finish her charting, Janet asked if everything was all right, which Christina answered with, "Hmm. Not really."

Janet frowned as she watched Christina return to the meeting room and close the door. Something was going on, and she wanted to know what it was—mostly out of curiosity, and partly wondering if the spell she had cast two days earlier was taking effect. She had called on powers to wreak havoc in Christina's life—not to cause harm to her or the children, but to make life uncomfortable—maybe enough to make her want to give up and go back to Michigan. *Yeah, right. It may take more than one spell to accomplish that,* she thought. *But I can be patient.*

When she had cast this spell before on her ex-husband's girlfriend Carmen, the girl ran screaming out of her apartment, tripped over her cat, and fell down a flight of stairs. When the paramedics arrived, they had to sedate her, as she kept insisting there were tarantulas everywhere in her apartment. None were ever found. Janet smiled.

Ronnie ended up dumping Carmen because he thought she was crazy, and Carmen moved to another town. *Served them both right,* she thought. She did what she had to do for her and Leelee's sake. *Couldn't have another woman in my daughter's life so soon after the divorce. The poor child suffered enough when her daddy left her, and then to have another woman try and take her mamma's place? Besides, Carmen was a bimbo. She was young and naïve and didn't have a lick of common sense. I did her a favor as well by breaking off that doomed relationship, because Ronnie would have left her somewhere down the line anyway when he tired of her. I'm doing Christina a favor too, whether she ever realizes it or not.*

CHAPTER 101

Larry was sitting at his desk, reading files concerning young women who had committed crimes between the years of 1975 and 1985. So far he had come up with twenty-five. Most were petty thievery—jewelry, candy, beer, cigarettes; others were domestic violence complaints—spats with girlfriends, boyfriends, parents, or siblings. No extended jail time was served. He had narrowed his suspect list down to five possibilities that fit the time line and description of someone who may hold a grudge against Christina—but the evidence was pretty weak. He sat pondering all this when his phone rang. Usually his secretary answered and screened his calls, but this came directly to him—someone he had given his personal phone number to. His heart accelerated a bit. His wife? Mom?

He answered a bit warily. "Hello? Sheriff Clifton speaking."

He heard sniffling and a choked "Larry? This is Cindy."

His hand tightened on the receiver. "What's wrong, Cindy?" He stood without realizing it—readying himself to what? Run?

"I'm at Christina's. Someone broke in and …" She stopped midsentence to blow her nose.

"I'll be right over." Placing the phone in his pocket and grabbing his jacket, he addressed his secretary. "Nancy, I'm going out for a bit. If you need me, call my cell phone."

"All right, Sheriff. Do you want me to call anyone else?" she asked as she looked up from a novel she was reading.

"Nope. I'll call *you* if I need any help." She shrugged and returned her attention to the book. She was vaguely curious about his sudden departure, but since nothing major ever happened in Alva, she figured it was nothing more than a family dispute.

He hurried out the door and into his patrol car, worrying that Cindy might have been hurt. Just in case, he called the EMS unit and instructed them to meet him at the Sanders residence. *Better to overreact than be caught unprepared,* he thought as his tires squealed onto Christina's street.

Even though he was married, he still had strong feelings for Cindy. They had been lovers once and had remained friends throughout the years, which he was thankful for but was a bone of contention between him and his wife. He had always wanted more from their relationship, but nothing ever developed, because they were either too much alike or too different. Neither one was sure why they couldn't seem to go further than friendship, but both were comfortable with the relationship as it stood.

Cindy took a deep, shuddering breath and let it out. She had to get a grip on herself. It wasn't like her to get so emotional. She wasn't hurt. Nothing was taken as far as she could tell. But she was scared. She hadn't felt this vulnerable since her dealings with her ex-husband so many years ago. She went to the family room and sat on the couch, drawing her knees up and wrapping her arms around them. She pulled the blanket around her shoulders and waited. *Larry will be here soon. He will take care of everything.* Benji jumped on the couch and lay next to her. Chloe tried to insinuate herself between Cindy's chest and knees, but Cindy wouldn't let her, so she jumped up on the sofa back, lay behind Cindy's head, and purred. Cindy was vaguely aware of the animals. She kept thinking about the face she saw in the mirror before she blacked out. It looked like Ed's face. *But how could that be? He wasn't in Alva. And even if he were, why would he be in Christina's house? No. It had to be someone who looked like Ed. But why would someone—anyone, for that matter—be in Christina's house? And who was in the closet?* She vaguely remembered two male voices as she gave into the darkness. A shudder went through her body.

There was a knock on the front door. "Cindy?" she heard Larry's voice call.

"Coming." Detangling herself, she hurried to let him in and was surprised to see two EMT guys with him.

He pulled her into his arms without thinking. She gladly returned the embrace. Security. That was what she longed for.

After a few seconds, he gently pushed her away and looked her over.

"Are you all right?"

Brushing the hair out of her face and wrapping her arms around herself, she said, "Yeah. I am now." He put his hand on her shoulder and guided her toward the couch in the front room.

"Here, sit down. Can I get you anything?"

She smiled shyly. "No. I'm fine. Really." Curling her legs under her, she sat on the couch, and he sat across from her in a wingback chair. One of the EMT guys took her blood pressure and pulse, which were both slightly elevated.

They reported their findings to the sheriff and then called it in to the dispatcher, who would call the hospital if it was deemed necessary. The two men left a few minutes later, satisfied that their patient would be taken care of.

Larry gritted his teeth and thought, *If I ever find the guy who scared this lady, I'll gladly beat the snot out of him.*

To her he said, "Okay then. Can you tell me what happened?"

Cindy recounted the events that had transpired from the time she had walked into the Sanders home to the present. He wrote in his notepad as she talked, nodding and making acknowledging sounds.

When she finished, he asked, "Did you see their faces?"

She hesitated. Part of her wanted to accuse Ed, but part of her wanted to protect him. She said, "No. Not really. I just remember thinking that the guy who snuck up behind me was so quiet to be so big."

"So, he was a big guy?"

She nodded.

"How big? Tall? Heavy set? Muscular?"

She made a face. "He was about your height, but twice as big. I think more muscle than fat, but I'm not sure. It happened so fast."

"Did you notice his skin or hair or eye color?"

She shook her head.

He nodded and looked at his watch. "Will Christina be home soon?"

"Yeah. She had to finish up some charting at work, and then she was coming home."

"Well, if you don't mind. I'll stay here till she arrives."

She sighed with relief. "Good. I don't want to be alone right now. I'm still pretty nervous."

"I doubt if they'll come back, if that's what you're worried about."

"Yeah, I know. But it's just nice to have some company." She smiled shyly.

Gosh I love that smile. He wanted so badly to reach over and take her in his arms and hold her close. Instead, he stood and asked if she minded if he walked around the house and took a look. She didn't.

"I could use a cup of coffee, if you don't mind," he said as he stood to inspect the den and adjoining bathroom where Cindy had said the incident took place.

She nodded. "Yeah, me too."

He didn't really want coffee but thought it was a good idea to get her occupied with something other than reliving the incident.

He put on a pair of latex gloves and walked around the room, noticing every detail. There was a fine layer of dust on the tabletops, and he checked to see if any object had been moved or was missing. Nothing was out of place. He walked over to the computer and felt the top. It was warm. *Hmm. That's interesting.* He touched the space bar and after a few seconds, the screen lit, welcoming him to the Sanders computer menu.

"Cindy," he called.

"Yeah."

"Did you use the computer today?"

"No. Why?"

"It was on. Do you know if Christina leaves it on during the day?"

She walked in carrying two cups of coffee, handing one to Larry.

"I don't know. You'll have to ask her when she gets here." Just then, they heard a car door slam, followed a few seconds later by the back screen door and then the squeak of the kitchen door being opened.

"Hey, Cindy?" Christina called as she threw her purse and keys on the kitchen counter.

"In here."

Christina hurried in and threw her arms around her friend, unaware of the coffee cup and Larry. Coffee splashed on both ladies. Larry quickly grabbed the cup from Cindy's outstretched hand.

"Christina!" Cindy squealed.

Releasing her friend and noticing Larry for the first time, she said, "Oops! Sorry." Catching her breath she said, "Larry! I didn't realize you were here. I was so worried about Cindy that when I saw her, all I could do was grab her." She smiled. "Guess I got carried away in the moment."

He smiled and looked at Cindy. "Yeah. I see that."

They all three stood awkwardly silent for a moment before Christina said, "Let me go get a towel to clean up that mess. Then you can tell me what happened." After cleaning up the spilled coffee and refilling the cup, the two ladies went to sit on the couch in the family room while Larry sat at the computer, bringing up files. Cindy, who had calmed down considerably, told Christina everything—except the part where she thought she saw Ed's face.

"Christina?" Larry called from across the room.

"Yes?" she answered, looking toward the voice and the squeaking sound of a chair as Larry sat in front of the computer.

"Did you use your computer this morning?"

"No. Why?"

"Do you know if one of your kids did?"

"No. We were all in a hurry this morning. Why?"

He still didn't answer her question, which made her a bit nervous. Instead he asked, "Did any of you use the computer last night and perhaps leave it on?"

"Well, Brad was on it for a while, but I'm sure he turned it off. He has never left it on when he finishes with it." She stood and walked over to where Larry sat.

"Why are you asking?"

"Do you know what Brad was working on?"

Exasperated, she said, "No, and for goodness' sakes will you tell me why you're asking these questions?"

He looked up at her. "Well, as I was walking around checking to see if anything had been disturbed, I touched the computer and it was warm—and it shouldn't have been if it had been turned off last night or before y'all left this morning. I decided to check the latest entry, and it looks as if your some of your personal files have been accessed."

"On? Personal files? What does that mean?"

"I'm not sure. Maybe whoever was here was accessing them and was interrupted. He shut down the computer before closing all the files."

"Can you tell which files were accessed?"

He nodded, punched a few buttons, and moved the mouse around. The screen lit up with a long list of files. He pointed to the right of the screen.

"See these dates?"

"Yeah."

"According to the computer, all of the files that were in David's folder have been opened today."

"What? Why?" she asked, feeling the first twinges of panic flow through her body.

Turning in the squeaking chair to look up at her, he answered, "Well, I was hoping you could tell me." *That squeak is annoying, and why haven't I noticed it before? Note to self—oil the hinges or whatever part is making the loud, protesting sound.*

She gave him a confused look, shook her head, and shrugged.

"What was David working on before he died?" he asked quietly.

Walking across the room to stand next to him, she answered, "I don't know. I never asked, and he never told me."

He nodded and returned his attention to the computer, punching a few more buttons, opening files, and quickly reading through a few of them.

"I don't understand most of this stuff," he admitted. Letting out a sigh, he said, "Tell you what. I'll call a buddy of mine who knows all about computers and have him come check this out. Maybe he can make sense of it, and maybe we can find out what these guys were looking for."

"So you really think they were trying to find something in David's files?" she asked, worry and fear shading her words.

Looking at her and raising his eyebrows, he said, "Seems that way. Although some of your other files have been viewed in the past month, these were the only ones that were viewed today."

She bent over and looked at the files and dates they were opened. "Look at that," she said, pointing to several files and dates. Those were all opened on the same day. She looked at Cindy.

"Wasn't that the day I had my job interview?"

Cindy shrugged. "Could have been. Get your calendar and check."

Christina quickly walked to the kitchen, retrieved the calendar, and returned to the family room, flipping the pages to September. She gasped as she pointed at the date and handed the calendar to Cindy.

"It *is* the day you had your interview," Cindy stated shakily.

Turning the page to October, Christina said, "Let's look at the other dates as well." Comparing the computer entries to the calendar, it was apparent that someone—probably those two men—had come when they knew Christina would be out of the house. Cindy gasped.

"What?" Larry asked, looking up from the computer.

"Oh my gosh!" said Cindy, on the verge of hysteria as she realized the implication.

Christina whispered, suddenly feeling dizzy, "Whoever was here today must have been here all those other days as well." Feeling a wave of dizziness wash over her, she said, "I need to sit down."

Larry stood and grabbed her as she swayed. He and Cindy led her to the couch, and Cindy gently pushed her friend's head down between her knees. After a few seconds, Christina sat up and took a deep breath.

Looking at Larry, she asked, "What's going on, Larry?"

He shook his head. "I don't know, but your family is being targeted by someone."

"Targeted? As in, dangerously targeted?" Cindy asked with a touch of panic in her voice.

"Not necessarily dangerous." He cleared his throat. "Whatever is going on, the guys doing the computer thing are being rather covert about it. It doesn't appear they mean any harm."

"No harm?" Cindy asked, holding Christina's hand. "What about what happened to me?"

He nodded. "I'm sure if you hadn't walked in on them, no one would have been the wiser. Believe me, things could have turned out a lot worse if these guys meant harm. I think you were an unplanned and unfortunate blip in their schedule." He sighed and looked around the room. "I just wonder if they got what they were looking for."

They all looked at the computer. So intent were they in thoughts about the computer that each jumped when Larry's phone rang. He answered and walked into the next room. After a few minutes he returned and stated that he had to leave.

"There was an accident out on I-35." Grabbing his jacket and heading to the door, he said, "I'll be back as soon as I can." When he saw the look of panic in the women's eyes, he walked over and, putting a hand on each one's shoulder, he added, "In the meantime, I'll get ahold of my buddy, and hopefully he'll come by today." He smiled at the two friends on the couch.

"You ladies try to relax. The worst is over."

Cindy jumped up and threw her arms around his waist. A bit embarrassed, he gently hugged her back and then disengaged himself and turned to go.

"Thanks, Larry," Christina called out.

He nodded and saluted her as he disappeared through the front door.

Cindy stood with her arms wrapped around herself until she heard his car leave the driveway. Christina watched her friend, wondering what was going through her mind.

She was pretty sure Cindy was fighting an emotional and mental battle about her feelings for Larry. But she was wrong. She had no idea that Cindy was thinking about Ed and wondering where he was and what he was doing.

Ed and Tom watched the activity at the Sanders house from their van, which was parked a block down the street. When they saw the EMT guys leave, minus a patient, they both breathed a sigh of relief.

Ed silently thanked God that Cindy was all right. He hated having subjected her to the chloroform, but sometimes unpleasant tasks had to be implemented to get a job done. He knew this in his head, but his heart ached anyway.

Tom asked, "So what do we do now?"

Ed was looking out the van window and sighed in relief as he watched the sheriff's car pull out of the driveway. He almost ducked when it drove by but remembered the tinted glass protected his identity.

"I think we'd best get back to headquarters, give them the information we have, and explain the situation. Who knows how far up the ladder the sheriff is willing to go." Tom nodded and started the van again. The two men sat in silence as Tom drove toward Dallas.

CHAPTER 102

When Larry returned to the Sanders house a couple hours later, the family, Cindy, and Samara were eating dinner. They asked him to join them, and not wanting to be rude or cause alarm in the children, he did.

"So Larry, tell us about the accident out on I-35," Christina said as she scooped up the last bite of her mashed potatoes and put it in her mouth.

"Accident?" Brad asked.

Smiling, Nicky said, "Yeah, tell us about it. Was there blood and guts everywhere?"

They all looked at him with disgust.

"Ew," Stacey said in response.

"What?" Nicky asked, giving his big-eyed, innocent look.

Christina shook her head.

Larry chuckled and reached over and tousled Nicky's hair.

"There wasn't any blood or guts, but there was a lot of broken glass."

"Cool," Nicky stated.

"Was anyone hurt?" Samara asked, taking a sip of tea.

"Just a few cuts and scrapes. Seems an older lady slammed on her brakes and swerved to miss a cat, and the person in the car behind her slammed on his brakes and swerved to miss her but ended up clipping her back bumper with his front one. Both cars ended up in the ditch—hers flipped on its side, his just nose down."

"Did she hit the cat?" Nicky asked.

"No, fortunately, the cat got away." Smiling, Larry said, "In fact, nobody saw it. Probably hightailed it out of there when it heard the screeching tires."

They all had a pleasant time, sharing stories of other accidents while eating meatloaf, mashed potatoes, green beans, and biscuits.

At the end of the meal, Samara boldly asked why he was there. He looked at Cindy, who avoided eye contact, wiped his mouth with his napkin, placed it on the table next to his plate, and stated that since his wife was out of town visiting her mother and he had no one to cook dinner for him, her mom and Christina had invited him over to share theirs.

Samara looked at her mom, who smiled and nodded. Christina did the same.

A half-truth was better than the whole truth, at least at the present moment, thought Christina as she stood and began removing plates, avoiding eye contact with her children. She hated the whole idea of keeping the truth from them but didn't want to worry or scare them either.

Samara furrowed her brow and said, "Uh-huh, sure." Then she shrugged and took the last bite of her biscuit as she handed her plate to Christina.

Once dinner dishes were cleared and loaded in the dishwasher and the kids had gone upstairs to do homework, the ladies and Larry went into the front living room and sat. Speaking softly so the kids wouldn't overhear, Christina showed him the bogus business card, and Cindy told him of her dealings with Ed Flores. Larry tried to keep his voice and face neutral even though anger, worry, and fear took turns running through his mind and emotions.

"So you called the number on this card, and it was out of service?"

"Yep."

"Hmm. This Ed Flores guy—you think he's legit, though?"

Cindy smiled sheepishly and said, "I think so."

"I think I'll run a background check on him to be sure."

Cindy nodded, hoping everything would turn out okay and Ed would be exonerated.

When nothing else could be asked or said, Larry left.

"I'm exhausted," Cindy stated as she stood.

"Yeah, me too. It's been a long day," Christina added as she joined her friend in a good stretch.

Cindy walked to the hallway and yelled up the stairs, "Samara, we need to go home."

"Okay, Mom. I'm coming."

Cindy sighed and rubbed her eyes. "I think I could fall asleep right here on the stairs."

Christina smiled and patted Cindy's back. "You've been through a lot today. I'm just so glad you're all right. I shudder to think what could have happened."

Cindy did shudder. "Yeah, me too, so I just try to block out those thoughts when they try to get in."

Christina nodded. "Good."

Samara exited Stacey's room with her backpack slung over her shoulder.

"Did you get your homework done?" Cindy asked, looking over her daughter's shoulder at Stacey, who was smiling and nodding.

Samara smiled. "Yep."

"She helped me with my math too," added Stacey.

"Good. Let's go home and get to bed."

Samara frowned at her mother. "Mom, it's only eight thirty! Why would you want to go to bed so early?"

Cindy smiled and sighed. "It's been a long day," she said, putting her hand up to her forehead. "Hope I'm not coming down with something."

Good cover, thought Christina.

Samara cocked her head, frowning. "Can I stay up till ten? There's a documentary about migrating birds I'm supposed to watch for science class."

Cindy smiled. "Sure. Now let's get our coats on and get out of here. The sooner we get home, the sooner I can hit the hay."

On the way back to the station, Larry rethought the day's events, trying to make sense of it all. He wondered if there was a connection between the things that had happened to Christina at work and the break-in. *The puzzle pieces just don't seem to fit together.*

When he returned to his office, he would check through the files of the men and women he had accessed earlier and see if he could locate any of them. It would be a difficult job, as many, if not all, were married and had changed their names or had moved elsewhere. Thankfully, with the aid of computers and modern technology, he could find just about anyone on the planet, no matter how many times they moved or changed their name, if he was willing to put in the hours of tedious searching.

He sighed. *Am I willing? Well, it's not like I don't have the time,* he thought. His wife was away for a few days, maybe longer if she decided to finally make good on her threat about leaving him. He felt a pang of regret in his heart. Part of him wanted their marriage to work out, but there was a part of him that was tired of the constant bickering and wanted peace and quiet away from her. Lord knew he tried to be a good husband, but it seemed no matter what he did or said, it was never the right thing or wasn't good enough. Maybe it would be better for both of them if they just called it quits and got on with their lives. His thoughts went immediately to Cindy. *Is there any hope for us?* He certainly felt a connection with her, and she seemed to still care about him—but a relationship? Well, he'd just have to wait and see. Couldn't let those thoughts cloud his thinking process right now.

And what about that Ed Flores guy? How does he fit into all this? What has Cindy got herself into?

CHAPTER 103

As Christina prepared for bed, the phone rang. It was Steven.

"Hey, how are you?" he asked when she answered.

She sighed as she sat on the bed, pulled her feet up to sit yoga-style, and leaned against the pillows.

"I tried calling you at work, and they said you had left early for a family emergency." Concern filling his voice, he asked, "Is everything all right?"

"Yeah, we're all fine. Hang on a minute." Realizing her door was ajar, she peeked out to see if Stacey's door was closed—it was—and then closed hers quietly and returned to the phone.

"Okay," she said quietly. "Now I can talk."

"What's going on, Christina?"

Christina told him of the day's events, and he asked if he should come over.

"No, Steven, you don't need to come over. It's late, and I'm ready for bed." She stifled a yawn, "I'm exhausted. Thanks for offering, though."

"Christina, do you think this break-in and the stuff that's been happening to you are related in any way?"

"Hmm." She considered the possibility. "I don't know. I don't think so, because today's events seemed to involve David." Pausing for a second, she said, "I just wonder who got into his files and why."

"Yeah, that is a bit odd, especially since he's been gone a couple of years. If there was something important in them, don't you think whoever it was would have accessed them by now?"

"That's what I was thinking." She rubbed her eyes. "Larry's going to do some investigating, and he's sending someone over tomorrow to check through the computer to see what those files contain."

"Have you ever looked through the files yourself?"

"No. Never felt I needed to and really had no desire to."

"I'm surprised you still have them in the computer. Seems you would have deleted them by now."

She sighed again. "Yeah. Just never thought about it. I don't use the computer much except to write e-mails and occasionally do some online shopping. It just never occurred to me to delete them. Guess Brad or I would have gotten around to it eventually."

"Do you know if David left any other discs or CDs with important information on them?"

"I think so. There was a box of discs and CDs somewhere near the computer. I kept them thinking that Brad or Stacey could copy over them." She sat up. "Maybe I should go see what's on them."

"Would you know what to look for?"

She leaned back again and sighed. "No, not really, but maybe something will just jump out and be obvious."

"Yeah, maybe. Maybe you should just give them to the guy tomorrow and let him check them all out."

"That's a good idea." She yawned.

"Hey, I'm gonna let you go. We can talk more about this tomorrow."

She yawned again and stretched. "Yeah. Sorry. I just can't think right now. I'm so tired."

"That's okay. Good night. Hope you sleep well. And Christina?"

"Yeah?"

"Try not to worry."

"Yeah, right." Smiling, she said, "Good night, Steven. Thanks for calling."

As soon as she replaced the receiver, the phone rang, making her jump.

"Hello?"

"Christina? It's Mom. I hate to keep bugging you, but I just need to know that you and the kids are all right."

"Hi, Mom. Yeah, we're fine. What's going on?"

"Well, I just had one of those nagging feelings all day. I couldn't shake the feeling that something wasn't quite right with someone in the family. I called Robert and Joyce and they are all fine, so I thought I'd call you. Are you sure you're all right? You sound tired or something."

Not wanting to worry her mother-in-law, she told her the half-truth. "It's been a very long, tiring day, Mom. I was just crawling into bed."

"Are you sick?"

"No. Just stress at work, and one of my friends is going through a difficult time right now."

"So the kids are doing well?"

"Yes, they're doing great," she said stifling a yawn. "As you know, they're getting ready for the holiday season and are busy at school with band and play practices."

She heard a chuckle on the other end of the line. "Oh yes, I remember those times with my kids. The holidays were always a busy time. As much as I looked forward to and enjoyed them, it was a relief when they were over." She let out a sigh. "Well, I won't keep you. I just needed to hear your voice and make sure you were all right."

"Thanks, Mom. I love you, and I appreciate your concern."

Christina felt her eyes filling. Maybe someday, when all this was over, she could tell her mother-in-law the truth, but now was not the right time.

"I love you too, dear."

When Christina replaced the receiver, she thought about her extended family, realizing she hadn't talked to David's brother, Robert, or their sister, Joyce, in quite a while. Every now and then she'd receive an e-mail stating they were fine, followed by a funny story or joke, but nothing very deep or significant. She needed to call them and start making plans for Thanksgiving and Christmas. *Wouldn't it be great if they could all come to my house for Christmas?* She fell asleep with that as her last conscious thought.

When Cindy and Samara returned home, she was true to her word. She took a long, hot shower, trying to wash away the fear, fatigue, and unease that she felt and then prepared herself for bed. She took two pain relievers to help ease the tension that had settled into her neck and shoulder muscles.

Thoughts kept whirring through her mind like a swarm of pesky mosquitoes. She wanted—no, needed—to talk to Ed, to clear her mind and ease her fears. *What if he was the man in the mirror? What do I do then?* She contemplated the answers as she turned down the covers and crawled into her soft, comfy bed. She heard the muffled sound of the TV as Samara watched the National Geographic special. Her last conscious thought was of Christina, hoping she would be able to sleep, considering the events that had taken place today and over the past couple of months.

CHAPTER 104

The next morning, Christina woke before the alarm went off, rolling over and staring at the red numbers on the clock—five thirty, five thirty-one, five thirty-two—letting her mind wander from one thought to the next until she finally turned to lay on her back and stare at the ceiling. She began to pray earnestly and passionately for the protection of herself, her family, and her friends and for wisdom, strength, and courage—and, most of all, for answers. *Who is causing all this strife in my life? Who was in my house? What did they want? Why now? Should I quit my job? Should I move back to Michigan? Should I move closer to my in-laws? What? What? What should I do? Will it ever end? Will I find the peace that I so desperately want?*

She jumped when her alarm announced that it was 6:00 a.m. and time to rise and shine. Well, it didn't say that exactly. It just buzzed annoyingly until she reached over and turned it off. She stretched and dragged herself out of bed and into the shower. More questions than answers flooded her brain. *What was God's purpose in all of this? Was there a purpose? Was this a test of some kind? If so, would she pass it, and at what expense?*

Her head hurt. It was too much to think about. Too much for her mind to comprehend. Too much. She got dressed, forcing her mind to be still. She had a cup of coffee, wrote the kids a note, and slipped out the back door when she heard Brad's alarm go off. She needed to be completely alone for a while before taking on the day's challenges at the hospital. It was supposed to be her day off, but Mrs. Ferguson had asked yesterday morning if she could fill in for one of the other nurses who had a family funeral to attend. She had agreed, not knowing what the day would hold or how exhausted she'd be. *Oh well, I gotta do what I gotta do,* she told herself.

As she drove toward the cemetery, the sun was beginning to light the sky, forcing the darkness to skitter away like a roach in a suddenly lit room. She parked the van in front of her parents' graves and stepped out into a crisp, fully illuminated fall morning. Her breath formed little smoky clouds as she breathed in and out. She took in a deep, cleansing breath and watched as it slowly dissipated into the atmosphere as she released it, making her realize that her life was like that—a vapor in the wind. Here today and gone tomorrow. *A depressing thought.* She sat on her parents' headstone and let tears fall. She missed her parents: their insight, wisdom, and laughter; their love, their comfort, and even their anger and disapproval. She wanted so desperately to talk to them both again. She was tired of being alone. She gave in to her self-pity for a while, sobbing. Good thing she had brought a box of tissues. Then she heard a whisper: "You're not alone, Christina." She stopped crying suddenly and looked around, listening intently. No one was there, but she was sure she had heard someone whisper in her ear.

"Lord? David?" she whispered.

She felt a warm embrace and closed her eyes, vaguely aware of the tears streaming down her face and into her collar. She saw images of her children, her in-laws, her friends. *No, I'm not alone.* But there was a part of her that still felt lonely. Then the image of Steven popped into her head.

"Lord, is he the man you want me to be with?" she asked. No answer came forth. *What did I expect? A chorus of heavenly angels? A sonic boom? A burning bush?* What she got was a buzzing in her pocket, which turned into a full-fledged ringing tone.

She fumbled with the wad of tissues in her hand and the ones stuffed in her pocket as she dug it out before the last ring.

Still wiping tears and snot from her face and hands, and taking a calming breath, she tentatively asked, "Hello?"

"Christina?" a worried male voice on the other end asked.

"Yes?"

"It's Steven. Where are you?" Before she could answer, he continued. "I called your house, and Brad said you had left early, but he wasn't sure where you were. Are you all right?"

"I'm fine, Steven. I just needed some time alone to sort through my thoughts."

She stifled a chuckle. *Lord, you work in strange, funny ways,* she thought as she asked Steven to hold on. She gathered her soggy tissues, stuffed them all into her pockets, said a quiet good-bye to her parents, and walked to her van. She agreed to meet him in his office and have a cup of coffee before their workday started.

David smiled as he watched Christina drive away. He and Jarrod had been sent to encourage and comfort her. It was David who had wrapped his arms around her, reminding her she wasn't alone, and Jarrod who had brought forth the images of her friends and family. David knew they couldn't interfere any further and was thankful that even though it seemed like such a small task, it had brought Christina comfort.

CHAPTER 105

When Tom and Ed left Alva, Tom drove directly to Dallas. There wasn't much conversation during the hour drive, as both were lost in their thoughts of how the day had transpired. Tom was mentally beating himself up for leaving the computer on—he had wanted to check one last file before they called it quits on the investigation. If he hadn't been interrupted, he would have turned it off, and no one would have been the wiser. *Sometimes things don't go as planned.* Tom looked over at his partner, who had laid his head back and closed his eyes. He broke the silence by saying, "I wonder where we go from here—regarding the investigation."

"According to our boss, we're finished. We got the information we needed and retrieved the bugs."

Silence. When Tom pulled the van up in front of Ed's apartment, he turned the ignition off and turned to face his partner—his best friend.

"What are you thinking, Ed?"

Ed looked out the window at the well-lit apartment complex, with its treelined sidewalks and flower-filled pots on the porch by the front door, and thought about how he dreaded going into his empty abode, greeted only by darkness and cold. After a minute or two, he turned to face Tom, determination in his voice.

"A lot of thoughts were zipping through my head, but I keep coming back to one in particular."

Tom waited for him to continue.

"I want to talk to Cindy. Tell her the truth."

Tom nodded. He knew that was what Ed wanted to do. That was what he would want to do if he was in Ed's position. Would it be the wisest and right thing to do? That, he didn't know. He sighed and blew air out through his lips.

"When?"

"Not sure. I need to think and pray about it. I know I'll wait till after the meeting tomorrow." Tom nodded. "I think I'll call her tomorrow night and see how she's doing. I can at least find out if she saw one of us before she blacked out. My gut feeling is that she *did* see me in the mirror when I put the rag over her nose, and all I can do is hope she'll forgive me when I explain everything."

"You think she will? Forgive you?"

Ed shrugged. Both men pondered the situation, and then Ed shrugged, saying,

"Can't say for sure one way or the other, but I just have this niggling in my gut that says she did."

"Niggling? You sure it's not just hunger pains?"

Ed gave him an exasperated look.

Raising his hands in a surrender gesture, he said, "Okay, seriously, that could complicate matters."

"Yeah. It sure could." Ed reached for the door handle. "Guess I'd best be going."

Turning the ignition key and bringing the van to life, Tom said, "I'll see you bright and early tomorrow, say around seven?"

Ed nodded. As he shut the van door, he turned and tapped on the glass. Tom pushed the button to lower it.

"Tom, thanks for not pushing me one way or the other about Cindy."

Tom nodded and smiled. "You'll do the right thing."

Ed raised his eyebrows and sighed. "Hope so." He patted the door and turned, swinging his backpack over his shoulder as he strolled up the sidewalk to greet his dark, empty, cold apartment.

CHAPTER 106

Cindy woke the next morning with a dull headache. She had had a fitful night's sleep filled with dreams of dark things chasing her through the woods, down the streets, and through big empty buildings. She turned and looked at her bedside clock. Seven o'clock.

Hearing Samara in the kitchen pouring cereal in a bowl, she rubbed her eyes, stretched, and forced herself out of bed. She was scheduled to work at the boutique today and needed to get herself together. Heading for the bathroom and looking in the mirror as she passed it on the way to the toilet, she stopped and backed up to get a second look. *Gosh, I not only feel older—I actually look older!* She splashed water on her face and patted it dry and then applied moisturizer under her eyes. She would turn forty in a couple of months and had noticed over the past year the gradual deepening of the wrinkles around her eyes and mouth. She looked down at her belly and saw the small roll of fat that she just couldn't seem to get rid of no matter how much she exercised or how little she ate. She told the reflection in the mirror, "My body is betraying me!"

Gosh, how she hated the aging process. She was determined more than ever not to give in. She would fight tooth and nail to keep her girlish figure and youthful looks for as long as she could. Putting on her jogging suit, she headed for the kitchen.

"Hey, Mom, you want some cereal or something?" Samara asked, not looking up from the paper she was reading.

Cindy patted her on the head. "Nope, I'm going jogging."

Samara looked up, surprise showing on her face.

"Do you know where I put my little tape player?" Cindy asked as she headed for the living room.

Samara stood and headed for her room. "I have it in my room. I'll get it for you."

Cindy grabbed her favorite Billy Ray Cyrus tape and popped it in the player when Samara returned. *One of these days, I'm gonna get one of those new iPod things that they've been advertising on TV.*

Hugging her daughter and kissing her on the cheek, she headed out the door. "See you later, alligator."

Samara replied, "After a while, crocodile." They both chuckled.

An hour or so later, after running all over town and listening to the tape twice, Cindy returned home, completely drenched in sweat but headache-free.

As she neared the front porch, she heard the ringing of the house phone. When she walked in the door, Samara handed her the phone and shrugged when her mother mouthed, "Who is it?"

Samara gave her mother a peck on the cheek and whispered, "Love you." Then she walked out the front door and headed to school.

"Hello?" Cindy answered breathlessly, grabbing a towel from the kitchen counter and wiping her face and neck.

"Cindy? It's Ed."

She sucked in air and was speechless for a few seconds. *Why is he calling? How come he didn't call my cell phone?*

"Cindy? Are you there?"

She cleared her throat, pulled up a chair, and sat.

"Yeah. I'm here. I just wasn't expecting to hear from you. Guess I was in shock." She could see him smile in her mind's eye and could hear it in his voice.

"I know. It's been awhile since we talked. How are you?"

She felt cautious and guarded, not sure if she could trust the man who may have been the one in Christina's house and may have drugged her. She had a quick mental argument with herself. *Why would he have been there in the first place? I have no tangible proof it was him. Can I trust him? How can I not trust him?*

"Cindy?"

"Oh, sorry. My mind was wandering."

"Are you all right?"

"Yeah, I just had a really bad night. Don't think I slept much." She yawned.

"How come? Are you sick?" He hoped the chloroform hadn't made her sick, knowing of people who had become quite ill after being exposed to it.

"No, I'm not sick. I just kept having weird dreams." She cleared her throat. "So why are you calling? How come you didn't call my cell phone?"

Ed sensed she was being cautious. She wasn't her usual bubbly, happy self.

"I tried calling your cell, but it went right to voice mail. So I tried the house number. Samara said you were out jogging?"

"Yeah, I just got back." There was a pause before Ed continued. "Well, I'm glad you're not sick. Do you want to talk about the dreams or anything? Maybe we could analyze them?"

She couldn't help but smile. "Analyze them? Are you a part-time psychiatrist or dream analyst or something?"

He chuckled. "No. I just know that talking about dreams or scary things that have happened sometimes helps to put our minds at ease—puts a new perspective on things."

Red flags went up in her brain. *Why would he say scary things? I didn't say my dreams were scary or that anything scary had happened to me. Okay, now I'm being paranoid.*

"Hey, Ed, where were you yesterday?" she asked suddenly.

He hadn't expected her to ask that, so he hesitated a second before answering, and did so cautiously. "I was at work. Why do you ask?"

"Where were you working?"

"In Dallas. Why are you asking?"

"All day?"

What could he say? He didn't want to lie to her, but he couldn't exactly tell her the truth either. "I was at work most of the day, then I had a couple of errands to run. Why are you asking?" He hoped that would satisfy her.

"You sure you weren't here in Alva?"

"Cindy, I don't know what's going on here. You're acting strange. I call to talk to you and see how you're doing, and you start grilling me about my whereabouts yesterday. Did something happen?" He needed her to talk about it, to reassure him that she hadn't seen him, even though his gut feeling that she had was becoming stronger by the second. *Why else would she be asking about his whereabouts?*

She let out a big sigh. "Ed, something happened yesterday that I don't understand. I tried calling you at the number on the card you gave me and it was a bogus number. My friend Larry, who's the police chief, checked out the business name, and it too was bogus. You want to explain that?"

He was silent for a moment, hoping she would continue—not wanting to lie to her again.

"What happened?" he asked quietly. She noticed that he hadn't answered her question.

"I'm not gonna to tell you anything until you answer my question."

There was silence on the other end of the line, long enough for her to think he had hung up. She didn't know that he was having a mental war with himself, deciding if he should hang up and walk away or be up-front and honest with her.

"Ed? Are you still there?"

"Yes." He let out a frustrated sigh. "Cindy, we need to talk. Can I come over this evening?"

She thought a moment before answering. Not sure she could trust him anymore, she didn't want him to come to her house and didn't want to be alone with him. Before yesterday's event, she could hardly wait to have him all to herself; she had dreamed and fantasized about it. Today, however, there was this nagging feeling that he wasn't the man she thought he was.

"Tell you what," Cindy said. "Why don't we meet at the Black-Eyed Pea? It's usually pretty empty on weeknights, and we could get a corner table in the back for privacy."

Yep, she's spooked. "Okay. What time?"

"Seven?"

"All right. I'll see you then."

"All right," she agreed, hearing the line click as their connection was broken.

After showering and readying herself for work, she called Christina and told her of the conversation with Ed.

Christina, having just arrived on the CCU, explained she couldn't talk long but managed to say, "I'm glad you're meeting him in a public place. Do you want me to come along?" Returning a chart to its proper slot, she said, "I can sit somewhere else and just keep an eye on y'all."

"I think we'll be okay. He doesn't seem the sort to follow me home or anything." *Follow me home and rape or kill me,* she thought, not letting those thoughts have a voice.

"Maybe you should call Larry and let him know your plans."

"No. Things between Larry and I are touchy right now. I don't want to encourage anything or even seem like I am." She paused a second, thinking about his possible reaction. "I'm concerned that he'll jump the gun and do something irrational."

"Irrational? Like what?"

"Like confronting Ed. Maybe arrest him for something. Follow him." She sighed. "I don't know. Maybe *I'm* being irrational."

Christina chuckled. "Well, maybe a little paranoid, but not irrational."

"Thanks. Anyway, I think I'll be okay just talking to Ed by myself."

"All right, I'll be praying that all this stuff gets settled between you and Ed. Gotta go!"

Cindy heard a voice in the background and then muffled words.

"I'll call before I go and when I get home," Cindy said before the phone line disconnected.

CHAPTER 107

True to his word, Tom was in front of Ed's apartment at seven.

"Hey, buddy, you look like crap. Didn't you sleep last night?" Tom asked as Ed entered the passenger side door.

"Thanks, Tom, you don't look so good yourself, and no, I didn't sleep well at all."

Tom chuckled. "I haven't had my three cups of coffee yet. Once those are in me, I'll perk right up." He saluted Ed with a large paper cup that read "Ken's Koffee."

Making a face, Ed asked, "You drink three of those?"

Tom nodded. "Yep, I'm on my second one now."

Ed shook his head. He didn't drink much coffee—just once in a while when he needed an extra caffeine boost, or when he didn't have any iced tea or ginseng.

"You know," Ed said with a grin, "that stuff will stunt your growth."

Tom patted his round belly. "Well, Lord knows I could use some stunting."

Ed shook his head and smiled. Tom pulled the van into traffic and headed downtown for the dreaded meeting with the head of internal affairs.

"So have you talked to Cindy yet?"

Ed looked out the window, chewing on his bottom lip, watching the trees, cars, and houses whiz by. He still hadn't decided how much information, if any, he would share with her. His mind and heart still felt conflicted.

"Yeah. I called her this morning."

"And?"

"And she sounded scared. I don't think she trusts me anymore."

Tom looked over at him with raised eyebrows.

Ed continued, "She told me she had called the number on the card I gave her." Ed sighed. "She knows it's bogus. When I gave her the card, I never thought she'd keep it or ever use it. She even had her policeman friend check out the business, and of course he found it to be bogus as well."

Tom blew out air through his teeth. "Not good."

Rubbing his eyes, Ed said, "You think?"

"What did you say?"

"Well, I couldn't exactly tell her everything over the phone, so I set up a meeting with her tonight."

"Tonight? Where?"

"In Alva at the Black-Eyed Pea. I think she's afraid to be alone with me."

Tom nodded. "She must have seen you or thought she saw you, or she wouldn't be acting so squirrelly."

"That's what I'm thinking."

"So you gonna tell her everything?"

"I've been up most of the night thinking about what I'll say. I'll tell her as little as possible, but I'm just gonna have to see how things play out."

Tom nodded. He wasn't sure what he'd do if he were in Ed's position.

He pulled the van into the parking lot. "Here we are. Are you ready for the crap to hit the fan?"

Ed smiled and shook his head. "Are you?"

"Nope."

Grinning, Ed said, "Alrighty then, let's go get crapified."

Setting the briefcase on the large mahogany desk, Tom opened it and extracted the CDs, printed files, and papers and the electronic bugs that he and Ed had extracted from the Sanders house. He placed them in front of his boss, Henry Steil.

"Well, here's what we have. As far as we can tell, that's all there is."

His boss, who seemed to wear a perpetual frown, narrowed his eyes and leaned forward in his chair to retrieve the pile. Tom sat across the room in a chair next to Ed and watched as the man looked through the papers. The squeaking chair, the rustling papers, and the grunts were the only sounds in the room for quite some time. Ed and Tom looked at each other with raised eyebrows and shrugged, occasionally adjusting their bodies to sit more comfortably in the large leather chairs on the opposite side of the room from their boss.

After reading through the papers, Henry turned with a grunt and put one of the discs in his computer. Ed pulled a magazine off the end table next to him and started flipping through the pages. Tom laid his head back and closed his eyes. They both knew this could take awhile. About ten minutes later, Tom was lightly snoring. Ed looked at him shook his head. Henry looked up from his computer screen and scowled.

"You guys have a late night?" he asked Ed.

"Not me," he answered, smiling. "I was in bed by midnight." He failed to add that he hadn't slept much because of tossing and turning—alternating between worry, fear, and prayer.

"Humph," Henry said, shaking his head and returning his attention to the screen.

Ed laid the magazine in his lap, and then he too laid his head back and closed his eyes. He didn't fall asleep, however. His mind was busy playing through scenarios regarding Cindy. *What am I going to do? What am I going to say?* He wanted so badly to tell her the truth—to be finished with this job and get on with his life.

Henry cleared his throat and slapped his palm on the top of his desk, which brought Ed out of his reverie and caused Tom to snort and rub his eyes.

"All right, you guys. Here's what we have." He turned the screen to face the two men across from him. They brought their chairs closer to get a better look. "It took some fancy deciphering on my part, but I think we have what we've been looking for."

"As you can see," he said, pointing to the screen with his sausage-sized finger, "there is a list of names, dates, and locations."

Ed squinted as he read the list. "Hey, aren't some of those guys already eliminated?"

"Look at those dates too," said Tom, pointing to the screen. "Most of them have already passed as well." He pointed to the screen. "Well, except this one." It read November 9, 2006. They all looked at the screen and then at each other.

"I wonder what that means," Ed said. "That's like five years from now."

Tom asked, "Do any of the names or locations correspond to that particular date?" Henry turned the computer screen to face him and typed in a few words. The computer went blank for a second, and then another list appeared.

This list consisted of the previously listed names, but next to the names were birthdates and locations, places they had been and were now, any illegal activities, and, by a few of the names, dates of death. Nothing, however, had the date November 9, 2006 by it.

"Do you think that could be the date of another attack of some kind?" Tom asked, leaning forward and frowning.

Henry rubbed his eyes. "I suppose anything is possible. Those terrorists are crazy. The date could mean nothing ... a decoy of sorts—something to lead us on a wild-goose chase."

"Or it could be significant?" said Ed.

"Yeah." Henry sighed. "I'll have to get some people busy checking it out." There was silence in the room for a few minutes as each thought about the possible ramifications of another attack.

Ed sighed and leaned back in his chair. "So, are we finally finished with the Sanders?"

Henry looked up and frowned, sighed heavily, and ran his fingers through his sparse hair. "Absolutely. I'm not even sure if this list will be of any use. It's been a couple of years since David's death, and most of this stuff seems to be outdated. I'll have some of our guys go back through it all with a fine-tooth comb to see if I've missed anything, which I doubt. In the meantime, now that you've removed the bugs, you two are officially dismissed from the case."

The two men across from him nodded in relief, Tom thinking, *Yeah, it's finally over,* and Ed thinking, *I still have Cindy to deal with.*

As Tom drove Ed back to his apartment, he asked, "So, you wanna get a bite to eat before I drop you off?"

Ed looked at his watch. Eleven thirty. "Yeah. I didn't eat any breakfast, and my stomach's feeling a bit empty."

"How's about that new Applebee's off Magnolia?"

Ed nodded. "That'll be just fine."

Tom tried to keep the lunch conversation light, knowing Ed was struggling emotionally and mentally with the whole Cindy thing.

"Hey, did I tell you what little Tommy said yesterday when I called?"

Ed took a large gulp of iced tea and, shaking his head, said, "No."

"He told me his kindergarten class at church was gonna be in the Christmas play, and he and his best friend Ayden were going to be little lambs. He was so excited. He told me his mom was sewing the costume as we spoke. He said, 'Daddy, it's all fuzzy and has little ears and a tail. I didn't know lambs had tails, but they do.' Isn't that cute?" Tom asked, taking a bite of steak.

Ed nodded and smiled. "Yeah. When is the play? I'd like to go see it."

"You know, I forgot to ask. I'll call Eleanor tonight and ask and let you know."

Ed nodded and moaned. "This is the best hamburger I think I've ever had."

Tom chuckled, "You said that about the last one and the one before that, and let me think … yep, the one before that too."

Ed just shook his head and continued eating. When he stopped chewing to take a sip of his tea, he asked, "Say, how's Eleanor's family doing? Didn't you say her dad had a stroke last year?"

"Yeah. He had a stroke, which the doctors figured must have done some brain damage. Either that or it's dementia. He has difficulty remembering events and, from what Eleanor says, tends to make things up or misinterprets things—things that make no sense."

"Hmm. Like what?"

"Well, the other day, he noticed the cable guys digging a trench to put an underground cable in for their new TV that Eleanor bought them and asked why the army was digging trenches on their property."

Ed stopped eating. "Really? That's odd."

"Yeah. His wife explained it was the cable guys, but he told her he thought they were probably looking for those 'little ground monkeys,' a term his unit in Vietnam used for the Viet Cong who lived underground. Eleanor thinks maybe some of his Vietnam memories are resurfacing and getting mixed up with his present thoughts."

Ed nodded. "I guess that's possible. I read once that the human brain is like a computer, and sometimes the wires get all crossed and shorted out and can wreak all kinds of havoc in the thinking process—especially after a stroke."

"Yeah, I've heard stuff like that too. It's just sad to see such a big, strong, intelligent man lose so much in such a short time."

Ed nodded. "My grandma had dementia before she died and was seeing animals and people who weren't there and would just wander off at times. My mom ended up putting her in a nursing home after she had wandered off in the middle of the night and ended up in a park two blocks away. They found her early the next morning curled up on a bench, cold, crying, and scared. That just about broke my mother's heart. She hated putting Grandma in a nursing home, but she couldn't chance another escape like that."

"Yeah, it's difficult watching your loved ones grow old and become like children again. Eleanor hopes the situation with her dad doesn't get any worse, or they may have to put him in a home. It will certainly devastate them all if it comes to that."

Tom added with a sigh, "I hope the good Lord takes me home before I get to that point."

Ed nodded. "Yep. Me too."

CHAPTER 108

Cindy had difficulty focusing on the task before her as her mind kept wandering back to Ed and tonight's meeting.

"Excuse me, ma'am." It wasn't until the second addressing and clearing of the throat that Cindy responded.

"Oh, I'm sorry. My mind was wandering."

The fiftyish-year-old lady looked at her watch and raised her eyebrows, scowling. "I don't have all day."

"I'm sorry. I'll check you right out."

She rang up the purchases, took the money, gave her change, bagged everything, and smiled sweetly, even though she received a scowl in return.

Walking over to rehang blouses that had fallen, she sighed heavily.

Her boss, who had witnessed the incident, asked, "Cindy, honey, are you all right?" She walked over and started hanging blouses beside her coworker and friend.

Mary, owner of the little boutique named Mary's Clothes Garden, was in her early sixties and had been owner and operator for at least twenty of those years since the passing of the previous owner—her mother, also named Mary. She was slim and petite, thanks to long walks in the morning and evening with her little poodle Muffy. At times, she had more energy than Cindy, who was twenty years her junior. She had short, dark brown hair—thanks to Miss Clairol—and twinkling blue eyes. Cindy loved Mary's smile that was nearly always present, and she desired to age gracefully like this woman was doing.

Cindy sighed and turned to face Mary.

"I have a situation that I don't know how to handle."

"Does it have to do with a man?"

Cindy rolled her eyes and smiled sheepishly. "Yeah."

"Don't most problems have to do with men?" Mary asked with a smile.

"Sometimes it seems that way."

"Want to talk about it?"

Cindy thought for a moment. *Should I tell Mary? I could use the wisdom of an older, mature lady, but do I want to bring her into this weird situation? I trust her, but why bother her with something she really doesn't need to know about?*

"Thanks, Mary, but I think I'll be able to get through this. I appreciate your willingness to listen, though." She reached over for a hug, which was quickly returned. They pulled apart when the bell over the door chimed, announcing another customer.

Larry stared at the computer screen. There were four lists now: two containing the names of all the men and women who had committed crimes and ended up in police database between 1975 and 1985, and two with names of men and women who worked in Alva Community Hospital. The men's list of lawbreakers was much longer than the women's, so he decided to start there. He typed in a few commands, and the computer promptly obeyed. There were seven names from each list that matched up. He looked over the names, recognizing at least five of them, and began to read, perusing through names, dates, and misdemeanors—details. The files that were of interest, he set aside to read later. After a couple of hours of this tedious task, he felt a need to stretch. Standing, he felt and heard his knees pop, causing him to wince in pain. *Man, this getting older stinks!*

Nancy, his secretary, poked her head in the door and said, "Excuse me, sir."

"Yes?"

"There's a call for you on line two."

"Oh, thanks. I didn't even hear the phone ring."

She smiled and nodded. She knew when he was concentrating on a case, a bomb could go off next to his chair, and he wouldn't even notice.

Picking up the receiver, he said, "Sheriff Clifton speaking."

"Hey, Larry, it's Steven. How're you doing?"

"He,y Steven. I'm doin' all right. What makes you take time out of your busy day to give me a call? Certainly not to inquire about my health."

Steven chuckled. "Actually, I'm calling to see how you're progressing with the search for Christina's mysterious tormentor."

"Funny you should ask. I was just going through a list of names from 1975 to 1985, and one seemed to stand out."

"Anyone I know?"

"Maybe. Do you know a Janet Washburn?"

Steven gripped the phone tighter as he heard the name. "Yeah. Is her name on that list?"

"Her name came up as a juvenile offender. Actually, she was questioned for shoplifting and released to her father when she was sixteen. No big deal, really, but a red flag went up when I saw that she works on the same floor as Christina." He paused, waiting for a response.

Steven sighed. "I know Janet. She's a good nurse—a hard worker. I can't imagine her doing anything harmful to anyone, especially Christina. The times I've been around them, they seem to get along well enough." He paused for a second. "Do you think we should be concerned?"

Larry thought for a moment. "Oh, it's probably nothing. I've still got a few names to check." He rubbed his eyes, feeling the exhaustion from hours of reading.

"Will you let me know if you come across anything else that might have a bearing on this situation?" Steven asked.

"I'll keep you informed." The men said their good-byes and disconnected.

Steven sat at his desk pondering the information he had received from Larry. *Could Janet be responsible for the heparin incident? I suppose it's possible. She certainly has access to the medications and knows their purpose. But why? Why would she want to harm Christina, whom she barely knew? Was it jealousy? She had wanted Christina's position as head nurse. Should I mention it to Christina? No. Why make her more paranoid? I'll keep an eye on Janet myself and see if she presents any suspicious behavior.*

He picked up the phone and dialed a number.

"Cardiac Care Unit, Christina Sanders speaking."

"Hey, Christina, it's Steven. How are you?"

Smiling, she answered, "I'm fine. How about yourself?"

"I'm fine and dandy. I see it's almost time for you to end your shift. Would you like to meet me in the cafeteria for a cup of coffee?"

Christina looked at the wall clock. Fifteen more minutes till punch-out time.

"Steven, I need to go home and let my dog out, but why don't you meet me there? We can either have a cup of coffee at my house, or we can go into town."

"All right, I'll meet you in the back parking lot in, say, twenty minutes?"

"Twenty minutes it is." Smiling, she replaced the receiver.

Removing her lab coat, she remembered the bank card she had put in the pocket that morning after going to the ATM. When she reached in her pocket to retrieve it, her hand touched the small tissue-wrapped vial she had also forgotten about. She pulled it out.

Slapping her forehead, she said, "Shoot. I forgot again!"

Janet was reaching around to hang up her own lab coat when she heard Christina's exclamation. She raised her eyebrows. "You all right?" she asked, noticing the small item in Christina's hand.

Christina quickly closed her fingers around the object and slipped it into her pants pocket. Stammering, she said, "Uh, yeah. I just remembered that I forgot to do something really important yesterday." She shrugged and gave a crooked smile.

Janet nodded slowly. "Uh-huh," she said, wondering what she was trying to hide.

The two women rode the elevator in silence down to the first floor and said their good-byes.

True to his word, Steven was waiting in the parking lot next to his silver BMW.

Smiling and waving as she exited the hospital, she met him at her van, and like a gentleman, he opened the door when he heard the lock disengage.

Giggling, she said, "Why thank you, sir."

"You're quite welcome, ma'am," he said with a playful smile and a bow as he backed away. "I'll follow you home."

She nodded and finger waved as she started the van and lowered the windows.

"I'll follow you home." It sounded so comforting. David had said that on a few occasions when they had driven separately to church or met somewhere for dinner.

She smiled, adjusted her rearview mirror, and watched as Steven followed her home.

Janet watched the interaction from her car and felt her pulse accelerate.

"I'll follow you home," she mimicked in a sarcastic tone. "Well, I'll follow you both home." As she pulled out a few cars behind Steven's, her mind knew she was acting irrationally, but her heart didn't care. She *knew* she should just go to her own home and stop this foolishness, *knew* she had lost Steven to Christina, and *knew* she had no idea what she would do once they had arrived at Christina's house. *Then why am I following them?* She gripped the steering wheel, and when they turned left, she followed two cars behind. "Janet, Janet, Janet," she murmured to herself, "you've got to get a grip."

She heard a voice in her head say, *Face it, you've lost—lost the job you wanted, lost the man you wanted. You're just a loser. You've never been good enough for anything worthwhile.*

She felt a tear trickle down her cheek. The voice continued to taunt her.

"Stop it!" she heard herself scream at the voice in her head as she pounded her forehead with the palm of her hand. It stopped, and it was eerily quiet for a moment before the taunting began again, reminding her of all her past failures. If another individual had been listening in on this one-sided barrage of negativity, they would have concluded that Janet had *never* done anything right in her forty years on this earth, which in reality was far from the truth.

She was so lost in her negative thoughts that she almost rammed the car in front of her when its brake lights suddenly came on. She watched as Christina's van left the road, and Steven pulled his car over behind her. She wanted to stay and see what was happening, but the car behind her honked, and she pulled around Steven's BMW. She glanced in her rearview mirror and saw Christina leap out of the van and run around. It looked as if she were screaming. Well, she'd have to find out tomorrow what had happened. *Maybe there was a wasp or bee in her van.*

Janet pulled her ten-year-old blue Chevy to the side of the street about a block from her house and beat the steering wheel as years of pent-up emotion found their way out. She cried and screamed and pounded until she accidentally hit the center of the steering wheel and was jolted back to reality by the blaring of the horn. She quickly wiped her eyes and face and took a few deep breaths to calm herself before driving the rest of the way home. As she pulled into the driveway, she saw Linda peek out through the curtain in the front window. She wasn't quite ready to face another human—even her own daughter—and pointed to the her ear and then to the car radio and put up a finger, indicating that she would be there in a moment. Linda would assume she was listening to something on the radio. The girl smiled and nodded, and the curtain closed. Janet sighed.

She was so tired—tired of struggling to make ends meet, tired of having to work every day, tired of not having a mate, tired of feeling inadequate, tired of seeming to always want things she couldn't have. She sighed again and thought, *If it wasn't for Leelee, I would just get a bottle of gin and a handful of sleeping pills and be done with it all.* She felt tears trickle down her cheeks and wondered, *If I'm such a despicable, worthless individual, why am I blessed with such a perfect child?*

She sat in her car for another fifteen minutes before finally going into her small home. She was greeted with a hug from her daughter. *Even if I've been a failure all my life, I did do something right by bringing this wonderful child into the world,* she thought as she hugged her girl and felt tears well in her eyes.

"Mom, you okay?"

"I am now."

CHAPTER 109

Once the boutique was closed and locked up, Cindy rushed home to shower, change clothes, and prepare for her meeting with Ed.

Her hands betrayed her nervousness by dropping the bottles of shampoo, conditioner, and body wash, as well as her lipstick, mascara, and eyebrow pencil. To avoid poking herself in the eye or smearing lipstick all over her face, she had to steady one hand with the other and hold her breath.

"Mom?" Samara called from her bedroom down the hall.

"Yes?" Cindy answered as she jumped and poked herself in the eye with the end of the mascara wand. She said a couple of expletives as she grabbed a tissue and held it over her eye, which she squinted shut until the pain diminished and she was able to open it and assess the damage. Her neatly applied eye makeup was all smeared, and she had to wipe off the mess and start over.

"Great," she mumbled.

"What time are you leaving?"

Cindy glanced at the clock on the wall next to the mirror.

"In about twenty minutes," she yelled so her daughter could hear.

She heard a mumbled reply.

"What?" she called and still couldn't hear a coherent answer. Frustrated she called out a little too harshly, "Samara, if you want to talk to me, then come in here so I can understand you."

A second later, her daughter was standing in the doorway with a frustrated look on her face. Cindy glanced her way. "What?"

Samara rolled her eyes and let out an audible sigh. Cindy put the mascara wand down and looked at her daughter. She asked more quietly, "What did you want, Samara?"

"I just wondered what time you'd be home and if I could stay up and watch a movie."

Cindy sighed and thought a moment before answering.

"I hope to be home in a couple of hours, and you can watch a movie or TV or whatever until eleven. Then you need to go to bed, whether I'm home or not." Samara crossed her arms across her chest and rolled her eyes.

"Mom," she whined, "I'm not a baby. Why can't I stay up until midnight?"

Cindy felt her pulse increase, her blood pressure rise, and her teeth clench. She didn't have time to argue with her daughter about bedtimes and the benefits of long restful sleep and such.

She almost snapped back at her, "Because I said so!" Instead ,she looked at her daughter—really looked at her. The girl standing before her was definitely not a baby anymore. She was wearing a tank top and pajama bottoms, and even with her arms across her chest, Cindy could see that Samara was almost as well endowed as she. Her honey-blonde hair, which was braided, lay across her right shoulder. *When had it grown so long?* Samara's olive complexion still held the summer tan and looked vibrant and healthy. Cindy looked at the pouting girl's face and saw breathtaking beauty. Her big blue eyes, small nose, full lips, and dark eyebrows and eyelashes shouted Cover Girl.

The only drawback, if one could call it that, was Samara's height. She was petite like her mom, standing a little over five feet. Cindy knew that even if Samara possessed all the criteria for a model, she wouldn't have ventured into that arena. Samara was not the competitive type. She was a behind-the-scenes kind of girl. The fourteen-year-old girl possessed a calm, mature spirit, which made Cindy feel that at times, her daughter possessed more wisdom and insight than she.

"Mom?"

Cindy shook her head. "Oh, sorry. What did you say?"

Samara sighed and rolled her eyes. "I asked if I could stay up till midnight."

"Oh. Yeah." Cindy sighed. "Well, if you think you can get up on time for school tomorrow, then I guess you can stay up." She blinked her eye and wiped it with the tissue and then asked, "What movie did you want to watch?"

Samara thought for a minute and shook her head. "I can't remember the name, but it's about some teenagers who get stuck on an island, and there are some bad guys there and they have to figure out how to escape."

"Sounds exciting. Maybe I'll be home in time to watch it with you. If not, why don't you tape it for me?"

"Sure."

Samara walked over and hugged her mom. "Thanks, Mom." Glancing at the clock on her way out the door, she said, "Better hurry, you've only got about five minutes."

Cindy glanced at the clock and felt her heart leap. She reapplied her eye makeup and ran her fingers through her hair.

"Whew! Well here goes." She left her room and walked down the hall, said bye to her daughter, and headed out the door.

Driving to meet the man she thought she was in love with and picturing him in her mind's eye, her thoughts traveled back to another man, another time, and another place—to a man she'd sworn she'd love for the rest of her life.

Stan, her ex-husband, whom she had been married to for seven years, was once very buff and handsome, like Ed, but when a car accident left him with a closed head injury, causing him to lose his job, he became depressed, which led to drinking. His toned six-pack was slowly replaced with a pudgy middle caused by too many, well, six-packs. It had been a very stressful time for all of them as they tried to adjust to his short-term memory loss, headaches, and mood swings. Samara had been too young to understand what depression was, but her parents' constant bickering was taking its toll on her physical and emotional development. When Cindy realized she couldn't make Stan take his medication or follow through with counseling, she made the heart-wrenching decision to leave, promising to return when he decided to take care of himself—which he did with a drug overdose three months later. She resented him not only for taking the coward's way out, but for leaving her and Samara with nothing but debts. A part of her heart still belonged to him, and it would remain so even if she fell madly in love with someone else. Stan was her first true love.

Jerk! How dare you leave us to fend for ourselves!

She let her mind wander back to the first encounter with and impression of Ed. She had been more than happy to entertain him while the other two men went about their business of checking the electrical wiring. She remembered her knees feeling weak as she handed him a glass of iced tea and watched his Adam's apple bob up and down as he swallowed.

Standing a little over six feet and approximately two hundred pounds of solid muscle, he could easily pass as a linebacker for the Dallas Cowboys.

He had a face that was strong and intense with its chiseled jaw and natural five o'clock shadow, reminding her of Stan, who had always looked like he needed a shave. On Ed it looked good. Real good. Ed's big brown eyes with their long lashes that almost touched thick dark eyebrows reminded her of an actor on one of those law shows she had watched the previous night. His full lips looked so soft and kissable, she bit her bottom lip as she wondered what it would be like to be held in those strong arms and kissed by those lips. *Whew!* She felt a flush go through her body and shuddered.

CHAPTER 110

Ed arrived at the Black-Eyed Pea about half an hour before his appointed time, asking the waitress for a table in the back of the restaurant as far away from curious eyes and ears as possible. Once seated, he ordered a sweet iced tea and thought about how he would tell Cindy the truth. He ran a few scenarios through his mind—her reactions and his counteractions. Once every possible scene he could think of was analyzed, he waited, his mind drifting to the past.

Before he had started working for the ATO, he had worked for the FBI, where he had met and married a fellow FBI agent named Celina. They were both thirty-two when they had met and had been working together on a kidnapping case. A little seven-year-old boy, the son of a prosecuting attorney in Dallas, had been kidnapped as he walked the two blocks home from school. Because the father was a lawyer, the kidnapper had demanded a large sum of money in exchange for the child. The attorney immediately called the Dallas police chief, who in turn called the FBI. Celina and Ed had been called in and, working together with the Dallas police department and the FBI, found the unharmed child seven hours later.

The kidnapper was captured and taken into custody, where he was serving the last few years of his twenty-year sentence.

Celina and Ed dated for another year before deciding to tie the knot. They had been married for two years when she had been killed. *The best two years of my life.*

She was almost as tall as he and pure muscle, reminding him of a gazelle when she ran, a cat when she walked, and a tiger when she was confronting the enemy, but she was gentle as a lamb when she was around children. They had hoped to have children someday. *Someday. That someday will never come.* He felt a lump form in his throat as that thought stabbed into his brain and heart simultaneously. He shook his head, mentally grabbed the thought, and stuffed it back in the box in his heart where he kept memories of Celina.

The desire to protect society and keep criminal activity at bay prompted him to enter law enforcement, which ultimately put him in the Sanders house, pretending to be someone else.

Thinking he would never find another woman that could replace Celina, he would not allow another female close enough emotionally to rattle the cage that he had so carefully built around his heart. The woman who was coming to meet him, however, sent a shiver through him that made the bars around his heart tremble. That scared him. He would rather face a firing squad than face the possibility of falling in love again. He wasn't ready, but his heart was showing signs of betrayal.

CHAPTER 111

Driving home, Christina sang along with the Beach Boys about a little Deuce Coop, taking comfort in knowing that Steven was right behind her. Glancing in her rearview mirror, she smiled, still finding it difficult to believe that after all these years he had come back into her life—that he actually seemed interested in her. Why now and not twenty years ago was still a mystery. Lost in her daydream, she jumped when she felt something move across her foot. Thinking it was a water or pop bottle, she moved her foot around to move it, but couldn't locate it. Glancing down, she gasped as a snake slithered under her foot to the passenger side of the van. She screamed and slammed on the brakes, driving the van onto the shoulder and jumping out before it had completely stopped. Steven, who was travelling about a car length behind Christina, almost rear-ended her when she slammed on the brakes. He shouted an explicative as her van left the road and watched in dismay as Christina jumped out and run away screaming. The car behind him swerved and blew its horn as it passed. *Was that lady laughing?* He screeched to a stop, backed up, and pulled his car behind Christina's van. Jumping out and running over, he grabbed her by the shoulders. She was screaming hysterically about a snake in her van. He looked her over to make sure she was all right and hadn't been bitten and then walked over to the van and cautiously opened the door. A few seconds later, he turned around and held up a limp, three-foot-long black snake. Christina, still thinking it was alive, backed away, and holding her hands over her mouth stifled a scream.

He called to her as he approached, "Christina, it's dead."

"What?" She exclaimed. "Are you sure? I could have sworn it slithered across my foot."

"It's dead. The head's been cut off. Come here and see."

She cautiously walked over to him and examined the lifeless snake.

Visibly shaken, she asked, "What kind of snake is it?"

Holding the snake between his hands and letting it dangle like a limp rope, he said, "Looks like either a cottonmouth or a water snake. Hard to tell without the head, though."

She shuddered. "Aren't they both dangerous?"

He held the snake up and looked it over once more before putting it in a grocery bag and tossing it in his car.

"Well, the cottonmouth is poisonous, but the water snake isn't. It'll bite if threatened, but it won't kill you."

She let out a sigh of relief and then stomped her feet and screamed.

"What the heck is going on? Who would put a dead snake in my van?" She stomped around a few more seconds, wanting to hit something or someone—needing to vent the rage building up inside her. Steven leaned against his car with his arms crossed across his chest and watched as she threw her tantrum.

"I could have crashed my van! I could have had a heart attack!" she screamed. She started crying. "What if the kids had been in the car? What if it had been alive and bitten me?" She leaned her back against the van, slid down to a sitting position, and held her head in her hands. Steven walked over, squatted beside her, and, putting his arm around her shoulders, drew her close.

At first she fought against him, pounding her fists on his chest. He took the blows and talked soothingly to her. After a few minutes the raging storm had passed, and she just let him hold her as she calmed herself. She finally pulled away and said, "I'm okay. Let's go to my house." She stood and brushed the dirt from her pants.

Steven looked at her skeptically and then nodded, sensing she was indeed okay. He opened the van door and held it as she climbed in and started the engine. Following her the rest of the way home, he wondered what crazy person had killed a snake and put it in her van. After they arrived, she went in to care for the animals, and he called Larry.

The sheriff arrived a few minutes later and sat with them in the living room sipping iced tea and listening as they retold the story of the snake. Steven handed him the bag that held the dead critter. Larry removed the snake and, after examining it, said he was sure it was a harmless water snake, but he'd take it to the local vet to make sure. Returning the snake to the bag and laying it by his feet, he turned to Christina and asked, "Where did you park your van this morning when you arrived at the hospital?

"In the lot behind the building."

"Do you always park there?"

She sighed. "Well, I usually park in the front lot and go in the front door, but this morning the lot was full, so I pulled around back."

Larry nodded and wrote in his notebook.

"Christina, was the van locked when you went out to the parking lot?"

"Yes. I pushed the automatic unlock button as I approached it."

"Did you notice the snake when you got in?"

She looked at him skeptically. "No. I think I would have freaked out if I had seen it then."

He nodded. "Okay. Where do you usually park your van at night?'

"In the garage," she answered, wondering where all this was going.

"Do you lock it at night?"

"Sometimes, but I'm not sure if I locked it last night." Realization dawning, she asked, "Do you think someone may have put it in there last night?"

"Well, I can't say for sure. I'd like to look at the van and see if there are any signs of forced entry. If not, we can assume it was put there last night." Everyone was quiet for a moment as the idea took root. "Say, does anyone else have keys to your van?"

She thought for a moment. "My son and Cindy."

"Why Cindy?" he asked, perplexed.

"Well, if I lock myself out, or lose my keys, which I'm prone to do," she said embarrassed, "then she can bring me her set."

"Do you have another set somewhere in the house?'

"Yeah, in the cabinet on the back porch."

"Could you see if they're still there?"

"Sure." She rose and went to fetch the keys.

While she was gone, Larry asked Steven to look through the van with him to see if there was any other evidence of foul play or maybe a note.

Christina returned a few minutes later, looking perplexed.

"The keys aren't there."

"What?" Larry asked.

"They're not there. I looked all over the back porch thinking maybe they fell out of the cabinet or something, but they're nowhere to be found."

"Hmm," Larry said, giving Steven a look.

"What?" Christina asked with alarm.

"It could be nothing. Why don't you check around the house, and when your children come home, we can ask if they've seen them."

She sighed. "All right. Do you think someone stole my keys and that's how they got into my van?"

Larry shrugged. "It's a possibility."

She nodded and said, "I'm going upstairs to change my clothes, and I'll look around up there. I'll be back in a few minutes."

The men nodded and, when they heard her bedroom door shut, headed out to the garage to check out the van.

Larry walked around the outside of the van looking for any signs of a break-in. He did find some slight scratch marks around the window moldings of the driver and passenger side windows. Rubbing the scratches with his finger, he thought, *They could have been made with a slim-jim,* thinking of a tool often used to break into vehicles. *Of course just everyday use, such as loading or unloading things through the window or a dog or cat jumping in and out of the window, could have caused the scratches as well.* When and how they were made could remain a mystery. He continued looking around the outside of the van as Steven searched the inside.

Looking under the seat, in the ashtray, up under the dash, in the console, and between the seat and console, Steven found only gum and candy wrappers, loose change, and miscellaneous receipts. He crawled into the back and continued his search. Finding more of the same items in and around the seats, he exited the sliding door and opened the passenger side door, searching every nook and cranny, sighing in relief that no ominous note had been left—until he saw the piece of paper sticking out from under the floor mat. He had looked under the mats on the driver's side and in the back and was so relieved to have found nothing that he had almost forgotten to look under the passenger side mat. Hoping it was one of the kids' misplaced papers, he pulled it out and carefully unfolded it. Reading the typewritten words, his breath caught and his heart skipped a beat. He called Larry over and handed it to him.

Larry frowned as he read, "If you don't leave, next time the snake will be alive, and you won't be. Go back to Michigan!"

He blew out air between his teeth. Looking at Steven, he said, "I think we have a real problem here."

"Yeah!" Steven said emphatically, running his hands over his face. "Whoever is doing this stuff is getting bolder and more threatening. I'm worried that something will push him or her over the edge."

Larry nodded. "Yeah."

"What are we gonna do now?"

Shaking his head, the sheriff said, "I'm not sure. I need to make a couple of phone calls." He refolded the note and stuck it in his pocket.

"Hey, don't tell Christina about this. No use upsetting her any more."

Nodding slightly, Steven said, "Yeah. That's what I was thinking.

Concern etching his face, Larry asked, "Can you stay with her for a while?"

Steven nodded. "At least until her kids come home, but Larry, I can't be with her 24/7."

Larry let out a sigh. "I know. I'll have my guys drive around the neighborhood every couple of hours for the next few days."

"Well, that'll help I guess. I can keep tabs on her at work," Steven said, unconsciously pounding his right fist into the palm of his left hand. Giving Larry a pleading look, he said, "I just want to punch whoever is doing this!" Sheriff Clifton nodded in agreement. He would have liked to punch somebody's lights out about now as well.

Steven said, "Look, if this person really wanted to hurt her, he would have done so by now. Right?"

Larry nodded slightly, not really sure how to answer. He said with more confidence than he felt, "I think he's just trying to scare her." But who really knew what someone else was thinking or could be capable of?

"Well, judging by her reaction today, it's working. Sure is scaring the heck out of me," Steven said, running his hand through his hair.

Buttoning the flap on his pocket, Larry asked, "Do you think she'll leave town?"

"You mean go back to Michigan?"

Larry nodded.

"No way. This is her home now," Steven answered, fear clutching his heart at the thought of her leaving.

Larry nodded again.

"If she doesn't leave, do you think this person will just give up?" Steven asked.

Larry shrugged. "Sure hope so. I'd hate to think he'd follow through on his threats." He sighed, and both men stood silent for a few minutes, thinking the matter through.

Steven broke the silence by asking, "What about the heparin incident?"

"Well, there is that. I'm not sure what to think about that." Larry shook his head. "Heck, I'm not even sure this is all related." He sighed. "Maybe it's one crazy person—or a couple of crazy people—doing this." He rubbed his hand over his eyes. "I need to get back to the station and think this through and try to make sense of it all." He removed his hat, ran his hand through his hair, and replaced it. "I still have a few profiles I need to read through."

Both men jumped when they heard the back door open and Christina call out, "Hey, Larry, I found something that I want you to look at."

He walked over to the back door and she handed him a small object wrapped in a tissue.

"Be careful. It's fragile."

Carefully unwrapping the small glass vial, he asked, "What is it?" He gave her a perplexed look. Examining the vial, he said, "Okay? Where did this come from?"

"I found it a couple of days ago under a shelving unit in the linen room. I just thought it might be the one used to poison me."

Larry nodded and held the vial up to the light. "There's still some in it."

Christina nodded and shrugged. "Yeah. I thought maybe there might be some fingerprints."

Examining the bottle closely and seeing a possible fingerprint, he said, "This may not be the vial that was used."

"I know. But maybe you can match the fingerprints to someone at the hospital?"

Larry sighed. "Maybe, but it won't prove anything. Even if we match it to someone, especially a nurse or doctor, who's to say they weren't administering it to a patient?"

"Yeah, but what if the fingerprints *don't* match anyone from the hospital? Or they belong to someone other than a doctor or nurse?"

Larry nodded. "Well, we'll have nothing to lose. I'll run it for prints and check them with the hospital personnel prints on file."

Christina let out a sigh and smiled. "Thanks, Larry."

"You know, if you touched the vial without gloves, this could be your fingerprint."

"Yeah, that is a possibility, but I'd rather err on the side of caution."

He nodded, touched the tips of his fingers to his hat brim in a salute, and turned to walk toward his waiting police car just as the Sanders children walked up the sidewalk.

"Hey, Mom, why was the sheriff here?" Nicky asked as he waved at the sheriff, who was backing out of the driveway.

"I'll tell you in a little bit. Why don't we all go in and have some milk and cookies?"

CHAPTER 112

Cindy walked into the Black-Eyed Pea and looked around for Ed. He smiled and stood when he saw her walking toward him, his heart feeling as if it were ricocheting off his rib cage.

"Hey, beautiful," he said as he pulled the chair out for her to sit.

She smiled and said, "Hey."

As soon as she sat, a waitress came up and asked for her drink order. She ordered sweet iced tea, and Ed asked for a refill.

Their eyes met, and they shared an intense moment before each looked away—she around the restaurant, he at the menu. Clearing his throat, he asked, "So how are you? You look great."

Cindy smiled shyly. "Thanks. I'm all right. And yourself?"

"Oh, I'm fine. Hungry as a bear, but fine."

Cindy chuckled. "You're always hungry."

Ed smiled and nodded. "Yeah, you're right about that." He patted his tummy. "Gotta keep this bad boy happy, or he growls at me."

Cindy laughed out loud. She was starting to relax.

He smiled, reaching across the table and taking her hand. She started to pull it away, but he held on, rubbing his thumb over her palm, which sent shivers up and down her spine. *Does he know how this makes me feel?* She felt her face flush and pulled her hand away, placing it in her lap. He started to say something, but the waitress returned with their drinks and an order pad.

They each ordered the house special. As they waited for their order to arrive, they shared a little small talk about the weather—how unusually warm it was for this time of year—and their plans for the upcoming holidays.

Their soups and salads arrived, and Cindy decided it was time to get serious and attack the real reason for their get-together.

"Well, Ed," she started as she poured ranch dressing on her salad, "you wanted to meet me here to talk, and I doubt if it was about the weather, holidays, and well-being of my daughter."

She looked at him and cocked her head. He was about to take a bite of his own salad, but before he stuck the fork in his mouth, he nodded and said, "I do want to talk to you about something important, Cindy, but why don't we eat our dinner first?"

She stared at him a moment, watching as he brought the forkful of salad to his mouth and began to chew. He was watching her watch him as he chewed and had difficulty getting the food past the lump that was forming in his throat.

She wanted to talk right then and there—get everything out in the open—but knew that if the information he revealed was disturbing, they would both miss out on a really nice steak dinner. She smiled, nodded, and said, "All right." He smiled back and took another forkful of salad.

After she told him about the fall clearance sale at the boutique and how she had to put in more hours, she mentioned Christina's near-death experience with the heparin—which he knew about but feigned interest in anyway.

"So Ed, tell me how the electrical business is going."

He coughed, almost choking on a piece of steak. He took a sip of water before answering.

"Um, it's been crazy busy lately," he said, trying to cover his nervousness by slicing off a large piece of steak and stuffing into his mouth. He couldn't talk if his mouth was full, and he was trying desperately to keep it that way.

Cindy smiled and nodded. "I see." She sliced off a small piece of steak and chewed it slowly, wondering if she should confront him with the truth. She looked at their plates, which were almost empty, and thought, *Why not?*

"Ed, do you remember when I asked you about the bogus business card?"

"Uh, yeah."

"Well, you never explained that. I want to know the truth." She pushed her plate over, put her elbows on the table, and leaned forward, resting her chin on her clasped hands.

Ed swallowed hard, took a sip of tea, wiped his mouth with a napkin, and pushed his plate off to the side. They sat across from each other, eyes locked as he mentally danced around the answer in his head. He had known this time would eventually come and had practiced different scenarios in his head and thought he was ready, but now he felt a panic rise within him.

She raised her eyebrows and cocked her head as if to say, "Well?"

This is it, thought Ed. *This is truth time. God help me.*

He leaned closer to her, putting his hands on the table. She did the same. He put his hands on top of hers. She didn't try to pull them free.

Clearing his throat and exhaling, he said, "Okay. Here's the truth. I'm not an electrician."

Cindy nodded. She knew that. "Okay. So what are you? An undercover cop, an FBI agent, a, a …"

Before she could continue, he said, "An agent. With the ATO."

She pulled her hands free and laughed. "Yeah, right. What is the ATO?"

"No, seriously, I am. ATO stands for Antiterrorist Organization."

She gave him a skeptical look. "Let me see your ID."

He reached into his back pocket, pulled out his wallet, and opened it. When she saw the ATO card with his picture on it, she gasped.

"Let me see that," she said as she reached for his wallet. She pulled the card out and read it. It looked real enough. She started to thumb through the rest of his wallet, but he plucked it out of her hand. Shaking a finger, he said, "No, no. Some of that stuff is personal. Maybe someday you can see it, but not right now."

"Why not now?" she asked, sounding like a petulant child who had just been told she couldn't have a cookie.

"Because it's not important now. The important thing is that you know who I am and what I really do."

"What do you mean who you are? Your card read Ed Flores. Don't tell me that's not your *real* name."

He shook his head. "I didn't mean my real name. I meant what I really do for a living." She looked confused. He sighed. "My name *is* Ed Flores, and I honestly do work for the ATO, which is a branch of the Department of Homeland Security."

She shook her head, trying to comprehend what he was saying. "Okay. So what are you doing in Alva?"

"I'm working on a case."

"What kind of case?" Then it was if a light bulb came on in her head. She looked at him with wide eyes. "Does it have anything to do with Christina?"

He nodded.

"What? How?" Before he could answer, she furrowed her brow and asked, "Why were you and those other guys in her house the first time I met you?"

Ed looked around to make sure no one was in the area. "We were installing bugs," he said in a whisper.

"Bugs? What kind of bugs?" She was thinking the six-legged kind and wondered why they would do that.

"You know, listening devices."

"Oh yeah!" She almost giggled because of her naïveté but sobered quickly when she realized what this knowledge implied. "Why?"

"We were working on a case involving her husband."

"David? He's been dead for two years. What could you possibly be looking for now? And how does this involve Christina?"

"Cindy, if I tell you, you have to promise you won't tell anyone, especially Christina."

"Yeah, or you'll have to kill me?" she said, smiling. Ed didn't smile. Panic flitted across her face. "You wouldn't kill me would you?"

"No! God, no!" he said emphatically reaching for her hands again. "It's just that this case just recently closed, and if anyone finds out we've been in Christina's home looking for certain information, she and her family could be in danger."

The panic returned to Cindy's face. "Danger?" she whispered.

Ed nodded. "David worked for the government before his death, helping track down terrorist groups around the country."

"David worked for the government? Christina never told me that."

"Christina didn't know."

"Didn't know? How could she not know? They never kept secrets from each other."

"Well, David *wanted* to tell her, but he had to sign a paper stating that he would tell no one, not even his family, what he was involved in."

Cindy leaned forward till their noses were almost touching and whispered, "So what were you listening for when you put the bugs in?"

"We thought maybe Christina might know something and let it slip or one of the kids may have come across something."

"How?"

"Maybe on a disc or some papers they found while packing and unpacking."

"But it's been two years!" she said emphatically. "Why now? What has happened to get the agency all riled up?"

Ed shrugged and frowned. "There's been some phone and e-mail chatter about another attack, and in one of the correspondences, David Sanders's name was mentioned."

"Whoa!" responded Cindy. "What was said?"

"I don't know. I was just informed that we needed to make sure we hadn't overlooked anything—make sure he hadn't knowingly or unknowingly tapped into some information he shouldn't have."

Cindy nodded and sat back, pondering the information she had just received. After a moment she said, "I have to ask you something, and you have to be honest with me."

Ed had a feeling he knew what the question would be. *Well, I've already told her more than I should have, so what would it hurt to continue telling the truth? She is handling it very well so far.*

"Okay."

"Were you the one who drugged me?" She didn't feel the need to say more, hoping he would ask what she was talking about, maybe look confused, but he did neither. Instead he closed his eyes and sighed. When he opened them, he looked directly into hers, sadness and resignation emanating from them.

"Yes," he whispered.

She nodded, feeling tears well in her eyes. She quickly blinked them away.

"Why?" she whispered, not really wanting to know but needing to.

"Tom and I were there getting the bugs and making sure we hadn't missed anything when you came in and caught us by surprise. Tom was in the den, and I was up in Christina's room. We thought you'd just leave, but then Benji brought your attention to the closet where Tom was hiding. I couldn't let you find him, so I chloroformed you." His heart ached when he saw a tear trickle down her cheek.

"I'm so sorry, Cindy. I didn't want to. You have to believe me. But I had no other choice at the time. It was as much for your protection as it was ours."

"What do you mean by my protection?"

Ed closed his eyes and blew out air. *How can I tell her that if she had surprised Tom, he may have come out of the closet swinging his fists—or, worse yet, with a gun? I don't want to frighten her or make her distrust me or Tom.*

He said, "It wasn't the right time for you to get involved."

She nodded and wiped the tears from her eyes.

"So now it's okay for me to know all this? What's changed?"

"We found what we were looking for, and we're finished here."

"What happens to me?" she asked quietly before pausing and looking at her hands. "Us? Now that I know all this?"

He looked at her, wondering what she was really thinking. *Did she think she would be eliminated? Did she think he was just using her to get to Christina? Did she think he would or could just walk away?*

"Cindy, I'm not sure what you're asking."

She looked at him, a frown creasing her eyebrows. "I'm just wondering if—" She was interrupted by the appearance of the waitress.

Cindy and Ed watched as a young woman with dark hair and eyes and a name tag that read Brandy cleared the table and asked if they wanted dessert. Cindy ordered a hot fudge sundae—her form of stress relief—and Ed asked for a slice of key lime pie.

With hope shining in her eyes, like a child looking at Santa when asking for a special gift, Cindy continued, "I was just wondering if there's any future for us."

He opened his mouth to answer when the waitress returned and set the desserts in front of them. Ed waited for her to leave and then looked at Cindy and sighed, unable to say what was in his heart and mind. He was still having such conflict with his emotions that he wasn't sure what he wanted to say. On the one hand, he really liked her and wanted a relationship, but on the other hand, he wasn't sure if he wanted to bring someone else into his chaotic and sometimes dangerous life.

She quickly looked away and focused on the ice cream.

"It's all right, Ed. We don't have to discuss this now."

He nodded. "Yeah." They were lifting their utensils to take a bite of their desserts when Cindy's cell phone rang. Christina's number registered on the ID plate.

"Hey, Christina," she said as she put the phone up to her ear.

Ed watched as Cindy listened for a few seconds, furrowed her brow, and said, "I'll be there in a few minutes." She returned the phone to her purse and looked at Ed with shock on her face.

With the fork halfway to his mouth, he asked, "What is it?"

"That was Christina. Someone put a dead snake in her van, and she almost had an accident on the way home."

"Is she all right?"

"Yeah, just really shook up." She looked at the ice cream and shook her head. "I need to go over there."

"Okay. Mind if I go with you?"

"Why?"

"I want to see for myself that she's okay and maybe get more information about the incident."

"Do you think this is related to your case?"

He shrugged and shook his head. "I doubt it but can't say for sure. Will it be a problem if I go along? Does Christina know about me?" he asked, taking a bite of pie and almost moaning from the sheer delight of the taste.

Cindy nodded. "She knows everything except for your ATO status. I'm sure she'll be happy to meet you." She stood to go. "Gosh, I hate leaving this ice cream."

"We can come back and have it later, or we can just come back another time?" he said as he stood and pulled her chair out from the table.

She smiled and nodded as she gathered her purse and sweater off the chair and let him put the latter around her shoulders. He threw a fifty-dollar bill on the table as they left.

Cindy rode with Ed to Christina's, wondering who would put a dead snake in her friend's van.

CHAPTER 113

The woman laughed when she thought of the incident earlier that day. She knew Christina had found the snake when her van left the road. She had pulled ahead and turned her car around, driving slowly past, noticing Christina behaving hysterically and Dr. Dawson pulling the snake out of the van. They had been so preoccupied that they hadn't noticed her, thank goodness. If they had, she would have stopped and asked if everything was all right—just like any concerned citizen would do.

All day she had nervously waited. It had been obvious that Christina hadn't found the snake on the way to work, or she would have certainly heard about it. She decided to follow her home to see if she would discover it then, and she had. It irritated her that Dr. Dawson had gotten involved. *Too bad for him.* She sighed. *Well, I gotta do what I gotta do to eliminate the problem. If he gets in the way, oh well. That'll be his own fault.* She had been instructed to use any means available to persuade Christina to leave Alva, the only stipulation being that she wasn't to physically harm her or the children. *But what if they accidentally got hurt? Like, if one of the kids had been in the vehicle, and Christina had run off the road and hit a tree? What was it called on TV when civilians got hurt or killed? Collateral damage? Yeah, that's what they would be—collateral damage. Surely the boss couldn't fault me for that.*

She thought back to the day she had been propositioned. Her back and feet had throbbed with pain from standing for eight hours on the hard cement floors in the laundry room at the hospital, and her arms and hands ached from constantly loading and unloading the washing machines.

As she entered her hot mobile home, she immediately went to her bedroom and turned on the small window air conditioner. After filling her kitty's food bowl and making herself a root beer float, she picked up the remote and had just sat down in front of her box fan when the phone rang. Thinking it was either a telemarketer or her supervisor at the hospital—because no one else had her number—she halfheartedly answered.

"Hello?" She pressed the button to turn the TV on, simultaneously pressing the mute button so she could hear the caller.

A gruff male voice had spoken her name. At first she thought it was a prank call and said, "I'm not interested," and replaced the receiver. The phone immediately rang again, and she answered it, ready to give the caller a piece of her mind. The same voice told her not to hang up, but to listen. It was then that the voice on the other end of the phone line asked her to do this job and said she would be paid a substantial amount.

Thinking it was still some kind of prank call, she asked what kind of job it was and how much money she would be paid. It was pretty straightforward and simple.

He said, "You need to convince Christina Sanders to leave town—preferably go back to Michigan. We don't need her kind here in Alva."

"What do you mean her kind?"

"That's not your concern. I will pay you ten thousand on completion of the job."

She nearly dropped the receiver as she whispered, "Wow, she must have done something pretty bad for you to want to pay me that much money."

"Again, not your concern. So do you want the job?"

"Can you call me back in about fifteen minutes after I think about this?"

"If you don't want the job or the money, I'm sure I can find someone else who does."

"It's not that. I just need a minute to wrap my mind around it."

There was an audible sigh and then a click as the phone disconnected.

"Oh, shoot! Hey mister?" Realizing she may have missed the opportunity of a lifetime, she banged her forehead with the receiver before replacing it in the cradle. *You stupid idiot! I should have told him yes. How could I refuse? Ten thousand dollars! The things I could do with that money!* As she resigned herself to the fact that she had missed out on the opportunity of a lifetime, the phone rang.

She grabbed it and answered, "Hello?"

"So what did you decide?" the voice asked.

Relief flowed over her. "Yes! Yes, I'll do it."

"Good." After a few instructions and the promise to keep in touch, he had given her three months to succeed, or he would find someone else to complete the task.

A month had already passed, and Christina was still around with no apparent desire to leave Alva. *Well, I'll just have to try harder.* Obviously, the things she had tried hadn't frightened her enough. She had to come up with more scary things to do to convince her to leave before Christmas.

She smiled. She knew scary. She was the youngest daughter of an alcoholic mother and father and the sister to four older brothers who had derived great pleasure in thinking of new and cruel ways in which to make her scream and cry with fright.

CHAPTER 114

Christina awoke Friday morning with her head feeling as if it had been in a vise all night. She hadn't slept well. In fact, she wasn't sure she had slept at all. When the alarm clock rang, she wanted so desperately to stay in bed but knew she couldn't. She *had* to get up and go to work. She *had* to pretend that she hadn't been nearly scared to death by a dead snake in her van. Cindy, Larry, Steven, and Ed had advised her to pretend that nothing had happened. *Nothing? Seriously? How am I supposed to pull that off?*

She lay in bed a few more minutes as her brain once again played the memory of those terrifying moments, wondering for the thousandth time why someone would put a dead snake in her van. Realizing for the thousandth time that she still had no answer, she crawled out of bed and dragged herself to the bathroom.

Undressing and standing under an uncomfortably cool shower—the only way she knew to completely wake up—she thought about Ed and understood Cindy's attraction to him. He was definitely one fine specimen of a man—not very talkative, but attentive. *I sure hope I can get to know him better.* Little did she know that her wish would soon become a reality.

Once the kids had come home and were apprised of the situation and all the questions and answers had been put to rest, Cindy, Ed, and Steven left, assuring her they would call her the next day.

Before sending them to bed, she asked her children once more what they thought about the situation and was relieved that they believed it was nothing more than a cruel prank and didn't seem very upset. *I bet they didn't lose any sleep over this!*

She shivered as much from pondering these questions as from the coolness of the water cascading over her body. As she reached out and turned the shower knob to increase the hot water output, the memory of a long-forgotten incident made its way to her conscious mind. *Could something that happened so long ago be the cause of all this chaos? Surely not,* she thought. She stood under the steamy water, allowing her mind to dredge up and remember the incident in question. A revelation struck her that made her gasp. She turned off the water and quickly toweled herself dry. She needed to call Cindy, Lisa, and Donna and run this new revelation by them.

She dressed and took a couple of pain relievers before heading downstairs, hoping they would kick in before the kids came down for breakfast.

She was sitting at the table, sipping her coffee and massaging her temples, when

Nicky entered and asked what they were planning to do for Thanksgiving—"Which, by the way, is in two weeks," he had added as a reminder.

She looked at him blankly for a minute before answering. "I don't know. What do you want to do?" With everything that had happened in the past couple of weeks, she had forgotten about Thanksgiving.

He sighed and said, "I want to be with Grandma, Grandpa, Aunt Joyce, Uncle Robert, and my cousins." He paused and gazed at her with his big hazel eyes. "I want to be with our family." He looked down at his fingers, stuck one in his mouth, and started chewing on a hangnail. "Isn't that what Thanksgiving is all about? Family?"

She nodded and motioned for him to come into her arms for a hug. He did.

When Brad and Stacey came into the room, Nicky proudly announced that they were going to go see Grandma and Grandpa and the rest of the family for Thanksgiving. Both Brad and Stacey expressed their pleasure at the news by giving high fives and shouting things like "All right!" and "Yeah!" and other words of joy that made Christina's head throb even more. She just smiled and nodded and wondered how she was going to pull it off. She hadn't actually said they were going to see the family—in fact, she was hoping to spend a nice quiet vacation at home. The excitement in her children's voices told her she needed to make some kind of get-together become a reality.

She watched the kids eat their breakfast, tuning out their chatter as she sipped her coffee and let her mind wander. Once the kids were out the door, she went to the kitchen and called her three best friends. When all she got were recordings instructing her to leave a message, she told each one to give her a call, as she had something important to discuss with them.

Stacey, Brad, and Nicky walked their usual route to school, unaware that they were being followed. Knowing they had plenty of time before the school bells rang, they walked slowly, enjoying the cool fall air and talking about their plans for the weekend.

Brad stated that since he didn't have any more football games, he had asked Melinda if she wanted to go to the movie with him. Saturday, he would be working at Safeway all day doing inventory and restocking shelves. Stacey told her brothers that she didn't have any real plans but hoped she could have a sleepover with a couple of her girlfriends. Saturday morning, she would go to church and practice for the Christmas play. Nicky said he was planning to spend the night at Danny's house.

"Tomorrow, we're going fishing on a big boat that has a sleeping area and kitchen and a bathroom!" he told his siblings excitedly. "I can hardly wait!"

He ran up to Danny's house and rang the doorbell, hoping his friend would be able to walk the rest of the way to school with them. He was disappointed when Danny's mom answered and said that Danny wasn't feeling well and wouldn't be attending school that day. Nicky asked if he could still come over for the night and if they would still go fishing.

Danny's mom frowned and shrugged. She squatted and looked Nicky in the eyes.

"I don't know, honey. He has a sore throat and is running a fever right now. I'm gonna take him to the doctor in a little while, and we'll just have to see how he's feeling later on. Why don't you stop by after school, and maybe I can tell you what the plans will be?" She smiled and tousled Nicky's hair. He nodded, finding it difficult to keep his disappointment from showing. Turning to go, he said, "Tell Danny I hope he feels better soon."

She smiled and nodded. "I will."

Stacey and Brad heard the conversation and shook their heads, feeling disappointment for their little brother. They each patted him on the back and told him not to worry.

"Things have a way of working out," Stacey said as they continued their trek to school.

The car pulled over behind a van and stopped, and the driver watched the activities of the three Sanders children. The body language of the youngest child indicated that something significant and disappointing had been said. He had run up to the door, talked to the lady, and then walked slowly back to his siblings with his head down. When the children continued on their way, the car followed at a distance. The driver watched as each one entered his or her particular school. After writing the information on a notepad, the driver sat for a few minutes and contemplated the next move. What was planned would be bold and possibly dangerous but would certainly bring the desired results. If all went well, no one would be injured, and everyone would return to a normal life within a day or two—traumatized for sure, but not hurt. The driver returned home to prepare for the day's events.

Standing under the hot steamy shower, Cindy smiled as the water pelted her face and body and the memories of the previous night ran through her mind once again.

After dinner, she and Ed had gone to Christina's house to discuss the day's events with Steven, Christina, and Larry. They had all come to the conclusion that someone wanted Christina to leave Alva and would continue threatening and terrorizing the Sanders family until that goal was accomplished. The question then was—should Christina leave? They all agreed that she shouldn't. Eventually, the tormentor would give up or be caught.

For the life of her, she couldn't understand why anyone would want Christina and her family to leave Alva. *Maybe I can do a little investigating of my own. After all, I know a lot of people who know a lot of people.* In a town the size of Alva, everyone seemed to know a little about everyone else's business. Surely someone had heard or knew something about this whole situation. It was just a matter of finding the right person to talk to.

As she soaped and rinsed off her body, thoughts of the conversation she and Ed had had during the drive back to the Black-Eyed Pea, where she had left her car, meandered through her mind. He had asked if she wanted to continue their relationship, and she had said yes—after she had reversed the question and he answered in the affirmative as well. They had sat in the parking lot next to her car for another hour discussing their future together. Before kissing her good night, he had said, "I'd like to spend more time with you and Samara—get to know you both better."

She agreed that that would be a good idea. When they parted ways, he had gently kissed her and pulled her into a tender embrace. She hadn't wanted to let him go and was pretty sure he felt the same. It had felt so right being held next to his strong, warm body, listening to his heart. She could easily imagine a long future together. Feeling a shiver run through her body, she thought, *It's been a long time since I've felt such a strong desire to be with a man.* She finished showering and decided to call and check up on Christina. *Poor thing probably didn't sleep a wink.*

CHAPTER 115

The police chief sat at his desk reading through old files, thinking how thankful he was that they had been put on computer discs. As he sat reading about an unsolved murder that had happened thirty years ago, the phone rang, making him jump and knock over his cup of pencils.

"Dang it!" he exclaimed as he grabbed for the receiver, thankful it hadn't been his coffee cup. "Hello, Chief Larry Clifton speaking."

"Hey, Larry, it's Steven.

"Hey, Steven. What's up?"

"I was just wondering if you'd come across any more information that might help shed light on this thing with Christina."

Larry leaned back in his chair and stretched. "Not since we spoke last night. But I'm going back through some files I found to see if I might have missed anything."

"Hmm."

"When I finish here, I'm plan to check at the hospital to see if any employees own a small white car and then go from there. I have a gut feeling that our perpetrator works at the hospital."

Steven nodded and said, "You know, I think you're right, considering that most of the incidents happened in and around there."

There was silence for a moment, and then Larry said, "Steven, I want to ask you a personal question."

"Um, okay."

"What kind of relationship do you and Christina have?"

"Excuse me?"

He repeated the question and then added, "Are you just friends? Is there more going on?"

"And why are you asking this?"

Larry smiled. Steven still hadn't answered the question.

"I'm worried about Christina and was wondering how much time you're willing to spend with her—you know, to keep an eye on her and the kids."

"So, it sounds to me like you're asking if we're sleeping together and if I would be willing to stay at her house."

Larry chuckled. "Well, you know how to see through the smoke screen, don't you?"

Steven smiled. "I *am* a doctor. We're trained to listen and read between the lines, because, as one of my instructors said at the beginning of my residency, everyone lies."

"Ah, yes, so true. So are you gonna answer my question?"

"All right. I like Christina, and even though we're becoming better friends, we are *not* sleeping together. She is much too …" He paused, trying to find the right word, and finally said, " … proper for that sort of thing." *That sounded downright Victorian.*

Larry chuckled. "Proper? That's an interesting word."

"Well, I'm not sure that's the right word, but I couldn't think of any other one that seemed right. I guess I meant that she wouldn't just sleep with anyone without some kind of commitment attached."

"That's what I thought. As I said last night, I just don't have the manpower to keep an eye on her and the kids 24/7, and I'm starting to get nervous. Up to now, the incidences have been prank-like stuff—something a teenager might do."

"Yeah," Steven said as he rubbed his eyes.

"I don't think we're dealing with teenagers now, though. The threats are getting more, well, threatening."

"Yeah, I know."

They both sighed and were silent for a moment.

"Say," Steven asked, "did you come across anybody in Christina's past who might be a suspect—besides Janet?"

"Oh yeah, I meant to tell you about that. In my researching, I found a couple of names of folks who were arrested or had misdemeanor offenses back in the early eighties *and* are employed at the hospital. I was planning on visiting them sometime this week. I don't think it'll lead anywhere, but hey, who knows? If one of them *is* the culprit, then maybe my questioning will convince them to quit harassing Christina."

"Hmm. Maybe. If you discover anything else, be sure and call me."

"Yeah. You do the same."

They disconnected.

CHAPTER 116

Christina arrived at work with her head still pounding, wishing she were anywhere but there. Looking at the clock and realizing it had been four hours, took a couple more pain relievers, washing them with a drink of strong coffee—and mentally kicking herself as her stomach rebelled. She went through the change of shift routine in a mental fog, knowing the staff was getting frustrated with her as she asked to have information repeated. The pills hadn't done their job of relieving her headache, the two cups of coffee were making the lining of her stomach feel like it was on fire, *and* she was running on less than four hours of sleep.

She just wanted to get through the day without harming anyone and go home to her nice cozy bed. Then she remembered. *Oh, shoot, it's Friday! I'm supposed to go out with Aaron tonight.* She rubbed her temples. *I hate to cancel, but I just don't feel like going out on a date. I sure hope he'll understand. Maybe I'll feel better as the day progresses. I won't cancel yet.*

When the briefing was over, Mary approached her.

Concern showing on her face, she asked, "Christina, are you all right?"

Christina sighed, rubbing her tummy and making a face.

"Not really. I had a rough night. Didn't get much sleep, and now I have a killer headache and my stomach is on fire."

Patting Christina on the arm, she said, "I'm sorry. Did you take anything?"

Christina nodded. "I took a couple of pain relievers, but they don't seem to be working."

Mary frowned. "Did you eat anything before drinking the coffee?"

Christina nodded slightly. "I had a piece of toast."

Mary nodded. "Hmm. Why don't I go get you some Tums? Maybe that'll help with the tummy."

Christina sighed and nodded. "Thanks. At this point, I'll try just about anything."

Mary returned after a couple of minutes with a little medicine cup full of extra-strength Tums. Christina smiled, popped two in her mouth, chewed and swallowed the chalky substance, and pocketed the remaining ones.

"Thanks, Mary, I appreciate this."

Mary nodded. "I hope they work." Making a face, she added, "I hate that acidy, queasy feeling. Just kinda ruins your whole day."

Christina nodded. "Yeah."

Mary glanced at the clock as she gathered her belongings and headed for the elevator.

"Well, gotta go. Feel better."

Christina smiled and waved.

Fortunately for her, there were only three patients on the floor, and each was in stable condition. *Should be a relatively calm day.* Once the night shift workers left and the nurses and aides started their morning routine, Christina was free to sit at the desk and peruse the files.

Mr. Anthony Perkins was a seventy-five-year-old white male who had come into the emergency room two days earlier complaining of chest pain radiating down his left arm. It was discovered that he had a 95 percent blockage in his carotid artery. Dr. Dawson had done an angioplasty the next morning, and Mr. Perkins was in stable condition. She looked at the papers that had his vital signs and blood work recorded. She checked his medications listed with those in his basket in the medication room. All was in order. She did this with the other two patients as well. *So far so good,* she thought as she sat at the desk and rubbed her tired eyes.

"Christina?"

She looked up and saw Janet Washburn standing beside her. "Yes?"

"May I talk to you?"

Christina looked around and, seeing no one else, said, "Sure. Pull up a chair."

Janet did and sat across from Christina, nervously massaging her hands.

Christina looked at her and asked, "Is everything all right, Janet?"

She sighed then shook her head. "Christina, I feel I owe you an apology."

Christina raised her eyebrows in surprise. *Janet Washburn, apologizing?* "Why?"

"Well, I've been …" Just as she started to say more, an alarm went off, and Christina looked up to see that the monitor in Mr. Perkins room had flatlined.

"What the heck?" She jumped up and pushed the intercom to announce a code blue in room 220. She and Janet rushed in with the crash cart and found Mr. Perkins face down on the floor. Immediately turning him over—which was no easy task, as the man must have weighed over two hundred pounds—they discovered that he had stopped breathing. Janet administered oxygen as Christina pushed on the man's chest to keep his blood flowing. They were both relieved when Dr. Dawson and Dr. Meils rushed in and took over. Between the four of them, doing CPR and administering drugs, they were able to revive Mr. Perkins and return him to his bed. Once he was stabilized and conscious, the four of them left the room and returned to the nurses' station.

Dr. Meils, shaking his head and smiling, said, "Well, that was exciting."

"Yeah," the others said in unison.

Christina excused herself and returned the crash cart to the storage room, where it was restocked and locked. When she returned to the station, the two cardiac doctors had left, and Janet was at the desk filling in pertinent information in Mr. Perkins's chart.

She looked up when Christina pulled a chair next to her and sat.

"So what did Dr. Dawson and Dr. Meils have to say?" she asked as she found stray pencils and pens and put them in the coffee cup designated for them.

"The usual stuff. Monitor intake and output; run an EKG strip every half hour for the next four hours; make sure he gets his meds on time." She looked at Christina and rolled her eyes. "The usual stuff."

Christina nodded. "Any different meds?"

"Nope. Same old stuff."

Christina nodded again.

"Janet, are you free after work?"

Janet looked up from her writing. "Why?" she asked.

"Well, I just thought we could continue our conversation that was so rudely interrupted." She gave a crooked smile.

Janet returned the smile and nodded. "Yeah, how dare Mr. Perkins decide to have a heart attack right as we were about to have a serious conversation? And yes, I am free after work. What did you have in mind?'

"Why don't we stop for coffee at Caribou by the outlet stores?"

Janet thought a moment then nodded. "Okay, that sounds good. I like their caramel lattes."

"Mmm. Me too."

"Excuse me," an unfamiliar voice cut in.

They both looked up to see the face of a troubled young woman.

Christina stood. "Yes? May I help you?"

"I'm Mr. Perkins's granddaughter, and he told me he had just had a heart attack. Is that right?"

Christina walked around the counter and extended her hand. "I'm Christina."

"I'm Angie."

"Nice to meet you, Angie. Let's go see your grandpa, and I'll tell you what happened."

Angie was petite with fine blonde hair pulled back in a ponytail, flawless porcelain skin, and big blue eyes framed with long dark lashes. *If she had wings, she would look like a fairy,* thought Christina as they walked toward Mr. Perkins's room.

"Your grandpa did have a setback, but he's all right now."

Angie looked up at Christina with tears in her eyes. "How did he get the big bruise on his forehead?"

"Well, when the cardiac alarm went off and we went into his room, he was face down on the floor." The girl brought her fist up to her mouth and gave a worried look. "We presume he must have tried to get up and passed out. We administered CPR, and he responded well within a few minutes."

She whispered, "His heart stopped?"

"There were a few seconds when we couldn't find a pulse, but as I said, once we started the CPR, his heart rate returned to normal."

The girl chewed on her thumbnail.

Placing a hand on the girl's shoulder, Christina asked, "Is anyone else with you?"

The young lady shook her head. "No, I came by right after school. My mom wanted me to check on Grandpa. She had to work and won't be able to get here till after supper."

Christina nodded. "I see. What grade are you in, Angie?"

"I'm a senior this year."

Christina raised her eyebrows in surprise, thinking she looked much younger, like a freshman. That would explain why she was here in the middle of the day—most seniors finished their classes by two, giving them time to work or study or whatever seniors did nowadays.

"Do you attend Alva High?"

"Yes, ma'am."

"My son's a sophomore this year. Maybe you know him. Brad Sanders?"

Angie's face lit up. "Well, I don't know him personally, but I've seen him at school and watched him play football. Didn't y'all just move here this summer from Michigan?"

Christina smiled. "Yes, we did."

"How do y'all like living here?"

"Well, it's been quite an adjustment, especially getting used to the heat, but all in all, I think we like it."

Angie nodded and smiled. "I've never been outside of Texas. Someday, I'd like to travel and visit different parts of the country—maybe even go up to Michigan. Is it always cold up there?"

Christina chuckled. "No. Believe it or not, it does get pretty hot in the summer. Granted, it's cold for about six months out of the year, but the other six months are quite pleasant."

"That's the opposite of here. It's hot for about nine months and cool or cold for the other three."

Christina smiled and nodded. "Yeah, I've noticed that."

Mr. Perkins moaned and shifted his large, bulky body. The girl walked over and took his hand, watching as he slept.

Glancing at Christina, she whispered, "Mrs. Sanders?"

"Yes?"

"Is my grandpa gonna be all right?"

Christina walked over and stood by the sleeping man, placing her hand on top of Angie's.

"Yes, Angie, I believe your grandpa will be just fine. He'll need to take it easy for a little while, change some of his eating habits, and take certain meds, but all in all, he's a pretty healthy man."

The girl sighed and nodded. "Good. I really love my grandpa."

Christina smiled and patted the girl's hand.

"Grandpas are pretty special people." The two women stood quietly for a few moments, watching the sleeping man—Christina remembering her own grandpas and the wonderful times she had with them, and Angie remembering wonderful times with her own grandpa and hoping for more.

CHAPTER 117

Nicky watched the second hand on the clock in the front of the classroom as it ticked off the seconds. *Only five more minutes,* he thought, vaguely aware of the teacher announcing something about next Monday's assignment.

"Nicky, did you hear what I said?" she asked, bringing his mind back in focus.

He looked up at her, wide-eyed. "No, ma'am," he answered, feeling heat on his face as his classmates snickered.

She nodded and smiled. "I didn't think so. You seemed awfully interested in that clock."

He nodded shyly.

She raised her eyebrows, as if expecting some kind of explanation.

"I was just thinking about my friend Danny. He's sick, and I'm supposed to go to his house for a sleepover tonight and go fishing tomorrow."

She smiled and nodded. "Well, I hope he feels better so y'all can do those things."

He nodded. "Yeah, me too."

She looked around at the other students. A few were gathering their books and papers; others were just waiting for the bell to ring.

"Don't forget to read chapters two through five in your science book for Monday. We'll be doing a couple of experiments and possibly taking a quiz." She heard a collective moan and smiled. The bell rang, and twenty students noisily left her classroom. She watched with interest as Nicholas Sanders gathered his belongings together and quietly left the room—alone.

He was an interesting child—not really an introvert, but definitely not as verbal and aggressive as his friend Danny. They were like yin and yang as far as personalities and looks went. Nicky was more of an observer—watching and thinking, weighing his options before getting involved in any given activity. Danny, on the other hand, was a jump-in-ask-questions-later kind of kid.

She had noticed over the past couple of months that once Nicky was committed to something, he stuck to it until it was completed and perfect, according to his standards. Danny seemed to go through life with a just-get-it-done-in-any-way-possible attitude. She smiled as she thought of Danny. He was the class clown, a doer without any thought of consequences, apt to tell jokes and do things to make his peers smile and laugh.

Nicky didn't seem to have many friends. In fact, she had only seen him hang out with Danny and wondered if maybe he was Nicky's *only* friend. She sighed and hoped in her heart that he would make more friends as the year progressed. A best friend was great, but a kid needed more than just one friend to get through the lonely times, didn't he? She looked out the classroom window and watched as he crossed the lawn and disappeared behind a hedgerow—appearing so small and vulnerable without his friend.

Nicky was so caught up in thinking about the fishing trip planned for the next day that he didn't see the heavyset woman approach until she was right in front of him. His breath caught as he nearly bumped into her.

"Excuse me, ma'am," he said as he looked up into her round face. She had a pleasant smile. Recognition slammed into him. *She's the lady that was staring at us when we were having lunch at the fried chicken place last Sunday after church. Why is she here?*

Smiling down at him, she asked, "Are you Nicky Sanders?"

"Yes," he said warily, stepping back. *How does she know my name?*

"I'm your mom's friend. She asked me to come pick you up and take you to the hospital."

"Why?" he asked as he pictured his mom injured or sick. "Is she hurt or sick?"

The lady laughed. "No, no. She just wants you to come. She has a surprise for you."

Nicky backed up a couple of steps. It wasn't like his mom to send a stranger in her place.

"Who are you?" he asked warily.

"I told you. I'm your mom's friend." She took a step toward him. He stepped back again and then asked something she didn't have an answer for.

"What's the password?"

She looked dumbfounded. "What?"

"What's the password?" he asked again, dropping his backpack and preparing to run.

His mom had given the kids a password that only they and anyone who was sent to pick them up knew.

The Sanders password was "fuzzy pickles." The lady didn't know it. He needed to run.

Realizing her mistake in not knowing this, noticing his facial expression change from concern to fear, and sensing he was about to escape, she reached out and grabbed his arm as he turned to run. He felt her other hand, which held some kind of cloth with a sweet-smelling chemical, close over his nose and mouth. He started to cry out, but all he managed was a muffled scream. He tried to kick and bite, but his vision blurred and his limbs went limp as everything went black. Thinking he was about to die, his last thought was *Mom will be so sad.*

CHAPTER 118

Janet smiled as she thought, *If I can win Christina's trust and confidence, she'll never suspect that I've been the one behind the chart incidences. I can continue discrediting her, and she'll never suspect me. Maybe she'll quit or be fired and I can get the job I deserve—and the man I want.*

Christina and Janet sat in a booth by the window sipping their iced caramel lattes, watching the people walk in and out of stores, and discussing the day's events.

"So, do you think Mr. Perkins will recover?" Janet asked.

Christina nodded. "Yeah. He seems like a pretty tough guy."

Janet nodded in agreement. There was an awkward silence before Christina finally said, "Janet, you wanted to talk to me about something?"

Janet sighed and nodded. Taking a sip of her latte and pushing it aside, she leaned forward and spoke quietly so no one else could hear.

"Christina, I owe you an apology."

Christina nodded and with a confused look said, "Yeah, you said that earlier, and I don't understand *why* you need to apologize."

"I need to apologize because I've been a real bitch to you lately."

Christina frowned and started to protest, but Janet held up her hand and said, "I have to admit that I was very angry and jealous when you came in and took the job that I had so desperately wanted."

Christina frowned.

"Now that it's been a couple of months, I can see that you are the right person for the job." Christina shook her head and started to speak, but Janet silenced her with an upraised finger. "Please let me continue."

Christina sighed, nodded, and took another sip of coffee.

"I've worked in the hospital on the cardiac floor for many years and for several different doctors, but Dr. Dawson was—or I should say is—special." She gave a little smile. "Can I speak honestly, woman to woman?"

Christina nodded slightly, wondering where all this was going.

"I have to admit that I have—had," she corrected herself quickly, "a crush on Dr. Dawson over the years." *I'm not telling her we dated.*

Christina raised her eyebrows in surprise.

"I know, I know, it's kinda childish, but you have to admit, he's pretty darned good-looking and fun to be around."

Christina nodded and gave a slight smile, not sure how to respond.

Janet nodded and rolled her eyes and then waved a hand, and continued. "Anyway, I've been jealous of you because of your job status, and because you and Dr. Dawson have hit it off. I had always hoped Steven and I would become more than friends, and I've tried *everything* in my power to make it happen, but ..." She paused and let out a sigh. "I've finally come to the conclusion that it's just not gonna happen. No matter how hard I try, it seems he only has eyes for you."

She looked at Christina and shrugged. Christina raised her eyebrows in surprise, having had no idea that Janet felt that way.

Shrugging and leaning back, Janet sighed heavily and said, "I don't *want* to feel that jealousy and anger anymore."

Christina cleared her throat and said, "May I speak now?"

Janet nodded.

Not sure what she was about to say, but hoping the right words would come out, she began.

"First of all, thank you for your apology, even though I'm not sure it was warranted. I haven't been aware of your being bitchy toward me. Maybe you were and I just chalked it up to hormones or thought that you were having a bad day, but I never gave it a second thought." Noticing Janet's frown, she held up her hand and added, "Okay, maybe once or twice I wondered what was going on." They both smiled. "But really, I haven't had a problem with you at all. You're a great nurse and colleague, and I think we work pretty well together." Shaking her head and looking down, she said quietly, "I had *no* idea that you felt that way about Dr. Dawson."

Janet looked down at her hands and nodded slightly, stifling a smile, thinking, *Gotcha! You don't really know me, Christina.*

Janet wiped her eyes and let out a big sigh. "It just feels good to get this all off my chest. I feel as if a huge piece of concrete has been lifted from my shoulders."

Christina nodded and smiled. "Good. Maybe we can start over. I certainly don't want you to be angry with me, and I don't want to make you uncomfortable."

Janet gave a crooked smile and nodded. They each sipped their coffees in silence for a few moments, and then Janet spoke. "Do you know I have a daughter the same age as yours?"

Christina nodded. "Yeah. I just recently heard that and have been meaning to talk to you about it."

"Do you also know that your daughter and mine are best friends?"

Christina looked confused. "What?"

"Leelee—I mean, Linda—is Stacey's best friend, and vice versa. Her name is Linda Lenore Lewis, and I started calling her Leelee when she was a baby. After the divorce from her dad, I changed my name back to Washburn. I didn't want to have his name anymore. It was bad enough that Linda had it."

"Well, I'll be danged," Christina said, putting her hand over her heart. "I wondered who Linda belonged to. I knew her mom worked at the hospital, but I never put two and two together. Guess I didn't give it that much thought. Well, geez, I feel stupid."

Janet smiled. "I knew from day one who Stacey belonged to." *And I hated that Leelee chose her as a best friend.*

"Leelee's so gentle and meek but doesn't have much self-esteem. She gets teased about her shyness, but Stacey came along and has helped her feel more confident." She paused and took a sip of coffee. "Ever since her dad and I divorced and her grandma died, Leelee has gotten more and more withdrawn. I can only do so much for her because I have to work so many hours. Stacey seems to have filled in that hole in her soul that had made her so sad." She stopped to wipe the genuine tears forming in her eyes.

"Anyway, even though I wanted to drive you away"—*and send you packing back to Michigan*—"I know how devastated Linda would be to lose Stacey's friendship."

Christina gave her a confused look. "And you're telling me all this now because …"

"I'm telling you this so we can start over." *And get any suspicions off me.* "Wipe the old slate clean, so to speak, and begin again. I just don't want any walls between us." She took a napkin and wiped up a wet spot that the latte had left.

Christina nodded. "Janet, I need to ask you something, and I hope you're honest with me."

Janet nodded warily.

"Did you have anything to do with the heparin incident?"

Janet looked shocked, blinked her eyes several times, and stuttered, "Why are you asking me that? I might be bitchy, but I'm not evil." *Well, maybe a little,* she thought as she choked back a smile and giggle.

Christina paused a moment and then sighed and said, "So who did?"

Janet shook her head and said, truthfully, "I honestly don't know."

Christina's phone rang, and she almost dropped it. She put it to her ear and said brusquely, "What?"

"Mom?"

She took a calming breath. "Hey, Stacey, what's up?"

"Are you all right?"

"Yeah, I'm fine. Just a little stressed at the moment." She looked across the table at Janet, who was sipping the last few drops of her latte.

"Mom, is Nicky with you?"

Christina looked at her watch. Four thirty. "No. Isn't he home with you?"

"No."

"Is he at Danny's house?"

"No. I called there, and they said they haven't seen him."

"Is his backpack or any of his belongings at home?"

"No. I've looked all over the house, and there's no sign of him anywhere, like he never came home."

"Did you call Brad? Maybe he's with him."

"I did and he isn't. Mom, I'm worried. This isn't like Nicky to disappear without telling us."

"I know, honey. I'll be home in a few minutes. In the meantime, walk around the block and up to the school and see if he may be with some friends and lost track of time."

"Mom, he doesn't have any friends except Danny."

"Stacey, just do as I ask, please." Worry started taking root in her soul. *Great,* she thought as she put the phone back in her purse, *another crisis.*

Janet looked concerned. "Is everything all right?"

Christina shook her said and said a bit too sharply, "No. My son is missing." She stood and gathered up her jacket and purse. "I need to go."

Janet nodded. Christina threw a five-dollar bill on the table.

"Janet, we'll talk later."

Janet nodded again. "Okay."

Christina rushed out of the building and, as she drove, called Larry and Steven.

CHAPTER 119

When Christina ran in the back door, Stacey, who had been crying, and Larry, who looked grim, greeted her. She hugged her daughter and told her to go call Cindy. She and Larry went into the family room.

"Okay, Larry, where's my son?"

He sighed and shook his head. "I'm sorry, Christina. I don't know."

"You don't know? Have you and Stacey called all his classmates and teachers?" He nodded. "We've talked to most of them. There were a few we need to call back."

"Well, when was the last time anyone saw him?"

"His science teacher said she saw him leave the schoolyard and disappear behind the hedges between the houses on Elm Street—you know, where the sidewalk cuts through the property so the kids don't walk on the yards?"

She nodded her head and started pacing around the room, chewing on her thumbnail. "Yeah, I know. I used to walk home that way all the time. Did you find anything there? His backpack? Anything?"

"I just returned from there, and I did see an area where it looked like there was a struggle, but geez, Christina, how many kids go through there in a day? Those scuffs could have been made by anyone."

Christina jumped when Benji barked and Steven walked in the back door. She ran to him and buried her face in his shirt. He looked at Larry, who shook his head.

Steven pulled Christina away and looked her in the eyes.

"What do you know so far?"

"Nothing!" she said, pulling away from him and crossing her arms over her chest. Stacey came back into the room and started crying again when she saw her mother. Brad, Cindy, and Samara walked in the back door at the same time. They all came together and hugged.

"Brad, what are you doing here?" Christina asked her oldest son.

"Stacey called and told me Nicky was missing, so I called Mrs. Murray and asked if she would come get me and bring me home. My boss was okay with me leaving."

Christina nodded and looked at Cindy and said, "Thank you."

"Oh, honey, I'm so sorry. How long has he been missing? Did you call all his classmates?" Cindy asked as she clung to her best friend and looked at Larry.

"There's no sign that he made it home from school, and yes, we called everyone we could. Right now, my deputy is going house to house asking if anyone heard or saw anything. So far, we've come up empty-handed."

They heard a knock at the front door, and Christina rolled her eyes and said, "Now what? Who could that be?"

Cindy went to answer the door and was surprised to see Ed standing there.

Opening the door, she said, "I didn't know if you got my message or would come."

"I was on the outskirts of town headed in to see you when I got your message. What's going on?"

She gave him a quick summary, and he nodded. They walked into the family room, and the men shook hands. He put his arm around Christina's shoulder and led her to the couch.

"I have something to tell everyone." The group followed him into the living room, found places to sit, and waited for him to speak. Once settled, he began explaining his true identity and his reason for being in Alva. Everyone sat in shocked silence as he explained his involvement with the Antiterrorist Organization, or ATO. He looked at Christina and told her of David's involvement with the government and that he and his men had entered her home on several occasions and had confiscated the discs and documents that David had left. Christina looked over at Cindy for confirmation. Cindy gave a crooked smile and nodded. Christina gave her a look that said, "Why didn't you tell me?" Cindy shrugged and looked down, not able to withstand the confusion and hurt in her friend's eyes.

"Even though most of the papers and discs had work-related stuff on them"—he shrugged and looked around the group—"there were a few that had pertinent information." Christina gasped.

"Wait! Let me get this straight. David worked for the government? Tracking down terrorist groups?"

Ed nodded.

With genuine hurt in her voice, she said, "He never told me about that."

"He couldn't tell you, because he had to sign an affidavit stating he wouldn't." Christina shook her head, brought her hand up to her mouth, and found a nail that needed chewing.

Brad, who had been sitting quietly in the background, stood and asked, "So my dad worked for the government? Do you think Nicky's disappearance has anything to do with that?"

"You think terrorists kidnapped Nicky?" Stacey asked, standing next to Brad.

Everyone else looked at Ed wide-eyed as the idea took root.

He put his hand up and said, "Well, I'm not saying that for sure, but it is a possibility. I don't know exactly what David was involved in or how deep into the terrorist network he went, so ..." He shrugged and sighed.

Looking around at the seven pairs of anxious eyes, he focused back on Christina, whose desperate look reminded him of the mother of the boy who had been kidnapped in Dallas several years ago.

As everyone began talking and noisy chatter filled the room, he tuned them out and let his mind recall that particular event with such clarity; it was as if it happened last week.

He hoped Nicky would be lucky enough to have an incompetent kidnapper and be returned safely, but knew that if this was terrorist related, the odds were stacked against him.

Christina shook her head, trying desperately to comprehend all that had been said as thoughts raced through her mind. *How could I have been so oblivious to everything? David's involvement with the government is certainly a surprise! How could he have kept that from me? And the recent break-ins? I guess that explains the deal with the computer.* She gasped as a thought occurred to her, and she looked at Cindy, who was looking at Ed like an adoring puppy. *Was he the one who drugged her? Probably so, but I'll have to ask her eventually.* She shook her head. *Geez, I feel so stupid!*

Noticing her distress, Steven pulled her closer. Stacey and Brad walked over and stood beside their mother.

With a trembling voice, Christina asked, "So what are we to do?"

Ed stood and blew out some air. "I'm going to make a few phone calls. I have friends in the FBI who can help locate Nicky. In the meantime, I need you to get a recent photo of him so we can have it copied." He looked at Cindy. "Could you run to town and get about one hundred copies made?"

She nodded. "A hundred copies?"

Ed nodded. "I want to paste his picture all over town. In a town this size, I could just about bet someone has seen something."

Cindy nodded. "Okay." She looked at Christina. "Where's the best place to go to get these made quickly?"

"Considering the time, I'd say go to Wal-Mart."

"Better yet, go to the station and use that copier," Larry said in response.

"Can I come with you?" Stacey asked.

Samara, who had been sitting quietly in the background, chimed in. "Me too?" Cindy nodded.

Christina ran up to her room and grabbed the most recent school picture of Nicky, taken a month earlier. Her breath caught and tears stung her eyes as she looked at his sweet, innocent face. She fell to her knees and begged God to please take care of her child.

Returning to the living room with the photo, she jumped when the house phone rang. Brad answered it and called out to her. Taking it, she gave him a questioning look. He shrugged, indicating he had no idea who was on the other end. Ed and Steven both came and stood next to her, hoping the caller would be the kidnapper.

She answered warily. "Hello?" Ed put his ear next to the receiver.

"Christina?" a male voice said.

"Yes?" She answered.

"This is Aaron. I tried calling your cell phone, but it went right to voice mail. Are we still on for tonight?" Ed shook his head and indicated for Steven to follow him back to the living room.

Christina sat in the nearest chair. "Oh, Aaron. I'm so sorry. I completely forgot about tonight. My son's missing."

"What? Your son? Which one?"

"My youngest one, Nicky."

"What happened?" She sensed the concern in his voice.

"He didn't come home from school, and he hasn't called, and no one seems to know where he is."

"Oh my gosh, Christina! Is there anything I can do? Do you want me to come over?"

"Oh, Aaron, thank you for offering, but really, there are enough people here. There's a guy here who works with the FBI, and of course the police chief and some of my friends." She paused, not wanting to offend him, but not wanting him to come either. *It would be very awkward to have him and Steven in the same room.* "I'll keep you informed."

"How did the FBI get involved so quickly?"

"You remember my friend, Cindy?"

"Yeah."

"He's a friend of hers who just happened to be visiting."

"Wow. That's good timing on his part."

She nodded and said, "Yep."

"Well, please don't hesitate to call if you need me for anything. I'll be glad to come by tomorrow if you want me to."

"Thanks, Aaron, but I don't think that'll be necessary. I'll keep in touch."

She replaced the receiver and turned. She hadn't heard Steven return and was surprised to see him standing so close. He was frowning.

"Aaron?" he asked.

Christina bit her bottom lip. "He and I were supposed to go out to dinner tonight."

He raised his eyebrows. "Oh, really? Were you planning on telling me about this?"

She frowned back at him. "I don't know." They looked at each other for a few seconds, not knowing what to say. He was thinking, *Why should I care who she sees?* She was thinking, *How dare he question who I see?*

Ed walked in, interrupting the silence. He looked at them both and then said to Christina, "Excuse me, but the FBI guys will be here in a few minutes. They're driving down from Dallas."

"What will they be doing?" she asked, looking away from Steven.

"They'll be setting up a phone tap to trace any calls coming in. I'm sure the kidnapper will call and ask for some kind of ransom. They always do."

Christina nodded. She felt numb with shock and fear.

"In the meantime, why don't you and Steven go sit in the front room and try to relax? Have a cup of coffee or some iced tea."

Christina gave him a confused look. "Relax?"

Steven put his arm around her shoulder and steered her into the front room. He whispered in her ear, "I think he just wants us out of the way."

She nodded slightly.

"Sheriff? Larry, is it?" called Ed from the breakfast room, where the home phone was located.

"Yeah?"

"Have you finished calling the teachers and classmates?"

Flipping his phone open, he said, "I have about a dozen I need to call back. I was planning on doing that right now."

"Good. Let me know if you get any more pertinent information."

"Sure thing."

CHAPTER 120

Janet left the Caribou coffee shop wondering what had happened to Christina's son. *What did she mean he was missing?* She drove home and asked Linda to call Stacey and inquire about the situation.

She was preparing macaroni and cheese when her daughter came in and announced that the youngest Sanders boy had been kidnapped. Janet almost dropped the dish in her hand.

"What? Are you sure?"

"That's what Stacey said. She was crying and said that Nicky didn't come home from school and they had called everyone they knew and he wasn't anywhere to be found."

Janet set the bowl on the counter, wiped her hands, and sat down at the kitchen table.

"Oh my gosh! Christina must be worried out of her mind. I know I would be if anything happened to you." She motioned for her daughter to come over, and she put her arms around her waist and drew her in close.

"Stacey asked if I could come over and spend the night. She's pretty freaked out about all this."

Janet nodded. "I can understand that. Are you sure it's okay with her mom?"

"I don't know. I didn't ask."

"Well, call her back and ask. If it's okay with her mother, then it's okay with me. A girl needs her best friend at times like this."

Linda smiled and nodded. "Thanks, Mom. I'll go call."

Janet finished preparing the macaroni and cheese and a salad and set them on the table. *Could the spell I cast the other day have anything to do with this? I just wanted chaos in Christina's life ... not for her child to be kidnapped. Could the powers that I tapped into cause this kind of chaos? Oh, man. What have I done?* She sat in a nearby chair and said a silent prayer to whatever powers might be listening that Nicky would be kept safe and returned quickly.

Linda returned to the kitchen looking crestfallen. "What's wrong, honey? Did you talk to Stacey?"

"No. I talked to her mom, who said that Stacey had run into town with Mrs. Murray to make some copies of Nicky's picture. I told her Stacey had asked me to come over, and she said okay. She said as soon as they returned, she'd tell Stacey to call me."

"Well, I'm sure her mom will tell her you called, but if she forgets, you can call her after dinner."

"Yeah. All right."

As they were finishing their macaroni and cheese, Linda looked at her mom and asked, "Mom, do you hate Mrs. Sanders?"

The question so surprised Janet that she choked on the sip of milk she was swallowing. Once her coughing fit had subsided, she cleared her throat and asked, "Why would you think I hate Mrs. Sanders?" *Was it that obvious?*

"Well, it's pretty obvious that you don't like her."

"How so?"

"Every time I mention Stacey or her family, you either roll your eyes or try to change the subject."

"I do?"

"Yeah. You do. So do you hate her or what? And if so, why? What has she ever done to you?"

Janet wiped her mouth with her napkin and stood to remove the dinner plates and utensils, wanting desperately to avoid this conversation. Linda reached over and put her hand on her mom's arm.

"Mom, please sit down and talk to me."

Janet sighed. "All right," she said, sitting down once again. "*Hate* is an awfully strong word, Leelee, and I'm not sure it describes what I feel about Mrs. Sanders." *Well, it does, but how can I explain that to my thirteen-year-old daughter, who is naïve enough to love and trust everyone?*

Linda gave her a skeptical look. Janet raised her hand in defense. "I know I haven't said very nice things about them, but to be honest with you, I just don't like Christina."

"What? Why? She's such a nice lady."

"Linda, I don't expect you to understand, and I'm not going to attempt to explain my feelings, so you'll just have to accept that Mrs. Sanders and I will *never* be good friends."

Linda shook her head and said, "Okay."

Just then, the phone rang, and Linda ran to answer it.

"It's Stacey. She said I could come over and spend the night. I'll go pack my bag."

Janet smiled and thought, *Good for her,* Then she felt a pang of jealousy, wishing she had a best friend—well, *any* friend, for that matter.

CHAPTER 121

Nicky woke with a dull headache, a queasy stomach, and a full bladder.

"Dad? Daddy?" he called out as he became conscious. He had been dreaming that his dad was in the room with him, telling him to wake up and not to be scared, because he was right there beside him. He slowly opened his eyes expecting to be in *his* room and see his daddy sitting in the chair next to his bed, and he was disappointed and frightened at finding neither, seeing only blackness.

Coming fully awake and hearing unfamiliar voices, he thought, *Where am I? Where is everybody? Why can't I move? Why can't I see?* Something was over his eyes. *A hood? A scarf?* He wasn't sure. He tried to put his hand up to remove the material, but his hand was caught on something. He yanked and tugged, soon realizing something metallic—*Handcuffs?*—had him attached to something. He moved his other hand and found it to be bound as well. Panic started to seize him, and he kicked his legs, relieved to find them free. He lay still for a moment, thinking about his situation. *This has got to be a nightmare. Wake up!* he yelled inside his head. *But wait ... I am awake.* Tears stung his eyes, and he gritted his teeth to keep from letting his fear and emotions get out of control. He smelled bacon frying and heard someone—not his mom—humming. His heart continued its galloping, and the tears he had tried so hard to keep in ran down into his ears. It was then that he felt a calming presence and heard a familiar voice in his mind. *It's okay, son. I'm here.* He whispered, "Daddy? I'm so scared!"

I know, but it'll be all right.

"Where am I and how did I get here and why am I tied up?" he whispered to his invisible companion. Just then, his memory slammed into him, and he knew.

A large lady had approached asking his name. When she was unable to give him the code word, he had turned to run away, but she had grabbed his arm, swung him around, and covered his nose and mouth with a cloth that contained some kind of sweet-smelling chemical. He wasn't sure but thought that it was probably chloroform. According to the TV crime shows, that was what bad guys used to knock out their victims.

He wondered how long he had been asleep. Lying very still and listening intently, he realized the voices he heard were from a TV sitcom show.

He thought of his mom, Stacey, and Brad and wondered what they were doing. *They're probably worried out of their minds.* The tears kept cascading down to his ears, making them tickle, and he tried rocking his head back and forth to dislodge them and get some relief. He gave a frustrated groan as he tried once again to free his hands. He needed to think clearly so he could get out of this situation alive. *Alive? Am I really in danger? Well, considering I was taken against my will, drugged, and tied up and blindfolded, yeah, my life is probably in danger.* His heart felt as if it was going to gallop right out of his chest. He took in a deep breath and released it slowly, trying to steady his nerves. *Okay. Think.*

Even though he couldn't see his dad or any angels, he knew they were with him, and that knowledge gave him a sense of hope and courage. As he was pondering his dilemma, he heard the door open.

"Hey, sleepyhead, it's time to wake up."

He lay very still, feigning sleep.

"I know you're awake, so you don't need to fake it." She walked over and pulled the blindfold off his eyes. He jumped at the touch. He hadn't even heard her take a step. *Wow, she's not only fast, but quiet too. Weird.* Squinting his eyes, he looked up at her smiling, round face. He did a quick assessment and decided that she reminded him of a very large baby with her plump face and body. Instead of fighting and trying to escape, which was what every instinct in him wanted to do, he decided to play it cool. He had learned from a self-defense class in school that the best way to escape a captor was to remain calm and think things through. Irrational behavior usually ended badly for the victim. *Okay. I'm gonna remain calm, gather information, and then hightail it out of here first chance I get.*

Mustering up a smile, he said, "Hi. I'm Nicky. I'd shake your hand, but I'm kinda tied up."

She smiled and tousled his hair.

"Aren't you the cutest thing? And polite, too. I know who you are, Nicky. You can call me Ruby. It's not my real name, but I've always liked it and wanted to be called that. If I ever have a little girl, I will name her that."

Oh, boy, he thought, *the lights are on, but nobody's home!*

Nicky nodded and smiled. "Hello, Ruby. That's a nice name. So why am I here?"

She ignored his question and asked, "Do you need to go potty?"

Potty? Not bathroom or toilet? Does she think I'm a baby? To her, he said, "Yes, Ruby, I do."

"Now, I'm gonna uncuff you, but you have to promise not to try and run away. I'd hate to have to drug you again and tie you up. I don't like hurting little kids."

Nicky nodded.

"You have to say it. You have to say, 'Ruby, I won't run away.'"

Nicky nodded again. "Ruby, I promise I won't run away."

She smiled and clapped her hands. "Good. I could tell you were a good boy when I saw you that first time."

First time? When did she see me? Oh yeah, at the fried chicken place. I wonder how long she's been watching me.

"Ruby, I don't remember meeting you before today."

"Oh, honey, I've been watching you for quite a while now—your mama, you, your brother and sister. Y'all are such a nice family."

Nicky felt a flutter of fear in his chest. *This lady isn't playing with a full deck of cards—that's for sure.* Then a terrifying thought occurred to him: *What if she has hurt them?*

"Thank you, but you know they're going to be worried sick about me," he said, not knowing what else to say.

Ignoring his last comment, she said, "Okay, now you might feel a little shaky, bein' you've been drugged and been asleep for a few hours, so I'm gonna hold on to you."

"Okay." *Oh God, please let my family be all right!* he screamed inside his head.

She led him down a dark hallway to a small bathroom. He wondered how she was able to fit in the tiny room, as he was barely able to walk in and turn around. Walking down the hall, he took in his surroundings. Noticing the width of the room and hallway, he surmised that they were in a trailer. *If we're in a trailer, then we must be in a trailer park, and there must be neighbors.* He wanted to look out a window, but they had curtains on them and it was dark outside.

He asked, "Could I have some privacy, please? I need to poop."

Ruby tsked. "All right, but I'll be standing right outside this door. The bathroom spray is by the toilet. Make sure you use it, 'cause I don't want it smell like a sewer in there."

Nicky nodded. He looked around the tiny bathroom for anything that could be used as a weapon. He found nothing. She must have cleaned everything out in preparation for his arrival. There wasn't a bottle of shampoo, conditioner, soap, razors, or even a toothbrush. Nothing. The only thing available was the bathroom spray. *Maybe I can spray that in her eyes and blind her. No, she'd see it in my hand. Maybe if I stuck it in my pants and when we're by the door to the living room, I could spray her and run out the door to a neighbor. That probably won't work either. She is so large that it would be difficult to get around her, and if she tripped and fell on me, well, I'd be a goner for sure. Oh, heck. I guess my best chance for survival is to play along and wait for an opportunity to escape.*

When he finished, he flushed the toilet, sprayed, and called for Ruby.

"I'm finished."

"Okay, honey." She opened the door and stepped back so he could exit the bathroom.

"Hey, what's that on TV?" he asked as they passed the living room door.

"Oh, it's *CSI: Miami.* Do you watch that?"

"No, but my brother does. It comes on too late for me to watch it." *Okay, it must be around ten o'clock. I was out a long time!*

She nodded. "It's a good show. You want to watch it with me?"

"Could I?"

"Sure. You don't have to worry about getting up for school tomorrow, so why not?"

He smiled up at her. "Thanks, Ruby." *Of course I don't have to get up for school, 'cause it'll be Saturday. Geez, does she even know what day it is?*

"Hey, why don't I pop us some popcorn?"

"That sounds great. I'm pretty hungry."

"Of course you are. Would you like a bacon sandwich too?"

"Yes, that'd be awesome," he said with enthusiasm.

Ruby smiled. She led him to the living room and secured his hand to the arm of the couch. He looked up at her pleadingly.

"I'm sorry, but I can't risk losing you."

He nodded, wondering why she had him in the first place and what her plans were.

She went to the kitchen, and he heard her open the refrigerator door and then the microwave. He watched TV and waited for his food, all the while praying for a way out of this situation. He knew if he tried hard enough, he could escape the cuff around his wrist, but he felt in his gut that it wasn't the right time to make a break for safety. He thought it would be wise to build up her trust in him, and then, when she least expected it, he would make a run for it. He just wondered how long it would take.

In the meantime, he would treat her with respect and try not to make her angry. He had a feeling that if she were to get angry, he'd be in a world of trouble. She seemed nice enough on the outside, but there was something that wasn't quite right about her. *After all, she did kidnap me.*

Ruby glanced over her shoulder at the boy. He was sitting quietly staring at the TV, one hand in his lap, the other cuffed to the arm of the sofa. She had bought the set of handcuffs from the local pawn shop, and although they were handy, she really hated using them and was careful to not latch them so tightly that they would cut off circulation or bruise his wrist. As distasteful as it was, she couldn't risk losing him now.

CHAPTER 122

As the evening progressed and word spread around town, more and more people dropped by Christina's house bringing food and encouragement. Her friends Lisa and Donna had stayed a while, keeping a list of the folks who dropped by. She grimaced when she saw the trays, bowls, and packages of food. *Surely they must realize this is more food than we can possibly eat. Unfortunately, most of that food will end up in the garbage, unless I can give it away.* She immediately thought of the soup kitchen downtown. *I wonder if they'll take some of this off my hands.* The whole atmosphere felt like a funeral gathering. *No! I will not allow myself to think of that!*

Steven, Larry, and Ed sat in the family room with the FBI agents and Tom, one of Ed's friends, discussing how best to handle the situation. In the front room, a group sat around and prayed, and in the dining room, a group talked quietly around the dining room table. Christina just paced from one room to the next in a daze, not knowing what to do or say.

Stacey, Samara, Brad, and a few of their friends were upstairs in Brad's room, talking and praying and trying to figure out what *they* could do to get Nicky back.

The people, the whispering, and the silences all reminded Christina of David's funeral. She was trying *so* hard to not worry—to *not* think the worst—to *not* picture her baby in a casket. When those thoughts bubbled up, she would say a prayer of protection and try to think of something else.

With everyone preoccupied, she quietly ascended the stairs and went into her bedroom. She didn't bother turning on the light as she crawled in bed, turned on her side, pulled her knees up, clutched her pillow to her mouth, and screamed into it.

A few minutes later, there was a knock on her door.

"Christina?"

Steven. "Yes."

"May I come in?"

"Yes." She sat up as he opened the door.

"It's dark in here. Can I turn on the light?"

"I'd rather you didn't."

"Okay. I brought you a cup of cocoa. Can I sit by you?"

"Thanks, and yes, you may sit by me."

She scooted over on the bed, and he sat down and pulled her close. They didn't even talk. What could be said? She drank her cocoa, curled into his body, and sighed.

The next thing she knew, a pale light was filtering through the curtains. She gasped when she looked at the clock and jumped out of bed. Six o'clock.

"Oh my God!" she exclaimed as she threw open the door and ran down the stairs.

She found a bleary-eyed Steven in the kitchen.

"Christina, you're up. I was just pouring a cup of coffee to bring up to you."

"How could you let me sleep?" she snarled as she punched him in the chest.

"Ow!" he exclaimed, rubbing his chest. "You fell asleep, and I couldn't wake you up." *Maybe because I put a strong sedative in your cocoa, and if you find out, you'll probably give me a black eye.* "You were exhausted, so I let you sleep."

"Is Larry still here? How about the FBI guys?" she asked as she walked briskly to the family room. Steven followed behind, carrying their cups of coffee.

When she entered the empty family room, she turned to him.

"Where the heck are they?"

"They left around one this morning. They said they'd be back around six thirty to reinstate the surveillance equipment on the phones in case the kidnapper calls."

"Why didn't they stay the night and listen for the call?"

"Honey, they figured the guy wouldn't call after midnight, and they wanted to be alert for today, so they left to go rest." He looked at his watch. "They should be arriving any minute now."

Tears sprang to her eyes, and her knees buckled. He set the coffee cups down on an end table and went to her. Helping her to her feet, he led her to the couch. She sat and pulled her feet up under her as he put a blanket around her shoulders and handed her the coffee cup.

"Here."

She wiped her eyes and sighed. "Thanks. Sorry I hit you."

He rubbed his chest and shrugged. "It's okay." He sat silently beside her as they drank their coffee until they heard car doors slam.

Glancing at his watch, he said, "Here they are, right on time." He stood, stretched, and went to let the two FBI guys in the back door.

She and Steven watched helplessly as the agents went about their business setting up the phone-tapping devices on her house and cell phones. One man, Curtis, was large with closely cropped blonde hair. *The name doesn't fit,* she thought. *It should be Bruno or Butch or something more menacing. He makes Ed look like a midget. His arms look bigger than both my thighs together,* she thought.

The other man had a much smaller frame; he was lean and wiry with short, curly brown hair, brown eyes, and a killer smile, looking like he had just graduated from high school. His name was Mike. They both wore dark suits with white shirts and black ties and had ear mikes wrapped around their right ears. She was reminded of the men from a James Bond movie.

"I thought those guys set that equipment up last night," she said, pointing to the men and their phones and other equipment.

"Well, they did, but when nobody called by one this morning, they disconnected it. I think they're reprogramming it or something." She nodded, though she didn't fully comprehend what they were doing.

"When did everyone else leave last night?" she asked Steven as they sat in the front room watching the activity.

"Around midnight. I came down after you had fallen asleep and told everyone there was nothing else they could do. I thanked them and sent them on their way."

"Where did you sleep?"

"On the couch in the family room. Stacey brought me a pillow and blankets. She said the FBI guys gave her the creeps and was glad I was staying." He smiled. "She's a cute kid."

Christina smiled and nodded.

"Yeah. I've got awesome kids. I'm glad you stayed too. Thanks."

He nodded and gave her a crooked smile.

"Did Cindy or the other gals say if they were coming back today?"

"Well, you know Cindy—she'll be here as soon as she's up and dressed. Her boyfriend from the ATO said he'd be back later today. He had to run up to Dallas for something."

Christina nodded and sighed. "Nobody's called?"

He knew she meant the kidnapper. "Nope. Just your friends and a few concerned neighbors."

"Oh my God!" she said as she sat up and threw off the blanket.

"What?"

"I've got to call David's parents and his brother and sister. They need to know what's going on. I don't want them to hear it on the news!" Just as she said that, there was a knock at the front door. Curtis went to answer it as Mike guided her and Steven from the front room to the kitchen, explaining that they didn't know whom they could trust. She felt as if she were in some crime show melodrama—which she kinda was.

She heard Curtis say, "Mrs. Sanders doesn't have any comment at this time." He then quietly closed the front door.

She looked at Steven and rolled her eyes. "The news media have arrived."

Once they were allowed back in the living room, she asked Mike if she could call her in-laws. When he nodded his permission, she did so. Her mother- and father-in-law were grief stricken and anxious with worry. They said they would be on the next flight out of Detroit and would rent a car. Hopefully they'd be there by the evening. She tried to talk them out of it to no avail and, after asking them to call Joyce and Robert with the news, finally said thank you and good-bye.

CHAPTER 123

Nicky woke with a dry mouth and a full bladder.

"Ruby!" he called.

Nothing. No noise of any kind.

"Ruby, I need to pee!" he yelled as loud as he could. He heard a groan and a thud as heavy footsteps headed down the hall toward his room.

"Good mornin', sunshine!" she said as she rubbed her eyes and stretched. "How'd you sleep last night?"

"All right, I guess. It's hard to move with my hand cuffed to the bedpost."

"Yeah. Sorry about that."

Yeah right, he thought as he crossed his legs and groaned. "I really gotta pee."

"All right, honey, I'll get you undone in just a sec." She dug the handcuff key out of her pocket and unbound his wrist. As soon as he was free, he jumped out of the bed and ran down the hall. She lumbered after him.

Standing outside the door and listening as he relieved himself, she smiled and thought, *It would be nice to have a little boy around here. I wonder if I could just keep him. We could go to another state and he could be my son and I could be his mama.*

As the thought started taking root, the phone in the kitchen rang. She listened at the bathroom door and called out, "Nicky?"

"Yes, ma'am?"

"I need to answer the phone. You stay in there until I come get you. Okay?"

"Okay."

He heard her walk into the kitchen and started looking around the bathroom again, either for a weapon or a way of escape. He looked up and saw an air vent in the ceiling and next to it a skylight. *Kinda small, but I might fit through if I can figure out how to get up there.* He opened the shower curtain and discovered a small window close to the ceiling. He hadn't noticed it the night before, probably because there had been a towel hung over it. The towel lay in a heap in the bottom of the tub. He could see light outside the window and knew it was morning. Climbing in the tub and balancing himself on the two ledges, he stretched up to take a peek. All he could see was blue sky.

Darn it! Maybe I can sneak a peek out a different window when she's not looking. I need to know where I am if I'm gonna run away. He looked around the bathroom once again and, not finding anything different, tiptoed over to the door and put his ear against it. He could barely hear Ruby speaking, so he quietly opened the door a crack.

Hearing only her side of the conversation, he deduced that she had ticked somebody off.

He heard her say to the mysterious caller, "Yes, sir. I know, sir. Well, I just thought—I know, sir. I'm not getting paid to think, but ... yes, sir. I'll take care of it. Can't I just keep him? He's such a cute little thing, and I always wanted ... All right, I'll give him back. Do I still get the money? Okay. I'll wait for your call."

He closed the door quietly and sat on the toilet seat, waiting for his captor to return.

She's talking like I'm a puppy or something. She wants to keep me? She did say she'd give me back. That's good, right? Fear started taking root in his belly again. He said a silent prayer and took a few calming breaths. *So it sounds like she kidnapped me for money. I kinda figured that, but geez, Mom doesn't have any extra money, unless she has it hidden somewhere. I just hope this crazy lady let's me go soon. Mom's gotta be worried sick.*

Ruby replaced the receiver and stood in the kitchen for a few minutes before returning to the bathroom.

When she opened the door, she had a sad look on her face.

"Ruby, are you okay?" Nicky asked in his most concerned voice.

She tousled his hair. Sounding like a reprimanded little girl, she said, "I just got yelled at by my boss."

"I'm sorry. How come? Can I help?"

She looked at him, and tears formed in her eyes. He was such a sweet kid. She wanted to keep him for herself.

"I'll be okay. I just need time to think. Are you hungry?"

"A little bit."

"How about a bowl of Cheerios? And you can watch TV while you eat them. Cartoons should be on."

He smiled up at her. "Thanks, Ruby, that'd be great. Thank you for being so nice to me." *Don't think I wouldn't knock you upside the head if I had to,* he thought as he watched her out of the corner of his eye.

She poured his cereal, watched as he ate, and smiled when he laughed at the cartoon antics. It was odd that he hadn't asked about his mom or what she was planning to do with him. Most kids would be scared senseless, but this kid was different. He had a calmness, politeness, and maturity that almost gave her the creeps. She was grateful that he wasn't freaking out and crying or pitching a fit. She wasn't sure what she'd do if he did that. She might have had to hurt him to get him to shut up.

She thought about her next move. *Should I do as the boss man said—give the kid back and hope no one will catch me? Or should I just take the kid and run? If I run, I'll never get the $10,000, and I really want the money. I don't think I can trust the kid to* *stay with me. I think he'd run away the second I let my guard down. Plus, he's big enough that I can't disguise him, and folks would recognize him from his picture, which I'm sure would be plastered all over the TV and newspapers. I could keep him drugged and go to Mexico or Canada. No, I don't have a birth certificate for him, and the border patrols are getting a lot stricter about such things since the 9/11 thing.*

The boss man said to phone Christina and tell her I have the kid and that I'll give him back if she promises to leave Alva. That's probably the best plan, but I need to think about this some more. She massaged her temples as she watched her moneymaker eat his cereal.

CHAPTER 124

The man on the other end of the line slammed down the phone receiver.

"What the heck was that stupid woman thinking? Kidnapping the kid? That was never in the plan."

His wife walked over and put her hand on his arm. Not having a clue as to what he was referring to, she said, "Tell me what happened, dear." She had never seen him so angry before, and it frightened her. "What woman are you talking about and what kid?"

"That stupid, stupid woman decided to take things into her own hands. She thought if she kidnapped the kid and held him for ransom, she'd not only get the money from me, but money from Christina as well." He paused and took in a deep breath before continuing. "And get this—she says she'd make Christina promise to leave Alva. Doesn't she know that Christina will promise anything to get her kid back? The question is—will she make good on her promise once the kid is back safe and sound?"

His wife put one hand over her heart and the other up to her mouth.

"Oh, dear," she replied. "Some woman kidnapped one of Christina's children? Why would she do that? *Who* is this woman, and how do you know her? What is all this about? What did you tell her to do?"

He gave her a blank look and then said, "I told her to take the kid back."

"Do you think she will?"

"I don't know," he answered as he sat on the couch near his wife and put his head in his hands. "It's a good thing she doesn't know who we are, or the cops would be all over our backs. She'd squeal in an instant."

His wife felt weak in the knees and sat on a nearby chair. *What has my husband gotten himself involved in? What money is he talking about? Who was the woman on the phone?* There had been times over the past year when he had ranted about one thing or another, and she hadn't paid much attention, but now—*What is he talking about now?*

She needed to fully understand the situation before she could determine her next move. She put her hand on his arm and gently asked, "Tell me again why it's so important for Christina to leave."

He gave her an exasperated look. "Woman, I swear, we've been over this a hundred times!"

She looked at him and said quietly, "I know, dear, and I'm sorry, but I still don't understand. I've thought about it a lot, but it just doesn't make any sense to me."

She shook her head and sighed. She did remember an argument a month earlier that had ensued after seeing Christina and her children at a local restaurant. He was convinced that she had been sent by the government to spy on the people of Alva. "Why would she be spying on us?" she had asked. He didn't have a reasonable answer. She had laughed at his story and told him that was a crazy idea. She tried to explain that Christina was *not* a government spy—she was just a widowed woman with three children to raise. He had argued with her and told her that someday she would see that he was right. She had shook her head and walked away chuckling.

During his next checkup, she had mentioned this behavior to his doctor, and he had informed her that after a stroke, it wasn't unusual for a person to have a distorted view of reality.

After examining her husband, he had called her into his office and, as she sat across from him, explained the behavioral manifestations of a stroke.

"Sometimes stroke victims become depressed, paranoid, and angry, or I've even known some folks who believe they are someone else all together. It all depends on where in the brain the stroke took place and how much damage was done. Strokes don't just affect the motor skills, as so many folks believe. Sometimes it's not even evident except in mood or cognitive behavior changes. I'll write a prescription for a new medication that has proven to help stroke victims regain some of their mental and motor skills."

It was certainly true that he wasn't the same man since his stroke the previous year, and even though the medication seemed to help with some issues, it didn't help with the paranoid episodes—especially at night.

She would hear him walking around the house a couple of times during the night, checking doors and windows to make sure they were locked, even though he had done the same thing before going to bed.

She also noted that the last several times he walked out to the barn, he carried his loaded shotgun under his arm. Granted, it only had buckshot, but she was afraid that if anyone or anything spooked him, he'd shoot first and then ask questions. Buckshot could do a lot of damage and could possibly kill if it hit in the right spot from the right distance. She had considered hiding or locking up the gun and pellets but was a little afraid of how he would react. She didn't want to push him over any sanity ledge.

Shuddering, she realized this thing involving Christina was more than a passing paranoid fantasy—especially if it involved another person, money, and a kidnapped child. She wasn't sure what to do. As she chewed on a thumbnail and contemplated her options, he suddenly stood and announced that he had to go check the horses in the barn. She frowned at him. They didn't have any horses. They had had a herd of them twenty years ago but had sold them all over the years. They only had a couple of cows and about twenty chickens.

"Honey, did you forget that we don't have any horses?" she said as sweetly as she could.

He gave her a blank stare as the comment made its way through his brain. He shook his head and smiled. "Oh yeah. I meant to say that I have to go milk the cows. We do have cows, right?"

She smiled and nodded. "Yes, we do have cows, and they do need milking."

He clapped his hands together and said, "Alrighty then, that's what I'll go do."

She stood and followed him to the door and watched as he walked to the barn, shotgun under his arm. Once he had disappeared through the barn door, she turned and headed for the phone.

CHAPTER 125

Christina jumped when her cell phone rang. The hulk held up a finger for her to wait, and then, after the second ring, pointed at the phone and nodded. She picked it up and cautiously said, "Hello?"

"Hello, Christina?" They all blew out a sigh of relief when the other voice announced that it was "Mom." She had called to say they would be arriving at the Dallas airport around three in the afternoon and would be at her house around five. Christina replaced the receiver and sat down. Her hands were shaking. Steven sat with her, holding her hands in his. His phone rang. Digging it out of his pocket, he looked at the caller ID and said, "I need to take this call. I'll be right back."

He exited the room, and Christina could hear him giving medical instructions to someone on the other end. He came and sat back down.

"Sorry, one of my patients had a question about his medication."

"This is so nerve-racking," she said as she rubbed her hands together.

"I know. Can I get you anything? Have you eaten anything yet?"

She smiled and patted his hand. "No. I'm fine. My stomach is in knots, and I can't fathom eating anything right now. I just wish someone would call and let us know if Nicky's okay."

Steven nodded. He felt a buzzing in his pocket and pulled out his cell phone again.

"Sorry, I have to answer this call."

She nodded. He stood and walked into the kitchen. She tuned out the chatter in the room, closed her eyes, and focused on thoughts of Nicky. She pleaded with God to protect her baby.

Her cell phone rang again, and she jumped. They went through the same procedure, only to hear Cindy's voice on the other end of the line. Christina wished she could just tell everyone to quit calling her. *Don't people know we're waiting for the kidnapper's call, for goodness' sakes?*

CHAPTER 126

When the cartoon was over and Nicky had finished his cereal, Ruby told him he had to go back to the bedroom. He started to protest but decided he'd better be obedient. She looked like she was in a sour mood, and he didn't want to upset her any more. He had watched enough police shows to know that people could be unpredictable.

"Ruby, I was wondering if it would be okay for me to take a shower. I feel pretty sweaty and sticky, and I kinda smell."

She looked at him and cocked her head. She had never known a kid who *wanted* to take a shower. Most kids would happily avoid a bath or shower, being content to wallow in their own filth. *Is he trying to pull something over on me?* She thought of the bathroom window. She didn't think he could reach it, and even if he did, he couldn't get through it. *The skylight? The ceiling fan?* He wouldn't be able to reach those either, nor fit through those small openings. Nope, there was no way he could escape.

"Sure. You can take a shower."

"Thanks," he said as he smiled up at her. He still didn't have a definitive answer as to why she kidnapped him and what her plans were. He didn't think she would harm or kill him, but that fear was always in the back of his mind. *I wonder if I should ask what she's planning to do with me.*

Once the kid was in the shower and she heard the water running and him singing, she went to the phone. She sat for a moment, composing her thoughts. She had never talked to Christina, so she wasn't afraid that her voice would be recognized but decided it wouldn't hurt to disguise it someway, like lowering her voice to sound like a man or muffling it with a towel—or both.

She wrote down what she wanted to say and practiced it a few times before making the call.

Again, everyone jumped when the house phone rang, and the FBI men readied themselves before Christina picked up the receiver.

"Hello?"

"Is this Christina Sanders?" the voice asked.

"Yes."

"I have your son. If you want him back safe and sound, you need to promise to leave Alva and never come back and also give me $5,000."

Christina listened and watched the FBI guys. The young one motioned for her to keep the woman talking, as they were trying to do a trace.

"I want to speak to my son," she said emphatically.

"He's in the shower."

"I won't promise anything until I speak to my son."

The voice hesitated and then said, "All right, I'll go get him." The FBI men were smiling. Obviously this was an amateur and a pretty dumb one at that. He or she didn't know they were being taped and traced.

Christina waited anxiously, pacing in circles. She could hear a knocking and a woman's voice calling her son's name. After a minute or so her son's voice came on the line, and she almost dropped the phone.

"Hello? Mom?" Nicky asked warily.

"Hi, baby. Are you all right?"

"Yeah. I want to come home."

Christina's eyes welled up, and she stifled a cry.

Suddenly the voice was back on the line. "Okay, lady, you heard your kid. Do we have an agreement?"

Christina heard Nicky yelling in the background, "We're in a trailer!"

"Shut up, kid, or *I'll* shut you up!"

"Of course. Just tell me where you want me to drop the money off, and I'll be glad to do it. I just want my son back safe and sound."

The voice hesitated for a few seconds and then said, "What about the other thing?"

"What other thing?"

"The part about you leaving Alva? You have to promise to do that before I can give him back."

"Oh, yes. I'll leave. In fact, I'll start packing today."

Christina heard an audible sigh. "All right. I'll call you back and let you know where we can meet."

"Good. Thank you for letting me speak to my son."

The line went dead. She looked at the FBI men, who were smiling, nodding, and giving each other high fives.

"We got it!" announced the hulk. "This person is really stupid. I can't believe he put the phone down and went and got the kid. I've never had a ransom call that was so easy to trace."

"So where is this idiot?" Steven asked, putting his arm around Christina. Brad and Stacey walked in and started asking questions. The FBI men called for order and told everyone to sit down.

The one named Mike said, "Obviously we're dealing with an amateur who doesn't know who they're dealing with—or someone who is very clever and just pulling our chains." Christina cocked her head and looked at him. He put up his hands.

"I can tell you the call is local. We have it pinpointed within a five-mile radius.

It appears to come from an area north of town about twenty miles out, probably a secluded farmhouse or trailer. I have some men who will be checking around that area. We have a helicopter that's coming in from Dallas and should be arriving in the area within the hour. What I need y'all to do is remain calm and talk to no one about this. We don't want this person to get spooked or get wind that we're on to them. As long as we can keep it off the evening news, we should be okay."

"What about the money?" Christina asked, worry etching her face. "I don't have $5,000."

"Don't worry about that. We'll provide the money." He smiled. "I'm sure we'll be getting it back. This idiot won't get far with it. That's for sure."

"Y'all aren't planning on shooting this guy, are you?" Christina asked, fearful for her son's safety.

Mike shrugged. "Well, I hope it doesn't come to that. We wouldn't do anything unnecessary, and of course we wouldn't put your son in harm's way."

Christina sighed. "So I guess now all we can do is wait for him to call back?"

The hulk nodded. "Yep."

Christina sat on the couch with Steven and her two children, and they silently watched the phone—as if watching it would make it ring.

CHAPTER 127

After the phone call, Ruby told Nicky to go get himself dressed. He reminded her of a little wet puppy. His wet hair hung in his eyes, and he was wrapped in a big brown towel. He looked up at her with his big dark eyes, which were rimmed with tears, nodded, and slowly walked back to the bathroom to get his clothes.

The kid had handled himself pretty well. Yeah, he'd yelled out, which had caught her by surprise, and cried a bit, but he didn't get hysterical. Now, if she were in his situation, she would have gotten hysterical. Maybe it was because she was a girl and girls tended to be more dramatic. At least that was what everyone said. She shrugged.

She had to pick a place where she could see Christina's car to be sure she hadn't been followed, get the money, leave the kid, and make a clean getaway. She figured that by now Christina had called Dr. Dawson and probably the sheriff. If she waited much longer, they'd probably call in other law enforcement agencies. She had watched enough TV shows to know it took at least twenty-four hours before the FBI would get involved.

Unfortunately for her, she had no idea whom she was dealing with on the other end of the phone line.

Ruby wished the boss man would call so she could tell him what had transpired between her and Christina. He would be pleased to know that Christina had agreed to leave Alva. Then he could give her the $10,000, and she could leave the dingy little trailer and the dull little town and start a new life as a rich woman—$15,000 rich. She smiled and imagined herself in a nice, big house on a beach in Mexico.

She was brought back to the present by a tug on her shirt. She looked down to see Nicky, dried off and dressed.

"Ruby? Are you gonna take me to my mom?"

She nodded. "Yeah. Pretty soon. I have to figure out where we can meet." She looked at him and frowned. "I sure wish I could keep you. I always wanted kids, but no one would want to marry a big slob like myself." She shrugged. Nicky wrapped his arms around her ample middle.

"I think you're a nice person, Ruby. You have a great smile and a nice personality."

She patted him on the head and felt tears well up in her eyes. "Thank you. That's the nicest thing anyone has ever said to me." She walked over, sat on the couch, and patted the cushion next to her. Nicky sat beside her, and she put an arm around him. They sat that way for a few minutes, and then Nicky asked, "Ruby, what was your family like?"

As soon as he asked, he regretted it. She tensed up and pushed him away.

"Now why did you have to go and ask something like that?"

"I … I … I …" he stuttered.

"You don't need to know about my family. Just because I didn't grow up in a nice, well-to-do family like you doesn't mean I'm a bad person."

"I never said you were bad," he answered defensively.

"I guess you think you're better than me, huh?"

Nicky shook his head and felt tears sting his eyes. She was scaring him.

She saw the tears and the fear in his eyes and let out a sigh.

"I'm sorry, honey. I didn't mean to scare you." She put an arm around him and drew him close. He tensed at her touch but decided he'd better relax or she might get angry again. He nestled into her side and silently prayed, *Dad, if you have any power at all, will you please send someone to rescue me?*

"You see, it's like this. My parents weren't nice people. My dad and mom both drank a lot of beer and would hit each other and me and my brothers whenever they got mad. My four brothers were mean too. I was the youngest and only girl, and they would have contests to see which one could frighten me the most or make me cry the hardest. The older I got, the easier it was to avoid them or pretend that what they did or said didn't hurt. But it did." She looked at Nicky, sadness filling her face.

"I ran away when I was fourteen and hitched a ride with some old trucker guy. I stayed with him a couple of months and then hitched rides with other guys. I lost track of how many men I was with and how many places I lived in. Finally, a few years ago, I decided that I'd had enough of use and abuse and settled down here."

"Did you ever go back home?"

"Nope," she said as she shook her head.

"Don't you miss your family?"

She chuckled. "You're kidding, right?" Nicky shook his head solemnly, thinking, *I sure miss mine.*

"When I left home, I swore I'd never look back, and I haven't. I couldn't even tell you where my family is—and to be honest, I don't care."

Nicky shook his head. "That's the saddest story I've ever heard." He reached over and patted her hand.

She nodded in agreement. "Yeah." She sighed and looked at her hands. Shifting her large bulk, she looked at the child.

"So Nicky, tell me how you and your family ended up here in Alva. Why did you leave Michigan?"

Ruby sat quietly and listened as Nicky told his own sad tale of how he had lost his dad and why his family had ended up in Alva. She was surprised to feel tears stream down her cheeks.

"Seems like you've got a sad story yourself."

He nodded and said, "Yeah, but not as sad as yours."

They sat a few minutes in silence, each wondering what was going to happen next. The phone rang, breaking the silence.

Ruby pushed herself out of the couch that had seemed to partially swallow her and managed to answer the phone on the fourth ring.

"Hello?"

The mechanical voice asked, "Did you do what I told you to?"

"Yeah. I called and told her I'd give her the kid if she'd agree to leave Alva."

"Did she agree?"

"Yeah."

"When are you going to give the kid back?"

"I haven't decided that yet. I have to figure out a good place to meet so I won't get caught."

"Hmm. Well, you'd better decide soon, or it will be too late. She'll get law enforcement involved."

"I know. Are you still gonna pay me?"

"What for?"

"Well, I got her to agree to leave."

"Yeah, but she hasn't left, now, has she?"

"No, but she said she will."

"Our agreement was that when she left, you'd get the money."

"So if she does leave, you'll pay me then?"

There was silence on the other end for a moment. "I don't think that will be possible."

"Why not?" she whined.

"Because when you give the kid back, you'll have to disappear, or you'll go to jail."

She stood silent for a moment as the reality of what he said sunk into her brain.

"If you'd just stuck to the plan and not gone out on your own and done this kidnapping, we might have been able to work out this deal, but you blew it."

She sighed audibly. "Yeah, all right. Well, at least I'll have the ransom money."

The voice on the other end chuckled. "Sure." The line went dead.

"Who was that?" Nicky asked, sitting straight up on the couch.

"It was the boss man." Her shoulders drooped and she made a pouting face.

"What did he say?"

"He said he won't pay me the money he promised."

"Money? What money?"

"The $10,000 he was gonna give me if your family left Alva."

Nicky raised his eyebrows. "You were gonna get paid if you made us leave?"

She nodded.

"How were you gonna pull that off? Did you do anything else besides kidnap me?"

She sat next to him and smiled sardonically. "I already did some stuff, but it didn't work."

Nicky looked surprised. "You did? What stuff?" he asked, though he had a pretty good idea of what he was about to hear.

CHAPTER 128

The Sanders house was becoming quite congested with people once again as Cindy, Samara, Ed, and Tom arrived. Introductions were made, and everyone was busy with some sort of task. Stacey, Samara, Linda, and Brad had left to go hang up pictures of Nicky and ask friends and neighbors if they had seen the boy. The FBI guys filled Ed and his team in on the information they had received. Christina and Cindy just sat and watched everyone else. Christina couldn't think or function, and Cindy was beside herself with worry as well. Steven had to leave and take care of a hospital emergency, and the sheriff was called out on a domestic dispute. The most difficult part of the whole situation was the waiting. They had to wait for the next phone call before they were able to move forward. In the meantime, the agents were busy checking phone records, car makes and models, possible suspects, and hospital personnel files and monitoring the helicopter's whereabouts. The FBI men assured Christina that Nicky would be returned to her before the day was over. She hoped and prayed they were right.

After confessing to Nicky about the devilish deeds she had instigated against his family—the snake, the rat, the flat tires, and the heparin—she told him to go back in the bedroom, and she re-bound him. He was in such shock and dismay that he quietly complied. She then left to drive around the area and find a suitable exchange site, returning about an hour later to find a sleeping boy. She sat on the couch and chewed on her thumbnail, thinking about all that had transpired and all that would transpire in the next twenty-four hours. If all went according to her plans, she would be sitting in a hotel by a beach somewhere in Mexico. If not—well, she didn't want to think about that.

Ruby looked at the clock. Almost noon. She had to decide what to do. She picked up the phone and dialed Christina's number.

"Hello?"

"Mrs. Sanders?"

"Yes."

"Do you have the money?"

Christina looked over at the FBI guys, who gave her a thumbs-up.

"Yes."

"Good. I want you to bring it to the old torn-down granary out on Palmer Road. Do you know where that is?'

"Yes. When?"

"How about in an hour. That should give us time to get there."

"Okay. I'll see you in an hour."

"Have you started packing?"

"Packing? The money bag?"

"No. Your stuff. Have you started packing your stuff so you can leave Alva?"

"Oh, yes. Sorry. Been packing all morning." She hoped she sounded convincing.

"Good. Well, I'll see you in an hour."

The line went dead. "Did you get another trace?" she asked anxiously.

"Yep. Same area." The phone rang again, and Christina answered it. It was the local operator. She handed the phone to the hulk. All she heard was "Good. Thanks."

She watched anxiously as he smiled and nodded. "The operator traced the call to a number belonging to a lady by the name of Lula Mae Halsey. And get this: her address is out on Palmer Road."

"Lula Halsey? That name rings a bell," Christina said, chewing on her bottom lip as she tried to recall where she had heard the name.

"Cindy, call Larry and see if he has any information on her name. I know that name from somewhere—maybe the hospital."

———

Ruby replaced the phone and sat back down on the couch.

From the bedroom, Nicky called, "Ruby?"

"Yeah?"

"I need to go pee."

She smiled. "All right, I'll be there in a sec."

After he did his business, they sat on the couch together, shared a bag of Fritos, and drank Dr Peppers from ice-cold bottles.

She sighed. "Well, I did it."

"Did what?"

"I called and set up a meeting place with your mom. She agreed to give me the money and then leave Alva." She pulled him close and twisted a ringlet of his hair around her finger.

"I'm gonna miss you," she finally said.

"Yeah, me too." *Not! I wanna go home and get away from you as fast as I can, you crazy lady!* he thought as he munched on his Fritos.

"Guess I'd better go grab a few things and pack up my car." She looked around the room. "I sure as heck won't be coming back here."

Nicky nodded again.

"Can I help?" Looking around the room, he thought, *I wouldn't want to come back to this nasty place either!*

She looked at him and shook her head.

"Man, you're something else, kid. I kidnap you and ask for a ransom, and you ask if you can help me pack. I don't get it."

"My mom and dad always told me to be nice to people—even those who hurt me or say bad things about me."

"Huh? You don't say? Where did they get ideas like that? My folks just taught us to do whatever we had to do to survive, whether it was nice or not."

"The Bible."

"What?"

"The Bible. That's where my folks got the idea. There's a verse in there that says, 'Treat others as you would like to be treated.'"

"Really? Huh. Well, I guess that would make sense. If you treat people nice, then they'll treat you nice? Sounds good, but I've found that the opposite is true most of the time. Seems like the nicer I was to people, the more they hurt me, so I quit trying to be nice and did what I *had* to do to survive: steal, cheat, lie."

Nicky shook his head. "We're not supposed to treat people nice so we can get niceness in return; we're supposed to do it because it's the right thing to do. Doesn't matter what other people do. We're not responsible for other people's actions and reactions—only our own."

"To be such a little kid, you sure got a lot of smarts in that brain of yours," she said as she tousled his hair and stood.

"Come on, you can help me pack."

CHAPTER 129

The elderly lady sat at the dining room table with her daughter and told her of her husband's involvement in something she knew was completely insane and illegal. The daughter listened in shocked silence and then said, "Mom, we've got to call the police. If dad is involved in any way with a kidnapping, we have to let the authorities know."

"Do we have to? He didn't sound like he was directly involved. Maybe it will all just pass, and we won't have to do anything." Her daughter reached over and took her mother's hands in hers. They were so tiny and shriveled. *When did you get so old, Mom?*

"Mom, I …" Just then, the back door swung open, and her father walked in, looking surprised to see his eldest daughter there.

"Why, Eleanor. What a surprise seeing you here. Is Tommy with you?"

Eleanor stood and hugged her dad. "He's in the family room, Dad." As soon as she had said the words, she heard a squeal and the pounding of little feet running into the kitchen.

"Grandpa!" shouted the excited little boy as he ran into his grandpa's arms. "Come look what I built with the Legos."

The old man reached down and picked up his grandson, and they walked into the family room.

"Excuse us, ladies, we have some building to do."

Eleanor took the teacups from the table and asked her mother to join her for a walk around the garden.

Almost in a whisper so her father wouldn't hear if he decided to come outside, she said, "Mom, I know you're worried about Dad. So am I. You're right that he hasn't been the same since his stroke."

"Well, Eleanor, I just don't want to see him arrested or taken to jail. It would just kill him." Eleanor stopped and picked a small red tomato and popped it in her mouth.

"I'm surprised these plants are still producing," she said as she chewed and swallowed the delicious morsel.

Popping a tomato in her mouth, her mother answered, "It's been a mild fall so far. We haven't had a hard frost yet."

Eleanor nodded. She had never been interested in gardening. She left that chore to her mom and younger sister. They did the gardening and canning, and she and

Tommy reaped the benefits of their hard labor. Her mom and sis were always bringing her bags of fresh fruits and vegetables and jars of jams and sauces, her favorite being her mother's tomato sauce. She had tried on numerous occasions to duplicate the recipe, but it never tasted as good as her mom's, so she quit wasting her time and money.

"Mom, Tom called and said he was here in Alva and wanted to drop by and see y'all. Is it okay if he does? I promise I won't say anything about Dad. Or then again, maybe I could tell him and get his advice on what to do."

Her mother nodded. "It'll be nice to see Tom. It's been quite awhile since we've seen him. I'm sure Tommy will be happy to see his dad." She paused and looked at her daughter pleadingly. "I don't think it's a good idea to tell Tom about this. No use getting him involved." She batted her eyes to help dry up the tears that were forming.

Eleanor smiled, nodded, and drew her mother into a hug. The two women silently continued their walk while the big and little man constructed a Lego city.

"What's Tom doing in Alva, honey?" her mom asked as they sat on the porch swing.

Eleanor was reluctant to tell her mother the real reason—he was there helping with the kidnap investigation—so she just said, "He's helping a friend do some work around here."

The elder lady nodded. "That's nice. He's always helping someone. Such a nice man. I don't know why you two divorced."

"Mom, we're not gonna go there. Remember? We agreed *not* to talk about our divorce."

Her mother shook her head and waved a hand. "Sorry. I know it's a touchy subject with you."

Eleanor sighed. "Mom, it's getting chilly. Why don't we go back in and start fixin' dinner?" They walked into the house, arm in arm.

Hearing them come in, Tommy ran in, shouting, "Mom, Grandma, come see what Grandpa and I built!" He grabbed their hands and pulled them into the family room. Eleanor smiled as she saw her dad sitting cross-legged on the floor surrounded by a Lego city. He looked up at them and smiled.

There's no way he's going to jail, she thought. *It would devastate Tommy, and it would kill him and Mom. God, I hope all this just plays out and no one will know my dad is involved.* She decided right then and there she wouldn't tell anyone, not even Tom, about the kidnapping incident. She knew her mom wouldn't either. In fact, she'd probably carry that secret to the grave. It would be their little family secret. After all, didn't every family have a secret?

CHAPTER 130

As the designated hour approached, Christina felt herself becoming more and more anxious. Tom handed her a black duffel bag that contained the $5,000. She looked at him, surprised that the money had been acquired so quickly.

"Where did this come from?" she asked.

Smiling, he said, "Oh the agency always keeps a little cash on hand for cases like this." She gave him a perplexed look.

He said, "Don't worry about it. I have a feeling we'll get it all back."

She nodded. "I hope you're right."

Ed walked over and put a hand on her shoulder. "Christina, our guys would like to put a wire on you."

"Why? Aren't y'all going to be close by?"

"Yes, we'll be close, but not in listening range. We want to make sure we're dealing with the right person. Plus we want everything documented." He sighed. "Hopefully we'll catch this guy and anyone else that may be involved." She nodded in understanding.

He pointed to a female agent whom Christina hadn't been aware of and said, "Agent Holmes will attach it, if you don't mind."

Christina nodded and asked, "When did you come in?"

"I got here a few minutes ago with the equipment. You were on the phone with your mother-in-law."

"Oh," Christina said. "So many people coming and going, I didn't see you. Sorry."

Smiling and gathering the equipment from her bag, she said, "That's okay."

She has a nice smile, thought Christina.

"Shall we go in the bathroom, and I'll attach the equipment under your shirt?"

"Sure," agreed Christina as she led the way to the bathroom.

When Steven arrived, he was informed of Christina's whereabouts and waited patiently outside the bathroom door, smiling when she walked out and into his arms.

"How ya doin'?" he asked, resting his chin on her head.

"I'm okay. Nervous as heck, though. My hands won't quit shaking."

He smiled. "Yeah, I bet. Where are the kids?"

"Upstairs. They just got back from canvassing the neighborhood. They're up in Stacey's room."

He nodded. "Is it okay if I go up and see them?"

She smiled. "Sure. They'd like that."

He hugged her again and left.

Ed walked over and asked her to join him and his team.

"We've got some last-minute instructions before you go."

CHAPTER 131

Ruby and Nicky loaded several boxes and bags of clothes and knickknacks that Nicky knew his mom would never have into the backseat and trunk of Ruby's little white Chevette and then went inside, sat on the couch, and drank lemonade.

"Aren't you gonna take your furniture and other stuff?" Nicky asked, looking around the still furnished trailer and remembering all the things they had packed when they moved from Michigan.

"Nah. I don't need this junk. When your mom gives me the money I asked for, I plan to go to Mexico and buy me all sorts of new things." She sipped her lemonade and said dreamily, "I've never had new furniture, so I plan to buy a new black leather couch and recliner and one of those fancy thin TVs that hang on the wall—and maybe a big brass bed." She closed her eyes and sighed, lost in her fantasy.

Nicky looked at her and shook his head, thinking, *You'll never get away with this, Ruby. You'll probably go to jail.* To her, he said, "That sounds nice, Ruby." They sat silently for a few minutes, and then she suddenly popped her eyes open and jerked up, looking at her watch.

Pulling herself free of the couch, she said, "Well, it's showtime, buddy."

Nicky furrowed his brow and looked up at her. "Ruby, I'm scared."

"What?" she said, looking at him with concern. "Scared? What for?"

"I'm afraid that you'll be hurt or caught and sent to jail."

"Oh, honey, I won't be caught or sent to jail, but it's sweet of you to be concerned."

He shook his head. "I don't know. All the cop shows I've watched show the kidnapper being caught or killed. I don't want you to be caught or killed." *I don't want to get caught in the middle either.* He encircled her waist with his arms and held his breath to keep from crying, all his emotions finally coming to a head. He had held everything in so tightly the past twenty-four hours or so to keep from panicking, and like a pressure cooker, his emotions threatened to explode out of him.

She patted his back and hugged him close.

"Well, I don't want that either." She was touched that he would be concerned for her well-being. No one had ever shown concern about what might happen to her. "I've thought about it a lot, and it should go pretty smoothly. We meet your mom; she gives me the money; I leave."

"But Ruby, what about the police? Don't you think my mom would have called them?"

"Yeah, but there's only a couple of cops in Alva, and I told your mom that if I saw any cops, I wouldn't make the exchange." She smiled and looked at him with a gleam in her eyes. "I disguised my voice, so she thinks I'm a man."

Nicky shook his head, still worried. *You poor, crazy woman!* he thought as she tousled his hair and lifted his chin so he was looking into her eyes.

"It'll be okay. You'll see."

All he could do was nod his head. He knew in his heart that it wouldn't be okay.

David and Jarrod went back and forth between Christina's and Ruby's houses, keeping an eye on the situation that was being played out. David watched as angels and demons gathered to battle for the very lives and souls of his family. He had been able to speak to Nicky while he slept and reassure him that everything would work out and he would be fine. He tried to speak to Christina, but there were demons blocking his access to her. Jarrod said sometimes God doesn't allow angels or loved ones access to the humans, because the humans have to choose which path to take without heavenly interference. During that time, all they could do was stand by and watch and pray that the humans would make the right choice and call out for heavenly help; only then could they intervene. David gave him a perplexed look. Jarrod shrugged and said, "That's what free will is all about."

CHAPTER 132

Janet dressed and drove over to Christina's house and was surprised to see cars and vans parked in her driveway, on her yard, and along the street. There were a great number of people milling about Christina's yard and standing in nearby neighbors' yards as well. She had to park about a block away and walk to the house, where a woman in a black pantsuit and a microphone in her hand—followed closely by a cameraman—intercepted her.

"Excuse me, ma'am."

"Yes?" Janet answered as a microphone was shoved in front of her face.

"Do you know the Sanders family?"

"I know Christina. We work together at the hospital."

"What is your name, ma'am?"

"I'd rather not say."

"Do you know anything about the kidnapping?"

"No."

"Why are you here, ma'am?"

"I'm here to pick up my daughter."

"Your daughter?"

"She's best friends with Christina's daughter. Now, if you'll excuse me."

"Do you have any comments about this situation?'

"No."

"Do you know the little boy?"

"No. I've never met him."

"Do you know of anyone who would kidnap the child?"

"If I knew something like that, don't you think I would have called the police? Now, if you'll excuse me, I need to get my daughter."

"Well, thank you," said the lady with the microphone as Janet reached out and pushed her aside.

As she walked toward the front door, she heard the woman in black say, "Delete that, Jim. That was worthless."

Janet smiled and shook her head as she knocked on the door. A hulk of a man who introduced himself as Curtis greeted her and allowed her to enter once she stated her business.

Christina walked in the front room and was surprised to see Janet standing there.

"Hi, Christina, I'm here to pick up Linda."

"Hey, Janet. You want to stay awhile? Have a cup of coffee or something?"

Janet smiled warily. "No, thanks, I'll just get Linda and go."

Christina nodded and walked to the bottom of the stairs and called up for Stacey and Linda. She heard Stacey call down, "In a minute, Mom."

She walked back in the living room, where Janet stood looking around uncomfortably.

"So what's happening so far? Linda told me a little this morning when I called her, but she didn't know much."

"I'm meeting the kidnapper around one. Hopefully we'll get Nicky back safe and sound."

"One o'clock?" Janet looked at her watch. "That's just a half hour from now. You must be scared out of your wits."

Christina nodded and made a face. "Yeah, but I have a lot of backup, so I'm sure it'll be fine."

Linda walked in with Stacey. "Mrs. Sanders, thank you for letting me spend the night."

"You're welcome, Linda. I hope we see more of you." She was surprised and pleased when Linda walked over, gave her a hug, and whispered in her ear, "I know everything will be all right. Stacey and I prayed all morning."

"Thank you, honey," replied Christina as she wiped a tear from her eye.

Janet walked over, and the two women awkwardly hugged.

"Let us know what happens," Janet said as she put her arm around her daughter, and they left the Sanders residence.

Ed pointed to his watch and said, "Christina, it's time."

She nodded, walked over to Steven's waiting arms, and held on to him as he said a prayer of protection for her and Nicky. She felt her heart swell and emotions bubble up. This was the first time she had heard him pray, and it gave her great comfort.

Christina gave her children, Cindy, and Samara hugs before walking out the door with Ed.

As they walked to the car, Ed reviewed the last-minute instructions.

"Okay, Christina, this is how it's going to work. You'll drive out to the mill by yourself, but be assured that our guys will be close by and out of sight. We've already deployed several agents who'll be ready to intervene if necessary." She nodded her head, took a deep breath to calm her nerves, and let it out slowly.

"Once you get Nicky and you're both out of harm's way, our guys will close in. It'll happen so fast the guy or gal won't even know what hit him."

She nodded. "All right. Let's go get my son."

CHAPTER 133

Ruby and Nicky sat in silence as she drove the five miles to the old abandoned cotton mill and grain elevator. Nicky thought it looked pretty creepy with its rusting metal walls, missing and broken window panes, and caved-in roofs—a great place to film a scary movie. He shuddered. Ruby looked at him and smiled.

"Are you cold, honey?"

He shook his head.

"Scared?"

He looked at her, and tears formed in his eyes.

"Ruby, you don't have to do this. You could just leave me here and drive away."

She looked surprised. "Now why would I do that?"

"I don't want you to be caught and have to go to jail," he pleaded.

She shook her head and patted his. "Now, we talked about this already. I'm not gonna get caught."

"But—"

"No buts about it. I'm gonna give you back to your mamma, get my money, and that'll be the end of it."

He sighed heavily. In his gut, he knew this wouldn't end well. He looked out the window and, as the tears fell, said a prayer for this poor, lost soul with grandiose ideas.

Ruby parked the car under a shade tree near the abandoned building, facing the direction she had just come from. She would be ready to take off as soon as she had the money in hand. She and Nicky rolled down their windows and settled in for the wait, thankful for the nice, cool breeze that wafted through.

As Nicky watched for his mother's arrival, he saw a movement in the distance—a flash of light reflecting off glass or metal and a dog or something moving through the tall grass. He sat up and squinted as he watched a man dressed in camouflage move from behind a rock to a pile of brush closer in. He looked over at Ruby, who had laid her head back on the headrest and had her eyes closed. He looked out the other windows and saw more movement in the distance. It was almost imperceptible because of the camouflage, but if he stared in one particular spot, he could see a slight shift as a body changed position.

Should I tell Ruby? He decided against saying anything for fear of making her panic and maybe doing something really stupid—like trying to run and getting them both killed. He looked at his watch. Five more minutes and hopefully this would all be over. He saw a cloud of dust before he saw his mom's van.

He reached over and shook Ruby's arm.

"Ruby, she's here."

Ruby sat up and rubbed her eyes. She opened the car door, stood beside it, stretched, and put her hand up to shield her eyes from the sun's glare.

"You stay in the car until after I get the money. I'll tell you when you can come out. Okay?"

Nicky nodded.

Christina pulled her van around the little white car and turned it to face back toward the road. She was surprised when she passed by the heavyset woman. *A woman? I could have sworn I'd be meeting a man.* She turned the engine off, pocketed the keys, grabbed the duffel bag, and stepped out of the vehicle.

"Mrs. Sanders?" the woman asked as she continued to shield her eyes from the bright sun.

"Yes. Where's my son?"

Ruby laughed. "He's waiting in the car, but we have some business to take care of before he's allowed to go."

Christina dropped the duffel bag. "Here's your money. Now let me have my son." She tried to sound authoritative but knew her voice betrayed her nervousness.

Ruby cocked her head and smiled. "My, aren't you the bossy one?"

Christina closed her eyes for a second and regained her composure.

"I'm sorry if I sound rude, but I just want to get my son and go home."

Ruby looked over her shoulder at Nicky, who had leaned forward in his seat, listening and watching the interchange.

"You know, Mrs. Sanders, you've got a great kid there. If I could have, I would have just kept him for my own, but ..." She didn't finish the sentence. She stood silent for a few minutes, remembering how nice Nicky had been to her and wishing with all her heart that someday she could have a boy like him to go along with the little girl she hoped to have. *Ruby and Nicky. Those are two great names I want to use for my kids.*

Christina stood silently, watching this strange woman. *I wonder where her mind is right now.* After a moment, she cleared her throat and said, "Excuse me. Can I have my son now?'

Ruby shook her head, returning to the present, and gave Christina a confused look.

"Oh yeah." She walked over, groaned as she picked up the duffel bag, and set it on the car trunk. Unzipping it, she looked in at the neatly stacked bills.

"Wow! I've never seen so much money before!" She took out a stack and flipped through it. Smiling, she said, "I have great plans for you!" She kissed the stack of bills and returned it to the bag.

Looking in the car at Nicky, she nodded her head. Christina squatted, and he immediately opened the door and ran into his mother's waiting arms. She smothered his face and neck with kisses.

He whispered in her ear, "Mom, are there cops out there?"

Christina nodded slightly.

"Please don't let them hurt Ruby," he pleaded as he turned to see her throwing the duffel bag in the passenger seat.

Ruby? I thought her name was Lula, Christina thought as Nicky pulled free from her arms.

"Ruby!" he called out as she opened the driver side door. He ran to her and put his arms around her waist. She returned the hug and patted his head.

"There, there, little man. You go with your mama. Ol' Ruby will be just fine." She gently pushed him away and entered her car.

Christina walked over and put her arm around Nicky, both silently watching as Ruby drove the little white car down the dirt road to what she thought was long-deserved freedom. Smiling, she turned on the radio and sang along with the Beach Boys about a little old lady from Pasadena.

Once the car was down the road, men in camouflage surrounded Nicky and Christina and insisted they ride with them in their vehicle to the hospital, where Nicky would be checked over. Nicky was surprised and overjoyed to ride in the Hummer. As they rode, he asked his mom what was going to happen to Ruby.

"I'm not sure, but I imagine she'll be arrested for kidnapping."

Looking up at his mom, he said, "I hope they don't hurt her. She really was a nice lady, even though she kidnapped me. She just wanted money so she could get away from here and start a new life." He paused and made a sad face. "Is that so bad, really?"

Christina hugged him close, resting her chin on his head. *Yeah, it is, son,* she thought, knowing that anything she said at this point would be useless.

CHAPTER 135

Three hours later, after Nicky received a clean bill of health from Dr. Carmichael, Christina and Nicky were sitting in the living room on a couch surrounded by family, friends, and government agents. Everyone was taking turns asking him questions.

"Who was the lady who kidnapped you?" Grandpa Sanders asked.

Nicky shrugged. "Just some poor, sad lady who needed money."

"How did she get you in her car without anyone seeing?" Cindy wanted to know.

"She put a rag with some sweet-smelling stuff on it over my mouth and nose. It made me feel all tingly and gooey."

"Did she hurt you?" Grandma asked quietly as she held his hand.

He shook his head. "Actually, she was pretty nice. She kept saying she wanted to keep me, like I was some kind of puppy."

"How are you feeling?" Christina asked, putting her arm around his shoulder.

He made a face. "I guess I'm okay. Just tired."

The questioning went on for another hour or so. Nicky answered them all as well as he could, but the stress of the day and the restless sleep he had had the previous night were starting to take a toll on him. He yawned several times and then told his mother that he was just too tired to answer any more questions. Everyone in the immediate area heard him and agreed that he should go take a nap. They would continue talking to him after he had rested.

When Christina came back downstairs after tucking Nicky into bed, Ed approached her and asked if they could talk somewhere privately. She looked around and, seeing that all the rooms were occupied, suggested they go up to her bedroom. He had expected to see the clutter of boxes and clothes that had been there on his first visit but was surprised to enter a very neatly organized, clutter-free bedroom—well, except for the box in the corner that had the *x* in the corner or it. *David's box*. He wondered when she had finally gotten around to cleaning and organizing it. He didn't know that a couple of nights ago, when she couldn't sleep, she had stayed up well past midnight de-cluttering her room.

When they entered, Christina shut the door and sat on the bed. He pulled out a chair from under her desk, turned it around, and sat straddling it, resting his arms over the back.

She raised her eyebrows and asked, "So what's up?"

Ed cleared his throat. "Well, I just got a call from your sheriff, and they have the lady down at the jail. They're in the process of booking her right now."

Christina nodded.

"Seems her name isn't Ruby. It's Lula Mae Halsey. Does that name ring a bell?"

Christina frowned and said, "Seems I've heard that name before, but I couldn't tell you when or where. Maybe at the hospital?"

"She did work at the hospital, in the housekeeping department. Did she look at all familiar to you?"

Christina's eyes widened. "When I approached her to give her the money, I knew I had seen her somewhere, but I couldn't place her face. Now that you tell me she was a hospital employee, I do remember seeing her there."

"Do you know if you and she have had any contact other than at the hospital?"

Christina frowned as she thought and then shook her head. "I can't think of any other time I've seen her. Oh, wait. A couple of weeks ago, she was sitting across from us at a restaurant. Nicky mentioned that she was staring at us."

He nodded and then asked, "Do you remember exactly when or where you saw her at the hospital?"

Christina bit her lip and frowned, trying to remember. After a few seconds she shook her head. "No, sorry."

"That's okay. If you do remember, let Larry or me know."

She nodded. "Did Larry or any of the other guys discover why she kidnapped Nicky?"

"Not yet, but I'm sure she'll tell us all we need to know. She doesn't seem to be the brightest bulb in the carton, if you know what I mean."

Christina half smiled and nodded. "When you find out anything else, will you please let me know? I'd love to get this all cleared up."

Standing and replacing the chair in its rightful place, he walked over and opened the door. "Are you coming down?"

She sighed and nodded. "In a few minutes. I need to take a few minutes to regroup my thoughts and emotions. This has been quite a traumatic two days."

He nodded and smiled. "You take all the time you need. I'm sure everyone will keep themselves occupied."

"Thanks."

Christina lay down and pulled the downy-soft comforter up around her tired, achy body. She lay thinking about the day's events and how it could have turned out so differently. She said a silent prayer of thanksgiving. Before she knew it, she had drifted off to sleep and was surprised when she was awakened by a knock on her door.

"Mom?"

Christina sat up and rubbed her eyes and glanced at the clock. *Good grief, I've been out for two hours!*

The person at the door knocked again, calling for her. "Mom?"

She got up and opened the door and was pleased to see Nicky standing there in his pajamas. He rushed into her, wrapping his arms around her waist. She hugged him back, holding him tightly, and kissed the top of his head.

"Did you have a good nap?" she asked as they stood in her doorway hugging. She felt his head bob up and down.

"Good. Me too. Are you hungry?" Again she felt his head nod.

"Alrighty then, let's go downstairs and see what we can rustle up." He disengaged himself and walked beside her down the stairs.

She was surprised to see Ed, Tom, Cindy, Larry, and Steven sitting around the dining room table. They looked up from their intense conversation and greeted her when she walked in. Steven stood and walked over to embrace her.

"Hi, guys. Where's everyone else?" she asked as she looked around the empty living room.

Cindy stood and walked over to embrace Christina. She said, "Your in-laws took the kids out for pizza. They should be back pretty soon."

"They went for pizza without me?" Nicky whined.

"They didn't know when you'd be getting up, so they decided to go on. They'll bring you some pizza back."

He sighed and nodded. "Okay."

"What about all the other guys?"

Ed smiled. "They're gone. They went down to the police station, and then they'll probably head back to Dallas. They said to tell you thanks and good-bye."

Christina nodded. "So, is there anything to eat around here?" she asked, smiling, knowing full well her counters and fridge were full of consumables.

Cindy said, "There's sandwiches and salad in the kitchen. Here, I'll go help you get it."

Ed started to speak, but Christina raised her hand.

"Wait a minute. Let me get something to eat, and then you can tell me what's going on."

Cindy went into the kitchen with Christina and Nicky and helped prepare bologna sandwiches for them. She then poured iced tea for them both and apple juice for Nicky.

"Christina, did you have a good nap?" Cindy asked as she opened a bag of Fritos and put a handful on Nicky's plate. "You can snack on those until your pizza arrives."

"Thanks," he whispered.

"Yeah, I was surprised to wake up and find that I had slept for two hours, though." Cindy smiled. "If Nicky hadn't knocked on my door, I might still be asleep." She took a bite of her bologna sandwich. "Mmm, this is good. I can't remember the last time I had a bologna sandwich. My mom used to fix these for my lunches all the time when I was a little girl."

Nicky took his plate and drink, headed for the family room, and turned on the TV.

"Who brought the sandwich stuff?" Christina asked as she devoured hers.

"Actually, I'm not sure. I lost track of who brought what," Cindy replied, sipping her tea.

"Well, I'd like to send everyone thank-you notes if I can. Maybe you can help me make a list of all the folks who dropped by and brought stuff."

Cindy made a face and nodded slightly. "Okay. But I don't think that's necessary. Folks around here are just happy to help out when they can."

Munching on her corn chips, Christina asked, "Well, maybe I could just write a general thank-you and put it in the newspaper? Do you think that would be all right?"

Nodding, Cindy said, "That's a good idea. It'll save you a lot of time, energy, and stamps." When Christina had finished the second half of her sandwich and refilled her tea glass, she and Cindy returned to the dining room, carrying a tray of the remaining sandwiches, a pitcher of sweet tea, and bags of potato and corn chips.

Steven brought her a chair, and she sat next to him in her new circle of friends. She looked at each one and smiled.

"Thanks for being here. You'll never know how much it means to me and the kids to have such good friends as yourselves." They all smiled and nodded at her, reaching for the sandwiches and chips.

"So fill me in on what's happened in the past couple of hours."

Larry cleared his throat and started speaking. "Well, we have formally booked Lula for abduction and endangerment of a minor. Right now we have a psychologist talking with her. Seems she has the emotional and mental development of a twelve-year-old."

He shook his head and looked at Christina. "She admitted to putting the heparin in your coffee and the dead snake in your car and something about a flat tire. She says she didn't mean to hurt you; she just wanted you to leave Alva and go back to Michigan. She figured if you got scared enough, you would."

Christina listened intently and nodded. "I see. Did she say where and how she got the heparin?"

"She says she got the idea from some TV show—ER, I think. Anyway, she knew heparin was a blood thinner, and one day when she was cleaning one of the medication rooms, the door to the medicine cabinet was left open while the nurse went to answer the phone. Lula saw the bottle of heparin and stole it. She was picking up the laundry from your floor one day when she overheard you tell another nurse you were having your period. She figured the best time to make someone bleed more was when they were already bleeding. She knew your schedule, and before you came in in the morning, she put a few drops of heparin in your coffee cup. She did this for about four days. Then, on the fifth day, you collapsed."

Steven looked at Larry and said, "I thought you said this lady was mentally incompetent? Sounds like that took some real thinking and planning to pull that off."

Larry shrugged.

"Did she name the other person involved?" Christina asked as she took a sip of tea.

Larry shook his head. "No. She says she just talked to him over the phone."

"Are you sure it was a man she was talking to and not another female using a voice modifier?" Christina asked, worrying that the other person was still out there somewhere and could still pose a threat to her family.

"Well, we can't be sure of that, as we don't have any concrete evidence—only the testimony of a mentally disturbed woman. For all we know, the other person could be a figment of her imagination."

Standing in the doorway, Nicky said, "No, there was someone else. I heard her talking on the phone to him. She called him 'the boss man.'"

Motioning for Nicky to come in, Larry said, "Hey, Nicky, come on in, son. How ya doin?"

Nicky walked over and stood by his mother. "I'm okay, I guess."

Smiling, the sheriff asked, "So can you tell us anything about this lady?"

Nicky looked at his mom, who encouraged him to answer by nodding her head. "She likes the name Ruby. That's what I know her as, so when I talk about her, I will call her Ruby."

Everyone around the table nodded.

"Ruby said she had an awful childhood. Her parents didn't really want her, and her older brothers used to hurt and scare her. She said she ran away from home when she was fourteen and has lived on her own since then. She never went to high school. She said she learned enough life lessons in the school of hard knocks." He paused, making a face and looking at his mother. "I'm not sure what that means."

"I'll tell you later," she whispered. "Go ahead and finish your story."

He continued to talk, and by the time he had finished telling the sad life story of Lula, everyone present felt sorry for the poor, pitiful woman being held in jail. After a few minutes of silence, Sheriff Clifton cleared his throat and said to Nicky, "Thanks for telling us about Lula. I'm sure all that information will be taken into consideration when she goes to trial."

Nicky looked shocked. "Trial? Why does she have to go to trial?"

"Well, son, when someone breaks the law, they have to go before a judge and jury and tell their story, and then—"

Nicky interrupted him. "I know about all that. I've watched some TV shows with judges and juries. I just don't understand why you can't just let her go. She didn't hurt me. I'm back safe and sound. You got your money back." He raised his hands palms up and looked around the table at the faces before him. They all shook their heads, looking down if they made eye contact.

He gave his mother a pleading look. "Mom. Can't we just drop the kidnapping charges? She really is a nice lady. I could just about guarantee she would never do anything like this again."

Christina put her arm around her son and drew him close.

"I'm sure you're right, Nicky, but she deliberately broke the law, and she has to face the consequences—like when you disobey or break my rules, you have to receive some kind of punishment to remind you not to do it again." She saw tears well up in his eyes. "Oh, honey, I'm sure the jury will have mercy on her, considering her mental and emotional state. Maybe she won't even have to go to jail or prison. Maybe she can go to a facility where they can help her."

"Like a hospital for crazy people?" he asked, worry etching his face.

Patting his hand, she said, "Something like that."

Tears spilled down his cheeks. "She'll be so scared and alone," he whispered.

Christina sighed. She looked at Steven for help.

He squatted beside Nicky and put his hand on the boy's shoulder.

"Look, Nicky, we know how much you care for Lula." He paused, frowning. "I mean Ruby. We feel compassion for her as well, but your mom is right. She *did* break the law and she *will* have to face the consequences. In the meantime, you can send her cards and letters and pray for her. I'm sure she'd love to hear from you now and then."

Nicky's face brightened, and he smiled, wiping away the tears that had made their way down to his chin.

"I think I'll go and make her a card right now."

Christina smiled at Nicky and then looked at Steven and mouthed, "Thanks." Steven stood and patted Nicky on the shoulder as the boy told everyone bye and ran up the stairs to his room to make a card for his new friend.

Once Nicky was out of sight, Christina breathed a sigh of relief. "I think that went well."

Everyone smiled and nodded.

Ed said, "That's one smart, tenderhearted kid."

Nodding in agreement, Christina replied, "Yes, that he is."

"So, she admitted to putting the heparin in my coffee and putting the snake in my van, but that doesn't explain the Halloween rat or chart discrepancies. I know she couldn't have done that," Christina commented as she unconsciously curled a ringlet of hair around her finger.

"No, it doesn't," agreed Larry, "but we haven't questioned her about those things yet. Personally, I don't think she's bright enough to have messed with the charts."

"Maybe not, but she did figure out the heparin dosage, unless that other person told her or gave it to her to give to me."

"Or it was just a lucky guess," Cindy added. Everyone looked at her. "Okay. Not really lucky."

Smiling, Christina reached over and patted Cindy on the shoulder. "I know what you mean."

Cindy rolled her eyes and nodded.

Sighing and rubbing her eyes, Christina said, "Well, at least it's over. Maybe we can all get back to a more normal life."

"Yeah, normal. Whatever that is." Larry chuckled as he stood. Walking over and patting Christina on the shoulder, he said, "Well, ladies and gents, I need to get back to the station and take care of some business." She started to stand. "You don't have to get up. I'll let myself out." He nodded at everyone, put his hat on, and walked out the front door, where a TV reporter immediately met him.

A woman with a microphone in her hand, followed closely by a cameraman, called out, "Sheriff?" *Darn it! I thought all these folks left!*

Larry stopped and waited as she approached. He was ready to give a statement.

"Hello, Sheriff, my name is Debra Metzer from channel four news. Can you give us a summary of what has transpired?"

Larry nodded and removed his hat before he spoke into the camera. "At this time, we have a suspect in custody. She's admitted to kidnapping the boy."

"I understand that there were other threats made against Mrs. Sanders and her family? Has this woman admitted to any of those threats?"

"I have no further comment at this time," Larry stated as he repositioned his hat on his head and started walking toward the squad car.

Ms. Metzer and her cameraman followed him.

"Sir, were there other people involved in this incident?"

After entering his vehicle and closing the door, he said through the open window, "As I stated, Ms. Metzer, I have no other comments at this time. So excuse me."

The woman shook her head and motioned for her colleague to turn off the camera.

Soon after he left, Christina's in-laws and the other kids entered the house through the back door.

"Geez, Mom. It was like driving through the middle of a circus out there!" Stacey exclaimed as she walked over to her mother and gave her a hug.

"Yeah," Brad agreed. "We had to run in the back door as some lady with a microphone and a guy carrying a big ol' camera came running up the driveway yelling questions at us."

"Where are your grandparents?" Christina asked when she noticed they hadn't come in with the kids.

Walking over to her mom, Samara said, "They weren't as quick as us, and that lady with the microphone blocked their way to the door and started asking all kinds of questions."

Christina stood. "I'd better go rescue them. Ed, could you please go tell all those news people to get off my property?"

Ed nodded and stood. "Sure thing."

Christina's house phone rang, and she excused herself to answer it.

Steven smiled as he listened in on the conversation. He remembered Christina mentioning the little old lady from church who called every now and then to encourage and pray for the Sanders family.

"Ellie! It's so nice of you to call. We're all doing well now. Nicky has recovered and is sending handmade cards to Lula. Yes, he is indeed a special child. Thank you so much for your prayers and encouragement, and yes, I'll see you at church or around town." When Christina replaced the receiver, she looked at Steven and said, "I want to be like her when I grow up!"

He chuckled and nodded, trying to picture Christina as a ninety-year-old lady. She would be cute—that was for sure.

CHAPTER 136

Janet sat at her kitchen table, idly staring at the newspaper laid out in front of her. Her daughter was sitting on the couch in the living room watching something on TV. She thought about all that had transpired over the past several months.

Well, she thought, *I'm not the only one who wants Christina out of the picture. Who is that lady that kidnapped Nicky, and why did she want Christina to leave? Was she the one that gave Christina the almost lethal dose of heparin? If so, why? And how did she get ahold of it? The meds are always kept locked up.* She unconsciously chewed on her thumbnail. *Is there any way I can be linked to any of this?*

She went over the conversation she had with Christina at the coffee shop. *Did I say anything that would incriminate me? No, I don't think so.* She looked in at Linda and bit her lip with worry. *What was I thinking? If someone does figure out that I was the one who changed the charts and put the rat in the box and almost gave her the heparin, I could be in deep trouble. I could go to jail!* She thought back on all the incidents and played them out in her mind. There was no way anyone could point a finger at her. She had been careful to always wear latex gloves. She sighed shakily. *I'll be all right. I just have to remain calm and cool till all this passes over.*

Al Conger sat in his easy chair sipping iced tea and watching the evening news. He almost choked on his drink when he saw the news story about the kidnapping of the Sanders boy. The screen showed a woman holding a microphone describing the scene at the abandoned granary where the boy was recovered. It showed Lula being put into a police car. The woman stated, "As you can see, the woman, who calls herself Ruby, is being taken into custody for the kidnapping of Nicholas Sanders." The camera turned to show Nicky and his mother embracing next to a group of soldiers.

"Nicholas was reunited with his mother and will be taken to a local hospital to be evaluated." The camera refocused on the woman speaking.

"We have also been informed that David Sanders, Nicholas's father, worked with an antiterrorist branch of the government before his tragic death two years ago, and that is why the FBI and the military were called in so quickly to help with the rescue of this child. There are rumors that this could be linked to a terrorist cell here in Texas. We'll keep you updated as we receive more information."

Al pushed the button on his remote control, and the TV screen went black. He sat in silence for a few minutes, wondering why anyone would kidnap a child.

CHAPTER 137

Thanksgiving

Two weeks after the kidnapping, Thanksgiving was celebrated at the Sanders home. David's parents, who had flown home the day after Nicky was reunited with his family, returned with their son and daughter and their spouses and kids to celebrate with Christina and her family. Cindy, Samara, Ed, Steven, Tom, Eleanor, and Tommy were there as well. The house was filled with food, fun, and fellowship. Tables had been set up in the dining and adjoining living room to accommodate the huge amount of food, dishes, and people. Not only were there two large turkeys, but there were also two containers of everything: potatoes (white and sweet), corn, beans, carrots, beets, salad, and several smaller bowls of mixed veggies and condiments. The only other place she had seen that much food was in a cafeteria.

The day had been a comfortable seventy degrees with clear blue skies. The kids and a few of the adults enjoyed indoor and outdoor games while the others sat around, talked, and enjoyed the food and companionship. As the day progressed, more and more friends dropped by to visit: Lisa and her family, Donna and her kids, and Larry sans his wife, who had informed him the previous day that she wanted a divorce. Christina felt her heart swell with joy as she watched and listened to all the activity. She was truly home.

"Christina? A penny for your thoughts," Ruth said as she walked up and put her arm around her daughter-in-law's waist.

"Oh, hi, Mom. I was just thinking about how blessed I am. I have such a wonderful family and so many dear friends."

Ruth nodded and smiled. "Yes, you *are* blessed. We are *all* blessed." The two women stood in the doorway watching the children and other adults play a game of volleyball.

Christina sighed and said, "I wish this day would never end."

"I know what you mean." Ruth sighed as well. "Well, we just have to make the best of every day we are given. So why don't you go and play a game of volleyball? I'll make sure the food and dishes are taken care of."

Christina smiled at her mother-in-law. "Are you sure?"

Ruth nodded. Christina gave her a hug and went to join the players. As she walked toward the group, she felt the unmistakable buzzing of the phone in her pocket indicating she had a text message. She flipped the phone open and almost dropped it when she read the warning.

Printed in the United States
By Bookmasters